THE QUEEN'S BOUQUET

INGA DUNBAR

THE QUEEN'S BOUQUET

HarperCollins*Publishers*

HarperCollins*Publishers*
77–85 Fulham Palace Road,
Hammersmith, London w6 8jb

Published by HarperCollins*Publishers* 1997
1 3 5 7 9 8 6 4 2

A catalogue record for this book is
available from the British Library

ISBN 0 00 225468 9

Set in Meridien by
Rowland Phototypesetting Ltd,
Bury St Edmunds, Suffolk

Printed and bound in Great Britain by
Caledonian International Book Manufacturing Ltd, Glasgow

This book is dedicated to the memory of
IAN GRIMBLE
Scottish Historian, Broadcaster,
and Gentleman.

ACKNOWLEDGEMENTS

With thanks to: my husband, Charles Dunbar, for his unfailing support and for living with *The Queen's Bouquet* for two years; to my doctor, Dr Catherine Legg, for sympathetic and generous advice on matters medical; to Mrs Jeannie Taylor, for her interest in the north of Scotland and her help; to my friend, Mrs Ruby Turberville, for access to her library; to Maureen Waller, for allowing me to read her research into the Stuart Dynasty; to Lucy Ferguson, my editor, for her kind and gentle guidance throughout; to Judith Murdoch, my agent, who suggested this book in the first place, and to Yvonne Holland and Linda Joyce, for their detailed work and help on the manuscript.

I greatly appreciate, and am indebted to, two major works on the subject of Queen Mary; Margaret George's magnificent novel, *Mary, Queen of Scotland and the Isles*, and Lady Antonia Fraser's *Mary, Queen of Scots*, a biography unsurpassed. Also *A History of Scotland* by Rosalind Mitchison.

AUTHOR'S NOTE

Although this novel is based on events surrounding the life of Mary Queen of Scots, many of the characters and incidents reported are entirely fictional.

PART ONE

ONE

As soon as George Gordon, Earl of Huntly, appeared in the castle door his piper struck up 'The Cock o' the North'.

Keeping time with his signature tune the Earl strutted out into the courtyard where his Gordon soldiers were already waiting astride their horses. His green velvet-clad paunch hung over his gold waist chain, and his backside was so massive that it seemed raised up in the air behind him.

'Jesus!' Captain John McCracken said to himself as he watched the Earl advancing towards him. 'Now, *there*'s a cock lording it over the midden if ever I saw one!'

'Look at that! He's just like our rooster! All he needs is a tail feather,' Donald MacLaren's childish treble pierced the air and echoed the Captain's thoughts out loud.

That boy needed a spot of discipline, John thought, but his eyes were sparkling with laughter as he struggled to keep his face dead straight. Lord Huntly might look like a figure of fun, but he was one of the most important men in the country, the great Catholic magnate of the north of Scotland, well able to raise an army of hundreds from any point of the compass with just one flick of his podgy fingers.

'So, McCracken, you're all ready?' Lord Huntly asked in the lilting Highland accent of everyone in the district.

'We are, my lord.'

'Well,' the Earl sighed, swaggering up and down the rows of the escort with his hands clasped behind him so that his unfortunate posterior was even more accentuated, 'she shouldn't be long now, God help us all.'

Copying him almost exactly, a large black bird cocked his head and stalked up and down the other side of the rows of men until some of the soldiers could contain their hilarity no longer. John heard the first infectious titter. It was coming from that little devil Donald MacLaren, of course.

'No, sir,' John said so loudly and firmly that the tittering stopped, and at that point Florrie, the head nursemaid, came out holding the hand of the baby, Adam. They were followed by Maggie May, younger and more able to run about after his older brother, John, already exhibiting all the signs of an irrepressibly skittish nature. The Earl grasped a son in each of his great paws. After a considerable delay his wife, Elizabeth Gordon, Countess of Huntly, made her dramatic appearance. Two ladies preceded her and two ladies followed her, dressed for riding in dun colours ranging from brownish grey to greyish brown, which combined with the dark green of the Gordons' uniforms was Lady Huntly's idea of camouflage when riding out into the dangerous wastes of Scotland in this year of 1538.

By comparison, and with all thoughts of camouflage forgotten where she herself was concerned, she glowed like an emerald, clothed in green satin and velvet, banded with gold and edged with fur. On her head she wore her favourite lettice riding cap, also of fur, which came to a peak at the crown of her head and fitted into the nape of her neck, while its sides curved inward over her cheeks.

Some of the baggage was in panniers, carried on either side of the waiting-ladies' horses, but the main bulk was in large baskets which four of the Gordon soldiers carried behind the ladies. John McCracken directed his men, four behind the row of luggage-bearers, four along each side of the procession, and prepared to take up his own position in the front, flanked by two of his best fighting men.

As he mounted his horse again he shot a warning, withering glance at young Donald – filthy, grinning and undaunted – who was hanging over the wooden gate leading into the Home Farm.

4

In the excitement of this fairly straightforward manoeuvre Lord Huntly could contain himself no longer. 'Here,' he said, thrusting his two little sons back into the hands of the nurse-maids, 'take them inside, away from the horses' hooves.'

The nursemaids held up each child to kiss Lady Huntly goodbye while her husband regarded her with some distaste. She had discontinued marital relations recently, complaining bitterly of headaches and sickness, which *she* of all people should have been able to cure. But no, she did nothing to help it, which meant he had to suffer, too. Also, she had allowed her waist to thicken. In fact, she had become fat, and that, on a figure as tall as hers, made her more imposing and formidable than ever. *And, frightening . . .*

Approaching her, he tried to summon a pleasant expression to his face. With all this resentment boiling up inside him it was far from easy, and made more difficult still when at last he caught sight of the large black bird, his wife's pet raven, stalking about on the grass and glaring at him with its head cocked to one side.

Lady Huntly took one last look around at Strathbogie, the stately castle of Huntly, the home of the Gordons for generations. The sun burnished its yellow stones to gold and made the trees surrounding it seem even more darkly green. Everything, in this instant of her leaving it, seemed more intensely beautiful than ever.

Brooding for a moment on her lot in this life, her eyes took it all in before they came to rest on the luxury of her own gown. Well, her husband was a very wealthy man, and he knew better than to stint her. She supposed that in spite of all she had to put up with she was a very lucky woman, even if she couldn't trust him as far as she could throw him. Where, for example, was he going today as soon as her back was turned? She scowled as his groom led out his horse.

She kissed her two youngest sons goodbye in a perfunctory manner, reflecting that she would have been happy enough to possess all her other innate abilities without this extra amazing gift she had been granted – *that of being a witch . . .*

5

Only a white witch, it was true. All her spells and sorcery were directed at healing people. But nobody believed that, looking at her jet-black hair and hooded eyes, least and last of all her husband, and that was the way she intended to keep it. It gave her a sort of power to add to her reputation of being the best midwife in Scotland.

But it also meant that very often she must leave home as she was doing today, this time to go to Aberdeen, where her delicate sister would soon be confined.

'Now, my lord,' she said, looking down at her husband severely.

'Yes, my dear?'

'In my absence you will guard all our sons with your life if need be. And,' she added significantly, darting a venomous glance at Donald MacLaren still perched up on the gate, 'you will remember that *they* are the legitimate Gordons and therefore the only ones who count.'

The Gordon soldiers were as used to these unpleasantries as the Earl was himself, and their attention strayed, for everyone knew that the Huntly lords fathered more illegitimate children than they did within wedlock. All the gentry were the same. King Jamie himself was worse than most. He had nine at the last count.

John McCracken's eyes wandered idly over the two lines of servants gathered to bid a respectful farewell, and he saw a girl dressed in blue at the end of the women's line who had not been there on previous occasions. She could only have been about fourteen, with a lovely fresh face and trim figure.

'Who's that, at the end?' he asked his sergeant, who took it for granted that the Captain could only be referring to a woman.

'Och, the one in blue? She's a new one. Her name's Abigail.'

Abigail . . . A gentle little name for a gentle little girl, standing there with her eyes downcast and a shy flush on her cheeks, he thought. But no one could have told to look at him that such tender sentiments beat in the breast of John

McCracken as the whole company began to trot sedately down the long tree-lined avenue from the castle leading into the town of Huntly. In his mid-twenties, John McCracken was at the peak of his manhood, large, fair and dauntingly masterful as he directed his troops and the whole cavalcade.

Donald watched them wistfully. His one and only ambition in life was to be a Gordon soldier. At the last minute Lord Huntly climbed up onto his huge chestnut stallion. As if by some prearranged signal, so did the raven, perching on the stallion's head and regarding his lordship with a beady, malevolent eye.

'Elizabeth!' the Earl bellowed after her. 'Tell this wretched bird to go away!'

Without turning her head Lady Huntly whistled shrilly and called, 'Nick! Nick! Come here!' and the raven flew to her and settled on her shoulder.

'That proves she's a witch,' Donald muttered in John McCracken's ear as he rode past. 'Another name for the Devil is Old Nick. I know. My grandmother told me.'

'And I'll have your guts for garters when I get back, see if I don't,' John muttered back. 'You'll show some respect by the time I'm finished with you, my lad!'

All the same he couldn't help smiling at the temerity of the boy, scarcely out of her ladyship's earshot too. Donald MacLaren believed in witches, as they all did, but he displayed neither fear nor respect even for them.

'A proper little shit, that one,' John said to himself.

Still smarting bitterly from his wife's latest public castigation the Earl watched them go, and as soon as they approached the first corner he cantered off in the opposite direction. He could hardly wait. Dimly, the old saying passed through his mind, 'When the cat's away the mice will play', and by God, the Chief Mouse was going to play today, all right.

What he couldn't understand was why the streets of Huntly were emptying so rapidly as he thundered through them. He saw a man clutching his wife and hurrying her along, their heads bent close together. Three women linked arms and scurried down a side street. The people seemed to melt away. Lord Huntly was baffled.

And out in the countryside the cottages had been hurriedly closed up and the fires doused, as he could tell by all the black smoke billowing to the ground. All seemed deserted.

He should have been the first to know that word spread like wildfire in this, his own territory, so vast that it seemed more like a kingdom in its own right. He depended on such a network of communication whenever he had to defend it, but this time the message flying before him was that the Countess was off on one of her midwife expeditions and the Cock o' the North was on one of his rampages again, so for God's sake – lock up the women!

He hadn't ridden far when he saw a large cloud of dust on the horizon. Immediately he reined in his stallion. Anyone could see that a company of horse was riding towards him very fast. He was about to turn back to the safety of Strathbogie when he made out the royal banners, and a few minutes later he was lumbering off his horse and bowing to King James V of Scotland, his monarch and his master.

'Your Majesty,' he stuttered, 'we did not expect you!'

'Of course not. It is a secret visit.'

Only then did Lord Huntly see the boxes and chests carried by the soldiers and ringed by guards in the heart of the escort. There must be more gold in them than usual for the King to be accompanying them in person.

'I have not been well,' King James went on, 'so I have let it be known that I have gone away for a few days' hunting. Between you and me, I am hoping that your Highland air will prove beneficial.'

'Strathbogie Castle and all of us inside it are at your disposal always, Majesty. But I regret to tell you that Lady Huntly left early this morning to attend a birthing in Aberdeen, and as you know, she is the mistress of medicines and potions.'

The King's slanting eyes smiled into Lord Huntly's, he

8

could have sworn in relief, and both men relaxed.

'Our Mistress of the Household will make you and your party both welcome and comfortable, sire, and there will be room in the barracks for your soldiers, since so many of the Gordons have gone to escort my wife.'

'Then we shall settle ourselves while you get on with the important business immediately, Huntly. You have always sworn that the gold is secure in the safest hiding place in Scotland.'

'No idle boast, Your Majesty,' Lord Huntly assured him.

But he was mopping his brow as he saw the King's party dispersing in Strathbogie, to be waited on hand and foot as his wife had well instructed their servants. Then the Earl scuttled off as fast as his legs could carry him to find George, the young Lord Gordon.

'George,' he said, when he found him, 'the King is here!'

'*The King?*' Lord George said incredulously. 'Why?'

'On the pretext of a hunt, but really to dispose of more gold. Come! You and I have work to do!'

TWO

Plump and pretty in her blue dress, carrying a tray of tiny plants, and quite unaware that she had an ardent admirer, Abigail Moncrieff left Strathbogie Castle almost immediately after Lord and Lady Huntly. She couldn't leave the precincts of the castle, of course, because as a mere servant she was virtually a prisoner inside them, but at least she was out into the sunshine of this morning in May, and walking along a path bordered by huge chestnut trees.

When she looked up she could see baby chestnuts on the lower branches in between the glossy five fingers of the leaves, and on an impulse she set aside her tray to reach up and pluck one. Its little burrs were already formed, pale green and pink. She put it in the pocket of her blue dress, for luck.

Leaving the path and climbing a gentle hill she looked down at the place where two rivers met. It was beautiful, she thought, not knowing that it was also a critically strategic place for Strathbogie to be built three hundred years before. All Abigail knew was that the two rivers were the Deveron and the Bogie, but which was which she couldn't tell.

Gingerly skirting the huge cannon which the Earl kept pointed towards the north for fear of an invasion of Highlanders she headed towards the Gardeners' Cottage. It was taking a long time to reach it. She knew she couldn't mistake it, because it was built out of the same glorious golden Moray stone as the castle itself, as well as all its outhouses and even the cobbles. Her grandfather had told her she was very lucky to be going to work in a golden castle when Lady Huntly appointed her to be a gardening maid. Most castles in the north of Scotland were grey.

Then at last she came upon the cottage through the trees. No one lived in it. It existed nowadays only to house the gardening tools and inside, it had a curious earthy smell. Abigail liked the smell, but it brought back the day the Countess had brought her here for the first time.

'I want a herb garden,' she had said, 'like the one at your grandfather's house. I want you to see to it right away. I need special herbs to make medicines for sick people.'

'Yes, my lady,' Abigail had said, trembling in absolute terror in case she put a foot wrong or said a word out of place for it was whispered that spells, not medicines, would have been a better word.

She would far rather have been living with her grandparents again in their cottage. It was surrounded by beautiful gardens which people came from far and wide to see. Her grandfather, Simon Moncrieff, worked in his gardens from morning to night and had instilled in her a love of plants, ignorant of the fact that this would prove to be his beloved granddaughter's destiny.

So here she was today, looking for pegs and string to mark out the ground and the spade to dig it, pausing long enough to think quite bitterly – for someone as gentle as Abigail – that this hut was a far better dwelling than her grandparents' where she had been brought up. And it was only for tools!

It took a long time first to find a suitable site for the herb garden and after several attempts, to mark it out. But at last she decided on something quite ambitious, an eight-sided figure, the eight sections of it running into a circle in the middle, and the reason for that was that she had got eight different bundles of herbs from her grandfather to plant out.

Then came the digging, but it was only half begun by the time the sun was setting and she was almost exhausted, reduced now to lying along the ground cleaning the edges of her octagon to plant in her plants before they wilted, unaware that her skirts had ridden up to her thighs. She was at the last one of that particular section, the last lavender plant, when she noticed that she wasn't alone. She looked up to see a party of men on horseback, all of them exquisitely dressed, and all of them grinning at her bare legs. Angrily, she smoothed her skirts down again.

'Go back to Strathbogie,' their leader said. 'I'll follow shortly,' and the others rode away, still laughing.

To begin with, Abigail was nervous, but the beautiful young man with the dark red beard and hair and all the golden chains around his neck couldn't have been kinder, and soon she found herself telling him all about her herb garden.

'You are prettier than any of the flowers, my dear,' he said, putting his arm around her, and to her surprise, giving her a kiss. 'You may call me Jamie. I am to be here for a week for the stag-hunting, and if I may I shall come back every day to see how your herb garden is progressing.'

'Oh, yes,' she said, tingling and thrilled with his kiss.

Every morning after that she was up early and working hard at the Gardeners' Cottage. Every afternoon Jamie visited her there. To her relief he came alone, because she hadn't liked those other giggling men. Soon the garden became unimportant, and their lovemaking all important, for she had fallen madly in love with Jamie and his strange slanting golden eyes and gentle ways.

The last afternoon he came to see her he took her face in his hands and kissed her tenderly, and before he rode away he promised to come back some day. Abigail really believed he would when she waved him goodbye.

Lord Huntly happened to be in the courtyard, and Donald MacLaren happened to be crossing it with his bucket of pig-swill, when King Jamie galloped back all alone and at such a speed that his velvet cap flew off. Donald darted under the horse's hooves to retrieve it, and handed it back up to him, with a bow.

'You certainly have your servants well trained, Huntly,'

the King observed, looking narrowly from the Earl to Donald, seeing the likeness.

'This boy *is* a little special,' Lord Huntly smirked.

'I know the feeling,' James grinned sympathetically, jumping down off his horse. 'I have a few little specialities of my own.' Then, turning to Donald, he handed him a tiny gold coin. 'Remember me,' he said.

'I'll never forget you, sire,' Donald assured him gratefully.

Lady Huntly sent a message to her husband at the end of May. The baby still hadn't come. There was no saying when it would, and in the meantime as well as not being able to leave her sister, she wasn't very well herself. In June she sent another message. It had been a bad birth, and the lives of both mother and child hung in the balance. In July a third message was sent to Lord Huntly, again by word of mouth, since he could neither read nor write.

'They're getting better,' the messenger told him, 'but Lady Huntly will stay on for a while yet.'

'Tell her to stay as long as she likes,' he was foolhardy enough to reply, since the messenger relayed every word back to her faithfully.

Strathbogie, in the meantime, grew dirtier by the minute. Now and then the Earl exploded, for his nose at least was delicate, and then the servants would shovel out the filth around the long dining trestle, mostly old bones and festering scraps he had thrown down on the straw himself, mingled with the excrement of the dogs never far from his side.

The bubble had to burst sometime, and it did, when on the second day of August the announcement came that Lady Huntly would return home the following day.

'The bitch!' he muttered to himself. She had never caught him short like this before. If anything, she delayed, presumably to give everyone time to give her a fitting welcome.

The Earl declared a state of emergency. The entire castle must be cleaned, and in a tearing hurry. He berated the servants and called in the garrison troops. The dirt from every floor must be shovelled out forthwith and fresh rushes strewn.

'Fetch lavender,' he bellowed, beside himself in his frenzy, while nasty little thrills of pain shot across his chest. 'I don't care where you get it. Steal it, if need be, but this whole place must be sweetened before any of us lays down a head tonight!'

Abigail Moncrieff had felt so sick and dizzy that morning that she was forced to leave the garden and go back to the castle. The cook, Mistress MacLaren and a young boy about seven years old were the only two in the kitchen.

Mistress MacLaren took one look at her face and turned to the boy with a pail in her hand. 'Off you go, Donald,' she said. 'Take this to the pigs,' and winking horribly at Abigail: 'Little pitchers have long ears, you know ... Well, lassie,' she said, 'what's wrong? Are you pregnant?'

Abigail looked up at the cook with an ashen face and began to cry. Such a thing had never crossed her mind.

'Well,' the woman said, 'you're sick in the mornings, are you not? We all know what *that* means! Who was it? Was it his lordship?'

Abigail shook her head, speechless at the absurdity of such an idea. What woman in her right senses would go near the Earl of Huntly?

'Well, everyone will think so, especially her ladyship. It's a good job she's away, but as soon as she gets back it will be only a question of time before she gets rid of you, you know – unless you are to be married to someone? No? Oh well, then ...'

'Gets rid of me? What does that mean?'

'Oh, it's happened before to many a poor girl on this estate. It happened to my own lassie, only she managed to hide her pregnancy – Donald, that boy you saw, my grandson – until the day he was born. *Then* they got rid of her.'

'What do you mean?' Abigail whispered.

'And here I am,' the cook went on in a bitter tirade, 'still working at my age – and with Huntly's brat to drag up any way I can! We all know that Donald's name should be Donald Gordon! But her ladyship ignores yet another of her husband's bastards. She won't have Donald near her. And as for his lordship, he wouldn't get rid of any of his by-blows that are living. He thinks too much of himself and what is his for that!'

'But where is your daughter now?' Abigail persisted.

'Dead, most likely! Taken away to the hills and left there to die. The wildcats and the wolves will have eaten her long ago.'

'Oh my God,' Abigail said, and slumped to the floor in a faint.

THREE

Abigail heard the cook's voice in the distance. She felt water splashing on her face, and then she opened her eyes again.

'Good!' Mistress MacLaren said. 'You're awake again. Now, take my advice. Act as though nothing has happened. Go round to the front door now and join the rest of the servants. They are cleaning the floors. Her ladyship is coming home tomorrow.'

Nausea overcame Abigail again as soon as she entered the Great Hall. The raising of the rushes had released the stench beneath them. She only had time to reach the vomitorium at the side of the hall before she was sick again. Then strong hands were helping her up to sit on a chair, and a man's deep voice was in her ear.

'Rest a minute, Miss Abigail. You don't know who I am, do you?' the man smiled down at her. 'You couldn't, because I have to go away so often, on duty.'

'No, sir.'

'But I know who you are, and I've admired you since I first saw you. I'm John McCracken, Captain of the Gordon Guard.'

He was very tall, very broad and very fair, and he had a kind face. But why was any of this happening to her? Terrified half out of her wits, Abigail stared at him dumbly.

'The Mistress of the Household is glaring at us,' he said softly, 'but don't worry. If she has anything to say, she'll have to deal with me. It's all her fault that the castle is in this state, anyway.'

'I feel a bit better now,' Abigail lied nervously. 'I'll come and help.'

He put his hand under her arm and helped her to take her place in the line of servants scraping the floor of the Great Hall, kneeling by her side and handing her a wooden board. 'Just do what you can,' he said gently. 'Push the straw towards the door, dirt and all. Then we'll take it all out to the midden.'

Abigail tried her best, crawling forwards bit by bit. It made her feel more squeamish still. John looked at her in concern and took her board into his left hand.

'Just crawl along beside me and pretend instead,' he said in a comforting tone. 'You're pregnant, are you not, wee lassie?'

'I fear I am, sir.'

'Have you told the father?'

'I can't. He was here with a hunting party in May. I've never seen him since.'

'What was his name?'

'Jamie.'

'Jamie? Last May?' he asked incredulously, and now it was John McCracken's turn to become ashen. All the fair young colour drained out of his face. 'Good God . . .' he said.

'Do you know him, sir?' Abigail asked timorously, yet hopefully.

There was a long silence before John answered her. Another bastard for the King, he thought, and in that case Abigail was in danger, if this came out. He shuddered, thinking what Lady Huntly might do if she discovered that this time the guilty man wasn't her husband but the King himself. Worse and worse . . . But, so long as Abigail herself was informed about who her royal lover had been and realised the gravity of the situation, he might be able to do something to help her. They might be able to do something together.

Abigail saw him shudder. 'Yes, I do know him,' he said gently. 'Your Jamie was King James, and you are not the first innocent country girl he has bairned. The only children born out of wedlock he keeps are those of titled ladies, as a rule. As it is, his wife, Queen Marie, has had to accept at least nine of those at Holyrood Palace in Edinburgh. So for *your* safety, Miss Abigail, and your child's, you must get married to another man and pretend the child is his.'

John saw that she was too shocked to speak. He dropped the scraping boards and put his hands on her shoulders. 'Would you marry me?' he urged her. 'I fell in love with you the first time I saw you. I can't hope for the same in return, not right away, but I'd look after you and your child and I'd never let you down.'

Abigail had no means of knowing whether she could trust John McCracken or not. She had thought she could trust her beautiful Jamie. Now she had learned that not only was Jamie the King himself, but that he had taken advantage of her. She was devastated.

'But you shouldn't be burdened with another man's child, sir,' she sobbed.

'We'll forget about the other man, Miss Abigail. From this day on we'll pretend he never existed. When your child comes it will bear my name. Do you agree, then?'

John McCracken smiled calmly into her eyes. Although so big and fierce-looking he seemed kind, and in a flash she knew she could trust this man. Besides, she could see no other way out. In desperation, she nodded.

'Tomorrow morning I have to take the escort to Aberdeen to bring Lady Huntly home,' John said. 'I'll ask her then for her permission, so that we can marry as soon as possible. In the meantime, don't worry. Just look as though you're working.'

Dumbly, Abigail bent to her task and shuffled forward on her knees as before, so overcome with relief, gratitude and the speed of her deliverance that she was on the very point of swooning again. She would have done if it hadn't been for a pain in her right knee. She was kneeling on something sharp, which must be in her pocket.

When she pulled it out she saw that although it was wizened and black its tiny burrs were still there, as sharp as needles. The chestnut had survived many washings of her blue dress. She vowed she would keep it for ever. It must be a luck charm to be protecting her guilty secret like this and saving her from certain death.

But all the same, convinced that nobody else in the entire castle of Strathbogie had ever faced such a desperate crisis and survived it, Abigail burst into a torrent of tears.

Later that night Lord Huntly sat by the side of his imposing fireplace now that it had been hastily swept and glanced up at the medallion portraits of his ancestors sculpted on it. He was exhausted by his efforts and the pains in his chest were back again. He called for a goblet and a bottle of wine to ease them, frantically going over all that had happened during the last three months . . .

He thought he had everything covered, everything except the King's visit. His wife would be furiously angry because she hadn't been there. He would have to try to convince her that by the time he would have got word to her in Aberdeen and she had returned, the King would have gone again, anyway.

With that little problem solved he really believed he could concentrate now on higher things. Like the King, for instance. He hadn't thought about James V much since the visit, except to feel fairly sure that the little man with the red beard had been doing a splendid job, as usual, of sapping the Catholic Church of funds and relaying them to more worthy causes. To the baronial dynasties such as Huntly's own, for instance.

Every now and then more gold, usually from cathedrals, and heavily guarded, would arrive at Strathbogie to be hidden away, but never so much as this last time. He reflected with slightly puzzled satisfaction that he must be one of the wealthiest lords in the country, for he had no intention of ever giving it back. It was all thanks to the King who spent most of his energies looking for money, raising enormous sums in taxation, and rumour had it that there were mysterious royal boxes tucked away in secret places all over the country, full of gold and jewels.

The question flashed through his mind – was he being bribed by this King? Were he and every other Catholic lord in Scotland being bribed to keep silent and act as royal repositories? Of course they were! And the King's bastard, young Lord James Stewart, would have got the lion's share salted away somewhere. There was no doubt of that.

Nobody was safe, that was a certainty, because when it came right down to it, almost every lord in Scotland was descended from a Stewart. Take the Douglases, for example. The Douglas dynasty had been one of the wealthiest and certainly the most powerful in the land at one stage of the game ... And look what happened to them! The King had simply wiped them out when it suited him.

And now, there was His Majesty's latest ploy of mixing business with pleasure. Ah yes, George Gordon thought, more than halfway down the bottle by this time, it all came down to women in the end. Two years ago King James had gone to France and managed to persuade Francis I to fulfil the Treaty of Rouen by giving him his daughter Madeleine. Within a few weeks of bringing the poor child to Scotland she was dead. But James got to keep the dowry. Not only that, the French King had allowed him to marry Marie de Guise immediately afterwards, and Marie de Guise carried an even larger dowry.

George Gordon, Earl of Huntly, reeled off to bed uneasy about his country, and certainly about his own lands, ruled by such a monarch, until the worry of his wife's return made him feel more uneasy still, and wiped all hope of sleep clean away. Had he seen to everything? What about his wife's cats? Now he came to think about her favourite creatures, he had not come across them all the time that she had been away. He hated them. They were so old that their black fur was now a rusty grey, but their age did not prevent the four of them from slinking along the corridors of Strathbogie, spitting and arching their backs and glaring at him out of their yellow slitted eyes.

It was too much to hope that they were dead and gone for ever.

The following morning three people watched the Gordons setting off from the courtyard for Aberdeen with vital interest and concern. Gloomily, Lord Huntly wondered what sort of reunion he would have with his wife. Abigail smiled at John McCracken through her tears, and felt lonely and vulnerable already without him. Donald MacLaren sighed enviously, and wished he was grown up so that he could go with them.

Because he was so happy at the prospect of actually marrying the girl he so admired, no matter what the circumstances, John McCracken was in a particularly good mood. He waved to Abigail and, feeling sorry for Donald standing there in his rags and tatters with such longing in his eyes, he gestured to the urchin to mount up in front of him.

'It's like all my birthdays have come at once,' Donald breathed ecstatically.

'Ay, well, behave yourself, my lad,' John said sternly, surprised to discover that the boy sat so easily on a horse. 'Have you ridden before?'

'No, but I always knew I could,' Donald said airily.

'Cocky little devil,' John said, although he couldn't help smiling.

The journey to fetch her ladyship went like clockwork. But on the way back to Strathbogie with the ladies, accompanied by Bishop Leslie of Ross and a youthful priest, Father Tiberon, the soldiers were ambushed by wild men from the hills.

John got the ladies' horses into a circle. Then he put the two clergymen with the ladies and Donald inside the ring while the Gordon Guards started to do battle.

'Watch out!' Donald yelled suddenly. 'Watch that bugger on your right!'

The Gordons disposed of the 'bugger on the right' and one

by one the rest of the tribe, but the greatest satisfaction John got from it all was to discover that the little pig-boy might make a soldier yet one day. He would bear it in mind.

'You did well, Donald MacLaren, for once,' he growled.

'To prove it, *you*'re still living, sir.'

'And you're still a wee shit. Don't think I've forgotten it.'

But John was smiling when they gathered themselves together to move on. He went first to attend to the ladies. The French priest travelling to Huntly with them clearly was not used to such encounters, and as for the Bishop, he was too old to act quickly.

'I don't know what would have happened but for you and the rest of the Gordons, John McCracken,' Lady Huntly said shakily. 'You must let me know if I can ever help you some day in return.'

'Perhaps you can, my lady,' John said calmly, holding her horse's head until her servants and the priests were mounted again, 'if you would grant me ten minutes of your time to discuss a very private matter?'

'I'll see you at four of the clock,' she said.

The rest of the expedition was peaceful until they reached the gateway in the castle walls. Here the Countess dismounted and found Lord Huntly coming out of the main door to greet her. She glanced at him, and read him expertly. Many times before she had seen this same expression of smug innocence on his face, and that usually meant he had been cheating her with some other woman and was pretty sure he had covered his tracks. In addition, the nearer they approached each other, the more clearly she divined that his bad temper had entirely disappeared, and he was contented, which probably meant that he had been sowing his wild oats over the whole of the summer.

She shrugged her shoulders. If another of her husband's bastards was waiting to be born, it would only add to a long string of such by-blows. Her own position was unassailable, as were the positions of her children when it came to the question of lawful inheritance.

No doubt her husband had taken some poor girl by force, for who would have him willingly? Her marriage to him had been arranged by her father. There had been no love lost on her side at least, and she couldn't complain about this latest misdemeanour so long as it kept him from her bed – all passion spent elsewhere, she truly hoped.

'My dearest George!' She smiled at him and kissed him on both jowls.

'Elizabeth, my dearest! It's so good to have you home again! But what has happened to you? Have you lost weight?'

'The weight of a baby,' she said sadly. 'I suffered a miscarriage in Aberdeen.'

That explained everything. It also changed everything, and it certainly affected Lord Huntly. He felt guiltier than ever, and was very subdued when he turned to the men standing behind his wife. 'And a welcome to you, Bishop Leslie and Father Tiberon,' he said.

They were welcome indeed. Their presence meant services in the chapel by day, so that they could pray for the soul of the child the Gordons had lost, and long religious debates in the evenings. The Earl welcomed anything that would occupy his wife's mind now, and divert her attention away from the state of the hurriedly half-cleaned castle.

As soon as she stepped in over the doorstep Lady Huntly smelled a rat, or rather a few sprigs of fresh lavender scarcely concealing a more pungent odour beneath hastily renewed rushes under her feet. So when the cat was away the mice had been at play, had they? A very fine time had been had by all as far as she could see. Her mouth set in a grim line, but she gave no other sign of her suspicions. In due course she would find out who the poor pregnant girl was. Time would tell. Yes, she sighed, it would all come out in the wash, eventually. It always did.

FOUR

'I needn't beat about the bush, my lady,' John McCracken said at four o'clock. 'I love Abigail Moncrieff, I want to marry her, and she is in the third month of carrying our child.'

Lady Huntly gazed at him open-mouthed. Abigail Moncrieff? Who was she?

'I'm sorry, my lady. I should have asked your permission to court her. But you were absent, and I'm afraid I was too carried away to wait any longer.'

'Abigail Moncrieff? Do I know her?'

'She began as a gardening maid just before you left, my lady.'

That sweet little girl! Simon Moncrieff's granddaughter! To arouse such passion in John McCracken, of all men! Lady Huntly never ceased to be amazed at human behaviour, especially men's.

'Do we have your permission to marry, Lady Huntly?' John looked at once very stern and very nervous, she thought. There was probably more here than met the eye. 'As soon as possible?' he added bluntly.

'You can arrange it this very afternoon. You will find the Bishop in the chapel. But that is only the beginning of your problems. You know there are no married quarters here, and the Captain is required to be on the premises day and night. Is it really worthwhile giving up such a position to marry this girl?'

'There *is* a way around it, my lady, if you will bear with

us,' John smiled, and ignored her inference. 'Abigail loves the Gardeners' Cottage. I will undertake to make it a comfortable dwelling before we marry. Also, I will build another small hut just for the tools.'

'You are a very determined young man, John McCracken.'

'Thank you, my lady,' he said.

What was the use of having a feast just for the inmates of Strathbogie? If there had to be one at all, Lady Huntly intended to invite half the countryside while she was at it. She hadn't entertained all summer, and she wanted to make sure of her welcome at the various other Gordon castles on a progress south, if she had to make one – should a summons come from Falkland Palace or Linlithgow or Holyrood itself, for instance . . . Her imagination ran riot.

'You presume too much, Elizabeth,' her husband said. Marie de Guise, the Queen, seemed to him to be a tight-lipped, self-contained creature – which perhaps, she needed to be from all he'd heard. The widow of a French duke, she was lonely here in Scotland with few friends and a husband who had little time to visit her, because most of it was spent visiting his mistresses.

Lord Huntly had more sense than to discuss any of this with Lady Huntly. However, his wife was fast becoming the Queen's closest friend and confidante, and that might be very useful to him some day. In the meantime there would be this very worrying wedding next week on his own estate.

All through the solemn Wedding Mass Lord Huntly barely managed to stay awake, although the feast afterwards, at which he was to be the host and John and Abigail McCracken the honoured guests, promised better entertainment. But Elizabeth relieved him of all that responsibility when she heard about the pains in his chest, which he was suffering again.

In fact, she panicked. The Earl must be preserved at all costs. Her plans were no use without him. *She* was no use without him. Although not a direct descendant, he was the one with the Stewart blood in him should anything happen to the royal family. And something very nasty *was* going to happen to the royal family, according to her familiars.

And then, who would wear the crown of Scotland?

Lady Huntly was determined that her husband would, and she would be his Queen. So she slipped away once the celebrations were underway, to make him up a potion to give him immediate relief, and another to be taken three times every day. And she knew she would make herself very unpopular with Mistress MacLaren when she put a stop to the menus of rich, greasy food.

Then, returning to the reception, she made the speeches, got the music going and afterwards arranged it so that her husband was left alone with the Bishop and the young priest, Father Tiberon, in the Great Chamber with bottles of light wine.

The more wine they drank, the more amusing a companion Father Tiberon became. Bishop Leslie tottered off to bed eventually, and Lord Huntly rang the bell for more wine. After a long delay, young Donald arrived with it.

'Where are the servants?' Lord Huntly asked him.

'I am the only one still awake, my lord.'

'Hm . . .' Lord Huntly said, looking at the boy's very black hair and blue eyes, and thinking that it was a wise father who knew his own son. 'Oh, very well. Sit in the corner, then, and wait.'

Donald chose a corner of the inglenook, and listened. A lot of the conversation he didn't understand, but it must have been funny, because the laughter and the jokes came faster and faster – jokes, that as the night wore on and the bottles became dead men, grew bawdier.

'But how do you manage, yourself?' Lord Huntly asked Father Tiberon in amazement. 'You're still a man, and young, after all.'

'Oh . . . usually with a little choirboy impaled, his head sticking out of my surplice,' the young priest said with a twinkle. 'Well, that's what you were thinking, isn't it?' he added, when at last Huntly saw it was a joke.

They slept where they fell down laughing that night and Donald curled himself up into a ball and tried to sleep, too, by the dying fire. He didn't want to go back to the kitchen, back to his cruel grandmother who wasn't beating him as much as usual, but was groaning in a way that frightened him even more. She was ill and could hardly drag one foot past the other. He didn't know *what* could be the matter with her, but it was very, very bad.

Next morning a servant woke them, whispering in Lord Huntly's ear.

'Donald,' the Earl said, 'your grandmother is dying. I want you to go to the barracks this morning and stay there. Tell John McCracken I said to find something to keep you busy.'

Later that day, alone in the Great Hall, Lord and Lady Huntly eyed each other across the table like two wrestlers, waiting for an opening to move. At the start of yet another domestic incident the threat of violence was in the very air, but as usual it all began quietly enough.

'Well, she's dead, and a good riddance too,' Lady Huntly said with great satisfaction. 'Why I put up with that woman all these years I do not know! Mistress MacLaren never *could* cook.'

'You put up with her because I said so,' her husband retorted calmly, 'and I'm the master here! Besides, I liked Mistress MacLaren.'

Lady Huntly's temper rose, along with her voice.

'You liked her daughter, you mean! Oh yes, I knew all about it – which reminds me – that boy, that Donald, will have to go now too! I cannot stand to look at him another minute! You have insulted me all these years with his very presence!'

'You shouldn't get so excited, Elizabeth! Your face goes very red – in fact, purple – and it does nothing to enhance you.'

'Bloody whoremonger!' she screeched, lifting the nearest object which happened to be his pewter tankard, full of ale, and throwing it at him. 'Get your bastard out of here!'

With an expertise born of many long hard years of practice Lord Huntly ducked and avoided the missile. 'Don't worry,' he said coolly. 'I was going to, anyway. Now that his grandmother has gone, who can tell what may happen to him here, where so many servants have conveniently disappeared over the years?'

'And what, pray, do you mean by that, George Gordon?'

'Oh, I think you know well enough. Do you imagine I've never heard your mutterings and incantations? Do you think I never knew that you were talking to people who weren't there – or if they were, disappeared into thin air whenever I approached? Who are these people, Elizabeth? What are your secrets?'

Lady Huntly tossed her head. So, he wasn't as stupid as she had thought after all. 'I never heard such nonsense,' she said acidly.

'Anyway, I have plans for Donald. If he takes after me, he'll be a bonny fighter. So, young as he is, he'll go and live in the barracks from this day on for his own protection, and in a year or two he'll be a Gordon soldier,' Lord Huntly said, swaggering out.

'Good! And I hope he gets killed in the very first battle,' she screamed as one of her very best dishes crashed against the door behind him and shattered into a thousand pieces.

The following February Donald helped the Gordons to dig a path through the snow to the Gardeners' Cottage so that Lady Huntly could get there and deliver Abigail's baby. Once inside, she divested herself of her furs and held out her hands at the brightly burning log fire, surprised to find the comfortable little home that John and Abigail had made it.

'A fine little girl, my dear,' she said a few hours later, busily wiping off the baby's eyes, nose and mouth, so she didn't see the look the young parents exchanged.

For months after their marriage Abigail had remained pale and subdued and it had taken John all his time to keep her spirits up. He was still at it. 'Isn't she a wee beauty?' he said firmly, taking the baby in his arms and marching up and down with her while a smiling Lady Huntly attended to Abigail.

'The proud father!' she said.

'Yes.' Abigail tried to smile back, but tears ran down her cheeks.

'And those are tears of happiness, I know. Every mother, from the highest to the lowest, sheds them at the birth. Even the Queen will, I expect. She has asked me to attend her confinement in the spring.'

Abigail felt duly honoured that by a strange coincidence she was being attended by the same midwife as Queen Marie herself would be. And, if either of those two ladies did but know it, the babies had been sired by the same man – another strange coincidence, and one that she must put out of her mind for her dear husband's sake.

For by now, Abigail loved John McCracken with all her heart and soul. He had proved his worth to her over and over again. All the same, when she dried her tears and examined her new little daughter, she was still fearful of finding her covered with gold dust. But no – she was just the prettiest little girl in the world and quite normal.

'What will you call her?' Lady Huntly asked.

'Abigail, after her mother – who better?' John said, laughing. 'But we'll call her Abbie, for short.'

FIVE

In April the following year, when the weather eased and the roads to the north became passable again, Lady Huntly set off with her retinue to go back home after the safe delivery of the second little prince, Prince Robert. She got only as far as Perth when the royal messengers caught up with her and told her the news that was to send all Scotland reeling in shock and distress.

Queen Marie begged her to come back at once. Both princes, James, the heir to the throne, and the new baby, had died.

Lady Huntly felt her heart plummet. She became icy cold and great tremors shook her body. Her hand went to her breast, trying to still a heart that was now racing, as somehow she redirected the messengers to Strathbogie Castle. Then she collapsed into her bed remembering all that her familiars had told her would happen, and which she had only half believed.

Lord Huntly was at her side the following day.

'Oh, my lord,' she wept, 'birth is one thing, but death is another. I cannot do this alone. I need your strength now, if I must go back to the Palace of Falkland to face it.'

Shocked and depressed though he was, her husband was so cheered by this appeal that he immediately assumed control, and together they made their way back south to Falkland Palace.

They wept together, as everyone there wept all through the interminable funeral services. Only King James and

Queen Marie shed no tears. They were like pillars of bleached stone.

Watching them, Lady Huntly could think of nothing but the births of those two infants – the pain, the joy, the blood and the tears that had been shed for them, and now they lay so still. At the end of that terrible day she sat alone with her husband. He was so bitterly affected, with his hand rubbing his chest, that she became concerned. Facing him, she took his hands in hers.

'Oh God, Elizabeth,' he wept, 'it might have been –'

'Don't say it,' she said. 'Of course I know what you are thinking, but don't say it. It's bad luck. I will give you more medicine, to help you to sleep.'

'I feel I will never sleep easy again. Don't let me sleep alone again tonight, my love,' he pleaded.

In that moment Lady Huntly realised she had only one life to live, and in it she would probably only ever have this one husband, with all his faults and with all his strengths . . . She would have to make the best of it.

'We will never sleep apart again, George,' she said, and took him in her arms.

Next day, after waiting endlessly, Lord Huntly was rewarded. The King would see him, but briefly. He entered the royal chamber and with some difficulty kneeled down.

'Your Majesty, please accept the sincere condolences of my wife and myself. We are devastated by your loss. All Scotland is devastated.'

A brief tremor crossed the King's face, a face that had aged overnight. His pointed sandy beard made it seem longer and thinner than ever, and his eyes were haggard. He acknowledged Huntly's sympathy with a brief nod. Apart from that there was no other reference to his sons' deaths.

'You received that last shipment of gold, Huntly?'

'Indeed, sire.'

'And you have it safely hidden away?'

'Of course, Majesty.'

'We may have need of it yet. Henry of England wants me to meet him at York in a supposed move for peace between our two countries. To go so far with all the escort I should need would prove a very costly exercise, as well as a dangerous one. Of course, I shall not go.'

'No, sire? I do not think Henry the Eighth is a man who can be snubbed with impunity. To meet Henry anywhere in England would be dangerous, of course, but in the cause of peace all our Scottish armies would support you. Not to meet him at all might be the very excuse he needs for open warfare – and war would be a very much more expensive exercise,' Lord Huntly argued, throwing in all his considerable weight.

Surely James would heed his caution, especially about money? But was the man even thinking straight? Of course not. He must still be in severe shock, Lord Huntly thought anxiously, while the King paced restlessly up and down, clutching his side as if in pain. Suddenly he stopped and confronted his visitor.

'Tell me, Huntly, what colour is your urine?'

'Why, clear, sire . . . or sometimes golden,' Lord Huntly stammered, taken completely off his guard by the sudden introduction of such a subject.

'Never dark red, even purplish, the colour of Burgundy wine?'

'No, sire.'

'Leave me now, Huntly.' James sighed deeply after a long pause. 'As you can see, many troubles beset me. It is not easy to know which way to turn next.'

Henry of England kept his side of the bargain. He moved his vast bulk north to York to meet with the Scottish King, and when James did not appear he took extreme umbrage. In fact, he was furiously angry.

Ever since his split with Rome, when the Pope would not allow him to divorce his wife and marry another, he had taken it upon himself as head of the Church of England to do more or less as he pleased. Above all, he hated and feared the French-Scottish alliance – the very subject he had intended to discuss with James. Well, now he would have his revenge.

By the following year, the prospect of being a father once more was diluted by James finding himself at war after all, just as Huntly had warned – and Huntly himself refused to join in the fight. So did most of the other Scottish lords, and it was a poor army James got to Lochmaben with the intention of crossing the Solway to attack the English.

The Scots were mustered in the bogs of the Solway Moss on a misty day in November. It was cold and clammy, and as the day wore on the blue mist thickened to white impenetrable fog.

The slaughter of the Scots continued all that night, and the next morning when the fog lifted a sight not unusual in the cruel, bloody borderland between England and Scotland was revealed – hundreds of dead bodies lying in the reeds and mud on both sides of the River Esk.

Three weeks later it began to snow. Within an hour the world outside Falkland Palace where James had retreated became a bitter white hell. He stared out of the windows, hopelessly. Surely he would hear soon the outcome of the Battle of the Solway Moss? Even now he dared not believe in total defeat.

But no one was coming no matter how much he willed it. No snow-clad figures were to be seen. Nothing was moving, and the scene looked like the end of the world. In the meantime his side was hurting him badly, and he was freezing to death.

'Fetch more logs, more logs,' he kept mumbling, pressing his hand to his side. 'It is too cold. The cold is killing me . . .'

He left the window and fell into a chair beside the fire while anxious servants fanned the flames. They saw that his eyes were closed and his face was indeed as white as death. Then, at last, men arrived at the door.

'What news?' he gasped. 'What of the battle?'

'We are defeated, sire.'

'Oh God . . .' He lurched from his seat. 'Then all is lost!'

33

He stumbled across the room towards his bedchamber, still clutching his side, but now openly screaming in pain. 'All is lost! All is lost!'

'No, not all, Your Majesty,' his physician said. 'Remember your Queen. Her hour has come. Even now she is delivering your child.'

The royal bedchamber filled with nobles, including Lord Huntly. They stood around his bed. The Earl of Arran was there, of course. He was next in line to the throne now that the two little princes were dead, and no doubt this infant would soon be dead too.

'All is lost,' James kept mumbling, as their faces appeared and dissolved and reappeared again. Then the physician spoke in his ear.

'Sire, your Queen has been safely delivered. She has borne you a fair daughter.'

'A daughter?' James smiled a ghastly smile. 'The Devil! Adieu, farewell, adieu! The Stewarts came with a lass and they shall pass with a lass!'

'What did he mean?' someone asked, and Huntly replied, 'He meant that the crown of Scotland came to the Stewarts through Marjorie Bruce, and it will pass away again through this new daughter when she marries. What is her name, anyway? Princess . . .'

King James turned his face to the wall. For a moment there was silence and then his physician looked up.

'My lords, the King is dead. The baby will never be a princess. She will be Queen, and her mother has named her Mary.'

Mary, Queen of Scotland, Lord Huntly and every other noble there thought. But for how long?

The deep gloom of December 1542 and the deep gloom of mourning had shrouded Linlithgow Palace, the traditional place for Scottish royal confinements, where Marie de Guise had not long ago given birth.

But as soon as she heard the news of her husband's death

34

she insisted on getting up. She had work to do. She went and sat by the cradle, rocked it gently and considered her position.

'Oh,' Lady Huntly said, entering the room, 'should you be up out of your bed so soon?'

'My daughter is already a queen. I must be ready to defend her, for there is no one else. But – come and look at her, my dear! Come and sit beside me.'

Outside, howling winds blew the snow sideways. Wind and snow battled to see which would penetrate the thick walls of the castle first, and both succeeded in gaining entry through the merest crack. But Marie had ordered fires to be kept burning continually, and now as the two women watched, a rosy glow outlined the tiny sleeping face of the new Queen.

'How fair-skinned she is!' Lady Huntly smiled. 'Her skin is so fair that it is almost transparent. You can even see the tracery of the veins beneath it.'

'Yes. Her skin is so delicate that it must always be clothed in the finest silk. I will see to that,' Marie said, gently pushing back the baby's cap. 'I have been trying to see the colour of her hair, but it is so very fine.'

At that, the little Queen woke up. She opened her eyes, those slanted Stewart eyes so like her father's, and let out a wail.

'She's hungry,' Marie said, lifting her out of the cradle.

'Hungry and healthy,' Lady Huntly laughed and took her out of her mother's arms. 'You want to know the colour of her hair? Look!' She held the child up between the Queen Mother and the brilliant snowy light from the window. 'What do you see?'

'A glow. A golden glow,' Marie said, calling for the wet nurse, and the baby was removed.

'She will have a fair complexion and beautiful red hair,' Lady Huntly said as they stared after her, 'and *of course* you want to defend her. All Scotland wants to defend her. But how are we going to do that?'

'Shortly I will put the arrangements in motion. We cannot

stay here in Linlithgow for long, without all our belongings. We cannot go back to Holyrood. That is a palace almost defenceless, while Henry of England is coming up from the Borders at this very moment. Soon he will be barking at the door, like the ferocious wolf he is. The best place to take the baby Queen is Stirling Castle.'

'Stirling Castle! Well, neither Henry nor anyone else will overcome it, perched on rocks so high that it seems like a castle in the clouds!'

'Mary may spend all her childhood there, if necessary. I want her to be a secure and happy child.'

'Can she be happy without other children to play with, Majesty?'

'Of course, I shall take all my husband's children with me.'

'You mean the illegitimate children?' Lady Huntly asked, scandalised. 'Forgive me, Your Majesty, but is that wise?'

'I believe it will be best if they enjoy all the privileges of a royal upbringing along with my daughter. In that way none of them will resent her. Also, I visualise the little Queen being brought up with other little girls of much the same age. They will come with their mothers to Stirling Castle, and they will all be Marys, rosebuds surrounding the Rose of Scotland.'

Lady Huntly felt as though the breath had been knocked clean out of her body. '*All Marys?*' she gasped.

And here she was, without a single daughter, herself . . . And with no prospect of one either. But she would put that right at once.

'Yes, my dear. *All Marys.* Now, can you stay on and then journey north to Stirling with us?'

'I beg your pardon, Your Majesty.' Lady Huntly, having thought quickly, lied through her teeth. 'But you see, we want to be back in Strathbogie as soon as you can spare me. My lord insists on it. He fears I may lose our next child, as I lost the last.'

'Oh, I hope the little Queen's birth has not been too much for you!'

'Thank you. I feel quite well, so far. Only I long now to be at home...'

'And when I get there,' she added to herself, 'I will pray day and night for a daughter to be one of the little Marys, for Marie is sure to choose a child of mine after all I've done for her.'

A little Mary could be next door to the very crown of Scotland itself. Crown fever was upon Lady Huntly. Crown fever had long ago been upon her husband, she knew that. Apart from women the one thought in his mind had always been to extend his lands and thus his power until he was master of all. He was no different from every other noble in Scotland. They all wanted to be near the helpless little Queen, with only a woman to defend her, ready to snatch the crown at the first opportunity. Now, without realising it, Lady Huntly herself was joining them.

And she possessed powers of her own.

SIX

The day was hot, like each successive day that summer of 1543. In the stone-flagged kitchen of the Gardeners' Cottage the door was set back on its hinges and the tiny window flung wide open in a desperate plea for the merest rush of air. As the morning wore on the heat became suffocating.

It was no cooler in the shade of the apple tree, either. When Abbie looked up through the leaves the sky had become strangely yellow. She pretended to be playing with her rag doll, but all the time she was watching her mother from under the lashes of her almond-shaped golden eyes, watching and waiting.

Mistress Abigail McCracken was watching too, though she had one eye on her young son at her feet. She was watching the weather anxiously as she continued to snip long stems of herbs and tie them up in bunches to be dried, but when the baby wailed she got up off her knees to go and attend to him, taking the toddler with her. As soon as she disappeared around the corner of the door Abbie seized her chance and squeezed out through a hole in the hedge. She had been eyeing it for days.

And oh, it was wonderful to be free! She ran up and down the gentle hills of the Strathbogie estate, and when she fell, which was often, she simply rolled and rolled until she came to the bottom. Somewhere her white cap flew off, but she didn't care. Abbie had never had so much fun in all her three and a half years and it got better and better when her latest roll took her to the edge of a path which went right round

Strathbogie Castle itself, which so far she had only seen from the back, and from a distance.

A boy appeared out of one of the side doors, carrying a wooden pail by its handle of string. He seemed quite old to Abbie, and far too big for her, but he was better than nothing when there was nobody else to play with, in any case. She bestowed one of her best smiles on him, for just lately she had found out that if she bared as many of her milk teeth as she could, people smiled back and she usually got her own way.

'You can play with me if you like,' she offered grandly. 'You can be my friend.'

'Friend? Ho, ho, you'd be lucky! I'm the best friend anyone could ever have,' he assured her, laughing. 'Besides, I have to work.'

So her best smile hadn't worked, after all . . . She gazed at him uncertainly. He was barefoot, the same as she, and his clothes were torn and shabby. But his hair was black and glossy, his eyes were merry and blue, and unhesitatingly she believed everything he said implicitly. For some reason she trusted him instinctively and wholeheartedly, so she tried again.

'I'll come with you, then,' she said. 'What's your name?'

'Donald.'

'Where do you live?'

'In there,' he jerked his head at the barracks and strode off.

She trotted after him until they came to a small shed, surrounded by mud and enclosed within a wall built out of the same yellow stone as all the other buildings at Strathbogie Castle. Enraptured, Abbie didn't notice the smell.

'What are you doing?' she asked him.

'What does it look like?' Donald demanded, tipping the contents of his pail into a trough and immediately, fat and filthy, the once-pink pigs were grunting over it. Abbie had never seen anything like it before.

'Is this your work?' she asked.

'Yes. I'm the pig-boy. Of course, I'm a very special pig-boy. Lord Huntly said so. After all, it's not every pig-boy who's spoken to the King!' Donald swaggered around the sty.

Abbie had heard her parents talking about the King, but she thought he was dead, and there was a baby Queen now. 'To the *King*?'

'He was here when I was seven, for a hunt.'

Not too sure what a hunt was, Abbie pursued the point of this conversation relentlessly. 'What was he like?'

'He was a very nice man. He spoke to everybody, but he gave *me* a gold piece,' he said, fishing around in his pocket and pulling out a few conkers, a shell, a twist of string and some grey crumbs which may once have been a cake. 'Yes, here it is,' he showed her a tiny golden coin. 'My grandmother wanted it, but she never got it, and I'll never spend it either, because every time I look at it I see King Jamie, with his red hair and all his golden necklaces.'

Abbie hung over the wall of the sty, smiling at the pigs and completely enchanted with this special boy until a terrible noise came from somewhere nearby. It seemed to be coming from high up. 'Listen!' she said. 'What's that? Is it thunder?'

'Thunder? No, that's not thunder. It's Lord and Lady Huntly, at it again, having a quarrel. You know – the master and mistress?'

She nodded her head uncertainly and Donald looked at her intently for the first time. 'What did you say your name was?'

'Abbie McCracken.'

'John McCracken's bairn? You've run away, haven't you? You'd better go home before your mother finds out you've been talking to the pig-boy!'

'No! No! I'm coming with you!' Trustingly, Abbie placed her hand into her new-found friend's grubby paw and pulled him as best she could towards the noise. She didn't tell him that her parents had expressly forbidden her to go anywhere near Strathbogie and to her delight, Donald dragged her right round the castle to the front of it where she had never been

40

before, where a lot of people were gathering. The towns-people were stopping in the street below to listen to the screams and roars and the crashing of doors that were coming from Strathbogie Castle.

Towering and golden on its hill, on this hot day its casements were flung back, with the result that every word that George Gordon, the Earl of Huntly, shouted at his wife and every word she yelled back could be heard a long way off, to the vast entertainment of the crowd.

Just when they had been thinking that the bad old days were gone for ever, they muttered to each other. When the Huntlys had been so lovey-dovey for so long! And her with a new-born baby too!

'Come on!'

Skilfully steering a path between the grown-ups' legs Donald dragged Abbie to the front of the crowd and pulled her up to stand on the wall beside him. In her excitement she jigged up and down, off one foot and onto the other, holding on to Donald's hand for grim death while the battle raged on inside the castle.

It had all begun softly and quietly with Lady Huntly gazing up at her lord from her childbed with tears of joy in her eyes. 'Oh, George,' she said. 'Just what I wanted, a little girl, fit to be the Queen's lady.'

Lord Huntly took the baby in his arms, opened the shawl, which was all she had around her, and examined her from head to foot. From her heart-shaped Gordon face down to her tiny toes she was perfect.

'You will grow up to be a very important lady yourself,' he told the infant, 'not only here in the north, but in all Scotland. Won't you, my little love?' He tickled her tiny chin and then kissed her. 'Yes, you will be Lady Jean Gordon, a very important person indeed.'

In the utter, awful shock of it Lady Huntly felt a great clot of blood falling from between her legs onto the drawsheet. One half of her mind considered that this was probably part of the afterbirth not properly released by the midwife. In that case, it was a good thing that it had come away now. At a higher level the other half of her mind tried to believe her ears, and the blood of fury rose to her head.

Had she just endured nine months of misery, weaving every spell she knew, and taking every hideous concoction she could think of to ensure the birth of a daughter – a little Mary – all for nothing, in the end?

Had she married a complete idiot, after all? Could he not see beyond the end of his own fat nose? Was he content to be a small king here in the north of Scotland for ever? When the whole country could be his, if they played their cards right? *Jean*? What next? She took a deep breath.

'*Lady Jean*?' she screeched. 'Her name is Mary! Of course it is Mary! I insist upon Mary!'

Lord Huntly clutched his daughter to him and reeled back against one of the windows. '*Mary*?' he roared. 'Wherever did you get that idea?'

'Don't you understand?' his wife shouted. 'She *must* be Mary! The Queen Mother is going to surround baby Queen Mary with other little Marys to be her ladies-in-waiting when the time comes. All the great Houses in Scotland are naming their baby daughters Mary to be in with a chance of being at court . . . What use is Jean? Ohhh!' she wailed and sobbed.

'*They* can all do as they like,' he bellowed, scarlet-faced and angrier than his wife had ever seen him, 'but the first-born daughter of a Gordon is always Jean, and our little girl will follow a proud tradition – the Gordon tradition!'

'There is more at stake here than the Gordon tradition!' Lady Huntly screamed, lifting the large jug beside her bed and aiming it at her husband, but even with so large a target she missed, and instead the jug crashed against the wall while the baby added her howls to the commotion. 'It is a place in the sun! A place next to the throne! Perhaps leading to the very throne itself!'

'And how do you make *that* out, may I ask?'

'The lords of Scotland are all Stewarts, are they not? Every

42

lord can claim the blood above or below the blanket, and they would slit each other's throats to get at the throne. The new little Queen is only the first among equals. The Queen Mother has lost two sons already in infancy. Who is to say what might happen to Mary, Queen of Scots next? And then, who will succeed?'

'Your imagination is running away with you, Elizabeth.'

'It could happen, and *something* must be done before any harm comes to the little Queen, and that bastard, Lord James Stewart, steps in. You have as much right as he has. It is a claim to the throne we should be staking, and if our daughter were already established in Edinburgh we should be halfway there!'

'I have my own ways of belling the cat,' Lord Huntly said coldly, and then addressed his daughter again. 'Never you mind, little lass,' he boomed. 'Your own mother has just missed murdering you with that jug, but nothing will come over Lady Jean Gordon so long as her father is here!'

With that he placed the baby back in her mother's arms and marched out, slamming the door so that the very roof vibrated and the baby screamed louder than ever. Within ten seconds he was crashing the door open again and coming back to his wife's bedside.

'Elizabeth,' he said, his face an even deeper crimson, 'I allowed you to name our sons. I have named our daughter, so let that be the end of it.'

'Let me out of here!' Lady Huntly screeched. 'I'm not staying here! I will go somewhere else where I can call my own daughter anything I like – and that will be Mary!'

With the baby in one arm she flung back the covers with the other and Lord Huntly saw from the blood on the bed and by the pallor of her face that this was now an emergency, and one that must be terminated at once before any more damage was done. He called for the midwife to remove the baby while he forcibly held his wife down.

'I'll hold her,' he then directed the midwife, 'while you get a sleeping draught. She is beside herself. Now,' he said when

43

the midwife came back, 'I'll prise open her jaws and you'll pour it down. It should work in a few minutes . . .'

With the last of her senses Lady Huntly made one last desperate attempt to make her husband see sense. 'Dearest George,' she flattered him drowsily, 'you are so powerful . . . And as a Catholic perhaps the only true and loyal lord the infant Queen possesses . . . She has so many enemies, and none worse than here in Scotland . . .'

'She's sleeping now,' Lord Huntly said. 'I shall take my daughter to the priest in the chapel of Strathbogie and have her christened Jean Gordon in the name of the Father, the Son and the Holy Ghost this very minute. After that there is nothing that my wife or anyone else can do about it.'

Abbie hadn't understood one word of the quarrel but she had enjoyed every moment of it, standing there with Donald. They watched as a very big, fat man with a red face, dressed in green velvet, crashed out of Strathbogie's doors with his baby in his arms and made his way across to the chapel.

As if in sympathy the heavens crashed too in the first peals of thunder, and opened to pelt down a deluge of rain. The people were scattering as Abbie was snatched out of Donald's hand by her angry, frightened mother who was clutching her own howling baby Jackson under her arm with the toddler, Jonathon, holding on in a piggyback.

She was panting, Abbie saw, and her cap was all askew. That meant she had been running, and she hadn't even taken off her gardening apron of coarse sacking in her haste. To appear in public like that, and her the wife of Captain John McCracken too, was something her mother would never normally have dreamed of doing, and Abbie's heart sank.

She was in trouble.

SEVEN

It hadn't mattered how much Abbie beamed and smiled at her mother for the next hour, even with the tears rolling down her face at the same time. Abigail refused to be charmed.

'You must never run away again,' she said sternly, stripping off her daughter's wet clothes. 'You must stay here at the Gardeners' Cottage with us. In particular, you must never go near Strathbogie Castle. I've told you before.'

'No, Mother, I won't . . . But why not?'

'Because, as you've found out for yourself, it only leads to trouble.'

'You mean, because of Donald? Is it because he's poor and dirty?'

Abigail sighed. 'No, Abbie. Donald can't help being poor and dirty. He has no mother or father to look after him.'

Abbie turned this over in her mind for a minute or two. 'He could come and live with us,' she suggested.

'No,' her mother said firmly, 'he could not. He lives in the barracks now. He used to live in the castle with his grand-mother before she died. She was the cook there before this one came. She hasn't got time to look after him – and it takes time and a lot of hard work to look after children, you know,' she added, clucking her tongue. 'Just look at your hair! I'll have to wash it too!'

But after Abbie was clean again, Abigail relented and took her in her arms. 'Oh, Abbie! Abbie!' she said, rocking her back and fore, while to Abbie's horror a great fat tear rolled down her mother's cheek before she dashed it away and tried to smile again. 'Always tell me where you're going, after this.'

'I will, Mother,' Abbie promised, quite frightened now, and sensing her mother's fear. There was something her mother wasn't telling her, she was sure of that.

'Well, little Jackson's gone to sleep at last, and Jonathon's having his nap. Take your doll and I'll sit outside with you until your hair dries in the sun. It's come out to shine again.'

Abbie dressed her doll with the tiny clothes her mother had sewed so painstakingly, and then she gathered leaves to make her a bed. Not content with that she looked for stones she could pretend were chairs and a table. She would make a whole house! She was absorbed in her game, and as she played her hair dried out from the wet brown it had been to a golden red, with glittering blue glints where the sun caught the edges of her waves and curls.

At the sight of it Abigail's tears threatened again. Her eyes strayed to Strathbogie, and her thoughts strayed to the first time she had ever come to the Gardeners' Cottage, nearly five years ago. How innocent she had been then!

She came out of her reverie to find Abbie still playing with her doll, and John coming down the garden path. 'Abbie,' she said, 'here's your father,' watching her child's sturdy little legs running to meet him, and listening to his beloved booming laugh.

'Who loves me?' he asked, picking Abbie up and swinging her round.

'I do, Father, best in all the world!' Abbie laughed back. 'And Mother! And Donald, too!'

'Donald?' John gave Abigail a questioning look.

'She ran away today, John, and I found her with Donald, just filthy. They had been at the pigsty. I've told her not to go with him again.'

'Don't be too hard on poor Donald, my dear,' John said gently. 'He's had a terrible life for a boy who is still only eleven years old.'

'Yes,' Abigail sighed sadly.

'Perhaps we may allow him to come here instead, now and

46

then? Lord Huntly has simply thrown him into the barracks. The boy doesn't know what a proper home is like.'

How could she resist her husband's kindly entreaties, and Abbie's pleading eyes? Abigail could not. 'What does he get to eat?' she asked.

'Not much, as far as I can see,' John said. 'Scraps from the soldiers, and perhaps the cook spares him some milk. He's very thin, as you saw, and stretching every day. He must often be hungry.'

It was more than Abigail's tender heart could bear. 'Then bring him whenever you can, John, and we'll see how we get on.'

'You'll mind your manners,' John told Donald sternly. 'And no swearing.'

'Yes, sir,' Donald said as he stepped into the Gardeners' Cottage for the first time, and straight into Abigail's heart, although she didn't show it.

But Abbie knew, by the way she called him 'dearie' and gave him small jobs to do about the place. If she was a good girl, she was sure her mother would allow her to play with him. So Abbie tried her very best, and as for Donald, there was a haven now occasionally for him with the kindly McCrackens. It was a privilege he was careful never to abuse. Mistress Abigail was a lovely lady, even if Abbie was a perfect little pest.

Donald became Abbie's dearest friend whether he liked it or not. She followed him about faithfully from pigsty to castle door and then back again, for even though he lived in the barracks, he still had to feed the pigs and do other work in the Home Farm. She shadowed him at every turn.

Then one day he was nowhere to be seen. Abbie searched all his usual haunts, all the barns and all the stables, but she couldn't find him until she climbed one of the little hills – and there he was! He was walking along the path bordered by huge chestnuts and talking to another youth of about the same age and height as himself.

47

Joyfully she ran to meet them, only to be waved aside by Donald's hand. He didn't even halt in his conversation with the other boy who was splendidly dressed in a dark red velvet doublet with a feathered cap to match over his black shiny hair. He wore black hose and black leather shoes with pointed toes, and he seemed to be the best of friends with Donald, who today was subtly different.

She realised that he was wearing different clothes. He was in a Gordon uniform that her father must have dug out for him. He almost fitted it. With a start, Abbie saw that Donald had grown at such a rate recently that he was halfway to becoming a man.

Of course, she told herself, it was only her imagination, but facially at least, the two youths were very alike. If they had let her speak to them she would have told them so, but they strode on, and talked on, and paid no attention to her whatsoever.

Abbie had never been so offended in her life, nor so wounded, when she crept back to the Gardeners' Cottage.

'What's the matter?' her mother asked, and offered no sympathy when she told her.

'That was Earl Huntly's son, young Lord George, who Donald was speaking to. I saw them too. What you must understand, Abbie, is that men and boys like each other's company,' she said. 'They have one life. Women and girls have another, and it's time now for you to be helping me, instead. You can start by weeding the pansies, and you know how to do it. You've watched me often enough.'

So Abbie began to help her mother from time to time and saw Donald less and less, until John McCracken came home one day and announced that there was a spare Shetland pony in the stables. He had given Donald the task of teaching John and Adam Gordon to ride.

'And it would be a good idea if he taught Abbie at the same time,' he told Abigail. 'Most people have to ride a horse at some time or other if they want to get about. It would be very useful to her, and she'll never learn younger.'

'Oh, *Father*!' Abbie said excitedly, flinging her arms around his neck and giving him a kiss.

It was a wonderful idea and a wonderful adventure to Abbie, especially when she would get to see her beloved Donald nearly every day now, although she still wasn't pleased with him for snubbing her.

'You don't look too happy,' she informed him coldly the first afternoon. 'I suppose that's because Lord George hasn't come out to play?'

'You're wrong, Abbie. Lord George hardly ever comes out to play. He is always too busy with his tutors – which is where I wish these two were as well,' he added in a whisper, nodding his head at the young Gordon boys. 'That day you saw me with him was one day in a thousand for us, worse luck, because I like him. He's the best of all the Gordons.'

'Oh, Donald!' she said, all her affection for him flooding back now that he had explained himself. 'Well, never mind. I won't give you any trouble.'

'This pony is called Misty,' he told her, lifting her up and leading her around very slowly. 'She's kept for the youngest Gordon children as a rule. But John and Adam are too big for her.'

Abbie soon saw that neither of the two boys was going to make a good rider whatever horse he rode. John was too rough, and his younger brother, Adam, was too scared, and as the days went on they all three fell off at one time or another. John roared and cried and stamped about angrily, Adam snivelled miserably, and Abbie pushed back her tears and kept going. Not for anything would she let Donald think she was a crybaby, and she got her reward when after six months he gave her his highest praise.

'You're not bad, for a girl,' he said.

Lady Huntly did not totally reject her baby, but she utterly rejected her husband again. If he came into the room she looked right through him and would not speak to him. She became sullen, and never addressed the child as anything other than 'Baby'. She spent long periods of time sobbing and in general plunged her husband and everyone else in the castle into the deepest gloom along with her, a gloom which Lord Huntly strove in vain to dispel. Just lately he had been adopting the habit of voicing his thoughts to his wife, speaking at her, even if she never seemed to hear, and certainly never answered. Today he was reminiscing about the Coronation.

'Queen Mary, only nine months old at the time!' he said. 'How they balanced the crown on such a little head, I shall never know. Even Robert the Bruce's circlet of gold would have been too much. But now it is enclosed by more gold, so it is heavier still and studded with jewels. And such tiny hands to grasp the sceptre!

'Of course, it was another Scottish act of pure defiance, another one after we broke Henry of England's betrothal of his son, Edward, with our little Queen. Now that we are showing Henry that we will have nothing to do with him or the English, let me tell you what is bound to happen next. He will unleash his fury – wait and see.'

They did not have long to wait and see. Henry sent an army north with orders to blaze a trail of havoc and waste all the way to Stirling Castle, and from there to capture Mary and bring her back to England. To Henry, it was all very straightforward, and his soldiers did as they were told, destroying all the Border abbeys on the way until they came to Edinburgh, to Holyrood Abbey itself.

They broke into the Stewart tomb, found the body of Mary's father, James V, in his coffin, tore it out and left it abandoned on the ground. Nothing was sacred to the English. But Stirling Castle proved too much for them. It was impregnable and in the end the soldiers were forced to go back empty-handed to a growling, ferocious Henry VIII.

Yet something rose up like a phoenix out of the appalling ashes of Scotland, something that its people grasped, for there was nothing else. The hand of God was held out to them directly. His missionary, William Tyndale, translated the

Scriptures in a new Protestant version, and from it God spoke to them directly, too, in a new dawn where there was a glimmer of hope, and help, at last.

Lady Huntly had had plenty of time to brood and think as events unfolded. Her own daughter would survive up here in the far north. The English would never get past the Gordons. But the infant Queen! That was a different matter. She might not survive to realise the Queen Mother's dream, to be surrounded by Marys . . . Not that there was another little Mary at Strathbogie to sit at the Queen's feet.

The Countess grew tired of brooding at last, when she looked out of her window and saw that the spring flowers were actually blooming now in May after the dreadful winter. As far as she was concerned this whole past year had been dreadful, ever since her daughter's christening . . . But life went on. The buds were bursting on the trees and fresh green leaves were peeping out. It filled her with a longing to get outside and go for a walk, perhaps as far as the Gardeners' Cottage, to see Abigail's gardens again. On a sudden impulse she sent for Maggie May.

'Yes, my lady?'

Even now, Lady Huntly could hardly bear to call her daughter by name. 'We will take Baby out for an airing this morning. Get her ready.'

'Yes, my lady,' the young nursemaid said, and a few minutes later reappeared with the little girl.

'Down to the Gardeners' Cottage,' Lady Huntly directed, walking on ahead.

Behind her, Lady Jean clung to her nursemaid's hand and toddled along as best she could. When she faltered Maggie May picked her up and walked quickly with her in her arms until she caught up with the Countess, when she set her down again.

'You may go,' Lady Huntly told Maggie May when they neared the cottage. 'I shall visit Mistress Abigail for half an hour. Then, come back for us.'

There was a young girl, perhaps four or five years old,

playing about outside the door. She must be John and Abigail's daughter. She was a pretty child with red-gold hair and slanting brown eyes that were at once innocent and yet strangely penetrating.

'Who are you, child?' she asked.

'Abbie McCracken.'

'Yes . . . I brought you into the world.' Lady Huntly looked down impatiently at her own child, grizzling miserably now that Maggie May had deserted her. She picked her up and sighed as Abigail appeared in the doorway.

'What's her name?' Abbie asked the one question which could not have pained the Countess more.

'Jean,' she replied shortly.

'Lady Jean Gordon,' Abigail interpreted. 'You must call her Lady Jean, Abbie. Won't you come inside, my lady? We have two sons as well now – Jonathon, and Jackson, who is about Lady Jean's age.'

'*Sons!* Oh, they are so much less trouble!'

'But not so pretty,' Abigail smiled nervously. 'Come away in. Perhaps Lady Jean will stop crying when she sees the children.'

Lady Jean howled on, paying no attention whatsoever to the two little boys, the younger now staggering about the kitchen, while Abbie stared at her longingly. Her mother was holding her so awkwardly and disdainfully away from her that both Abbie and Abigail suspected the same thing. Lady Huntly didn't really like her baby.

'I wish I could hold her,' Abbie said.

'Oh, Abbie!' Abigail said reprovingly.

'Here, take her!' Lady Huntly offered Abbie the baby.

'Then sit down first,' Abigail said, and in a flustered apology, 'She's quite good with babies, my lady. She's had plenty of practice.'

'Yes, but this one is different,' Abbie said, cuddling the little one, and almost at once Lady Jean stopped crying, cooing and prattling up at Abbie in her baby language instead. 'She's so dainty.'

Lady Huntly gazed at Abbie in surprise and with suspicion, and she examined her face more closely. What was the reason for her immediate bonding with Lady Jean? Abbie McCracken would be about the right age, conceived about the time when she had gone to help her sister, and she had had her own miscarriage. Could this be a bond of blood? Were these two girls half-sisters? Had Abigail been the unfortunate girl her husband had bairned while she was away?

But Abigail looked back at her, clear-eyed, and Lady Huntly recalled how proud a father John McCracken had been. Abbie had some of the look of Abigail about her, although there was absolutely no resemblance to John McCracken. Lady Huntly supposed, looking at all that red hair, that Abbie must be a throwback to someone in John's or Abigail's parentage, and she recovered a little and accepted a cup of buttermilk and one of Abigail's cakes while she watched Abbie's inexplicable rapport with her daughter.

They were in a world of their own, the baby waving her little hands and laughing, and Abbie persistently patting her shawl and tucking it around her more securely before she looked up again. 'She likes being cuddled,' she said. 'I wish I could cuddle her and look after her all the time.'

'*Abbie McCracken!*' Abigail said, scandalised, when the visitors had gone.

Abbie hung her head all the way through her mother's reprimand. Then she raised her tear-filled eyes. 'I couldn't help it, Mother. I just loved that little baby. I wish she was my sister.'

But on the way back to the castle, Lady Huntly was brooding again. She no longer suspected that Abbie McCracken might be one of the Gordon bastards, but the child had disturbed her and stirred up a lot of mud again. There could never be another royal child for her to deliver now. She didn't think Queen Marie would ever marry again to have more.

So bang went her one last chance and excuse to be at court again.

She had fought and fought for it – and more for Lord Huntly's sake than for her own. But she had lost the battle, thanks to that bloody husband of hers.

EIGHT

Eighteen months later, when Lady Jean was running about everywhere, her favourite ploy was to escape from Strathbogie and make her way to the Gardeners' Cottage along the path her nursemaid had taken her many times to visit Abigail and her children.

'Look, Mother!' Abbie cried. 'She has come herself again! Oh,' she said, running out to lift the little creature into her arms, 'look at her, Mother!'

'I see her,' Abigail said. 'And now, once more, you must return her immediately to her mother. When she discovers that Lady Jean is missing there will be trouble.'

Lady Jean kept going back to Abbie, and every time Abbie faithfully returned her to Strathbogie Castle.

'Why does she do it when she has two perfectly good brothers here to play with?' Lady Huntly demanded.

'Because they are too rough, your ladyship,' Abbie said bravely. 'She is too little to want to ride horses yet, or climb trees. She wants to make mud pies instead.'

'Mud pies? I never heard the like! And down by the river, I suppose you will tell me next?'

'It's a place where there's hardly any water,' Abbie pleaded.

'Well, well. But she's got to learn to ride sometime, you know. In the meantime I shall send old Florrie to watch over the pair of you. It would never do if the Earl of Huntly lost his precious daughter, would it?'

Abbie knew this was meant to be a joke, but there was no smile in Lady Huntly's eyes when she said it, and a cold shiver of fear for Lady Jean went down Abbie's back. But she held her ground, even if she wasn't yet six.

'I'll look after her, my lady,' she said. 'Sometimes we collect pebbles from the edge of the Bogie and put them under the bushes for the fairies to find. Lady Jean believes in fairies.'

'Does she, indeed?' her mother sniffed.

'And witches, as well,' Abbie said innocently, not for a minute dreaming that she had just set one of her small feet on the very perimeter of the paranormal before she turned away.

That girl! Lady Huntly thought, watching her running off. Well, she's only a child, and the child of two of our own tied servants, at that. If and when the time comes, I'll soon put Abbie McCracken in her place!

Abbie was seven when her mother proudly placed her third son in the cradle John McCracken had originally made for her, and called him Johnny.

'Jonathon, Jackson and now Johnny?' Abbie asked, leaning over the cradle to examine the new baby.

'All after your father,' Abigail agreed, 'and they couldn't be named after a better man. The only pity is that he has had to go away on another escort, and us with a new-born child in the house.'

'Where has he gone this time?'

'To Holyrood Palace in Edinburgh where the Queen Mother is holding a garden party. Lord and Lady Huntly have gone and taken all their children with them, Lord George, Mr John, Mr Adam and even Lady Jean.'

'What's a garden party?'

'A great big party, so big that the guests spill out of the castle or palace and onto the lawns. All the most important people in Scotland will be there, to pay their respects to the little Queen.'

'Well, I'll go and play with Donald, then.'

'Donald has gone with your father and the rest of the Gordons.'

56

'Oh . . .' said Abbie, deeply disappointed. 'He'll see the little Queen then – and I won't!'

'I suppose so, along with her ladies-in-waiting, the four Marys.'

'There's nobody left to play with,' Abbie moaned.

'There are always your brothers,' Abigail reminded her.

'Mother, they don't want to play with *me*. They only want to play with each other. They think I'm different,' Abbie frowned.

Abigail took a deep shuddering breath. So the time and the opportunity had come at last, and she had a duty to do.

'Yes,' she said, 'you *are* different from them, and by now you must have seen it for yourself whenever you look in the mirror.'

Abbie had never thought about it, and now suddenly, seeing the tears in her mother's eyes, she didn't want to know. But Abigail carried on gently, even relentlessly.

'This is a dead secret I am going to tell you now, Abbie. We wouldn't want you to tell anyone else. But you see, dearie, although John McCracken is the father who loves you so much, he is not your natural father.'

'Then who is?'

'A beautiful young nobleman who came here once. I loved him and he said he loved me. But then he left me.'

'Who?'

'I didn't realise it at the time,' Abigail wept, 'for he called himself Jamie. But it turned out he was King James. James Fifth of Scotland – the dead King now.'

Abbie considered this for a long time, and her mother saw with utter relief that she did so quite calmly. 'But does it make any difference?' she asked at last.

'Dearest wee lassie – none at all to me, or to John McCracken!'

'Then it doesn't matter at all.' Abbie wound her arms around her mother's neck and kissed away her tears. 'But it still means I've nobody to play with!'

* * *

No sound of her father's return woke Abbie that night, or the next night or the one following that, and every morning she sighed along with her mother when he didn't return, until at last, a week later, tired and saddle-sore, the Huntlys came back and John McCracken and the Gordon soldiers and Donald with them.

'Did you see Queen Mary?' Abbie asked eagerly.

John laughed wearily. 'I did catch a glimpse of her, although the garden party was cancelled at the last minute because of terrible news –'

'What is she like?' Abbie interrupted.

'Almost as tall already as you are, child, but as thin as a wisp of hay, with long red hair, a long thin face and very long hands, to match.'

'And she squeaks like a mouse when she talks,' Donald added.

'Stop pestering the men,' Abigail said. 'They're tired, and they're needing something to eat. What terrible news, John?'

'From England – where else? Henry the Eighth still wants the little Queen to marry his son, Edward, and unite the two kingdoms, though the marriage of our Catholic Queen to a Protestant prince would be a blasphemy and a black day for all Scots of the True Faith. The Queen Mother's spies reported that English soldiers were on the march north again to come and get her.'

'You mean coming to snatch the Queen of Scotland? Our Queen?' Abigail asked incredulously.

'Yes. So the Queen Mother stopped the party, and decided then and there to decamp out of Holyrood Palace for good, bag and baggage, and take Queen Mary and her little court to Stirling Castle. No English soldiers will get to her there! It's up on the top of a very high rock. There were hundreds of other Scottish soldiers, but the Gordons were at the edge of the escort to Stirling.'

'The dangerous edge,' Abigail said fiercely. 'The outside edge. Why is it always so?'

'So, you see, I hardly saw the little Queen, Abbie,' John

smiled at her. By now, he had given up all hope of having a real daughter of his own. All their children would be boys, fat and fair, just the same as these three. It made him love Abbie all the more.

'Well,' he laughed and picked up his new son, 'we're going to need a bigger house at this rate. I'll ask permission to extend the cottage.'

'Where will you get the stones, Father?' Abbie asked a week later, trailing behind him, for that day she had nothing better to do. Lady Jean had failed to turn up since her trip to see the Queen.

'Down by the Bogie. There are plenty of boulders by the sides of the stream. I'll get a horse and two panniers to put them in first.'

Abbie dogged her father's footsteps but there wasn't much she could do to help. Then the next time they came back with the boulders they found Donald lying on the grass taking his ease and sucking a blade of grass. He took the grass out of his mouth and grinned at John.

'It's my day off,' he said. 'I thought I'd come and watch.'

'Or you could play with me,' Abbie said. 'I've nothing to play at today.'

'Oh? Where's Lady Jean, then?'

'I don't know,' Abbie said miserably.

'Well, cheer up!' Donald smiled. 'You can run and fetch something for me instead.' He whispered in her ear and Abbie came back with a stonemason's hammer.

'Oh, yes,' John grunted as he heaved up one of the heavy stones. 'And what do you propose to do with that, Donald MacLaren?'

'My father was a stonemason.'

'Oh, *was* he?' John smiled. 'How do you know?'

Immediately, he regretted asking such a cruel question. Poor Donald, he thought, the illegitimate son of Lord Huntly and a mother he couldn't remember! He must have been very unhappy sleeping in the straw under the kitchen table of

Strathbogie. That terrible old Mistress MacLaren berated him every day for ever being born, for being a millstone around her neck.

John believed that, helpless in the teeth of it all, Donald's only self-defence had been in the cultivation of a second skin, a hard veneer. It was the only way that Mistress MacLaren's verbal and physical abuse had bounced off him, and it was still standing him in good stead, for he was proving very popular in the barracks, keeping the men laughing with his antics and his impossible stories.

'Well, anyway,' Donald answered him, not in the least put out, 'I know how to build a wall, which is more than you do, by the look of things. You'll have to chip the stones into some kind of shape before you begin. Here,' he got up lazily, rolled up his sleeves and winked at Abbie. 'Let me show you.'

By the end of the day they had got three walls almost built and Abbie was exhausted running about and picking up the chippings.

'I've got another day off tomorrow,' Donald said casually, and John didn't argue. The boy had never taken a day off in his life before, either from the Home Farm or from the troop.

'Well, *I* haven't,' he said heavily as they parted company.

The next evening when John came back wearied by his duties there was milk on the table and newly fired and crumbly oatcakes thickly spread with butter, fresh-churned by Abigail that morning.

'Donald said to tell you to come with straw tomorrow morning, Father,' Abbie said. 'Lady Jean still hasn't come, so I was helping him most of today when you were away. Now that he's a Gordon, I like him best of all the soldiers, Father. He's cheeky, but he makes me laugh.'

That was an accurate assessment, coming from a child of seven. John gazed at her, astonished.

'He's finished the walls, Father.'

'Finished the walls? Already?'

'And besides that, he knows how to thatch the roof as

60

well. He says his uncle was a thatcher,' Abbie said importantly, turning away to wash the platters.

'And he's full of shit, as usual,' John muttered to Abigail.

'He's an expert with the weather, too,' Abbie added from
the other side of the room, quite annoyed with her parents
for whispering and laughing. 'And he said to tell you to hurry
with the straw, Father. He had a look at the sky and saw
rain coming!'

'Oh, I can see he makes a deep impression,' John smiled.

'Don't tease her,' Abigail warned in a whisper. 'Some
impressions go very deep with our Abbie.'

'Oh yes, he has,' Abbie replied airily. 'I'm going to marry
him when I grow up.'

'Oh, yes? And does Donald know that?'

'Not yet, but he will.'

Lady Jean did not appear all the rest of that week, and every
day Abbie became more and more alarmed. 'What can be
wrong, Mother?' she kept asking.

'I don't know. She could be ill, a wee lassie like that, trailed
all the way to Edinburgh for that garden party.'

'Something's wrong,' Abbie agreed. 'So if she hasn't come
by tonight I'm going up to the castle to see what it is. Please
say I may, Mother.'

'Well, I don't suppose you'll rest otherwise,' Abigail agreed.

It took for ever to gain admission to Strathbogie that night,
and it was only because her name was McCracken that Abbie
got past the night guards who had never seen her before.
From there it was easy to find her way to the first floor and
the sleeping quarters of the Gordon family, by way of the
burning tapers in the passages. She was drawn to the open
door of a brightly lit room, and she knew she was in the
right place when she heard the rasping sounds coming from
a child's chest. Summoning up all her courage, Abbie knocked
on the door.

'Child, how did you get here?' Lady Huntly asked. 'What
do you want?'

'Just to see her, my lady.' Uninvited, Abbie rushed across to the bed where two little arms were outstretched at the sound of her voice. 'I'm here, Lady Jean. Abbie's here now.'

Later that night Lady Huntly stood looking down at the sleeping faces of the two girls side by side in the bed. Her own daughter didn't have glorious red hair, like Abbie, though red hair was common in Scotland, she thought. The best example of it could be seen in the Stewarts. Mary, Queen of Scots had inherited it from James, the seventh Stewart king.

She paced about, feeling more and more agitated. The cause was something to do with this girl Abbie, and she tried to puzzle out what it could be.

Failing in the attempt, for she had brought her into the world herself, a very ordinary child of very ordinary parents, her thoughts went back to James V and the last time he had visited Strathbogie Castle. It had been for a hunting holiday, she recalled. About eight years ago . . . And the child had that red hair . . .

James V had nine red-haired bastards who had lived with him and Marie de Guise. She was too soft-hearted, that woman . . . Goodness knows how many other bastards he had fathered before he died, who went unclaimed. She went across to the bed again. At that moment Abbie opened her eyes, those slanting golden eyes, and suddenly Lady Huntly knew.

She had stumbled on the truth.

NINE

With her hands shaking and her mind confused Lady Huntly went back over to the bed and saw that her own daughter was sleeping peacefully and the girl Abbie was lying perfectly still although her eyes were open. Perhaps she was one of those who slept with their eyes open, the Countess thought, and sat down on a chair by the bed.

She was aware that she had made a momentous discovery. But what to do about it, if anything? She needed time to think. Leaving the door wide open she walked through to her sitting room and sat down at her embroidery frame. It had always soothed her up to now. Marshalling the silken threads helped to marshal her thoughts, and she began to stitch with hands that were gradually steadying.

In reality she was spinning a web. Those all-important long silken strands flung as far as the Scottish throne were swiftly and easily in place. It was the intersections, the steps and bridges to get there which kept tangling. They wouldn't come right however many times she tried, and she saw that she would need help of a sort that she resorted to only in times of the direst need.

This was one of them, if ever there was one.

'Meenie! Queenie! Beenie! Teenie!' she muttered so low that only her four grey cats could hear her in the sleeping castle.

They rose up, dusty from lying in the warm ashes of the fire, and four old women shawled in grey sat down beside Lady Huntly. When they appeared, so did a man in black,

63

and they all huddled around her, hissing from time to time. Every now and then the man in black threw a powder in amongst the ashes so that flames leaped up, purple and red and green, and threw off swirling coloured plumes of smoke.

But Abbie was not asleep.

She was watching and listening, terrified.

Donald was always telling her that Lady Huntly was a witch, and worse than that, there was a coven of witches at Strathbogie.

'What's a coven, Donald?' she had asked once, icy prickles on the back of her neck despite the sunny afternoon.

'I don't know *everything*, you know. Anyway, it's bad luck.'

'Yes, you do. What's a coven?'

'Curiosity killed the cat, but if you *must* know – and this is the last thing I'm going to tell you – it's a meeting of witches. They gather together and chant black magic and cast their spells.'

'Ooh . . .' Abbie shivered deliciously. 'What's a spell? What's black mag – ?'

'No, you don't, Abbie McCracken! That's all I know. It's all I want to know. But you could ask your father.'

It was one thing, chatting amiably with Donald about it out in the safety of the farmyard, but it was entirely another here in this huge, dark, cold castle. Lady Huntly seemed to be sliding down in her chair in a sort of trance when the soft chanting began. The coloured haze was drifting through the door almost to the bed, and when the chanting grew louder Donald's words flashed into her mind.

Were these the witches? Was this the black magic? Or was she dreaming? She put a protective arm over Lady Jean and lay still, rigid with fear. One voice was louder and more insistent than the rest, rising to a wail:

> 'Paths are running,
> Straight to the Queen.
> Use all thy cunning,
> Bind the girl to Jean.'

The voice repeated these words over and over again, but Abbie could make nothing of them. Lady Huntly didn't understand either.

'What do you mean, Nick?' she asked the man in black.

Abbie's sharp ears heard his first few words, but his whispers were too low for her to pick up the rest.

'Abbie McCracken is in the bond of manrent to your husband already, along with the rest of her family, so she is yours for life, to do with as you will. Use her.'

Something about Abbie McCracken? What could they be saying about her?

Stumbling footsteps sounded along the passage, and when they staggered to a halt at the door Abbie saw that they belonged to Lord Huntly. She had never seen witches before and she had never seen a drunk man before either, and all she hoped was that they would all go away and leave her and Lady Jean alone. Her father had always told her that a little prayer could help any dangerous situation and silently, she repeated the one that seemed most appropriate to her now.

> Matthew, Mark, Luke and John,
> Bless the bed that I lie on.
> Four angels to my bed,
> Four angels round my head,
> One to watch and one to pray
> And two to bear my soul away.

Lord Huntly was indeed very late going to bed that night, and at that stage of intoxication when his thoughts were all of his wife's voluptuous body. It was half-past midnight when he shambled along the passage towards the light of her sitting room and finally staggered to a halt.

And there were those four old women again! He had caught glimpses of them before. Now he saw them distinctly although it was through a coloured mist and somewhere in his fuddled brain he wondered how they ever managed to get into Strathbogie. He never saw them coming and he never saw them leaving, and even now as he stood there swaying they had disappeared in the blinking of an eye. His wife's pet raven was flapping up onto his perch and only the cats were moving, hissing and coiling in the ashes of the fire, and fixing him with their yellow eyes.

He came to the conclusion that he must be drunker than he thought, when his wife smilingly led him to bed. She didn't often do that. He thought she must be pleased about something, but before he could find out what it was he fell into a drunken stupor.

When he woke up the following morning he found that she continued in a surprisingly good humour, considering that there were two little girls running about the castle now, when she had made it plain that she didn't like little girls, not even her own. Then, looking out of the window he saw a royal messenger galloping into the courtyard. He hoped very much that whatever message this was, it wouldn't alter her frame of mind.

'It is from the Queen Mother, my dear,' he said, handing the letter over, for she was the clever one. She could read.

'Yes,' Lady Huntly said, scanning it, while Lady Jean and Abbie sat still and listened. 'She is sending the Secretary of State, Sir William Maitland of Lethington, to see us next week.'

Abbie stored these difficult words in her memory as best she could, repeating them under her breath to make sure she'd got them right. As soon as she saw him she'd ask Donald what they meant.

'Maitland? The Secretary of State?' Lord Huntly said. 'I wonder why.'

'She is so sure that there will be a battle when the English come to Edinburgh, that she wants him in safekeeping in the meantime.'

'Well, he couldn't be in safer hands than mine,' Huntly boasted, and strutted out to dismiss the messenger.

His wife glared after him. He had never had the least idea of diplomacy. She would have to speak to Maitland herself, for the beginnings of a desperate plan were forming in her mind.

A few days later she left Jean and Abbie playing happily together in the castle and took her way to the Gardeners' Cottage.

'How is Lady Jean?' Abigail asked anxiously.

'She has recovered.'

'Then send Abbie back home. She should not have stayed so long. She will be in your way, my lady.'

'Not at all. In fact, I have decided to keep her.'

At once Abigail felt a great sadness and an even greater anxiety fall upon her. This woman had the power to do as she liked with them all. But what could she want with a seven-year-old child?

'I'm afraid I don't understand you, my lady,' she said, with a tremor of fear in her voice. Above all, she wished John would only come home at this moment.

'It is quite simple.' Lady Huntly's hooded eyes were impossible to read. 'You know how good Abbie is with Lady Jean, and it seems she is good *for* her as well. I have decided to keep her at the castle so that she can be a companion for my daughter.'

Was that all? Abigail almost laughed in relief. Why had she panicked, even for a moment? Her Abbie was going to be a companion to a child who would one day be a great lady!

'How can I ever thank you for such an honour, my lady?' she smiled.

'By understanding that if my daughter ever has to go away, to Edinburgh or Stirling or for any other reason, Abbie must go with her.'

'I understand, my lady. I hope she won't be a nuisance to you, for Abbie has been a very poor sleeper all her life. She seems to be able to exist on only a few hours of sleep every night.' Then Abigail remembered her manners. 'Now, what can I get you to eat or drink? There is only ale, I'm afraid, but I baked some oatcakes today.'

67

'I thank you, but no. I must go back now, but this evening I shall send Abbie home for an hour so that you may explain my plans to her yourself.'

There was some sort of dreadful finality in all this which Abigail could not put into words when John came home.

'Why should you worry so much?' he asked her.

'Because I have this feeling that if Abbie goes now, we may not see her again for years.'

'She will be only a stone's throw away, up at Strathbogie.'

'All the same I want to prepare her for what may lie ahead as best I can, John.'

'You've done a good job already, Abigail, preparing her for life. No girl could have had a more caring mother.'

But John's words did little to reassure Abigail, and Abbie herself, when she came bursting into the cottage later, only made her feel more apprehensive than ever.

'I should be proud of you,' she said with a sigh. 'It isn't every girl who is chosen to be a lady's companion. As such, Abbie, you must never forget your place or your manners. You will remember to curtsy when any of the Huntlys speak to you, and always say, "My lady" or "My lord"?'

'Of course, Mother. I do, anyway.'

'The Countess says you may have to go away sometimes with Lady Jean.'

'One castle will be much the same as another, I expect,' Abbie said cheerfully, and Abigail sighed.

'But will you be happy, dearie?'

'Looking after Lady Jean? Of course, Mother.'

'All the same, I want you to come through to the other room with me. I've made up a bundle for you. John, keep the boys in here with you for a few minutes until I talk to Abbie.' Abigail closed the bedroom door behind them and sat Abbie down on the bed beside her, taking both her hands. 'I'm worried in case you may be away for longer than we think, dearie,' she said. 'I think Lady Huntly knows more than she told me. I'm sure she expects you and Lady Jean to have to go away soon.'

'Don't worry, Mother. We are bound to come back home in the end.'

'Of course you will. But when? You are leaving home at such an awkward time in your life, Abbie. We hope, if it happens, that it will only be for a few weeks or at the most a few months. But I have this dreadful feeling that it could be for years, even.'

Abbie had never seen her mother's face so sad. She put one of her arms around her waist and gave her a little squeeze.

'I'm nearly eight now. You mean I could be eleven or twelve before I see you again? Surely not, Mother!'

'Eleven or twelve, or even thirteen – and that's what I want to talk to you about. I've put these cloths in your bundle for a special reason. They're called month-cloths. Any day, as you grow up, you may find a little blood coming from between your legs, and these cloths are to stem the flow so that your petticoats are not soiled. You mustn't be frightened if this happens when you are away from home. It happens to every growing girl, and it happens every month. It is healthy, dearie, and means that you are changing into a woman. It means that one day, you could have a child of your own.'

'Oh, we'll be back long before I'm a woman, Mother,' Abbie laughed, 'but I understand what you've told me. Don't look so troubled! Let me remember my mother's face smiling, as usual,' she added as they returned to the kitchen, and she took up her bundle. 'Everything will be all right.'

'Well,' John said, hiding a pang of doubt himself as they waved goodbye to their daughter, 'we have no choice but to let her go, in any case. We are all tied servants to the Huntlys here. At least she seems quite happy, and I'll be in a position up at Strathbogie to keep an eye on her myself. Come inside, Abigail, and stop worrying.'

TEN

'A very important visitor is coming here soon,' Lady Huntly told Lady Jean and Abbie. 'If he speaks to you, smile and curtsy and just answer, "Yes, sir," and "No, sir." Don't bother him.'

'Lady Jean hasn't learned to curtsy yet,' Abbie said.

'Then teach her.'

'Yes, my lady.'

Feeling very important herself, Abbie set about it, but the lessons quickly deteriorated into the hilarious when four-year-old Lady Jean almost always fell over with her legs sticking up in the air. Still, Abbie persevered.

When the visitor arrived at last she felt very let down. His hair was black, his pointed beard was black, and his clothes underlined his great importance, for they were also black, with touches of silver. Even his long thin legs were black-clad. Abbie already knew his name was Sir William Maitland, although she still hadn't found out what a 'Secretary of State' was, but to her he looked just like a spider.

A few days after his arrival Lord Huntly galloped off to another of his estates with a few of the Gordons, and the Countess took Abbie to one side in a furtive fashion. 'Take Lady Jean out to play,' she commanded. 'I am going to talk to Sir William now, and I want no interruptions. It's a fine day, and you may stay out as long as you like, so long as you go no further than the Gardeners' Cottage and bring her back by bedtime. I will post one of the Gordon guards on the top of the hill to watch you and see that you obey my instructions.'

On that fine, lazily warm day in late summer the two girls were only too delighted with their unexpected freedom. They had time to play all the games which were usually cut short, and there was a surprising bonus when they met Donald crossing the courtyard to go into the barracks.

'There's a visitor in the castle,' Abbie muttered to him out of Lady Jean's earshot. 'He's Sir William Maitland of Lethington. He's the Secretary of State. What's a Secretary of State, Donald?'

'I never met such an inquisitive girl! I'm sure I don't know. But some of the soldiers will know,' Donald replied.

'Well, will you ask them – now?' Abbie asked. 'We'll play around here, if you're quick. Lady Huntly's got a spy posted to watch us.'

Donald was back out in a flash. 'He's *only* Queen Marie's most important minister of state,' he reported. 'The Gordons say that every other adviser she has must do as he says. Why is he here? they are wondering.'

'I think the Queen Mother is expecting war,' Abbie whispered. 'He's here for safekeeping. I'm sure that's what they said.'

Then she led Lady Jean away again to play in the parks. They stayed out all afternoon and at last went to visit Abigail who gave them a cool drink and laughed when they showed her how they could curtsy.

'But why does her ladyship want you to practise so much, dearie?' she asked Abbie. 'Anyone would think you were going to see the Queen! Bairns, are you hungry? I've made some honey cakes . . .'

When, regretfully, they thought it was time to go back to Strathbogie, Abbie was taken aback to see a tear rolling down Lady Jean's face, especially since she thought they had had such a happy afternoon.

'What is it?' she asked gently.

'I don't want to go back,' the little girl said. 'My mother

never calls me "dearie", and I don't like when you always call me "Lady Jean".'

Abbie felt so sorry for her, realising for the first time that while her own parents had given her a very happy childhood, wealthy, highborn parents didn't always do the same for their children. She felt a great upsurge of the same feelings with which she loved her rag doll, as she hugged the little child to her.

'All right, then,' she said. 'When nobody can hear us I'll call you Jean and sometimes Jeannie, if you like.'

'And dearie,' Lady Jean smiled through her tears.

But the nearer the castle loomed the more Abbie felt a sense of foreboding herself. She tried to dismiss it when they got inside, surprised to see that the door of the Great Hall was still shut, and to hear the murmur of voices inside. She was just thinking that Lady Huntly and Sir William Maitland must be having a very long talk indeed when the door opened, and they both stood there, looking at her very closely. Abbie didn't like the way they were staring at her like that, and to make matters worse she had never liked black spiders, although she tried not to show it now.

'My daughter, Lady Jean, you already know, Sir William,' Lady Huntly said as Jean tried her best to curtsy. 'And this is Abbie McCracken, the girl I have been telling you about.'

'Ah . . . yes, I can see it for myself,' he said. 'The likeness is remarkable.'

Abbie curtsied and smiled politely.

'Have you enjoyed this fine afternoon out playing, my dear?' he asked her. 'Where did you go?'

'Just around about, sir. Then we went to see my mother.'

'And where was she?' Sir William asked, and listened intently as Abbie answered, while she wondered why he was prolonging a conversation with her. He couldn't possibly be interested in her or her home.

'At the Gardeners' Cottage, sir. My home.'

'It's nearly bedtime, girls,' Lady Huntly said as the two nursemaids appeared.

72

But when Florrie and Maggie May led them away Abbie's sharp ears heard the Spider speaking again before the door of the Great Hall closed behind him and Lady Huntly, and she wondered what he meant. 'She could be a godsend in these troubled times,' he was saying.

Inside, he continued to voice his thoughts. 'She may not turn out to be as tall as the Queen, who is growing at such a rate that I believe she will not stop until she is six feet tall. Also the girl's voice is certainly of a lower pitch – although, of course, it could be trained. We shall have to wait and see.'

'These are dangerous times, Sir William. Would it not be better to have the girl in place beside the Queen while you wait and see? She would need training in every department, and the sooner the better.'

'You are right. Abbie McCracken may eventually double for the Queen in many a dangerous situation in the future. I will think about it, and discuss it with the Queen Mother. Leave it with me, Lady Huntly.'

Abbie could not help noticing that as soon as Maitland departed Lady Huntly began a flurry of unusual activities.

'Jean is growing so fast that she must have new gowns made, six for day and six for night wear,' she informed her husband. 'I shall have to call in the seamstresses.'

'*Twelve* new gowns? All at once?'

'Furthermore, Abbie McCracken, her companion, must be dressed in green as befits a Gordon maidservant.'

'Abbie McCracken seems very young for a maidservant, to me. Will she be all right for Jean?'

'None better, I assure you,' Lady Huntly said firmly, and turned her head away to hide a sly smile.

Lady Jean's new gowns of silk and satin were measured, fitted and sewn within days. New caps, a size larger than usual were made for her in an effort to give her spiky straw-coloured hair more room under them, although in the end Abbie was the

73

only one who could tie them on with any semblance of security.

She herself got two new dresses, dark green servants' dresses made down for her, and after a lot of thought Lady Huntly had narrow white ruffs and cuffs sewn on to them to relieve the stark colour. Next she gave Abbie stockings and her first pair of leather slippers, so that the two girls had been fitted out from top to toe, their new clothes hanging up and ready to wear at a moment's notice.

It was all for a purpose, Abbie was sure of it, and it was all done in such a hurry that she wasn't surprised to see a royal messenger galloping up to Strathbogie again. Taking Lady Jean by the hand she arrived at the door of the Great Hall in time to hear the news.

The messenger handed Lady Huntly two letters. Abbie was sure he had handed her *two* letters, but one seemed to have mysteriously disappeared.

'I thought by the way Maitland spoke that there was something in the wind,' Lady Huntly smiled at her husband, as she opened the letter with its heavy seal. 'I half expected this! Marie de Guise says here that Queen Mary was so taken by our little Lady Jean when she was down for the garden party that she wants her to come and play with her at Stirling Castle. Isn't that wonderful? What an honour! And she isn't even called Mary.'

'I'm not going anywhere without Abbie.' Jean stamped her foot.

'I shall send a message back to the Queen Mother,' Lady Huntly said, ignoring her daughter. 'Let me see . . . This is Saturday. I want it arranged that Jean goes on Monday, and of course she will be accompanied by her maidservant.'

So that was what she was now, Abbie thought. Not a companion, but a maidservant.

'Ho! Not only by a little maidservant,' Lord Huntly boomed. 'They are only young girls, you know. The two nursemaids, Florrie and Maggie May, will go with them, and I will arrange for a full Gordon escort. I'll go and see John

McCracken now. I'm not too sure about our little daughter stravaiging over the countryside to Stirling at a time like this,' he frowned as he stamped out.

Abbie could see that he didn't approve of any of this by the way he shrugged his shoulders at the retort his wife flung after him.

'It is by royal command,' she said firmly.

Abbie played at dolls with Jean and watched what Lady Huntly did next. The Countess went over to the window and took out the second letter she had concealed from her husband in her cuff. Abbie wished she could only read. She would have given anything to know what was in it, because she sensed that it concerned her.

It certainly did concern Abbie. In reality it was she, with her beautiful red hair and her true father's eyes, who had proved to be Lady Jean's passport into the court of Queen Mary, and it was irking Lady Huntly very much that her own daughter should have to play second fiddle to a mere maidservant to get there. But it was that or nothing, and one way or another, she gloated, she had achieved her ambition.

Lady Jean Gordon would be another flower in the Queen's bouquet – and as for Abbie herself, she was expendable – for when she read the second letter it was unsigned and contained only one word in spidery handwriting.

'*PROCEED*.'

On Monday morning everyone at Strathbogie Castle and on the estate came out to see the two girls off. Lord Huntly still looked worried, and barked more orders than usual at John McCracken, while John himself remained tight-lipped.

Lady Huntly looked triumphant. By whatever means, she had manoeuvred her daughter into court at last. It had been very hard to do, and she could never have managed it without her familiars to guide her, as they had guided her all along. Now Jean would be there for the rest of her life. No doubt she would marry some lord of the realm. No, the Countess would have no more worries about Lady *Jean* Gordon. The important thing was that the excuse was there for Lord Huntly to be at court any time he liked now, on the pretext of seeing his daughter, whatever the real motive.

Abigail and her little boys waved at Abbie forlornly. Watching her, Lady Huntly's lip curled.

As for Abbie's fate, she didn't give that a second thought.

ELEVEN

Donald wrapped a sheepskin around Abbie and set her up in front of him on his horse. Only John McCracken was entrusted with Lady Jean, and the two rode side by side followed by the two nursemaids and surrounded by Gordon soldiers on the long journey south. For many miles Donald kept Abbie entertained with his stories, but as the light faded so did his voice, and lulled by the unwavering rhythm of the horses' hooves, she dozed off.

Only when the rhythm changed abruptly, and the pace became jerky and different, was she dazedly aware that they were climbing. Peering out from the furs around her she saw that they were struggling up a rough road – up and up for ever ... Up and up right into the sky – or so it seemed to her.

She recognised the straining grinds of a portcullis being raised, the groans and clangs of heavy gates opening and then shutting behind them and after that the clattering of hooves as the horses streamed over cobbles before they came to a steaming halt. She saw that they were in the forecourt of another castle, far larger, blacker and grimmer than Strathbogie ever was.

There were still a few streaks of red left in the darkening sky. The flames of the torches lighting the ramparts flared first this way, and then that in the fickle night wind and Abbie's eyes were drawn to them as though hypnotised. Then as his strong arms lifted her down Donald spoke in her ear.

'We're here,' he said gently. 'Are you awake, Abbie?' She

had been like a young sister to him, a perfect little nuisance, but now that the moment of parting had almost come he realised how empty Strathbogie would seem without her. 'Wake up, little Abbie! This is Stirling Castle.'

Blinking, Abbie looked around for her travelling companions. Florrie and Maggie May had already dismounted and were standing shivering beside the horses while the soldiers who had been escorting them rolled up their sheepskins and strapped them back onto the saddles. John McCracken was lifting Lady Jean down and as soon as her feet touched the ground she ran towards Abbie and clasped her hand.

The great doors of the castle were flung open by the guards who took up their positions to right and to left. In the light streaming out Abbie saw outlined the figure of a lady – a great lady, to judge from the splendour of her dress, its black underkirtle gleaming in the torchlight, its over-gown of black and silver brocade open down the front, while the sleeves were close-fitting to the elbows before they opened out to very wide cuffs, turned back to show a lining of cloth of silver.

Marie de Guise, widow of James V of Scotland stepped forward, her face framed in a standing collar of pearly gauze.

'Your Majesty,' John McCracken said, bowing low. He took each girl in either hand and muttered, 'The Queen Mother. You must curtsy.'

'But where's her crown?' Jean asked in a childish, penetrating voice that brought everyone there to a halt before they laughed politely.

Nobody answered and the Queen Mother looked from Jean to Abbie, her gaze lingering on Abbie so long that John McCracken pushed Lady Jean forward, and put his hand on her head. 'This is Lady Jean Gordon, Your Majesty.'

'Yes, of course. I recognise Lady Jean. And the older one?'

'Abbie McCracken, my own daughter. Lady Jean's companion.'

'So this is Abbie McCracken . . . The companion?'

'Well,' John said, and looking up into his face Abbie could

78

see that he was frowning, 'they don't like to be parted, that's true.'

'And how old are you, Abbie McCracken?' Marie de Guise addressed her directly.

Abbie curtsied, and replied gravely. 'Seven, nearly eight, Your Majesty.'

The Queen Mother smiled when Lady Jean made a wobbling attempt to copy Abbie's curtsy but then stiffened when she felt a little hand creep into hers. Clearly, Lady Jean had never been told that ordinary people were not allowed to touch royalty. The child's cap had come off during her efforts, to reveal her long hair, strangely the colour of straw and just as straight and spiky. It made the two innocent grey eyes looking up at her somehow very appealing, even pathetic, and the infant smile on her heart-shaped face was quite enchanting . . .

Or was it *bewitching*? Jean Gordon was her mother's child, the Queen Mother reminded herself, and Lady Huntly had the reputation of being a witch. She became uneasy, and more uneasy than ever to be thinking such thoughts about a little girl who was only a little girl, and an innocent, pathetic one at that. Lady Huntly had been so anxious to get her daughter to court that she had more or less thrown her in along with this Abbie McCracken, according to Sir William Maitland.

After the first few encounters of the kind, the Queen Mother had given up feeling affronted and insulted when confronted by her husband's bastards. It was not their fault. The children were blameless, after all. Now, as she regarded Abbie, she saw the Stewart likeness all too clearly. And yes, she sighed, she *did* resemble her own beloved daughter to a marked degree, although not nearly so delicately made in face or in figure. She saw, to her relief, that nobody would look at Abbie McCracken twice, dressed like that, as a maidservant. It was an excellent disguise. But then she had never underestimated Lady Huntly's intelligence. On the whole she approved of this wild plan – *any* plan to protect the little Queen.

'You must both be tired,' she said, unclasping Jean's hand and ushering the girls and their servants inside. 'We will put you to bed now, and you will see Queen Mary in the morning.'

It was only then that Abbie realised that she was parting with her hero, Donald, and she couldn't believe it, nor the terrible thud of her heart. She hesitated and looked back at him beseechingly, but all he could do was to smile encouragement, wave his hand and wait in the courtyard with the rest of the Gordons.

Only John McCracken was allowed to go in with them. The Great Hall of Stirling Castle was dazzling, even in his eyes, with torches burning all around and spilling their grease, lighting up the large number of people moving about, some dancing, in their glittering clothes, and others sitting at the long tables up and down the middle.

But Jean's face paled, her eyes filled with tears and she clutched Abbie's hand, moaning, for in front of them a monster was prancing. She had never seen anything like it before. Why had no one told her such horrors existed? She stared in fascinated horror at two men joined at the waist but with only one set of legs. It had four arms, and in all four hands there was a stick with feathers on the end.

The monster was singing with two voices, and when the four hands ran the tickling sticks over the children, Jean's face became convulsed with terror.

'No! No!' she screamed. 'Take them away! Make them go away, Abbie!'

Shuddering and sobbing she turned her face up to Abbie who put both arms around her protectively, although it was plain to be seen that she was shocked and frightened herself.

John McCracken took Jean up in one arm and put the other around his daughter's shoulders.

'Oh,' Marie de Guise laughed, 'you mustn't be frightened, my children! These are the famous King's singers, Ferdinand and Frederick. They are twins. They will sing a song especially for you.'

Ferdinand burst into song, singing bass, and Frederick did his best to harmonise in his tenor voice until he started to cough with a deep, hacking cough, and the song had to stop until he got his breath back.

'Come, children.' Marie spoke again over Jean's sobs. 'You should be in bed. My ladies will show you the way. It is straight past the bear cage.'

The nearer they came to the huge black iron cage the stronger and more revolting the stench became. Still in John McCracken's arms, Jean drew level with the evil red eyes of a huge brown bear. His coat was mangy, hanging off in strips, and he stood up on his hind legs and rattled his cage violently as they passed. Cringing, Jean saw the claws on the end of his paws, two inches long, filthy and murderous.

'That's old Hercules,' one of the ladies laughed. 'Don't worry. He never gets out of his cage. Come, it is this way,' and a few minutes later Jean and Abbie were ushered into a bedchamber where a servant was waiting with warm water to wash in and hot milk to drink.

The two nursemaids took charge immediately. Maggie May began to peel off Jean's clothes in front of the fire.

'You poor wee lass,' she said, and gave her a cuddle. 'Don't worry, Lady Jean. You're safe up here with us. Look, Florrie,' she said to the other nurse, 'her eyes are closing already, after all that crying.'

'Ay, Maggie May,' Florrie sniffed. 'No child should have been given a shock like that! But I suppose it's different with royalty. They don't care. They're a law unto themselves.'

Down below Captain John McCracken was taking leave of Marie de Guise. 'I must apologise for them, Your Majesty,' he said, although he didn't look sorry at all. 'They are not used to a royal court and all its wonders.'

'The twins were a legacy from my husband's father, James the Fourth,' she told him coldly, sensing his disapproval once again. 'My husband took a fancy to the twins when he was visiting the court in France, and when he married me had them brought to Scotland as part of my retinue. They are twenty-eight now, and in all that time they have been a great asset to the court and a wonder to all who have ever seen them. Of course I had to bring them with me from Holyrood – as well as old Hercules, banging about over there – although I fear Hercules may not have much longer to live.'

'No?'

'He gets angrier as he grows older, and he smells abominably now.'

'Indeed,' John agreed fervently, well aware that the Queen Mother would probably take more exception than ever. But the sickening stench hung over the Great Hall like a foul cloud, enough to make him marvel that people were actually eating there.

'But – to Lady Jean Gordon,' Marie changed an uncomfortable conversation, 'do you think she may recover, and smile again? My daughter, the Queen, saw her at the garden party which had to be postponed, and she loved her for her smile. That is why I invited her here, to play with her and the other little Marys.'

Somehow, John didn't believe this for an explanation, not for a minute.

'And Abbie, too,' the Queen Mother added in an after-thought, eyeing John sideways.

John McCracken looked the Queen Mother straight in the eye. 'Oh, Lady Jean will recover *and* smile,' he assured her, 'so long as she doesn't have to face the animals again – and so long as she has Abbie beside her. The girls are devoted to each other.'

'I understand that you do not wish them to be separated, Captain McCracken. I shall see to it. You and your men will not stay the night?'

'No, Majesty. We had to ride here slowly with the children. We will return much faster now, and more safely under cover of darkness.'

But as he galloped back north to Strathbogie at the head of the Gordon soldiers with Donald MacLaren beside him,

John's face was very grim. He had taken note of the wining and the dining going on in Stirling Castle, and he had recognised many of the other nobles of Scotland enjoying it, men with greedy eyes, men jostling for position around the little Queen with only her foreign mother to protect her, a woman who was ignorant of Scotland and Scottish ways.

He wondered if Marie de Guise felt the hot breaths of the carrion-eaters circling her and her daughter every day, panting in anticipation of something – anything – happening to the child Queen.

The Earl of Arran, James Hamilton, had been there, of course. If Mary had never been born, he would now be king. Next to him had been Matthew Stewart, the Earl of Lennox, who claimed he, and not Arran, was the true heir.

And not far away sat Lord James Stewart with his clever green eyes, only a boy as yet, it was true – but a boy to watch, since he was the King's oldest bastard son and had been his favourite.

There were dozens of these Scottish lords there and, of course, there was no show without Punch. Inevitably, the most dangerous one of all in John's opinion, Patrick Hepburn, the Earl of Bothwell, was there as large as life and twice as ugly, and had even brought along his young son, James Hepburn, whose face was maturing into a rough mask, a dog's face, on top of a rough, tough body. James Hepburn would turn out to be an even worse Lord Bothwell than his father. John was convinced of it.

John McCracken's own master, George Gordon, Earl of Huntly, happened not to be there himself, but he had sent his small daughter, Lady Jean, instead – and her only four years old! It was a cruel disgrace. Only four and already a pawn in the game, John thought gloomily . . . Oh, they were all the same, these lords of Scotland! And hadn't he had first-hand experience of them himself? His face became even grimmer when he thought about his own little Abbie and her sad story. At least he had saved her and her mother from *one* of the pack.

But had it been only so that the Huntlys could throw her back in again? He felt a wave of helplessness wash over him, as it washed over every man bound in manrent sooner or later.

'Bastards!' he cursed them out loud as Donald galloped up alongside him. 'For that's what they are! A pack of wolves, the lot of them!'

'You don't need to tell me. I know all about it.' Donald's face was as grim as John's under his steel bonnet. 'And, considering my parentage, more than most.'

John looked across at him, at his helmet gleaming in the moonlight, and cursed again. 'Damn this moon,' he said. 'We could do without that.'

But Donald's eyes were looking past him. He seemed to be listening, and then all of a sudden he roared, 'Watch out, John!'

A gang of ruffians had appeared from behind the rocks at the side of the rough road, armed with sticks and cudgels. Already they had one of the Gordon soldiers torn from his saddle, and two of them were beating him into the ground. Donald wheeled about to deal with them and to rescue the soldier, while John made short work of another. The ambushers had the advantage of surprise but their victims were trained and organised, and after ten minutes with their swords drawn, the Gordons had killed the ruffians, leaving only two to take to the hills.

John McCracken realised that but for Donald he might be dead by now. He also realised that although he always called him the bad boy of the barracks, Donald was a boy no longer. He was nearly sixteen years old, and a man. John looked at him with fresh respect, but even as he did so Donald began to laugh.

'Well, which is it, sir?' he asked. 'A medal or more money for saving the Captain's life?'

'Just my thanks, Donald MacLaren. I would have done the same for you.'

'And now you can see for yourself, it was a good job you

had me with you on this escort, after all. I'm the best friend anyone ever had.'

'I wonder . . .' John asked, looking at him speculatively. He signalled to the soldiers to stop and rest, then took Donald to one side so that he could speak to him quietly and privately. 'I wonder, Donald . . .'

'You can trust me, sir,' Donald said soberly.

'You know, son, one day I might never come back from an escort. I would like someone to watch over Abbie if that ever happened. At least I would like someone to know all about her. You see, she is not my daughter.'

'Not your daughter?' Donald said incredulously. 'But it's plain to be seen that you love her as your own daughter!'

'I do. But although Abigail is her mother, it was James Fifth who got her with Abbie.'

Donald thought this over for a while before he spoke. 'And now she's gone into the vipers' nest, you mean?'

'That's exactly what I mean.'

'It's a pity one of us couldn't be there to keep an eye on her,' Donald said as they rode on again, more thoughtfully now, until one of the soldiers shouted, 'What about one of your stories, Donald? We could do with a laugh!'

Donald managed to oblige, laughing and bantering all the way home, so that when they got back to Strathbogie nobody outside the troop ever knew that the trip to Stirling Castle had very nearly ended in tragedy.

TWELVE

So as to avoid the Great Hall and all its horrors, Abbie took Jean down a back staircase she had discovered. It led out onto an enclosed lawn where children were playing.

'Mind you do your curtsy properly when we see the Queen, Jeannie, and call her "Your Majesty".'

'Yes, Abbie, I'll try. But how shall I know her?'

'Father told me she is very tall for her age, and thin. I suppose she will be wearing a beautiful gown.'

'And a crown?'

'I don't know about a crown,' Abbie said doubtfully, 'but she has red hair. Ah, yes...' she added when they got out into the sunshine, 'there she is!'

Jean held on to Abbie's hand while they stood and watched for a few minutes. It was easy to pick out Queen Mary. Not quite five yet, she was even taller than Abbie was at seven. They could not take their eyes off Mary's long, slender hands which she waved about continually as she spoke. Such long, thin fingers, just skin and bones!

Then Mary turned and saw her visitors. 'See, my Marys,' she said to the four little girls who were with her, 'they have arrived!' Her voice was as thin as she was, and high-pitched. 'It is Lady Jean Gordon come to play with us. Look at her! Is she not pretty?'

While Mary was looking their way and laughing her tinkling laugh Abbie seized the opportunity to push Jean forward before she retreated to the doorway again herself. Nobody paid any attention to her after that. Thankfully, she hung back and watched. She was not alone. From a window high up in Stirling Castle Marie de Guise was watching too.

Lady Huntly has schooled her daughter to be biddable, at least, she thought. She seems happy to join in any game my Mary wants to play. That girl Abbie knows her place too, I am glad to see. She is not pushing herself forward. It is true that from this distance she could indeed pass for my Mary, given the right clothes . . . In fact, she is more like Mary than any of her half-sisters or half-brothers, and the implications of that are enormous. We must look after Abbie McCracken, but she must not know that any special attention is being paid to her. Then there should be no trouble.

Trouble, she sighed, as always, comes from England. Henry VIII is dead, but nothing improves. If anything, it gets worse. Edward's Regent, Somerset – that bloody butcher who desecrated my husband's tomb – will attack us again. How far will he push up into Scotland next time?

'Can you ride a horse?' Queen Mary asked Lady Jean a few days later. 'My Marys and I all ride little horses sent down specially from the Shetlands. Did you know I am Queen of the Isles, as well?'

'No, Your Majesty,' Jean answered, her eyes on the small shaggy horses being led out by the grooms. 'But there's Misty!' she cried excitedly. 'Look, Abbie! There's Misty!'

'No, that grey one is called Cloud,' Mary told her.

'Please excuse her, Your Majesty,' Abbie hurried forward, 'but he is very like her own Misty at Strathbogie.'

'Well, you may ride Cloud,' Mary smiled, trotting off with the little ladies-in-waiting. 'But perhaps,' she flung over her shoulder at Abbie, 'you should get one of the grooms to take charge of him on the long lead.'

'Would you rather just play a game with me?' Abbie whispered when the other girls had gone.

'Oh yes, Abbie. Tell the man to take the horse away. Don't you think it strange that the Queen calls the four Marys by their second names? But sometimes she has another name for

Fleming. She calls her Flamina. She's the prettiest one.'

'I don't know why they call her Flamina,' Abbie wrinkled her brows, 'unless it's because of her flaming red hair, just like her mother's, with all those ringlets and spirals. But I do know that she is the most important one although she gets into the most mischief. She has the royal blood of the Stewarts in her veins. Her mother is Lady Fleming.'

'Then there are the two in the middle, called Beaton and Seton.'

'Their mothers came over to Scotland with the Queen Mother. They were ladies-in-waiting to her in France before they married here.'

'How do you know all that, Abbie?'

'Florrie and Maggie May told me. They go down to the kitchens every night when we're asleep. They hear all the gossip there.'

'What do they say about the last one, then? What about Livingston?'

'Oh,' Abbie laughed, 'there's no gossip about Mary Livingston. She has a nickname too, you know. They call her Lusty because she dances so high and lustily. When the others are naughty, Mary Livingston takes the blame.'

'So who are those two boys we play with sometimes, James and Robert?'

'Lord James and Lord Robert Stewart, sons of King James the Fifth, but their mothers weren't married to him so the boys don't count.'

'I don't believe that, Abbie. Lord James Stewart thinks *he* counts, anyway.'

'And what makes you say that, Miss Cleversticks?' Abbie teased.

'Because he looks at Queen Mary, when he thinks she isn't looking, in a nasty sly way. I've seen him doing it.'

Abbie was amazed that Lady Jean could have seen that at her age. But it only confirmed what Abbie had been seeing for herself, that out of all the court the little Queen's worst enemy was her own half-brother, Lord James Stewart.

'That's because he thinks he should be king, I suppose. Anyway, you should be playing with them all, and not worrying about such things.' Abbie set Jean's cap more firmly on her unruly hair and sighed. 'Just you leave the watching and worrying to me. You are only a little girl – and with all this wind and rain something will have to be done with your hair to stop it flying about like this. It is getting quite long enough to plait.'

'What does that mean?'

'I can weave it into a long tail like a pony's tail. Then it will pin up under your caps, so that we don't have all this trouble.'

'Oh . . . Let me go now, Abbie. The Queen and the Marys are back. I hear them calling for me. They said we will tell fortunes with the cards,' Jean said, scampering away.

While the little Queen and her Marys were playing at Stirling Castle, outside, rebellion was in full swing. Reformers carrying their new bibles had brought their outlawed messages to willing converts, and at the head of a militant group defending them was a man called John Knox who had once been a Catholic priest, but who no longer kneeled in front of crucifixes. Instead, he carried a two-handed sword.

Those protesting against the Catholic faith and all things Catholic had risen up, and invaded the castle of St Andrews, killing Cardinal Beaton, a friend of Marie de Guise.

Marie had sent a message to France, begging the help of the new king, Henry II, and Henry, who wanted above all to please the powerful family of Guise, had dispatched a fleet of fighting men to lift the siege of St Andrews, and force the rebels to surrender. Its principal defenders were sent to France as prisoners. Its inhabitants, including John Knox, were sent to the galleys.

Outraged at such French impertinence, and spitting fire at the mere idea that another French-Scottish alliance was impending, Somerset, Regent of England, marched with an army of 18,000 well-equipped and well-drilled English soldiers, hacking and burning all the way to Musselburgh, to Pinkie just outside Edinburgh. There he was briefly halted by 36,000 Scots – Scots without a gun amongst the lot of them, but only spears and bows.

Lord Huntly was there, pompous as ever and magnificent in gilt and enamelled armour, but he had no gun to defend himself with either. He laid down his arms and fled. One by one the other Scottish magnates followed suit and the result of the Battle of Pinkie was a total rout of the Scots.

Inside Stirling Castle a horrified Queen Mother paced up and down. Her horror was intensified when she was told that Malcolm, Lord Fleming, husband of Janet, her favourite lady-in-waiting, and father of little Mary Fleming, was one of the 10,000 dead at the foot of the rock on which the castle stood. Tragedy touched the little Queen and her playmates. Reality was too close for comfort any more. Waves of panic washed over Stirling Castle.

Lady Jean Gordon, tired out with the games of childhood played in the fresh air, slept like the baby she virtually still was. But Abbie, standing by and watching every move, slept only a very few hours before she woke up refreshed and immediately restless.

On the night the Queen received news of the defeat of the Scots, bored with lying still, Abbie rose up out of her bed silently and flitted like a ghost through the castle. People were talking and moving about in the Great Hall although there was no sound of music. What were they talking about? She couldn't go in there. She only wished she could. *Surely* there must be some way that she could see and hear them without their being aware of it?

Stealthily but determinedly, she poked around the area at the entrance until she found a very narrow space between the wall and the arras. She could walk along it, and not only that, but there were chinks of light coming through the rich tapestry hangings where they must have rotted in places. The stone floor was icy on her bare feet, but minutes later Abbie was shivering, not with cold, but with excitement.

Only inches away, on the other side of the tapestry, Marie de Guise was sitting with one of her henchmen. He was big and burly and had come over with her years ago from France. He was her most important manservant and she was talking to him now. By closing one eye Abbie could see her face through the little hole she'd found, and she could hear every word.

'It is an emergency, Guillaume, you understand?'

'Yes, Majesty,' he answered, his English heavily accented.

Abbie wasn't surprised that he spoke in English. The nurse-maids had told her that Marie insisted on English in common usage. She rarely spoke in French herself, even to her daughter.

'It is Hercules. I have made up my mind, at last. He must go. How will you do it? How will you even manage to get into his cage? We must think of a way, Guillaume, and at once.'

While they pondered this the saddest and most macabre sight that Abbie had ever seen came into view. The Siamese twins were not dancing now. One of the men joined at the waist must have died – poor Frederick, with the bad cough – and now here was Ferdinand, carrying his brother's corpse around on his back, and crying as he pleaded with the Queen Mother.

'How can I ever be merry again? Frederick sang with me and talked to me, and comforted me when I was sad. I did the same for my beloved brother, but now I have nothing but the grief of carrying so heavy a burden dead and cold on my back, and that has taken all the pleasure of living away. Therefore I pray day and night to Almighty God to deliver me out of this present life, as now I beg your dear Majesty, that we may be laid in the earth together, from whence we came.'

With that, Ferdinand trailed away, anguished and sobbing, and Marie gave a deep sigh.

'That settles it, then,' she said. 'It must *all* be done tonight, as quickly and quietly as possible.'

'I will pour wine into Hercules' drinking vessel, as we have done for sport many a time before. He likes wine. If he drinks enough he will fall down and then we can get into his cage.'

'Very well, Guillaume. Let it be done. But don't tell me what you will do to Ferdinand. I have been fond of him and his brother. Do it as painlessly as possible – but do it. I must get rid of all excess baggage, for we leave later tonight. Somerset is too close for comfort.'

The Queen Mother rose up sadly from her seat, and now Abbie had a better view of the hall. For hours, it seemed to her, the men poured out gallons of wine for Hercules. She could hear him gurgling and grunting and swallowing it greedily, until once he tried to stand up on his hind legs as usual and instead fell down flat on his face with a tremendous crash.

Immediately the bolts of the cage were flung back and men went in and tied thick ropes around his legs and neck. They dragged him out over the passage towards a back door, followed by a silent crowd which Abbie saw included Florrie and Maggie May. She was left in darkness, for everyone who could snatch one had taken a taper from the walls. Suddenly frightened, Abbie headed back upstairs.

Lights and noise outside made her stop running, to look out of one of the slits in the walls of Stirling Castle. Flickering torches were ringed around a huge black pit dug in the very lawn that the Queen and the Marys and Lady Jean had played on so often, and the men had got the bear to the very edge of it when Hercules showed signs of life. So many spears were hurled into him that he was soon a pincushion of thrashing, roaring pain, and to stop the terrible noise Guillaume and his men used their clubs to bludgeon the wretched animal to death.

Hercules' body was lowered into the pit. The sides of his cage were flung in after him. Last of all the limp remains of what had been once the showpiece of the Scottish court,

Frederick and Ferdinand, the famous King's singers, were thrown in on top of the lot.

Shuddering in horror, Abbie crept back to bed. It wasn't long before she was shuddering in fear. 'Excess baggage,' the Queen Mother had called it. Up to now, Abbie had always thought that meant too much luggage, too many boxes and bags, but now she understood that it could also mean animals and even human beings.

So who next?

THIRTEEN

The Queen Mother's ladies-in-waiting brushed her hair, placed her lace bed-cap over it and departed, begging her to sleep for an hour or two – but how could she?

The candles made long shadows on the walls, jumping, ghostly shadows in this ancient, haunted castle on the rock where men with blood-stained hands walked side by side with ghosts. But then, in Scotland, people live with ghosts and witches every day.

So many of the nobility are witches themselves, she thought. She had always known that James Stewart's mother, Lady Douglas – that whore – had cast a spell over her husband, the King. But she had borne their bastards no grudge. Hadn't she taken them all under her own wing and brought them up as royalty?

And now she must worry about another witch, Lady Huntly. What was she to do with her daughter, Lady Jean Gordon? If she sent her home she could be attacked on the way. If she left her here, the castle could fall, and the child could be killed. Then all the Scottish lords would rise up against her and Mary. She didn't trust one of them.

No . . . There were enough enemies from the south, from England, she brooded, and tossed and turned. Lady Jean Gordon would have to go with them in order to keep Abbie McCracken close by the Queen. Lady Huntly possessed brain power, as well as her other more dubious powers, as Maitland had not needed to point out.

Marie's mind was going round and round and back to

these Scottish lords again. Arran had been elected Regent by those same lords at Mary's birth, to govern Scotland for her in her minority, but Arran was the most inconstant man Marie had ever known. The slightest breeze could sway him this way or that. So she must act for Mary politically as best she could, as well as looking to all her other needs.

She should rest – but how, when she knew that she must send Mary to France, where there was the most wicked witch in all the world? The Queen of France herself . . . Catherine de Medicis, Satan's disciple, who had sold her soul in return for children to inherit the French throne.

Now Marie must sell something too, her own dear daughter, to the French. In return for their shelter she must agree to Mary's marriage with the Dauphin, so that in the end he would share the Scottish crown. It was the best solution she could find. France was her native land. Mary was half French herself. The French were their only allies.

And France is Catholic. Marie de Guise crossed herself. *Above all, it is Catholic.*

She would send Janet, Lady Fleming, to be a governess for Mary and her own daughter, Flamina, and the other children. Janet Fleming had taken her widowhood badly.

Brother Thomas, the Prior of Inchmahome, would have got her message hours ago. He would be prepared to receive them already at the secluded island retreat. She could lie here no longer.

It was time to go.

In the heart of the night, when it was darkest and coldest, and Abbie was still rolled into a ball of misery in her bed, she sat up in alarm when a candle was quietly lit. In its glow she saw Florrie and Maggie May, both fully dressed, scurrying about and peering into the chests and presses.

'What are you looking for, Florrie?' she asked.

'Clothes, especially warm ones. Here are yours. Get dressed quickly.'

'But why?' Lady Jean objected, rubbing her eyes when in

95

turn Maggie May dragged her from her bed and began to dress her.

'You are going on a secret journey,' Florrie answered, and then pursed her lips. That meant there was to be no argument about it.

'Where to?' Jean persisted, and Abbie understood when the child began to wail in fear of the unknown.

'Sh! Maggie May and I are to go back to Strathbogie,' Florrie conceded grudgingly. 'The Queen Mother has ordered two riders to take us there. But you and Abbie are to go with Queen Mary.'

Then Jean sobbed in real earnest. Abbie felt angry, for she could tell that the nurses were more interested in themselves than in trying to reassure the little girl. She put a comforting arm around Jean. 'Tell us where we are going,' she demanded.

'There's no use asking *us*,' Maggie May put in nervously, with her hands full of bundles. 'We have not been told. It is the little Queen's secret. But she wants the Marys and you two to go with her. So we'd better get downstairs.'

'Yes,' Florrie said, picking up the rest of the bundles. 'We are all to be ready in the Great Hall as fast as we can.'

'I'm not going down there!' Jean screamed. 'Not with that bear and those two queer men!'

'That was only a bad dream you had, dearie,' Abbie said steadily, while she smoothed Jean's brow, rubbed her back and glared at the two nurses. 'Come with me and see for yourself. There's no bear, and no queer men there any more, I promise you. Trust your Abbie. Come, take my hand.'

Gently coaxing, she persuaded Jean down to the Great Hall where all was bustling activity. The two nurses were the first to be sent out, escorted by two horsemen. Oh, they were so lucky to be going back home to Strathbogie, Abbie thought. She wondered, not for the first time, why had the Huntlys left Lady Jean here without visiting her? They hadn't even sent her a message . . . Or did they know that she was on her way to somewhere else? They were cruel, cruel people.

Abbie felt no such pangs about her own family although

there had been no contact with them either. She knew all she needed to know, that they loved her, as solid as a rock. So solid, that she felt guilty herself to be leaving Stirling Castle without being able to tell them.

She felt worse than that about Donald. She had sadly missed the friend she could always confide in, all the time she'd been in Stirling. There was no one else in the world who would listen to her questions and never fail to come up with answers which she always believed. Would she ever see him again?

The little Queen was just as confused as Abbie. 'Are we going alone?' she was asking Mistress Sinclair, her personal maid, while she pulled on the last of her heavy clothes.

'No. Your mother is going with you, and so are all your playmates.'

'Shall we be coming back?'

'Some day, perhaps.'

'So it is a great adventure?' Mary laughed excitedly.

'Yes, a great adventure,' Mistress Sinclair smiled tearfully, wiping her eyes. 'May God speed Your Majesty.'

Outside the night was cold and moonless. Dim torches lit the courtyard while they foregathered, but for fear of English enemies still lurking at the base of the rock the torches were extinguished while they descended the long steps from the castle. At the bottom horses and soldiers were waiting for them in the darkness. The children were settled in front of the soldiers, for safety, and then they were riding, galloping through the misty, murky night.

It was not nearly such a long ride as the one from Huntly. It stopped when they came to water, and in the early dawn Abbie could make out that this was a lake. They stepped into little boats and boatmen rowed them across the lake towards an island. Now that the light was coming in, Abbie saw that it was a green island and in the middle of it was a white building like a church. Down at the water's edge to meet them was a figure dressed in a long black robe.

Queen Mary was handed out first, and the man fell on

one knee. 'Welcome, Your Majesty,' he said. 'I am Brother Thomas, the Prior here. Welcome to Inchmahome.'

The children ate at the long refectory table with the monks, they slept on clean beds smelling of lavender, and sometimes when they were sure that nobody was looking they peeped in and watched one of the eight services of the day in the church.

Queen Mary loved the place. She loved the soft chanting of the monks, the perfumed smoke of the incense, the stained-glass panels of the windows glowing like jewels in the sunshine. Most of all she loved the beauty of the Virgin Mary, carved out of alabaster, her robes softly reflecting red and yellow and violet and green as the light caught the colours of the glass.

'I wish I could be a nun, Mother,' she said, ecstasy in her eyes. 'I could be happy for ever then.'

'You are a queen, my child. Queens cannot be nuns. They must grow up and have children to inherit the throne.'

But Marie de Guise was worried. Mary had been to Mass at the Chapel Royal in Stirling Castle many times. Admittedly, it was a colourless affair. But now she seemed to have seen magic. Her soul had been aroused, too aroused. She was forgetting her true purpose in life.

The royal party stayed only three weeks before Marie de Guise took them away on other wild night rides over the moors, to other refuges. Once they went to Dunkeld, and now and then, when all was quiet, she would hide them away in Stirling Castle again. But she remained alert and very suspicious, her worry intensified when Mary suddenly fell ill in March.

She had smallpox. She was dying. The rumours spread like wildfire, and it was true that Mary was very ill. But the spots faded away and she could get out of bed again after a bad bout of measles so that in a few weeks came the very last ride of all, west until they came to Dumbarton Castle, another castle perched high on a rock, overlooking the sea.

When daylight came they saw a painted fleet riding at anchor in the rocky port below, the galleys of Henry II of France come to rescue Mary of Scotland.

'We are all going to France,' she told her playmates excitedly, 'and I am going in the King's own galley! See, it is that one with all the lovely flags. All our belongings are going with us, even our ponies! What a great adventure!'

That was that, then, Abbie thought unhappily. They were going across the sea to France. Now she knew for certain that she would never see Donald again. She had never given up hope until that terrible minute.

FOURTEEN

John McCracken, summoned to Strathbogie, was quite prepared to hear of the Earl's latest quarrel and what the
Gordons were expected to do about it. That was not unusual.
But when the Earl was not in the courtyard to bark out his
orders for all to hear, John was wary.

He was not summoned into the castle itself unless it was
for something of extreme importance, something secret.
There was always the dread in the back of his mind that he
could be sent far away one day on a mission that could last
for months.

Well, he wasn't going. Somebody else would have to go
instead.

There was one man bold enough for anything, who wasn't
married, who had no ties, and that man was Donald Mac-
Laren. John was putting all his faith and trust in Donald in
whatever emergency this would turn out to be.

He passed the sentries at the door of the castle, and
marched along the passage to the Earl's door, his face relaxed
in a smile, for only this morning Donald had had all the men
laughing when he made an announcement in the middle of
the serious business of donning the uniforms and checking
the weapons.

'Boys,' he said. 'I feel a dance coming on,' and proceeded
to kick up his legs and leap about the floor.

'Would you just look at that idiot!' one of the soldiers
exclaimed, starting to laugh.

'For Christ's *sake*, Donald, give it up!' another one

wheezed and crowed, doubled up with laughter. 'You're making my stomach sore!'

In a few minutes the whole barracks was helpless.

'Let me show you a few of my latest steps,' Donald insisted, while the men howled all the louder.

'If I were you I wouldn't give up my real job,' John advised him. 'Now settle down, the lot of you, and be ready to go by the time I get back.'

But Donald had been like a breath of fresh air in the place, John admitted it. He had grown up to be a real man's man. Still walking along the corridor as all these thoughts passed through his head, John McCracken would have been genuinely surprised if anyone had told him that he had done most to shape the boy.

It was a pity the Huntlys never shut a door, John thought next. Standing outside it, he could see and hear everything inside, where Lord Huntly was pacing up and down and arguing with his wife while she sat beside the fire as adamant and commanding as ever.

'You cannot mean it, Elizabeth! The Queen is being shipped off to France, and our daughter with her – yet you will not go to Dumbarton to say goodbye?'

'*You* may go if you wish, but I can tell you now it will only unsettle her. Jean should not come back here. Her place is beside the Queen.'

'Where you have left her, without a word, all this time!' Lord Huntly said indignantly.

John knocked, before it got any worse. 'You sent for me, my lord?'

'Yes, McCracken. The Queen is to be sent to France. She and the rest of the royal party are at Dumbarton now and will embark any day. The Queen Mother has ordered that the best soldier from each loyal clan should form a Scottish Guard and go with her.'

'I see . . . How long would this assignment last, my lord?'

'Weeks, months, years perhaps. How can I tell?'

Years perhaps? In that case, John McCracken decided

instantly, the honour would not fall to him. Abigail was twenty-three now, in the prime of her life and more beautiful than ever, in his opinion. He could not allow her to be a grass widow, alone and defenceless at the Gardeners' Cottage, anywhere near Lord Huntly with *his* dubious reputation with women.

'Of course,' Lady Huntly put in, 'Abbie will accompany Lady Jean.'

It got worse by the minute. The mistress had laid down the law, and there was nothing to be done about it, except bend it a little if he could. Well, thank God Abbie liked Donald MacLaren.

'I myself will escort the Queen Mother back to her rightful place in Holyrood Palace,' Lord Huntly said pompously. 'There will no longer be any need for all this chasing around, with the child Queen gone.'

'There should be no difficulty with any of that,' John said smoothly.

'Then you will join the Scottish Guard?' Lord Huntly asked. 'It is within my power to order it, you know,' he added when John hesitated, and narrowed his eyes already so creased in fat that they were almost out of sight.

John's eyes flickered only once. His mind was racing, but he kept the muscles of his face carefully schooled. Lord Huntly was a bully and a brute. He was also strangely weak in many ways, and very easily flattered. John decided to play on that as he looked him straight in the eye, man to man.

'You did say "the best soldier", my lord, and you are in the happy position of having the two best fighting men in Scotland here at Strathbogie. Naturally, I should prefer the honour of remaining in your service here, but there is another man who would not hesitate to go to France.'

'Who?'

'Donald MacLaren.'

'Donald . . . ?' The Earl's eyes lit up, while his wife glowered. 'Indeed, no one would recognise him as the pig-boy of a few years ago.'

Now, the Earl thought, Donald was bursting into manhood, tall, broad and extremely handsome in a dark sardonic way, very like himself when he was younger. He wouldn't like to get in his way, and he easily imagined that Donald MacLaren could turn very nasty in a crisis, very nasty indeed. After all, he was his own son.

'I have come to know him, my lord, and he has grown into a very good soldier and an expert fighting man.'

'Like his father before him!' Lord Huntly puffed up his chest proudly, regardless of his wife's finer feelings.

'He has saved my life twice now, and is the only man I would willingly trust with my own daughter's life, let alone Lady Jean's,' John added firmly.

'Wonderful! Then let it be Donald, by all means!'

'Shall I have the honour of escorting you, too, my lady? Are you coming to Dumbarton with us?'

'I am far from well.' Lady Huntly put a hand on the healthiest bosom in the north of Scotland. 'My husband will say goodbye for me.'

'We leave in two hours, McCracken,' the Earl announced, glancing at his wife angrily. 'You will detail MacLaren?'

'We'll be ready,' John said, and went home to comfort Abigail as best he could, knowing what her reaction would be.

'*France*, John? Oh, I had a terrible feeling about all this from the beginning,' Abigail wept.

'Yes, you did, and I should have listened to you. As it was, I had a bit of fast talking to do, or I should have been going as well as Abbie.'

'What?'

'I managed to persuade Lord Huntly that I should stay here, and that Donald was the man for the job.'

Later that day he turned to the man riding at his side. 'I'm trusting you, Donald MacLaren, and you'd better not let me down. I talked you up to the Earl, which is why you've been chosen to go to France, in case you start getting big-headed.

Above all, no harm must come to a hair of Abbie's head. You must promise me that, absolutely.'

'Och, cheer up, John!' Donald smiled his quirky smile. 'I'll look after her like my own sister.'

'You haven't got a sister, you young devil.'

'No. Abbie will be my first. I haven't been on a ship yet either. But I did have an uncle who was a sea captain, so I'll have my sea legs along with the best of them, never fear – and we're going to need them by the look of that sky!'

So, laughing at him all the way, John arrived with Donald in Dumbarton. The royal party were ready to depart and the two little girls from Strathbogie were standing by themselves on the pier. John squatted down in front of Abbie with his arms around her.

'You won't be alone, my wee lassie,' he told her. 'Donald is coming, too. He won't be living in the same house as you when you get there, but he'll be watching over you. He promised.'

With a great thud of her heart Abbie smiled and her cheeks became pink again. If Donald were coming, nothing else mattered.

'Your mother sends you her fondest love. She says you have always been a good girl and she can trust you now to be a good girl in France.'

'I will, dearest Father.'

During this conversation John saw Lord Huntly saying a few stiff words to Lady Jean who howled louder than ever as a result. John put his arms around her next and gave her a cuddle, diverting her attention by pointing to a group of boys also on the pier.

'Look!' he said. 'You're going to have plenty of boys to play with! The Queen Mother sent for them, because she thought there were more girls than boys. Shall we go and meet them?'

Lady Jean's eyes followed her father, who was marching off to the Queen Mother without a backward glance, but once again John distracted her attention by introducing her to the boys.

'This is Lady Jean Gordon,' he told them, 'and she's looking for a friend to play with. She's feeling a bit lonely.'

Then an arm went around Jean's shoulders and a fair-haired boy was at her side. 'I'm going to France, too. I'll play with you. Oh, we'll have a fine time, you and I. Come on, Lady Jean, let's go aboard!'

'Who's that?' John asked Donald when he found him in the crowd again. 'Go and find out.'

'Och, I've found out already. All these boys are the sons of noblemen, specially chosen to balance the Queen's court. That particular one is Alex Ogilvie of Boyne, one of the richest boys in Scotland. Not even the Huntlys could object to *him*. I was talking to him, and he seemed very pleasant. Slow, but pleasant.'

Abbie gave her father one last kiss, then put her hand in Donald's quite happily and went on board the ship where Jean and Alex Ogilvie were already chasing each other around excitedly. Lord Huntly prised the child Queen, weeping now that she realised her mother wasn't going with her to France, out of the Queen Mother's arms.

Half an hour later Mary was running about the deck with the others, but in the bowels of the French ship John Knox and the other rowers were flexing their aching muscles for another gruelling trip. For a year now, after he had been captured by the French when St Andrews Castle fell, he had been rowing in the galleys.

Ever since, he had been carefully nursing his bitter hatred of all things Catholic. Now, out of a porthole he caught sight of the object of his bitterest gall, the small figure of Mary, Queen of Scots.

'There she is!' he cursed. 'The tragedy of Scotland! God grant that this ship sinks to the bottom of the sea with her, even if we all go as well, for Scotland's sake!'

'Shut your bastard mouth!' roared the overseer, lashing him as hard as he could.

Marie de Guise stood on the edge of the rocks and waved her handkerchief forlornly before she turned and swung onto her horse.

When John McCracken looked back the French ships were almost dots on the horizon.

'God help them all,' he prayed. 'God help them.'

FIFTEEN

'I suppose we'll see Alex Ogilvie and the other young Scottish courtiers every day,' Abbie said, once she had got over her initial seasickness, 'but when and how will I ever see you, Donald? Where will you be?'

Her eyes told her that he had grown in stature, and she sensed that he was changing in other ways too. Donald, who had always laughed and teased her unmercifully, was treating her more seriously and gently now.

'The Scottish Guard are here to guard Queen Mary, Abbie. Day and night we can never be very far away from her.'

'But where?'

'There will be soldiers' quarters in all the French castles.'

'Good! Then I'll come and visit you, the same as I did at home.'

'No, Abbie. The Gordons get a lot of freedom around Strathbogie. It will be quite different in France. We won't be allowed to wander about there – and wee lassies will definitely not be allowed into the barracks, believe me.'

'Then I'll never see you!'

'Yes, you will. Your father has seen to that. He knows the Captain of the Scottish Guard, who promised that any messages to and from the castles will be one of my duties. So I'll look out for you every time I'm sent.'

So it was a happy and reassured Abbie who saw the journey end at Roscoff, and who embarked with the others on the French King's huge decorated barge which had been sent for Queen Mary, to take her and her court up the River Seine to the Château of St-Germain-en-Laye. It glided along slowly, fitted with unimaginable luxuries.

When they could tear themselves away from these, Abbie and Jean hung over the railings with the other young Scots, trying to catch a glimpse of their own Scottish Guard marching alongside up the river. Their bagpipes reminded them of home, delighting all who saw and heard them on the way. The French people clapped and waved and shouted a welcome to them, and Abbie's heart swelled with pride, fit to burst each time she saw the tall figure of her beloved Donald.

'The Queen is getting very excited,' Jean whispered, as the leisurely journey was drawing to an end and Mary joined them at the railings, straining to see their destination.

'That's because she is going to meet the French royal children, whom everyone calls *Les Enfants de France*, in particular Francis. He will be her husband some day,' Abbie whispered back.

Letters from Marie de Guise arrived at the French court before the Scottish children did. One in particular interested Marie's brother, Charles de Guise, Cardinal of Lorraine.

> In this desperate gamble to preserve the life of my child and her realm, there is only one ace up my sleeve, in the shape of Lady Jean Gordon's young maidservant, Abbie McCracken, whose striking resemblance to my Mary you will see at a glance. It is my wish that in any present danger or emergency Abbie McCracken should be used, even now, to impersonate the Queen. My long-term aim is that she, a rough country girl, should be groomed to that end for Mary's eventual triumphant return to rule Scotland. It is therefore to Mary's advantage that Abbie McCracken should be educated and instructed, up to a point and as far as she is capable. We do not expect her to possess Mary's intelligence, naturally, but the

fostering of any glimmer of understanding would be desirable.

My dear brother Cardinal, you will understand that not one of us of the family of Guise would wish Queen Catherine to be acquainted of this plan. I have not thrown my dearest child upon any mercy of hers, but only on that of her husband, King Henry, with your inestimable assistance.

Having committed the whole letter to memory, the Cardinal burned it at once. It was too dangerous a missive to fall into the hands of Catherine de Medicis by chance, or into those of one of her minions, and her spies were everywhere. The information it contained provided him with yet another trump card to add to others he was keeping up his own sleeve, for he hated Catherine and was determined to overthrow her at the earliest opportunity.

In justice, since she was a wicked witch and he was a distinguished man of God, he should succeed. Good would triumph over evil.

But the English interpretation of his name, Guise, fitted this two-faced man like a glove. If Catherine was the mistress of intrigue, he was undoubtedly the master of it.

The King and Queen of France were away when Queen Mary and her court arrived. In their place, the most beautiful lady Abbie had ever seen received them. She was Diane de Poitiers, the King's mistress – not that Abbie or any of them had understood *then* what a mistress was, and Mary certainly didn't care, because Diane introduced her to Francis.

Dear little Francis, with his pursed-up rosebud mouth! He did not seem very strong. Abbie saw fear and uncertainty on his face before he looked away from Mary shyly with tears in his eyes. Abbie felt sorry for him at once, and obviously, so did his future bride.

'Dearest Francis,' she said, putting her arms around him. 'I am so happy to meet you! I love you already.'

Then he smiled. 'I love you, too,' he said, and everyone was happy, especially Diane de Poitiers.

With her silver hair and pale luminous skin Diane was kind, unhurried and serene. She seemed to glide along the marbled floors of the château, out of one magnificent salon and into the next, showing them the way to the nursery. She was the complete opposite of Queen Catherine of France, when in due course she returned to St-Germain.

They were all playing a delightful game inside one day when the door opened and in stepped a short ugly woman, fat, black-haired and pug-nosed, followed by a servant who turned out to be an interpreter. The nursery floor was littered with toys and the clothes the children had been dressing up in, and silence fell as the woman stared around haughtily until her eyes fastened on Mary and looked her up and down.

So, she knows perfectly well who the tall red-haired child is, Abbie thought.

'You should all bow or curtsy to the Queen of France,' the woman said in overbearing, guttural tones.

The Scottish children did so at once, all except Mary.

'And *you*?' the French Queen frowned.

Mary stood up proudly, tall and slim. 'I am a queen also, madam, as I think you know. I am Mary, Queen of Scotland and the Isles.'

Inwardly, Abbie shrank. From her days at the Scottish court she understood that the little Queen knew no better. She had been brought up and flattered into thinking, and often saying in this imperious fashion that the very sun rose and set on her, and on her alone. Marie de Guise should have trained her better than to put her first foot down so wrongly on French soil.

There was a tear in Abbie's eyes when she realised that Abigail would have warned *her* in a similar situation, and she hardly needed to glance at Queen Catherine's face to see that Mary had made an implacable enemy in just that one minute.

It seemed a long time to them all before Francis shouted,

'*Maman*!' and followed by the Princess Elisabeth and the other French royal children hurled himself into her arms.

When she looked up Queen Catherine was still glaring at Mary. '*Maman*!' Francis cried. 'Here is dear Marie from Scotland!'

'I am honoured to meet Your Majesty,' Mary said pleasantly, curtsying low.

'Hm . . . And do you like her well enough, my son?' Catherine ignored that pretty speech and turned to Francis.

'I love her,' the little Dauphin said.

'Then that will have to be good enough for me, I suppose.'

'And I am going to marry her,' Francis added firmly, and at that Queen Catherine bethought herself.

'Yes, you are welcome here, Maria,' she said in a lukewarm fashion.

The door opened again, and in stepped a handsome man impressively arrayed in satin robes. Abbie knew by them that he was a man of the Church, although up to now she had only ever seen sober black robes. These were silver and blue, the very same blue as his brilliant eyes. Abbie took an instant and unreasonable dislike to the man, his robes and the jewels he wore on every finger of his hands. It was as if he were trying to be the King.

He swept in, accompanied by Mary's own Scottish priest, Father Mamerot, and addressed her first. 'I am your dear mother's brother,' he smiled at her – falsely, in Abbie's opinion – 'Charles de Guise, the Cardinal of Lorraine.'

Mary ran forward with arms outstretched. 'Dearest Uncle Charles!' she cried, but the Cardinal stepped back.

'No,' he said. 'You may call me Uncle Cardinal,' and then Abbie knew her instinct had been right. Mary was amongst enemies.

The French Queen listened as the Scottish priest introduced all the young people of Mary's court. Her black heavily painted eyes slid around first to Abbie whom she ignored, and then to Jean. 'And who is this?' she asked next.

III

'She is one of Queen Mary's playmates, Your Majesty,' the interpreter said. 'Lady Jean Gordon.'

'*La pauvre petite* . . .' Catherine said, half in French and half in Italian, softening unexpectedly. '*La bella*! . . . Jeanne, is it? But – look at her hair!' Jean's cap had been long cast aside and her corn-coloured hair wildly dishevelled. But it seemed to touch a maternal chord in the Queen's heart. 'Jeanne, your hair could be so pretty! I will make it so.'

'That's done it,' Abbie whispered to Jean when the Queen left, dragging Francis, protesting, with her. 'She's taken a fancy to you, all over that hair of yours!'

Jean looked across the nursery at Alex Ogilvie for approval. By now he had become her closest friend next to Abbie, and Alex was smiling encouragingly when the Cardinal silenced them all with an imperious wave of his bejewelled hand.

'These are the arrangements that have been made for you,' he said. 'The young gentlemen will be allocated tutors. The Marys and Lady Jean will take lessons in the royal nursery under the supervision of Lady Fleming. Queen Mary herself must be specially trained. She will study with me, and because she is so young it may be less tedious for her if she studies with a companion.' He looked directly at Abbie. 'I understand that you have acted as a companion already?'

'Yes, sir.'

'But Abbie is *my* companion,' Jean objected tearfully.

'Of course she is,' the Cardinal said in a soothing voice, 'and she will be gone from you only for a few hours each day. You will have the other children to work and play with while she is with me.'

He swept out again, leaving Jean in tears and Abbie with the uncomfortable feeling that someone masquerading as God had just spoken.

'Never mind,' she comforted Jean. 'Come and see what a wonderful dolls' house I've found. You and Alex can play with it.'

And it was indeed wonderful. It was a wooden model

château which opened up on hinges to reveal miniature rooms and furniture inside. Jean rushed over to it and peeped in its tiny windows. Inside was a magical world.

'Look,' Abbie said, 'here are the doll-people that live inside it. You can dress them and put them on their little horses in the courtyard, or you can undress them and put them to bed. It will be a little world of your own where you can do what you like.'

So Jean's tears dried and she was playing quietly with Alex in the corner when the little Queen was introduced to her grandmother next, the Duchesse Antoinette de Guise. Antoinette hugged her and Mary clasped her arms around her neck, weeping and thanking her over and over again for always supporting her mother, Marie, although so far away in the barbaric country of Scotland where now she appeared a lonelier figure than ever, protecting the throne for her only surviving child.

SIXTEEN

Those early years in France were bathed in a rosy glow where it was always summer, the meadows were always bright and the air was always laden with the perfumes of flowers and the sharper scents of ripening fruits. From the beginning Queen Mary seemed completely at home. As far as she was concerned the grey dourness of Scotland was a thing of the past.

So Abbie confided to Donald the next time she saw him, which happened to be one afternoon when she was waiting for Lady Jean to come out of her classroom.

'What have you been learning in there?' Donald asked Jean when at last she escaped.

'The same old things. Reading and writing. It's boring.'

'You don't know how lucky you are,' Donald said sternly. 'I wish I could read and write, but it's too late for me now.'

'I wouldn't say that,' Alex Ogilvie said, coming to join them. 'We have a wonderful tutor, Father Tiberon. I'll speak to him.'

A few days later when Donald was in the château Alex waylaid him. 'Of course, you and the rest of the Scottish Guard hear Mass in the chapel, Donald?'

'Yes. It breaks the monotony of nothing to do. This sojourn in France is a waste of time for us soldiers. There are no battles to fight here.'

'Well, the next time Father Tiberon is taking the service, he wants you to stay behind to talk to him. Do you know Father Tiberon?'

Donald laughed, remembering the night the priest got drunk with Lord Huntly and told dirty stories. 'I know him. And thank you, Alex.'

'I know you, don't I?' Father Tiberon peered into Donald's face.

'I was the boy at Strathbogie who plied you and Lord Huntly with wine, Father, on the evening of the wedding of John McCracken and Abigail Moncrieff.'

'Dear me, so you are! *Tempus fugit*,' the priest said with a sigh, noting Donald's height. 'Alex Ogilvie tells me that you would like to read and write.'

'I would, Father.'

'Hm . . . You would not be permitted to join the young Scottish nobles at their studies in the château, I'm afraid. Would it be possible for me to come to your quarters in the evenings, perhaps?'

'You would be welcomed, Father, and not only by me. Many of our soldiers are keen to learn.'

'That is a Scottish characteristic, I believe.'

So Donald learned to read and write, and it was only the beginning of boredom relieved both for the soldiers and for the priest on many evenings which inevitably ended in hilarity after that.

Queen Catherine kept her promise to Lady Jean. Almost immediately the order came.

'You are to attend her Majesty, Queen Catherine, this morning,' the interpreter came to tell her.

'Not without Abbie,' Jean said, grasping her hand.

The man shrugged indifferently and led them through the rooms and passages to the Queen's apartments. 'She will receive you in her parlour,' he said, opening the door to a mixture of silken tassels, beaded curtains and walls painted with fat cupids cradled in the arms of Venus. Over all hung the smell of suet, mixed with heavy Italian scent.

Queen Catherine jumped up from her purple love seat with

alacrity for one so stout, scattering astrological charts and lapdogs right and left. 'Ah, yes! The oil for the little one's hair,' she said, flapping her arms and ushering the girls before her like a hen with two chickens down more passages and out into the gardens. 'There are my perfumers,' she told them, pointing out several hard-working men. 'They gather the flowers, first of all. But it must be done at the height of the day, when the dew is off the petals – except the jasmine, of course. Jasmine is picked at night when its perfume is at its height. That is why it is so scarce and so expensive. Then,' she shooed them back indoors again, 'the petals are dried and crushed, and the oil distilled from them – like this!'

Abbie and Jean found themselves in a large room where more men were busily working with jars and tubes and glass bottles. 'Now,' Queen Catherine said, 'you know where the oil comes from! My ladies will wash your hair with it. It will become soft and beautiful, like mine.'

Perhaps, Abbie thought, the Queen's hair was indeed the best part of her. It glistened jet-black under her cap. She was obviously very proud of it, and very proud too, of her legs. She lifted up her skirts whenever she walked so that everyone could admire them, but they only reminded Abbie of John McCracken's legs, muscled and powerful, and not a lady's legs at all.

Jean's hair was gently washed in another of the Queen's rooms, and the oil rubbed into it. Then it was brushed and brushed by one of the Queen's ladies, and during this process Jean became so restless and bored that the lady opened a drawer and took out a box.

'What's in it?' Jean asked, taking off the lid.

Abbie was as mystified as Jean until she saw that it contained tiny arms and legs, heads and bodies and even feet and hands. 'Let's try joining them together,' she said. 'We might make a doll.' It was a fascinating pastime and before they knew it Jean's hair was brushed dry and shining.

'That's better!' the Queen exclaimed, coming into the bou-

116

doir. 'You will come back every week, on Wednesday afternoons, and repeat the treatment.' Abbie may not trust the Queen, but so far she had proved herself a woman of her word.

Nothing much has changed in so many months, Abbie thought, looking back. She sat behind Queen Mary and gazed across the desk at the Cardinal's robe, noticing how well the blue satin set off his fair hair and blue eyes. If only he would shave off his silly, wispy beard! Abbie was intelligent, interested in people and quite capable of assessing the good and bad points of their appearance. She enjoyed learning the lessons along with Mary. One day, however the little Queen argued with the Cardinal.

'My Marys miss me so much while I am closeted in here with you, Uncle Cardinal,' she fretted, seated at the desk in his study.

'They have other duties, my dear, while you are studying. And study you must, if you are to be our Queen.'

'But what can they find to do all day long?'

'They are to be your ladies-in-waiting, are they not? So they must be able to sew and attend to your wardrobe. It takes up so much of their time already that it has been decided that they shall each be given a French maidservant. Lady Jean Gordon has a maidservant of her own, after all,' the Cardinal glanced at Abbie, 'and she is only a little Scottish girl.'

Abbie fumed inside. Lady Jean Gordon – only a little Scottish girl? But Mary was smiling, pleased at the arrangement for her Marys.

'In fact, the maidservants have already been chosen, and you, Abbie, will move into other quarters with them.'

'Lady Jean and Abbie like to be together, Uncle Cardinal,' Mary protested.

'And so they shall be, my dear, except to sleep. You'll see! Everyone will be happier than ever!'

The sun glinted in the long window and lit up the Cardinal's eyes, eyes which Abbie could never fathom. They often took on different shades of blue. Today she thought what a beautiful colour they were, the colour of the turquoises she had seen in Queen Mary's jewel box, and for a second a little shiver passed over her. They glittered just as cold and hard.

But Mary adored him.

'He is so good and kind,' she said as they walked back along the passage from the study. 'But then, he would be. He is my mother's brother, but he feels more like a father to me,' and after that small confrontation she obeyed his every suggestion without question.

Abbie agreed that what he had said was true.

Everyone was happy, very happy indeed, even the King. Although he had a mournful disposition, he really believed the court flatterers when they told him that he resembled the sun, so that they basked in his rays. Diane de Poitiers was a stylish woman whose beauty also flattered his ego. She never wore colours, only black or white. She never wore jewels except diamonds, usually in her silver hair and often in the shape of a crescent moon, the symbol she had adopted.

Just lately, however, his eye had fallen on the Scottish woman Lady Fleming, with her long red hair and crimsoned pouting mouth . . .

Catherine de Medicis, or the Italian Woman, as the Queen of France was sometimes called, was also very happy.

When she was not actually giving birth to one of the royal babies she had every year now – at last, after so many barren years, and after so many consultations with her 'advisers' – Queen Catherine was a busy woman. Each day she studied the charts that Nostradamus prepared for her, foretelling the future. Together they consulted the stars. Together they concocted the receipts for their potions, and together they oversaw the scientists who had to brew them.

Catherine was also a connoisseur of art and had brought Leonardo's pictures with her from Italy, and to regale the royal nostrils she produced the heady perfumes of the roses, hyacinths, lilacs and jasmine. The scents, the sights and the sounds went on and on like the never-ending cascades of water tinkling from the fountains.

Yes, Abbie thought, childhood in France had passed by in a dream of gold, eternal and unchanging. The sun shone every day, dusk fell every evening like warm milk and at nightfall the coloured lanterns were lit in the court gardens, dancing like fireflies in each passing breeze, making St-Germain-en-Laye a magical place . . . making it a fairyland.

There, the children were pampered by royal right, fed on the luxuries of strawberries and melons, delicate pastries and trout as pale and pink as the wine they washed it down with.

Their eyes saw only beautiful things, gold and crystal at the table, rich velvets and silks to wear, and wonderful paintings by great masters hanging on the walls.

It had been a happy conspiracy to bewitch the senses, a fluffy cocoon to shelter them from the world outside, but now into the boundless azure of this heaven came the first tiny cloud of change.

Mary's half-brother, Lord James Stewart, left the French court and hurried back to Scotland, saying that he had business there and could dally in France no longer.

'And what a relief that is!' Lady Jean said to Abbie. 'I never liked him, right from the beginning in Stirling.'

Abbie agreed, and so when she told him, did Donald. 'A very nasty, sly creature,' he summed him up. 'He would have Mary's crown if he could get his hands on it, there's no doubt of that. I wonder what "business" it is he has in Scotland?'

Then, one morning, after he had tried to explain to Queen Mary, with Abbie in attendance, what was happening in Scotland and the continuing problems with England, the Cardinal told her that he had good news for her, and bad.

'Which shall I tell you first?' he asked.

'The bad. I hope it is not very bad?' Mary asked, bracing herself.

'I'm afraid it is. I have here a letter from Lord James Stewart. As soon as he got back to Scotland he declared himself a Protestant. He does not say so here, but my emissaries have told me that John Knox was the man behind that. He has converted James to the New Faith. Since he was released from captivity he is trying to convert all Scotland – John Knox, your mother's bitterest enemy.'

'*James, a Protestant!*' Mary gripped the table in front of her until her knuckles went white. She swayed where she sat and Abbie jumped up in concern to go to her. 'I don't believe it,' Mary said. 'Not James!'

'Read it for yourself, my dear.'

While she read it Mary collected herself swiftly. Then she looked up. 'Yes,' she said, 'and he has signed it James Stewart. But I am not like him. I shall never be like him. This is how I sign *my* name,' and, reaching for a quill, wrote 'MARIE STUART'.

'Well,' she said after a pause, 'now that I have dealt with the bad news, please let me know the good.'

'You have done well, Marie. Everything changes, you know, as everything must. But this time you will welcome it with open arms. Yes, my dear,' he smiled at her, 'we must prepare to entertain an important embassy from abroad. It is the Queen Mother of Scotland's embassy . . . Marie, your mother is coming to France!'

Abbie remembered how Mary glowed with the most perfect happiness long after the Cardinal had left the study.

'Oh, Abbie,' she said, 'I have been truly, truly blessed,' and burst into tears.

Mopping up those tears of happiness, Abbie felt surprised that she had been allowed to remain present during such a personal conversation, for there had been many times when the Cardinal had made her wait outside the door while he held private sessions with the little Queen.

In fact, it was during one of those occasions recently that Abbie had begun to ask herself questions. Why had *she*, in particular, been chosen to be educated along the same lines as the Queen of Scotland? Why did the Cardinal always make a point of telling her, as well as Mary, all the political news, and the implications of it, from Scotland and England?

Why was she, a very ordinary maidservant, being groomed almost like a queen? She saw at once, when she asked him, that it had not escaped Donald's attention either.

'What do you think, Donald?'

For the first time he was evasive. 'Perhaps it's just a coincidence, Abbie. Perhaps they just wanted a Scottish girl in attendance during the Queen's lessons with the Cardinal.' Then he tried to dispel any more anxieties she might have. 'Can you understand all that the Cardinal is telling her, and you?'

'It's very interesting, especially when he tells the Queen the real motives of different countries. Not that she pays enough attention, I think. She's really only vitally interested in herself,' Abbie said sadly.

'Then cheer up! You'll finish up better educated than she is!'

But when she left him he looked back at her with a worried frown on his face. He was sure that Abbie's instinct was quite right, although he had tried to dismiss it. He wished that there was some way he could have discussed it with her father. John McCracken would be as suspicious as he was, and as Abbie was herself. As things were, he would have to help her and try to reassure her as best he could, for he had noticed that during the past six months there were times when she seemed unwell.

He didn't realise at the time that Abbie was in the turbulent throes of changing from a girl into a woman, when her instincts were developing and with them a heightened intuition. She *knew*, no matter how Donald had tried to shrug it off, that she was being watched, she was being used and that there must be a reason for it all . . . But what?

SEVENTEEN

'We go to Amboise tomorrow,' Queen Catherine told Nostradamus one Wednesday when Lady Jean and Abbie were in her apartments. 'It is that time of year.'

'Ah yes,' Abbie said to herself. 'You mean St-Germain is in dire need of freshening. Then, in a few months, after the court has dirtied Amboise, it will be time to go to Blois. After that we will all move to Chaumont and finally to the huge white Palace of Chambord with its four hundred and forty rooms. It's a wonderful way to live.'

But of course, she kept her mouth shut. Abbie was becoming quite cynical, and determined on a career as a spy. She had never given up the practice of rising from her bed and gliding like a shadow between the darker shadows of night in whatever château they happened to be. The secrets never changed, she discovered. They only moved with the people from château to château.

There was the fat count who always paraded around in red velvet. Abbie derived enormous entertainment from his exploits with any silly maidservant he managed to tumble to the ground while he pulled down his hose, unbuttoned his breeches and wheezed and grunted on top of her.

There were endless secret assignations to follow up in the middle of the night. The ladies were as promiscuous as the gentlemen, but to keep Abbie busiest of all were the constant movements of the King himself, flitting between Diane de Poitiers's bed and Queen Catherine's. This was the activity that puzzled her most. Relations between the two women were far from cordial, but in the end Abbie supposed that at least the Queen of France knew – as all the court knew – where her husband would be when he wasn't with her.

On the whole, her sympathies lay with Queen Catherine. People called her cunning. They called her cruel. They were frightened of her supernatural powers which so far Abbie had never witnessed. In fact, all she had seen was the mother of *Les Enfants de France*, doting, jealous, over-protective, but above all a mother, and there was no doubt that her maternal emotions spilled out to include Lady Jean who had scarcely known a proper mother in her life.

That was good enough for Abbie.

She began to make a close study of Catherine de Medicis. In her opinion Catherine, who seemed to adore her son, poor little Francis, was quite the most interesting person in the French court. In a few years Francis would become the husband of Mary of Scotland, and that union would have repercussions, for better or for worse, on the Scottish people. So, in Abbie's reasoning, Catherine – the power behind the French throne – was the lady to watch.

Abbie thought up an excuse to be in her company more often. She begged permission to join the perfumers amongst the flowers, explaining that her mother and her grandfather before her had been gardeners. Then she set about her real purpose in very small ways, always there to run errands for the Queen, always paying attention to every word the Italian Woman spoke, or when in a bad temper, screamed.

And always, she remained silent herself and kept a plain face whatever happened in the day-to-day crises. Then, when tempers cooled, she would beg the Queen to tell her any way that she could help. It had taken weeks of patient hard work to achieve it, but gradually Catherine, always temperamental and suspicious, came to trust Abbie as she would an unfailing part of the furniture around her.

By now, they had left Blois and were at Chaumont. Chaumont had a large tower on the top of it, where another of Queen Catherine's 'advisers' worked. Carrying a box in each hand Abbie toiled round and round up the steep steps of the tower behind Queen Catherine. At the top they entered a stiflingly hot room, a fug of strange gases hanging in the air.

'This is Monsieur Ruggieri,' the Queen introduced her. 'He is the astronomer here – or is it the astrologer?' They both laughed at some secret joke, and Abbie thought she must find out the difference between those two words. 'At any rate,' the Queen went on, 'he can tell your fortune by the stars.'

'Would you like me to tell you yours?' he asked Abbie, polishing a large glass ball.

'No, thank you, sir. I would rather not know.'

Again the Queen and Ruggieri laughed, but Abbie was finding the atmosphere in the tower very oppressive. She longed to get out, away from the heat, the strange smells and the smoke. While the Queen was having a long whispered conversation with Ruggieri Abbie wandered to the side of the room and into a large cupboard lined with shelves from floor to ceiling.

What she saw on the shelves took her breath away altogether. There were hundreds of little waxen models, effigies of everyone at the court. One section was devoted to the Scots. Mary, the Queen, was there, dressed in white, her favourite colour. The four Marys were behind her. And behind them Abbie saw herself, holding Lady Jean's hand.

She didn't like it. It was as though their lives had been taken from them and transplanted into these replicas. She began to feel frightened. She had entered another world. Then, away to one side, she found Lady Fleming, unmistakable with her red hair rippling down her back . . . But Lady Fleming had a long black pin stuck into her breast, and another between her legs. It was all unreal, vibrating with passion and hatred, although all her eyes saw were beautifully sculpted, painted and dressed dolls.

'Your face has gone pale, child,' the Queen said suspiciously when she found Abbie back at her side. Then she spoke to Ruggieri. 'See what has happened! A third party now shares our secret. Keep that cupboard door shut at all times from now on!'

Then, her black eyes as menacing as a snake's, she grasped Abbie's arm and propelled her down the spiral staircase and mercifully back into the fresh air. 'You will forget what you saw up there,' she hissed.

'It is forgotten already, Your Majesty,' Abbie said meekly.

But of course, it wasn't forgotten. They both knew that, and as if in some way to bribe her to forget, the Queen began to give Abbie little presents, usually bottles of perfume all to herself.

Queen Mary remained very fond of Lady Jean. One afternoon she met her with Abbie.

'Lady Jean? Abbie? Where are you going?'

'This is our day to see Queen Catherine, Your Majesty,' Abbie said. 'She is still oiling Lady Jean's hair once a week.'

'Then I'll come with you and watch,' Mary laughed. 'I've nothing better to do,' but instead of walking along with them she gave a gasp and fell down suddenly on the floor.

'She's fainted again,' said Lady Jean. 'That makes three times in as many weeks,' and they dragged her back along to her own bedchamber.

Mary opened her eyes to the delicately painted ceiling. She was lying on the floor, a cushion under her head, and Mistress Sinclair was holding a vinegar cloth to her nose while Lady Jean and Abbie gently chafed her hands.

'Thank God,' Mistress Sinclair said, kneeling beside her.

'Remember your promise,' Mary said, and the nurse nodded.

The physician was not to know about these fainting spells she was having. Her mother, when she came, was not to know. Fortunately they were always of very short duration, a mystery and a very great nuisance.

'It is probably your age,' Mistress Sinclair soothed her. 'You are growing so fast and so tall. You will be having your bleedings soon. Girls often faint at such a time.'

Recovering, Mary lay in her bed and thought about Francis. Thinking about Francis always made her feel better. In a few years he would be her dearest husband. She fell into a peaceful sleep, dreaming about him.

There was nothing Abbie would rather do than go out into the flower gardens and help the gardeners. She told Donald that she always called them the Perfumed Gardens to herself, and that every time she went into them she thought about her mother, and Abigail's gardens.

'Oh, so that's where you spend your time, is it? I'll have to get the soldiers to ride that way when we're out exercising the horses.'

He was as good as his word. Every day after that the Scottish Guard would ride past, and Donald would wave, and Abbie would tingle all over with joy, to think he went to so much trouble over her.

The ladies of the court sometimes went for a stroll in the gardens, although they never looked at Abbie or the other servants, and it wasn't long before they noticed the Scottish Guard riding past. In fact, they quivered with excitement when they rode past, especially one named Veronique.

If Veronique had not been able to walk and talk, Abbie thought she could easily have been mistaken for the most beautiful doll in the world. She was a tiny but exquisitely formed woman, with a painted face and blonde hair which curled around her face and down to her waist at the back. Usually she wore pink or blue. Any other colours would have been unthinkable on such a dainty creature.

It got to the point where it seemed to Abbie that Veronique was never out of the Perfumed Gardens, fluttering about like a butterfly, and only hovering when she saw the soldiers. She was positively dizzy when Donald waved as he rode past, and at last it dawned on Abbie that she believed he was waving at her.

It was a small step from there for Veronique to be actually

outside the hedge and walking about on the fields the Scottish
Guard were galloping over, and one morning Abbie watched
as Donald got down off his horse and disappeared behind
the hedge with her. What were they doing? She couldn't see.
All Abbie knew was that she was in a turmoil as a result.
She didn't wait for him to remount, to see if he would wave
at her again. She ran back into the château, more miserable
than she had ever been in her life.

Abbie had never been attacked by the green monster of
jealousy before. Now it tore through her. It devoured her,
and she made up her mind that she would never look at
Donald MacLaren again. She should have known this would
happen to him some day, she berated herself. He was surrounded by beautiful women, and he had certainly picked
one of the loveliest when he chose Veronique.

If only she could see her mother, Abbie pined. Or her
father. All she wanted to do was go home and curl herself
up into a corner, and cry. She hated France now. It had
brought her nothing but unhappiness.

Excitement was at fever-pitch the day Marie de Guise arrived
in France. Accompanied by a number of Scottish lords and
ladies her party was escorted by the Scottish Guard, for they
had gone to Edinburgh to fetch her. Mary simply flew into
her mother's arms while Lady Jean and Abbie scanned the
faces of the other visitors. Their hearts dropped when they
caught sight of Lord and Lady Huntly, but Jean put on a
brave face and smiled at them.

The years had taken their toll. Lord Huntly's face was
mottled red and purple as he swaggered towards them, and
Lady Huntly's best flame-coloured dress was at odds with
the heavy face paint she had used for the occasion.

'What on earth have you been doing to the child's hair?'
she greeted Abbie unpleasantly. 'I did not give you permission
to flatten it like that.'

'Her Majesty Queen Catherine herself has been oiling it,

Mother,' Jean said quickly. 'Now it is smooth enough to go under my caps – '

'Her Majesty Queen Catherine? Oh! Oh . . .' Lady Huntly interrupted. 'Well, it is quite nice, I suppose. But you look different, daughter. So do you,' she frowned at Abbie, fingering the silk of her dress and beginning to grumble. 'These were paid for with Scottish money, I hope you know.'

'No, Mother, we did not know,' Jean said with tears in her eyes.

'We do as we are told,' Abbie said firmly. 'We were given these clothes and told to wear them.'

'Your mother is quite right,' Lord Huntly boomed, clearly giving vent to strong feelings on the subject. 'The Queen Mother is supposed to supply the money for the upkeep of the Queen's court here in France, but she fights so many battles that she is always short of gold, and begs from us,' quite forgetting about all the gold her husband, James V, had deposited in Strathbogie.

'She is only over here to beg from the King of France next,' Lady Huntly put in. 'We shall not be staying long at the court to watch it.'

'Indeed!' Lord Huntly's eyes were popping with indignation. 'Your mother and I are going to tour the Continent, Jean. I am going to renovate Strathbogie as long as we have any money left to do it. We are going to look for inspiration in all the great cities.'

'I can hardly wait,' Lady Huntly told them before she wandered off with her husband, leaving the two girls stunned. 'In fact, we shall probably go tomorrow.'

'Oh, Abbie – I don't even like them now! In fact, I hardly know them!' Jean sobbed when her parents had moved off. 'I'm glad they're going away.'

'Don't you worry about it, dearie,' Abbie said wearily. 'Perhaps we'll never see them again. Perhaps our lives are in France with Queen Mary for ever, now. Anyway, here's Alex Ogilvie.'

'Let's all go and meet the Scottish Guard,' he said. 'Donald will have been glad of some action, at last.'

As if I care about him, Abbie thought sourly. All she hoped with all her heart was that her father had come across with them, and then, despite what she had told Jean, she would beg him to take her home again.

But when the soldiers laid aside their steel bonnets she saw at a glance that John McCracken wasn't there. They all wore a leather cuirass embossed with the fleur-de-lis. Their jewelled leather gauntlets were tucked into red tartan sashes, and their black velvet cloaks with facings of silver were impressive.

Under the cloaks she caught glimpses of ruffs and wide, silver-slashed sleeves – and with her heart almost stopping Abbie picked out the face of the most handsome soldier of all, more handsome than ever in full dress uniform.

It was Donald MacLaren, and to her horror he was heading straight towards her. She wanted to run away, for now she knew that she didn't just love him best in all the world any more, she was madly *in love* with him as well, and that was breaking her heart.

EIGHTEEN

'Did you miss me?' Donald asked.

Speechless at such effrontery, Abbie couldn't answer. She pretended not to have heard and kept on leaning over the white balcony, watching the people still arriving.

'Oh, I was keeping a very close eye on *you*, Abbie McCracken, before we went away!' His eyes danced into hers. 'Every time we rode past the Perfumed Gardens I thought you were the prettiest flower there.'

'But still, you never got off your horse for *me*.' The words were out of her mouth before she could stop them.

'Get off my horse?' he asked, clearly mystified. 'What are you talking about, Abbie?'

'Don't try and get out of it, Donald MacLaren! I saw you!' And now the tears were in her eyes, though she kept looking past him for her father.

He followed her eyes. 'No, Abbie. John isn't here,' he said gently, 'but men from Strathbogie coming down with Lord and Lady Huntly told me that all is well at the Gardeners' Cottage . . .' He gazed at her face anxiously. 'Ah! Now I know what you were meaning! You meant I had to get off my horse to help a lady one morning.'

'Veronique.'

'Veronique – was that her name? I never asked her. She had lost a slipper in the rough grass, and I helped her to find it.'

'You'll never change! You, and your silver tongue! Now I suppose you're going to tell me that you never kissed her?'

'*That* silly little painted doll? Oh, Abbie! Give me some credit,' Donald said, laughing now. 'You're jealous!'

'No, I'm not!'

'Yes, you're jealous . . . Thank God you're jealous. Does that mean you love me as much as I love you? I adore you, Abbie McCracken. I always have.'

'Oh, Donald . . .' Abbie smiled, with the tears still in her eyes. 'So you haven't changed, after all! Don't ever change, because I love you, too – just the way you are.'

The balcony was a very public place for what Donald had in mind next, and besides, he saw they had friends approaching.

'I see Lady Jean and Alex Ogilvie have never changed, either,' he said when they rode up on their ponies. 'Still sweethearts?' he teased them.

'Oh, yes!' Jean was smiling now.

'Yes,' Alex agreed. 'We'll get married in the end, perhaps.'

'It's all wine and roses in France,' Donald winked over their heads at Abbie as all four of them leaned over the white marble balcony and watched the bright throng milling about below. 'I suppose you've learned a lot since you came here?'

To her great annoyance Abbie giggled and blushed before she could stop herself.

'Ah . . .' said Donald, knowingly.

'Oh! Did you see that boy kissing that other boy just now?' Jean squealed, pointing them out, her eyes round. 'I always thought boys only kissed girls.'

'Where?' Donald asked. 'Oh, you mean that tall skinny one? That's Lord Darnley. We call him The Powder Puff.'

'*The Powder Puff!*'

Screaming with laughter Jean and Alex Ogilvie mounted their ponies again and trotted off.

'Explain that to me, Donald,' Abbie said. 'The Powder Puff? After living at the French court I thought I knew everything there was to know already.'

'You're a wicked little spy, Abbie McCracken! You want to know everything!'

'I know I am, and you're the very man to tell me.'

'I *am* the very man. I'm your man. So when can I see you again, then?'

'Oh, my dearest! My dearest, beloved daughter!' Marie de Guise rained kisses on Mary's face. 'Oh, you have grown! How tall you are! Take me to your rooms at once and show me all your things. Then we shall send for Mistress Sinclair, so that I may ask her all about your health.'

Proudly Mary showed her mother the chests of beautiful gowns she possessed and the jewels in her jewel box, and then Marie opened a velvet box she was carrying with her. Something red glowed inside.

'This belonged to your grandmother, Margaret Tudor,' she said, showing Mary a huge brooch of diamonds and rubies. 'You will wear it on your wedding day. King Henry will keep it safe here for you.'

'But that is a long way off!' Mary cried. 'Why didn't you wait to give me it then? You *will* see me married, Mother?' she asked anxiously. 'I should not like it if you were not here.'

'Of course I shall, dearest. But a lot could happen between now and then, and so I have made sure.'

Marie de Guise stayed a year in France, and during that time Mary was happy to see that the tired, drawn look was leaving her mother's face, although no one could fail to observe that all was not well at St-Germain. Thunderous, mutinous mutterings were coming from the direction of the Queen of France.

They erupted one evening just before one of the farewell banquets to the Queen Mother was about to begin. Abbie flattened herself against the wall in a deep curtsy, confronted by the very unusual sight of Queen Catherine, accompanied by Diane de Poitiers, sweeping down the passage to the banqueting salon.

The Queen was dressed in crimson satin, to match her mood. She stumped along beside Diane, who for once was showing signs of extreme strain on her porcelain face.

It was all too much for Abbie.

She crept to the door of the salon in time to hear Lady Fleming addressing the company in a loud, defiant voice. 'Yes,' she was saying to the hushed audience, 'it is true! I am expecting the King of France's child! I'm proud of it! I love him, and he loves me.'

It was better than a play to Abbie, to see the Queen in all her splendour, and Diane with her beautiful nose in the air, transfixed like statues. A pin could have been heard to drop. The silence went on and on until the King's eyes signalled the guards to come forward. They dragged Lady Fleming out unceremoniously and the musicians struck up again, faltering a little with the shock.

'Such rubbish!' the Queen spluttered, going up to the King and putting a possessive arm around him. Diane stood on the other side of him, silent and graceful, her face smooth again.

Lady Fleming had dared to invade these two ladies' territory. She should have known better. Abbie shook her head. Now, Lady Fleming would be banished in disgrace, she thought, and she was quite right.

'My mother doesn't like Lady Fleming any more,' Francis confided to Mary one day. 'We are to have a new governess, Madame de Parois. I've seen her and I don't like her. She's old. I wish we could have Lady Fleming back again.'

'Yes,' Mary agreed, absently winding around her finger a tendril of hair from under her gold lace snood. 'Lady Fleming is my favourite aunt.'

'My mother called her a bloody Scottish whore. What's a bloody Scottish whore, Mary? You're Scottish. You should know.'

Mary shrugged. 'I don't know.'

'Perhaps it means a Protestant?'

'My aunt would not be a Protestant, Francis,' Mary said vehemently and then sighed, looking at her future husband. It would be a long, long time before he was a man.

* * *

Lord and Lady Huntly had returned to France to accompany the Queen Mother home to Scotland. They got an appointment with the Cardinal for an hour after Queen Mary's morning lessons.

Mary was impatient to get away. Her mother would be leaving tomorrow. As soon as she left his study she took to her heels, leaving Abbie to pick up the books she had left behind. Abbie was still gathering them when the Huntlys entered, and after the Cardinal seated them she made her retreat, unashamedly leaving the door open a crack behind her.

They exchanged pleasantries for some time. Lord Huntly handed over a heavy bag of gold, to judge from the loud chinking noise Abbie heard when it was dumped on the Cardinal's desk.

'You have seen my sister, the Queen Mother?' he asked.

'We have,' Lady Huntly said. 'I am particularly anxious to know if the plan I suggested to her through Sir William Maitland is working out.'

'The girl, Abbie McCracken, has been given every chance.'

At this, Abbie froze. What were they saying about her? She held on to the bundle of books for grim death, the whole corridor swaying before her eyes.

'She has grasped all I have been trying to tell the Queen. In fact, she has probably grasped it better. The Queen's span of concentration is not as long as hers, I fear. Next, we shall be giving the girl some voice training exercises, to try to raise her pitch.'

'I see,' Lady Huntly said.

'Have you used her yet?' Lord Huntly put in.

'There has been no need, so far. There have been no dangers for Mary to face here in France. There has been an uprising of Huguenots, but nowhere near any of the royal palaces. No, the greatest disparity is in their heights. Mary is taller already. Her mother is a Guise, the same as I am, and we are all tall. Mary takes after us, I'm afraid. But we will work out a plan for all that when the time comes.'

By that time Abbie had heard enough. She tiptoed away unsteadily. Being a companion for Lady Jean had only been a cover-up for something much more sinister – to face up to death on Queen Mary's behalf, perhaps. She wouldn't put it past any of the nobility.

Then, she began to wonder – was Mary in this plot too?

Marie de Guise left for Scotland, and the lives of her daughter and her entourage returned to their former routines. Mary missed her mother, but as the months passed she was content. One morning as she and Abbie went for their usual lessons in the Cardinal's study, as they kneeled to kiss his ring he patted Mary's cap and said, 'I have a surprise for Your Majesty. Your mother wants you to be declared of age.'

'You mean, of age to marry?'

'No, not yet. You are still too young. But she wants you to have your own establishment in a separate wing of the palace, away from Queen Catherine and the nursery down the corridor. You will have your own court, and that move means that you are old enough to make some decisions about Scotland.'

'Yes?'

'We must strive for a Scotland united against Protestantism, and that is impossible with Arran still acting as Regent, bribed as he was by Henry the Eighth to be Protestant.'

'How can he be displaced, Uncle Cardinal?'

'The new English Queen Mary is strongly Catholic, murdering every Protestant she can lay her hands on and earning herself the title of "Bloody Mary", so I hear. She will get rid of Arran for ever, her way, if we do not do it diplomatically first. He would be satisfied with a French dukedom. The King of France would create him Duc de Châtelherault if he gave up without a struggle. Then we would appoint a new Regent.'

'My mother!' Mary cried.

'An excellent choice.'

So they were going to get away from the stifling nursery at last! Abbie thought with relief.

'But you must remember one thing,' the Cardinal went on instructing Mary. 'Do not parade your new authority outside your own court.'

'I wouldn't!'

'Perhaps you would never mean to. But Queen Catherine is ... touchy. When the King dies, Francis will be King of France and you will be the Queen – not Catherine. Also, when you marry Francis you will be taking away her first-born child. Be tactful.'

NINETEEN

A year later, with Abbie present again, Mary had another disturbing talk with the Cardinal.

'The New Religion is spreading,' he told her. 'Not only is Queen Mary Tudor doing her best to suppress it by killing Protestants in England, her husband, Philip II, is killing them in Spain. Protestant refugees flee to Scotland, and although your mother accepts these refugees out of the kindness of her heart, she holds a tottering Catholic throne. Her nobles, now turned Protestant themselves, plot to overthrow her. Only one noble upholds her and does his best to help her.'

'Who?' Mary asked.

'The Earl of Bothwell.'

'My mother has already told me that,' Mary said, as she embroidered a shift for her trousseau in her lilac and silver parlour. 'I will not forget the Earl of Bothwell.'

Catherine de Medicis was brooding in her own salon, and she was brooding over Mary. The Scottish Queen was as shallow as the waters of the fountain, riding and hawking with Francis, rolling about the lawns whispering childish foolish jokes with him – but yet, she could not see the obvious: Francis was a child still. Where were the broadening shoulders, the sidelong glances at pretty women?

'Have you seen my son?' she asked Abbie. 'Go and get him wherever he is.'

'Must I, Abbie?' Francis wailed. 'Oh, not again!'

'I'll come with you as far as the door,' she smiled encouragingly, wondering why the Queen had to have all these private consultations with her son lately.

'I can't bear it,' he sobbed and snivelled all the way, until Abbie pushed him into the Queen's parlour and closed the door on them both.

She could still see through a crack, but even Abbie was unprepared when Queen Catherine tore down Francis's breeches and felt about at his private parts. 'Has it got up yet?' she demanded. 'Does it have a bone?'

'No, Maman,' he said with great fat tears rolling down his cheeks.

'What? Even after that girl in Paris? Even after all the women I've sent to you?'

'No, Maman!' he shouted, struggling from her clutches and rushing out, flinging the door ajar with such a bang that Abbie had to invent stories for days afterwards about her blackened eyes.

But it was worth it, to find out something else. Francis was not a proper man, not yet, although he was trying to prove that he was by riding his horse too hard and too fast every day.

'How did you get those black eyes?' the Queen asked suspiciously.

'A door did it,' Abbie answered truthfully.

'Some face paint will easily disguise them. It is high time you were learning the art of painting, anyway. Come with me and I will show you.'

When the lesson was over the Queen pressed the little jars into Abbie's hands, clucking her tongue in annoyance. 'But how are you to carry them all?' she wondered, and before Abbie could reply, continued, 'You must have boxes for them. I shall send for the cabinetmakers.'

'Thank you, Your Majesty. And thank you again for all the perfumes and creams you have given me already.'

'Hm! I suppose you will need boxes for them, too?'

'Your Majesty is too kind,' Abbie smiled and curtsied.

Later that day four flat wooden boxes, all compartmented,

polished and beautifully made to fit one on top of the other with carrying handles at each end, were delivered to Abbie's bedchamber. They were embossed with the fleurs-de-lis and the men carrying them presented her with a different key for each box on a silver keyring. Later that evening she and Lady Jean and the four Marys entertained each other trying out the face paints, while Queen Mary watched them and laughed.

'Oh, you will need them too,' Mary Fleming told her, 'and before long, on your wedding day.'

'So far you are the best at face painting, Flamina. If you keep that up I may allow you to teach me!'

But although Mary struggled to present a happy appearance, her heart was heavy. Francis had taken his horse from the stables a few weeks ago and ridden its heart out. Frantic attendants had found him crumpled on the dead animal, and for hours he was unconscious. The last rites were given him. It seemed a miracle when he recovered, and when he did he would scarcely speak to Mary. There was something far wrong.

'What is it, Francis?' she asked him gently. 'Is it your mother?'

'No,' he said.

But his eyes avoided hers and Mary knew he was lying. She must see the Queen herself. She sent Abbie to request a private audience, and in the meantime she examined herself critically in her long looking glass. She was still too slim, and taller than Francis by a head. In an effort to give some width to her figure she fluffed out her wide mink-lined sleeves. She smoothed down her pointed bodice of pale gold velvet, and adjusting the peak of her pearl-edged coif to the exact middle of her forehead she saw the beginning of beauty in her face. That face stared back at her, looking so young! She must look more grown-up for a mission such as this.

Desperately, Mary outlined her lips with rose salve as Flamina had shown her, rubbed a little rouge on her pale cheeks and smoothed her eyelids with smoky kohl, but she was intensely nervous when Abbie came back to say that the Queen would receive her in her parlour.

'Come with me, Abbie,' she said.

Catherine nodded when they were ushered in, but said nothing. Her attendants withdrew and closed the door, but still she said nothing. She only waited with her black, snake-like eyes on Mary, and knowing her so well, Abbie dreaded what was to come. She was going to bite.

'Francis is behaving strangely,' Mary said. 'Can you tell me what is wrong with him? I want to help him.'

'Can you not see?'

'No,' Mary answered, bewildered.

'Then you are more stupid than I thought. Why do you think he rides off every day as he does? He *wants* to die.'

'What do you mean?'

'He wants to die because he doesn't want to marry you. God knows you keep men at a distance.'

'You would have even more to say if I didn't,' Mary said, with a spark of anger. 'But I am not here to quarrel with you, Madam. I only want to help Francis. If he doesn't love me any more I shall release him.' She said that proudly, but Abbie saw that she was shaking at the mere suggestion of parting with her beloved Francis.

'Nothing would please me better, I assure you. But the King and the Cardinal are set on this marriage. If Francis had a dozen mistresses you will still be his wife. Never fear,' Catherine sneered, 'you will be Queen of France, if that is what's worrying you.'

'Mistresses?'

'He is thirteen, is he not? His father was no older than that when Diane de Poitiers snatched him from the nursery to her boudoir. Perhaps she is doing the same with Francis.'

'*No!*' Mary's face went white beneath the patches of rouge, and a fine film of sweat appeared on her upper lip.

'After all, Diane de Poitiers had always an eye to the future. If my husband dies, Francis will be King. He would be her next choice.'

'God forgive you!' Mary sobbed, rushing out. 'How can you be so cruel?'

Outside, Abbie held her while she gulped in great breaths of air. Then Mary began to shiver. Somehow they staggered back together to Mary's own apartments, where the young Queen collapsed in a heap of despair.

The life of the court went on as usual, but now the changes the Cardinal had warned of came fast and furious. Some Protestants who had incited a mob in Orleans were dragged to the palace and tied to stakes in the courtyard, whereupon the Cardinal changed into a monster before their very eyes.

He ordered faggots to be lit at the foot of each stake, and as the poor victims writhed and screamed and burned in agony he laughed and waved his scented handkerchief under his nose to dispel the acrid smell. The more he waved and laughed, the more compassion Mary and her ladies felt for them, even if they were Protestants, before Mary fainted clean away again.

From that day on, Abbie could scarcely bring herself to look at the Cardinal, the man Mary had loved and trusted like a father for so many years.

But Mary found a new protector. The King of France took her under his wing and, after that, Mary and her ladies were invited to all the King's parties and all the French ladies paid the Scottish Queen the compliment of imitation. Her heart-shaped caps became all the rage. Bosoms were bound, hips flattened and high-heeled shoes worn to give the illusion of slender height. She blazed like a star at the centre of the court, and all the men were as moths attracted to the flame.

But Mary had eyes only for Francis. Of course, he loved her. Of course, she saw it all now. She should not have run from Queen Catherine's apartments. She should have laughed at her instead, and ridiculed her lies.

Unaware of many of these undercurrents, Abbie continued to visit Queen Catherine every Wednesday afternoon. Sometimes

Lady Jean went with her, although no longer for the attention to her hair which had become smooth and thick and golden, thanks to the Queen. These days Jean was spending most of her time with Alex Ogilvie, her intended husband, for she was now thirteen and fast approaching the marriageable age.

Abbie remembered the uncomfortable interview Queen Catherine conducted with Lord and Lady Huntly at their request, before they returned to Scotland laden down with treasures from all over Europe.

One witch had eyed the other with the utmost dislike.

After Lady Huntly had finished boasting of their new acquisitions, which Abbie and Jean knew paled into insignificance when compared with the Queen's vast collections, she began to extol the virtues of her daughter, Lady Jean.

Listening to it, Abbie and Jean raised their eyebrows at each other. Seeing that glance the Queen suddenly sat up straight, very interested.

'Tell me, Lady Huntly,' she asked, with deceptive sweetness, 'how was it that you were fortunate enough to employ Abbie to look after your daughter?' As she asked it, she kept looking pointedly at Abbie, scrutinising her face. Too late, Lady Huntly realised the Italian Woman knew exactly how delicate that question was, and tried to bluster her way out of it.

'Abbie's mother was my gardening maid,' she said haughtily, 'with a great interest and aptitude for growing the herbs I use so often for my medicines.'

'Then that explains it,' Queen Catherine smiled. She almost licked her whiskers, and shortly afterwards the Huntlys withdrew. They could hear the furious voice of Lady Huntly upraised all the way down the corridor.

'That woman knows too much! She has the power to divine secrets! Besides that, she knows more about medicines than anyone else in the Western world, and I have learned nothing! Nothing! It's all your fault!'

'*My* fault? How is it *my* fault?' they heard an injured Lord Huntly exclaiming, and then they were gone out of earshot.

But ever since that day the Queen looked at Abbie differently, and invited her into the rooms where two apothecaries worked alongside two herbalists. 'This is how my medicines are made. Are you interested, Abbie?'

'Oh . . . more than you know, Your Majesty!' Abbie said, gazing at the herbs hanging from the roof in bunches to dry, at all the rows of chemicals laid out on the tables, and at the four men busily mixing and pounding the extracts together with mortars and pestles, and sometimes boiling them.

'It was not the King's fault that I was childless for so many years,' Catherine said. 'These men helped to cure my infertility.' She waxed enthusiastic on the subject. 'Look! Here are the receipts for everything that was tried and used until they hit on the magic formula! And here it is in these little bottles, although I don't need it now.'

Those little bottles, Abbie thought, would be worth a fortune, although none of them contained a cure for Francis, otherwise his mother would have used such a medicine long ago. They had found nothing that could change a boy into a man. But Abbie kept her thoughts to herself while sometimes the men allowed her to help. They explained how they had made their medicines and what they could cure. And, once again, the room had a secret cupboard, the same as the astrologer's.

'What's in there?' Abbie asked the Queen, anxious to avoid the embarrassment and the Queen's anger which she had suffered before.

'All the bottles are black. That is for poison. Come, I'll show you,' Catherine said, leading the way quite amiably. 'You must never touch them, Abbie, unless one of us is there.'

'Of course not, Your Majesty.'

'But you must not think that these poisons are here only to kill. Some, in certain doses, are medicinal also.'

'How?'

'Well, there is this one,' the Queen held it up. 'This one is for the Pox. Used properly it can protect a woman from a diseased man. It can even prevent her from becoming with child.'

That, too, would be worth a fortune.

'In fact,' the Queen said, suddenly generous, 'I shall give you some of this. You never know who you might meet, and syphilis spreads its ugly, deadly fingers all over Europe every day and night. Yes, I shall give you some of this, and also ointment and pills. There may be someone close to you some day – *someone very close* – whom you can help. This one,' she held up a black bottle labelled with a skull and crossbones, 'is the deadliest poison I know. You may find a use for it, too, if some day you find you have an enemy.'

Surely she didn't mean Queen Mary! Surely she didn't mean that Abbie might want to poison her! So *that* was what all this was about! How she must hate the Scottish Queen! Did she mean that they should enter into a conspiracy against her together?

'But you must never tell anyone I have given you these medicines,' Queen Catherine added.

'No, Your Majesty,' Abbie said, and escaped before any more was said.

So, in time, another box – the deepest one yet – arrived in Abbie's bedchamber. At first glance only the bottles, some of green glass and some of black, were revealed when she lifted the lid. Then she discovered two drawers under the top layer for the bottles, one containing jars of ointment and the other little boxes of pills. Everything was carefully labelled, with directions for use, and the lids for the bottles and jars were made of finest kid and tied with golden string.

This was a box Abbie showed to no one. She carried the key with her at all times.

TWENTY

The years of happiness in France sped by, and at last, when Mary was fifteen, the marriage that was her destiny was imminent. While Mary of Scotland was being fitted for trousseau gowns the Cardinal set about arranging a wedding fit to dazzle international eyes. Paris swarmed with workmen, hammering theatres and pavilions throughout the windy days of March. Goldsmiths, jewellers, wigmakers and dressmakers worked far into the nights by candlelight. Flowers by the cartload were waxed and sewn to satin ribbons to decorate every balcony. The second week in April a huge blue carpet edged with gold was stretched over the cobbles, and above it an open pavilion of blue Cyprus silk was raised, spangled with fleurs-de-lis.

'You may tell Queen Mary that I shall be providing your gowns for the wedding,' Queen Catherine told Lady Jean and Abbie. 'I have decided on a Scottish theme for you. Come, let me show you the swatches of silks. You may choose your own colour scheme.'

'Perhaps this lilac and green?' Lady Jean asked.

'Yes. They are the colours of our thistles,' Abbie agreed.

The court slept by day and danced by night, while wedding gifts, the treasures of Catholic Europe boxed in ivory, ebony and mother-of-pearl, piled up in the palace storerooms. Excitement was building to fever-pitch when Mary's page announced the arrival of the Scottish commissioners. She dismissed the embroidering nuns and seamstresses and sent Seton to request Lord James Stewart to come to see her.

'Of course he is misguided by the New Religion,' she told her ladies, 'and no doubt the Cardinal will not be pleased that I am receiving him, but I don't care. He is my brother.'

When she heard his footsteps along the corridor she ran to the door, her hands outstretched in welcome. But as his half-sister served him with wine, discussed his journey, the health of her mother and the plans for her forthcoming marriage, Abbie became aware that James's eyes were watchful, as green and spiteful as a cat's, and her blood ran cold.

'Yes,' he said, 'your marriage will be marked in Scotland. Bonfires will be lit up and down the country.'

'And the people will dance and sing and feast?'

'The people will celebrate according to their means, madam.'

'It costs nothing to dance and sing . . . But that is not what you meant, is it?'

'No. The people do not like an alliance with France.'

'Why? God knows Scotland needs help from somewhere.'

'Because it is Catholic.'

'But you are sitting there, a prior yourself! The Prior of St Andrews, although you do not wear your robes, I see.'

'Merely an honorary office inherited from our father, madam.'

'But it must be bringing you fine revenues,' Mary said, gazing at the rubies on his fingers and the heavy golden chains about his neck.

'I would gladly exchange it.'

'For what?'

'For the Earldom of Moray.'

Mary laughed. 'You are nothing if not direct, sir! And ambitious! That is the richest earldom in Scotland!'

'And should I not be ambitious, when my name is Stewart, the same as yours?'

'Not quite the same as mine. I have adopted the French version of Stuart. Yes, it is French and it is Catholic – and yet I hear you flirt with Protestantism yourself, sir?'

For the first time James grinned, and his eyes were more

cruel than ever. Abbie sensed that he was going to hit Mary hard now, and that he was going to take great pleasure in doing it.

'My flirting days are over, madam. I have married it now.'

And it did hurt. They all saw that, as Mary stared at him, shocked. 'You mean, you follow John Knox? I had heard a rumour but did not believe it. You would destroy the faith of your father and your Queen?'

'The Catholic faith is the faith of self-indulgence,' he said primly.

Pointedly, Mary stared again at his rubies and his golden chains. 'And does Knox wear precious jewels, also?'

'Of course not.' James was becoming impatient. 'But I am different. Let me repeat, I am a Stewart, of royal blood.'

'A Stewart . . . of royal blood . . . yet you would deny me my Mass?'

'Naturally, I would defend Your Majesty's right to Mass,' he blustered, 'so long as you never pushed it down Scottish throats.'

'Does my mother know your views?'

'She does. She also knows that no one is more loyal to the Crown.'

'*Except the Earl of Bothwell*, she tells me in her letters.'

It darted out, and Mary and her ladies saw that the barb had driven home. His pale cheeks flushed angrily. He tensed in his chair. 'Bothwell? Bothwell? Bothwell is a depraved adventurer!'

'And the only man to come to my mother's aid against her enemies. For that reason he has my respect. You may not belittle him in my presence, sir, ever again. I welcomed you as my brother. Now I understand that you leave me as my enemy, and it has broken my heart,' Mary said, getting to her feet.

Abbie, Jean, and the Marys rose with her. It forced him to do the same.

'You may go,' Mary dismissed him.

After he left there was silence. Nobody dared to say anything. What was supposed to be a happy meeting had turned into a nightmare family quarrel. But that was the point – it was a family quarrel. Lord James and Queen Mary were still brother and sister.

Sleepless in bed that night, Abbie reflected that if she were in Mary's shoes she would not deny the people their New Religion, as Mary Tudor, Queen of England was doing, trying like King Canute to stem the waves of the sea.

But all of that was not what James had been meaning. He was clever. He had not turned to the New Religion himself out of conviction, not at all. He was using it, riding on the crest of its wave – for what?

It was because it was becoming so powerful that its believers could topple the Scottish throne. The Earldom of Moray was only the first rung on his ladder of ambition. At the top lay his desire, the crown.

She lay there, listening to the sounds of the night. Usually she liked to lie snug in her bed and listen to the howlings of the wind outside. But tonight she shuddered and felt afraid, fancying that it was not only the wind she was hearing. Far in the distance was the howling of wolves.

When the news of the impending marriage between Mary and Francis trickled through to her, Elizabeth Tudor, Princess of England, recorded it in that neat and tidy brain of hers. One of her many qualities was that she never forgot anything. One of her many failings was her foul language, and she used it now to curse Mary.

When her solitary rantings subsided she was almost in tears, and she took to brooding, remembering that awful consultation with Dr Wendy. She could still remember every detail of that day, how she had pulled on her stockings that morning, exchanged her white nightdress for a shift, slid out softly on the floor and without pausing struggled into the black cloth dress she wore for the dead King, her father, Henry VIII. The gown was shabby, but its open collar had been lined with satin once. It rolled back in wide wings from her throat, which rose white and small like a child's.

Her long red mane slapped heavily across her face as she bent to the fastenings. She pushed it back with an impatient hand, reddened with menial work, and pattered to the window in her stockinged feet to open the casement.

It was warm and bright in the August sunshine and the birds sang in the garden which sloped down to the riverbank under fine old trees. Dew sparkled on the grass, the air was gay with the scents of flowers, and her gaze caressed the green land of her birth. There were many such gardens as this along the Thames between the dower house here at Chelsea and the big Strand palaces in London. England itself was a garden in the summer.

For the moment she had almost forgotten the appointment with the doctor . . . But only for a moment. Her mind soon reverted to thoughts of Thomas Seymour. Only a few months before he had caught her in bed and set her squealing by his boisterous threats to strip off the coverlet and drag her out. Nobody had heard her, and handsomer than ever dressed only in shirt, trunks and hose, he quickly fulfilled his threat.

His arm around her waist, he had pulled her over to the window seat and sat close against her, his knee on hers dragging at her nightdress, his knowing eyes never leaving hers, nor her pallor and the droop of her lips. He began to whisper the things he knew all too well how to say until she turned in his embrace and her arms crept slowly around his neck. She was burning with desire.

Under the nightdress his hands chased all over her undeveloped body, down to her buttocks. She shivered with delight. Then his hands began to creep around to the front, to her innermost temple of womanhood. It was a temple she could not afford to have explored . . .

With a sob, she had snatched herself out of his grasp just as her tittering maids burst in – but then, they were used to seeing Admiral Thomas Seymour in the princess's bedchamber. When Mrs Ashley, her governess, arrived next, however, she was so utterly scandalised that she turned to remonstrate with Elizabeth's stepmother, Catherine Parr, who came in last.

But Catherine's eyes had been soft with love for her husband. It was not long since she had been widowed by King Henry VIII's death and, pregnant to Thomas Seymour, had married him. 'She's only a child still,' she said easily, 'barely fourteen. My Lord Admiral means her no harm.'

Her throat tight with worry and terror, Elizabeth had not been able to eat at all since then, and her bony frame grew thinner than ever. Mrs Ashley had sent for the physician. So there she was, leaning against the casement, watching for the arrival of Dr Wendy, who had been her doctor since she was a little girl.

From the gardens Dr Wendy saw her boyish figure standing there, and frowned. She should have been filling out a little by now . . . Up in the bedchamber he dismissed the maidservants, bade Mrs Ashley stay, and told Elizabeth to take off all her clothes and lie down on the bed.

'It's time I was giving my Lady Elizabeth a proper examination,' he said. 'Draw the bed-curtains, if you please, Mrs Ashley – and see that no one enters the room while I am here.'

He ran his cool fingers over Elizabeth's shoulders – a little too broad for a girl – and then down her skinny arms to her long, long hands. Her breasts were so far undeveloped and her hips were very slim. He glanced for a second at the black slippers, patched and worn, which she had kicked off her long feet beside the bed.

Money must be tight in this household, then. He would not be surprised if food were short, too. Sometimes that explained a slow development. But this girl was strong and healthy enough. By rights she should have been eating like a horse, growing as she was. The doctor concluded that her problem must be much more deep-seated than at first appeared. She was worrying about something. Determined to find out, he proceeded to the examination of her legs and the lower part of her body, alarmed when he found two soft swellings, one in either groin.

'Are these painful, my lady?'

'Of course not! They've always been there! Are you nearly finished?'

'My dear,' he said, 'I want you to spread your legs for me next. Spread them wide now.'

'No!' she said. 'What for?'

'Have you had any bleedings yet?'

'No,' she sighed impatiently.

'I thought not. So you must allow me to investigate. There are only two people now between you and the throne of England. Perhaps one day you may be our Queen, and queens must have heirs. I must examine you inside.'

At that, Elizabeth turned her face back towards the doctor, regarding him with a little more respect. He was no fool, then, to have worked out the succession, no matter how improbable. She had done so already, but had kept her conclusions to herself.

She must have bleedings, she knew that, before she could conceive a child, and as she knew from the antics of her own father, the Glorious King Hal who had executed her mother for not giving him a male heir, to produce a son was of vital importance. Nevertheless, she didn't want the doctor to examine her private regions, child or no child. She knew herself that all was not well. Very reluctantly, and with her face averted again, Elizabeth spread her legs and felt the doctor's prying fingers inside her vagina.

Almost immediately they touched the membrane she knew was there, and she began to cry.

'Hm . . .' he said at last, sounding puzzled. 'I have finished in the meantime. You can put your shift back on, my dear.' He walked to the window while she dressed again, and looked out unseeingly. Hermaphroditism had been known about since Greek times. It was a freak of nature sometimes found in animals and in plants. He hoped he had not discovered it in a human being of such importance.

151

'Are you finished?' Elizabeth asked impatiently, and he turned to face her again.

'Not quite. Is there anything you wish to tell me?'

'Get rid of Mrs Ashley,' Elizabeth whispered tearfully. 'She will have her ears, if not her eyes, to the bed-curtains.'

'Now, tell me,' he said, with Mrs Ashley dismissed.

He listened with dismay to her account of her ordeals at the hands of my lord Admiral. Why was she telling him this? Was she trying to dismiss her malformity, trying to impress him with her budding sexuality? It was a serious matter. The child had been quite right to worry ... And unbeknown to her as yet, more worries were to come.

'The problem of the Admiral is easily remedied,' he said unsmilingly. 'You must have a change – go away to another house. Doctor's orders!'

'And my health, sir?'

'You are a strong, healthy girl and hopefully, when you are away, and left in peace to grow up, you will develop naturally. I will see you again in a month, and after that, every month.' He went to the door and took Mrs Ashley back in. 'A holiday will do you both good,' he told her. 'My Lady Elizabeth must get out into the fresh air. Let her ride her horses. She must eat to put the roses back in her cheeks.'

But as he rode away, Dr Wendy's mind was in a turmoil. He had just examined a little girl *on the outside*, but he was convinced that she was genetically male. How else could the suspicious testicular appearance in the groin be explained? How else could the shallow vagina be explained, or the clitoris lengthened to a tiny penis so that it actually protruded beyond the lips of the vulva? The lack of bleedings meant that she had no womb and no ovaries. She would never menstruate. She would never have babies.

And it was as he had hinted. Her brother, Edward, would not live long. Her sister Mary, some seventeen years older, hanging like a creaking gate with all her ailments, would not last much over forty. It was highly probable that Elizabeth would be Queen of England before long. It was no wonder

152

that the poor girl had been in a state of hysteria. And as for that brute, Thomas Seymour! But what else could he be, when he was the brother of the Protector, Somerset, who had butchered and ravaged Scotland? Oh, they would get their just deserts one day, both of them!

In the meantime he had never had to deal with a condition like Elizabeth's before. His suspicions could be unfounded, but he doubted very much that they were. He must consult with other physicians who may have had this experience. Of course, it couldn't be done in England. Too many people knew Elizabeth was one of his patients. He would have to go further afield, to the Continent, and what was more, he would have to go in disguise . . .

TWENTY-ONE

Abbie was becoming as impatient with her education as Queen Mary, and when the Cardinal insisted that she should have voice exercises it was the last straw. In fact, she was beginning increasingly to dislike the Cardinal, as he sat on the other side of his desk, preening himself in his silks and satins while he burdened Mary with more and more bad news.

'I want you to look at this,' he said, handing her the pamphlet John Knox had written entitled *The First Blast of the Trumpet Against the Monstrous Regiment of Women.* 'As you see, I have blacked out many words of it too gross for a lady to read.'

'Who does he mean – the monstrous regiment of women?'

'Mary Tudor, who has banished him from England, and your own dear mother who has thrown him out of his church at Berwick.'

Mary threw the pamphlet down in disgust. 'If there is nothing else, Uncle Cardinal, may we be excused? I am very busy.'

'Before you go, be good enough to sign these three documents,' the Cardinal said.

'What are they?'

'The usual marriage contracts between the husband's side and the wife's. I have been over them. They are all in order, and if you would act as witness,' he glanced at Abbie, 'sign your full name after the Queen's. Abbie McCracken.'

'My full name is Abigail McCracken, sir,' she said, doing

154

her best to cause a diversion, and pretending that she was a slow writer as she took each document out of Mary's hand and skimmed through it at lightning speed. She did not trust the Cardinal now, not after all she had seen.

Before she signed her name under the Queen's she saw that by signing them Mary was bequeathing Scotland to France, should she die without a child. It was monstrous. Why was not someone in authority here to oversee the signing of such momentous documents?

'I think you should read them carefully, Your Majesty,' Abbie protested. 'It is a trick.'

'Abbie, don't argue about it now,' Mary said, already half-way to the door. 'Pray excuse me. I have summoned Balthazzar for a final fitting of the wedding dress. Every meeting with that tailor is a fight to the finish.'

'You should have heeded his advice from the start. You should not have chosen white for your wedding dress. Here in France white is the colour of mourning. I only hope it will not bring you bad luck,' the Cardinal smiled slyly and then glared at Abbie.

All the way along the passage Abbie tried to explain to Mary just what she had signed, but she waved her words aside impatiently.

'Forget all that, Abbie. Tomorrow is my wedding day. Don't spoil it. Come with me, and we will peep at my dress.'

All political thoughts were wiped clean from their minds at the very sight of it. It had turned out even more exquisite than Mary had dreamed, of dazzling white silk with its bodice gleaming with pearls like the morning dew, and the only thing to mar her happiness was that her mother could not come from Scotland after all to see her wear it and the huge ruby brooch.

Diane de Poitiers had not made any such mistake of colour. Her gown was black, encrusted with crescent moons of jet and sparkling diamonds. It hung ready, and her jewels were laid out.

Catherine, the Queen, was also ready for the marriage the following day, her magnificent gown of the blue of France stamped and jewelled with fleurs-de-lis. She had overseen what her children would wear and had commanded Balthazzar to make adjustments to the ermine of Francis's cape. It had seemed too wide and heavy for his puny shoulders. That done to her satisfaction, she sent for Lady Jean and Abbie.

The green and lilac checks of their silks were entirely satisfactory. So was the darker shade of their blue-purple underskirts, exactly matching the silk thistles nestling among the lilies of France in their coronets and posies.

'Now, Jean,' she said proudly, 'are you not glad that we attended to your hair so many years ago?'

'Thank you, Your Majesty,' Jean curtsied gravely and looked in the looking-glass. Her hair hung gleaming and golden down to her waist. The Queen, the four Marys and the two from Strathbogie would all wear their hair loose and unbound as a sign of virginity. 'Our dresses are beautiful.'

'And so Scottish,' Abbie said quickly. 'The thistles were an inspiration.'

'I can always rise to an occasion,' Queen Catherine said grandly, easily flattered and easily diverted, as Abbie had found out long ago.

At last the great day dawned, bright and sunny, 24 April 1558. All Paris milled and scuffled for space in the square of Notre-Dame, and people leaned from windows and balconies and scaffoldings to get a better view. It had been two hundred years since anyone had been able to witness the wedding of a dauphin and the whole city was in a fever of anticipation, for not only would there be this magnificent spectacle, but also largesse would be scattered afterwards – ducats, half-crowns, douzains – and anyone could scramble for the coins of silver and gold.

First in the procession came the musicians in crimson and yellow, piping and drumming for the Scottish Guard who followed them, resplendent in black and silver. Then came a hundred princes, princesses and their attendants. Next came the princes of the Church, wearing jewelled mitres and carrying their crosiers, headed by the Cardinal of Lorraine in his golden cope.

The procession took half an hour to pass by. And then came the Dauphin, his two younger brothers, Charles and Henry, on either side of him. Francis shuffled along slowly as if he were going to a terrifying ordeal, looking straight ahead. But the crowd cheered him until they were hoarse, and then they fell silent in anticipation. The bride was coming.

They saw her in the distance, a glow of white . . . And they gasped. A dress of mourning – for a wedding? But their mutters were hushed in awe as Mary appeared with the King at her side. She was sheathed in a flame of sunlight from the brilliant crown of sapphires, rubies, emeralds and diamonds on her head, to the diamond necklace around her throat, to the huge ruby brooch pinned to her breast, to the blue velvet robe glittering with silver lilies, sapphire thistles and ruby roses, to the massed jewels of her six-yard train – right down to her golden slippers.

Her ladies followed behind her. Abbie felt the tears in her eyes as she watched Mary plodding along anxiously under the weight of her crown and her heavy jewelled clothes. The crown kept slipping down. Abbie imagined the muscles of her throat must be getting sore with holding her head up straight to keep it on. She was only a young girl . . . Her mother should have been here for her. It was a shame.

But as Mary walked to the entrance of Notre-Dame the crowd broke its silence in a roar of approval, pelting her with blossoms. The people strained their ears to hear the vows being taken on the open-air platform, but all anyone heard were whispers. All anyone saw was the flash of jewels as the rings were exchanged when the Archbishop of Rouen married them. Mary and Francis walked on a cloth of gold to the sanctuary. The air was heavy with incense and the scent of lilies.

And when it was all over Mary was Queen-Dauphine of France.

After the banquets, the masques and the pageants, and the youngest children were taken home to bed, the dancing began. Boats with silver sails seemed to float on the ballroom floor, each big enough for two wedding guests to 'sail'.

Abbie waited until she had seen Alex Ogilvie handing Lady Jean into one of them before she made her escape into the night. And it was a night just made for love. In the moonlight the flowers of the palace orchard looked bleached, but their perfume wafted down every little side street. An occasional firework still flew and sparkled into the sky. The moon shone on some departing guests, stealing away into the dark. It shone on the tall figure of a man in black.

'Oh God, Abbie,' Donald MacLaren said, holding out his arms. 'I thought you weren't coming . . .'

'You knew I'd come,' Abbie said, and lifted up her face to his, 'and as you say yourself, my Donald, you're never wrong.'

In a bedchamber of the Palace des Tournelles hung with white pearled brocade, Mary waited for her husband, dressed in a white transparent gown of gauze. She longed to lay down her aching head and sleep, but she willed herself to stay awake for him, and at last there was a timid knock on the door and Francis came in. His face was as pale as his white damask robe and he looked everywhere but at her.

'I am so tired, Mary,' he said in a low voice, sitting on the satin bed. 'Could we sleep for a few hours?'

'I wish we could, but we dare not risk it,' she whispered back. 'You know the Cardinal will be listening outside that door until dawn. Did he explain to you what is expected of us?'

He nodded miserably, still not looking at her.

'Well, we cannot lie to the Cardinal from a bed blessed with holy water.'

'All right, then,' he said. 'Come here.'

158

At last he looked at her, and his eyes were soft with wonder. She bent her head and kissed his lips. Together they moved shyly to the bed, for although they had embraced before like two puppies, kissed as playmates and clung together through nine long years of secrets, it was never grown-up like this . . . Not like this.

After a few minutes she knew that whatever it was, this wasn't love. For her it was an utter collapse of dignity and the threat of pain. For him it was a blundering frenzy. She seemed paralysed beneath him, and then she felt his tears spilling down her neck before he rolled over to the far side of the bed.

'Oh, Francis,' she said. 'What is it? Is there something wrong with me? Can't you love me?'

'There is nothing wrong with you, Mary. It's me. My mother told me long ago that I would be incapable. Magic, second sight – oh, whatever it is, she knew. Oh, Mary! I am not even a man!'

'You mean we can never have children?'

'Never.'

In utter despair Mary remembered Abbie's desperate appeals after the marriage contracts were signed. Catherine would know that Francis wasn't a proper man. The Cardinal would know. It *had* been a trick, after all, a cruel, cruel trick. Never again would she trust the Cardinal of Lorraine. Least and last of all would she ever trust Queen Catherine. But even yet, perhaps it wasn't too late, she thought angrily and desperately.

'I don't believe it! I won't believe it!' she cried. 'It is the fault of your mother. She has put a spell on you. She has cursed you. But promise me that we will never show her that she has hurt us. In time you will grow to be a man, and I will help you. We will be happy yet.'

Francis put his arms around her and kissed her again with his sweet childish lips. 'No one can take you away now,' he agreed happily, and drifted off to sleep.

But Mary remained awake until dawn. There was a tap

on the door, a long pause, and she closed her eyes. The Cardinal pulled aside a bed-curtain and smiled at the two children clasped close in the tumbled sheets. Mary pretended to stir and opened her eyes.

'My child,' the Cardinal said, 'we have prayed for a fruitful union. Is all in order?'

'All is in order, all is as expected,' she looked him squarely in the eyes and smiled. 'Your prayers have been answered.'

Nothing changed, just because they were married. Everything went on as before except that Mary's household and Francis's became merged. They avoided Queen Catherine at all costs, and they took great pleasure in dismissing Madame de Parois.

The Marys remained with them, as did Lady Jean and Abbie, Father Mamerot and the physician, Bourgoing. It was a household of young, pleasant people. The lazy days flashed by, when Mary helped Francis to lay out his toy soldiers for battles, or hunted and hawked with him in the parks and the forests. The nights were not so happy, but Mary and Francis prayed they soon would be.

In November couriers arrived, gasping out the news. Mary Tudor, Queen of England, was dead. The Cardinal and indeed all the French court were plunged into mourning – not for Mary Tudor herself, but for the last hopes of a Catholic Europe.

At the end of January the King of France sent for Mary and Francis to attend an interview. Mary took her ladies with her and Francis a few courtiers. They entered the audience chamber to find the English Ambassador bowing backwards from the throne. Henry waved Mary and Francis to a love seat below the dais, and her ladies sat at her feet.

'Your Majesties,' Sir Nicholas Throckmorton addressed the royal party, 'may I say first that your ladies-in-waiting in their pretty dresses look like a ring of roses, the flowers in Queen Mary's bouquet.'

The ladies smiled politely, and Mary inclined her head.

He went on. 'My mistress, Queen Elizabeth, was crowned

at Westminster on January the fifteenth to the joy of all her people. Already she has snatched hundreds of innocent Protestants from the stake, condemned there for their religion by her half-sister, Mary Tudor. Having been imprisoned herself in the Tower on charges of Protestantism, her sympathy for that religion will come as no shock to you. She has appointed Sir William Cecil Secretary of State. She has surrounded herself with wise men. I believe she will be a truly great queen, for her mind is as keen as a man's.'

There was a chilly silence for several minutes before the King of France replied. 'Please convey to Her Majesty our congratulations and best wishes for a long and prosperous reign,' he said, with no enthusiasm whatsoever in his voice. 'We shall present gifts.'

'And I shall send her a golden heart surrounded by sapphires,' Mary added, 'in the sincere trust that she will not persecute Catholics as her sister persecuted Protestants, and in the hope that she will not encourage John Knox.'

'You do not mince your words, madam,' Throckmorton replied suavely, 'and I can assure you that she will not persecute anyone –'

The interminable interview minced along and finally dragged to its end. Throckmorton bowed himself out.

'Don't go,' King Henry detained Mary and Francis. 'There is something I wish to discuss with you.'

They sat down again, and waited.

'Elizabeth is a bastard,' he reminded Mary. 'She is not England's rightful Queen. She is no more entitled to rule it than James Stewart is entitled to rule Scotland. But *you* are the granddaughter of Margaret Tudor and great-granddaughter of Henry the Seventh. Therefore by legal right, as well as by divine right, *you* are the true Queen of England.'

Abbie had sensed that no good would come of this interview. It could only mean war. Queen Mary thought the same. 'You mean war?' she asked.

'Not yet. We shall simply proclaim you Queen of England.'

'And infuriate Elizabeth? Isn't that the same as war?'

161

'We aim to sow the seeds of rebellion in the English Catholics.'

'And cut the ties of friendship between England and Scotland? They are frail enough as it is. I cannot understand how anyone could suggest such a thing! Does the Cardinal know of this?'

Does the Cardinal know of this, indeed . . . thought Abbie.

'It was the Cardinal's idea.'

'And my mother?'

'Your mother will certainly agree. In the meantime I shall order your coat of arms to be combined with England's on the top half of your escutcheon, with Ireland's and Wales's on the bottom.'

'You really mean it,' Mary said, dazed. 'You really wish that I should be Queen of England?'

King Henry nodded, his eyes shifty.

Mary stood up. 'Please tell the Cardinal that instead of being joyful and triumphant at this turn of events, I feel unutterable dread and disapproval. I disagree absolutely with his idea. Surely Queen Elizabeth has suffered enough already without this? The Cardinal himself told me that Elizabeth was imprisoned in the Tower of London by her own sister, just for being suspected of Protestantism. She was almost beheaded.'

The King stared at her and for the first time the Scottish court saw dislike on his face. 'I am the King,' he said, dismissing them. 'You will do as I say.'

On the way back the corridors seemed colder and eerily darker to Abbie as she tried to understand the implications of this latest French plot. The truth did not come to her until she had her hand on the handle of her own door.

Nobody here was interested in Mary as a person, nor Francis either. To the King and the Queen and the Cardinal the young couple were not human beings with ordinary human feelings to consider.

Queen Catherine had cruelly baited Mary with Francis, giving Scotland over to France if the marriage did not yield an heir, and Francis was not robust and seemed yet such a child. And there were rumours that he was impotent. Was it that Catherine's second son, Charles, might be a better prospect for the throne than Francis had ever been? He might rule both France and Scotland.

And the Cardinal . . . He was as double as men came. He had manipulated Mary from the beginning, since she was a little child.

Now, standing at the door, Abbie saw it all. The young couple and their court all might as well be blocks of wood, to be carved into pawns on a chess board as far as the French were concerned. They were useful only as long as they could be moved around to French advantage. Perhaps they were only still living so long as they could be moved around to French advantage. Kings, queens, bishops, knights – it was all a power game.

In the service of Mary, Queen of Scots, they were surrounded by enemies.

TWENTY-TWO

In the state bedchamber at Whitehall, curled snugly round
the comfort of a hot brick in the middle of the great bed,
Queen Elizabeth lay awake. Her sister, Mary, had lain in this
bed. Her brother, Edward, had slept here too, a weary child
of nine. And Henry, the great loud man who had fathered
them all – she supposed that he had died here.

Well, now his 'little red wench' was Queen of England
after all, and it was her turn to sleep here, and she so young
and strong and not afraid of anything . . . Not any more, not
now the first terrible twenty-six years of her life were over.

Her very earliest memory, when she was almost three, was
when her father had her mother's head cut off. From then
on, depending on her father's politics and marriages, she had
been a princess one minute and a bastard outcast the next.
Then, when she was fourteen and thought herself in love
with the Lord Admiral Seymour, he had plotted her downfall.
For his pains he had been flung into the Tower and beheaded,
leaving her, a mere child, to explain everything away. It had
been an awful warning.

Next, she (who had never had a religious conviction in her
life) had landed in the Tower herself, sent there by her own
sister, Mary. That bitch! That Catholic tyrant! Only by the
grace of God had she been pardoned, but not before she had
caught another glimpse of that gorgeous man, Robert Dudley,
who had been Edward's tutor in happier times.

She supposed that it was about this time that Dr Wendy
began to break it to her gently that she was not made as

other women are made. He explained, he drew diagrams, she ranted and raved, she went into hysterics and although that was how it continued for the next five years or so, nothing changed and nothing could be done.

For all these twists and turns of fate Elizabeth blamed her father, and she blamed him not merely bitterly but virulently. She blamed him also for her life of poverty, of always living off and with other people, but never with him. He was too busy searching for a woman who would give him a son to think about his daughter.

A son! A son! If Henry VIII had only known what he had bred! It had taken her nearly ten years to come to terms with the masculine and the feminine within herself and to live with the duality, but during that time she had come to some surprising conclusions as she watched other people around her.

It seemed that in time most husbands became tedious. So, if she could never have a child, why burden herself with a husband? Better by far to indulge herself in love affairs, the sport of the chase, for long ago she had found out that in some things it was better to journey than ever to arrive.

Better in some things, but not for the Crown. Oh, no! The coronation – the long blue-carpeted path to the high altar amid the pealing bells and the voices singing *salva feste dies* – her own voice, strangely repeating the Lord's Prayer aloud alone – the coronation oaths, more awesome by far than the marriage vows – the oil for the anointing – the ring made to fit her slim finger – and then – and then, at last the Crown! Nothing could ever get better than that . . .

No, it was much better as it was, herself upon the throne, quite alone, Queen in her own right, for she had no doubt that her tortuous brain was sharper than most men's. She could hold her own with any of them, and while she was at it she could always fall back on her femininity in times of doubt – and just not be able to make up her mind . . .

Oh, it was a wonderful prospect! And behind the throne there could still be Robert, merry and laughing – and fond.

* * *

No sooner was Elizabeth on the throne but a strange anomaly declared itself and it came from the direction of that red-haired, arrogant, half-French bitch Mary Stuart, no less.

Throckmorton, newly arrived back from visiting her at the French court, had dined off freshly engraved plates showing the arms of England quartered with those of France and Scotland, the heralds had proclaimed Mary's appearance with, 'Make way! Make way! For the Queen of England,' and the whole company had cheered, 'Long live the Queen of England!'

For a few seconds it took Elizabeth's breath away. When she got it back she gave full rein to her spectacular temper and her foul language. Underneath it all was her secret worry, that her childlessness put a premium on her murder. She knew it, but after ten minutes of ranting and raving in her high raucous voice, she smiled. Mary Stuart had not had a child yet. According to rumour she would never have a child, and in one of her lightning changes of moods Elizabeth laughed and hugged her own secret to her heart.

Early summer in Paris, and the royal Valois family had three reasons to celebrate. The first remarkable piece of good fortune was the forthcoming marriage of the King's sister, when all hope had been abandoned long ago. The Princess Marguerite de Valois was to marry the Duke of Savoy.

And fourteen-year-old Princess Elisabeth, Mary's dear friend, had been persuaded to accept Philip of Spain in marriage. She had never seen him, and everything she had heard about him was bad, but such an alliance would mean the end of the wars with Spain at last. No one worried about how the brides felt when they heard that both bridegrooms had been Elizabeth of England's suitors before she had laughed them out of her court.

Nevertheless, in honour of all this, the King arranged three days of tournament and jousting, and now on the third day in the city's heat the French court were beginning to feel jaded and not a little bored.

'What a waste of time and money!' Jean whispered to Abbie as they took their seats on the balcony. 'One day of this would have been enough.'

'Yes,' Abbie agreed and nodded to the right. 'Look over there! There's Princess Elisabeth, sitting on her own. Philip of Spain should have been here to join in the celebrations with her. He'll never win her heart that way.'

'Oh, Abbie! What has her heart got to do with it?'

'Ah . . . so you haven't just been playing with Alex Ogilvie of Boyne, after all.'

It was true, Abbie thought. Lady Jean Gordon had grown up fast here in France. She was no longer the little girl with the flyaway hair, but almost a woman, displaying more and more in little flashes such as this that she had a mind of her own despite her quiet exterior.

'Between what you have told me, and what Alex's told me, and what I've seen for myself, marriages are all arranged for land, money and power, Abbie. Can you show me a marriage that hasn't been arranged? Even my own mother had an arranged marriage!'

So had mine, Abbie thought, but for a different reason, and no doubt carried out much faster.

'Doesn't anyone marry for love?' Jean persisted. 'Oh, Abbie, it makes me wonder what will happen to Alex and me –'

Just then the trumpets sounded, and Queen Catherine arrived dressed in grey silk which made her pudgy face look very white and her black hair even blacker. She sat down at the opposite end of the balcony from Diane de Poitiers, for once not casting a single baleful glance in her direction.

'What's wrong with her?' Jean whispered.

'When I ran along this morning she was coming out of her room with both Nostradamus and Ruggieri. Goodness knows what they had been saying to her. None of it could have been good. Her eyes were staring, but she didn't see me.'

Heralds drowned out anything else Abbie had to say, blowing their trumpets, then crying, 'Make way for the Queen of

Scotland and England!' The girls saw that Throckmorton, the English Ambassador, leaned forward at that, watching with interest.

When Mary arrived with Francis in a coach with gilded wheels he stumbled out with his hand over his ear and ran straight to his mother. Catherine put an arm around him but kept on staring straight ahead, while a shout rose from the great field for Mary. Smiling, she kissed her hand to the people.

Again the trumpets sounded and King Henry entered the lists on a big bay warhorse, flaunting the black and white silks of Diane de Poitiers. The Queen's expression didn't change, but her sinister eyes followed every move the King made all afternoon until the shadows lengthened, and it came to the last joust of all.

The King and Captain Montgomery, a soldier of famed courage, faced each other from opposite ends of the field, their lances levelled. They charged each other, but missed. They pounded close again and again in the swirling dust, and missed. The last time they charged there was a clatter and a crash, and both lances splintered.

The jagged edge of Montgomery's lance had pierced the King's visor, and in a deathly hush the people watched as the King reeled on his saddle and his blood spurted out.

Queen Catherine jumped to her feet, throwing Francis aside so that he thudded to the ground, moaning and weeping. 'I warned him,' she screamed in a terrible voice that hundreds could hear. 'I warned the King – but would he listen?'

Screaming and crying, she was there when the grooms rushed to lay him out on the ground and lift his visor. Diane remained in her seat without moving a muscle. Queen Catherine saw her husband's face drowned in blood, with the splinters sticking out of his temple and eye. Completely distraught, she ordered that he should be taken to the nearby Palace de Tournelles, where for ten days he screamed in vain for Diane de Poitiers and then died in agony.

Lady Jean and Abbie were among the young attendants when Mary and Francis were hurried to the Louvre and proclaimed King and Queen. Catherine paid them homage, but she looked ghastly. After the ceremony the new King and Queen led the procession through the huge cobbled courtyard to the street where the royal coach awaited and Mary stepped aside for Catherine to enter it first.

'No,' Catherine said, but she said it with hatred and venom in her voice, 'you take precedence now.'

Francis liked being King François II of France. It meant he could do as he pleased, and his pleasure was hunting. Sometimes he was twenty hours in the saddle, racing – racing – racing – and lashing his weak body to race again, until his attendants dragged him from his horse and poured wine through his blue lips.

'It's the Devil in him,' Queen Catherine said to Mary one day. 'He should be exorcised again.'

There was a dangerous note in Mary's voice when she replied. 'Indeed? And just how do you propose to do that, may I ask?'

'The same as last time. Hang him up by the heels and let the doctors beat the demon out of him. It's the only way.'

'It's a wonder Francis is still living,' Mary said furiously. 'If there is a devil in the gentlest creature in the world, it is you who put it there with your black magic. I forbid you and your doctors to go near him.'

'*You* forbid *me*, madam?'

'I am your Queen, which you have very quickly forgotten. You have given up Francis for lost, as well. But perhaps that is what you want? To allow your doctors to kill him? Then you could rule France again, through your second son, Charles.'

'And have you not seen the way Charles looks at you although he is only ten? He is almost a man already!' Catherine looked at her slyly. 'I mean a proper man, this time – one who could –'

'Get out of my sight,' Mary interrupted her furiously. 'I love Francis. I will not listen to such filth.'

'You would dismiss me, madam? As you would a maid? Oh, you will pay for *that*,' Catherine said, striding to the door.

Mary had managed to dismiss Queen Catherine for the moment, but she could not dismiss the fresh worries she was plunged into so easily. In Scotland the Protestant cause was sweeping forward like a great tide, and the news from Edinburgh was that John Knox was spreading rebellion against her mother.

'If only I could go to Scotland to help her . . . If only Francis would get stronger . . . I cannot leave him in this nest of vipers . . .' Mary wept, and her ladies tried to comfort her.

From the pulpit of St Giles', John Knox swayed the Lords of Scotland to depose Marie de Guise as Regent. He encouraged Elizabeth of England to send troops against Leith, the port of Edinburgh.

Leith fell. Marie de Guise, surrounded by traitors, locked herself in Edinburgh Castle and fought with her back to the wall. Only the Earl of Bothwell remained faithful to her, and somehow he and his Borderers recaptured Leith and drove the English back.

Mary faced the Cardinal with tears of fury in her eyes. 'You have done this! I told you Elizabeth would be enraged when I displayed the emblems of England! I should not have listened to you! God knows I had more sense myself.'

'You, a girl of seventeen?' he sneered, his face as thin and evil as the Devil's, his eyes flashing and glittering poisonously. 'What do *you* know?'

'Enough to tell you that Francis is your King and I am your Queen. From now on you will carry out our orders. We rule France, not you.'

'Silly child,' the Cardinal said in a gentle voice. 'Queen Catherine and I have ruled France for years! But you didn't even know that, did you?' he asked contemptuously.

* * *

Months of mourning passed, during which Mary's health was precarious. In June she fell ill again with a sudden sharp pain gnawing at the right side of her stomach. The doctors didn't know the cause and were powerless to relieve it. She lay in her bed, not daring to move. If she lay very still, the pain was not so severe.

She closed her eyes and drifted off into an uneasy doze, and awoke to whispers, whispers, whispers all round her bed. Yet she couldn't make out one word of the whispers until the Cardinal's face materialised above her and she tried to sit up.

'What is it? What are they all whispering about?' she asked, feeling suddenly so very frightened that she knew the answer in her heart of hearts already.

'Very sad news from Scotland,' he replied.

'No . . . No . . .' Mary moaned.

'Our dear sister and your dear mother has died. She died of the dropsy.'

Mary wept for hours.

Unable to speak or eat or sleep, she remained in her bed for the next ten days. Worse than her grief was her feeling of guilt. The burden of holding Scotland for her daughter had driven Marie de Guise to her death, and she was only forty-four.

On Mary's first public appearance in mid-August she wore black. The Cardinal was gently reproving. 'Black?' he raised his eyebrows.

'Do you forget I mourn my mother? Your Eminence will respect my grief,' she said, turning away from him, sickened by him.

He was quick to appear sorry. 'Of course I respect your grief, Your Majesty. Your grief is mine, also.'

There seemed to be no end to her problems. Francis was ill again. The pain in his right ear was worse, this time accompanied by excruciating headaches, and Mary felt increasingly helpless in a world that had changed completely. All her life she had been used to the best that life could offer. Crowns had simply dropped into her lap, and she had cherished them much as she would have cherished rose petals.

Now she saw that they were far from that.

The crown of Scotland was another Crown of Thorns, and just as bloody. The crown of France was only borrowed, and looking at Francis with pity, she did not think it could be for long . . . And as for the crown of England, rightfully hers, it was sitting upon the head of a Protestant bastard.

TWENTY-THREE

By now Abbie had become tired of the political moves here in France, and abroad in England and Scotland. There was something a good deal more personal to worry her than any of that, and it was worrying her more and more every day.

She was by now very suspicious of everything. Her life seemed to be a melting pot where she believed nothing she had ever been told and trusted nobody to tell her the truth – except one man, Donald.

The Marys were too bound up in themselves, each other and the Queen to discuss it with, and besides, although they were always pleasant and friendly, in some subtle way they all let her know that they were ladies, born and bred.

Only Lady Jean never did that, but Jean could think of no one else but Alex Ogilvie. More than once Abbie had tried to broach the subject nearest to her heart to Jean, but no matter how the conversation began, it always came back around to Alex Ogilvie and stayed there, while Jean's eyes shone and she became quite animated. Abbie sighed. It was hopeless. Jean was the closest friend she possessed, except for Donald, and just lately, since Abbie had started to worry in earnest, there had been no chance to meet him in private, and on no account could she risk being overheard.

And then, the court moved to Orléans, so that Francis could pursue his favourite hobby of hunting boar. Although he could rarely eat any of it, one of his great pleasures was when a fanfare heralded the servants bearing aloft a boar he had hunted, bringing it to the table on a vast silver salver with an apple in its mouth and cherries in its eyes.

Mary would sometimes set off with him, although she didn't always stay the pace, and some or all of her ladies accompanied her. One day, Abbie trailed behind the hunting party, thoroughly bored, and slowed her horse to a gentle amble near the edge of the wood. To her delight, the Scottish Guard were going in the opposite direction, one of its riders peeled off, and then Donald was at her side.

They dismounted, tied their bridles around a tree, and in the shelter of the trees he took her in his arms and kissed her. They sat down and he kissed her again. Abbie could see that nothing sensible was going to be achieved unless she took a stand, and it wasn't easy to look as worried as she felt deep down when he looked at her like that.

'Donald,' she said, 'I want to ask you a question.'

'Fire away. You know I'm the best at answering questions that anyone ever knew.'

'Do *you* think I resemble the Queen?'

'Which one?' he teased her. 'Well, she's shorter and stouter and her hair is black and she kicks up her legs a lot, but otherwise –'

'You're a devil, Donald MacLaren! Be serious for once!'

'If you resembled Queen Mary I wouldn't be sitting here with my arms around you. A man likes to feel some flesh in his arms, not a long skinny drink of water.'

'I meant, in the face?'

He looked at her critically. 'Your hair is the same colour, your eyes are like hers, but you haven't got a long thin face with a pointed chin. You have a sweet face, like your mother's ... And a very sweet mouth ...'

'It always ends up like this,' Abbie said breathlessly, grabbing her cap and sticking it back on her head.

'Besides, you don't speak with a squeaky voice.'

'If she really tries, any woman can speak with a squeaky voice,' Abbie squeaked at him.

'Good God! Where did you learn to do that?'

'Oh, I've been well trained, believe me. They've been training my voice for years so that I can speak just like her.'

'Why?' Donald's face was serious at last.

'I don't know. That's what I was hoping you could tell me . . . And besides that, the Cardinal has been instructing Mary all these years in my company. He arranged it that way. He didn't bother with me for the Greek and Latin lessons, and there were other times when he excluded me from the study, but he saw to it that I was kept in touch with current affairs, the same as the Queen.'

'Enough to be able to converse with statesmen, perhaps? And this has been going on all along? Abbie, why did you not tell me this long ago?'

'Why? What are you thinking?'

'The same as you have been suspecting, sweetheart. They have been preparing you to stand in for the Queen, to take her place in some emergency. Have they asked you to do it already?'

'No! Anyway, she's six feet tall!'

'Hm . . .' Donald looked at her fixedly for a few seconds. 'But anyone could mistake you if you were sitting down, wearing her face paints and her clothes.'

'I don't like it. I like it less and less every day.'

'But you're a brave girl, Abbie. You can't help looking like the Queen. You and she had the same father, as John McCracken confided in me. Oh, yes . . .' he smiled at her. 'I've known about it for ages, and even if your father hadn't made me promise to look after you here, I would have anyway. I love you, and whatever happens, I'll always look after you, I promise. We're just a couple of bastards together, little Abbie! But,' he hugged her close, 'it isn't sore! Now is it?'

Laughter rippled from deep inside her. 'Oh God,' she said, 'you could always make me laugh, Donald MacLaren!'

'If that's who I am.'

For a long time they laughed and cried together until Abbie recovered enough to dry her eyes. 'Oh, thank God you're here, Donald! You'll never know how much I was needing to talk to you today.'

175

'There's a happy day coming, and I pray to God it won't be long in coming, when you can talk to me all day long and all night long, Abbie.'

But despite his reassuring words, when they parted, he watched her going with a very worried frown on his face.

Two days afterwards, Francis set off for the hunt as usual, and within an hour he was hastily brought back and laid on his bed.

Mary did as she always did when this happened, gently warming a mixture of egg yolk, oil of roses and turpentine and pouring a few drops of it into his ear. Then she took her place at his side as she had done so many times before, holding a cool damp cloth to his forehead to ease the pain.

In a few minutes he opened his eyes and tried to smile at her. 'Oh, Marie, you always make me feel better,' he groaned, and turned his head to the side. To her alarm she saw that now there was a large swelling behind his right ear, his face was completely white except for great blotches of red across his cheeks, and he was in a rising fever.

Queen Catherine hurried to the room where he was lying. 'Just the same as his grandfather, François the First,' she pronounced with a sniff. 'He was named after him, against my wishes. I thought it bad luck to name a child after a man who pursued hunting right up to the end, when he fell off his horse in the last stages of syphilis.'

'Syphilis?' Mary looked at her as though she were mad. 'How can a swollen ear be syphilis? I must send for the physician at once.'

'Don't bother. This is beyond a mere physician. It is a surgeon we must have here. I shall call for Ambroise Paré, the King's surgeon.'

Paré lanced the swelling, but Francis did not improve. Over the next few days he grew worse.

'There is more there . . . Probably an abscess on the brain. The only hope is to operate,' Paré said, looking at Mary. 'You are his wife, Your Majesty. Do I have your permission?'

'Please! Do what you must! Only save him!' Mary cried.

'And I am his mother!' Catherine shrieked, elbowing her aside. 'I will not allow you to cut open his head. You will make him an even bigger idiot than he is already. Have neither of you any respect for the Crown? What sort of king would France have then?'

'Something must be done to ease his agony,' Mary appealed, in tears. 'Is there anything you can give him so that the pain is dulled, at least?'

'Opium, madam.'

'Then administer it at once.'

Catherine shook her head and retreated to the furthest end of the room, away from the putrid smell of Francis's ear, and soon afterwards she was joined by the Cardinal, waving his scented handkerchief under his nose. But Catherine and the Cardinal grew impatient as Francis hovered for days between life and death, and only visited the sickroom at intervals.

Mary held Francis's hand all the time, scarcely eating or sleeping, and now and then when she saw a flicker on his face she would murmur, 'I love you, Francis. I love you.'

For the most part, the Marys were no help. Beaton refused point-blank to go near the sickroom, Livingston was no better, and Seton told Mary in her quiet voice that she could do more good by praying for Francis in the chapel. Only Flamina, Lady Jean and Abbie kept Queen Mary company in a twenty-four-hour rota. The atmosphere became worse all the time as the yellow pus ran down his neck. The girls wore nose masks, but Mary refused. She wanted to kiss her beloved husband. She wanted him to see her smiling at him.

Abbie was on duty, and the Cardinal and Queen Catherine happened to be in the stuffy room when Mary thought she would surely choke if she could not slake her throat. She dropped Francis's hand for a minute to pour herself some wine. Her back was to the bed when she heard a gasp and a rattle and then the Cardinal's voice, bright with relief.

'The King is dead.'

The wine cup dropped to the floor. Mary rushed back to

the bed. *Dead*? How could he be? He was not even seventeen years old yet! Catherine flung her violently aside.

'No, you don't, madam! I take precedence now! *I* am Queen of France!'

In Edinburgh such a golden opportunity was not to be missed. 'The French King died of a putrid ear as he sat at Mass – that deaf ear that would never hear the truth of God,' John Knox brayed from his pulpit.

On her eighteenth birthday, Mary attended her husband's burial and then retreated into forty days of mourning and of prayer. At the end of it the black candles were snuffed and the window tapestries parted to admit the wan winter sunlight.

From a deep chair by the hearth the Cardinal said, 'Your Majesty's mourning is officially over. Now we must go on to settle your future and arrange another marriage. The Kings of Sweden and Denmark are asking for your hand. So is Don Carlos, the heir to the Spanish throne. But we would suggest your brother-in-law Charles. If you marry him you would be Queen of France again. You would no longer live in Queen Catherine's shadow.'

'I do not intend to live in her shadow, nor yours either. If – God forbid – I married Charles, we would be your puppets, as Francis and I were. And that's what you want, isn't it? *You* want to rule France.'

'I am France,' he said. 'Didn't you know?'

'So you are France?' said a voice from the doorway, and Catherine stalked in. Her eyes were glittering with fury. 'You are wrong, Your Eminence. *My son is France*, and as Regent I shall rule through him. I am ruling already. Neither of you,' she looked from the Cardinal to Mary, 'is welcome any longer at my court unless you obey my every wish. Otherwise, you may leave as soon as you please.'

Speechless, the Cardinal left the room. Catherine turned to Mary.

'Downstairs the public room is thronged with ambassadors awaiting an audience with you. Do as you please. Marry whom you like, but remember, you have only six months in which to make your arrangements. In six months it will be summer, and travelling to wherever you choose will be easy.'

'I beg leave to remain in France, Your Majesty. Many times I have contemplated becoming a nun.'

'Not on French soil, you won't,' Catherine said as she left.

Not knowing any of this, Abbie did not understand the Cardinal's chastened demeanour. It was clear that Mary no longer trusted him, not an inch, but he was still her official adviser. All her foreign dealings were still filtered through him, and one day he waved a document under her nose saying, 'You had better read this very carefully.'

'What is it?'

'A copy of the Treaty of Edinburgh. Under the terms of peace between France, Scotland and England, all foreign troops shall be barred from Scotland. Your Majesty shall "in all times coming abstain from bearing the title, emblems and arms of the Kingdom of England and Ireland."'

'That would also apply to my children, if I were to have any in the future. It would be throwing away their birthright. What else?'

'The Scottish Parliament, mostly Protestant now, recognises Elizabeth's claim to the English throne. They do not admit yours. Elizabeth knows her power now. The Scots bow to her bidding.'

'Thanks to you and your bungling, they might as well give her Scotland and be done with it,' Mary said bitterly. 'But I will never give her Scotland, not after all my mother did to keep it for me. She died to keep Scotland for me!' she cried passionately. 'And I will never sign that treaty!'

The young people of Mary's court tried to comfort and amuse her but, pale-faced, she spent her days asking God for the answers to her questions. What should she do? Where should she go?

God didn't answer. He gave her no sign.

The wearisome, dull days of winter dragged on until one day Flamina tapped on her door and entered. Her eyes were shining with excitement. A gold curl had escaped from her cap and her breast was heaving. 'Madam, James Hepburn, the Earl of Bothwell is here! He arrived from Flanders an hour ago and has taken lodgings at the inn of The Three Brothers. He desires private audience.'

Mary jumped up. 'My mother's friend! He has come, at last! Get a page to find him and tell him I'll receive him in half an hour. You will help me to dress, Flamina.'

Flamina helped her to change into a stiff black velvet dress and spread the long sable-lined train. Mary smoothed the high silver-lace ruff that flared back from the gown's deep neckline.

'What does he look like, Flamina?'

Flamina giggled and blushed. 'Like a wolfhound, madam.'

'An attractive wolfhound, to judge from your blushes.'

'Yes, madam, attractive . . . But we have heard of James Hepburn's reputation! It is worse than his father, Patrick's, ever was! He can't be over twenty-five, yet they say he has been a rake for ten years. They say no woman is safe alone with him. Perhaps I should stay with you?'

'Oh, they say, they say!' Mary smiled. 'Thank you for your offer of protection, *chérie*, but I think I can manage him myself.'

Reluctantly, Flamina left her. Almost immediately there was a tap at the door and Mary turned as it opened. In the dim hallway, in the flare of a guard's torch, she saw his shadow first.

Then she saw the man.

'James Hepburn, Earl of Bothwell, Your Majesty,' he said, 'Lord High Admiral of Scotland, Keeper of Hermitage and Edinburgh Castles, Lieutenant of the Borders – at your service.'

Of middle height, but of great bodily strength, he was certainly not handsome. Mary saw at a glance what Fleming had meant when she described him as a 'wolfhound', but there was also something apelike about the shape of his head with its close-cropped red hair. His ears were large and protruding, his nose must have been broken once, his skin was leathery and weather-beaten and his lips under the carefully trained moustache with its curling ends were full and sensual.

She met his eyes, the smoky green eyes of a watchful animal. Despite his appearance Bothwell simply oozed sexuality, and that was something that Mary had never met before . . . But her body didn't interest *him*. She knew it instinctively and was shocked by her own resentment.

'Well?' she asked finally. 'Am I indeed your Queen? You are silent. Do I dazzle you?'

'You're not old enough to dazzle a man. They say in Scotland that you are only a doll, a puppet here. What is the purpose of your life in France now, when you are a widow? You need your own country and your country needs its Queen.'

'I hear differently,' Mary said. 'That James Stewart, my half-brother, rules Scotland.'

Bothwell laughed contemptuously. 'He thinks he does, along with John Knox, and the longer you leave them to believe it, the quicker it will happen. *You* are our rightful Queen. Your dear mother died upholding you as our rightful Queen. Are you going to let her down now?'

'No.'

'Then, are you coming to Scotland, or not?'

'I shall come,' she said, almost hypnotised.

'When may I fetch you?'

Nobody had ever spoken to her so directly – God certainly hadn't – but now suddenly, Bothwell was showing her the way.

'In the summer,' she said.

'The fleet will be at the ready.'

And her decision was made.

He smiled and bowed, holding out a bundle of papers. 'Before I take my leave I must carry out the other part of my business with you. These are the last letters your mother wrote before she died. She begged me to deliver them in person.'

'Thank God for you, James Hepburn,' Mary said slowly. At the very sight of that dear lacy handwriting the tears were in her eyes. 'I shall summon you when I am ready.'

'Scotland will rejoice,' he said, and left.

She looked tenderly at the pile of her mother's papers he had left behind him, and began to read. Among them was Marie's last will and testament, the bequests pitifully small and few. But, Mary thought, she bequeathed to the world a matchless example of courage. For seventeen years she had been one woman against thousands of rebels, opportunists and fanatics.

Another paper was a document of Scottish treachery. Her mother had made out two lists of names. The one headed 'Traitors' was heartbreakingly long. James Stewart was first, with a question mark. She had added a note: 'There is evidence that he is another tool of Queen Elizabeth's, as are the others here.'

Under 'Allies' the list scarcely covered a page. Bothwell's name headed it. 'Trust this man with your life. He is irreligious and immoral, but forthright and honest.'

Mary read and reread those lines, feeling oddly comforted. Then she came to her mother's last words to her. 'I forgive my enemies, but they do not forgive me. I leave you a heritage of hatred.'

Lady Jean and Abbie were returning from their afternoon walk as Bothwell mounted his horse to depart. It was getting dark already, and a chilly wind had sprung up. They clutched their cloaks more firmly to them and held on to the deep hoods drawn up over their caps as he trotted past, going to join the rough men waiting in a line.

'Did you ever see such an ugly brute of a man?' Jean whispered.

'And you know where they are all going from here.' Abbie glanced back. 'That's where they all gather to go into the brothels of Paris on a Saturday evening. Who was that man?' she asked Flamina when they got inside.

'James Hepburn, the Earl of Bothwell, from Scotland. Isn't he gorgeous?'

Gorgeous?

The girls stared at her, and Flamina ran off, giggling.

'She becomes more like her mother, Lady Fleming, every day,' Jean observed.

'Man-mad,' Abbie agreed.

TWENTY-FOUR

Now her husband was dead, Mary was forced to return many of her jewels and belongings to Queen Catherine as property of the Crown of France. Thoroughly depressed, she received Throckmorton, the English Ambassador, who was calling with the official condolences of Queen Elizabeth.

With those preliminaries out of the way, he coughed. Plainly, he was coming to the crux of the matter.

'Yes, Ambassador?'

'I should warn you, Your Majesty, that my mistress is extremely displeased that you have not yet ratified the Treaty of Edinburgh.'

Mary was so tired of this argument. She had given her answer so many times. Why would the English not leave her alone? 'Everything has changed with the death of my husband,' she prevaricated.

'In what way?'

'The treaty was drawn up when Francis and I were King and Queen of both Scotland and France. Now there is only a Queen of Scotland.'

'That has nothing to do with it. The question is of your claim to the English throne, or your successor's. King Francis was not concerned.'

'When I go to Scotland I shall consult with my Scottish council.'

'Perhaps you should not wait so long. This delay hinders your relationship with your most noble cousin, Queen Elizabeth.'

'It grieves me that it is so. But I know that your Queen would not really expect that anyone would allow hereditary rights to be set aside. She did not allow it herself in a similar situation.'

'We must resolve this somehow,' Throckmorton groaned.

'It might help if your mistress would give me a guarantee of safe passage past England when I sail,' Mary smiled. 'I await her letter of authority upon your return.'

Lady Jean and Abbie were among the Scots who watched Francis's young brother, Charles, being crowned in Rheims Cathedral. Mary of Scotland wept throughout the ceremony, but Queen Catherine smiled. She had come alive again. Abbie glanced over at her and saw how excited she was, straining to see every detail of the coronation.

Her eyes were glittering. That is because she will be the real ruler of France, thought Abbie. She has waited a long, long time for this, and now she has come into her own at last.

Since the court mourning for Francis Abbie had seen very little of Queen Catherine. Now she wondered if she would ever talk with the strange little Italian Woman again. Yes, she was strange, Abbie mused – half bad in most people's estimation . . . although half good in hers.

The trumpets roused her from her reverie, sounding forth to announce that France had a new king, His Most Christian Majesty Charles IX.

Afterwards Jean and Abbie joined the Marys at Queen Mary's feet. Her white lips blurred into her white face under her white widow's veil and her eyes looked almost black, circled by deep grey shadows. But she had stopped weeping now and seemed to have reached some sort of decision.

'Oh, my ladies,' she said. 'My dear friends, all of you – how would you feel about going back to Scotland?'

For a few seconds there was a stunned silence. Then Fleming spoke. 'If you go, I go,' she said.

'Yes,' Beaton and Seton said together. 'Oh, yes.'

185

'If it is truly your wish, it is mine also,' said Livingston.

Mary sighed, and then smiled at Jean and Abbie sitting together. 'It would not be to Strathbogie, my dears, although you must feel free to go home to Huntly if you wish. My destination must be Holyrood Palace in Edinburgh.'

'We would rather be with you, Your Majesty,' Jean spoke quickly for them both.

'There will be many arrangements to be made,' Mary said, 'and I would wish to take all the good people of my household with us – Father Mamerot, Bourgoing, my physician, Balthazzar, my tailor – oh! And of course, our faithful Scottish Guard. I could not imagine life without any of you! But if I knew you would come . . .'

'We will come,' the girls assured her excitedly.

Of course, our faithful Scottish Guard – Abbie's heart lifted.

Only a few days later Queen Catherine sent for her and Lady Jean, as she had half expected.

'Now, what?' Jean asked nervously as they walked along the corridors.

They found the Queen directing servants in the clearing out of her apartments. 'I am moving into the King's rooms, to be with my son. I am needed at the helm now,' she said triumphantly.

She broke off to bark out more orders in her guttural voice and then came back to them.

'You are wondering why I have sent for you? But you always knew I took a special interest in my two little Scottish girls. I cannot say goodbye to you without giving you a little memento of your time in France,' she said, holding out a small black velvet box to Jean. 'Go on, open it!' she commanded.

'Oh,' Jean gasped. 'This is too much, Your Majesty.'

'I have had the fleur-de-lis fashioned in sapphires and diamonds for you, Lady Jean.'

'You have been so kind to me already,' Jean said quietly and curtsied deeply. 'Memories of that would have been enough to take back to Scotland.'

186

'Nonsense, my dear. Let it remind you of France – and me,' Queen Catherine said. 'And now,' she kissed Jean on both cheeks, 'you may go. I have something to say to Abbie.'

When Jean had bowed herself out, Catherine held out another black box. 'For you, Abbie, the brooch is a ruby heart surrounded by pearls. That is because I thought you always had a kind heart to me.'

Abbie looked into Catherine de Medicis' eyes. She had seen so many expressions there. Suddenly, she felt sorry. She would have liked to believe in this moment of parting that Catherine was sincere, but too often she had seen flashes of cunning and even evil in those black depths, and now she thought she detected a mocking flash. What was Catherine's intention? she wondered, and at the same time chided herself for ingratitude.

'It is beautiful, Your Majesty. But you have given me so many gifts already,' Abbie said, and as she dipped in a curtsy she suspected that most of them had been to bribe her to silence about the Queen's strange hobby of making dolls and sticking pins in them. As she kissed Catherine's outstretched hand, she suddenly knew that the dolls were part of this witch's black magic.

'You have all the boxes of perfumes and medicines safe?'

'Of course, Majesty.'

Abbie wondered how far and for how long Queen Catherine's black powers would stretch.

All the way to Scotland, perhaps? Abbie became convinced that they had not felt the last of this woman's hatred.

'I have another for you. The last. This time it is a small trunk. It will be delivered to you, with the key, as you embark for Scotland. And now you may go. As you see, I am very busy.' Catherine turned away.

'Yes. Thank you, Your Majesty. And farewell,' Abbie said.

Four galleys rode at anchor in Calais. Two were loaded with Mary's silver, furniture, tapestries, china and wine, along with many other items. Another stood by for her animals, her palfreys, the royal stud, hunting dogs and falcons. The largest and most splendid ship of all was the white one for the passengers, flying the flags of France and Scotland.

But still, Mary delayed and delayed, waiting at an inn near the docks surrounded by her retinue which included her ladies, priests, altar boys, pages, musicians, chefs, tiring women, doctors, her secretary, and two French poets, Branthome and Pierre de Chastelard. The small court passed the time playing music and chess, or walked about followed by the anxious Scottish Guard, including Donald, who never took his eyes off Abbie.

Pierre de Chastelard was the latest addition to the court. Tall, handsome, with golden hair rippling in waves, he embarrassed Mary by pestering her with love sonnets – graceful enough, but her grief for Francis did not allow her to take any other man seriously.

However, Beaton especially, was fascinated. She kept speaking about 'Pierre', and her smouldering eyes followed him wherever he went.

'Perhaps I was wrong to allow that young man to come with us,' Mary frowned.

'Oh, but just think!' Beaton said swiftly. 'What a wonderful dancing partner he will make!'

'If I ever feel like dancing again,' Mary sighed.

Abbie overheard them. Beaton had not been talking about a dancing partner for the Queen but for herself, and Mary was too distracted to notice it.

The captain of the little fleet was next to ask permission to speak to the Queen. 'Good weather is wasting,' he growled.

'We are not quite ready to sail yet,' Mary told him, 'but I will send word to you when we are.'

'Why are we hanging about like this?' Donald muttered to Abbie, having taken it upon himself to be her personal escort as she walked in the little orchard behind the inn. 'I'm tired of it! The sooner we get home, the sooner I can ask your father's permission for us to marry. Will you marry me, Abbie?'

'Do bastards marry, Donald?' Abbie teased him.

'This one will, if you will have me.'

'Nobody *has* to get married,' she said playfully, 'as you well know.'

He swung her round, almost angrily. '*We* do,' he said. 'I want you to belong to me only, and I to you, and I want the whole world to know it. Now, will you marry me, Abbie?'

'Considering that I decided I would before I was four years old, Donald MacLaren, you've taken a long time to ask me. Of course I will. I'll die if I don't. I love you with all my heart.'

'And I adore you.' Donald kissed her again passionately. 'Oh God, why are we waiting?'

'It's Mary. She's waiting for something,' Abbie told him. 'Or someone . . . Perhaps it has been this man riding up now, Throckmorton, Elizabeth of England's Ambassador.'

'Well, he's ridden fast and hard. Look at the dust on him!'

'Look at his face, Donald! Whatever he's got to say, it's not good news. Come with me.' Abbie took his hand. 'If we hurry we might hear what he has to tell her.'

Donald laughed, and together they strolled as nonchalantly as possible up to where Mary was sitting in the sun on a wooden bench outside the inn.

'Her Majesty Queen Elizabeth refuses safe-conduct,' Throckmorton was saying miserably. 'I could do nothing.'

Abbie saw that Mary's face went snow-white before she rallied.

'She would grant it if you would ratify the Treaty of Edinburgh,' Throckmorton went on desperately. 'Not only that, but she would offer you a haven anywhere on English soil. She would receive you at any port you care to mention, and entertain you as a sister.'

'I shall not sign until she acknowledges me as her successor.'

'*Please* sign, and sail with her blessing, madam.'

'No. The seas are free, and the only blessing I ask is God's. We sail at dawn tomorrow.'

*　　*　　*

But at dawn the following day everyone saw that the captain had been quite right to worry about the weather. A stiff wind swept the harbour, tugging at the tall masts, filling and flapping the sails. It whipped the cloaks of the ladies and gentlemen about their legs, and they looked at the gangplank leading up to the deck with grave misgivings and apprehension.

Mary was the first to embark, shortly afterwards giving herself into the hands of the Marys, who hastened her below. Her entourage followed, all except Abbie who held Donald back.

'Look! There's another coach coming,' she said.

She had seen that it was Queen Catherine's coach, the fast one, and it must have been timed to arrive at the very last minute. Catherine's intelligence service had always been good, Abbie thought. Nothing ever escaped her – but who on board this ship had got news of the time of departure to her so fast? And between last night and early this morning?

Two servants carried a small trunk from the coach, laid it on the deck and gave Abbie the key before they departed hurriedly again. Then the gangplank was lifted and they were off, the green hills of France receding with frightening rapidity and the view to the north grey and dour over the cold sea.

'Abbie, where shall I put this trunk?' Donald asked, but at that moment someone screamed from across the harbour and they rushed to the side. They saw that a huge wave had dashed a fishing boat on the rocks. Men were struggling and screaming in the water before they went under, and the boat vanished.

'That's a very bad omen,' Donald said, throwing himself on the trunk as another huge wave hit the royal galley and the trunk slid drunkenly towards the rails.

'No! No, Donald! Let it go!' Abbie screamed, holding him back.

The trunk disappeared over the side with a splash. 'Well, it's gone now,' he said ruefully. 'What was in it?'

'I don't know. I didn't have time to unlock it and see.'

'The sea has unlocked it. It's burst open. Look!' Donald pointed.

The box floated upside down, its contents scattered on the waves. Dazedly, Abbie recognised them. They were the waxen images of the Scottish court, the dolls Queen Catherine had got made, which had filled Abbie with terror and repugnance.

Abbie saw Lady Fleming bobbing past, and beside her, her daughter, Flamina, before their long red wigs came off and they disappeared. She saw the four Marys, stripped of their finery by the waves. One flash of them, and they were gone for ever, sunk to the bottom of the sea.

Last of all Mary of Scotland's effigy floated by, long and thin, her white gown ballooning before it was whipped off. Her black heart-shaped cap came off and even her golden hair floated like seaweed for a second before the sea claimed it too.

Abbie and Donald stared in horror at what was left. They could not mistake that beautiful young face before it disintegrated . . . nor that Catherine de Medicis had been practising the most vicious of her black arts upon it.

'Oh God!' Abbie whispered, her flesh crawling when she saw that it was not a necklace Mary had been wearing around the stump that was all that was left of her neck.

It was a ring of long, black pins.

PART TWO

TWENTY-FIVE

Driven before the wind like a great white swan Mary's galley ploughed northwards, and on the evening of the fourth day as it neared Leith the notorious haar of the east coast of Scotland enveloped it in a thick impenetrable fog. All night long, floundering drearily outside the harbour, the galley announced its position in the Firth of Forth with monotonous drumbeats.

Up on deck, peering through the pall and seeing nothing, with Chastelard at one side and Beaton at the other, Mary recognised the Scots-French accent of Arthur Erskine, her equerry.

'Jesu! How long will this last?' she asked him.

'Perhaps for weeks,' he answered gloomily. 'You may as well go to your bed, Your Majesty. In this weather we can move neither forwards nor backwards. We are marooned until it lifts.'

No one slept that night. The drums beat loud and persistent, the wreaths of fog swirled down even into the cabins, and the feeling was one of blind suffocation.

But at dawn there was a glimmer of light. The Captain could see the pier for a brief moment. He steered the galley straight towards it and docked before the choking yellow curtain, stinking ferociously of rotting fish and tar, descended again.

'You don't remember the haar, do you, Jeannie?' Abbie asked her in their cabin. 'No, of course you couldn't. You were too young when we left Scotland to remember it, or the way it seeps into your very bones. It's a mercy that I had our cloaks at the ready. Wrap up as warm as you can.' She handed Lady Jean her cloak and hurriedly fastened her own. 'We are to disembark.'

Up on deck the ladies and gentlemen of Mary's French court had tried to do the same. Huddled into their warmest clothing they walked down the gangway and into the yellow oblivion. Dressed in a white satin gown under a white velvet cloak trimmed with ermine, the young Queen hesitated a moment at the rail, shuddering, her face blue with cold.

'*Mon Dieu!* What hell is this?' she asked herself. 'For so long I have visualised landing in Scotland to a radiant home-coming, with the sun shining and flowers massed, the crowds cheering and the flags flying – with Francis at my side, of course – and the mounted council lords with my mother at their head to welcome me into Edinburgh. Not like this . . . Not like this, with both Francis and my mother in lead coffins, while I step down alone into this terrifying blankness, as silent and chill as the grave . . .'

Chastelard saw the sadness and the fear on her face. He pulled his cloak more tightly about him and murmured into her ear, 'Is it possible that Your Majesty's messages never reached Edinburgh – that they don't expect us?'

'My brother, Lord James Stewart, acknowledged my messages a month ago. Of course he expects us,' she answered coldly.

But for a second she actually welcomed the yellow vapour all round them. It would hide the tears in her eyes. Of course her brother wanted her to come! He had said so in his letters. The lords wanted her to come. The people of Scotland wanted her to come. James had said so, and he would not betray her. He was her brother . . . At least, her *half*-brother.

'Come, my ladies,' Mary said, forcing herself to be cheerful, 'we will go ashore,' and led the way down the slanting plank, a tall slender figure in white, followed by four tall figures in black, and moments later by the two smaller figures of Lady Jean and Abbie.

'Oh God,' Abbie said with her teeth chattering. 'Fasten your hood, Jean! It was raw enough already but now, here's the rain as well.'

'Do you not feel something else, Abbie? It is worse than all the fog, all the cold and all the rain put together! I feel spite. Pure, evil spite. We never should have come here.'

Shuddering, Abbie looked around for the Scottish Guard, Donald in particular, but her eyes could not penetrate the fog. Her ears picked up the voices of men nearby, but that was all. She sneezed as their feet touched the quay, and respectfully believed every word that Lady Jean was saying. After all, her mother was Lady Huntly, so it followed that she would have second sight. Besides, Abbie herself felt that something was far from right.

Arthur Erskine returned and hurried to where the Queen's party were huddling together on the quay. 'Your escort is not here, Your Majesty,' he said, 'but I took the liberty of sending a messenger to Edinburgh Castle. It is only a few miles away from here, so your nobles should not be long. In the meantime I asked a friend of mine to shelter you while you wait. His name is Andrew Lamb, and he will be honoured to receive you.'

'We shall be grateful,' Mary said as she and her retinue followed Erskine through the war-torn town of Leith.

'The English left scarcely a building standing.' Erskine could explain the blackened ruins and the atmosphere of desolation to them, but he could not explain why there was no cheering, no greetings from the Scottish lords, no pipers piping, no arches of flowers over a gold cloth for the Queen to walk on, as Abbie had expected. Instead, the haar intensified to pouring rain and the cobbles under their feet gave way to mud.

Mary and her ladies held up their skirts and splashed through it, and Abbie squelched along at Jean's side. She could feel her very toes wet, and Mary's white satin slippers were black by the time they reached Andrew Lamb's small stone house and were shown into his meagre parlour with its rock walls and earthen floor. In the inglenook the Queen removed her shoes and stockings and placed them near the hearth to dry.

'You must all do the same, my ladies,' she said, 'before you catch your deaths of cold.' Then she sighed with bitter regret, for as they all knew, Mary's clothes were very important to her. 'I swear I'd sooner enter the city barefoot than in dirty shoes . . . A queen – in dirty shoes?'

'As soon as they are dry I will try to brush them,' Livingston said.

'It is outrageous of your brother to make you wait like this,' Flamina protested hotly. 'It would have been more like it if he had been here early to wait for *you*.'

'I agree,' Mary smiled, 'but I cannot afford to lose my temper, or I might lose my crown. Remember, in Scotland I am Queen in name only, which is the point they are trying to make. That is why there is no one to meet us. It will be a battle to win back my rights . . . And I have been thinking that I should not expect any of you to share the hazards of such a life.'

Mary stretched out her bare feet to the fire while Abbie and Jean and the four Marys sat in shocked silence. Never before had their Queen confided her troubles, but now here in this dour parlour, in this strange country, they all came tumbling out.

'Perhaps you will wish to leave me and return to your families,' Mary went on. 'If so, you must not be shy to tell me, and I will arrange for it and provide suitable dowries for your future marriages.'

Abbie looked across at Lady Jean, and knew exactly what she was thinking as she sat there, frozen with horror at the Queen's words. Go back to Strathbogie – *oh, no! Never!*

Jean was the first to speak. 'I would sooner die,' she said. 'I will never leave you until you marry again yourself,' and one by one the others fervently agreed. 'Forgive me, Your Majesty,' Jean continued, 'but I cannot help thinking there may be more substantial worries than that to face, and immediately. If this reception at Leith has been deliberately insulting, as we suspect, will Edinburgh be any better?'

'Oh, my brother will have the Palace of Holyrood readied for us, I'm sure! There has been plenty of time for that.'

'There was plenty of warning for him to meet you here too!' Flamina pursued her theme. Her freckle-dusted nose tilted dangerously in the air and she stamped her foot angrily.

Mary smiled at her, when with every stamp Flamina's red curls bounced entrancingly from golden side combs. 'Don't worry, *chérie*,' she said.

'All the same, Lady Jean is quite right,' Seton put in. Usually the quiet and deeply religious one, immersed in her prayer books, she always referred to herself as 'the weed in the Queen's bouquet', for she was not as pretty as the others and kept well in the background, rarely voicing any opinion. Now, she got immediate attention. The other ladies fell silent. 'What if Holyrood is *not* fit to receive you, Your Majesty?'

'What do you mean, Seton?' Mary asked, looking at her in surprise. Once plump, Mary Seton had become statuesque and it seemed, all of a sudden quite formidable.

'That you must not forget that we, your ladies, are prepared for the worst. If your life will be harder in Scotland, then so will ours,' Seton said resolutely. 'There were so many servants in France that we never needed to use our training, but you can rely on us to fulfil our duties here. Since you yourself will be concerned with matters of state you should not have to worry about your household. With your permission, Majesty, I shall be the Mistress of the Royal Household myself.'

'Have you thought about that, Seton? That is a very big task, to be in charge of all the servants, the overseeing and allocation of rooms and all the linen?'

'I was well tutored for it in France. It will be my pleasure, madam,' Seton smiled calmly.

'Well, I shall look after the food,' Beaton volunteered and they all laughed, for Mary Beaton's appetite was prodigious for one so slim and seductive in her low-cut gowns. Only her brown, rather bovine eyes under her blonde mane gave her away. 'And the cooks, and the tables besides!' she added indignantly. 'I was well trained, too,' and they all laughed again.

'Then at least we can be sure of being properly fed, dear Beaton,' Mary said gently as footsteps and dishes chinking together sounded outside the door. 'And speaking of food, is this some coming now, do you think?'

Queen or no queen in his parlour, Andrew Lamb saw no reason to knock at any door in his own house. He opened it with a flourish and stood back to admit his wife, a small, bustling, wiry woman carrying a large tray. On it was a covered tureen, seven bowls none of which matched another, and seven spoons. Mistress Lamb laid down the tray on a small rickety table and her husband set down a jug beside it.

'Nae doot ye'll be hungry, Yer Majesty,' Mistress Lamb said briskly, 'so I've made ye some porridge. Noo, it's come right off the fire. Ye're to sup it while it's hot, and here's the milk to go wi' it.'

'Ay,' Andrew Lamb said proudly, 'there's nothing like porridge to put a right grand lining on yer stomach in the mornings!'

Then, with more smiles and nods they departed as suddenly as they had come, while Mary and her puzzled ladies gazed after them and then at the tureen in astonishment.

'What did they say?' Mary asked. 'Porridge? What is it?'

Abbie went across to the tureen and lifted the cracked lid. Steam and a strange but pleasant smell of hot meal wafted out. 'It's oatmeal boiled with a pinch of salt, Your Majesty. I remember my mother making it every morning for our breakfast.'

'Well, let's see you eating it first then,' Beaton said, peering into the tureen. 'It looks horrible. It's a sort of pale brown jelly, with lumps.'

Abbie put a ladleful into a bowl, covered it with milk and took up a spoon. 'I've never seen lumps in it before. But,' she announced, biting into one of them, 'they taste like soft nuts. Delicious! I wonder how Mistress Lamb managed to make them?'

'All I know is that I'm dying of hunger,' Beaton said, and went to sit on the window seat beside Jean and the Marys. 'I could eat anything! At least, let us try it ... Abbie, you dish it out, since you know all about it!'

They all tried to eat the slippery rough brown jelly, and Mary who had never been faced with anything so elemental as pure grain before in her life spoke up. 'When in Rome do as the Romans do, my ladies. We must try to eat their food, and although Mistress Lamb did not know it, she taught me a lesson this morning, for I did not understand a single word she said. It was like English, but with such a very different accent that it seemed like another language!'

'It was broad Scots, madam, which you couldn't be expected to remember,' Abbie told her. 'No wonder you found it strange. You haven't heard it since you left Scotland as a child, whereas we young Scots of your court still spoke it privately among ourselves.'

'Well, from now on we must all cultivate it,' Mary sighed. 'I cannot be a proper Queen of Scotland until I understand the language, at least – if not learn to speak it.'

'Oh dear – must it be all learning, again?' Livingston asked with a twinkle. 'Won't you still want dancing and music at your Scottish court, Your Majesty?'

'Lusty, you know we must have music and dancing – and fun! I command it!' Mary laughed back.

'Then I shall be Mistress of the Dance,' Livingston promised, 'and when I am not dancing I shall look after your wardrobe and your jewels. What does that leave for you, Flamina?'

'Your Majesty's hair, and your wigs,' Flamina said. 'I was always good with hair – and with face paints. Also, I shall be Mistress of the Bath.'

'I am grateful, Flamina,' Mary smiled at her first cousin, her closest relation in the gloomy little parlour, the one she would have chosen herself for such private matters.

'And you must not forget that when you have tedious letters to write I can copy your handwriting perfectly at your dictation, which is more than your secretary can do,' Flamina added.

'You will have little time for your embroidery, madam, but I could help you with that, and look after your holy ornaments,' Lady Jean offered.

'I think you have covered everything,' Queen Mary smiled at them all, touched by their eagerness to stay with her and serve her. 'I see you are quite determined to keep the crown of Scotland on my head.'

The crown ... The crown ...

The words spoken in Mary's thin voice echoed round the room and round and round in Abbie's head. Sitting cross-legged on the floor, for there were no other seats, Abbie listened to the ladies surrounding the Queen, swearing their loyalty and offering their help, and as usual the ready tears were in Mary's eyes when she clasped each of their hands in turn.

Abbie asked herself fiercely what about Donald and the promise she had made to him already? All she wanted to do in the world was to marry him. Deliberately, she sat still on the floor. She did not rise to her feet and offer the Queen her hand and her promise. And Mary didn't even notice, Abbie thought wryly.

Yet, she wondered, what had her ladies promised her, after all – apart from staying at her side until she married again? To look after her plumes and petticoats, her ruby-heeled slippers and sparkly buttons, her dainty menus and satin sheets. Were these woman's weapons to be her only defence in this rough country?

The Queen would need much more than these fripperies to keep her crown on her head ... *to keep her head on her shoulders* ... Abbie shuddered at the memory of the waxen effigy of Mary battered by the waves so that her poor little head was knocked off to leave a ring of long black pins that looked like daggers.

No, what she needed were strong right arms to defend her from the daggers – or at least *one* strong right arm – and as Flamina had pointed out, it would certainly not belong to Lord James Stewart, her bastard brother. Whose arm would it be, then?

Abbie had no idea, and she realised that the Queen could have no idea either, here in this strange land where she knew virtually no one, and could trust no one. *The crown, the crown, the crown* . . . The words were still ringing in her ears when she looked up and saw that Mary must have been speaking to her.

'You've been far away, deep in your thoughts, Abbie! A penny for them!' Mary demanded gaily. 'I was saying that between them my ladies will look after everything perfectly.'

'Not quite everything, Your Majesty,' Abbie said.

'No? What can possibly be left for you, Abbie?'

'What I am best at, if you will permit me. I will be your eyes and your ears in the corridors of Holyrood and beyond,' she said, and they all laughed again.

'Our little spy,' Mary teased.

But Abbie did not join in the laughter. Her face was serious when she said, 'I have a strange feeling that you will need a spy more than anything else here, madam, and it would be better if I were to be known as the Queen's Messenger.' As she was speaking a knock came to the parlour door.

'You may as well begin now, then.' Mary was still smiling. 'Open it, and tell me who's there.'

Abbie opened the door and then closed it smartly in the visitor's face. 'It is Lord Bothwell, madam,' she said. 'Will you receive him?'

'Give me a minute,' Mary said, and to Abbie's amazement the Queen was blushing and tucking her bare feet under her on the chair in the inglenook. 'Yes, now you may admit him.'

Bothwell stooped to avoid the low doorframe, spattering raindrops as he swirled off his blue cape and dropped it carelessly on the hearth. He bowed deeply to Mary and nodded to her ladies. 'Welcome to Scotland, Your Majesty,' he said.

'You are the first to welcome me, my lord. Come to the fire.'

'I bring bad news, I fear. The animals' galley is missing.'

'Missing? But we sighted it yesterday morning, just east of us!'

'So did I, before the fog came down.'

'You mean, you were at sea also?'

'Where else, madam, as Admiral of your fleet? I sailed to meet you, and when I saw you three days ago I swept the seas before you and behind you in case of English warships. Although I saw none, they could have been hidden in the fog and they may have trapped the animals' galley. In any case, it has not arrived.'

The corners of Mary's mouth went down. She looked very disappointed. 'My beautiful white palfrey was on board. I had hoped to ride into Edinburgh on him – but I'm sure my brother will provide horses for us,' she rallied swiftly.

'Your *brother*!' Bothwell paused. 'If I may suggest, do not allow him or the other lords to trample you. They were not here to welcome you?'

'As I said, you are the first to do so. But thank you for the warning and for your protection at sea.'

'I must not linger, Your Majesty. My messengers tell me there is trouble brewing on the Border.' Bothwell's eyes flickered over the flimsy white cloak draped over her chair. 'But you cannot mean to ride into Edinburgh in that, surely?'

'I had not bargained for your summer weather, my lord.'

'Then I shall leave you my cape. At least it is warm,' he said, bowing and closing the door as he went.

Flamina rose up from the window seat and pretended to fall down in a swoon. 'What a fascinating man,' she said dreamily. 'I suppose all the ladies fall at his feet!'

Livingston attended to her first task as Mistress of the Wardrobe, spreading out Bothwell's cape to dry. 'The clasp is interesting, Your Majesty! See, it is really a locket.'

They all gathered round to look inside it at the tiny portrait of a woman with olive skin, black hair and a lush red mouth.

'I wonder who she is?' Mary asked, and Abbie detected a note of annoyance in her voice. 'She looks Spanish or Italian.'

'No. She is Anna Throndsen, a Norwegian,' Beaton said. 'She was Lord Bothwell's mistress, and it was when he was looking for funds to marry her that he came to see you in France, Your Majesty. But when he did not get them he threw her aside.'

'Well, you should know about his mistresses, Beaton,' Flamina said tartly, 'considering your own aunt, Janet is one of them.'

'Enough!' Mary said and shut the locket again swiftly with a snap, and Abbie saw with amazement a brand-new expression on her face. There was a bright spot of colour on each cheek, her lips were compressed into a thin line and she was scowling. *She was jealous!*

Queen Mary – jealous? Surely not on Bothwell's account? She hardly knew him. Yet Abbie saw that it was so. Of course, they all knew the Queen must marry some royally suitable person again and produce an heir for the throne of Scotland. So what was she doing becoming emotional over the likes of Bothwell?

'Enough,' Mary said again. 'I am tired. Let us try to rest a little while we wait.'

The rain beat steadily against the window and Mary closed her eyes. The girls fell silent, the fire crackled soothingly in the quiet room, but Abbie could not sleep. She got up silently to look out of the window. The Scottish Guard were waiting patiently and miserably outside in the wet gloom. Her eyes searched them for Donald, and when she saw his face suddenly, in this strange, rough little room, everything was different, different and fierce and frightening, when all the other men's faces seemed to melt away and only Donald's remained. In that moment Abbie knew it would be in front of her to her dying day.

All she wanted to do then and there, and it took the most

205

tremendous effort of her life so far to resist it, was to steal out to his side, take his hand and run away with him for ever. It didn't matter where – even if it were only to his old pigsty.

With Donald, a pigsty would seem like a palace to her.

TWENTY-SIX

By nine o'clock in the morning Sir William Maitland, Laird of Lethington, had been up for hours. His black velvet clothes embroidered with silver accentuated his slim height, which along with his long, narrow face with peaked hairline and pointed black beard gave him the crafty look of a fox. When he looked in the mirror he had to admit he could see for himself why his appearance had given rise to his common nickname in Edinburgh, 'Michael Wily'.

His gaze travelled down to the onyx necklace he wore around his neck, left to him by his father. It was very important to him that his whole appearance should be elegantly understated, and well satisfied that it was, he proceeded downstairs to breakfast.

Nowadays he was rarely at his ancestral home of Lethington Towers. Today, and most days, he was in his spacious town house, and as he tucked a snowy white napkin carefully under his chin he permitted himself a quiet pride when he looked around it.

He had brought the ox-blood leather chairs with him from Spain, and they were as soft and as beautiful today as the day he had bought them. Of all the finely bound books in his bookcase he loved those containing his father's poems best. So long as he had them to dip into he was never alone; his father was still with him, guiding him, and admonishing him in his kindly way, for his father had been in public service all his life.

'William,' he would say, 'neither a flatterer nor a scorner

be! Remember that Fortune is a fickle lady and do not be over-confident in a world as capricious as the moon or as changeable as the sea.'

He smiled at the memory now as he bent to his small bowl of porridge, dredged with sugar and topped with cream. What part of the world was as changeable and as capricious as this country of Scotland?

William Maitland, gifted at birth with great sensitivity and a natural finesse, could almost smell the changes of the moon and the sea, and then changed with them in whatever way was expedient. For that reason his fellow politicians, who did not possess his almost psychic abilities, called him by his other nickname, 'the Chameleon'.

His home, his person and his affairs were all in order, the way that this thirty-three-year-old, very precise man liked them to be. If only Scotland could be so neat and tidy too, he sighed. But Scotland was in an uproar. Scotland's nobles were vying with one another to be her ruler. *Vying?* Rather they would tear out each other's throats, given half a chance – and none more dangerous and bloodthirsty than Lord James Stewart who was fast becoming the most powerful noble of them all, ready to take over the country if the Queen of Scotland did not come soon.

But she was dithering and dallying in France, waiting for Elizabeth's assurance of safe-conduct across the sea, when William Maitland knew perfectly well that Elizabeth would never produce it, and certainly not in writing, if she could help it. She was too astute for that.

He smiled thinly at the thought. He had always enjoyed the cut and thrust of dealing with Elizabeth of England. With her he was at his very best, a politician and a diplomat first, last and always. Elizabeth he understood entirely. She never made decisions. She allowed events to happen first, and then took whatever was the safest path to tread in the protection of her crown. That was *her* first, last and only consideration.

A knock at the door interrupted these reflections. 'Two messengers, Sir William,' his servant said.

'From whom?'

'From Arthur Erskine, the Queen's equerry.'

Maitland cast his napkin aside, unfolded for once, and stood up in consternation. 'Show them in, man! At once.'

'We were sent to Edinburgh Castle,' one of them explained, 'and from there we were directed to you, sir. They said you were the proper person, being the Secretary of State.'

He *had been* Secretary of State in Marie de Guise's time. Now there was no Privy Council, no officers of the court. But he didn't voice such details. Instead, he nodded briefly. 'Your message?'

'Mary, the Queen, has landed at Leith, sir. She awaits an escort into the city and horses for sixty of her court. The galley containing her animals has not arrived.'

Stunned as he was, Maitland was too controlled to give himself away. 'Thank you,' he said. 'Go back and tell Arthur Erskine that the lords will be there as soon as possible, and they will bring horses.'

After that, all was feverish activity while he sent out more messages and while every available horse in Edinburgh that could put one foot past the other was pressed into service. Riding down to Leith in the afternoon alongside nobles he would not have chosen for this very important occasion, but were the only three he could find at short notice, Maitland was not exactly *nervous*, but he was certainly extremely uneasy.

He didn't like, or trust, any of the three of them. If it came to that, he didn't trust one single noble in the whole of Scotland. To a man, they all resented the young Queen. They resented her for being a Catholic, for being young, for her foreign upbringing, for being female and most of all for being James V's only surviving legitimate heir. But she was the rightful Queen.

Maitland could positively *feel* the brains of all three men whirling around, trying to find some way round the fact that Mary was Queen and she was now in Scotland. Take Lord James Stewart: he possessed the greatest punch in Scotland today, and Maitland did not doubt that Lord James had known to the minute when the Queen had departed from France, but he had chosen not to pass on such information to him.

Then there was John Erskine, kin to the equerry Arthur Erskine, but not nearly such a fine fellow. John Erskine was the son of that two-faced 'Brother Thomas' of Inchmahome, now turned Protestant. But the Erskines had always been in the forefront, so-called Protectors of the infant royals.

Lastly, there was James Douglas, Lord Morton – as if anyone could trust a Douglas, least of all this monstrous man!

So here they were, four Protestants all in a row, riding to meet their Catholic Queen! Although he had no particular interest in religion himself, Maitland had professed Protestantism when it became obviously politic to do so in the teeth of the sweeping tide of the Reformation. One religion or the other, it was all the same to him.

The four rode silently. It was impossible to hold a conversation anyway with the thunder of the hooves of over sixty horses behind them – sorry nags all – but Maitland was glad of it. It gave him a little more time to wonder if there was *any* way, any way at all, to persuade the young Queen, very quickly now, out of one religion and into the other.

Could she not be persuaded to see, somehow, how desirable it would be for her own sake as well as for Scotland's, to subscribe to the Protestant religion at least publicly, no matter how she chose to worship in private? How it would please Elizabeth! And more importantly, how it would pave the way for Scotland to join with England! Then Mary would inherit England. Her children would inherit England. Everything would be in order and there would be peace at last.

Oh, if only he could achieve such a circumstance! He would die a happy man the very next day. But that vow itself met a sudden death when they arrived at Andrew Lamb's house, he led the way inside and his eye fell on Lady Fleming. Sir William found himself quivering at the very sight of her. She had been a lively girl with glorious red hair, but now she was a fully grown and absolutely stunning woman.

Something happened to him in that instant, something totally unexpected to shatter his quiet, well-ordered existence. He was still trying to pull himself together when Lord James strode past him to where Mary was standing by the fire.

'Your Majesty!' he said. 'You have arrived!'

She stepped forward to embrace him, but he kept his distance, bowing low instead. Seeing that, her ladies bristled disapprovingly and moved closer to her as if to protect her. 'Yes, brother, I have come at last,' she replied.

There were so many people now in the tiny parlour, and most of them so tall that Abbie could neither see nor hear what was going on. She got up on the vacant window seat. From this vantage point she saw at once the hurt on Mary's face at her brother's subtle rejection.

To make the comparison with Mary's stained and grimy appearance much worse, he was regally attired in dark blue velvet, severely elegant. His only ornaments were a thick gold waist-chain and a miniature pinned to his chest, painted on a golden brooch edged with diamonds.

Abbie saw the situation at a glance. Lord James was trying to give the impression that he was every inch the rightful king, a king who was extending hospitality to a bedraggled poor relation.

'It is difficult to estimate these sea voyages,' he said. 'Really, we did not expect you until the end of August.'

And that was a black lie, Abbie thought, as another of the lords bowed to the Queen. He had a vaguely familiar face.

'John Erskine, Your Majesty,' he said.

'Of course,' Mary smiled. 'We played together at Inchmahome, a long time ago.'

'I do not go there now, madam, but I'm sure you will be welcome any time you wish to visit.'

'No,' Lord James put in suavely. 'He left Inchmahome behind him long ago, along with all his other Popish superstitions.'

The tall thin man in black velvet stepped forward hastily to cover this awkward moment and spoke quietly and pleasantly. 'William Maitland of Lethington, Your Majesty.'

Maitland of Lethington ... The man her mother had described in her letters as 'the most intelligent man in Scotland.' 'We are pleased to receive you, Sir William,' Mary smiled at him. 'You were my mother's Secretary of State when she was Regent. I hope you will be mine.'

Her smile wavered a little when the fourth lord pushed himself forward to make a nondescript bow, looking at her with small, greedy eyes out of a florid face under a thatch of red hair. His hands were not only pudgy, but positively filthy, and his speech was so slow that for a minute everyone seriously wondered if he were fully *compos mentis*.

'So ye're here, after a',' he acknowledged her. 'I'm James Douglas, as I suppose ye ken. Earl o' Morton.'

Once again Sir William Maitland stepped into the breach while Mary was clearly wondering what to say to the man. 'We have brought what horses we could procure, Your Majesty. After your long wait you will not wish to delay any longer.'

While the other ladies gathered together their belongings, Livingston swiftly and jealously attended to the Queen, dressing her first in her white cloak and on top of that Bothwell's blue cape.

'Yes, we are ready,' said Mary.

'Isn't that a man's cape?' Lord James asked, his eyes narrowing.

'Lord Bothwell lent it to me,' she said, and with the slightest edge to her voice, 'since he was the first to welcome us to Scotland.'

At last Queen Mary had scored a small point, although Abbie felt quite put out that it was the wolflike Bothwell she had to thank for that.

'Bothwell?' James asked. 'How did *he* get here?'

'He is our Admiral, after all,' Mary smiled sweetly and then burst into a laugh. 'My lords, you must forgive my appearance! I had hoped to be so elegant for you, but look! Look at my slippers! And my petticoats! Are they not disgraceful?'

Deliberately she lifted her skirts high above her ankles to show them her stained shoes, and silence fell in the small parlour. Lord James looked positively shocked. Morton licked his thick lips.

'Ay, they're black,' he said, 'but yer legs are bonny.'

Mary made her way to the door, followed by her ladies and then the lords, but she kept them all waiting until she had spoken to Andrew Lamb and his wife. 'Thank you, good sir and mistress, for your kind reception and your hospitality. I shall not forget.'

They smiled and waved and shouted, 'Good luck, Yer Majesty! Thank God for our Queen!'

Abbie brought up the rear, in time to hear the commands of the Captain of the Scottish Guard. 'There are no horses for us,' he told his men. 'We shall march. Fortunately, the pipers are all Edinburgh men. They will lead the way, with one section of you behind them. The other section will bring up the rear behind the Queen's procession.'

Mary was staring at the ludicrous array of decrepit old horses. Lord James was already seated on his own lustrous stallion, holding a wretched sway-backed bay for her. 'I would gladly lend Your Majesty my own horse,' he said, 'but I fear he would be too spirited for you.'

'Rubbish!' Flamina darted forward. 'No horse is too spirited for her! She rides as well as any man! It is disgraceful to allow her to ride into Edinburgh on that bag of bones!'

Sparks were almost flying out of her red hair, and her temper was matching it when Sir William Maitland smiled and moved to her side.

'As you say, Flamina,' Mary said resignedly as she climbed into the scarred saddle, 'I can ride anything –'

'Of course she can,' Flamina interrupted her in a blaze of fury, glaring indignantly at the lords. 'Her Majesty can ride anything and *still* look like the Queen of Scotland!' She

213

fastened her eyes on Lord James in particular. 'She cannot be humiliated! Queen Mary's dignity is inbred – and *pure*, you see.'

There was a murmur of agreement from those of Mary's court near enough to hear, as the last man of her party in a fur-lined robe was mounted.

'Who is that?' Lord James spat. 'A priest? Your confessor?'

'Father Mamerot,' Mary nodded, and sat up tall in the saddle. 'Now we are complete. Pray, let us go. I am longing to see Holyrood Palace, my new home.'

TWENTY-SEVEN

'What?' John Knox cried.

'It's true, sir,' his secretary panted. 'I've come as fast as I could from Leith. The Queen has arrived.'

'Already?'

'And she is beautiful! I saw her as she was leaving Andrew Lamb's house. So tall! And with such a fine complexion! She moves with such grace, sir!'

'Have you gone mad? A French Catholic whore – beautiful?' Knox rounded on him.

'Sir!' the secretary protested. 'I am only the bearer of news! I do not make it! She will pass by your window in less than an hour.'

'I beg your pardon,' Knox sighed. 'Go on, man! Who met her?'

'Lord James, Erskine, Morton and Maitland of Lethington.'

'All Protestants, thank God! And now I understand this fog, this corruption of the air, this mist so thick and dark! It is Heaven itself telling us what she brings to this country – nothing but sorrow, darkness and impiety! It is God's warning to us all.'

The men of the Scottish Guard marched in front of the royal party. Seated on the frailest specimen of horseflesh there, Abbie could just make out Donald's tall back through the mist. She caught a flash of his silver gauntlet when he turned and waved at her, and took heart. But she still had a sinking feeling that this fog was a symbol. She feared that it could only mean a murky future in Scotland.

The next time Abbie looked up she saw to her dismay that Erskine was riding on one side of her and the awful Earl of Morton on the other. What was worse, Morton was leering at her, and it seemed in that horrible moment, cloaked in fog, that she was alone in the world with him.

How she managed to infuse some enthusiasm into her poor old horse she never knew, but it tottered forward obligingly until she had caught up with Lady Jean and Alex Ogilvie.

'What happened to you, Abbie?' Alex asked in concern. 'We looked for you, but couldn't see you in this mist.'

'This horse happened to me,' she said, and laughing, expelled a long breath of relief to have got free of Morton. Alex took hold of her bridle and helped to urge the animal on.

Just ahead of them Mary was riding with Lord James. If Abbie could hardly see them, at least she could listen to their conversation.

The rain stopped and a chilly wind got up as the royal party left Leith, but penetrating as it was, the wind could not cut through the fog. It merely blew it about, so that one minute they caught sight of the dreary moor they floundered over and the next saw a ruined monastery. Crossing themselves, they shuddered when the swirls of fog parted as they were passing a gibbet where the corpse of a man swung to and fro.

The damp and bitter wind blew Bothwell's blue cape and underneath it Mary's white cloak apart, and for a moment Abbie saw her gleaming gown exposed, and watched as Lord James leaned towards her.

'That is a most magnificent brooch you wear on your breast, madam! The rubies in it flash like fire even in this fog!'

'I wear it only on great ceremonial occasions. The last time was when I married Francis. I had hoped that today would be another great occasion, when I came as Queen to Scotland.'

'Scottish haar can obscure anything . . .' Lord James said smugly.

And just what did he mean by that? You would think he had ordered it specially. Abbie scowled angrily at his back. She wouldn't have put it past him. She had taken a great dislike to the Queen's brother.

'Let me see,' he went on, 'is it in the form of an H?'

'That is why it is called the Great Harry. King James Fourth gave it to my grandmother, Margaret Tudor, when they married.'

'Yes,' James said sourly. 'I *do* know the history of our lineage.'

For a while they rode on in silence, and Abbie could tell by the droop of the young Queen's shoulders that she was distressed at the way her brother was pushing away every friendly advance she was making towards him.

'I see that you are wearing a very beautiful miniature yourself, James.'

'It is a portrait of my father, James Fifth.'

How ridiculously formal he was being! As if everyone didn't know his father! But Abbie remembered Marie de Guise pinning that miniature on one of the little Queen's childhood gowns, many years ago. That was before she lost it, running about in Stirling Castle. Lord James must have found it and kept it.

'*Our* father, dear brother,' was all Mary said. 'Please let us be friends, as we used to be,' she added, touching his gloved hand with hers.

But he turned his face away and they rode on in silence until a red and orange glow tried to pierce the fog, and as they climbed uphill smoke was choking them and making their eyes smart, so that Mary hid hers in the collar of Bothwell's cape. The higher they climbed the more they felt the heat of fire on their cheeks.

'This is Calton Hill, madam,' Lord James said. 'These bonfires heralding your arrival will be seen all over Edinburgh. The capital lies before you.'

Mary reined in her horse and opened her eyes. 'I am so disappointed,' she said, after a minute. 'I can see nothing of it.'

But through the smoke and fog they heard people running towards them into the light of the fires, and saw their rough brown clothes, their blue eyes and fiery hair. These people were different from the mobs Abbie had seen in Paris. There was nothing light and gay about them. They did not flaunt their tatters as the people did in France. They wore their rags defiantly, like armour, staring at Mary's flashing diamond earrings and white kid gloves encrusted with pearls. She turned in the saddle to smile and wave, but they were gone. It was as though they had seen ghosts, creatures of the mist, Abbie thought with a shiver.

They rode down the other side of Calton Hill, skirted water which James called the 'Nor' Loch' and began to climb again as they approached the muffled city. A huge rock loomed up in front of them and at the very top was perched the grimmest castle they had ever seen.

'Edinburgh Castle,' Lord James said unnecessarily. 'The Royal Mile runs down steeply from it to Holyrood Palace.' He waved his hand to right and then to left. 'Which one is Your Majesty's pleasure?' he asked mockingly.

'Let us go to Holyrood,' Mary shuddered.

'Neither one is properly prepared for you, of course, although I sent servants to both this morning. They cannot have made much impression in the few hours since then.'

His rudeness was meant to be demoralising. Instead, it was putting Mary's back up, Abbie was glad to see.

In a little act of pure defiance Mary swept off Bothwell's cape, tucked it in her saddlebow and rode on resolutely in her gleaming white. She was in Edinburgh's Royal Mile now, where so many of her ancestors had made history before her, and if any of her subjects could see her through this frustrating fog she determined that they should see a real Queen, another Stewart, even if she died of cold in the endeavour.

'Holyrood was one of my father's favourite palaces,' James said as they approached it.

'*Our* father's,' Mary corrected him again wearily.

It wasn't until they rode under the portcullis and the sentries had saluted and unbolted a massive iron gate that they actually saw Holyrood, with the round tower James V had built for Marie de Guise, its conical cap looking like the palaces on the Loire.

There, the resemblance ended. The windows were small and mean. The stone walls were grey. There was only a dim glow from within and not a welcoming blaze of torch and candlelight. It was like a prison, and Abbie saw that Mary hesitated to enter.

Inside the icy cold and almost empty palace, Lord James's voice echoed hollowly.

'Welcome to Holyrood,' he said, and he sounded grimly pleased. 'Wait here until I send someone for torchbearers.'

When they arrived they lit up the figures of servants gathered in the entrance hall, men and women in poor, shabby clothes. Mary smiled at them, and they bowed and gazed at her in awe.

Lord James snapped his fingers. 'Mistress Clarihew!' he said, and a plump, middle-aged woman stepped forward. 'I appointed her housekeeper this morning, to direct the servants,' he explained.

'And a gey poor lot they are, Yer Majesty,' Mistress Clarihew pronounced them cheerfully. 'And little wonder, rounded up so hasty!' She cast a scathing glance at Lord James, which in Abbie's present mood endeared the woman to her immediately. 'But dinna worry! I'm on top o' them noo!'

Whatever she had said, Mary knew it to be reassuring and she pointed to Seton. 'Lady Seton will oversee you tomorrow,' she smiled at her, and walked on, followed by her weary, shivering courtiers, under Gothic arches green with mould. Everywhere there was the rank smell of damp decay.

Lord James said, 'Only a caretaker and the Master of the

Hunt have lived here since your mother died. Towards the end, when she was well enough, she came only to hunt. The royal falcons and staghounds are kept here . . . But now Your Majesty will wish to see your apartments? I thought you would prefer the suite your mother occupied in the west wing.'

'I would. Is there room there for my ladies?'

'No, but the King's suite below yours is prepared for them. The courtiers may occupy the east wings,' James said, having appointed himself the director of operations.

He separated the torchbearers into two groups, one to lead the courtiers across the yard, the other to precede Mary and her ladies up the wide staircase.

At the top of the first flight they caught a glimpse of a long, narrow room hung with the banners of Scotland. 'The Great Hall,' he told them. 'Next to that are the King's rooms, prepared for your Marys. Mistress Clarihew will conduct them there. If you will follow me, madam? Your rooms are directly above.'

The four Marys, Lady Jean and Abbie followed Mistress Clarihew. Her thick waist was belted with jangling keys, and her round rosy face under the white cap puffed atop her grey curls was bursting with importance. 'Ye'd better choose yer ain rooms,' she invited them, unlocking the first door.

Beaton stepped inside the tiny room. The others trooped behind her over to the window. They could just make out the great gates of the courtyard, and though they could see nothing beyond, they could hear the bustle of the Canongate. The room promised to have an entertaining view when the fog went away.

'This one will be mine,' Beaton said.

Fleming took the second room, Livingston the third, Seton the fourth, and now only the fifth remained. When Jean and Abbie looked inside they saw it contained only one bed. Mistress Clarihew beamed when Jean addressed her in Scottish accents.

'You've been very kind, Mistress Clarihew,' she said.

'I'd better light a candle tae ye afore I go,' she smiled. 'We dinna want any ghosties, not on yer first night, do we?' and she sped off, taking the last torchbearer with her.

Left alone in the dim flicker of the candle Jean and Abbie looked around fearfully. The window was broken, and through the hole the fog wafted in mournfully. What rushes there were on the floor were filthy and stinking with rot, and the walls were running with damp.

'I didn't think there could be such a room in a palace,' Jean said. 'What are we going to do?'

TWENTY-EIGHT

Along with another young courtier, his close friend Sir Patrick
Spence, Alex Ogilvie was conducted to a shabby room in one
of the east wings, and took a brief look around at the dismal
surroundings. There were no beds, but there were two straw
pallets on the floor.

'Good God,' said Sir Patrick with a shiver. 'Well, Alex, I
would rather not take the one next to the window, if you
don't mind. Already, after France, this cold is getting me
down.'

'I'll take it, Pat, don't worry,' Alex smiled at his portly
friend, and wondered if it was a true saying: fat freezes.
'Anyway, I'll leave you to it for the time being. I have to see
a lady.'

Sir Pat nodded glumly and began to unpack his bag. Out
of it he took a large fur cloak which had been rolled into a
ball, and some books, before he tucked himself in. 'I'm going
to try and heat myself up by reading about Italy's warm
climate,' he said. 'Give Lady Jean my regards. Do you think
there'll be anything to eat shortly?'

'If there's any sign of it I'll come and tell you,' Alex laughed
and departed, hoping to find that Jean had fared a lot better.

The Scottish Guard must have been shown their quarters.
There were a few lights burning now in the barracks. They
helped him to find his way back across the courtyard, and
Alex was just surmising that if the palace was in a terrible
state of decay, the quarters assigned to the Scottish Guard
were bound to be a lot worse, when a man bearing a torch

appeared at his side. He saw that it was Donald MacLaren.

'What are the barracks like, Donald?'

'Don't ask.'

'Well, the main buildings can be little better, believe me. God knows where Lady Jean and Abbie have been placed.' Alex sounded worried.

'Or the Queen, even.'

'We must investigate.'

Donald laughed. 'Follow me! Amongst other things I am the world's best investigator! We'll start on the ground floor and work our way up.'

The sentries paid no attention to them. Alex and Donald walked around quite freely, looking at the cooks working to set up the kitchens, watching the maidservants rushing around with linen and following them up the wide staircase, two flights to the Queen's apartments.

They paused at the open door of her antechamber and, fascinated, watched and listened as Lord James showed Mary her suite. It was clear that she was not impressed.

'Your bedchamber is smaller, but you may find it cosier,' James was saying.

'Cosier?' they heard the Queen's high voice. 'It is as cosy as a tomb, covered with cobwebs and green mould! And as for the bed! It sags! And what are these red berries on the pillow?'

'Rowan berries, madam. Obviously, Mistress Clarihew is superstitious. She must have laid them there in order to ward off ghosts, and the spirits of the dead.'

'Jesu Maria!' Mary said, while outside in the corridor Donald and Alex crossed themselves. 'Who are these dead?'

'They say that Queen Madeleine, our father's first wife, rises from her vault and moans with the cold she perished of on winter nights. In the full moon a monk can be seen walking the herb garden. But neither of them will bother you in here. No, it is our great-grandfather, James Third, whom no door can bar. He was stabbed by a *priest*,' James emphasised the word, 'and as he walks he drips blood.'

223

'You do not frighten me, James,' Mary said, but her voice quivered, 'and see to it that these stories are not spread among my court . . . what is behind this curtain?'

'Private stairs, madam, leading below to the King's apartments,' Lord James replied with a smirk in his voice.

'My ladies will use it until I marry again,' Mary said coldly as she moved along. 'And this room? Or is it a cupboard?'

'I believe it is possible to set up a table in here. Your mother used it as a supper room for her intimates. Of course, I was never invited,' Lord James sniffed. Before Mary could answer he rushed on. 'It is so small because it is in the round turret. The rest of the public and ceremonial rooms are in the front.'

Now he was leading her into the largest room, the audience chamber, and Donald and Alex could see them plainly in the light of the dripping rushlight he fastened to a wall. They could also see the clumsy wooden furniture, a round table and five chairs with worn velvet cushions.

'*Mon Dieu!*' Mary cried. 'Am I to receive visitors in here?'

'It was good enough for your forebears, madam. Scotland is not France, remember.'

'Fortunately, we shall have brought a bit of France with us when my cargo ships get here,' Mary said. 'Which reminds me, so far you have not mentioned the Chapel Royal.'

'It has been purified.'

'What do you mean?'

'It has been stripped of its idols. John Knox does not tolerate idols,' Lord James said sternly.

'But it is where I am to have my private masses? As you promised?'

'I gave you my promise, and I shall keep my promise, regardless.'

'Regardless of what?'

'Regardless of Master Knox.'

'Knox! Knox!' Mary cried. 'I am tired of him already! He does not rule this country – I do! I can see that I shall have to have a meeting with this Master Knox, and put him in his place!'

'By all means meet him, Your Majesty. He looks forward to it.'

People were approaching down the corridor and Donald and Alex moved away.

'Bastard!' Alex Ogilvie smothered a vehement exclamation on the way back down to the landing below. 'Did you hear that, Donald?'

'I did. He's a real dyed-in-the-wool Protestant bugger, that one! And her enemy! But will *she* ever believe it? No! She is convinced that because he's her brother he must be her friend.'

'Well, from what the Queen said about the private stairs, the ladies must be somewhere here on the floor below.'

'We can't stay here,' Abbie was saying when she and Lady Jean heard the tramp of footsteps and saw a light coming along the passage. 'Is this Mistress Clarihew coming back? Quick! Let's make up an excuse.'

'I heard that!' Carrying a torch, Alex Ogilvie took one step inside the room. 'An excuse for what?'

Donald was right behind him. In the light of the torch they saw his face grow paler and paler until it was absolutely white. Abbie had never seen him look like that before. It took a minute or two for her to realise that she had never seen him angry before either.

'Christ Almighty!' he said, and then to their terror he suddenly whipped out his dirk and threw it at the window, so fast that they never saw the flash of his blade. There was a bloodcurdling scream as it found its mark in a huge black rat, and to Jean and Abbie's horror – utter, dumb horror – more ghastly screams as the rat twitched itself to death.

'They're coming in that broken window,' Donald said grimly, 'and that finishes it. You can't possibly sleep tonight or any other night in a rat-infested room. Besides, it's freezing cold.'

'I did see a few swansdown puffs for the beds going into the packing cases,' Abbie ventured.

'A few swansdown puffs!' Donald snorted. 'It's wool, and plenty of it, as well as sheepskins that are needed here! Her Majesty must have forgotten what Scotland is like. Anyway, come with us. Alex and I saw other, better places when we were scouting around for you,' he assured them.

Clinging to each other, Jean and Abbie followed the men downstairs to an alcove beside the kitchen where a fire had been burning and there were ovens for baking, still warm. Donald kicked out of the way two dogs sleeping on the dirty, dusty rushes, and they retreated yawning and whining.

'Now,' he said, 'wrap yourselves up in your cloaks and wait here with Alex. You should be warmer here, and the dogs will chase any stray rat away. I won't be long,' and within ten minutes he was back with two soldiers, each carrying a bale of new straw.

'*Straw*?' Jean gasped when she saw it.

'Straw,' Donald agreed. 'It will be warm and clean. We carried some with us, for a good job. After a childhood spent at Strathbogie's Home Farm I know how to make up a bed of straw, and Abbie will help me. So if you two would kindly remove yourselves we can get on with it.'

Hand in hand Alex and Lady Jean wandered off along the corridor. Very soon they stopped, when he took her in his arms.

'Jeannie,' he said, 'we're back in Scotland – at last! It's a happy, happy day for us, fog or no fog! And we've landed just at the right time, now that you are old enough to marry.'

'No, Alex,' Jean said, drawing back. 'Please, let us not discuss marriage at the moment.'

'Why not? For years we have discussed it. For years we have looked forward to it . . . Jean, you do still love me, don't you?'

'With all my heart, and I always will. But I can't marry you yet. I gave the Queen my word that I wouldn't leave her until she married again. We all did, this morning.'

'But that could take years! She might *never* marry again. And then, what would happen to us?'

'She was talking about sending us back home.' Jean dissolved into tears. 'I just couldn't face that prospect. It was a promise made in desperation, to stay on at court – to stay with you, dearest Alex.'

'It was a promise you should not have made,' he said angrily. 'What were you thinking about, Jean? Do you think I would have allowed you to go back to Strathbogie after the way I've seen your parents treating you? You know I have a castle in the north, and a mansion here in the town! You didn't have to stay in Holyrood!'

'I have made the promise now,' Jean sobbed. 'I can't go back on it.'

'She should not have accepted it,' he said furiously. 'But then I have always observed that she is a very selfish person. She would accept it as her divine right to come first, last and all the time, and let the Devil take the hindmost.'

'*Please*, Alex, don't be angry! Please be patient. She must marry again, and soon.'

'Show me a man in Scotland fit for her to marry and be our King! There isn't one, Jean.'

'There are other royals in other countries, and she is so beautiful that she can take her pick of the suitors who will come knocking at her door. I don't believe she will wait long to choose one of them.'

'I hope not,' he said gloomily.

Meanwhile, Abbie and Donald set to work as though the Devil himself drove them. Every time their hands touched she felt a thrill throughout her whole body. She could hardly bear to look at him across that vast, terrible abyss of four feet. Within five minutes they had the fastest bed in the world made up, and she was in his arms at last, clinging to him and kissing him as she had never returned his kisses before. She was almost in tears. 'I just feel so desperately in love with you! I want to be with you always, Donald.'

'Oh, my darling little Abbie! You don't know how long I've waited to hear you say that!'

Roughly, he pulled her to him. She almost fainted with desire when she felt him hardening against her. His kisses were driving her frantic. The more he kissed her the more she wanted him to love her, and it seemed the most natural thing in the world when they fell down together in the straw.

'Besides,' she murmured in his ear, 'how can I resist you? Your hair is blacker, your eyes are bluer, and your mouth –'

With a groan Donald rolled over on top of her, and now that they were stretched out together for the first time, Abbie marvelled, with every pulse racing, that their bodies fitted together so perfectly. Then his hands were pulling at her bodice and her breasts were rearing up to meet them.

'Oh – *Abbie*!' said Lady Jean's voice from the doorway. 'Oh, Abbie!'

Donald kissed Abbie again, a long lingering kiss. To her it felt like goodbye, a little death, before he pulled her up to stand at his side.

'Yes,' he smiled at Lady Jean and Alex Ogilvie, 'you may congratulate us! We will be married as soon as it can be arranged.'

'But –' Jean said.

'In fact,' Donald interrupted her, 'I'm leaving for Strathbogie tonight to ask for her father's permission.'

'Oh, you'll get it,' Abbie said, her eyes shining.

'There's just one thing I haven't told you, Abbie,' he turned to her. 'Arthur Erskine gave me the news when I went for the straw. The Scottish Guard is to be disbanded. The soldiers drawn from diverse Scottish regiments will go home. They will enlist Edinburgh men to guard the Queen in future.'

'You mean, you are going back to Strathbogie for ever?' she asked.

'Yes – except for when I come back here to collect you.'

'Donald,' Lady Jean's voice was firm, so firm that it cooled the atmosphere considerably, 'there's just one thing that Abbie can't have told you. We have all given the Queen our

228

promise not to marry until she does. I'm sorry, but we took that vow as lately as this morning.'

'*You* did, Jeannie,' Abbie said, 'but I did not. I did not kiss the Queen's hand and give her any such promise. I couldn't. I had already promised Donald to marry him.'

Lady Jean looked absolutely stunned. Alex Ogilvie remained silent.

'She's a romantic!' Abbie laughed. 'When she learns that Donald has to go back to Strathbogie, she will allow me to go with him!'

'Don't worry about it,' Donald put a comforting arm around her. 'The sooner I go, the sooner I'll get back, and then we can ask her together.'

When the men had left, Abbie lay down on the bed of straw beside Lady Jean and almost immediately fell into a hazy, dreamy sleep of pure happiness with Donald at the centre of it. If she could not be with him in the flesh, then this was the next best thing, and she was just sinking into a deeper, dreamless sleep when something woke her up. It was Lady Jean, choking and sobbing.

'What is it?' Abbie sat up, fully alert and alarmed.

'Oh, Abbie,' Jean sobbed. 'I've made a terrible mistake! I should not have promised the Queen. But I was so desperate to stay here, to be near Alex. And there's something else,' Jean wept harder than ever.

'What?'

'Didn't you notice? Alex didn't say one word. We are to be married ourselves, but when?' Jean cried out in the darkness. '*He* never suggests going to Strathbogie to ask for *my* father's consent! He could have gone with Donald tonight!'

'But you told him of the vow you made to the Queen, Jeannie.'

'Yes, I did.'

'Well, then . . . He's just waiting, that's all – and you know Alex! He's never in a hurry, like the sun on the wall. But one day . . .'

'I suppose you're right.' Jean sighed deeply and lay down

again. 'But it was two blows in one day. First Alex's lack of enthusiasm and then the possibility of losing you, though you know I love you dearly, Abbie, and I truly hope that all goes well for you and Donald.'

'If it does, the idea of parting with you will be the only cloud to mar my happiness, Jeannie. Swear to me tonight that if I go, and you ever need me in the future, you will send for me. Swear it, on your honour!'

'I swear it, but I hope I can let you go in peace. The Marys are all our friends. And Alex will always look after me . . . so he says.'

'Well then, let's go to sleep,' Abbie yawned.

TWENTY-NINE

'Such a filthy disgrace!' Fleming stormed, as the Marys inspected the Queen's apartments. 'And so small!'

'My brother tells me that the rooms in the castle are even smaller and darker,' Mary sighed, 'so we must just make the best of it tonight, for we are all tired, too tired even to eat, and tomorrow there is much to be done. The whole palace must be cleansed from turret to cellar before we unpack.'

'God bless you and keep you, madam,' the Marys curtsied, and left.

That night, as the Queen lay in bed it was eerily quiet. Outside the fog billowed and swirled – a witch's brew, Mary thought, and she longed with a physical ache to be back in her beloved France.

There, the walls were sunny and smooth and palely painted – not clothed with these ragged tapestries swaying and moving continually to terrify her. There, the fountains tinkled their lullabies and the night noises were comforting – not like these rasping whisperings, these flutterings and croakings.

The yellow fog outside her window darkened gradually to black. Far up in the sky she thought she saw a star twinkling. It was all in her imagination, she told herself sleepily when suddenly, with a blast that felt like a rock crashing through the roof there was an eldritch, weird, unearthly shrieking, a moaning and a screeching and a wailing, and she thought her heart must stop altogether.

*   *   *

The four Marys came running.

Fleming ran to put her arms around the Queen. Beaton stood beside the bed, trembling, and Seton fell on her knees to pray.

Livingston ran to the windows, peered out, and laughed. 'No, it is not the banshees or the werewolves, madam! It's people with bagpipes and fiddles and drums! They have come to play you their tunes, to welcome you.'

The noise rose louder and louder. Mary went to one of the windows and looked out. There must have been five hundred people there or more. When they saw her they waved their torches and shouted, 'Welcome, dear Queen! Welcome, sweet Queen! Welcome! Welcome! Welcome!'

At last the Marys managed to open a window and the Queen leaned out. 'Thank you,' she called to the serenaders. 'Play on! Oh, please play on!'

Tears streamed down her face. She was touched to the heart as she turned to her Marys. 'Listen to them! Their music has come from Hell itself, but they are greeting me the only way they know how. Send the servants out with wine! But I should be raining gold on them instead!'

She stood at the window for fully forty minutes, for as long as they blew and scraped and banged, until her eardrums were throbbing. When they stopped she called to them again. 'You have made me so happy! Please, come back again!' She was still standing there with her arms outstretched when the very last person disappeared into the gloom.

From his house in the High Street, further up the Royal Mile, John Knox had heard the commotion.

'So the festering sore has opened again, O Lord!' He thumped his Bible and roared to Heaven. 'And I prayed to You, I begged You to help me to stamp out evil paganism and whoreish revelry!'

He was almost in tears.

Next morning Mary awoke refreshed expecting to see dancing sunshine to match her feeling of exhilaration, but there was still nothing to be seen but a grey blur at the windows.

Servants brought her breakfast in bed. She was very hungry, and very disappointed to find a plate of porridge on her tray. This time she sprinkled a little sugar on it, but that only made it taste worse and she pushed the plate away.

They came next with a fish she had never seen before. It was dark yellow and when she speared a morsel of it on her fork she thought it had all the salt of the sea captured in its flesh. It was impossible to eat it.

Then she was presented with a bun and a large dollop of butter. 'Spread it on thickly,' Mistress Clarihew advised, and left her. Mary did as she was told, took one bite and realised that only one half of all the salt of the sea had been in the fish, after all. The other half was in the butter.

Flamina helped her to wash and dress as quickly as she could and as soon as Mary left her bedchamber Seton sent in an army of servants. Her ladies were waiting in the audience room.

'It is not weather to go out,' she said, 'and we are only in the way, here. But I wish to explore the Palace in any case.'

It was still desperately cold when the five ladies climbed to the topmost turrets, to find them dripping with damp, their ceilings black and strangely quivering. For a while they gazed upwards, trying to understand this.

Then, 'Bats! Bats!' Beaton shrieked, and they all ran out screaming, and hastily wound their way back down again through the draughty corridors. They peered into mildewed rooms disused for centuries, so melancholy that they all shuddered again, and eventually came to the King's apartments where the walls were peeling and the tapestries shredded by rats and moths, and the Marys showed the Queen where they had spent the night.

'*Mon Dieu!*' She was horrified. 'And what happened to Lady Jean and Abbie?'

But nobody knew, and Mary shrugged. 'We must start our transformation of this place with the kitchens.'

'Lord James has been here already, madam,' Beaton said

233

when they reached the lower floor. 'He came to order a banquet for tonight in your honour, and he brought the food and drink. The cook has already embarked upon the preparations.'

'That should be interesting,' Mary smiled, 'because it will be the Scottish cook's last offering. He must go. Thankfully, our own chefs are with us. Henri and Gaston will be in full charge of the cooking tomorrow.'

While this discussion was going on within hearing distance, Jean and Abbie saw their chance to escape from the warm hiding-place Donald and Alex had found them.

'They don't need to know about this place, or else they'll all try to come here,' Abbie said. 'We'll hide here every night. Anywhere is better than that rat-filled room.'

They joined the others unobtrusively, and the party of ladies, now swelled to seven, continued along the corridor and down steps at the far end.

'What is down there?' Mary asked when along the narrow black passage they came to another flight of steps.

'Oh, please, madam – don't go down there,' Beaton pleaded, her candle trembling in her hand. 'Those are the dungeons, down there.'

'Nonsense! I want to see all the nooks and crannies of my new home!'

Unwillingly, Beaton led the way. There were instruments of torture, an iron boot with clamps, a body press and thumbscrews, all rusty with age propped up against the green walls, and on the floor the whitened bones of men held them transfixed in horror. The ladies ran back the way they had come and up a passage that led to the wine cellar where bottles lay flat on high shelves. They squeezed past barrels of ale and climbed more steps leading into the kitchen which was surprisingly large and well-appointed, with a stone-flagged floor.

Huge fireplaces were at opposite ends of the room. One was fitted with hooks and cranes where soup simmered in large-bellied pots. Underneath, three lambs had been speared end to end onto a spit and from them fat dripped into flat pans on the hearth. A woman servant, dressed in dun-brown clothes covered by a large white apron, sat at a table nearby preparing rushlights, peeling off the green fibre from the rushes and then dropping them to soak into a pan of sheep-grease. Another woman removed them to dry off on the hearth, and the ladies watched as she fastened the dried rushes onto wooden holders for little nightlights.

At the roasting fire a little dog was running round and round with his front paws up on the wheel, turning an ox on a long spit. 'See,' Mary laughed, 'he enjoys his work,' and bent to pat the little creature's head. He cringed away with his tail between his legs.

Abbie, the last in line, could not believe her eyes or her ears. She looked at the desperation in the dog's eyes, at his pitiful, scrawny body, unable to understand how the Queen could be so callous or at best, mistaken. She thought of Mary's own fat little white dogs, all of them spoiled, all in their blue velvet coats. But except for a glance from Lady Jean, nobody else seemed to have noticed, and not for the first time a doubt flickered through Abbie's mind.

Queen Mary was kind and gentle – wasn't she? She should not doubt it. It was disloyal to doubt it . . . And of course the Queen would release her, when Donald came back to fetch her.

Unbeknown to Abbie, Lady Jean was having similar thoughts as they stood there in the kitchens of Holyrood Palace. She couldn't help agreeing with Alex Ogilvie when he commented on the Queen's selfishness. Jean began to fret. How long would it take for the Queen to choose another husband? But Alex would wait for her – of course he would wait for her, wouldn't he?

At the long oak table in the middle of the kitchen scullery maids were rolling dough under the direction of the cook, a rough-faced man with a beard. He bowed and the women curtsied, while under the table a cat toyed with a mouse. Abbie could not help shuddering at the huge flitches of bacon hanging from the black-beamed ceiling, wondering if the mouse had been there already, or if the creature had eaten its fill of the dried herrings hanging there also.

'The vermin must go,' Mary told the servants. 'We shall hire every rat-catcher in the city with packs of ferrets.'

'As long as that ruined abbey stands, there will be rats,' the cook said sullenly. 'That's where rats breed.'

Abbie did not like his tone. She knew instinctively that he was a Protestant and a militant one at that, to dare to use the equation of rats in the abbey with the Catholics who had worshipped there, in the presence of the Queen. It was clear that Mary was quite sensitive to *that* though.

'Who ruined it?' she asked icily. 'Master Knox?'

His eyes fell beneath her clear golden stare. 'No, madam, the English did, in your mother's time.'

'I shall have it swept and cleaned, and the floor laid with my gold carpet. We will hear Mass on Sunday.'

'Mass?' The cook lowered his voice to a whisper. 'It's forbidden, madam. The people would murder a priest if they caught him holding Mass.'

'Not my priest,' Mary said grimly.

'You'd best keep him guarded, then, madam. Master Knox is terrible hard on priests – and witches,' he added, glancing at her slanting eyes, and trying to avoid them.

'Witches? Does Master Knox say I am a witch?' Mary asked.

'Last Sunday he said you would come here and cast spells. He said you were an enchantress.'

'He's a silly old man,' Mary laughed, turning to go back up to the main building again. They heard the sound of heavy wagons arriving. 'Good,' she said. 'Here are some of my crates, at last.'

That evening Mary declared herself delighted that items of her furniture had been unpacked. Abbie helped Seton to find satin sheets to spread on her bed, and Lady Jean and Livingston had managed to find a box containing a few of her gowns. She selected one of black and grey, and was ready to

236

go downstairs in it when Mistress Clarihew saw her.

'Oh, that's beautiful,' she said, admiring the tight-bodiced, square-necked velvet gown with its sweeping train. 'But ye shouldn't be wearing black, madam, not a young lassie like you. It makes ye look as thin as a rake.'

'I am a widow,' Mary reminded her sharply.

'Oh, not for long!' laughed the irrepressible Mistress Clarihew. 'And in the meantime, dinna let that old goat, John Knox, catch ye in that dress with tails. He calls them "Satan's tails", ye ken.'

'John Knox! John Knox! That's all I ever hear!' Mary fumed all the way down to the Great Hall, where Fleming and Abbie left her.

THIRTY

The lords stood up when she entered. Lord James came forward to show her to the top of the table and to seat her on a gold throne under a moth-eaten canopy that bore the emblems of Scotland and Lorraine.

Then Lord James sat down on her right, and next to him the Duc de Châtelherault, an old man now. Mary remembered him as Arran, the Regent. She remembered how, long ago in France, she and her Uncle Cardinal had appointed her mother to be the Regent instead of him. Did he resent her for that? It ran through her head like a red thread of warning that he might have spent the last eighteen years not just resenting her, but hating her, for if she had never been born, he would have been next in line to the throne.

On her left sat Sir William Maitland, and beyond him the old Duc's son, now the Earl of Arran, a boor of a man. He had had the impertinence and the insensitivity to travel all the way to France to propose marriage to her only a few days after Francis's death. She had refused him audience then, and she wished she could do the same now. It felt like an insult to be forced into the same room as him. She glanced at him coldly, and he leered back as though they shared some secret.

She was the only woman there in this company of Scottish lords and suddenly, she became sharply aware that except for the French courtiers, she was also the only Catholic. Her eye caught Chastelard's, seated further down the table, and he smiled at her sympathetically as the first banquet in her honour in Scotland began.

'I see you have adopted our French fashion of wearing hats at meals,' she said to James.

'Not at all. It is a fashion of our own, madam, to stop head-lice falling into our food.'

A bowl of soup was set down in front of her, and she looked at it suspiciously. A myriad little indefinable things were floating about in it, and she left it untouched. Sir William poured her a glass of wine.

'Elderberry, Your Majesty,' he smiled. 'I think you will like it, and you must not worry about the cleanliness of your immediate neighbours,' he chuckled. 'Lord James and I, at least, are quite fastidious.'

She drank a sip of the wine while the maids came in with wooden platters heaped with great chunks of roast pork and mutton, oozing grease. More servants laid down bowls of rabbit stew and boiled pigeons on the scarred oak table, devoid of cloths or flowers.

To her horror the Scottish lords, ignoring the cutlery, took out their dirks and speared the meat, grabbing it, tearing at it, and gobbling it down. The French courtiers looked helplessly at the running grease and waved their hands about.

'We must have napkins,' Mary demanded.

After some debate the servants brought strips of Holland cloth, and at the same time claret, and pint leather mugs of ale were set down at each place. The noise of conversation and laughter grew louder, and Sir William leaned towards her.

'They grow rowdy, madam – too rowdy?'

'No. Let them be. My policy is tolerance. They will soon find that out, and understand that they must be tolerant, too.'

Sir William bowed his head. 'Exquisite worldliness, madam, for one so young.'

'You have eaten nothing so far,' Lord James accused her from her other side. 'But perhaps you will now – if you are a true Scot,' as the thin screeching wails of the bagpipes burst into the Great Hall itself.

The Scots cheered to a man and then there was a hush. In the hush Sir William poured some golden liquid into a small goblet and set it in front of her. '*Aqua vitae*, madam,' he whispered.

The water of life? What did he mean?

Marching around the room, the piper began his caterwauling again, and in came the cook proudly bearing aloft a huge silver platter. Everyone rose. So did Mary. Everyone gazed at the steaming object on the silver salver with admiration. No, it wasn't only with admiration, Mary saw. It was with positive reverence.

'What is it?' she whispered to James.

'The haggis. Only true Scots appreciate it. It is the heart, lungs and liver of a sheep packed into its intestine with suet, oatmeal and spices.' He put a steaming spoonful of it onto Mary's plate.

She became uncomfortably aware that all the men's eyes were on her, waiting for her to taste it. She was forced to lift a little of it on her fork to her mouth. There was no getting out of it. But to her surprise it had a pleasant taste, although it was greasy.

'It will taste even more wonderful when you wash it down with a sip of the *aqua vitae*,' Sir William whispered. 'That's how haggis was meant to be consumed – along with whisky.'

She took a small sip and shuddered as she felt a run of fire from her throat to her stomach. Perhaps a little more haggis would soothe her throat. When she drank another sip it didn't feel so raw this time. Soon she had finished all the haggis on her plate and sipped all the whisky.

The men bobbed up and down proposing toasts, and Sir William filled up her goblet again. They drank to Scotland, to the Queen of Scotland, and to all the strong sons and beautiful daughters she would have, and one by one hurled their glasses onto the stone hearth where they shattered.

'They mean their glasses will never be used for a lesser

toast,' Sir William explained as the singing began in between more toasts in ale and whisky. The songs grew bawdy, but no bawdier than she had heard at the court of France.

Nevertheless, the French poet Chastelard hastily sent for his lute and the noise died down a little, while he sang a charming tribute to Mary's beauty. All the way through it Arran grinned and peered and leered at her again, wiping his greasy beard on his sleeve.

'The Earl of Arran is not only drunk, he is stupid,' Mary observed to Sir William, hoping that he might control his offending neighbour.

'Is it stupid to admire a beautiful woman?'

'Certainly, I am a woman. But I am a queen first. Yet not once have they asked me to speak.'

'Why waste your breath on drunkards, madam? Your face and form are all that concern them tonight.'

'You are clever, Sir William. You remind me of the English Ambassador, Throckmorton. He was my friend.'

'So naturally, Elizabeth assumes he is in love with you. She is a jealous cat, which explains why she is not sending Throckmorton to Scotland. She is sending Randolph, instead.'

'But why is she so jealous?'

'Because you are younger than she is, more beautiful than she is, and she is frightened not only of that, but because you would not sign the Treaty of Edinburgh. Besides that, you are a Catholic. She would like Scotland and England to unite in every way – as I would, Your Majesty.'

'I long for peace, Sir William, but she sets a high price.'

Mary finished her whisky which was now travelling through her veins back up to her head. She waved her hands to the men when she rose to depart. 'Enjoy yourselves, my lords,' she said smiling, for in spite of herself she had enjoyed the evening, too. In fact, she felt very, very happy.

Lord James escorted her to her rooms. 'You are remembering your ceremonial entry into Edinburgh planned for Saturday?' he asked her. 'You should wear a crown when we make the journey up the hill to the castle, for crowds will line the Royal Mile hoping to see their Queen.'

'Yes. And then?'

'The leading men of the realm will be waiting at the castle to swear allegiance. Afterwards there will be a state banquet. You should be back down to Holyrood by nightfall.'

He left her to her Marys. After they had attended to her she dismissed them all, except Abbie. 'Wait, Abbie,' she said, 'until I write a short message for you to deliver.'

But before she got to her desk there was a knock on the door, and when Abbie opened it Sir William Maitland was standing there, smiling. He looked past her to the Queen.

'I have just received this from England,' he said, holding out a scroll, heavily sealed.

Mary ripped it open.

'It is from Elizabeth, the passport I asked for before I left France. It must have been delayed, somehow.'

'Do you think so?' Maitland smiled. 'May I see it, Majesty? Ah, yes – it is dated the day of your departure, so that you could not possibly have received it in time.'

'Oh, I am sure she meant it kindly!' Mary cried. 'She wants to be my friend after all. I have had such a happy day! This has crowned it all.'

'I am glad, madam.'

'And when the ceremonial entry is over, I want you to go to London and tell her that I wish for no more misunderstandings between us, and please, let us become loving sisters! You will know how to say it,' Mary said confidently. 'You know her so well.'

'I thank you for choosing me to deliver such a happy message, Your Majesty,' Maitland said, bowing himself out.

'I just have this feeling tonight, Abbie,' Mary said as she took up her quill. 'It is of goodwill to all men, especially my own people. I must let them know that I mean them no harm.' She scribbled something swiftly on a parchment. 'Take this to one of the guards. It is a proclamation. He will know where to post it. Then you may retire.'

242

'Good night, madam,' Abbie curtsied, and ran straight down to Lady Jean in their kitchen hide-out. By the light of their rushlights they read the proclamation.

> My good subjects, it is the command of the Queen that there shall be no alteration or innovation in the religion of the country as she found it upon her arrival in this land, nor any attempt against the form of public worship in use, upon pain of death.
>
> At the same time, Her Majesty commands that the French people in her service who wish to practise their own faith in private may do so without molestation.
> Signed, Marie R.

'Should I take it to the guard?' Abbie asked doubtfully. 'I smelled strong drink on her, and you know the old saying – when the drink's in, the wit's out.'

'You must,' Jean said. 'It is by royal command.'

'But it will antagonise both Catholics and Protestants alike!' Abbie protested. 'And the sad thing is, she means well.'

'Oh God . . .' Jean sighed. 'Can you imagine what my father will say when he hears of this?'

What, indeed, would the Earl of Huntly say about it, the great magnate of the north of Scotland, staunch upholder of the Catholic faith? For that matter, what might Lady Huntly *do* about it in her own mysterious ways? Abbie's very blood ran cold just thinking of it.

Why had not the Queen slept upon it first, before she ever put quill to parchment? Instead of antagonising such a powerful noble as Huntly, as ardently Catholic as she was herself, Queen Mary should be enlisting his support. Then she would have the whole northern bloc of her realm behind her in time of trouble . . . And Abbie felt it in her bones that trouble was coming over this religious divide, without doubt.

'How could she think so dangerously – far less *publish* such thoughts?' Jean demanded. 'Dangerous for the country, and dangerous for herself? Now that the Protestants have such a firm foothold, they will never budge, and the Catholics

243

will resent her flourishing their Faith like this at the very outset. It's as if she is waving a red rag at a bull!'

'It was the whisky talking,' Abbie sighed.

THIRTY-ONE

With every mile that Donald rode north to Strathbogie he cursed himself for a fool. He should have taken Abbie with him. At the very least he should have warned her – and Lady Jean and Alex Ogilvie – not to spread the glad tidings of their impending marriage in the court.

By now he was very uneasy. There was no doubt of Abbie's resemblance to the Queen, once it was pointed out. Donald thought it would have to be pointed out, since Abbie was so much shorter and plumper, and her face was round, whereas Mary's was long and thin.

Still, she could be dressed up to look like the Queen, and after all these years so close to the Queen she could no doubt act like her too. Besides having the intelligence to follow the ins and outs of the European political lessons which the Cardinal had insisted she should attend along with Mary, she would be able to converse about them with anyone, if he knew Abbie. But it was the high-pitched, even shrill voice that Abbie seemed able to adopt at will that finally convinced him. Such careful training had not been for nothing. She was to be used to impersonate the Queen.

But why and when? Donald forced himself to address the issue, worrying more and more the further north he rode . . . The answers were obvious: when some occasion arose where circumstances were dangerous enough to threaten Mary's life.

The next question he asked himself was why the impersonations had not begun in France, and once again the answer was obvious. Mary's person had not been in danger there.

But, as he and his colleagues of the Scottish Guard had debated endlessly, tedious, involved and underhand as European politics had been during their stay in France, they were a mere minuet compared with the complexities of what went on in Scotland – many of which were resolved only by the hatchet.

Even so, they had just got out of France in the nick of time, in Donald's opinion. The religious reformation which was sweeping Europe was bound to lead to more bloodshed. He had heard of a Protestant minister, John Knox, who was continuing it in Scotland, inciting the people to overthrow Catholicism.

Then Queen Mary was certainly in danger *here*, where retribution was swift and bloody, and Abbie, masquerading as the Queen, would be even more at risk than he had at first realised.

And, worst of all, none of them, not even the Queen herself, was well enough acquainted with the ever-changing, fast-moving feuds and coalitions of the Scottish players in the power struggles. They had been too far away, too long, in France.

No, he never should have left Abbie behind. She would have to be got out of Holyrood before anything happened to her. It was imperative to get to Strathbogie with all speed, enlist the aid of John McCracken and get back to Holyrood as fast as possible. That was his best bet now. He rode hell for leather all night and well into the morning, and was just slithering down from the saddle in the courtyard of Strathbogie Castle when he found the Earl of Huntly at his side.

'So you're back, my boy,' he observed kindly.

'I am, my lord, and looking for John McCracken.'

'You won't find him here, then. McCracken has not long departed on a mission of mine to rescue the young Earl of

246

Sutherland, imprisoned by the Caithness tribe in his own castle of Dunrobin.'

'Dunrobin Castle? But isn't that miles and miles north of Inverness?'

Beaming, and clearly delighted to see him, Lord Huntly ignored Donald's startled questions. 'You've been away too long,' he said, 'and now that you've come back, here you will stay. I shall send another Gordon down to Holyrood to take your place.'

'That won't be necessary, my lord. The Scottish Guard are to be replaced in any case.'

Lord Huntly laughed. 'Oh, yes! I've heard all *that* before! It'll be a good two years before that is accomplished, believe me. But in the meantime I do need a Gordon at Holyrood. The next best man is Geordie Brand. You remember Geordie Brand?'

Geordie Brand, John McCracken's best friend, and about the same age. Geordie, who had never got married, who lived only for the Gordons, who never uttered two syllables if one could do – and then only if it was the truth. Otherwise he never spoke at all. A hard man, but one you could trust.

'Oh yes,' Donald said. 'I remember Geordie Brand, all right.'

'With McCracken away, he's in charge here. I'll go and see him now.'

'But before you do, my lord, I must ask your permission to ride one more time to Holyrood. It is with sheepskins and warm clothing for Lady Jean and Abbie McCracken. They have landed from France with the flimsiest clothing into a palace that is filthy, rat-infested, running with damp and freezing with cold.'

Lord Huntly's eyes narrowed, and his high colour deepened to an unhealthy puce. 'Do you mean to tell me that Lord James Stewart did not have the place readied for them?'

'He did not.'

'That is one Protestant shit . . . Well named the Bastard.' The Earl paced about, fuming, and Donald smiled faintly and a little bitterly to himself, for here was one of the great lords of Scotland speaking to one of his own bastard sons.

'Yes, my lord, he's a bastard, right enough.'

'By all means collect warm clothing for Lady Jean. My daughter, a great Gordon lady, must be looked after,' Lord Huntly boomed grandly. 'But I want Geordie Brand to go to Holyrood immediately. Come with me, and I'll tell him now.'

Geordie's eyes gleamed with pleasure, but he didn't bat either of his eyelids, nor did he allow his mouth to stretch into a smile when he received his orders. 'Yes, my lord,' he said, and as he and Donald watched Lord Huntly swaggering back into Strathbogie and out of earshot, 'Well, that's the Cock o' the North for you.'

'Oh, come on, Geordie! You know you like him, really,' Donald coaxed a smile. 'Anyway, I've got to speak to John McCracken – not that the Earl troubled to find out why! But Abbie and I want to get married, so I've got to find him. First I'll go and see Abigail, and ask her to gather some things together while I'm away looking for him. Where do you think he'll be by this time?'

'Christ knows. Somewhere between here and Dunrobin, and rather him than me mixing with that Caithness lot.'

'A fat lot of use *you* are, Geordie Brand!'

'And rather him than me, if the weather breaks,' Geordie Brand was further moved to say, with a shudder.

'Well, cover for me as long as you're here, in case the Earl asks any questions.'

'Oh, ay,' Geordie said.

Totally reassured by that promise, Donald went first to talk to Abigail in the Gardeners' Cottage, a tearful and emotional experience for which he was prepared. What he was not prepared for, was to find Abbie's two younger brothers, almost grown men, striding down the path to meet him.

'It's Donald MacLaren,' Jonathon said to Jackson, who was only slightly shorter, but much broader. 'Is Abbie with you?'

'Not this time, boys. Where are you off to?' Donald eyed the bundles on their backs.

'We're leaving, Donald,' Jonathon told him. 'It's farming, not fighting, for us. Mother's cousin has taken us on in his farm. We're fee'd to him for a year.'

'I wish we could have seen Abbie before we left,' Jackson said, and hesitated strangely. 'Donald, when you go into the cottage, don't seem surprised. Johnny is not well, and Mother is at her wits' end.'

So Donald was half-prepared, but very shocked, when he found Abbie's youngest brother a pale-faced cripple hobbling about on two sticks.

'Of course, he will get better,' Abigail wept as they regarded him. 'In time, he will be just like the other two, just like their father, you'll see. And as for getting the warm clothes for you, you can depend on it. I would do anything for any one of my beloved children – for my sons, for my dearest Abbie . . .'

Donald was glad to get away from the claustrophobic atmosphere of the Gardeners' Cottage. He walked through Abigail's gardens now that summer was drawing to a close, and thought how beautiful they were in their very artlessness, compared to the rigidly formal clipped hedges and geometrically designed flowerbeds around the palaces of France.

Under the changing trees the lupins still stretched tall in clumps of haphazard colour, late roses bloomed and scented the air, and the vivid blue of the tiny forget-me-nots had not faded yet. All of it only reminded him of Abbie in France in Queen Catherine's gardens, and spurred him on.

Riding out from Strathbogie he soon found himself in unfamiliar territory, where the only thing to do was to follow the drovers' roads. Often they were only discernible by the trampled grass a herd of sheep or Highland cattle had passed over recently. The drovers could not drive their animals over difficult terrain, he knew that, and certainly not over any of the towering hills he found himself surrounded by after leaving Inverness.

249

He tried to mark his direction by fixing his sights on one of the hills to his left, and the occasional glimpses of the sea through the hills to his right, and rode like the wind to the shelter and safety of the next foothill, and the next, and the next.

He still had no idea where he was, or if he was anywhere near Golspie, as the people in Inverness had directed him, and by now it was late afternoon. He slowed to a walking pace, thinking it was time for a rest, anyway, when suddenly from out of nowhere rough hands seized him, pulled him off his horse and threw him to the ground.

On Friday Holyrood Palace was in an uproar. Bothwell, patrolling down the east coast, had seized the last of the Queen's cargo ships out of English hands and sent her word to expect them. More and more of the Queen's belongings were arriving, cartloads of boxes, wagonloads of furniture, and at last in ones and twos, her animals. Mary dashed out to see what state her beloved white palfrey was in, and once she saw him settled in his stable she dashed back inside again to find his trappings of blue silk and his jewelled bridle and saddle for the ceremony tomorrow.

The Marys were in the throes of unpacking, driving the servants who were trying to clean the palace to distraction, and Mary herself was in everyone's way, unwrapping her miniatures with Lady Jean's help and setting them out on a shelf. Abbie found the Queen's ivory cross inside protective covers and hung it in a small shrine-like box on the wall near the royal bed beside the window.

'Madam,' she said, 'I think the fog is thinning.'

'Let us go out, then, and see the abbey. I hope to hear Mass there on Sunday.'

They were not expecting the abbey to be in such a state. Its ruins, joined on to the palace, rose up before them like a spectre through the trailing wreaths of mist. The roof had gone, and the windows, and they could walk through a hole in the wall on to the abbey floor, now weed-grown. But one wall was still standing intact, and in it was a door. When they pushed it open they saw the steps leading down to what had once been the crypt, steps where rats slithered and swarmed. Mary shut the door quickly again with tears in her eyes.

'There will be no Mass here on Sunday,' she said, 'nor any other Sunday, thanks to Henry the Eighth of England. How could anyone do such a thing to the house of God? But the Scottish cook spoke the truth about one thing. The rats are breeding here, and no doubt there will be passageways into the palace dungeons for them to run riot.'

'There is the Chapel Royal inside the palace itself,' Abbie tried to comfort her by reminding her. 'We could look out your gold carpet for the servants to lay down on Sunday morning.'

'Yes,' Mary said, drying her eyes, and listening to the sound of hammering above the rest of the usual commotion in the Canongate. But they could see very little beyond the palace gates, except the outline of what looked like a stage being erected.

'The people are getting the city ready for the ceremony tomorrow,' Abbie said, and Lady Jean added, 'They must be going to enact tableaux for you, Your Majesty.'

'Yes,' Mary sighed again. 'I suppose it is very exciting . . . if only we could see.'

But right on cue, on Saturday morning, the last of the fog fled away in shreds and the sky was brilliantly blue when Mary set out with a magnificent company to make the mile-long journey to Edinburgh Castle, still dressed in mourning. Her gown was black under her grey mantle. On her breast her huge ruby brooch glowed red, and on her head she wore a crown of gold and pearls.

The Marys rode behind her accompanied by their distinguished fathers and brothers, and behind them Lady Jean and Abbie headed the rest of the Queen's household, her French guards and servants in black livery, and the Scots wearing red and yellow. The slow procession climbed the gentle slope of the Royal Mile, cheered on by the crowds. The castle loomed larger and larger until it seemed to Abbie that its melancholy filled the whole sky, that it wanted to topple over and brutally crush them all.

She followed Jean and the Marys into the Great Hall of Edinburgh Castle to stand in their customary semi-circle behind the Queen, and watched as the leading men of Scotland came forward, one by one, each to state his name and title and to swear allegiance. Abbie recognised only a few of them. James Douglas, the awful Earl of Morton was the first man to kneel, which he did with difficulty. His great sword got in the way.

'He inherited it from his ancestor, Archibald "Bell-the-Cat" Douglas,' Jean passed on the whispered information from Flamina.

'And do you see who is behind him?' Abbie whispered back. 'It is your father.'

The Earl of Huntly had eyes for no one except the Queen, and they were filled with scorn and anger. 'Why did you issue that proclamation?' he spat furiously when he came forward. 'Now you have given John Knox a foot in the door!'

Mary's mouth dropped open in astonishment. She had thought that the Earl of Huntly, her own Lady Jean's father, was her friend and ally. He had interpreted the proclamation wrongly, and she was just about to open her mouth to explain it to him when the next man hastily elbowed Huntly out of the way. 'James Hepburn, the Earl of Bothwell, Your Majesty,' he said.

'Bothwell . . .' Her golden eyes smiled into his green ones.

Then came the rest of the Douglases, the Red Douglases and the Black Douglases, then Erskine, Argyll, Atholl . . . The list went on and on, and Abbie lost count. Afterwards, the ceremonial meal went on and on too, but at last they were outside again, mounted on their horses, and waiting for Mary to be mounted last of all.

The procession back down to Holyrood began when they

wound their way around the spiralling courtyard towards the castle gates. It was like a snail's shell, Abbie thought, and the theme had been repeated inside the castle, winding round and round to get to anywhere, through the tiny rooms. But up here on the rock, on this glorious day, they could see the countryside in all directions, and as far north as the sparkling waters of the Forth.

Then they rode out slowly into the town proper where it seemed that all thirty thousand of its inhabitants were waiting to cheer their Queen, and all along the way there were children up on platforms, singing their welcoming songs, and more children in the street, scattering flowers.

They passed by St Giles' Cathedral and then continued down into the High Street where the houses, sometimes in as many as eight storeys, rose up steeply like walls on both sides of the Royal Mile, until they came to a very handsome house of two storeys protruding into the street on its left-hand side.

In fact, it was just like an elbow, sticking out and attracting attention to itself. It offended Abbie's sense of proportion. It was just a nuisance. Whoever lived there loved to be in the centre of the stage, she thought sourly, when Bothwell rode up behind the Queen.

'That's John Knox's house, Your Majesty,' he said, and Mary, who had been looking at the house curiously, sniffed and turned her head away deliberately.

But Abbie tried to peer inside the windows, although it was difficult because of the reflection of the sun on the glass. She saw a face, and underneath it a long grey beard. So that was John Knox! She must remember to tell Donald that he looked like the old billy-goat she had known at Strathbogie, the bad-tempered one.

On Sunday morning the Queen got her ladies to look out the candles and candlesticks for the Mass and give them to a servant to carry. Queen Mary went on ahead, the court followed, and just as the servant was mounting the stairs behind them a mob burst open the palace gates. They

253

swarmed up the staircase and made a grab at the terrified man who ran into the chapel and locked and bolted the door behind him.

'They must all die!' yelled the mob right outside the door, and Mary rose from her knees in alarm when she heard them and saw the door straining to hold them back.

Then Lord James Stewart's voice rang out from the corridor right outside, the voice of authority. 'Are you not good Scotsmen?' he shouted at the mob.

'Yes!' came the answer.

'Then keep away from the evil and wickedness inside this door! It is the Mass, the Devil's trap! Do you want to go back to that?'

'*NO!*'

His words worked like a charm. The mob retreated and dispersed. His words worked wonders to open Abbie's eyes, finally. It was as she had suspected. No fair, conciliatory words of Mary's were going to sway these Protestant bigots – which included Mary's bastard half-brother, Lord James – as she had tried to win them over in her proclamation.

THIRTY-TWO

It was a whole week since that Sunday, and the weather in Edinburgh had continued fair. But even so, Mary could tell that her French courtiers, especially her de Guise cousins, were bored to tears. She had brought four of these young de Guises over with her, hoping to keep her French connection alive, although nobody here seemed to like them. She couldn't understand why . . . They were so tall, so handsome and so beautifully dressed! The same as she was herself, in fact.

They had plodded obediently and wearily with her around the dusty, overgrown weed-gardens of the palace every day, and visited the royal lions who were just as sullen as they were, not yet accustomed to their new cages. They had half-heartedly tried to hunt in the forest behind Holyrood, but still they yawned and lay about, complaining.

'There are no games to play here,' they told Mary, 'except croquet, and we can't play croquet for ever.'

'Perhaps we could play Pall Mall,' she suggested, 'once the cleaning is over and the servants have time to set it up for us.'

'Ah, yes – *the cleaning*!' they sighed, and Mary remembered that none of them had ever been in a castle that was not already cleansed and ready, waiting for them.

'And I have heard that there is a game called golf in Scotland,' she went on brightly. 'Perhaps we could have a course laid out here.'

'Not here, madam,' Lord James intervened. 'Golf requires a particular turf, short and springy, such as is found beside the sea. The Links at Leith are the nearest to here.'

'Well then, we shall go to Leith! This very afternoon!'

'Not on a Sunday,' Lord James said grimly. 'No games are allowed on a Sunday.'

'Who says so?'

'John Knox and the Lords of the Congregation. Even if you went to Leith you would be resisted. By force, if necessary.'

'I cannot tolerate this!' Mary burst out. 'John Knox! John Knox! I hear that name at every turn! You would think *he* ruled this country!'

'He does, madam,' Lord James smiled triumphantly.

'What rubbish!' Mary shuddered. 'I wish to hear the last of him!'

'You will never hear the last of him, Your Majesty. You would make your life here much easier if you would listen to more of him instead.'

'Nonsense!' She flounced off and went to sit beside Fleming on one of the marble benches of the palace gardens, noticing that her favourite Mary was looking despondent, but failing to connect that with the fact that Sir William Maitland had already gone to London to see Queen Elizabeth on her behalf. 'Sometimes, Flamina, I wish the French courtiers would go back home,' she murmured, 'especially my cousins de Guise. They cannot adapt. There is nothing for them here in Scotland. I don't know how to entertain them any more.'

Flamina smiled at her. 'You could pass some time for them by taking them on a progress, Majesty. Sir William says that Queen Elizabeth goes on a progress every year about this time, before the winter sets in, when she tries to visit different parts of her far-flung realm.'

'Oh, Flamina!' Mary clapped her hands. 'You have solved the problem! We shall arrange a progress! Now, let us decide where we shall go.'

Thoroughly glad and relieved to see them go, the servants headed by the indomitable Mistress Clarihew lined up, smiling falsely, to wave goodbye to Queen Mary and her sixty-strong cavalcade as they trooped away, escorted by the Scottish Guard.

The Scottish Guard, all except Donald, Abbie thought.

Mary rode with Lord James on one side and on the other was James Melville, who had been in France with her, and was a particular friend, besides being the man Sir William had chosen to enter the diplomatic service as his apprentice.

'Thank God they've gone,' said Mistress Clarihew. 'Noo, we can get on, which we were never able to do as long as those Geese were under oor feet. Dirty Frenchmen! Never lifted a finger in their lives! Just dropped their dirty clothes on the floor behind them for someone else to pick up! Naebody could get ony work done wi' them around.'

'Ay, that's right, the Geese were the worst,' the other servants agreed, and one piped up, 'How long are they away for, onyway?'

'Twa weeks,' Mistress Clarihew told them, 'for a round trip o' castles and palaces, Lady Seton said. All the places the Queen knew as a bairn – Linlithgow, Stirling, Perth, Dundee, St Andrews and Falkland Palace.'

'A grand holiday,' another servant sighed enviously.

'Ay, but not for us.' Mistress Clarihew bustled about and chivvied them into their work for the day.

Abbie could tell that the progress was not an unqualified success right from the start. Linlithgow was beautiful, but Stirling brought back terrible memories of Hercules the bear, Frederick and Ferdinand, the King's singers, and the awful night when Marie de Guise took them all away in a wild escape to Inchmahome.

Perth was devastated by the English, Dundee they hardly saw because they passed through it so quickly, and the Queen shed tears when she saw St Andrews Cathedral.

'It was here that my parents' marriage was blessed,' she wept.

No, Abbie thought, as they rode on to the last stop at Falkland Palace where they would stay for almost a week, it had not been a happy holiday at all. Wherever they went they had been reminded of the Protestant revolution and the English threat. From Scone, near Perth, the Coronation Stone of Scotland had been carried off by Edward I of England to Westminster Abbey, and it was in Perth itself, in St John's Church, that John Knox had preached the sermon which had started the destruction of the abbeys and all things Catholic. Lord James had been right. There was no getting away from John Knox.

And although she tried hard not to show it, Flamina was pining. Abbie knew it was for Sir William Maitland far away in London. Lady Jean and Alex Ogilvie, too, showed little enthusiasm for this trip. For the first time they seemed a little at odds in each other's company, with Lady Jean often bursting into unaccustomed tears.

As for the young de Guises, they were more bored than ever until they discovered a tennis court at Falkland Palace, a large high-roofed black box with a net stretched across the middle of it, and open windows all along each side to let in the air. Then Mary found a billiard table with little coloured balls and long pointed sticks to push the balls about. She had brought the de Guises to life at last. They could stay here for ever, they told her.

How long could the Queen of Scotland go on amusing herself playing silly games while the whole country was in a state of anarchy, its population poor, starving and crying out for help? Abbie wondered. Did she not understand that behaviour like this was only providing John Knox with further ammunition to hurl at her?

Worried as Abbie was on behalf of the Queen, she was even more worried about Donald. She had expected to hear from him by now. Where was he?

Absolutely helpless, Donald lay on the ground.

'Christ's *sake*!' said a voice over his sprawling figure. 'I thought it was you, Donald MacLaren, dressed up in that black uniform. I couldn't believe my eyes!'

Donald saw that a man was running his horse up the hill and into the trees, and then he was being rolled over and over until he fell with a thud into a ditch, completely winded again.

'These hills are full of the bastards!' the voice continued. 'You could have been killed!'

Donald got his breath back and gave vent to his injured feelings. 'What bastards? And what way is *this* to treat the father of your future grandchildren, John McCracken?'

John pressed Donald's face into the sludge at the bottom of the ditch. 'Keep your head down,' he hissed in his ear. 'They must have seen you. They're coming back to look for you. Keep down!'

The thunder of horses' hooves burst upon them, wave after wave. The Highlanders whooped as they rode, and along with the jangling of their harnesses the noise, almost over their heads, was deafening.

'But who are they?' Donald spluttered, spitting out mud.

'Some of the local bloody scum. Enemies of the Earl of Sutherland, spies and watchdogs from Caithness. Here they come back again!'

They lay low while the riders passed by, slower this time, beating about the undergrowth, searching, searching. They lay low until Donald could bear it no longer, and came up for air.

'They've gone!' he protested, but once again John's heavy hand pressed him down.

'No they haven't! There's still another murderous lot to come. Now, shut up, Donald!'

Men got down off their horses, swearing and cursing and laying about with their swords up above their very heads. Weeds and undergrowth were scythed on top of them, and then Donald knew for certain that he was going to choke to death after all, here on a mountainside God alone knew where in the Highlands of Scotland.

'Ah, well,' John McCracken said, ten suffocating minutes later, 'that's the end of them for this day. They've gone back to their cave further up the hill. You can come out now, Donald MacLaren. What was that I heard about you wanting to marry Abbie?'

'Huh! You'd be *very* lucky,' Donald assured him bitterly out of a face plastered with mud.

'Well,' John McCracken laughed, 'it all depends on how well you do when you help me to flush out these outlaws, for there's no doubt I need every man I can get.'

'And how do you propose to do that, may I ask?'

'Smoke them out. But first we've got to get above them to the top of this mountain, and by stealth.'

He hadn't come here for any of this, Donald told himself a thousand times over as he crawled silently through the heather with John McCracken and two or three other Gordons, inch by desperate inch to the top of that hill where the rest of the Gordons were dug in and tying up bundles of heather with strings of ling.

'Not that I can see properly out of the mud caked on my face, but what are they going to do with the bundles of heather?' Donald asked.

'Set fire to them and throw them in the cave when they're all sleeping. And never mind the dirt on your face,' John said. 'If anything, it improves you. Now put your head down and get an hour's sleep. We'll make our move before the moon comes up.'

The Queen and her court arrived back at Holyrood only hours before Sir William returned from London. She took him into her private room at once.

'What did Elizabeth say?' she asked.

'She will not name you her successor, Your Majesty.'

'Why not, when I was prepared to sign a modified Treaty of Edinburgh?'

'She is too superstitious. She says that if she ever names a successor she will have one foot in the grave. But she has suggested a meeting with you, and she sends you this.' He handed her a box. Inside was a velvet pouch, and inside that was a diamond ring. 'She calls it a friendship ring, Majesty. It is in two halves, and she has kept the other half. If ever you are in trouble, send her this ring and she will come to your aid.'

'I see ... Thank you, Sir William,' Mary sighed in disappointment. 'Please feel free to go. You must be tired. How long did it take you to ride back?'

'Four days, madam.'

'Then I wish you goodnight.'

He bowed and left her. Flamina was waiting for him outside the door.

One morning a few days later Lady Jean and Abbie discovered to their horror that Holyrood was buzzing with Abbie's happy news. How had it got around? It could only have come from Alex Ogilvie, who must have dropped a careless word to Flamina, with whom he was friendly. In that case, Sir William would soon know, too – and then the Queen.

'I had better try to speak to the Queen myself and ask her for permission to leave and marry Donald,' Abbie said.

'The sooner the better. I hope she hears it from you first,' Jean warned her.

But at such an early hour there was no question at all of invading Mary's privacy in her bedchamber, as Sir William Maitland told her when he barred her way in the antechamber. He was there, as immaculate as ever in black and silver, inviting her to sit down to talk to him.

'May I ask for what purpose you wish to speak to the Queen, my dear?' he asked kindly.

'I am to be married to Donald MacLaren, one of the Gordon soldiers. I wanted Her Majesty to be the first to know.'

'My dear Miss Abbie, may I offer you my congratulations? Please do not concern yourself. I shall inform the Queen as soon as she comes through after her breakfast – that is,' he added in silken tones, 'if you really think it wise?'

'I don't understand you, sir.'

'I believe all the Queen's ladies gave her a promise not to marry before she does.'

'That is true, Sir William. They all did, except me, if you count me as one of the Queen's ladies.'

He placed five thin fingers of one hand precisely up against the five fingers of the other, and Abbie saw that his eyes were suddenly icy cold.

'Do you honestly doubt it, Miss Abbie? Were you treated as anything else all those years in France? Or are you now, for that matter, back in Scotland?'

'No, sir,' she was forced to agree.

'No, indeed . . . Perhaps we should not bother Her Majesty with the news of your betrothal just yet, after all. She has so many other worries,' he swept a spidery arm around the room as though all around the desolate country of Scotland. 'But there is good news on the way, I assure you. Good news not only for you, but for all the Queen's ladies.'

'Yes, sir?'

'Would-be husbands for Her Majesty are lining up in droves. She must choose one of them, and very soon. She cannot be expected to rule Scotland alone, so young – even younger than you are yourself. *You* would not like to under-take such a task yourself, would you?'

'No, sir,' Abbie said miserably. 'I would not.'

'Then,' he said, with the hard look gone from his eyes, 'believe me, we shall all rejoice for you when the time comes. In the meantime, please bear with our little Queen like the brave girl you are. I am sure you would never desert her, but wish to help her all you can.'

For a minute Abbie regarded him, her eyes bright with tears. There was no arguing with him. She *did* wish to help the Queen all she could, but only until Donald came back. Sir William was just like a spider, sitting there spinning his silken, mysterious webs. But although they were silken they were even more impenetrable than the fog had ever been, threatening to choke her off from Donald.

With a sob Abbie rushed from the room.

* * *

Sighing as she left, Sir William Maitland remained seated waiting for the Queen, for he had a very thorny proposition to put to her. He waited patiently for another hour, debating how to phrase it in another set of carefully chosen words, but in the end, when she did finally arrive, he found that the best way was to come straight out with it.

'Good morning, Your Majesty,' he bowed. 'I trust you slept well?'

'I thank you, Sir William. I fear I have slept late, still suffering from the effects of our progress. But I am wide awake now and fully recovered, so you must say your worst. What is it I must face next?'

'Your Majesty, dearest Queen, I am afraid it is a case of *who* you must face! You can put it off no longer. He has been clamouring to see you, and it would be best to get it over and done with, once and for all.'

'Who?' Mary asked, but with a sinking heart she already knew the answer, because it was true – she had been dreading and delaying this evil hour until she could delay it no longer.

'John Knox, Your Majesty.'

THIRTY-THREE

Queen Mary had dressed carefully to receive John Knox in a gown of black Spanish lace. Its square neckline was bordered with pearls, pearls outlined the heart-shaped brim of her head-dress, and there were pearls again, buttoning her wrists. Otherwise she wore no ornaments save the tiny pearl butterflies holding her hair in place.

The man could not question her sombre dignity. The dark gown and the smoky kohl deepening her eyes to blackness, contrasted with her white-painted face and the pearls. Flamina had crimsoned her mouth, outlining its curving underlip voluptuously, and that was colour enough. Whether he approved or not was no concern of Mary's.

'Now, my ladies,' she said, sprinkling scent on her hair and her wrists, 'you had best go on ahead to the audience chamber and join Master Knox and Lord James.'

The four Marys, Lady Jean and Abbie curtsied and left, and ten minutes later Mary followed. She opened the door of the audience chamber and smelled the fragrance of the juniper wood she had ordered to burn day and night in the wall braziers. If she could not eradicate the stench of the green slimy walls behind her silk tapestries, then at least she could mask it.

Her ladies, sitting on the window seat behind her chair, rose and curtsied, and Lord James and Knox turned to face her. Knox bowed low, sweeping off a black velvet hat.

Because his great stature in Scotland had been so impressed upon her Abbie had expected him to be a big man, and was

264

secretly pleased that he was forced to look up to Mary out of deep, blackly burning eyes. His brows were heavy and grey, and his limp grey beard streaked with yellow flowed to the waist of his rusty black doublet. His lips were very red and very full, his skin was like parchment and he wore a black Geneva cloak from which, apparently, he had refused to be parted.

'Please sit down,' Mary said.

At that moment Abbie recognised more completely than ever that the Queen of Scotland's life was not to be envied. It was a terrible life, Sir William had been right about that, and Mary should be given all the help she could get. The tension rose in the room, and Abbie hoped with all her heart that whatever was expected of her in the future, in some small way, for the sake of Scotland and to further the Queen of Scotland's ends, she would never seriously have to impersonate Mary in such a difficult task as this, to deal with such a person as this awful John Knox.

He was staring at the Queen in an unflickering stare that travelled slowly from her lacy head-dress down to the tips of her slippers and back up again. Surely, Abbie thought, no man of God should examine a woman so boldly? But Mary remained calm, and her voice was soft and sweet.

'Master Knox,' she said, 'I am glad to meet with you. Although we differ in faith, we both have Scotland's good at heart –'

'The heart, madam, is of the body, and thus inclined to evil. We will consider the soul.' He leaned forward pointing a long finger at her. 'What of yours?'

The impertinence of the man! Abbie hissed in disbelief. So did the other ladies. So did Mary.

Knox seemed grimly pleased. 'I dare say your Romish tutors neglected to verse you in sophistry?'

'You are wrong, sir. But I wish to speak of Scotland –'

'The Scottish people will not tolerate Mass, madam,' he shouted, half rising from his chair. 'Nor will I! You shall not poison this land!'

The argument descended into a slanging match of religious quotations and technicalities and Abbie found herself sitting there with glazed eyes. She came to life again when Knox started to pace the floor booming long passages of doctrine, arguing the rights of the people to rise up against a ruler. He expounded anarchy and insurrection, and Mary was speechless with the shock of it. She sat there in silence for so long that Lord James stirred uneasily, then rose and went to her, touching her arm.

'Madam,' he asked anxiously, 'are you all right?'

She looked up and nodded. Tears trembled in her eyes, but she flung her head up high while Knox ranted on as though the audience chamber were St Giles', oblivious of her attempts to break in. He was past stopping. He was in another world. Perhaps he was not mad, but only shelled with self-righteousness. At any rate, he would never hear another point of view.

Abbie could not detect any sign of spirituality in the man's face. The storm-black eyes were fierce, the mouth sensual, and the prophet-like beard had a pagan, goatish look. She wondered if there were not two sides to John Knox, and shuddered to think of the other.

Mary had been studying him quietly too. She pounced as Knox caught his breath. 'Master Knox,' she said sweetly, 'I read your blast against *The Monstrous Regiment of Women* and so I know in what low opinion you hold my sex. But in writing that book you unwittingly spread before the world your intense jealousy of women. It is obvious that you feel beneath us, perhaps because some woman once rejected your love? In France we used to speculate about it.'

For a moment Abbie thought he was going to strike the Queen. His face was grey with rage. Perhaps Mary had not been able to penetrate his theology nor his conceit by argument, but she had certainly succeeded by womanly spite. He spluttered, incoherent with fury, and she was still sweet when she rose and said, 'I am very sorry if I chanced to revive a tragic memory . . . Good day, Master Knox.'

266

She nodded coolly to him, smiled at Lord James and trailed slowly into the bedchamber. Flamina signalled to Abbie to come and help her, for by now it was accepted that any of the Marys could call on her if Lady Jean did not need her.

'Madam!' Flamina burst out. 'You were magnificent!'

'No.' Mary sank down on her bed, clutching her side. 'I was no match for him in theological argument. I could not even defend our faith, and that has upset me. I shall lie down for a while.'

As they talked, Flamina disrobed the Queen and handed her clothes to Abbie to put away. 'But you had the last word,' Flamina insisted, slipping Mary's white silk shift over her head. 'He was speechless!'

Mary smiled wanly and lay back. 'I enraged him. But since he is ruthless, I must be just as ruthless, starting now. I shall not get up again today.'

'Shall I send Abbie for Dr Bourgoing, madam?' Flamina asked anxiously.

'Perhaps you had better, Flamina. The pain in my side is getting worse.'

When she came back with the doctor, somehow Abbie was not surprised to see that Mary was sitting up again and speaking quite animatedly to Flamina. Nor was she surprised to see that Sir William was by the Queen's bedside as well. After a short examination Dr Bourgoing agreed that the Queen should continue to rest in bed, and he would visit her again in the evening. As the door closed behind him Abbie rose to follow him out of the bedchamber, thinking that she would not be required to stay any longer.

'No, Miss Abbie,' Sir William said, and she turned to find three pairs of eyes staring at her. Immediately, she knew what was coming next. *What she had been dreading for years, and never really believed would happen, was happening now.* 'We were wondering if you would do Her Majesty a little favour. As you see, she is not well, but there is a meeting she should attend this afternoon.'

267

So, Abbie thought swiftly, they want me to impersonate the Queen this very afternoon, do they? Yet in a way, she was almost relieved. She was also quite curious to see how they would achieve such a transformation of herself, as well as being apprehensive of what would happen when she tried to do as they wished. With any luck, she would be useless to them. But whatever happened, she must not show any fear or displeasure. She must not betray the fact that as soon as Donald came for her, she would run away with him, if necessary – out of Holyrood, this terrible hotbed of intrigue and danger.

'Of course, I shall do anything I can to help Her Majesty,' Abbie said with a smile.

'You won't even have to speak,' Sir William said, understanding that Abbie knew exactly what he was talking about. 'Just nod your head at the appropriate times. I will be at your side throughout, but let me go through it with you now.'

For several minutes he instructed Abbie. Then Mary laughed her tinkling laugh. 'You'll be very bored,' she said, 'but you'll manage our little secret. If you are successful it will save me from endless boring pageants and masques on draughty daises. Abbie, you will buy me leisure and freedom.'

'Then come with me,' Flamina said, 'and I'll prepare you.'

'Strip down to your petticoat,' Flamina flung over her shoulder while she busied herself with the face paints. 'Now, the shading of the contours will be gentle enough, but the white paint for the centre of your face might sting a bit. I'll make the solution weak.'

So Abbie sat, gazing into the mirror, while Flamina went to work. Soon the width of her face was narrowed by the shadow, and the highlighting of the central panel was nothing less than amazing. Flamina was certainly the mistress of the face paints, Abbie thought, while before her very eyes Mary, Queen of Scots looked back out of the mirror at her.

'Hm,' Fleming sighed. 'It might pass. Let's see what you look like, dressed.' One of the Queen's black velvet gowns

268

was tight, and far too long. 'Never mind that,' said Flamina. 'We'll put on the head-dress,' and she fitted the black heart-shape on Abbie's head and drew the gauze of the coif down over her cheeks. 'Oh yes, Abbie! It's wonderful! But you'll have to remain seated and keep that extra foot of velvet well tucked under your feet. Then no one could tell that you aren't the Queen herself, I'm sure!'

Sir William thought the same, as he settled Abbie on the chair of High Estate, where the canopy lent further shade to her face. He tucked in the hem of the gown, and the meeting began. 'Just smile,' he muttered from time to time. 'Smile and nod here,' he guided her throughout the never-ending afternoon.

But as the burgesses prepared to file out at long last, Abbie reverted to her adventurous self. 'I thank you, sirs,' she trilled.

They all halted, smiled and bowed. Sir William expelled a very deep breath and wiped his brow when they were alone again. 'You did well, Miss Abbie,' he praised her, 'although you were not required to speak.'

She smiled sadly and lifted up her skirts as they went to show the Queen Flamina's handiwork. Abbie knew herself that she had not only passed the test, but far surpassed it. Queen Mary and her advisers could rest assured that they had indeed nurtured a perfect cat's-paw, a perfect dupe.

Mary beamed to see her. 'Nobody beyond this room shall know that it was Abbie McCracken who received the town's burgesses today. It shall be our secret. Do you agree, Abbie?'

'I do, Your Majesty.'

'Such a small intrigue, so harmless, will pass the days most agreeably and break the monotony of state matters,' Mary smiled happily.

Abbie looked from one to the other, the laughing Queen, the secret face of Sir William, the Spider, and Flamina, who could not keep the adoration out of her eyes every time she looked at him.

An uneasy dread told Abbie that it would not always be like this, light-hearted and amusing. Some day, someone would try to gain by her imposture, for she knew that the Queen's wish to keep it a secret was folly. Sooner, rather than later, all secrets became public property within the walls of Holyrood Palace.

THIRTY-FOUR

'As far as we can make out, there are twenty-two or twenty-three of the Caithness men,' John McCracken told Donald. 'We started out a party of twelve. They surprised us, as we surprised you, and they killed two of our Gordons . . . So now we are only eleven, counting you.'

'Then it would be stupid to try and take them on head to head.'

'It would be suicide. We've been stuck here for two days frozen half to death, waiting and watching their movements, and found out that they sleep all together in that cave.'

'But surely they post a sentry?'

'No. They feel so secure in their mountain fastness that they don't bother. That's what gave me the idea. You see all these bundles of heather?'

Donald nodded. The Gordons had the bundles upright now, in little stacks for the air to blow through them and dry up any bits that were damp. 'How deep is the cave?' he asked.

'We think it's pretty shallow, although we can't get a proper look. But by the sound of their voices, they're not far from the entrance. I'm banking on it being not much bigger than an average room.'

'So what's this plan?'

'To crawl above it, and throw in the burning heather as far as we can. That should provide plenty of smoke, and with any luck they will be blinded when they rush out.'

It was pitch dark, and hampered by their bundles of heather it was a dangerous manoeuvre, with only an occasional

271

Caithness voice from the cave to guide them. Donald felt the adrenaline rising as they waited and waited for the signal to move, when John would scratch a light for the tarry torches each Gordon carried with him.

But John was waiting until snores replaced the voices, and the waiting seemed to go on for ever. The blood would have frozen in their veins with the cold if the excitement hadn't kept it pumping. Then there was a tiny rasp, a pinpoint of light, and they crawled around him to light their torches. One by one, their hands stiff with cold, they set fire to the bundles of heather, and when they were well alight flung them over the lip and as far into the cave as they could.

Nothing happened. All they had achieved, Donald thought, was to give themselves and their position away.

But a minute or two later one Caithness man spluttered and choked, then another and another, and by the light of their torches the Gordons saw the smoke billowing out of the cave. It had worked, after all.

'Now, boys! Down!' John McCracken shouted.

The Gordons leaped down to the mouth of the cave and caught the Caithness men as they stumbled out, coughing and trying to clear their eyes. The loss of their two friends hardened them for revenge. At the end of it all, twenty-four Caithness corpses lay on the ground.

When they got their breath back, John spoke again. 'We'll take the best of their horses with us, one each. That was only the first line of their defence, the first round of this battle. Golspie is on the other side of this hill, and Dunrobin Castle not far from that, filled with crack Caithness soldiers. That won't be so easy.'

Donald laughed as he tied a Caithness horse on behind his own. 'Well, after all that smoke you don't have to worry about blacking out your faces now! You all look as bad as I feel.'

'Ay, but not so ugly, Donald,' one of the Gordons teased.

They rode on as long as it was dark, along the winding road passing Golspie. Nasty little flurries of hail chased them into the comparative shelter of the forest surrounding Dunrobin Castle. For most of the next day they took it in turns to sleep wrapped up in their sheepskins, and in between times they admired the castle with its beautiful towers and spires, and watched the movements to and fro.

In the afternoon a young man came out, guarded by four soldiers.

'That's him!' John McCracken said. 'That's Alexander, the young Earl of Sutherland. Somehow we've got to get him out of there and back to Strathbogie. We'll wait and see if they take him out at this same time tomorrow.'

The next day it poured with icy, sleety rain, which trickled down through the trees and down the backs of the Gordons' necks and made them thoroughly bad-tempered. But raining or not, the young Earl was taken for his walk again.

'That seems to be the pattern, rain or shine,' John said a week later. I think we'll chance it. Tomorrow morning, I'm going in.'

Donald flung himself down beside him. 'How did the Earl of Sutherland manage to allow himself to become a captive in his own castle – tell me *that*,' he sniffed.

'Ah, well . . . That's a long story.'

'I wasn't planning on doing much this evening, anyway,' Donald sighed resignedly as they huddled around their small fire, 'so you might as well begin.'

An hour later John was still relating the complicated story of inheritance and treachery.

'What has it got to do with the Gordons, anyway?' Donald asked.

'The old Earl of Sutherland was a Gordon, too, a kinsman of our Lord Huntly. And now, it seems, Huntly has heard that all the charters and papers entitling Alexander to his inheritance have disappeared, and the Earl of Caithness with them. Huntly thinks that Caithness has taken himself off because there's a plot brewing to do away with the young Earl, and he doesn't want to be implicated.'

*　　*　　*

273

Whatever the momentary lift in her spirits at the success of the imposture, Abbie noticed a distinct change in Queen Mary when she got up after her disastrous meeting with John Knox. She was peevish and demanding and as she had threatened, quite ruthless.

'Madam, I beg you, rest another day in bed,' Flamina pleaded.

'There is too much to be done,' Mary snapped. 'To begin with, I must answer this latest letter from Elizabeth of England. She wants me to allow the Earl of Lennox to return to Scotland and inspect his forfeited estates.'

'Then at least let me help you with that, Your Majesty,' Flamina persisted. 'You know I can copy your handwriting perfectly. I could do the tedious writing at your dictation.'

'I suppose so,' Mary sighed drearily. 'Abbie, go and fetch Sir William to me. The question of the Earl of Lennox will have to be discussed, and then tell my courtiers to amuse themselves today. I am too busy to bother with them.'

The de Guises and the other Frenchmen were hanging about in a knot at the foot of the staircase when Abbie delivered the message. They burst into a torrent of French cursing she was ashamed to say she understood. It all boiled down to the fact that they were tired of Holyrood Palace, tired of Edinburgh and tired of Scotland. There was no fun here, and now they had heard that this Knox fellow did not allow entertainment of any sort in this cold, accursed country, even at Yuletide. It was too much.

Abbie said nothing to the Queen when she returned to the audience chamber. She and Sir William were arguing, and neither of them looked well.

'Matthew Stewart, the Earl of Lennox?' Sir William almost choked. 'That traitor? He deserved to lose his lands and his titles when he sold himself to Henry the Eighth! And all out of spite because your royal father did not adopt him as heir, and did not need to after you were born. Lennox has been your enemy since birth!'

'First Arran, and now Lennox,' Mary said wearily. 'Can

we not have an end to this never-ending feuding? Matthew Stewart, the Earl of Lennox, is still a second cousin to me! He committed his sins twenty years ago. Twenty years . . . May not a sin be forgiven after twenty years? I think twenty years is long enough, and so I shall pardon the Earl of Lennox and restore him to his estates as Elizabeth requests.'

'It is folly,' Sir William said flatly. 'Please, Majesty, give me time to consider this, to think what Elizabeth is up to. It is too serious a matter to dismiss in five minutes.'

'You may go,' Mary said coldly, 'but I will not change my mind.'

Sir William Maitland left the Queen's apartments and hurried off to find Lord James. They whispered in the corridor, two Protestants together.

'Queen Elizabeth wants leave for the Earl of Lennox to return! And I cannot persuade Mary to refuse it! Will *you* talk to her? She might listen to you! You are her brother, after all.'

'Oh, Jesu!' Lord James said. 'Oh, Maitland! If that man comes to Scotland he will assert his claim to the throne again! He will bring that pretty-boy son of his, Lord Darnley, with him as well!'

'*Ah* . . .' Sir William said. 'So *that*'s it, is it? Of course! Of course! How could I have forgotten Darnley? Elizabeth does not care a fig for the Earl of Lennox! She only wants to use his son to dazzle Queen Mary. Now I see it. Well, if I cannot stop it altogether, I will delay it and delay it. For years, if necessary. Let's hope something else turns up to divert the Queen's attention in the meantime.'

But the only thing to turn up was the departure of the French courtiers. One by one and two by two they said their farewells to the Queen and hastened back to France before the weather got worse. Pierre Chastelard was the only Frenchman to remain, to Beaton's great satisfaction.

'He stays on my account,' she purred.

Nobody believed her.

Lightning flickered through the broken arches of Holyrood Abbey and thunder growled, rolling along the Canongate and bombarding the massive rock of Arthur's Seat. The winds had pounded Edinburgh for months on end, throwing down sleet and snow all that winter and now, early in the New Year travelling was difficult, if not impossible.

Sir William Maitland's well-ordered life had been turned upside down these last few months. Gone were the days when he could anticipate anything. They had gone when he fell head over heels in love with Lady Mary Fleming. Now he never knew what would happen next.

She shuddered in his arms at every roll of thunder as they lay together in bed in her darkened room, and he saw with every flash of lightning that she was genuinely terrified. The thunder must be affecting him as well. His head was thumping when he held her closer still.

'Flamina! Flamina! My darling, nothing will happen to you as long as I am here,' he said, and kissed her passionately again.

'But you will not be here much longer, William. That's the trouble. It's not only the thunder and lightning. It's the long, dangerous journey ahead of you to London and back that worries me! When are you going?'

'In two days,' he sighed, 'with this latest letter and gifts from Mary to Elizabeth. I could do nothing to stop her. She can be as stubborn as a mule. But I should be back ten days later, although I don't know how I shall exist without you, Flamina.' He sighed deeply. 'It seems we have been waiting for ever.'

'But you haven't been waiting,' Flamina giggled as he rolled over her again. 'Have you?'

'Oh, I wish you had never made that idiotic promise to Mary, Flamina! I mean, I can't wait to marry you! We can't carry on like this.'

'I hope not, or else the same thing will happen to me that happened to my mother in France, when she was sent home pregnant and in disgrace. In fact . . .' Flamina forgot the thunder and lightning and everything else for the next few ecstatic minutes . . . 'I think it might have happened already.'

'Oh God! If that was so I would demand your release myself,' he said, lying back with his arm over his eyes.

'You wouldn't be the only one, William. Lusty and John Sempill are courting strong, as well . . . What's wrong? There's something wrong, isn't there? Is it your head?'

'I feel dreadful, Flamina, dreadful. I cannot go to London, like this. I must see Melville first thing in the morning and brief him.'

Melville, honoured to have been chosen as envoy, and still wondering if his elevation had only been due to Sir William's illness, followed his instructions to the letter. He went first on a secret visit to Lord and Lady Lennox. He found his lordship genuinely anxious to return to Scotland. Her ladyship was even more anxious that their son should go with him. After some discussion it was agreed that once Queen Elizabeth's permission had been granted, and passports, it should take place in the end.

Leaving them, he arrived in London in time to see Queen Elizabeth dancing with Sir Robert Dudley, and was shocked to the core when she leaned over him, put her hand inside his ruff and tickled his neck. In such a public place! They must be lovers, and she was proclaiming it to the world.

Mindful of his new and exciting office, Melville immediately fell to wondering how this development would affect Scotland, and was amazed when he saw the great Queen approaching him, instead of making him wait in turn with the rest of the ambassadors.

'Tell me, Mr Melville,' she said directly, 'are you come to see me about the succession?'

'Partly,' he replied, missing an opportunity that Sir William would have grasped with both hands. 'I bring you heartfelt greetings from the Queen, my mistress, your good sister and cousin.'

277

'You are new to the game, are you not? We have not met before, Mr Melville.'

'Sir William Maitland is ill, Your Majesty.'

'Then, since you see me for the first time, what think you – are we alike, your mistress and I?'

Two Queens, he thought. Cousins, even. But oh, the difference! The English Queen was much shorter, and her broad shoulders made her appear shorter still. She had shaved her forehead to make her face seem longer and more important, and she was wearing a red wig, as magnificent and as ostentatious as the rest of her apparel of gold and glittering jewels.

But it was the eyes that said it all.

Mary's soft golden eyes, slanting and gently provocative were as different from Elizabeth's as chalk from cheese. Elizabeth's eyes were the eyes of a fox, dark and hard, infinitely calculating – and it seemed, they could read somebody else's mind, as well.

'She is more beautiful than I am,' she said. 'I see it in your face.'

'Madam, she is the most beautiful Queen in Scotland, but you – *you* are the most beautiful Queen in England!'

Elizabeth laughed. 'Well done, sir! You will make a diplomat yet!' She took his arm and stood with him watching some young men of her court. 'What think you of yonder long lad?'

'That he *is* a long lad, Your Majesty,' Melville said, gazing at the tallest young man there, exquisitely dressed with a beardless face and long, waving golden hair.

'Taller than your mistress, perhaps? I hear she is very tall. Too tall, in that case, since I am exactly the right height.'

'Indeed, madam, she is tall. But the young gentleman is taller.'

'You do not know him? He is Queen Mary's cousin, Henry Stewart, Lord Darnley, son of the Earl of Lennox.'

Elizabeth left him and when they all went in to dine she took Robert Dudley's arm. All through the feast Melville

278

dwelled on his strange conversation with Elizabeth, his eyes drawn constantly to Darnley.

Melville was intelligent, and it wasn't long before he saw it all. His visit to the Lennoxes would not have been the secret that he thought it was. It would have been reported to the English Queen long ago. And she had not pointed out Darnley for nothing, either. He had a lot to learn about the diplomatic life. Now he saw that Elizabeth had manoeuvred it all. When he went to bed that night he realised that she had run rings around not only him, but all the Scots, and she still had not spoken of the succession. Sir William would not be pleased.

THIRTY-FIVE

Never before had Elizabeth, his Gloriana, permitted Dudley's hand on her thigh. It was the opportunity he had waited so long and so hard for, he had prayed for, and without further ado he slipped his fingers into her vagina. At the same time – at this, the most crucial moment in his life – he discovered to his horror that his member was refusing to stiffen. He should never have had that last glass of wine.

Elizabeth was drunk, but not as drunk as he was. For a happy moment she let his fingers stay where they were, before she remembered . . . For a happy moment he tried to penetrate further, before he met an obstacle . . .

'Get off me!' she screeched, and pushed him away.

He fell on the floor at the side of the bed. His eyes closed, and everything went black until the following morning when groaning, and with his head pounding, he awoke to find himself lying on the floor in the Queen's bedroom, and Elizabeth was nowhere to be seen.

It was two days later before Queen Elizabeth granted Melville another audience. She took the package Mary of Scotland had sent and glanced over the letter first. It was full of the usual innocuous platitudes. Cecil could interpret it later, and would certainly advise her as to her next move.

In the meantime she tore open the coverings of Mary's latest offering, to reveal the latest Paris fashion, a curious short garment with two legs, made of silk.

'What is this?' she asked Melville.

He coughed delicately. 'A lady's undergarment, Your Majesty. My dear Queen called them drawers, and bid me to tell you that soon all ladies will be wearing them. She thinks it is a fashion that will catch on.'

Elizabeth looked at them for one furious moment before she hurled them to the furthest corner. If she had been wearing those, her beloved Robin would not have discovered the secret above her thighs. Oh, Jesus Christ – she loved him so!

'Send Sir Robert Dudley to me,' she commanded, dismissing Melville, and for half an hour reviled her favourite, swore and cursed at him in her raucous voice, finishing up in tears of utter frustration.

'But I love you, Elizabeth, and you love me. We *should* be married.'

'Hear me for the last time. I shall die the Virgin Queen. And you must go away.'

'Go away?' Dudley said. 'Ah, Majesty, please don't send me away . . .'

'Oh, I'll find a reason,' Elizabeth said with a cruel smile.

Moretta, the Italian Ambassador, managed to scuttle into Leith with his retinue of twenty-two courtiers, singers and jesters as soon as the weather temporarily eased a little. They arrived at dawn one winter morning, only hours before Melville got back from London and reported to Sir William.

Holyrood's great open-mouthed fireplaces roared from kitchen to turrets day and night, but the creeping cold lurked just beyond the hearthstones. These days nobody ventured across a room or down a corridor without good reason and certainly not without a cloak and shawls.

Wrapped up in everything she could lay her hands on, Abbie obeyed Flamina's instructions to come and help her with the Queen, since the other Marys were evidently unwilling to brave the freezing dawn. She warmed the woollen undergarments for Flamina to dress her with. She warmed the long-handled spoon in the fire for the Queen to sup her porridge with, while with teeth chattering, Mary moaned, 'I never thought to receive a suitor's ambassador in a wool kirtle.'

Abbie walked behind Flamina, who walked behind the Queen into the audience chamber. A slender, elderly man turned from the fire when they entered and announced himself. 'Conte di Moretta, Ambassador of Savoy, greets Your Majesty in the name of the Duke of Ferrara.'

Mary extended her hand and he kissed it. 'Sit down, sir,' she said, 'and let us come to the point. It is too cold for shillyshallying.'

Thankfully, he agreed, and pulling out a portrait of his master embarked on the familiar pattern of persuasion. The Queen of Scotland could do no better, he assured her in a hundred different ways, than marry the Duke of Ferrara.

The Duke of Ferrara was very ugly, Abbie thought, gazing at the portrait. The poor Queen did not have much of a choice when it came to suitors. This would be only the start of a long procession of them. She heard Mary inviting Moretta and his retinue to a banquet that evening as the interview dragged to an end.

Eventually, it was Donald who came up with a plan to rescue the Earl of Sutherland. He bribed one of the Caithness guards, patrolling the border of the estate, with a bag of Lord Huntly's money and the promise of high rank among the Gordon soldiers, to take a message to Sutherland secretly. The Earl was to take a longer walk than usual the next day, right to the bridge at Golspie, and lead his guards into an ambush.

The plan worked perfectly and the Gordons made off with Alexander into a worsening weather knowing that soon there would be a hue and cry.

'To Dornoch! To Dornoch!' John McCracken led them on, as the Caithness men roared up behind them. The Gordons abandoned their horses and their belongings and leaped aboard a waiting ship to face a tempestuous journey. They landed at Portsoy into a world that was white and thick with snow.

'Now, *how* can I get back to Holyrood for Abbie through this?' Donald groaned.

'You can't. You know as well as I do,' John McCracken said sadly, 'we're banged up here until the spring. You'll just have to wait.'

'But will she?' Donald looked at him, his whole miserable heart in his eyes.

Sometimes it was kinder to be cruel, John thought, and his future son-in-law might as well face all the facts now, since he still had a few months of the winter to come to terms with them. 'Oh, she'll wait,' he said. 'You can trust Abbie. If she loves you she will wait for you.'

'John, she swears she loves me as much as I love her, and I would die for her, God knows. Do I have your permission to marry her?'

'You have my blessing, as well, and Abigail's. We always hoped that one day the two of you would marry. But there's one thing you've forgotten, Donald. As I said, you can trust Abbie – and so can Lady Jean. Abbie won't let her down, either. She'll always be loyal.'

That was true, Donald thought, and worried more than ever.

THIRTY-SIX

Late in the afternoon of the very day Mary had received the Italian Ambassador, Bothwell arrived in Holyrood. As he tossed his dripping cloak on a chair Mary and her ladies saw that he was wearing his sword, and his dirk was at his belt. Abbie concluded that he must also be wearing armour when she saw the stiff breadth of his chest under his doublet, and scowled ferociously at his muddy boots, jangling with spurs, as he walked over the Queen's pale carpet to bow before her.

Livingston whipped his dirty, wet cloak off the velvet chair, and stared at his boots and the muddy prints they had made in horror, but the Queen did not seem to mind.

'Sit down, my lord,' she said. 'I am writing to Queen Elizabeth now that she seems quite amiable.'

Bothwell settled down more comfortably in his chair, looking for once as though he would hold a conversation with her. 'And your nobles, madam? How do you find them? Do they seem quite amiable too?'

'How strange that you should ask! I have had to dismiss Arran from court. I think he is mad.'

'Arran has a maggot in his brain,' he agreed. 'And what do your nobles say of me?'

'That you are a rogue, a knave, an adventurer,' Mary said with sparkling eyes, nodding to her ladies so as to dismiss them.

Abbie wished that she could be dismissed, too, as far away from Bothwell as she could get. But she was never dismissed. She was always required to stay at the Queen's convenience, with her eyes and ears shut except when there were messages to run. But by nominating herself as Queen's Messenger she had brought it upon herself, she reflected sadly, as she retreated to a window embrasure and endeavoured to make herself as invisible as possible.

Now that she was to all intents and purposes alone with Bothwell, Mary smiled and continued. 'Lord James says you are ruthless with women and incapable of fidelity.'

That was blatant flirtation, in Abbie's opinion. Bothwell must have thought so too, for he was trying not to laugh.

Mary blushed as if to cover her girlish confusion. 'Perhaps you should marry and dispel such notoriety.'

She was showing her hand now. She was showing it far too much, if this was all only a game. But was it? Bothwell was leading her on from one pitfall to the next, dangling a dangerous carrot in front of her nose.

'Have you a lady in mind for me, madam?' he asked. 'I have always admired the beautiful Lady Fleming. Is she attached?'

'No, she is not!' Mary snapped. 'Besides, she is a devout Catholic.'

'Devout Catholics marry, I believe.'

'Not outside their religion – and I hear you are now interested in the new religion, my lord.'

'A kiss has converted many a lass,' he taunted her.

'And yes,' Mary sighed, 'she is very beautiful, and very talented . . .'

'You are displeased, madam?'

'Only to find out that Knox has another of my lords now – *you*, my Lord Bothwell . . . And I trusted you, as my mother trusted you.'

Bothwell did not rush to throw himself at her feet, as many another noble would have answered her pathetic appeal. 'Knox does not have me, madam,' he said. 'Nobody owns me. I am the master of my own soul.'

'Perhaps. But all I know is that when I appoint my Privy Council, Huntly will be the one and only Catholic on it.'

'Good! Then Knox will mistakenly believe the rest to be

on his side, when they are not. They are on yours, as I am.'

'If I can believe that, then I shall tell you my plans. Tonight I shall make the appointments of Lord James, Sir William Maitland and seven or eight others, including you, to my Privy Council.'

'My presence will infuriate the others, madam, and anyway I should not wait. I have been here too long as it is. There is trouble, as always, on the Border.'

'Trouble can wait until you have supped with us, at least,' Mary said gaily. 'I command you, my lord – be here at nine.'

After he left Mary went to her writing desk and reread the letter she had been writing to Elizabeth. Abbie watched her trying to continue it, but after a few minutes she threw down her quill, spattering ink over the page she had already written. Frustrated, she crumpled it up angrily and remembered Abbie at last.

'Come here,' she said imperiously, and Abbie stretched her limbs after crouching so long in the window seat and went to stand at her side, all the while feeling quite resentful. 'Go and tell Livingston to unpack the black satin ball gown.'

Abbie knew the gown she meant. It was daringly cut and totally unsuitable for mourning, but then mourning for Francis was no longer in Queen Mary's head. Consideration for her servants was no longer in her head either.

Only Bothwell was.

But surely she could not be attracted to that horrible man! After debating it all the way to give the message to Livingston, Abbie came to the conclusion that Mary, in this new mood, would flirt with any man – however unsuitable.

That evening Mary cunningly placed Bothwell on her right with Flamina, whom he had admired so much, next to him, and watched them and their reactions to each other like a hawk.

But the black satin ball gown, baring her shoulders and sloping into long skin-tight sleeves, ensured that the eyes of every man there were glued to her. Hovering behind the

Queen's chair, as usual, Abbie couldn't remember when she had seen her looking so very beautiful. Her hair waved low at her neck and was caught in a mesh of rubies. Long ruby earrings matched her lips and caught the fire of the candlelight.

Mary had many reasons to hold this banquet in the Great Hall where huge fires had burned all day long and, lately renewed, blazed up around the oak logs again. Randolph, the new English Ambassador, had not been formally welcomed. She would do so along with her extension of friendship towards the Italian Ambassador, Moretta.

She had planted Beaton, Seton, Livingston and Lady Jean strategically at the table among the English and Italian courtiers, where they would make little pools of conversation, having been well trained to take the onus off her.

The hall was now draped with red velvet. A portrait of Marie de Guise hung above one fireplace, and a portrait of James V hung above the other, so that Lord James was sitting at one end of the table under the face of his father, and Mary sat at the top, under her mother's.

Whenever Mary lifted her eyes she looked straight at James V. She glanced several times from him to Abbie, and back again. Oh yes, her father whose blood coursed hot in her veins had enjoyed life and he had enjoyed sex. She intended to enjoy all these pleasures herself, and that did not necessarily mean within marriage. She smiled with a strange, cruel twist of her lips.

Watching her, a horrified Abbie could almost read her thoughts, and she despaired. This woman had no intention whatsoever of marrying again in a hurry. She was going to have a good time, and if Bothwell believed that a good time could only be had with him, he was mistaken.

Just as the Queen had dillied and dallied in France before she finally set sail, she was going to dilly and dally here in Scotland for as long as she liked, Abbie was convinced of it – and where did that leave at least three of her ladies waiting desperately to be released from their promise to her?

Mary didn't care. But Abbie did, especially for Lady Jean, whom she could never desert in such a predicament. Gradually, Abbie's heart sank to the soles of her slippers. When Donald came to fetch her, what could she say except 'No'? If Donald ever did come . . .

When she came to herself again the banquet was continuing serenely. Tonight the tablecloth of Brussels lace glittered with silver plates and goblets, and white lilies bloomed between tall silver candelabra, all a pleasing background for pleasant conversation.

But Lord James spoke to no one. He kept darting baleful glances at Bothwell from his end of the table, which Bothwell returned. Even Sir William was not his usual urbane self. Flamina prattled valiantly against the weight of this masculine moodiness. She might have been an ugly old crone, for all the attention Bothwell paid her.

Up and down the table nobody else seemed to notice. Randolph, Moretta and Chastelard were laughing and conversing with the ladies, but Abbie saw how nervous and agitated the Queen was becoming by the minute. She pleated the tablecloth constantly between her fingers. Then at last she turned her face to the side, Abbie bent down and Mary whispered in her ear.

'These awful men!' she said. 'I can scarcely bear them! Go and tell the servants to send in the tarts and sweet wines right away so that I can put a stop to this.'

In a few minutes the *tartes au sucre* were brought in, tarts that were filled with figs steeped in white wine and wonderfully decorated with clouds of spun sugar. Mary waited impatiently for everyone to finish eating. Then she looked down the table at Lord James.

'Would it make you happier, my lord, if you knew that I intend to appoint you chief adviser on my Privy Council?'

'Happier?' he stammered. 'Why –'

'And you, my lord,' she said, turning to Sir William, 'could you manage a smile at the prospect of being Secretary of State?'

'Madam, I am honoured. I have no words —'

'*Mon Dieu*! Are you to remain wordless all evening? But, before any of you speak, I demand complete tolerance for my faith in return for tolerating yours.'

Lord James and Sir William bowed their heads.

'And now that you have the plums you both have coveted,' Mary went on, 'there are two other appointments I have well considered. Lord Huntly, for one, and I shall send word to inform him immediately. He will be my Chancellor, and advise us in matters concerning the northern parts of my realm . . . And another appointment — Lord Bothwell, who is most fortunately present tonight, and whom I am appointing along with you to my Privy Council. I trust you will find it expedient to co-operate with him.'

Lord James frowned and scowled more than ever.

Mary said, 'The plain truth is that in years past Lord Bothwell outmanoeuvred you. He tricked you by seizing arms and gold sent you by Queen Elizabeth. Oh yes, brother, I know that you have been in the pay of the English Queen! Lord Bothwell upset your conspiracy with her and defended my mother against you. But this is a new age, one in which to patch up old differences, if you have it in you.'

Bothwell rasped, 'For Her Majesty's sake I'm willing to forget our enmity.'

'And I pledge you my friendship,' Lord James said stiffly.

'We will drink to it,' Sir William said, and the three men rose, met together at James's end of the table and clinked goblets. After they drank the pledge they shattered the goblets in the fireplace.

'Thank you, gentlemen,' Mary said. 'We will leave you to talk in private.'

It was some time afterwards that the three men came to join the party in the audience chamber and gathered about the buffet table where spirits and wines stood in crystal decanters. The court musicians began to play and the guests seated themselves on chairs and cushions. Mary sat on a sofa beside Chastelard and watched Bothwell carrying a glass of wine over to Flamina, sitting in a window seat. She tilted her head towards him provocatively, and Abbie, watching the whole scene, wondered how long the Queen would put up with that.

Mary clapped her hands for silence. The music stopped and she called for the travelling minstrels who brought with them news and gossip from all over England and Scotland, singing it in doggerel verse accompanied by ill-tuned lutes.

To Randolph's acute embarrassment, the Scottish court learned that Queen Elizabeth had been publicly pinched on the buttocks by Sir Robert Dudley,

> and none could find
> that she did mind.

A jury had pronounced Dudley innocent of murder when his wife, Amy Robsart, was found dead at the foot of a flight of stairs, but even months later,

> most people thought he had caused her death
> so that he could marry Eliz-a-beth.

When they were finished the court musicians resumed playing. Bothwell whispered something to Flamina. Abbie watched her dimple and smile, and the Queen turned her head away jealously, unable to watch any more. She listened to Chastelard prattling on about the Dudley scandal. Then she listened miserably to his love talk. So did Abbie.

'In all your life Your Majesty has never looked more beautiful,' he said. 'Always before you have had the beauty of springtime, of April buds, but tonight you are midsummer, as lush as an opened rose . . .'

Bothwell and Flamina were leaning towards each other now.

'Do forgive me, Pierre,' Mary said. 'I have important matters to discuss with Lord Bothwell. Will you ask him to come here beside me?'

Bothwell took Chastelard's seat. 'I was just coming to speak to you anyway,' he said. 'I beg your pardon, madam, but I really must take my leave of you now. I should have gone long ago.'

'You are still determined to leave tonight for the Borders?'

'I must, madam.'

'There is something you should know.' Abbie thought that Mary cast around desperately for some excuse to detain him. 'As soon as possible Queen Elizabeth and I will have a meeting, and it is likely to be somewhere on the Border.'

Bothwell's eyes gleamed. 'Wherever it is I shall be there to protect you,' he said. 'But now I must go. Lady Fleming proved quite irresistible. I could not tear myself away.'

'Oh . . .' said Mary. 'Then when shall I see you again?'

'As soon as possible,' he said, and bowed.

Moretta came to speak next. 'I should like to present my most talented musician to you, Your Majesty. He is a singer from Piedmont. May I ask him to perform for you now?'

'Of course,' Mary said, and called for silence again. Then she turned her back on the court and faced Abbie directly behind her, who saw all too clearly the disappointment she felt at Bothwell's treatment of her on her face. For once, the Queen had been thwarted. She sat gazing into the fire.

Lute strings were softly plucked and a deep velvet voice sang of a lover's loneliness, and soon tears were raining out of Mary's eyes. The last notes of the song died away, she brushed the tears from her face and turned to applaud.

He should have been big and deep-chested, to match his bass voice, but instead a small man – a very small man – was bowing to the court's applause. Mary beckoned to him and Abbie saw that his shoulders were hunched, his legs were too short for his body, his face was black-jowled and his lips were very thick. He looked like a goblin. He kneeled before the Queen and drew the hem of her skirt to his lips.

'Thank you,' she said, 'for the finest music I have heard since I left France.'

'Your Majesty does me great honour,' he said, and looked up at her with great luminous black eyes.

Abbie remembered that in just such a way Francis had

looked at Mary with his humble heart in his eyes. There was the same spaniel-soft expression, the same shy smile, the same poor, malformed body.

'Your name, sir?'

'David Riccio, Your Majesty.'

Mary was well aware that all her court were watching them in amazement. A musician was little better than a page or a servant, eating with the other servants in the kitchen and often doing the most menial tasks. She had three other singers who washed her windows, swept her carpets and tended her fires. But this man was different.

He was educated and intelligent. In that way he was different from Francis, too. He had a mind, the sophisticated mind of a European, and she had longed for conversation such as his, no matter how heavily accented his English. She broke into French, and as they laughed and joked together Abbie wondered if at last the Queen had found a soul mate.

At the same time Abbie was feeling the pangs of hunger. Everyone else had eaten, but she had not. She could see that Mary was enjoying herself. Her conversation with Riccio could go on for a long time, so she waited no longer to go down to the kitchen. Gaston, Mary's favourite chef, was in charge. He seated her and cut her a slice of the gilded goose.

'I haven't seen gilding before,' Abbie said.

'Oh, it is quite common in France now,' he said. 'The difficulty is to get someone who is an expert to do it, so I sent to Paris for Philippe. Look – he is over there, making the spun sugar for your tart.'

While she ate, Abbie watched Philippe spinning the sugar. He had boiled it until it was very hot, and now he was dipping his fork into it and waving it backwards and forwards over the tart in a fine mist.

'It looks easy,' Gaston smiled, 'but it is not, believe me.'

'What makes the sugar form a mist like that?' Abbie asked.

'It is the contact of the sugar with the air,' Gaston was explaining, when suddenly Philippe lunged out and cracked a little scullery boy over the head so that he fell to the stone floor, stunned and bleeding. 'I'm sorry you had to see that, Miss Abbie,' he added. 'Philippe may be talented, as he certainly is with herbs and flavourings as well as decorations, but he is also very hot-tempered.'

'And cruel,' Abbie frowned, and refused the fig tart.

When Abbie returned to the audience chamber to stand behind the Queen, she saw that Mary was still chatting to David Riccio. Fascinated, she had forgotten about the dancing, about her other guests, about the late hour, and impulsively she was asking him, 'Would you accept a permanent post here as musician after Conte Moretta leaves? I need a bass for my quartet.'

'It would be an honour, madam. Do I take it that you will not be going to Italy, then, to marry the Duke?'

'I was sure,' she whispered, 'when I saw his portrait,' and they both laughed again.

But, all the same, when she went to bed that night Mary detained Lady Fleming. 'Flamina,' she said, 'I noticed that Sir William was quite attentive. Are you melting our block of ice?'

'He is thawing,' Flamina smiled. 'I told him he has a fascinating mind. He agreed, so we have a lot in common.'

'You're a minx!'

'Eventually I hope to gain his confidence,' Flamina added, without a blush.

Abbie, who had never given up her practice of walking about the corridors silently when she had slept long enough, knew all about Sir William's visits in the night. She wondered how Flamina could lie like that and still keep a straight face. But, she supposed with a sigh, she would do the same for Donald.

'And Bothwell,' Mary said casually, removing the ruby earrings. 'Did you find him amusing?'

'I found him terrifying.'

'Why?'

'Women should be very wary of that man. He could make any woman follow him clear to Hell, but only he would come back again.'

All the ladies-in-waiting laughed at that, and when the Queen dismissed them Abbie thought that Flamina had summed up all her own feelings about Lord Bothwell.

She also thought that instead of toying with such an impossible man, Mary should be looking for someone more appropriate, someone she could marry. With all her heart Abbie wished that such a husband for the Queen would come soon, and put them all out of their various miseries.

THIRTY-SEVEN

In the far north of Scotland it was almost pitch dark by three o'clock in the afternoon, and at Strathbogie the Huntlys were plotting again.

'After all these years in the service of the Queen, Jean has brought us no nearer to our goal,' Lady Huntly fretted.

'I kept telling you she never could,' her husband replied coldly. 'Certainly, it has given us access to the palace, but I am becoming weary of the battle when the Queen forever tries to conciliate with the Protestants.'

'We sent a child of the wrong sex,' Lady Huntly continued along her own theme, 'although at the time it seemed the only way towards the throne.'

'And *that* was only thanks to Abbie McCracken,' Huntly said acidly.

Lady Huntly ignored this, and struggled on valiantly. 'Yes, Jean was of the wrong sex,' she said, driving it home again, 'but now, when they are all full-grown, our John is of the right sex. And so handsome, my lord! So dashing – just like you!'

'Yes?'

'Yes. So Jean may have been only paving the path for him all this time. We should think of something else for her, and send John to Holyrood instead, to beg for the Queen's hand in marriage. She will adore him. Anyone would.'

'Oh God ... and then he would be King of Scotland!' Huntly almost melted in his own sweat at the enormity, at the audacity of it all. 'Of course! It shall be done! Right away!'

Lady Huntly joined him at the window and watched a royal messenger galloping up with the Queen's appointment to her Privy Council for the Earl.

'It's all beginning to happen at last,' she whispered to her husband and then turned to the messenger. 'If you go to the barracks and ask for John McCracken, he will look after you.'

'My daughter, Abbie McCracken, is at Holyrood with Lady Jean Gordon,' John began, settling the messenger down with a large plate of cold meat, some bread and a mug of ale.

'I know them both,' the man said. 'Miss Abbie is Donald MacLaren's sweetheart, is she not?'

'Yes, and she will be wondering why, if you have managed to ride north, Donald hasn't managed to ride south to see her. Will you give her a message?'

'Of course.'

'You will have to be discreet, I'm afraid.'

'Part of the job,' the messenger grinned. 'Besides, one good turn deserves another. I'm enjoying this fine meal. Messengers are not treated like this everywhere, I can tell you! I'll be discreet, never fear.'

'Then explain to Abbie that Lord Huntly has got the wind up about the speed of the Protestant advance up here. He is sending the Gordons to remove the valuables from the abbeys all around, and bring them back to Strathbogie.'

'Is he, by God? Now, who would have thought of that?'

'Oh, Lady Huntly, no doubt! She's the brains behind the brawn here. But unfortunately for Donald, he is Huntly's blue-eyed boy at present. The Earl is putting him in charge of one expedition after another, as fast as the roads clear of snow.'

'Let me see if I've got the story right so far,' the messenger said and repeated it back to John.

'That's right. Warn Abbie also, that we'll all be off to

Sutherland again to fight another phase of the Earl's battle there when the weather eases. Donald is tied up here at the moment with all these duties, but he will be coming to Edinburgh as fast as he can.'

'Thank you for your hospitality, John McCracken,' the messenger said, pushing back his chair. 'Now, is that all?'

'Not quite all,' John smiled. 'Most importantly, give her our love as well.'

By now, Abbie was accustomed to interviewing tiresome applicants on the Queen's behalf. This one was a little different. Donald had taught her to ride alongside John Gordon. He might recognise her as Abbie McCracken. She was very apprehensive, forced to rely entirely on the face paints and the royal clothes to mask her.

Her heart was beating uncomfortably when John swaggered in merrily, confident that no woman, not even the Queen, could refuse him. Abbie could see that this was going to be as difficult as she had been dreading. She glanced up at Sir William, standing at her side, and saw that he understood perfectly.

John kneeled at her feet, and when he looked up she gazed into his cunning, drink-laden eyes. 'Your Majesty, I have come to plead my cause. I offer you my hand in marriage. Not only would you have me for a husband – although that must be tempting enough – but also there is the prospect of the great wealth and Catholic manpower of the northern territories,' he boasted in booming tones, so like his father's.

'My dear sir,' Abbie replied, 'I cannot accept your hand, nor any other. I am far from ready to marry again.'

'You must be! It is over a year since you were widowed, and we all know what widows are,' he sniggered. 'They long for the beauties of a man again.'

'You are impertinent, sir.'

'But above all, I am a *man*,' he said, grinning knowingly and clasping Abbie's hand in his hot sweaty paw.

'Take your hands off Her Royal Majesty,' Sir William

snapped, coming forward, while the guards bristled menac-
ingly. 'That is treason.'

'You had better go, sir,' Abbie said hastily.

'And, if you value your head, do not show it again in this
palace,' Sir William said grimly. 'It is only by Her Majesty's
grace that it still remains on your shoulders. Begone!'

John retreated, crestfallen, and Abbie slumped in the chair.
'It is getting more difficult, Sir William,' she said.

Recovering from the interview, Abbie did some heavy thinking. Just as she had decided that Queen Catherine was the
one to watch at the French court, she now decided that Queen
Mary was the one to watch at the Scottish court.

She lay on her bed and remembered when the dirges began
for the memorial requiem Mass for Francis, last December.
The Queen had been a widow for a year then, but still she
wept all the way through the service conducted by Bishop
Leslie of Ross in the Chapel Royal.

And Abbie had been thoroughly sick and tired of it, of the
drag of the long period of mourning. It was not that she
didn't respect Mary's feelings, she told herself angrily as she
had kneeled and bowed and prayed along with the rest of
the court – but there was something artificial about it, as if
it were only for show.

She became convinced of it remembering the evening Riccio's mellifluous voice hit the rafters, Mary's tears dried up
and her face became radiant with joy. Suddenly, the Queen
was a different person. It had been too sudden for Abbie's
liking.

Abbie's suspicions had been confirmed when within a week
Mary had cast off her widow's weeds, then ordered the black
hangings to be removed from the walls. Her thoughts were
further reinforced after eavesdropping on a conversation the
Queen had had with Riccio in the audience chamber, while
the two of them were poring over maps of Scotland.

'He hasn't been here five minutes,' Abbie muttered to Lady

Jean, 'yet look at him, asking who is the power in which part of Scotland.'

'Where are Lord Bothwell's lands? How far north are the Earl of Huntly's lands? And Crichton, that I hear you speaking so much about, what is it and where is it?' Riccio enquired.

'That is Crichton Castle,' Mary pointed to the Lothian region. 'It is one of Lord Bothwell's castles, where my brother John was married to Janet Hepburn, Lord Bothwell's sister. Why are you so interested, Davy?'

'I am interested in power, Your Majesty.'

'Did you hear that?' Abbie hissed in Jean's ear. 'First it was "David", now it is "Davy".'

'And he is interested in power,' Lady Jean whispered with a grave expression on her intelligent face. 'That's strange, for a musician.'

It *was* strange, Abbie agreed. Everything about the little man was strange, from his sunburst explosion into the Scottish court to his immediate rise to the top of it, like cream on milk. Didn't he have people of his own in Italy, that he leaped into Holyrood society without a backward glance? Mary's almost fanatical love of music was well-known all over Europe. Had all this been planned from afar? Was there something sinister?

Abbie's imagination, always vivid, was positively snowballing when Arthur Erskine, the Queen's equerry, suddenly appeared with Lord James in the doorway, with Sir William not far behind them, all wearing expressions of extreme alarm.

Mary excused herself from Riccio and went to them. 'What is amiss?'

'There has been a plot!' Lord James cried. 'Bothwell urged young Arran to kidnap you and take you to Dumbarton Castle – and to kill me!'

Mary sounded frightened. 'How do you know?' she quivered.

'Arran wrote it in a letter to Randolph, the English Ambassador.'

'Where is he now?'

'Arran is in his father's custody, and Bothwell is under house arrest at Crichton. They must be brought before the Privy Council, for treason.'

Two days later, Mary took her place at the head of the Privy Council and looked around six of her councillors already seated, Lord James, Sir William Maitland, and the Lords Morton, Huntly, Kirkcaldy and Erskine. They sat there looking glum, with every appearance of being at a funeral.

She could understand why, when the seventh, Lord Bothwell, was brought in to answer the charges of young Arran ... Arran, Mary sighed, of the House of Hamilton, the noblest blood in the land, second only to herself. 'James Hamilton, Earl of Arran,' she said, 'explain yourself.'

But Arran could not. He pointed a shaking finger at Bothwell and gibbered, frothing at the mouth. He jumped, he danced and finally ran to Mary's side. 'My wife!' they made out from his grunts.

'Yes,' Kirkcaldy said, 'he imagines himself to be the Queen's husband, and wanted me to flatten the four corners of his head so that he could get the crown on.'

'My wife! She is! She is!' Arran cried, and tried to paw her. The guards dragged him off.

'He's mad,' Bothwell said contemptuously. 'What am I doing here, answering the ravings of a lunatic?'

'Because,' Sir William said icily, 'even a lunatic has to have the seeds of an idea planted in his mind.'

'Not by me, they weren't,' Bothwell protested. 'Acquit me at once and let me go about my business.'

'We cannot acquit you,' Sir William said.

Mary could not believe her ears. 'Why not?' she asked, bewildered.

'To acquit Bothwell would be to convict Arran, making him a traitor, and traitors must die. How can Arran be put to death? He is clearly raving mad and in no position to defend the accusations. And his powerful family would publicly condemn his conviction.'

'Of course we cannot acquit Bothwell,' Lord James put in slyly. 'Here is a letter from Queen Elizabeth, pleading for him. Now, how did *she* get to know about this, unless Bothwell had been in league with Randolph? Oh, it has been a plot, all right! Treason, without doubt! And for that he must be thrown into Edinburgh Castle.'

'Edinburgh Castle?' Bothwell roared. '*Never*! Let me go!'

He reached for the sword the guards had removed from him before he entered the chamber. Mary had no doubt, when she saw his contorted face, that if it had still hung at his side he would have killed Arran and half her Privy Council there and then, and she jumped up, terrified of his glaring temper.

'Remove him!' she cried. 'He is becoming as mad as Arran!'

'You cannot see the wood for the trees!' Bothwell shouted at her. 'Lord James is lying! You cannot see that he is your bitterest enemy! Where will you be, without anyone to help you, when I am in prison?'

'Where indeed?' Lord Huntly roared, glaring all around and then fixing his furious eyes on the Queen. 'There is no justice here – none at all! I will not stay here and be party to such corruption!'

He stamped out behind Bothwell and the guards, and Mary collapsed back into her chair. 'This has been incredible!' she said.

Lord James exchanged a superior smile with Sir William. 'I shall send a message immediately to Edinburgh Castle with orders to prepare cells for both Bothwell and Arran, and a strong force to escort them there,' he said.

Mary was sorely tempted to slap his sneering mouth. Yes, she thought, you will be rid of Bothwell for years, rid of my only defender, my only friend. As my mother wrote in her last letter to me, 'Trust Bothwell.' And now I see that sooner or later you will get rid of me, too, unless I *appear* to conform to your rule – for despite your fair words, you consider your-self the King of Scotland.

'You plan to hold them indefinitely?' she asked.

'Until Arran recovers and Bothwell confesses,' James snig-gered, for both were impossible.

And Edinburgh Castle was a living death. It had always horrified her, mean-roomed, iron-barred, and so high up. She knew that in over five hundred years of its history only one man had ever escaped.

In bed that night she lay sleepless, wondering if she could get a letter to Bothwell, assuring him of her secret support. She would miss his guidance through the darkness ahead, for he was more than a watchdog for the Borders. He was the one strong thread in the rotting tapestry of treachery that was her kingdom. Lord James, Elizabeth I and John Knox manoeuvred Scotland cynically. The Border lairds knifed its weakest spots. God alone knew what would happen without Bothwell there to keep order.

And worse, far worse, Lord Huntly was straining at the seams, setting up a northern Catholic hierarchy with himself and his sons as rulers.

Something would have to be done about Huntly, and soon.

Mary was tired, tired and weary in her spirits. She longed for some small release from the feuding and politics, some merrymaking, some love ... One evening, after they had danced the Skip, the Fling and the Canary over and over again Mary was more bored than ever, and taking Chastelard's arm went out into the picture gallery to sit in the window seat and admire the moon.

They sat down and she said, 'I wish I could get away from here *now*.'

'And where would you like to go?'

'Anywhere.'

She thought it best not to mention Spain, not yet, and the fact that she was contemplating Don Carlos of Spain for want of a better suitor – for who could tell? Perhaps in another year she may be shedding this grubby kingdom of Scotland for an empire.

'If only I could take you back to France with me,' Chastelard said.

'Oh, Pierre! You are returning?'

'I may as well. I have failed to reach your heart.'

'But you know I must marry for power, Pierre.'

'You could have love, for all of my life.'

'I cannot be too careful, in my position. Even if it were not sinful, I –'

'Even if it were,' Chastelard said, drawing her into his arms.

She welcomed his kiss with her head tipped back and her eyes closed. She could even see in her mind's eye what a pretty picture they made.

'It is best that you return to France,' she said.

'That is because you love someone else,' he said sulkily.

'No,' she said. 'Nobody. And I must go back to the dancing now.'

But the dancing was twice as wearisome when she went back. Shortly after midnight the party dispersed and Mary retired to her bedchamber.

Livingston removed the Queen's gown and petticoats and Abbie drew the bed curtains. When she turned back, Mary was slipping out of her shift and turning to take her night-gown from Livingston. Then, over Livingston's shoulder, Abbie saw a closet door suddenly opening, and she gasped as Chastelard emerged.

Clutching the nightgown to her nakedness Mary stared at him, too stunned to move. Livingston ran into the corridor, screaming. Abbie rushed to the Queen and tried to drag her to the door, but Chastelard pushed her aside and caught Mary in his arms, throwing the nightgown to the floor. She struggled fiercely as he kissed her mouth, her shoulders and her throat. She tried to reach the dagger at his belt, but he twisted her arm behind her and with his other hand held off Abbie.

At last they heard shouting in the corridor and there was a rush of men through the doorway. Lord James seized Chastelard, smashed his fist against the Frenchman's jaw and sent him sprawling. Standing over him Lord James unsheathed his dagger.

'No!' Mary screamed. 'Please, let us settle this some other way!'

She made to dart between Lord James and Chastelard. Abbie threw a blanket around her, but by that time at least fifteen people crowding into the bedchamber had seen the Queen naked – and with a man . . .

Lord James kicked Chastelard savagely. 'Explain yourself! What are you doing in the Queen's bedchamber?'

'I, also, demand an explanation,' Mary said.

'Do you deny that you asked me in the gallery tonight to hide in the closet until your ladies left?' Chastelard demanded. 'Only *this time* I came out too soon.'

'*This time?*' She staggered back.

'Your Majesty prefers to forget the other times?'

'Have you lost your mind, Pierre? If you persist with these lies you will lose your life. Confess, and I will send you back to France unharmed.'

'Never!'

Shocked as she was, Abbie was more shocked still to see the fanatical hatred in his eyes. What would happen to the Queen now as a result of all this? John Knox would revel in spreading a tale of scandal throughout Britain. Queen Elizabeth would gloat and gossip over it. Only if Chastelard confessed would Mary be absolved of blame. But would he confess? No, Abbie did not think so, because someone else was behind him, but who that was she could not imagine.

'He must be executed, Your Majesty,' Lord James said, 'or else everyone will say you were lovers.'

A week later in St Andrews, Chastelard followed a Protestant minister up the black-draped steps of the scaffold.

'*Please* don't let this happen,' Mary whispered, so that

only Livingston and Abbie heard her. 'Please, God, let him confess . . .'

But Chastelard did not look at her. He bowed his head and said, 'May God forgive me as I forgive my enemies. I die a loyal subject, faithful unto death to my Queen.' Only then did he look up at Mary directly, and added, 'Queen Catherine of France.'

So he was Queen Catherine's spy, sent to Scotland to disgrace its Queen! Abbie sagged, almost fainting.

Suddenly Chastelard shouted and pointed straight at Queen Mary.

'Cruel mistress!' were his last words before his head rolled.

'*Mistress!*' hissed the crowd behind them, and when Abbie turned to help Mary away, she saw speculation, condemnation and contempt written on every face.

Abbie felt sick. The enemies of Mary, Queen of Scots were crawling out of the very woodwork, and not only in her own country. They came from overseas as well. She shuddered from head to foot at the thought of Queen Catherine's tentacles of evil reaching out over hundreds of miles, over land and sea, and she hadn't finished squeezing Mary's neck yet.

Worst of all, nothing and nobody could make Mary see all the dangers that surrounded her. She was determined to dance on down her primrose path to Hell, without any thought for those whose chance of a happy life elsewhere depended on her.

THIRTY-EIGHT

After this horror, Mary took to her bed again. The Scottish court were used to it, and depression settled over Holyrood like a black cloud, while outside the snow lay stubborn, not sparkling white any more, but dirty shades of grey and brown to add to the general misery.

Abbie was sad and weary, waiting for Donald who never came. She knew perfectly well that he would be walled in by snow in the far north, but still she fretted impatiently while she fetched and carried for the Queen, and flattened herself against the door when Lord James and Sir William brushed past her to Mary's bedside.

'Bothwell has escaped,' Lord James came to the point immediately.

'What?' cried Mary, with a quickly suppressed smile at the corners of her mouth. 'Escaped from Edinburgh Castle? I thought nobody could.'

'Well, *he* has,' Lord James glared, and Abbie had a picture in her mind's eye of Bothwell recklessly swinging out over the edge of that vast rock, preferring to die rather than be caged any longer like an animal. 'He burst the bars of his cell. God knows where he may be by now, but I have men posted all around the city.'

They trooped out. Mary demanded a hot bath and her perfumed oils. Then, dressed in a golden gown, she gathered her court around her. 'Oh, my dears, we must cast off gloom and be merry again! Who will show me just one sign of spring? One sign, and we shall have a revel, the best party ever!'

Rain came first, laying down the wind and washing the snow away. Then came blinks of sunshine when everyone watched for the first blades of the daffodils to show. All except Abbie, who watched the north road for Donald.

After his spectacular escape from Edinburgh Castle James Hepburn, Lord Bothwell, had been in hiding in France. Adventurer or not, he was an educated man with many friends in high places in Paris. While he was there gleaning the news and absorbing the political climate, he also took the opportunity of visiting his erstwhile ladies of the night along with some new ones in the brothels of his acquaintance.

At the same time, he was closely observing Queen Mary's two uncles, the Cardinal of Lorraine and his brother, the soldier Duc de Guise. Between them they were slaughtering the Huguenots left, right and centre. *That* would not go down well with the Protestant Queen of England, and it would do the blossoming friendship between her and the Scottish Queen no good at all – if friendship it was. Bothwell did not trust it to be so. All in all there was no doubt about it: Mary, Queen of Scots, needed his advice and guidance.

It was time to go back to Scotland and put his plans into action, and the minute his spies told him that they had secured his safe sea-passage and a protected route back to Hermitage Castle, he was off.

By the most extraordinary stroke of luck, or by chance, or by Fate, or by the decree of God he had run into an English courier on his way, and invited him to stay the night at Hermitage to break the long journey to Holyrood. He spared nothing on the feast for his new friend, even less on the drink, and before midnight the Englishman had been carried toes up to the most comfortable bed that Hermitage could boast.

Then Bothwell found the key and unlocked the man's dispatch bag. Inside he found a letter to Lord James, promising English soldiers at Kershopefoot 'to assist him in the venture.'

It was unsigned and marked Private and Confidential. Bothwell smiled at that and laughed outright to have discovered the plot.

The letter from Queen Elizabeth to Queen Mary was of little account. In fact, it was cool, which did not surprise Bothwell after seeing the cruelty of the de Guise family to the French Protestants, and did not refer to any future meeting. It could be added to without any trouble. The main difficulty would be her signature, squiggly, flowery and absolutely individual. Who could copy *that*? But, being Bothwell, he had supreme confidence in himself as he removed his doublet, rolled up his shirt sleeves and settled down to a long night with his quill. I'll beat the bastard thing, he promised himself.

It had taken the first half-hour even to slit the red waxed seal in such a way that it could be joined again unobtrusively. It had taken him the rest of the night to complete – in his opinion – a perfect jewel of forgery. Mary, Queen of Scots was a long, thin, silly young girl, a queen in dire need of a husband ... Kings, princes and nobles from all over Europe were clamouring to do her the favour. Not for love, nor even lust, of course, but to become the King of Scotland.

Bothwell sat back in the dawning, his quill at rest, the great seal resealed, in the sure and certain conviction that he was the only man for the job. Already the young Queen fancied him, and him alone. She wanted his body. Women did. It was a fact of life.

Because of her neat and almost invisible stitches, the task of making a collection of fine undergarments to be worn next to the English Queen's delicate skin fell to Abbie. Mary had brought exquisite linens, silks and lace from France, and Abbie was instructed to make a petticoat and a shift. These she must embroider with the English rose and the Scottish thistle, to match the drawers Mary had already sent.

'Elizabeth will be pleased,' Mary smiled. 'By all accounts she did not hesitate to show those drawers to her courtiers – while she was wearing them! Sir William says her coarse tongue and shocking behaviour cause her ladies to wilt.'

Relieved to be excused from the preparations for the revel, Abbie worked quietly on. Her spirits were too low to join in when the Marys practised the *chansons champêtres*, or pretend to laugh at the very explicit sexual gestures used by the Queen's female jesters. She was glad to retire to a corner with her sewing and dream of Donald instead.

The Queen's excitement rose as the weather improved, and kept on improving right up to the date set for the revel. Evening came, the good weather held, and such a crowd of guests had been invited that they could not be accommodated within the palace.

'Open the gates!' Mary cried. '*Au jardin – au jardin!*'

The dancers clung, laughing, to the waist of the one in front to make a great winding human chain spilling out into the gardens, where small torches hanging on the walls marked the boundaries. In the twilight when the first stars rose into the sky the ladies looked like moths in their fluttering dresses, and the night breeze blew the courtiers' velvet and satin cloaks apart like strange, exotic wings.

A small crowd of Edinburgh folk, encouraged by the open gates, ventured in to join in the dancing and the kissing games. The only pause in the revelry was when everyone had to stand back to allow a messenger access to the door of the palace. He sat motionless astride his small, shaggy horse, but something in the very lines of both horse and rider suggested that they were capable of great speed.

'A message for the Queen,' he said, waving a letter between the forefinger and thumb of his right hand, and everyone saw that the other three fingers were missing. With his left hand he held his bridle.

Lord James stepped forward to take the letter.

'I'm sorry, my lord,' said the messenger. 'It is for the Queen alone.'

Lord James stepped back. He did not attempt to argue with such a man, and Abbie stared at the rider. Not in uniform, although she knew in her bones that he *was* a soldier and a rough, tough one at that, he made her feel uneasy. When the Gordons knew they were going to war they wore a mail-coat which they called a jack. This man's jack was of stout quilted leather, sewn with plates of horn for added protection against cuts or thrusts, and so of course, much lighter. This man was a mercenary, she decided, and his watchword was speed.

The Queen took the letter and almost sobbing with excitement, ran inside. The messenger turned his wiry little horse in the space it had occupied, and was galloping off again. It was all done in a flash, in the twinkling of an eye, and it left Abbie thinking that she had just seen one of the most dangerous men of her life.

The incident marked the end of the revel. The guards showed the uninvited guests the way out, and locked the gates behind them. The dancing and the singing continued inside, but the Queen did not join in again. Half an hour later she sent for Lord James and Sir William.

'Queen Elizabeth wants us to meet almost immediately,' she said, her eyes shining. 'In ten days, in fact. She will be in Carlisle and our meeting will be somewhere on the Border. She will send word later as to the exact time of day and the place.'

The two men stared at her. Sir William said, 'But, Majesty, the English Queen would never go on a progress so early in the year! She does not attend her various Courts of Justice until June at the earliest, just as you will do.'

'Let me see that letter!' Lord James snatched it from her hand. 'It is certainly her signature,' he said doubtfully, after studying it minutely. He passed it over to Sir William. 'No one else could sign "Elizabeth" like that, with all its frills and furbelows.'

'It must be genuine,' Sir William agreed.

'Of course it is genuine,' Mary laughed. 'It is wonderful!'

During the three days following, Mary behaved like a small, excited child. She consulted her mirror a dozen times a day, exclaimed anxiously over her hair or over an imagined blemish on that flawless skin of hers. She frowned and sighed and hoped that she would not have any of her tiresome fainting fits. She hoped that she might look her very best, so that her 'dear sister' would love her all the more.

Her ladies shook their heads at such innocence, and behind her back Fleming whispered, 'Does she not understand that her legendary beauty is what makes Elizabeth resent her most?'

Livingston sighed. 'She has changed her mind twenty times this morning about which gown she will wear for this meeting. Please come with me, Abbie, until she finally decides.'

The Queen was trying on the dove-grey velvet riding costume again, and darting questions at them as to whether her gifts for the English Queen were safely packed.

'Did you remember the diamond earrings? The necklace of Scottish pearls?'

'Yes, madam.'

'I do not recall seeing them.'

'They are in your velvet casket.'

Mary frowned and bit her lip. 'I am not sure I put them in.'

Exchanging an exhausted look with Abbie, Livingston fetched the casket and showed Mary the jewels. When she was satisfied that they were there after all, she turned to Abbie.

'And now, Abbie, which gown shall I wear for this meeting? Shall it be the purple velvet here? Or the black? You may decide, for none of the rest of us can.'

'It is an informal meeting, madam. You do not want to look too regal, so perhaps not the purple nor the black. That beautiful claret gown, with its lighter underskirt was always most becoming to Your Majesty.'

'Of course, you are right! And its skirt is less extravagant, should we walk. It would not become entangled with the briars.'

'Perhaps the dove-grey you are wearing at the moment would be more suitable still,' Abbie ventured.

'Oh no!' Mary frowned. 'It is too masculine by far.'

*　*　*

311

A few days before the meeting excitement rose to fever pitch in Holyrood. Unfortunately, so did Beaton's temperature, and she had to go to bed with a strange, sweating fever. It was not cholera, and it was not typhus, which they all knew. This was something new and, greatly worried, the Queen brought Dr Bourgoing to Beaton's bedside.

'I'm afraid that when you opened your gates to all and sundry at the revel, Your Majesty, you also welcomed in the "New Acquaintance" as the people of Edinburgh call it so quaintly. This new influence is rife in the city,' he said, shaking his head.

'Ah,' said Riccio who was also standing by. 'You mean *la influenza*? It was rife in Italy also before I left – but I did not bring it here!'

Lord James looked at him with the utmost dislike. 'No?' he said frostily. 'Who else, then?'

'Gentlemen, gentlemen,' Dr Bourgoing intervened, 'it is another pestilence spread by the wind blowing over the putrid odours of the middens, and carried by filthy flies. I have always advocated the use of flypapers, as you well know, Your Majesty.'

'But will she get better?' Mary cried.

'She is young, and strong, and well-fed, so she should get better in about a week, although she will be left feeling very weak. In the meantime allow only one lady to look after her, so as to contain the illness.'

'I will look after her,' Seton volunteered calmly. 'The rest of you – stay away.'

In the frantic activity of the short time left now before the Queen's departure, Abbie sewed from dawn to dusk, putting the last stitches into Her Majesty's gifts. Her task was almost at an end, and she did not envy Lady Jean and the Marys when the Queen's moods no longer varied from day to day, but from hour to hour. Tempers flared, and the ladies looked exhausted, especially Seton, who had rejoined them now that Beaton was recovering.

Mary looked at her sharply. 'Are you well enough, Seton?'

'It is just a sudden pain in my head, madam. It will go away.'

But it didn't go away. It got worse, and Seton was the next one to take to her bed, sweating and sick.

'I'll nurse her,' Lady Jean said and although Abbie was not surprised at that, for Lady Jean and Seton were close friends, both serious-minded, religious and gentle, she missed Jean sorely, more than she would have imagined.

But in a way, she was glad of this new alliance for Jean's sake. She and Seton drew and then painted patterns, and afterwards copied them in their embroidery. It occupied Jean's mind, Abbie sighed, while she herself was busy helping the Queen.

On the evening before the departure the Queen ordered an early bedtime for everyone. She summoned Riccio to her private apartments. She had discovered that he made a far better secretary than the one she had, and there were some pieces of business still outstanding to be cleared up.

'Come and help me, Davy,' she said. 'If we can get through this very quickly you may still play and sing a little to me, and soothe me to bed.'

But it wasn't long before she threw down her quill. '*Mon Dieu*! Such a headache! I feel quite dizzy . . . I shall lie down now for a minute or two.'

Five minutes later her coughing worried Riccio enough for him to peep in at her. She was burning up with the fever, and he sent for the doctor.

'Yes, yes,' Dr Bourgoing sighed. 'This is what you get for too many kissing games. You always were too free with your kisses, madam! And that is how the pestilence spreads from one person to another.'

'Nonsense!' Mary spluttered. 'I haven't got the New Acquaintance. I shall be as right as rain in the morning.'

Although the palace was very quiet that night, for a change, Abbie could not sleep. The bedchamber she shared with Lady Jean seemed eerily empty without her and her little sighs, her soft snores and snuffles. Except for a very short time in

313

France, they had always slept together, and now Abbie wondered if she would ever get to sleep without her. She had hardly closed her eyes when Flamina was standing over her, shaking her gently.

'Wake up! And get dressed – quickly! You are wanted.'

Reluctantly, Abbie followed Flamina along the corridors until they came to the antechamber, guarded as usual. When the guards saw them, they let them in. Lord James and Sir William blocked the way, their faces very serious.

'The Queen cannot go to the meeting with Queen Elizabeth,' Sir William said. 'This morning she cannot even stand.'

'Nevertheless the meeting must go on as arranged,' Lord James said, 'or else Queen Elizabeth will take the gravest offence. She will be our Queen's enemy for all time.'

'The whole course of British history depends on it,' Sir William agreed.

A horrible silence fell. The ticking of Mary's little musical clock on the mantelpiece seemed as loud as the ponderous ticking of a grandfather clock, and the hairs stood up on Abbie's neck.

The awful time had come.

'It is very fortunate that you were so well trained, and are so experienced in taking Her Majesty's place in an emergency,' Sir William went on inexorably.

'How could I speak to the Queen of England?' Abbie cried.

'The same way as you spoke to Queen Catherine of France and to the Queen of Scotland, I imagine,' Sir William was icy. 'All you have to do is pass the time of day. Let Elizabeth do all the talking. Believe me, she likes to talk. And if the worst comes to the worst you could always cough a lot and point to your throat.'

'Oh, Abbie – *please*! Please help our little Queen!' Flamina begged tearfully. 'She's so very ill . . .'

Abbie looked down at the carpet. There was no getting out of the plan, but what worried her most was the thought of Donald arriving at last, and she might not be there.

'How long will it take?' she asked.

'Two days. Three at the most. It has been arranged for the Queen to sleep tonight at Melrose, and go on refreshed to meet Elizabeth tomorrow. The meeting is at the bridge at Kershopefoot, at three o'clock. You may even be back here tomorrow night if you are not too tired.'

Abbie groaned inside herself. She had to steel herself even to reply. 'Very well,' she said.

'First, Abigail McCracken, you must take the oath,' Sir William said so coldly and formally that once again shivers of fear ran down Abbie's spine. 'This is a state secret. Nobody must ever know of the impersonation on pain of death. Do you understand?'

'Yes, sir.'

'As it is, only four people in the whole world know about it, apart from the Queen herself, and we are gathered here – Lord James, Lady Fleming and you and I. Now, put your hand on this Bible and repeat after me . . .'

Yes, Lord James as well, now. Abbie almost laughed. And no doubt everyone else in Holyrood knew about this as well, if not the half of Edinburgh. But she took the vow of secrecy. She did so under duress, and all the time she clung on to her last line of defence thinking, Ah, yes, but there is one other person in the world who will realise the truth if anything happens to me on this harebrained venture.

Donald MacLaren.

THIRTY-NINE

It still was not quite daylight when Abbie sat down with the claret gown and took up another hem by candlelight. She used huge tacking stitches, and she sewed desperately, as fast as she could. Lord James had been speaking about carrying her out to the white palfrey to disguise the fact that the gown was ten inches too long, and she wasn't going to allow that whatever happened.

It was not a large retinue that rode out of the palace, clattering across the drawbridge when daylight came in. It might have been a rich merchant's party, riding out to his country house. It would not excite curiosity, especially as they all wore black hooded cloaks to cover the finery of the courtiers and the uniforms and the weapons of the soldiers, and Abbie herself also wore a mask.

By mid-morning they were making good time, galloping briskly towards Crichton Castle. If she could deceive the Queen's newly wed half-brother, Lord John Stewart, who was in charge of Crichton meantime, she could deceive anybody, Abbie told herself grimly. That would be an important test to pass.

Lord James did not allow anyone to dismount. It was not in his interests to allow anyone to see how tall Abbie was standing on the ground. But he did allow some swift refreshments and a stirrup cup before they continued on the long haul to Galashiels.

Unused to long hours riding over harsh moorland, saddle-sore and weary, Abbie was delighted to see the towering ruins of Melrose Abbey coming into view. There, in the Abbey House they would rest overnight. After all, the Abbot was another half-brother to the Queen and Lord James, another of prolific King Jamie's illegitimate offspring. As they approached Melrose, Abbie dwelled on how strange it was that she was yet another of those illegitimate children herself, although nobody except Donald had ever discussed it with her.

'No,' Lord James broke into her thoughts, and turned his face away from the Abbey House. 'I will not stay here. We will ride on to Jedburgh.'

Of course he wouldn't stay in an abbey of all places! A faithful follower of John Knox in a holy Catholic place? Lord James was an inconsiderate, self-centred bully, Abbie thought indignantly, for by this time she was becoming very uncomfortable after the long ride with no stops for comfort.

'Is it far, still?' she asked in the Queen's high-pitched voice.

Lord James didn't answer her, and she leaned towards the man who had been riding on her left all this time.

'Not far now, Your Majesty,' he bowed from the saddle.

She saw that he was one of the Scottish Guard although he must be a new addition, because she had never seen him before. At least, she *thought* she had never seen him before . . . yet his face was vaguely familiar.

'You are an Edinburgh man?' she asked him.

'No, madam. A Huntly man.'

'A Gordon?' Abbie asked with a wildly beating heart.

'Yes, a Gordon,' he smiled.

'Your name, sir?'

'George Brand, madam.'

Geordie Brand! Her father's friend! No wonder he had seemed familiar, although it was years since she had seen him. But he had not recognised her. She longed to tell him who she was, to talk with him, to ask him for news of Donald and her family at Huntly, but Lord James was frowning across at them and she didn't dare.

In an inn at Jedburgh Abbie could attend to herself at last.

317

She washed and changed her petticoats and dined wearily on cock-a-leekie soup and fresh-caught trout baked with herbs before she climbed the stairs to bed.

An owl called after her mournfully and she shuddered at this omen of disaster, but she was asleep almost before she fell into her warm, soft bed to sleep the sleep of the utterly exhausted.

It was half-past two in the afternoon when the royal party, led by Lord James, stared down at last over open moorland to a stream winding its way into a small wood.

'On this side of that river we are still in Scotland,' he said. 'On the other side, it is England.'

It was a perfect meeting place for the two Queens, Abbie thought – quiet, secluded, but still in open country. The drizzle of rain had stopped and the sky had cleared so that she could see for miles across fields bare of trees or even bushes, except for those which lined the little river.

'The bridge is hidden amongst those trees,' Lord James told her. 'When you meet the English Queen no one will see you. You will be private.'

They rode on down the track towards the stream. In the silence they could hear it rushing along, tinkling over its bed of pebbles. From the other side of the hill a horn sounding once, and then twice, blasted the air and Lord James became very excited.

'There they are,' he said, and Abbie saw a group of horsemen with a litter in their midst rounding the hilltop and beginning their descent towards them. 'Queen Elizabeth is here to meet you.'

Abbie moved forward, seated on the Queen's white horse, determined to play her part to the best of her ability. When the English saw her they cheered. She held her reins proudly and held her head high as the Queen would have done, acknowledging their greeting. For one dazzling moment she knew how it must feel to really *be* the Queen, before she decided she would rather be herself, after all.

The track narrowed and Lord James, his face expression-less, dismounted and led the white palfrey by its leading rein. Its hooves kicked up last year's fallen leaves, and Abbie shivered at their acrid smell of decay. For an instant she thought of those ill-fated Stewart kings, prone to sudden violent death. Some of that same blood beat in her veins, too. She stared over Lord James's shoulders, her scalp prick-ling with fear, telling her that something was terribly wrong.

It was too still, too quiet, like the calm before a storm. But a minute later they caught sight of the bridge, an empty, innocent little bridge, just waiting. Lord James was also wait-ing, leading her horse round and round in circles on the Scottish side.

Suddenly he stumbled and gave a cry. Abbie saw him sprawling, helpless and cursing on the carpet of leaves. The white horse whinnied, scenting danger, and immediately it seemed all hell was let loose.

The English soldiers threw aside the empty litter and rushed across the bridge. From behind every tree and bush rough Bordermen wearing steel bonnets appeared and made a ring around Abbie, their swords drawn. Daunted, the English picked up Lord James instead, threw him across a horse and carried him away. At a word from their leader the Borderers gave chase, while he, wrapped in a cloak with a hood so deep that she couldn't see his face, seized Abbie's bridle and galloped her away.

She screamed and screamed and looked all around her in terror. Then, right behind her she saw Geordie Brand, the only man of the Scottish Guard who hadn't fled, still faithfully following. She stopped screaming and smiled at him briefly. With Geordie Brand still there she might have a chance – of something . . . That hope was swiftly dashed by a voice out of the deep hood.

'Queen Elizabeth never left London, Your Majesty, angry because of the cruelty of the de Guise family towards the Huguenots. She, and the Protestants, grow weary and impatient to be rid of you. This was all a plot between her and Lord James to capture you! But I have you, instead.'

The hood was thrown back, and Abbie saw to her horror that the voice was coming out of the lips of the apelike Lord Bothwell.

Oh God! There was no hope for her now . . .

FORTY

At last Donald set off from Strathbogie with another horse
tied on behind laden with rolls of sheepskins and bags of
woollen garments of every shape and size.

Abigail had shown him the warm, finely knitted shifts to
be worn under silken gowns, knitted petticoats, sheepskin
insoles for little slippers, gloves, shawls, thick cloaks, rugs
and blankets.

'Can you think of anything else?' she had asked anxiously,
and he had laughed and waved at her as he left the Gardeners'
Cottage. He had been away for so long that the warm things
would hardly be needed now.

In only hours now, he and Abbie would be together, and
the sheer happiness of the thought spurred him on his way.
He arrived at Holyrood at eight o'clock in the morning to
find the palace with a doleful air about it, strangely empty
of the people usually going about. Nobody came to give him
a hand when he toiled up and down the staircase with his
bundles to the room Abbie shared with Lady Jean, and neither
of them had appeared by the time he had piled the last bundles
on top of Queen Catherine's boxes in the corner.

The doors of the Marys' bedchambers were tight shut, and
there wasn't a sound from any of them. The corridors were
deserted. Mystified, he climbed the next stair to the Queen's
apartments, entered the antechamber unchallenged and had
progressed halfway across the audience chamber when he
heard a voice, light, scratchy and querulous, but undoubtedly
Mary's coming from her bedchamber.

Lady Fleming hushed it at once. '*Please*, Your Majesty! Your throat is too sore to speak! Take this posset to soothe it, and remember – no one must know that you are here, and not on the Border!'

'Oh, Flamina! I *should* be at Kershopefoot to meet my dear sister,' the Queen half croaked and half squeaked. 'What will happen if she finds out that I have not gone after all? Worse still, that I have sent someone to pretend to be me?'

Worse still, she fretted inwardly so that her temperature shot up, what would happen when Bothwell found out she hadn't kept what she just *knew* was to be a romantic assignment at the same time?

It didn't cross her mind to wonder what would happen to Abbie as the result.

'Oh, *sh*! SH!' Fleming tried to stop her speaking.

'I am not sure that Abbie McCracken will manage the deception . . .'

'Let me close this door.' Flamina shut it with a bang.

But Donald had crept out anyway. Down in the courtyard he met Alex Ogilvie walking with another Scottish courtier whom Donald recognised as Sir Patrick Spence. The old friends greeted each other warmly.

Then: 'The Queen has gone?' Donald asked.

'It was a sudden call to meet Elizabeth in the Borders.'

'Where in the Borders, Alex?'

'Some place called Kershopefoot. I've never heard of it, myself. Have you, Pat?'

'Of course I have,' Sir Pat said. 'It's near to my own territory, a ride of three hours from Jedburgh.'

Donald thanked them and without another thought leaped on his horse again, this time with terrible forebodings instead of the happy expectancy he had felt all the way from Strathbogie down to Edinburgh. Once again he was in unfamiliar territory. He had never ridden so far south in his life before, but the terrain was easier and faster than the Highlands had been, and there were more people going about if he had to ask the way.

He stopped only once, at an inn that looked hospitable at Jedburgh. There he changed his horse for a fresh one, agreeing that he would change it back again on the return journey, and called for food and drink.

'This is the best that I could do at such short notice,' the landlady dashed in and put a ham omelette in front of him.

'It smells wonderful,' Donald assured her, and a minute later, 'it *is* wonderful!'

'It's what I gave a very important party for their breakfast earlier,' she sighed proudly, lingering to discuss her omelette. 'They liked it.'

'How much earlier?'

'Oh . . . let me see. Perhaps two hours ago?'

'Can you direct me to a place called Kershopefoot, madam?'

'That's funny! That's where they were going, too! My husband gave them directions. I'll go and fetch him.'

Donald arrived above the bridge at Kershopefoot in time to witness the uproar. From the hill above where Abbie had ridden so recently he saw the battle for himself, and Lord James, obviously in league with the English, being spirited away with the rough Borderers in hot pursuit.

And worst of all, he saw Abbie with Bothwell's grinning face towards her as they galloped swiftly away. From where he was, Donald could not see that Bothwell held her reins. All he knew was that Bothwell's reputation was such, that he would go with any woman, and many women were only too anxious to go with him. During his long enforced separation from her, Abbie must have been ensnared by Bothwell's charms. He saw her face smiling back at Geordie Brand.

Jesus Christ! Even Geordie Brand had betrayed him!

For a long time, long after the noise of battle, long after the noise of pounding hooves had faded away, Donald sat there with the tears pouring down his face . . . Then he wheeled his horse about and headed back like a wounded animal to the only refuge he knew, the Gordon barracks at Strathbogie Castle.

Leading Abbie's bridle rein, Bothwell rode on and on until the lonely hills all around stood blackly against the sky, and there was only a blink of sunshine left. Here narrow streams cut into the hills to make deep hollows, natural hiding places for stolen cattle.

'The beef-tubs,' Bothwell grinned and rode carefully through the dead heathland with its writhing skeletons of dead roots, and the gleaming treachery of emerald bogs surrounding a dark, deep lake. 'Hermitage Water, Your Majesty,' he said, 'and those are the Druid Stones where long ago Lord de Soulis sacrificed people to the Devil. Later, he was boiled alive in a great cauldron – but look! Over there is Hermitage Castle!'

In such a sinister place, Hermitage must be the most sinister-looking castle ever built, Abbie thought, staring up at the huge, granite fortress with its large square towers projecting at its four angles, its tiny window-slits high up watching her like evil eyes, and its massive stone archway leading in to the cobbled courtyard. Once inside these powerful walls she would never get out, just as now in Bothwell's powerful arms she would never get away.

He swept her off her horse and carried her inside and up the narrow stone staircase as easily as a piece of paper. Halfway up, knowing she didn't stand a chance against the brute strength of the man, she fell silent in the grip of icy terror.

But somehow she forced her frozen brain to work, to reason. He would not abduct Abbie McCracken, only a serving girl whom he had probably never looked at twice. He seriously thought he had carried off the Queen, already attracted to him as Abbie had witnessed. Therefore the charade must go on.

She did not lift her veil nor remove her mask when he sat her down on a wooden settle. She merely waved her gloved hands about as Mary always did, and uttered little squeaks in French.

Bothwell stood in front of her, legs apart, triumphant. 'This is what you wanted, madam,' he said, 'and now you've got it! You've got me, and we are alone at last!'

Now Abbie's hands were fluttering agitatedly. '*Je suis malade*,' she kept saying, and then in case he hadn't understood her imperfect French she added, 'Oh, I am so ill, so ill,' for good measure.

'Ill? How can you think of illness at a time like this?' he was saying when Abbie leaned forward suddenly, and under her veil so that he couldn't see what she was doing, stuck her fingers down her throat. 'This is the most important moment of our –'

'Ugh . . .' Abbie vomited all over his right leg. 'Ugh . . .' This time she aimed at his left leg, and he leaped back.

'My God, you really *are* ill!'

'The New Acquaintance,' she gasped. 'The terrible fever . . .' She coughed from the bottom of her lungs. 'My lord, I fear I may have passed it on to you in my splashes,' she shuddered and gazed pointedly at his boots before she fell back moaning on the settle. 'I am burning, burning . . .'

Through her veil she saw that he was furiously angry. He looked down at his soiled boots and breeches and stamped out without another word. If he had only known it, Abbie had just made the greatest sacrifice of her life for Scotland. The one thing she hated more than anything else was to be sick – and she had actually induced it! Her mother used to say on the rare occasions when Abbie was sick as a child that her face went positively green.

It felt green now, and cold and wet with sweat while she agonised in case Bothwell came back. She heard his feet tramping back down the stairs, heard his yells and curses from below, heard servants running to him and minutes later heard his voice rapping out staccato orders before there was the sound of a horse being ridden furiously away. After a few minutes she allowed herself to hope that he had been the rider, that he had gone.

But she still had to escape somehow.

Outside on the cobbles of the courtyard Geordie Brand was waiting astride his horse, holding the white palfrey. He and Bothwell's followers had been there four or five minutes now, near an open brazier of burning peats, and Geordie had used the short time to observe his companions.

He supposed that they were Hepburns or relations of the Hepburns, and they were a murderous-looking lot. Every one of them was scarred somewhere. One of them wore a leather mask, no doubt to hide some terrible wound to his face. Another man who closely resembled Bothwell, but who was bigger and black-haired, had three fingers of his right hand missing.

'How long are we supposed to wait here, Fobie Fingerless?' one of them asked him. 'Some of us have homes to go to, you know.'

'You'll do as I tell you, and my orders are to wait.'

'But how long –'

'Shut your face, you moaning bastard!' Fobie Fingerless made a threatening move towards the man, and he fell silent.

The trouble was, Geordie thought, that they formed a barrier between him and the gates and any possible way out, once he had regained possession of the Queen.

But, right opposite the front door as he was, he had an excellent view of Bothwell rushing downstairs, peeling off his boots and breeches and cursing when he threw them into a corner.

'Burn the buggers!' he roared. 'Fetch me clean ones!'

Standing there naked, he looked exactly like the pictures Geordie had seen of apes. Bothwell was an ugly apelike bastard, he thought. God help any poor woman he forced to lie under him, but there was one great mercy. He hadn't had time to damage the Queen.

'Forbes Hepburn!' Bothwell yelled as he struggled into fresh breeches, and the man they nicknamed Fobie Fingerless got down off his horse and went running. 'Fobie, you will wait here, however long or short it is, until that damned lady wants to go to Edinburgh. Then you will escort her there unharmed.'

'Yes, my lord.'

'Take five of our men with you. I am not waiting for her. I shall ride on to Huntly tonight, alone.'

Geordie grudgingly conceded that dressed, and certainly on a horse, Bothwell was no longer a figure of fun. He wheeled away, and once he was gone the Hepburn tribe dismounted, grumbling, and dawdled about.

Bothwell was scarcely out of view when to the amazement of them all the lady appeared in the doorway. Bothwell had not called her the Queen, but Abbie looked every inch a queen when she lifted her hand imperiously.

'I wish to return to Edinburgh,' she commanded. 'Master Brand, you may lift me onto my horse.'

'Your Majesty,' Geordie was at her side at once, and looking down into her face instead of up, as he had expected, when Abbie lifted her veil and took off her mask, pretending to adjust it. She put her finger against her lips – and then she winked. Geordie gasped and bent down, pretending to fix her stirrup. 'You're a right wee madam, Miss Abbie,' he whispered. 'What would your father say about this?'

'You'd better not say a word to him or anyone else, Geordie,' she murmured in his ear as he lifted her on. 'They could have our heads.'

He nodded and climbed back onto his own horse alongside her in the darkness, eerie now in the light of the smouldering brazier. Fobie Fingerless and five other Hepburns gathered around them, guarding them, every one with a burning peat snatched out of the brazier on the point of his lance to light their way.

They were used to long, hard riding on moonless nights with only their torches to help them. They seemed to spark to life at the prospect of the treachery of the bogs and pit-falls ahead, and as they trotted away from Hermitage with

Geordie and Abbie in their midst, and then broke into a gallop, they were yelling their battle cry.

'A-Hepburn! A-Hepburn!'

Geordie Brand shuddered at the bloodthirsty, blood-curdling sound.

God alone knew what Miss Abbie was thinking.

The ride down to the Border had been bad enough, but Abbie didn't think she was going to survive the ride back to Holyrood. It was rough, it was fast, and she was terrified of the Hepburns. In fact she would *not* have survived it without Geordie Brand helping her all the way. All she knew when they got to Edinburgh and the Hepburns wheeled away, too cunning to ride in further than the outskirts, was that she was filthy and exhausted, too exhausted even to resent what the Queen, Lord James and Sir William had put her through. That would come in the morning.

She flung herself down on her bed just as she was, and came to in the early hours of the following morning, dazed. To be clean was the first essential, but although she washed every part of herself in ice-cold water she still was not functioning properly. She was too tired.

Was it really only two days since she had left? It felt more like two weeks. Where was Lady Jean? Of course, she would still be nursing Seton. And how had all these bundles of wool got here? Did it mean that Donald had come, that he was actually here?

The excitement of it wiped away all traces of tiredness. She ran out into the corridor and met the same blank doors that Donald had met, until she came to Seton's. Lady Jean staggered out.

'Are you all right, Jean?' Abbie asked. 'You have not got the New Acquaintance, have you?'

'No,' Lady Jean smiled faintly. 'I didn't sleep, that's all. Seton has sent me to lie down for a while.'

They walked back together to their room. Jean had been told that Abbie had gone with the Queen. When Abbie removed the bundles of wool from her bed Lady Jean said, 'I knew Donald was here, but I didn't get a chance to speak to him. I only saw him yesterday morning when I looked out of Seton's window.'

'What was he doing?' Abbie asked, turning down Lady Jean's bed for her.

'Talking to Alex. Then he rode off like the wind.'

'What?' Abbie's heart dropped. 'Which way?'

'South,' Lady Jean yawned, and fell into bed.

Abbie searched the palace until she found Alex Ogilvie. 'You spoke to Donald?' she asked. 'Where did he go?'

'To a place I've never heard of until recently. Kershopefoot, on the Border.'

'Yes, yes,' Abbie said impatiently. 'But why?'

Alex had not needed to know Abbie had even been absent from the palace. 'He seemed very anxious about the Queen. Of course it is an open secret that she set off to meet Queen Elizabeth the day before yesterday. Abbie, is there something wrong?'

'I don't know. Where is he now?'

'The Queen is back, I believe, so he must be, too.'

'No, he's not, Alex.'

'Then he must have gone back to Strathbogie.'

'Without me? Why?' Abbie was almost in tears as she ran off to search the palace again.

It was useless. He wasn't there. He might be in the barracks, she thought. It was the last hope, and she was lucky when Geordie Brand came to the door.

'Has anyone seen Donald MacLaren, Geordie? Is he in there?'

But Geordie Brand shook his head. 'They say he went off to the Borders, too, but he didn't come back. At least, he didn't come back here. God knows where he is. Probably at Strathbogie.'

Abbie went to sit on one of the marble benches in the gardens in a torrent of tears. She had no doubt that he had followed the royal party to Kershopefoot, knowing that she was impersonating the Queen. He could have been killed in that terrible skirmish. He might be lying dead at this very minute, all alone at the side of that dangerous little bridge on the hillside. But somehow, she didn't believe that.

She stopped crying and cast around for some other explanation. She sat there until she felt frozen, until another possibility gradually took shape in her head. It was like a cold, horrible dawning. He must have seen Bothwell carrying her off. But surely, he could not have imagined that she went willingly? Even although, acting the part, she had been forced to make it look like that?

But that's exactly what he *had* imagined! The more she thought about it the more convinced she became. Yes, he actually believed that she had gone off with Bothwell and spent the night with him! A great tidal wave of anger engulfed her, and she was cold no longer. She was burning with resentment at the way Mary and the court had used her so cruelly, and then for Donald to mistrust her so completely on top of it!

It was a terrible insult added to a very grave injury.

For that, Abbie vowed she would never speak to Donald MacLaren again.

FORTY-ONE

It was a very different Donald MacLaren who returned to the Gordon barracks at Strathbogie, tight-lipped and grim-faced. He confided in no one, not even in John McCracken. Least and last of all in John McCracken. He avoided him at every turn.

The only person he spoke to with any degree of normality was Lord George, who had been his friend from childhood.

'I see Bothwell has arrived,' George told him soon after Donald himself had arrived. 'I wonder why?'

Donald's heart plummeted to his boots. In the shock of it he almost betrayed himself. 'Is he alone?'

'He hasn't brought any of his Borderers with him, if that's what you mean,' George said in his mild way, 'so it seems he's come in peace. He's closeted with my father on some private business as we speak. Something's afoot, mark my words.'

No doubt in the first place he was asking Lord Huntly's permission to release Abbie from bond. Only then could he ask her father's permission to marry her, Donald thought jealously.

'Bothwell seemed furiously angry about something, to me,' George went on unconcernedly. 'And of course, my father is always angry, anyway. They're hatching a plot, believe me.'

'A plot? Against whom?'

'The Queen.'

'*The Queen?*' Donald was staggered.

'My father, on the Catholic side, has never forgiven her

for that proclamation. And neither has Bothwell on the Protestant side.'

'Oh come, George! I don't believe that Bothwell would turn against the Queen, whatever their religious differences. He is too cunning for that. He is more likely to worm himself into her good graces. He and your father must be hatching up some other plot. Besides, aren't they very unlikely bedfellows?'

'Ho!' George laughed. 'They'll get into bed together all right if it means increasing their lands and their power! But Queen Mary stands in their way. I'm afraid I don't have a very high opinion of my father, Donald. And as for Bothwell, my opinion is lower still.'

'No lower than mine,' Donald sighed.

He tramped back to the barracks in a state of complete confusion. Why wasn't Abbie here with Bothwell? What had he done to her? Had he ravaged her and then left her? Where was she now? Both their lives had been turned upside down by that man, when not long ago they had seemed set so fair.

But the evening meal was delayed when Lord Huntly called George, John and Adam to a private family meeting. Lord Huntly was in a different mood from any that his sons had ever seen him. He was not red-faced, roaring and shouting this time. His face was grey and the quiet ice in his voice impressed them more deeply than any of his blustering could have done. Even the ebullient John was silent before it.

'I have just been served with the greatest insult of my life. Indeed, it is the greatest insult ever handed out to us in the whole history of the Gordon family ... Mary Stuart – I will not call her my Queen – has seen fit to end my stewardship of the lands of Moray. As you know, they yielded immense sums of money. But now she has named Lord James Stewart the Earl of Moray over my head.'

John hissed. Adam looked quite indifferent, and in order not to make his father angrier than he had ever seen him before, George did not say a word. But he was not surprised.

In his opinion his father had been helping himself illegally to the Moray revenues for years. He waited to hear what was coming next, and it was as he dreaded.

'It is time for war, boys,' Lord Huntly said, and John's eyes sparkled with glee. 'I will not tolerate that woman interfering in our affairs any longer. Say nothing to your mother in the meantime. I know how to handle her, and I'll tell her when the time is right. John and Adam, you may go. George, remain behind.'

'Now, George,' his father said, 'you will go to consult with your uncle, old Arran, the Duc de Châtelherault, as he calls himself nowadays. If he is not in Edinburgh he will be at his house near Dover. We must enlist all the aid we can get. Remember, he is still next in line to the throne. He may be very useful – but we will talk later, before you go.'

Dressed in her favourite emerald green, and looking more than ever like the big-bosomed figurehead on a galleon, Lady Huntly was at her formidable best as she presided over the meal and the gentlemen. The salmon were going down well, she was happy to see. Even her youngest son, Adam, was eating a little.

She was quite worried about Adam. He had been a quiet, withdrawn infant who had never laughed and seldom smiled. Now he was forever with his nose in a book and becoming most dreadfully thin. One day, if things did not improve, he would fade away altogether, and that was a pity because he was so clever.

But she had other sons, she sighed, and then smiled in spite of herself at John, her second youngest son. He was so handsome! So like herself! Perhaps he was a little too high-spirited, but that's what ladies liked. She smiled at him indulgently, knowing that he was a devil for the women and had left a trail of broken hearts behind him already – even the Queen's! He had been to Holyrood and had come back smartly. Whatever the reason for that, he didn't have a good word to say for Mary now . . . A shame, for such an alliance would have solved everything. A Gordon child, the issue of such a marriage, would have inherited the throne.

There would have been no more need for all this plotting and fighting! Why could his father not have brought John up to be a little more circumspect, she asked herself angrily, switching her gaze to her husband and shuddering at the sight of his bad table manners.

Her gaze passed on hastily to young Alexander Sutherland, eating quickly and nervously. He was living at Strathbogie now. He still had not recovered from all his ordeals and he clung to George, steady old George, the oldest son still left at Strathbogie.

George was so placid. Although he had been named after his father, he was his very opposite. There would be no pomp or swagger with George!

Then she came to the sixth and final man at the table. Everyone always saved the best until last . . . James Hepburn, Lord Bothwell . . . She didn't know what to make of him, but she had to admit that in his rough ugliness lay his monstrous attraction. She could easily understand why women were drawn to him.

She was well aware of his discussions with her husband. The Earl of Huntly had, of course, the greater power, not to mention the greater wealth. He ruled the Highlands. But Bothwell's lands extended from the Borders almost to Edinburgh. Between the two they could squeeze and squeeze – until they joined together.

Lady Huntly's eye roved over Bothwell's well-worn clothes and his frayed cuffs as she sipped a glass of wine reflectively. Now, if *she* had had the power of Huntly all to herself, if *she* had only been twenty years younger! She and Bothwell could have ruled the world – never mind the country!

As if he had guessed her thoughts, Bothwell grinned at her and she could not mistake the impudent message in his eyes. At her own table, in front of her family of men too! Lady Huntly hadn't blushed for many years, but she blushed now, in a tide of heat that began between her legs and finished at the roots of her hair.

Silly old cow, Bothwell laughed to himself. Look at her! She's on fire for me! She would lie down for me in a minute . . . Well, there's many a good tune played on an old fiddle, and he thought of an old paramour of his, Lady Janet Beaton, aunt of Mary Beaton, who was twenty years his senior. He had taken her to Hermitage one day and they had been lovers ever since.

Lady Huntly saw that his thoughts had wandered elsewhere. Well, if she had not been born at exactly the right time, her own daughter had. She had always known that her daughter would be their saving grace one day, somehow or another. All was not yet lost. It was just such a pity that Jean did not have the fire, or the spirit, or her mother's sexual charms, Lady Huntly thought, preening herself. But then, very few women did.

She started from her reverie to discover the men well in their cups. It was time for her to go. They were still sober enough to get to their feet when she bade them good night, and she went thoughtfully to bed with this exciting new idea running around in her head. She would think about it, although she knew that in the end, to come to such a momentous decision, she would have to take *the ultimate advice*.

In the early hours of the following morning Lord Huntly and Bothwell were the last two who were still drinking hard. They talked and laughed and sometimes shouted, and in the end Bothwell fell back on the long dining bench, out for the count.

Lord Huntly staggered his way up to bed, weaving from side to side of the passage, bringing up with a curse every time he reeled against the walls. To make it all more difficult, some of the wall-tapers had burned themselves out, and there were pools of darkness on the floors.

In one such pool his right foot fell on something soft with claws on, and there was a hideous yowling scream. Then his left foot fell on another screaming, biting, scratching softness.

'Elizabeth!' he thundered, so that the very walls echoed, and there was a hasty scuffle in the blackness while the biting and clawing continued on both his legs. 'Elizabeth!' he yelled again, and when his wife appeared with a candle he saw that not two but all four of her grisly cats were gnawing at his legs. 'Get these buggers off me!' he exploded. 'Get these buggering beasts out of here! Do you hear me, Elizabeth? From now on they are banned – *banned*!'

In the commotion two of Lady Huntly's ladies and one of the guards arrived on the scene.

'But, my lord,' Lady Huntly removed the cats and stood there while they coiled and hissed around her feet. 'You know they are my pets!'

'Pets be damned!' he bellowed, so furious that he was frothing at the mouth. 'I've put up with them for far too long! I always hated them. If I ever see them again I'll kill them with my own bare hands!' He wept genuine tears of pain and fell on the bed.

Lady Huntly didn't hesitate for a second to decide that her cats were far more important than her husband. She left instructions with her ladies to attend to his legs, and then with a cat clinging to each of her ample breasts and the other two in her arms she ordered the guard to light her way outside.

She chose the barn that was back to back with the kitchen, took the torch, put it in the iron holder on one of the walls and dismissed the guard. Inside the barn it was warm, and the smell of the hay as she climbed the short ladder to the hayloft was inviting.

'Now, my darlings,' she murmured, putting the cats down gently on the hay, 'you will have fine, soft, warm beds here. You did not think that I would put you away, did you? No matter what his lordship says, my little beauties! Never mind him. He will be asleep by this time, anyway. So – Meenie, Beenie, Teenie, Queenie – will you come to me now? Come, my ladies . . . I need your help.'

The four cats crouched where she had laid them down, resentment in every line of them, and deeply, deeply offended.

'You will be very comfortable here,' she assured them anxiously, 'and every day I will see that you get the thickest cream and the best of fish.'

Still they were motionless, except for ominously waving tails.

In desperation, Lady Huntly tried to coax them once more. 'It will not be for ever, my pets. Lord Huntly will soon forget.'

But she saw by the light of the torch that their eyes were slits of evil spite telling her that *they* would not forget, not ever.

They had never looked at her like that before.

'I will come and see you in the morning,' she promised, and went back into the castle bitterly condemning her husband for a bigger fool than she had ever realised. She cursed as she went to another bed to lie awake for what remained of the night wrestling with her problem.

Alone.

Next day her mind was made up. Bothwell was sheltering here at Strathbogie, still a wanted man – but it might not be for long. Feuds, quarrels, battles and treason were everyday affairs, but then so were pardons if they were politically expedient, and Lady Huntly did not imagine that a professional fighting man like Bothwell would waste his talents shut up here much longer. She must arrange things as swiftly as possible, but to her dismay, he was nowhere to be seen as she and her husband sat down to breakfast.

As usual, Lord Huntly's indulgences of last night had not affected his appetite in the slightest, and he was chomping his way through a slab of mutton.

'George!'

'What is it now? I hope it's not about those bloody cats –'

'It is not about the cats,' she said coldly. 'There is something else, if you have come to your senses.'

'Senses? Senses?' he said irritably. 'What is it, woman?'

'We should bring our daughter back home now,' she said quietly, feeling her way. 'Lady Jean.'

'Lady Jean! Lady Jean! What do you mean, Lady Jean? Do you think I don't know my own daughter?' he boomed. 'What about her?'

Lady Huntly sighed, but managed to hold on to her temper. 'She should come home,' she repeated. 'Are you listening? Our John did not like Queen Mary. We cannot proceed with *that* plan, and Alex Ogilvie of Boyne has never asked you for a marriage contract with Jean.'

'No.' His little pig-eyes were focusing now.

'So what is the point of her staying on at Holyrood?'

'Hm.'

'And Bothwell has not married.'

'No.'

'What if Jean and Bothwell were to marry, my lord? In such a way his lands would be joined with yours, for what bond is stronger than a marriage bond?' She touched his hand tenderly.

Lord Huntly gazed down at the unusual sight of their two hands together on the table. What his wife was insinuating had been in the back of his mind all along. It was a great wonder that Bothwell had not suggested it himself, long ago.

Why not? he wondered. And why had he never married before this, anyway? Of course, rumour had it that he had never needed to. There was that scandal about Lady Janet Beaton. Lord Huntly toyed absently with his wife's hand, now that his wits were clearing, and she squeezed his fingers almost in sympathy. She could see by the creases on his brow that he was making a great effort to concentrate, and he was not a fool altogether. She kept very quiet, almost seeing the cogs of his brain slowly revolving.

Lord Huntly concluded at the end of this that Bothwell hadn't married for the simple reason that he had been waiting to land some very big fish of the female variety.

Well, female fish didn't come bigger – or richer – than his own daughter, Lady Jean Gordon. His eyes widened at the thought of what a bargaining tool *she* would make! And if she were married to Bothwell, he would provide the backup to the rebellion he was planning. Everything was working out splendidly. Elizabeth was right, as usual.

'By God, Elizabeth, you're a wonderful woman! Haven't I always said so? Bothwell and I have been searching for a way, but I never thought of that one! He would do anything for money!'

'I know that.'

'When do you think I should get Jean back here?'

'The sooner the better, before he disappears altogether. Before the end of the week, if possible. And, of course, you will not state a reason other than we have been missing our daughter so much.'

'And that's the truth! I'll send a messenger to Holyrood now, this very minute,' he said enthusiastically, rushing away.

Lady Huntly sat on, deep in contemplation. She had managed the first hurdle. Now to the next one, and that might be more difficult.

'No.' Donald flatly refused to co-operate. 'I *will not* go to Holyrood to escort Lady Jean back home. Geordie Brand is at Holyrood, isn't he? He can have that pleasure.'

John McCracken noticed that Donald didn't mention Abbie. Clearly, there had been a quarrel, or some misunderstanding between them. Well, that would soon be put right now that Abbie was coming home, for where Lady Jean went, so did she.

FORTY-TWO

Queen Mary sent for Lady Jean and Abbie. When she told them the news that they were to be sent back to Strathbogie Jean swayed where she stood, all the colour drained out of her face. Always so composed as a rule, she began to cry. Abbie put her arm around her and appealed to Mary.

'If you will forgive me, Your Majesty,' she said, 'you don't know what you are asking of her –'

'Please, madam,' Jean cried desperately, 'I beg you to keep me in your service until I marry! Once you are settled with a husband Alex Ogilvie and I intend to wed. I have kept that promise to you faithfully, not to marry before you do . . . All this time,' she added piteously.

'My dear Jean!' Mary seemed almost as distressed as she was. 'I release you from such a promise today, and Abbie as well, whether I marry again or not! Only, in the meantime, go and see your parents. You have been away from them for such a long time and they are pining for you.'

Jean turned to Abbie helplessly. 'Do *you* believe that?'

'No, I do not,' Abbie said firmly. 'They are not pining at all.'

'They do not really want to see me,' Jean sobbed. 'Abbie and I know better than that. There is some ulterior motive.'

'If you discover such a thing you may return immediately to my court,' Mary smiled. 'That is my promise to you. In the meantime it is my wish that you should please your father, my Lord Huntly. Remember, he is a Catholic ally and my Chancellor, although he has not attended the Privy Council lately. I do not wish to offend him. Go to Strathbogie today.'

'Yes, Your Majesty.' Jean and Abbie curtsied sadly, and withdrew.

Jean was still sobbing as they trailed back to their room and Abbie tried to comfort her. 'It may only be for a few days, Jeannie. A few weeks at most, so I won't pack too many things. While I'm doing it you could go and explain to Alex and say your goodbyes.'

When Jean shut the door behind her Abbie sat down on her bed in abject misery, for the news the Queen had given them had pierced her heart like a dagger. Strathbogie was the last place she wanted to go to. She did not even want to *see* Donald MacLaren.

Geordie Brand received his orders for the escort north and at the same time his release from duties at Holyrood. He had seen enough of the goings-on, the intrigue and the never-ending and corrupt plots of court life to last him all his lifetime, and it came as a great relief to be taking the two girls back home. There, at least it was straightforward feuding and fighting, things a plain soldier could readily understand.

They arrived at Strathbogie just as it was getting dark. Lord and Lady Huntly came out to greet them, and Lady Huntly made a great fuss of showing the two girls to their respective bedchambers. Lady Jean objected at once.

'Abbie has always slept in the same room as me,' she said, adding pointedly, 'ever since I was four years old.'

Lady Huntly tried not to stare at her daughter. She had grown into a proper Gordon, with her long nose, her grave face and her ladylike manner. This was no time for any unpleasantness, and the Countess could see that she would only cause it if she tried to separate her from her maidservant.

'My dear child,' she said, as they stood in the larger of the two rooms, 'by all means! I shall have another bed brought in here for Abbie. Now, there is hot water for you to wash off the grime of your journey. When you are both ready, come down to the dining hall.'

The two girls washed and changed their riding habits for pretty gowns in silence. Lady Jean led the way downstairs, and Abbie could see that she was very apprehensive – and no wonder with such a mother – so she stayed closer to her than ever.

'I won't know Adam and George, my own brothers,' Jean whispered.

'We'll face them together,' Abbie said, her face relaxing into a smile when she curtsied to George. *He* was just the same as she remembered him, only older, with his kind face and black hair. *So like Donald*, her heart smote her for a minute.

It was a terrible state of affairs when a brother had to introduce himself to his sister, but Adam had been only a child when Jean last saw him. John was away in Edinburgh, Lady Huntly told them, and Abbie had no doubt that he would be roistering and brawling in the taverns there, if his short appearance in court before he was thrown out, was anything to go by.

And then there was this interesting stranger, Alexander, Earl of Sutherland, with his handsome face, his shy smile, and deep lines already etched on his young face. Lady Jean and Abbie took to him right away and when they sat down Lord Huntly explained what he was doing here.

'He's here,' he boomed, 'until we win back his lands for him and his seat, Dunrobin Castle. The Earl of Caithness has overrun them.'

'And it will be a long, hard battle,' George put in. 'It could go on for months. We are gaining ground, although it is only inch by inch.'

Was Donald MacLaren engaged in that? Abbie wondered. A tiny flicker of alarm melted a small crack in the ice around her heart.

But such a worry, and indeed all coherent thought, was wiped clean out of her head when a footstep sounded at the door and another guest came smiling to the table. Abbie could scarcely believe her eyes. But there he was, in the flesh.

Lord Bothwell. To her immense relief his glance only flickered over her disinterestedly. He had not connected her with Hermitage Castle, or the Queen.

Geordie Brand came upon Donald skulking in the darkest corner of the courtyard eyeing with a savage glare the party from Edinburgh going into Strathbogie. 'What's the matter with you, Donald MacLaren?'

'I might have known!' Donald snorted. 'If Bothwell's here, Abbie McCracken wouldn't be far behind him.'

Amazed, Geordie watched Donald sloping off tragically. What on earth was the matter with the boy? This was not the Donald MacLaren he had known from the time he was a small pig-boy, faithfully shadowed by an even smaller Abbie McCracken. And it was Abbie that Donald had been watching in the courtyard. Light dawned on Geordie Brand.

Next morning he buttonholed John McCracken. 'Don't ask, and don't argue,' he said. 'Just bring Abbie, by force if necessary, to meet me.'

'To meet *you*, Geordie Brand? Why?'

'I've got a very good reason as you'll see. I'll be down at the gate of the Gardeners' Cottage at midday.'

'Well, that shouldn't be too hard,' John smiled at his old comrade-in-arms. 'She likes you, God knows why.'

Abbie took her father's arm as they walked through Abigail's beautiful gardens. They had matured over the years since she had left Strathbogie, especially the roses. They were climbing up and over all the walls now, and their perfumes were intoxicating, reminding her of Queen Catherine's scented gardens on this summer morning.

Did the sun really shine all day, every day, then? Perhaps it had only seemed so, because she and Donald had been falling in love, because they were so happy together . . . Tears sprang to her eyes. The scent of the roses was suffocating her, she thought angrily, and dashed her tears away as John McCracken opened the gate for her.

343

Then, suddenly the world stood still. She felt as if someone had just poured a bucket of icy cold water over her. Donald MacLaren was standing in front of her, face to face, held tight in Geordie Brand's iron grip.

'You're a bloody fool, Donald,' the big man assured him. 'You think Miss Abbie went willingly to be ravished by Bothwell. Well, I'm here to tell you, in front of her father, that she couldn't have been.'

Donald simply stared at Abbie, his blue eyes anguished and dark with longing.

'She was not alone with him any longer than five minutes. Whatever she did, she got rid of him fast,' Geordie added. 'By the way, Miss Abbie, what *did* you do? I've wondered ever since.'

Abbie glared furiously at Donald. 'I put my fingers down my throat and made myself sick all over him,' she said.

'By God,' John McCracken said admiringly, 'for you, that *was* something!'

'It was heroic,' she insisted, stamping her foot, the sparks flying out of her red hair and her golden eyes. 'Nothing short of it!'

John McCracken started to laugh. Geordie Brand laughed with him and they released their prisoners.

'Oh, Abbie,' Donald cried, 'what a fool I've been!'

The ghost of a smile began at the corners of her mouth. 'You always were an idiot,' she agreed.

Donald leaped forward and took her in his arms. 'But you love me all the same?' he pleaded breathlessly.

'You *know* I love you, and only you, God help me. I always have, and I always will.'

'Well,' John said to Geordie as they strolled back to the barracks, 'we'd better leave these two lovebirds to their own devices. They've got a bit of making up to do. Abigail and I saw at once that there was something sorely grieving Abbie, as soon as she came home – and as for Donald, he's been like a bear with a sore head, in the barracks.'

'Well, they're curing each other now,' Geordie said,

glancing back. 'They're still billing and cooing. Love is a wonderful thing, right enough!'

'Get away, you old hypocrite! How would *you* know?'

'Och, I've had my moments,' Geordie said, winking and smiling and digging John in the ribs.

Abbie and Donald were married quietly in the Gardeners' Cottage by gracious permission of the Earl and Countess of Huntly because Johnny was in bed all the time now, too ill to walk to the chapel. With so many other plans brewing at Strathbogie, Lady Huntly was only too glad to be relieved of such a burden as a wedding, but she sent the priest down to marry them and Lord Huntly sent bottles of wine and barrels of ale.

But that was not all he sent. There was something else. The delicate part was getting it handed over without his wife knowing anything about it. He found Lady Jean and Alexander Sutherland taking their daily walk in the gardens of Strathbogie.

'You are both invited to this wedding?' he asked.

'Yes, Father,' Jean replied warily.

'You have wedding gifts?'

'I am going to give this to Abbie.' Jean showed him a prayer book, bound in white leather. Inside it was gilded and illuminated.

'Where did you find such a beautiful book?' her father asked.

'In France. I was just showing it to Alexander.'

'I'm afraid I have nothing,' Alexander said sadly. 'You know how I left Dunrobin – with nothing but what I stood up in.'

'Now, Alexander,' Lord Huntly beamed at him, 'you will get back your castle, your lands and your money before too long. Trust me. In the meantime I will lend you some money for a gift to the bride and groom. Here it is in this small bag.'

'That is very kind of you, my lord. That will make me feel much better.'

Lord Huntly took another, bigger and much heavier bag out of his other pocket. 'Donald MacLaren has been a faithful servant here all his life,' he explained to Alexander, and then turned to Jean. 'You may leave us, my dear. I have a lot to say to Alexander, and you must have plenty to do.'

'I have, and so has he. Please don't keep him too long, Father. We must get dressed. We leave in an hour,' Lady Jean said and hurried away.

'I won't keep you, my boy,' Lord Huntly lowered his voice to a muted roar and winked ferociously, 'but, you see, Donald is a particular favourite of mine, and I do not want my wife to know about this gold, nor how much of it I am giving to him. Do you understand?'

'Perfectly, my lord. I shall hand it over in private, and tell him it came from you,' Alexander murmured as they walked back into Strathbogie, and he left the Earl to go and change his clothes for some of her brothers' which Jean had laid out for him.

Jonathon and Jackson McCracken got a day's leave from the farm. They arrived with a pretty little partner each and they all carried baskets of cooked chickens, cold meats, freshly baked cakes and eggs and honey, presents from their uncle.

The cottage was abuzz with excitement when, after the ceremony, the whole party all gathered around Johnny's bed and began the feast. Abigail, dressed in a new blue gown, had decorated the house with banks of flowers, and everyone laughed and sang and toasted the bride and groom until it was time for them to go.

'I sent three barrels up to the barracks,' John told Donald. 'The Gordons want to drink your health.'

When Abbie and Donald arrived at the barracks the atmosphere was thick and all the men were happy. 'Oh Jesus,' one of them staggered up to Abbie, 'just to have him back, our old Donald, laughing and joking again! And it's all due to you, Miss – Mistress Abbie! A toast to Donald and Mistress MacLaren, boys!'

Already happily drunk, the Gordons raised their glasses.

'Lang may your lum reek!'

'May all your troubles be little ones!'

They were still uproariously inventing more toasts when Abbie and Donald slipped away, their excitement mounting as they neared the little house in one of the streets of Huntly which Donald had bought.

'Here it is, Abbie,' he said proudly. 'It cost all of my wages from France. Well, nearly all,' he added apologetically when he unlocked the door and they stepped inside. 'I'm afraid they only ran to a bed, besides.'

'That's my Donald,' Abbie laughed. 'First things first!'

That same night, in Strathbogie, Lord Huntly handed over another gift of gold, but this time there was so much of it that it was in an iron chest. Two guards carried it between them to Lady Jean's room.

'Now then, Jean,' her father beamed at her, 'when the time comes for you to marry, here is your dowry and much more besides. Half of it must be handed over to your husband on your wedding day. The rest is yours, from your father who has always loved you, no matter how it may have seemed. Here is the key. I think you should hide it, even from your mother.'

'Thank you, Father,' Jean said.

She kissed him on his cheek and hugged him, thinking sadly that she would have loved him too, if she had ever been given the chance.

FORTY-THREE

These happy, happy times for Abbie and Donald were in many ways an extension of their childhood together, only now they played at grown-up games. He made her laugh no matter what small disaster occurred as they were setting up their home, and when he was away with the Gordons, Abbie proudly cleaned and polished until there wasn't a speck of dust to be seen on their newly acquired table and two chairs, or on their bed, or on Queen Catherine's boxes sitting one on top of the other in a corner of their bedroom.

Outside, it was different. Ruefully, Abbie surveyed the overgrown little patch of ground at the back. Queen Catherine's boxes had reminded her of France again, and all the glorious scents of her flowers captured in her tiny bottles. Well, even if it took her weeks to make this patch into a garden again, she vowed that she and Donald would have herbs and flowers of their own.

In fact, she would make a start right now, this very minute. The first thing to do was to clear out the weeds and the rubbish, and she was busy at it when a woman's face appeared at the other side of the fence.

'Mistress MacLaren?' she said, and laughed. 'I *thought* it was you, Abbie! I said to Jack, "That's Abbie McCracken that was, for sure!" Do you remember me? Lizzie Sproat. Here's Jack come out to speak to you as well.'

'Of course I remember you, Lizzie. And you too, Jack.'

'Once seen, never forgotten, eh?' Lizzie laughed.

That was true. They had always reminded Abbie of one

of the nursery rhymes her father used to teach her.

> Jack Sprat could eat no fat,
> His wife could eat no lean,
> And so betwixt the two of them
> They licked the platter clean

For Lizzie was as round as a barrel and Jack was as thin as a rake.

'Your garden is so neat and pretty,' Abbie complimented them. 'It puts this one to shame.'

'Jack'll give you a hand, don't worry,' Lizzie said.

'You notice that my wife thinks nothing of volunteering my services,' Jack Sproat cackled, but his eyes crinkling up in his weatherbeaten face looked at her lovingly.

'Pay no attention to *him*,' Lizzie said, opening the gate in the fence between the two gardens. 'Now that all our bairns are grown up and gone he spends his time gardening. I spend mine cooking and baking. Come inside and try one of my fruit scones.'

In the mornings Abbie visited her mother to do what she could to help with Johnny. Any free afternoons she had, she spent with Lady Jean up at Strathbogie, and she almost always found her strolling with Alexander Sutherland.

'I've been here two whole months now,' Jean fretted. 'Why are they keeping me here? I wish I could go back to Holyrood.'

'What – and leave me?' Alexander teased her.

'Are things any better for you?' Abbie asked him.

'They're getting better. The Gordons seem to be succeeding.'

Lady Jean took his arm and smiled at him comfortingly. 'Dear Alexander,' she said gently, 'we'll get there in the end. My father will see to it.'

Even then, Abbie noticed the calming effect Lady Jean had on him. He stopped frowning for a minute and smiled. 'Who else gives me hope, Jean, if it is not you?'

They matched each other. Abbie fell one step behind them on the narrow path and watched them. With all his worries and problems he seemed to Abbie to be a far better prospect for Jean than stick-in-the-mud Alex Ogilvie.

She took Jean's arm when Alexander left them to ride off with Lord George. 'Can you not think of him instead of Alex Ogilvie, Jeannie?' she asked. 'He is very taken with you. In fact, he is enamoured.'

'I cannot, Abbie. I love Alex with all my heart and soul, and I always will.'

They both scowled at Bothwell, mounting his horse at the front door of Strathbogie, with Lord and Lady Huntly waving him away.

'He has got the royal pardon,' Lady Huntly told them. 'He's going home to Hermitage in the meantime. But he'll be back.'

Jean did not deign to comment. 'Abbie will be staying to supper,' she said curtly instead. 'Donald is in Sutherland with the Gordons, as you know. She will be staying with me until he returns.'

'As you please.' Lady Huntly's eyes flickered over Abbie but she didn't really see her. She was bursting with some inner excitement of her own.

That night there were only the four of them at the table, Lord and Lady Huntly, and Lady Jean and Abbie. Once again Abbie found herself just part of the furniture as the Huntlys ignored her and addressed themselves exclusively to their daughter.

Lord Huntly was perfectly sober and perfectly sensible. As such he was imposing, and for once Lady Huntly was taking a back seat and allowing him to do most of the talking. That could only mean that she had made whatever cannonballs were coming, and his job was to fire them. Suddenly Abbie became very, very alarmed for Lady Jean.

Nevertheless, it was Lady Huntly who fired the first shot when the nature of the evening's business became apparent.

350

'Daughter,' she said sweetly, 'your father and I have been considering your future.'

'In Holyrood, I trust,' Jean said, her lips white and compressed.

'What is there for you in Holyrood?' her father demanded.

'My future husband, for one very important thing.'

Lord Huntly's face darkened to purple. 'If you are referring to Alex Ogilvie of Boyne, I must tell you that he has never bothered to come here and ask me for your hand in marriage.'

'Marriages, especially one as dynastically important as yours, must be very carefully arranged,' Lady Huntly slipped in. 'Besides,' she added, 'he isn't even good-looking! His face is round and flat. Certainly, he has any amount of money –'

'Not as much as we have,' her husband cut her short. 'We don't need Alex Ogilvie's money. So what else has he to offer?'

'Love,' Jean said quietly.

Her father looked from one corner of the room to another and then another, completely bewildered and trying to find some explanation from somewhere for this extraordinary statement from his offspring.

'Love?' he gasped. 'What has love got to do with it?'

'Everything, I should say.' Jean sat her ground and addressed her mother. 'How is it possible to live with a man all the years of your life and not love him?'

'Well, I'll tell you a secret.' Lord Huntly leaned forward. 'Believe it or not your mother didn't love *me* to begin with.' He smiled at such an absurdity. 'But she learned – oh yes, she learned! Take a leaf out of *her* book, my dear child. Marry the man we consider vital not only for your future happiness, but also for the political best of all concerned. Learn to love him afterwards, as your own mother did.'

'It will be easy,' Lady Huntly said smoothly, 'and in any case, it will be too dangerous for you to go back to Queen Mary's court just now. She has betrayed us Catholics disgracefully. Your father plans an uprising against her. So Alex Ogilvie or no Alex Ogilvie, you will stay at home meantime.

351

Now, about the arrangements we have made for your wedding –'

Jean half rose from the table. Abbie followed suit. She could actually feel Jean's tremors. She saw her hands clutching the edge of the table, the knuckles white. 'What *is* this?' she demanded. 'What are you talking about? *Who* are you talking about?'

'My dear,' Lord Huntly said, 'the negotiations have already been agreed with your future husband, the Earl of Bothwell.'

'Oh God – no!' Lady Jean screamed, and fainted.

That August in Edinburgh was a beautiful golden month, when the days were warm and softly lit with the late summer sun and the evenings came early and colder, with little puddles of mist swirling between the street-tapers, perfect for lovers' meetings and hilarious outdoor games in fancy dress. The Queen bundled up her hair under a man's hat and donned her satin breeches, laughing as she ran with her courtiers in and out the taverns of the town in disguise.

Beaton turned up her nose at such childish capers. They were not for her. She had just presented a supper of cold meat, pastries and Spanish wine and eaten her fill. But now, watching the throngs in the Canongate from her window on this dreamy, misty, romantic night, hunger pangs of a different kind attacked her.

When she crossed her arms with a little shiver, her hands brushed across her nipples under her silk low-cut bodice – and there it was again, this yearning that melted her insides. Her excitement mounted when she pulled up her skirts and put her hand between her thighs.

It was no use. She wanted – she needed a man. She had never recovered from the loss of Pierre de Chastelard when he was executed, nor the humiliation of finding out that he aspired to be the Queen's lover, not hers . . . Now, there was nobody.

Suddenly, rebelliously, her mind was made up. She pulled off her gown altogether, and clad only in her undergarments raked in the back of her cupboard for her old dark green cloak. She wrapped it around herself and pulled up the hood. In the pocket she found a key, still there where she had hidden it, a copy of the key for the postern gate.

She had been thinking about this for months. Now, quivering with a mixture of excitement, trepidation and flaming desire, she flitted out of Holyrood and hid, waiting until the guard marched up to the corner of the palace with his back to her. Then she was out, merging into the green-black darkness around the palace, just a moving shadow in her soft slipper-soles.

Oh God, it was all happening, at last!

She kept well back against the grey walls of the buildings down here in the lower part of the Royal Mile, creeping along. Then she bumped into someone else who was doing the same. Instinctively she knew it was a woman. A hand shot out. Long talons narrowly missed her face and raked her hood.

'What are ye doin' here, ye dirty whore?' a voice rasped. 'This is my patch! A'body kens it's Kitty Trotter's patch! Get yer arse off to some place else!'

For answer, Beaton lifted her plump and powerful arm and punched the woman in the face. *WHAM!* She went down like a sack of straw and lay there motionless. Beaton waited until she sat up, prepared to give her another where that one had come from, but the woman only shook her head dazedly before she scuttled away. It may have been Kitty Trotter's patch once, but now it was Mary Beaton's, and she sidled out to stand under the streetlight when she saw a man coming, a likely-looking man. He was big, and he was on his own.

After fourteen adventurous nights on the street, nights when she punched any man who looked like threatening her, she discovered that she liked hitting people. It gave her the next best feeling to sex, better even than eating. She knocked one man to the ground, stamped on his face and disarmed him of his knife. It was wonderful. Word soon got around. There was a new whore in the Canongate, a Woman in Green, and she was the best one in the town . . . But, watch her!

After every encounter, two or three times a night, she found herself well satisfied for the moment – but it was only for the moment. Lonelier and more frustrated than ever, she always contrived to return to the palace before the dancing and the music ended, and one particular night when she had washed her face, but no other part of her, and had put her silk gown back on again, she ran through to find the Queen dancing a galliard with Sir William. After a while Lord James and Livingston joined them on the floor, and then Morton and Flamina. Morton had always flirted with Flamina.

Beaton could bear it no longer. She *must* get a man who was permanent, one who would be there for her each and every night – in other words, a husband – and the dregs of humanity she had been consorting with in the Canongate could not provide that. She cast desperate, flashing eyes around the assembly as she had done so often before, in despair. Up to now they had always glanced over Alex Ogilvie of Boyne and dismissed him, but now they lingered. Lady Jean was away in Strathbogie and he looked lonely and vulnerable.

He was startled when she approached him. She was not his sort of woman, not at all. He preferred the modest ones who covered their curves circumspectly yet alluringly, like Jean. He had never been so close up to a woman's almost exposed bosom before. When he looked down at her he could plainly see her swollen, scarlet nipples peeping out. His eyes were drawn to them, they were hypnotised by them, and his arms felt achingly empty when she ran away. But within minutes she was back, with wine, and quite suddenly he was on fire with longing . . . for Jean. She had been away for such a long time.

Why had she made that stupid promise to the Queen the minute they had all come back from France – just as he had been about to ask for her hand in marriage? She would never have made such a promise if she had loved him truly, as he thought she did.

After a few gulped glasses of wine his bitterness and resent-

354

ment of Jean's treatment of him intensified to boiling point, and then Beaton was pulling him along, half-drunk, to the dark of her room. With a cry he tore down her bodice, grasped her breasts and kissed her passionately. She lit a candle, and undressed him so quickly and expertly that he had no time to do anything more than lift her skirts before he entered her.

Alex Ogilvie was a virgin, and the release of the pent-up, unfulfilled desires of years for his sweetheart, Lady Jean, was unimaginable. Within half an hour Mary Beaton had aroused him again. The third time she had taken off all her clothes, and for the first time in his life he was seeing, and holding, a real-life naked woman in his arms, instead of one of his fantasies of Jean. He was in Heaven.

Next morning, in the early hours, with his head bursting, he could not believe that any of it had actually happened. Beaton soon showed him that it had not been a dream. It certainly had happened, and it was about to happen again.

'Now,' she said afterwards, 'you know that this means we must get married?'

'Oh, yes,' Alex said, dazed and greedy for more.

FORTY-FOUR

On his way back down to his castle of Hermitage on the Borders, Bothwell made a quick trip into Holyrood Palace. His mission was entirely mischievous. He wanted to see the Queen's face when he told her of his intended marriage to Lady Jean Gordon, and with Riccio at her side she reacted to the news exactly as he had told himself she would. Her eyes flashed fire and jealousy.

'I see,' she said coldly, and added even more icily, 'Well, Lady Jean will bring you a magnificent dowry. The Earl of Huntly is very rich.'

'And powerful, Your Majesty.'

'So you are marrying for wealth and power, my Lord Bothwell?'

'For love, besides. All in all, it should be a successful union.'

'*Love*? Here at court, and even as far back as during our stay in France, we were under the impression that Lady Jean was in love with Alex Ogilvie and wished to marry him. Has she agreed to your proposal?'

'As I believe I told you once before, a kiss has converted many a lass, madam.'

At that point Riccio began to strum a love song, and Mary's eyes softened when she looked at him. Bothwell could actually feel any anger or heart-burning she had been harbouring positively flowing out of her. Instead of making her jealous, he had only succeeded in finding out this change in her attitude to him. Of course, it was all due to that hump-backed little Italian.

356

Bothwell made a mental note then and there to get rid of him, when he was ready – when he was ready, with enough money and power to overcome the Queen with love, and become the King of Scotland. Marriage to Jean Gordon was not his ultimate aim.

Sir Patrick Spence found Alex Ogilvie weeping bitterly in their room. 'So you have heard the news, Alex?' he asked sympathetically. 'What on earth happened to make Lady Jean change her mind?'

At that, Alex stopped crying. A hard expression, such as Sir Pat had never seen before in all these years, came over his face. 'Bothwell changed her mind. He has that reputation,' he said bitterly, 'but I never thought that Jean would fall for it. Well, it has certainly hardened my heart.'

'What do you mean?'

'I am to be married myself, immediately, to Mary Beaton.'

'To Mary Beaton?' Sir Pat echoed incredulously, for he had heard rumours about Mary Beaton.

'She is asking the Queen now for her permission.'

For the moment Sir Pat said no more. He merely shook his head.

The Queen sighed, and admitted Beaton for a private interview. She supposed that this would be another moan about the French chefs, but to her surprise Beaton started off on quite a different tack.

'Your Majesty, if you will pardon the allusion . . .'

Mary sat up. She had not credited Beaton, the least bright of all her ladies, with such a grasp of the English language. 'Certainly,' she said. 'What is it?'

'If you were the pot and I the kettle, there would be no point in the pot calling the kettle black.'

'What *is* the point, then?'

'Madam, I have lain with Alex Ogilvie, not once, but many times.'

The insolence of it! Was this girl saying that she was no

worse than the Queen of Scotland? Was she insinuating that she knew, and all the court knew, of Mary's budding love-affair with Riccio?

'I see . . .' Mary said slowly, and when she did not at once condemn her, Beaton's eyes became quite bold. 'Are you asking me to release you from your promise, Beaton? Do you want to marry Alex Ogilvie?'

'We must marry,' Beaton said defiantly, 'and as soon as possible.'

'Then I shall arrange it, of course, and see to your wedding gown and your dowry.'

Beaton did not thank her. 'Alex Ogilvie has plenty of money,' she laughed contemptuously.

It was the second time in as many days that Mary had heard that reason for a marriage, and it enraged her. She got to her feet. 'You forget yourself, Mary Beaton! It is not a question of mere money! It is a question of betrayal all round, and daring to ignore my command. You will be married here, and you will be married when I say so.'

She considered for a minute or two before speaking again. 'That will be on September the twenty-ninth. I am doing nothing else that day. Balthazzar will begin the fittings for your wedding gown this week. Is all this understood?'

'Y-yes . . .' Beaton said uncertainly.

'Then you may go,' the Queen said, and turned her back on her.

After these shocks and disappointments, worst of all the cancelled meeting with Queen Elizabeth, Mary decided to go on a progress of her own, and on 11 August she rode north on her first visit to the Highlands. She had some good reasons for doing so and they all spelled GORDON, which meant nothing else but mischief.

In June, after an Edinburgh street brawl and his scandal with a woman, she had thrown the outrageous John Gordon with his dashing good looks into prison. He had escaped, and she intended to recapture him and bring him to justice.

His father, the Earl of Huntly, was also behaving in a very unstable manner. Her spies had warned her that he was planning an uprising and a Catholic coup. He would try to inveigle her and her party into Strathbogie, kill the Protestants of her party – Lord James, Sir William Maitland and Morton – and then marry her off to his son John whom she had already refused.

She brooded for some time on the latest development in the Gordon family, this marriage proposed between Lady Jean and Bothwell, but she could make nothing of it. She simply didn't understand Jean – or Bothwell. But perhaps she would, long before the actual wedding day dawned.

Queen Mary hoped that her party would give the harmless appearance of a hunting and hawking progress into the northern wilds, and that all these extra soldiers were with her for nothing more than help over the difficult terrain. She carefully bypassed Strathbogie and headed for Inverness where she knew another of Lord Huntly's sons, Alexander Gordon, was the keeper of the castle. When she arrived he refused her entrance.

'All Scotland is yours,' Sir William said indignantly, 'and every castle in it. This is treason.'

'Many Highlanders are gathering to your flag,' Lord James reported. 'There are other clans besides the Gordons in Scotland, you know. We should camp here and wait to see what happens.'

While John Gordon was dodging northwards after his prison escape he heard about this. Strathbogie Castle was thrown into an uproar when he arrived home with the news. 'Alexander has locked the gates against the Queen,' he told his father, 'and the rest of the clans are rallying around her.'

Lord Huntly was thoroughly alarmed. 'Send a message to the stupid bugger,' he roared. 'He's got to let her in!'

So the gates of Inverness Castle were opened and the Queen rode in. Her soldiers ran to capture Alexander Gordon, and before the day was done they hanged him over the battlements.

*   *   *

For days the screams and sobs of Lady Huntly rang through Strathbogie and alarmed the people of Huntly. When she calmed down she took stock of the very explosive situation. Most explosive of all was her husband. His colour was dreadful and she feared for his health. She had just lost one son, her Alexander. Another son, John, was on the run. She would lose her husband as well, if she did not take charge.

'Leave it to me, my lord,' she restrained him. 'The Queen has gone to Aberdeen next. She is staying there for a few days and visiting the university. You will not go and try to reason with her. I shall go instead and speak to her, woman to woman. She will listen to me.'

Lady Huntly arrived in Aberdeen with a large retinue of attendants, and Mary regarded her with the utmost dislike, even if the woman had delivered her into the world twenty years ago. Quite clearly, nowadays Lady Huntly fancied herself Queen of the Highlands, which no doubt she had been for far too long. She would be fancying herself Queen of all Scotland next.

'Your Majesty,' Lady Huntly said. 'I beg you to be merciful to both my husband and our son John.'

'You have no business here, Lady Huntly,' Mary said coldly. 'Any business I have is with Lord Huntly. Where is he?'

'Oh, dear Queen, because you have ignored his invitation to visit us he feels he is being punished for his Catholic zeal.'

'His failure to present himself to me at the Privy Council and the indiscipline of his sons is an insult to me. Not only is he a childish coward, I hear he is a rebel too.'

'A rebel, madam? When he is waiting to welcome you to Strathbogie?'

'He waits in vain,' Mary assured her. 'Go home and tell your husband to mend his ways.'

'It is all-out war then,' Lord Huntly said when his wife reported back to him.

But it was not quite all-out war just yet. Characteristically,

John Gordon set out immediately to prick and harry the Queen's soldiers whenever and wherever he could find them, while his father planned his campaign by day in Strathbogie, but by night slept for security in one of his many other castles round about, always a different one.

The Queen soon got to know about this and one day Sir William Kirkcaldy of the Grange, who had served James V so loyally as Treasurer, set out from Aberdeen with twelve men to surprise Huntly at his midday meal in Strathbogie. The noise they made clattering up the long avenue from Huntly to the castle alerted the Gordon guards and Lord Huntly was forced to abandon his dinner. It was unthinkable.

'Where are you going?' his wife screeched when he rushed past her without his boots on and minus his sword.

'Where do you think I'm going? To get on a bloody horse before somebody kills me!'

'But what about me?'

She was left speaking to herself, and she swore and cursed with every obscene word she had ever heard uttered by her better half. Her better half? Every bully was a coward at heart, and that bastard had shown himself in his true colours. But *she* wasn't finished yet, not by a long chalk!

She ran out of the kitchen door as Kirkcaldy and his men ran in through the front door, and hid herself in the barn where she had put her cats. She could hear them growling and hissing. She was so angry and frightened that she growled and hissed along with them.

It worked like a charm.

Before her startled eyes the cats appeared, swishing their tails and looking every bit as angry and evil as when she had seen them last.

'Meenie, Beenie, Teenie, Queenie,' she said soothingly, 'I've looked for you every day and missed you so much!'

She put out her hand to catch one of them, to stroke it. All four flew at her with their claws extended and only the sleeve of her gown saved her arm from the worst of some very nasty scratches.

'No, no, my pets!' she screamed. 'It was my lord, not I, who banned you from the castle!'

The cats changed into the four old grey women she hadn't seen for many a long day, and from one of the beams her pet raven fluttered down and stood before her, having changed into the man in black.

'Yes,' he snarled, 'you forgot about me, didn't you? You forgot old Nick.'

'No! Never!'

'Listen,' he said, and as the chanting of the old women began, coloured plumes of mist wafted out from the hay.

Lady Huntly thanked God that she had never missed a single day of sending out cream and fish to her darlings. As if they would desert her in her time of need! Although they had not condescended to appear to her since that little unpleasantness with her husband, she always knew her familiars would come back. Little by little their message was coming through to her.

'The best defence is attack. Face up to the Queen at Corrichie, and by nightfall Huntly will be lying in the Tolbooth at Aberdeen, unmarked.'

Oh, it was wonderful, wonderful! Miraculously, unable to find their quarry, Kirkcaldy and his men rode away. Huntly rode back from the wilds of the Badenoch where he had been lurking, and his wife assured him that no harm would come to him if he did battle with the Queen, and if he did it now. She directed him to a commanding position on the Hill of Fare above the field of Corrichie and watched him go in his pink and gilt armour at the head of his troops, with their sons John and Adam at either side.

But something went horribly wrong when the royal harquebus-fire raked through Huntly's followers on the hill, and they were forced into the swamp at the bottom. Lord James hacked them down and captured Lord Huntly and his two sons, John and Adam.

The indignity of it! The humiliation of it! Lord Huntly felt himself swelling with indignation inside his glittering armour.

At the last minute he thought in a flash that he must burst altogether.

Queen Mary and her followers watched in stunned silence as the great Earl began to sway on his horse. He rocked from one side to the other, and then – and then, he rocked too far left and fell off with a dreadful crash.

The very earth seemed to move. The air resounded with the grinding of metal on metal. Great clouds of dust rose up and then fell back, covering the glorious pink and gilt.

'Remove his armour!' Mary commanded.

But it was too late. The Earl of Huntly was stone-dead. The royal soldiers treated him with scant respect. They threw his body over a couple of fish creels and took it to the Aberdeen Tolbooth for the night. There wasn't a mark on it, just as the witches had promised.

They had got their revenge.

FORTY-FIVE

At one point during the wedding celebrations for Alex Ogilvie and Mary Beaton Sir Patrick Spence had found a moment alone with the bridegroom.

'So it's goodbye, Alex, after all these years! But I hope not for ever, although you are taking your bride north to your castle, and I have made up my mind to go south – all the way to Italy!'

'What?'

'You know I always fancied it. Besides, I can't stand the cold here.'

'Whereabouts in Italy?'

'I thought you would ask me that,' Sir Pat laughed, 'so here is a map, and the directions to get to it. You can't go wrong.'

'Perhaps I already have, Pat,' Alex sighed in deepest dejection. 'But since she is determined to have a castle of her own, I suppose we'll go north and try to make the best of it.'

'Well, if it doesn't work out, come to Italy and stay for as long as you like with me. *And* my wife, I hope, when I find one – and our fat little babies!'

'Oh, I'll miss you, Pat! I'll miss our chats and our games of chess,' Alex said sadly, shaking his friend's hand.

'And John? What has happened to John?' Lady Huntly asked her youngest son, Adam, in floods of tears.

'The Queen has executed him, Mother.'

'Oh . . . Not John! Not John!' she wailed. 'Not my John!'

'She has spared George, since he was not even there, but she has thrown him into prison down south. And she spared my life, too.'

'Your father's body . . . Where is it?'

'In Edinburgh. I am sorry to have to tell you this, Mother, but the doctors are disembowelling it and embalming it.'

'What?' she screamed, and fainted.

'Now then, Mother,' Adam brought her round, rubbing her wrists and smoothing back her hair, 'you *know* that is the law! He must stand trial for treason, alive or dead. Queen Mary has demanded it, and she has demanded that the cannon in the courtyard must be handed over to her as well.'

'Then we shall not be here to see it. We shall go to France, Adam. She may have squashed the uprising, but never the Gordons!'

'I can't believe it,' Abbie said to Jean, observing the Countess's anguish. 'Can the Queen not see further than the end of her nose? Instead of fighting your father, she should have been behind him, supporting the Catholic cause. Now, she is all alone, surrounded by Protestants. She will pay for this.'

'She will pay for this,' Lady Huntly echoed her grimly the following day, thinking that there were a few people who must pay – four ladies all in grey, for example.

She went to the barn to look for the cats. She would wring their necks if she could catch them. But they had vanished, and she was never to see them again.

Now she and Adam prepared to depart for Leith to board a ship for France.

'We shall return when George gets out of prison,' she informed her daughter. 'And as for you, Jean, Bothwell is exiled so you won't be getting married yet a while. You may do as you like!'

'I intend to,' Lady Jean replied. 'Here is a letter from Her Majesty. She is distressed at my misfortune, and wishes me to go back to her court.'

Lady Huntly snorted. 'She is distressed at *your* misfortune, is she?'

Lady Jean said nothing. Her mother glared at her and delivered her parting, spiteful shot. 'Go back to Holyrood?' she sneered. 'What for? Alex Ogilvie has married Mary Beaton. You won't see *him* again!'

Abbie felt like cheering when Lady Jean did not betray her tremendous shock by one iota. But alone with Abbie afterwards it was a different story as Jean sobbed and railed against her fate. 'Oh, God – I don't want to go, Abbie! There's nothing for me now. In the end I'll have to marry that awful man!'

Abbie looked around the empty, deserted castle. 'You have no choice, Jeannie,' she said sadly. 'But you won't go alone. I'll come with you. When Donald left last night he told me the Gordons have only one last task now in Sutherland, to take Dunrobin Castle – but at the same time he warned me that it could take all winter. I would rather be at court with you than alone.'

Abbie said her goodbyes to her parents and Johnny, and gave the keys of her house to Lizzie Sproat next door along with instructions for Donald should he return before expected. Then, with the few straggling Gordons still remaining in and around Strathbogie, she set off to Edinburgh with a heart almost as heavy as Lady Jean's.

The castle was abandoned, left to the Queen's soldiers to destroy and to sack as Her Majesty commanded.

Queen Elizabeth had the perfect plan to extend her influence to Scotland, and Sir Robert Dudley eventually found himself on his way there with the courtiers, *valets de chambre* and guards she had sent with him. Now, arriving in Holyrood, he was shown to his quarters. His big moment was almost upon him.

His valets bathed the dust of the long ride off him in scented water, powdered him, shaved him, and working very hard at his direction began the laborious business of dressing him in the glistening pale blue satin of his latest suit of clothes, attending to his top half, first. The silk shirt went on, then his short doublet and the masculine pleated ruff.

Now came the dubious part, when they pulled up the blue silk hose over his legs, muscular and bandy from a life spent in the saddle. On top of that would be the breeches, the very latest fashion . . .

'You are sure you have relieved yourself, my lord?' the head valet whispered in his ear. 'After this, there's no going back.'

'I am ready,' Dudley barked. 'Get on with it, man!'

Gently, inch by inch, they eased him into the breeches, fastened the codpiece and tightened the waist-strings. 'You are ready now,' the head valet pronounced him, and smoothed down his apparel all the way to the door of the antechamber. It was very difficult to walk, but he managed it, and for a few seconds took a deep breath after he was announced.

Scarcely had Abbie returned to Holyrood but she was pressed into service in her old role of standing in for the Queen. As the months went by, the task became no less nerve-racking and it was with a very heavy heart that Abbie saw Sir William Maitland rushing towards her down the corridor one morning, having guessed why she would be wanted.

'Her Majesty needs you at once, Mistress Abbie,' Sir William said in a fluster. 'Queen Elizabeth has sent Dudley, her favourite, to ask for the Queen's hand. What her motive is, God alone knows. At any rate, Queen Mary will refuse him. I will stay with you, as always, and I know you will do your best, my dear.'

'I will try, with Flamina's help.'

'Then she will be with you directly.'

Flamina painted Abbie's face, dressed her and helped her into the chair of High Estate, and no sooner had Abbie composed herself for the task ahead than the latest applicant was announced.

'Sir Robert Dudley, Your Majesty.'

'Sir Robert!' Abbie's silvery Mary voice welcomed him

from the audience chamber. 'Please, come in!'

He managed to reach the door of the audience chamber, and there was a pause while he manoeuvred the door in his ridiculously wide pantaloons. He managed another three steps inside it, and then came the biggest moment of all when the Queen of Scotland would be completely bowled over at the sight of him.

'Your Majesty,' he said, bowing elaborately, so elaborately with a great waving and flourishing of his arms that the whole court was hushed. As he bent there was an ominous rip of silk and a roar of bran cascading on the floor. It made a very vulgar noise, and it did not stop there. He went on bowing and bending. There were more rips and roars and obscene noises as the bran poured out of his pantaloons, so that they were padded no longer, but hung limp in folds. Everyone there burst out laughing. Abbie wiped her eyes, fearful of the paint running.

'Approach, Sir Robert,' she gasped.

At last he kneeled before her, and his eyes looking up into hers were entirely unembarrassed. In fact, they were smiling.

'Come and sit by me,' Abbie said, exactly as Mary would have said. 'You are a monkey. You did that deliberately, did you not, to look like a monkey-suitor?'

'Thank God for you, Your Majesty ... My whole life depended on your ability to see the joke!'

'You love Queen Elizabeth so much?' Abbie asked him.

'To eternity, and that was my dilemma, since my mission was to offer myself to you.'

'Brave Sir Robert,' Abbie smiled. 'Go and tell your mistress that she is very lucky. I dismiss you.'

Dudley left for London that night, wearing his usual leather stream-lined riding breeches and tossing his silly pale blue satin cap with the feathers in it over the nearest hedge. He had done what was asked of him. Now he could go back with a clear conscience to the woman whom he knew had something to hide. They would never be lovers, but that

368

didn't matter. There were plenty of fish in the sea, just for sex.

None of that need stop the Queen of England marrying him for love, for he knew they loved each other for ever and ever. He truly believed that if he watched what he was doing, if he turned a blind eye to her little night excursions with her pageboys, she *would* marry him.

And then he would be the King of England.

Not the cleverest of Elizabeth's courtiers, Dudley brooded about it on the long ride to London. He had looked at it from his point of view. Now he began to wonder about hers.

What would be the point of her marrying him – or anyone else, for that matter? There could be no fruit of any union she made with a man. In other words, there never would be an English heir to the throne, and, as far as he knew, the only one who could be the next monarch was Mary, Queen of Scots, if she survived Elizabeth.

He began to groan. He never should have worn those blue satin pantaloons.

Elizabeth would marry no one, and he had lost his chance.

After Dudley had departed Sir William took Mary aside and whispered that there was something that Melville had found out that concerned her and, indeed, the whole of Scotland.

'Yes, Sir William?'

'He spoke to Dudley's physician. Dudley told him that Queen Elizabeth only plays at love.'

'I have heard that she is not like other women, Sir William.'

'She is malformed, madam. She can be neither mistress nor mother. She cannot bear children. You need not fret that she will have heirs! And that means that any child of yours must inherit England as well as Scotland.'

Mary smiled at him. She had just refused another suitor, and she was still unmarried, still free to do as she pleased. When the right man came along she would make love and have babies, but not till then. So far she hadn't seen one man she could even make a friend of, except Davy. As his music started softly again she thought that her only true friend in the world was David Riccio, attending to her faithfully, singing to her, advising her and caring for her. Without him she thought that she would die.

'I love you, Davy,' she whispered and kissed him, when full of wine and carried away by his divine music they sat together alone, dreaming into the fire.

At last, at last, she had said it! For a tenth of a second he sat stunned . . . And then his brain raced on.

By now he was well acquainted with the geography and social life of Scotland. He was well aware that an Italian musician might have a struggle to be accepted as the Queen's husband by everyone else in the country, but the important thing was for *her* to accept the idea. It all depended on the next half-hour.

'And I adore you, my beloved Queen. Oh, Mary, Mary . . .' he returned her kisses hotly, but with his mind clinically cold.

'Don't leave me tonight, Davy,' she pleaded.

'I'll never leave you,' he swore savagely, and small and hump-backed though he was, carried her like a long slim leaf through to her bed. 'Let me lie with you. Please, let me lie with you, Mary.'

She had never known lovemaking like that. In fact, she had never known lovemaking at all. In the guttering light of the candle she looked deep into the eyes of David Riccio, and believed that they belonged to Francis, but a Francis she had only dreamed of all the time she had been married to him, as she arched up to her lover again and again.

'Don't ever leave me, Davy,' she begged him.

'Never,' he promised, 'as long as I live.'

FORTY-SIX

Dudley arrived back in London in the evening four days after his audience with the Queen of Scots, and went straight to see Queen Elizabeth.

'Robin! Robin! Back so soon?' she cried, and ran to meet him. Then she wagged a finger. 'Reeking of horseflesh too, you naughty boy!'

'Forgive me, Your Majesty. I could not wait to see you.'

'Then tell me. What happened at Holyrood? Did the Queen of Scotland accept you as her suitor?'

'I never got so far, madam. She dismissed me.'

'*She dismissed you!*' Elizabeth's hand crashed down on the table angrily. 'What impertinence is this?'

'There was no impertinence, Majesty. Queen Mary was very kind and gracious . . . And I tried my best.'

'You will tell me more, sir, and in private.' Elizabeth nodded good night to her court and waved even Cecil, her Secretary of State, away impatiently. He closed the door behind him, and they were left alone. 'Now, Robin, explain yourself. Why did she dismiss you? Did you present yourself properly to her?'

'In pale blue satin. In the latest fashion. But it made no difference. She simply didn't like me.'

'I can't believe that . . . No, I cannot – but I like you, and that's all that counts! And now, by offering yourself to the Scottish Queen, you have shown my people that there cannot be anything between you and me. You have been very brave, and you shall not go unrewarded.'

371

'Oh, Elizabeth! The only reward I hoped for was to see your dear face again!' Dudley said, and meant it sincerely. He kneeled at her feet.

'In two days I shall make you my Earl of Leicester at Westminster.'

'But that is a title reserved for princes!'

Elizabeth drew him up to sit beside her, and smiled into his roguish brown eyes. She had never been able to resist them.

'Exactly,' she said.

Mary prayed for guidance day and night. The people around her would certainly advise her, but with their own ends in view, be they political, religious, or in the cases of the Marys and Riccio, romantic. Riccio loved her body, but only God loved her body and soul. Only He could help her now.

Sir William had made his point in the end, after all. It burned in her, and burned and burned. Her children, when she had them, would inherit the crown of Scotland, and of England too in the long run, and there must be no hindrance. They must be of pure royal blood. They must be legitimate. Riccio could not be their father, however fond she was of him, however much he loved her and comforted her every night.

From now on she must take this whole question of the succession more seriously. It was imperative, as she saw for herself now, that she should marry suitably as soon as possible. If only Riccio had been of royal blood ...

All around Mary there seemed to have been weddings in recent years – her brothers, Mary Beaton, Abbie McCracken and within a few weeks Jean Gordon too. Poor Jean Gordon, Mary thought. She had had a lot to bear. Her father and brothers dead, her mother fled to France. And Alex Ogilvie had gone off suddenly and married Beaton ... Perhaps she was so calm and tranquil because she looked forward to her eventual marriage with Bothwell. Who wouldn't?

A savage pang of jealousy ripped through Mary's heart.

She knew then that Riccio was only a stop-gap for the real thing.

And she knew for certain that she was tired, tired, tired and sick of it all – all the enigmas, of John Knox's constant bombardment of vituperation, of a million other problems. She had to get away.

In December she moved her court across the Firth of Forth to Wemyss Castle where they would spend Christmas, leaving her stuffy advisers like Lord James and Sir William behind her.

Besides, worried about their association, she wanted to change the routine of Riccio's nightly visits. In Wemyss they were impossible to continue. Furthermore, she needed time to think clearly about what was rapidly becoming an obsession with her – her future husband.

But her bitterness and jealousy of the happiness of others followed her. One afternoon she could bear the jollity no longer. Suddenly she thought she was going to faint, or scream, or both.

'I must have air,' she said breathlessly. 'I shall go out into the gardens. I wish to be alone with my thoughts.'

Once outside she pulled her mantle close and put up its hood to cover her heart-shaped head-dress. The wind blew in from the North Sea over the silent gardens, bearing speckles of snow to cloud the air like mist. The further she walked, the thicker grew the icy mist until she was lost. She couldn't find the way back.

She thought there was a movement somewhere – for a second a glint of metal, then a tiny clanking noise. She felt no fear. She followed the direction of the noise. It led her to the figure of a tall man in a dark hooded cape with a sword jangling at his belt.

She touched his arm and when he turned to look at her she gave a little cry. 'Why are you here?' she asked.

'To present myself to a Queen.'

In the breathless hush it seemed to Mary that a brilliant, radiant light fell upon the gardens. It seemed that fireworks burst and fizzled and popped their gorgeous colours up into the sky – for here he was at last, her knight in shining armour!

'I know who you are,' she cried. 'You are my cousin Henry! I expected your father, but you have come instead! You have come at last . . .'

They talked for a little while and never noticed that the wind had dropped and the snow had frozen solid. They only saw that the gardens, rimed with frost and sparkling when they turned to go inside, had become a fairyland.

Mary was exultant. At a stroke this tall Greek god – taller even than she was – wiped the memory and the thought of any other man clean out of her head. It was as though Francis, Riccio, or Bothwell himself had never existed. And best of all, she knew that this man would be her husband.

The music and the dancing stopped when she came back arm in arm with a strange man. Gradually the conversation died down and there was silence in the court. All eyes were on the beautiful couple. Coming in out of the frosty air they seemed frosted themselves, glittering and radiant, the Queen actually looking up, for once, at this handsome, smooth-faced man who wore the hair on his head like a golden crown.

As they stood there gaping, some thought that it was a sign. The Queen had met her match at last. They looked so perfect together.

Others, the older ones, thought it was an omen and shuddered at the sight of them, so young, so helpless, so hapless.

Abbie and Lady Jean shuddered, and drew closer together in the weird silence. They both recognised the golden ringlets falling about the pretty-boy face, even now, when that face was more than six feet above the ground on a man's shoulders.

It was the Powder Puff.

PART THREE

FORTY-SEVEN

Such a pretty little ship she was! In the dying rays of the winter sun her sails seemed made of silk, her decks trimmed with gold, and Abbie dreamed of the paradise of spice and jam in the bins, and rubies and pearls in the chests down in her hold.

Nearer and nearer she came, her sails white against a sapphire sky now that the sun had gone in. Abbie's eyes filled with tears when the ship stopped opposite Wemyss Castle's tiny pier.

It wasn't *her* ship coming in. The only ship she could be interested in was one to bring her own true love to her. She turned away blindly to walk back to the castle, so lonely without Donald that she wanted to die.

It was late afternoon on Christmas Eve and she had taken this walk to gaze out over the waters of the Forth and wonder and worry about what he was doing, while she filled her lungs with fresh air. She had not been able to endure the antics of the Queen's puppets another single minute in the stuffy Great Hall, its air thick with the smells of rich food mixed with the cloying perfumes of the ladies and gentlemen.

She didn't want to go back inside again, and she turned back longingly to look at the magic ship and say a reluctant farewell.

And, it was a magic ship ... A small boat was pulling away from it, and the next minute Abbie was racing down to the pier to meet it with her heart pounding and her arms outstretched. One man was rowing to shore.

And the man was Donald.

After that, everything was different. Now, Abbie smelled only the fresh greenness of the great swathes of cypress and fir which the Queen had ordered to be cut from the forest, because Donald was at her side to dance with her and play with her, and listen to the magnificence of David Riccio's beautiful voice.

The Queen had ordered a tableau of Mary and Joseph in the manger with the infant Jesus for Christmas Day. They all worshipped and prayed before it and Abbie thought it couldn't be wrong to wish for her own baby in her arms when she looked at the Virgin holding hers.

All the week following was devoted to the revel, the dancing and the frolics, and the party games which the Queen adored – and for Abbie it was fun now that Donald was there. Even the puppets made her laugh now, because they made him laugh.

'But how did he get here?' Lady Jean asked.

'The Gordons pushed the Caithness men to Golspie Bay, and there he spoke to the captain of a ship going to Leith who promised to drop him off here when he heard that the Queen and her ladies were at Wemyss.'

'Trust Donald to think of that one,' Jean laughed. 'Anyway, you look radiant, Abbie.'

'If only he and I could be together always, Jeannie,' Abbie sighed. 'These last ten days have flashed past like a dream but tomorrow I must wake up. Tomorrow, he has to go back.'

Later that night Donald tried to reassure her. 'We are weeding out the last of the Caithness men now. There are only a few left, still here and there in pockets of resistance. As soon as we get rid of them and the Sutherlands come back to defend their Earl, our task will be done.'

'How much longer, Donald?'

'Two or three months, that's all.'

'But you *still* look worried. What's wrong?'

378

'Because so many of the Gordons won't be coming back with us. They like it there. More importantly, they get paid there. They say they can't afford to go back to Strathbogie when there is no longer a Gordon to pay them their wages.'

'No . . .' she said. She had never thought of that.

'But when I come home you and I will manage somehow, Abbie. We'll live on love!'

At that moment, she believed him.

The court moved back to Holyrood and Abbie took up her duties again, duties which had never been clearly defined. Sometimes she was the Queen's dresser along with Flamina, usually she was the Queen's Messenger, and always she was expected to step into the Queen's shoes and impersonate her at any given moment.

But her holiday with Donald had invigorated her. Secretly, she was pleased at being privy to most of the Queen's business, both public and private, and she watched and she listened by day and by night.

'Abbie, you do not mind that I spend so much time helping Seton and keeping her company, do you?' Lady Jean asked one day. 'You are so occupied with the Queen's affairs.'

It was a subject that had been worrying Abbie for a long time. It pained her that she could not confide in Lady Jean. 'I am only too pleased that you have found another companion, Jeannie, while I have to attend to so much rubbish.'

'But you are still my Abbie . . . ?'

'Always, dearie. That will never change, you know that.'

'So what do you have to do today?'

'Oh, she is going hawking with Darnley! I suppose Flamina and I will have to trail around behind them,' Abbie said disgustedly.

Three hours later she watched Darnley binding the leather thong on Mary's wrist for the bird's talons, and saw how the Queen quivered and blushed at his touch. She watched as they danced together through the February nights while Mary became more and more besotted by the hour. For her, nobody else existed in her dream world but Henry, Lord Darnley.

Of course, it was only another dalliance, Abbie tried to reassure herself. Mary couldn't possibly be serious about such a shallow, vain man. But it was going on and on . . .

Perhaps Riccio's reactions might throw some light on the situation, Abbie thought, but he was as clever as ever, smiling throughout, while he appeared to step gracefully aside and allow Darnley to take his place in Mary's affections.

How much of that was because he knew he was being watched, as always, by the Scottish court? To have betrayed his resentment by look or word or deed would have been the same as betraying his erstwhile relationship with the Queen.

He took to going out in the early evenings, and that was a new departure. Time after time Abbie's curiosity prompted her to follow him. Every time she was frustrated by someone or something requiring her attention. But whatever Riccio was up to, he was always back in the palace in time to sing the duets, his fine bass voice blending pleasantly with Darnley's tenor, which were the Queen's latest pleasure.

They had just finished a song, and Mary was clapping, when Abbie became aware that Mary Livingston and John Sempill were standing before the Queen, holding hands.

'Your Majesty,' Mary Livingston said, 'John has asked me to marry him, and I have told him that I wish for nothing else.'

'Dear Lusty,' Mary smiled at her, 'you will be the second of my Marys to wed! I release you from your vow at once. Just be very, very happy.'

'Thank you, dear Queen.'

'You will be married at court. Oh, this is only the beginning of happy times! There will be weddings, and love, and births for all of us – for now,' Mary got to her feet and raised her voice, 'I wish everyone to know that I shall be married soon, too. Henry, Lord Darnley, will be my most beloved husband.'

Abbie's heart sank while everyone else stood up and clapped and cheered and raised their glasses. Then the happy

380

couple danced. Darnley moved exquisitely, and Mary looked up into his handsome face as if he were a knight from a dream. Indeed, he was so tall, so straight, so golden, that he seemed like a miracle.

When they sat down to supper, Darnley seemed to be all things to all men – deferential to Lord James and flattering to James's wife, Lady Agnes. The Marys warmed to him. They were won over at the first dance. Only Lady Jean and Abbie were a little stiff, but Mary convinced herself that they would come to like him too, in time.

She was almost ready for bed before she thought of Lady Jean and Abbie again, and with difficulty forced herself to concentrate on them for the first time in months. Abbie, now a happily married woman herself, though so often away from her husband, only looked unhappy at Holyrood if Lady Jean was unhappy. So what could be wrong with Lady Jean Gordon? Mary sent for her to find out. Before she kneeled down in prayers of thankfulness and gratitude for such a lover at last as Darnley, her mind must be free of such niggling little worries.

'My dear Jean,' she said, waving her to a chair, 'all these celebrations must be especially hard for you to bear.'

Jean smiled nervously and raised her eyebrows. 'Not at all, Your Majesty. I am very happy for you, and for Lusty.'

'I mean, here we are at February the twelfth and you should have been married yourself on the twenty-second. But unfortunately Lord Bothwell is still in France, outlawed.'

'He must pay the price, madam, just as my own father and brothers did. At this happy time in your life I beg you not to be concerned about Lord Bothwell – or me. I am in no hurry to wed.'

'No?' Mary looked surprised. 'Then tell me what is troubling you. Something is. You have always spoken plainly to me.'

'I fear I may sound impertinent, madam.'

'Out with it, Jean!'

'Some people who were at Queen Catherine's court with us are talking about the young boys there who used to stroll about hand in hand in the gardens, kissing each other.'

'I remember,' Mary said. 'They were amusing. We called them Powder Puffs.'

'Madam, they are saying that Lord Darnley is like them.'

'Oh,' Mary laughed, 'I believe many young boys go through that stage of youth before they mature. Please do not allow such rumours to upset you, my dear. Lord Darnley is a full-grown man now. I should know,' she added, blushing. 'He has kissed me.'

'You have relieved my mind, madam.'

But Jean was unsmiling when she curtsied, sensing her dismissal.

'So you promise – not another cloud on your brow?'

'Not one, Your Majesty,' Jean said, and went to report to Abbie. 'There was no arguing with her,' she said sadly. 'But at least my conscience is clear. I tried to warn her.'

'And was that all?' Abbie asked.

A smile broke out on Lady Jean's face. 'No. There was something else. Bothwell is still in France. She shows no sign of pardoning him.'

'Thank God for that,' Abbie said. 'Now we can look forward to Lusty's wedding on Shrove Tuesday without a care in the world.'

FORTY-EIGHT

Lord George Seton arrived in Holyrood to take up the post of Master of the Household, thus setting his sister, Lady Mary Seton, free of its arduous tasks. Instead, after the wedding, Seton would take over Livingston's duties of looking after the Queen's clothes and jewels. That morning the two ladies were making a detailed inventory with the help of Lady Jean and Abbie.

'So much of her youth has been spent in mourning,' Seton sighed piously while she and Lady Jean counted all the black dresses, some of camlet, some of damask or serge.

Livingston laughed. 'Don't you think she knows very well what a wonderful setting black – or white – makes for her glowing complexion and red-gold hair?' she asked. 'Abbie, let us begin on the white gowns.'

They separated and counted the Queen's loose dresses 'à l'Espagnole', her riding skirts and cloaks mostly of Florentine serge edged with black velvet or fur. Next they went on to the *vasquines* – petticoats or farthingales stiffened with hoops of whalebone to hold out her skirts. Then they counted her underwear of silk doublets, bodices of black or white silk, woven silken hose of gold and silver, hats and caps of black velvet or taffeta, and lastly her veils of white or black lace.

In the afternoon they tackled the Queen's glittering ceremonial clothes and recorded 131 entries.

'Let's leave the rest until tomorrow,' Livingston begged, stretching her arms.

'I hear she is having a masked ball at your wedding on Tuesday, Lusty. Are you becoming very excited?' Lady Jean asked.

'Oh, yes!' Livingston jumped up and down. 'John and I are dressing up as Punch and Judy.'

They all laughed. 'That should give you plenty of scope,' Seton said.

'But wait until you see the cake, dear Seton! Philippe, the Queen's French confectioner, has iced it. You will marvel at what he has done with sugar! There are little gardens with birds and animals on each tier, all garlanded with flowers and all made of sugar so they can be eaten! And there are sugar pigs for the children.'

At the banquet after the marriage ceremony, when Lusty and John cut the wedding cake, it was Queen Mary who found the Bride's Bean in her slice.

'That means you will be the next bride,' Darnley murmured in her ear. 'Let it be soon,' and he led her onto the floor to tread a stately measure to the sweet music of the lutes and recorders.

Afterwards Mary clapped her hands. 'Now for the masking!' she laughed. 'Anyone who wants to, may retire and dress up.'

'She never tires of such games,' Abbie said to Lady Jean, who preferred to sit and watch the others. 'What costume, this time?'

Most of the men reappeared in fantastical costumes – Romans in their togas, knights from the court of King Arthur, wondrous birds and animals – and then, there was the ludicrous sight of the fanatically Protestant Lord Ruthven who had been invited, his cadaverous form dressed as a Highland chieftain, his sallow skull-like face almost hidden under a steel headpiece, his yellow, evil eyes glittering through the eyelets, waiting . . . Waiting for something.

'What is he waiting for?' Lady Jean wondered, and shuddered.

384

Then the trumpets sounded again. 'The Harlequins, ladies and gentlemen – or the Harletwins, as they prefer to be called!' And in came Mary and Darnley, to hush the court, to bring them to a standstill.

They wore silver masks and tight-fitting plain black caps pulled down over their ears, covering their hair. Both very tall, their one-piece spangled suits patterned with coloured diamonds were identical. *They* were identical, except that their skin-tight costumes outlined the difference of the sexes. Darnley's shoulders were broader and his genitals conspicuous, while the nipples of Mary's small breasts stood out like berries, and as they paraded across the floor the sexual overtones suggested at the sight of them shocked everyone there.

Taking advantage of the stunned silence, Lord Ruthven marched up to Darnley with his dirk pointed at him. 'Get back to where you came from,' he shouted, and made a lunge at him. 'We don't want any more bloody Roman Catholics here!'

The guards rushed in as he was making another determined attempt, pulled him off Darnley and dragged him away. The Queen and Darnley stood still for a few minutes. Then she ran her hands all over him to see if he had been hurt. Oblivious of the fact that this gesture only made the whole scene more shocking still, Mary smiled and waved to the musicians for the dancing to go on.

But each of the following three days was a simmering cauldron of scandal, anger and blundering plots for a great many people. There was constant muttering behind closed doors. Couriers rode up to Holyrood in a lathering sweat. More couriers streaked away, and Abbie overheard Sir William saying, 'It is unfortunate that Lord Darnley is Catholic, Your Majesty.'

'Everyone likes him – and I am in love with him,' she said defiantly.

'Then my advice to you is to bed him, but for God's sake

not to wed him, madam. You will never unite Scotland under a Catholic king.'

As if that had not annoyed the Queen enough, Randolph was telling her the latest news from England the very next day. 'Elizabeth is furiously angry. She is demanding the return of Lord Darnley. She claims that you have tricked her by choosing a Catholic suitor. She is hinting at war.'

'Nonsense!' Mary cried. 'She sent Darnley to me herself.'

'She did,' Sir William agreed as they gazed at Randolph, perplexed. 'What can be in her mind, next?'

They did not have long to wait for an answer. Sir William was called out of a session of the Council to receive a message and came back shaken, excited and smiling.

'Incredible news, Your Majesty! Elizabeth will acknowledge you her successor if you will give up Lord Darnley and marry Robert Dudley!'

Abbie was stunned. Had she not, disguised as the Queen, dismissed Dudley herself? And was he not delighted to go?

Queen Mary was even more stunned. She was absolutely speechless. Lord James came and put an arm around her. 'Your dream has come true. If Elizabeth were to die tomorrow you would be the Queen of England. If she outlives you, your heirs are assured of her throne.'

Tears sprang to Mary's eyes, which Abbie wasn't surprised to see. The Queen had waited so long for this, plotted and hoped and prayed ... And now it came too late.

'No,' she said. 'I will marry Darnley.'

Suddenly the simmering cauldron boiled over, and all the mutterings exploded into a shouting match between brother and sister. Lord James snatched his arm away. 'Darnley?' he roared at the Queen. 'What use is *he* to any of us? I will not tolerate him!'

'*You* will not tolerate him? What does that mean? You are my subject!'

'I rule Scotland! Everyone knows that, whatever you may think, and I will choose its king! You will marry Dudley!'

'My lord, take care,' Sir William whispered nervously.

'Be quiet, damn you!' Lord James glared at Sir William and turned back to Mary. 'Marry Dudley or legitimise me! One or the other!'

'Legitimise you! So that you can call yourself King?' Mary's glance travelled contemptuously from his eyes down to his boots and then all the way back up again. 'You were born a bastard. You will die a bastard.'

'That insult will cost you your kingdom,' James hissed.

'And that remark is treason,' Mary said coldly. 'I'll have you brought to trial, for that.'

'Easier said than done,' James sneered. 'I am returning to St Andrews today. You have three months in which to marry Dudley or legitimise me. Otherwise I shall seize Scotland and establish absolute rule.' He bowed mockingly. 'Your humble servant, madam.'

After the door closed behind him Sir William said, 'Your Majesty, I implore you to marry Dudley!'

'Didn't you understand Robert Dudley?' Mary cried. 'I thought *you*, of all men, would have understood him! Dudley didn't want to marry me any more than I wanted to marry him. Why do you think I ordered Abbie to receive him instead of me? Why do you think he made himself look so ridiculous at that audience? He is far from a fool, Sir William, and he is in love with Queen Elizabeth.'

'God help us, then, Your Majesty.' Sir William was almost in tears. Abbie wondered if they were sincere, even when he went on to voice his loyalty. 'But if it comes to war between you and Lord James, I will not turn traitor.'

'Thank you,' she smiled wearily, and dismissed him.

'Oh, Abbie,' she groaned. 'Is there anyone, anywhere, I can trust? I should have been able to turn to Darnley in this predicament – but he is so new to this game. He would not understand.

'You know that I pardoned Huntly's son, Lord George Gordon, long ago,' the Queen continued to voice her thoughts. 'He could rally what is left of his clan and command a Highland army to win back his lands which I foolishly handed over to Lord James . . . I see now that I should not have been so generous to my snake of a bastard brother.'

Abbie did not dare to speak, and the Queen went on, 'Of course, Elizabeth will have thought of all that already. No doubt she engineered most of it. And Lord George Gordon is in an English prison . . . Oh no, Elizabeth will not let him go.

'Edinburgh and the whole central belt belongs to John Knox. He has turned it Protestant. It only leaves the Borders. The Borders? *Oh God – Bothwell!* Only Bothwell can control the Border lords and the lawless rabble of the south of Scotland. Bothwell is an experienced leader with the audacity to win against all the odds.

'And I expelled him myself,' Mary went on sadly. 'I should have realised that was another Protestant plot. Bothwell even tried to tell me so when he was being dragged off to Edinburgh Castle. Now he is so very far away. But,' her mouth tightened, 'I have committed myself to Darnley, and from now on I shall devote myself only to him, and to educate him in the ways of the land he will one day – soon – rule at my side.'

'We are to go to Stirling Castle,' Abbie told Lady Jean. 'The Queen is taking the whole court. She says she needs fresh air, and space – and I can't say I'm surprised at that,' she added tartly. 'Let's hope the fresh air will clear her mind, and she uses the space to come to her senses. In the meantime I must get word to Strathbogie, to let Donald know where I shall be.'

So on a bracing March day, proclaiming an early spring, Mary and Darnley led the way to Stirling. Perhaps the hunting and the hawking would be good there. In any case, they would be out of the stifling gossip and intrigue of Edinburgh, and they had not ridden many miles along the Firth of Forth before it became obvious that Mary's spirits were lifting.

Soon the Firth of Forth became just the River Forth and

shortly after that Stirling Castle came in sight, on top of its high rock with its head in the clouds.

'Now we are crossing Stirling Bridge,' they heard Mary telling Darnley, 'where –'

'I know! I know! Where William Wallace defeated the English in 1297. Must we always have these history lessons?' Darnley frowned. 'You sound like a tutor. I know you are three years older, but I am not your pupil. I learned all I need to know years ago,' he added arrogantly.

'But if you are to be King of Scotland –'

'I would wish to be King of the present, not of the past. Oh, Mary, we should live, and love, in the present.'

Abbie snorted. So he knew all there was to know – at nineteen? She glared at Darnley's back in front of her and thought that in taking on Darnley the Queen was only taking on another huge problem, probably her worst. But to judge from the way she was smiling up at him, she couldn't see it.

They rode into Stirling Castle and the company waited patiently to be assigned to their rooms, but they had to wait their turn. On her way to lead Darnley first to his, Mary stopped to speak to David Riccio.

'When you are ready, come and sing to us, Davy.'

She had given Darnley the King's apartments, with a connecting door through to her own. She knew it would cause more gossip and speculation, but quivering with excited anticipation of love she didn't care. She sent servants to show the others of her court to the crowded west wing of the royal apartments. Darnley, her beloved, must have the best.

And it was the best in all the land, aired and fresh-painted, gilded, sumptuous and inviting. Mary allowed Flamina and Abbie to help her out of her riding clothes and unpack some of her bags. Then she dismissed them, saying they could settle her in later, but they had hardly dipped in a curtsy before she ran to the connecting door. She couldn't wait.

Darnley opened it, and took her in his arms. Riccio, entering her bedchamber softly with his lute, as Flamina and Abbie were going out, was just in time to see the white whisk of her skirts before the door to Darnley's room closed in his face.

FORTY-NINE

They raced across the royal deer-park after game, and day after glorious day took their hawks and threw them into the air. Mary had never been so happy, day and night, for a very long time, and it showed as the roses bloomed in her cheeks once more.

One afternoon the Earl of Atholl rode up alongside Darnley and gestured him to stop. 'I could not give you this at the gallop,' he smiled, pushing a bottle into Darnley's saddlebag. 'It is very breakable.'

'What is it?'

'I thought you might like to sample my whisky. It is specially distilled for me, and very strong.'

'Indeed,' Darnley laughed. 'I was wondering where to obtain some whisky. I have heard such a lot about it.'

'There is plenty more where that came from,' the accommodating Earl replied. 'Just let me know.'

Later that night, when he was sure that everyone else had gone to bed, Darnley took the top off the bottle and swallowed a large gulp. A moment later he was coughing. It felt as though a fist had smashed into his chest. How could it do that? It was only liquid! The next minute the whisky was racing from his stomach to his brain. What would happen if he took another gulp?

This one didn't burn as much going down as the first one had, but his head was lifting off his shoulders and a beautiful feeling began, that he was floating off into another world . . . A world where there were no women.

He had hated his mother, always fussing over him, always keeping the wine away from him, always pushing him here and there. He had hated Queen Elizabeth and the orders she was always giving him. It was all Elizabeth's and his mother's fault that he was here tonight, miles away from civilisation and the friends he liked best, men of his own sort.

He drank a third time, and his mother faded away. Elizabeth faded away. Mary faded away. Thank God! He was free of the lot of them, free of women. Other young men would come to him. They always did. He could not imagine why he had felt so afraid, before ... Before he drank the whisky.

In only two weeks Darnley was addicted to whisky. Not that he could hold it. The lords could drink pints of the glorious golden stuff and never seem to be drunk. The only thing to do was to practise, and he was doing his best even if in the mornings he felt dizzy and his head ached terribly.

Riding out with Mary and the others sometimes cleared it, but today it was only getting worse and worse. They were returning across the courtyard on foot when he stopped suddenly, screaming with the pain. Mary ordered servants to carry him into his bedchamber, wringing her hands when he collapsed onto the bed, and calling for Dr Bourgoing to come at once to attend him. Taylor, Darnley's servant, undressed him, but by evening he was delirious.

'The fever is mounting,' said Dr Bourgoing. 'We must keep the light from his eyes, or they may be affected. I think it is measles.'

'He doesn't know me,' Mary wept, 'but Flamina and Abbie and I will take it in turns to stay with him.'

'You would do better to rest, Your Majesty, and wait for the spots to appear, if they are going to appear.'

'And if they do not? Oh, how can I rest, Dr Bourgoing? Tell me he will not die! I could not bear that, after Francis.'

'Measles, if it is measles, will not kill him, unless he already has some other affliction, such as syphilis . . . That may be different.'

'Syphilis? Syphilis?' Mary cried. 'They said that about Francis, too. Am I never to hear the end of that scourge? Lord Darnley is only nineteen. How could he have syphilis – at his age?'

'Hm,' said the doctor, drawing down his brows, terrifying her. 'Well, we must wait and see.'

Day after day Darnley kept vomiting, although the white eruptions inside his mouth surrounded by red, swollen tissue prevented him from eating or drinking, and it wasn't until the sixth day that the spots broke out, the fever began to subside and he opened his eyes, groaning to find Mary still holding his hand.

'I love you, Henry,' she said. 'I would not let you go.'

'I didn't think you would,' he croaked, and started to cry.

There were only two Marys left, now that Livingston and Beaton were married and gone. Lady Jean and Abbie took their places for the time being. In a fortnight Darnley was up on his feet again, and the Queen wept tears of gratitude to see her beloved restored to health although so thin and pale, and calling for wine. In those days of his convalescence she drank goblet for goblet with him, and a little under the influence one evening Mary could wait no longer.

'Ah, Davy,' she said, turning to Riccio who was singing softly in the corner, 'we release you from your duties tonight!'

For an instant there was a look of shock on Riccio's face. Then he smiled briefly in understanding and turned away, trailing his lute, its ribbons fluttering forlornly across the silk carpet behind him. Mary grabbed Darnley's hand, pulled him into his bedchamber and slid the bolt in the door. When she turned around he was standing there in the middle of the floor as if carved in wood, and stone cold sober again.

'What?' she laughed. 'You are not frightened, are you, Henry?'

But he was. He was terrified. 'Some whisky would help,' he said desperately.

'There is no whisky here, only wine. We shall both have some,' Mary smiled and poured it out.

He drank his in one gulp. 'I shall undress in my dressing room,' he said, grabbing the bottle and disappearing through the door.

How long he was taking! Mary removed her clothes and lay down on the great royal bed. Her father's bed, she reflected. From time to time she heard the gurgle of the bottle as he had another drink, and another, and another. But at last he emerged from the dressing room unsteadily, white-faced and naked.

'Oh, you are beautiful,' she breathed, and threw back the covers to welcome him into the bed. 'Oh, Henry,' she murmured, feeling his body all along hers, 'only now do I truly feel I am a queen.'

He entered her clumsily, as if he wanted to get it over quickly. 'Oh! Oh! Oh!' he cried out, and he was finished. But it didn't matter to Mary, smiling into the darkness. They had all the rest of their lives to get it right, and she spent the next few hours holding his precious body close to hers while he slept.

She thought it must be three or four o'clock in the morning when she slid out of his bed naked and tiptoed through to her own, finding another silk nightgown to put on. Something was making it stick to her body, but exhausted, she slept until the sun streaming in through the window woke her.

Flamina was bustling around the room.

'Please, I must have a bath,' Mary said, and within minutes warm water was brought by the servants and poured into the large tin bath over by the fireplace.

Abbie arrived with the last jug of water, and positioned the screen. Behind it Mary removed the soiled nightgown. Abbie and Flamina held the large bath-sheet over the bath while Mary slid under it into the water.

Immediately a strong, familiar odour filled Abbie's nostrils.

It must have filled Flamina's, too. They glanced at each other and quickly looked away again. Flamina's face was on fire.

Yes, Abbie thought, Flamina has recognised it too – that unmistakable odour of semen.

But in that speculation Abbie was wrong, for it was not the first time that Flamina had smelled that same odour on the Queen when attending to her most intimate toilet, and she had gossiped and giggled about it to Sir William only three weeks ago, telling him that Riccio stayed too long in Her Majesty's bedchamber at nights. 'And they are not making music, all the time,' Flamina had added. 'So you know what else they are doing, William. Making love . . .'

'Your Majesty,' Flamina asked hastily now, still blushing, 'shall I pour in some oil of sandalwood?'

'Please. And now you may both leave me. I can manage myself.'

'Go! Go!' Mary was screaming inside. 'Leave me! Let me think about what has happened . . . My beautiful secret.'

A few minutes later she resolved to hold the ceremony of the Order of the Thistle. She must marry at once, and her husband must be at least an Earl. She would make Darnley the Earl of Ross. Later, she would bestow on him a higher title still, the Duke of Albany. By then, he would be the King of Scotland.

She had never been so happy in her life.

All Fool's Day came in as merry and playful as its name, with the sun dancing in a bright blue sky and a little teasing wind. It was just the sort of day that Donald *would* arrive at Stirling Castle! Looking over the ramparts for him, as she did every morning, Abbie laughed and raced to meet him. 'Are you really here? Or is this an April Fool's trick?'

'I'm really here,' he beamed. 'It's not a trick.'

'Oh, Donald, it was so lonely without you! Don't go rescuing anyone again for a long time.'

'I'll rescue nobody except you and me, I promise you, and our honeymoon. When can you be ready to go home?'

'I'm ready now. But first I'll have to see the Queen, and say my goodbyes. I'll be heart-glad to leave this suffocating place with all its scandals, and go with you to live an ordinary life again.'

'Is that all you have?' he asked, eyeing her two little bundles, packed and ready to go.

'There are Queen Catherine's boxes.' Abbie pointed to the corner.

'I love you, Abbie. Don't waste any time on your goodbyes. In the meantime I'll be tying your boxes onto my horse.'

The Queen and Sir William exchanged alarmed glances when she asked permission to leave the court, glances that were not lost on Abbie. For a minute she had a sinking feeling that permission was going to be refused.

'How could I stop any wife from going to live with her husband?' Mary sighed dreamily. 'It is only natural.'

So she had managed to strike while the iron was hot! Abbie felt quite triumphant, after all. She was almost free . . .

She curtsied to the Queen and was beginning to walk backwards to the door when Sir William spoke in silken tones.

'Yes,' he said, 'it is only natural. Enjoy it, Mistress Abbie. The time has come to wish you every happiness, as we part . . . *If* we part. Huntly is not at the other side of the world, is it?'

Uncomfortably, Abbie didn't feel quite so free any more. She might only be escaping by the skin of her teeth.

She lingered longest with Lady Jean. 'I'll write to you, Abbie,' Jean said, 'and tell you what's happening here. There are always riders going north to take letters.'

'And you won't forget your promise to me, Jeannie, at the first hint of trouble?'

'I haven't forgotten. But there's no sign of Bothwell, and no mention of him at all. I feel safe enough, now.'

So Abbie and Donald returned happily to their little house in Huntly, hoping to settle down for ever. Lizzie Sproat from next door knocked and waved a plate of fresh-baked oatcakes at the window, and when she went to the door to let her in Abbie saw that Jack Sproat had been looking after their tiny garden at the back.

'Oh,' she smiled. 'You've even planted daffodils! What a lovely welcome, Jack,' and kissed the old man.

'He's not bad, considering,' Lizzie agreed. 'And he caught a rabbit yesterday. I've made a rabbit stew, so you'll both come round and share it with us this evening.'

They had plenty to talk about. Donald regaled them with stories of how the Gordons had finally recaptured Dunrobin Castle, how they had installed Alexander Sutherland back in his ancestral seat, and how badly damaged it was now, after all the fighting.

'He's going to try and restore it,' Donald said, 'but it will take time and a lot of money. However, we left him with the Sutherland clan massed around him again. He'll have plenty of help.'

'And what about our own Strathbogie Castle, and the Gordons?' Jack asked.

'Ah, well,' Donald's face clouded over. 'That's a different matter. It will never be right until Lord George gets out of prison and comes home to rally the clan and repair the damage caused by the Queen's men, if he has the money.'

'*If he has the money?*' Jack snorted. 'The money must be somewhere in Strathbogie. Huntly was one of the richest men in Scotland.'

'Is there nothing can be done in the meantime?' Abbie asked.

'Your father and Geordie Brand are trying to recruit more men, but it's not easy when they can offer no wages. No money has been found in the rubble. But some of the faithful are volunteering, and we hope other Huntly men will come and try to do something with the castle. The furniture is still lying there in bits. It could be mended while the rest of us are trying to patch up the walls.'

'I'll come,' Jack said.

'You'll need women too.' Lizzie's eyes sparkled. 'It'll be a rare ploy for us in our old age.'

'It's too late now to go and see my mother,' Abbie yawned.

'She'll be in bed,' Donald said. 'Where you and I are going right now, Abbie MacLaren.'

'Ay,' Lizzie smiled and sighed sentimentally. 'Meetings are aye sweetest after long partings. God bless you both.'

'I don't know how I kept my hands off you all evening,' Donald said when they went back home and shut their door.

'Lizzie was right,' Abbie whispered later. 'It *was* sweeter even than I remembered.'

FIFTY

Next morning Abbie went down to the Gardeners' Cottage and was shocked at the deterioration in her youngest brother's condition. She was further shocked when Abigail still would not admit that Johnny was seriously ill, and refused point-blank to talk about it.

'I don't know which of them worries me most,' John McCracken told Abbie outside in the garden.

'I wish you wouldn't worry so much, Father,' she said, her heart sinking at the sight of him. His hair had turned snow-white and he looked ten years older than when she had seen him last.

A month later the first letter arrived from Lady Jean, still at Stirling Castle.

> I have received very sad news from my mother in France. My dear brother, Adam, took ill and never recovered. He died on 15 March. She says that she will go back to Strathbogie, but she doesn't say when.
>
> The Queen has conferred titles on Lord Darnley, amongst others the title of Earl of Ross, which as you know is a royal title, borne only by a Scottish prince. From that we deduce that she is determined to go ahead with the marriage.
>
> Darnley is very often drunk and always very demanding. Mary heaps honours and jewels on him as a doting mother would heap sweetmeats on a spoiled child. She has had some of her priceless rings

widened for him and he now wears ten of them, five on each hand.

Abbie felt uneasy after reading this letter. It seemed that as long as she lived Queen Mary would continue to dominate their lives. In fact, everyone felt uneasy that summer, for so many strange omens were reported in Scotland.

There were shooting stars. Fishermen fled from enormous sea-monsters, the likes of which had never been seen or heard of before. Trees withered all around the north of the country. The earth trembled and ravens croaked. In the Mull of Galloway a blue light was seen moving swiftly over the waves, but when it came ashore the people saw that it was not a boat at all, but a carriage lit with blue lamps and drawn by six white horses and inside, it was full of witches.

It was an uneasy, unhappy time for many people, but Alex Ogilvie must have been one of the unhappiest of all, as he took up his quill to write to his dearest friend.

> To Sir Patrick Spence, on 14 June this year of Our Lord 1565, from Boyne House, Edinburgh.
> Pat, my dear friend,
> As you see, we are now domiciled at the above address. Going to Boyne Castle was a big mistake. Our hasty marriage was a disaster. It is now at an end, although for appearances' sake we still live under the same roof.
> I shall go into it no further than this. We had not been at the castle six months before my wife had seduced every man in the place, even the menservants, but when she set about my friends coming to visit me, I was forced to put a stop to it all.
> Realising that she suffers from some sort of madness

Here, Alex Ogilvie broke off in tears, remembering amongst other things the magnificent chess set Sir Pat had sent him from Italy, made of Venetian glass, the pieces etched in gold

400

and always kept high on a window-sill to allow the light to stream through their glorious jewel colours. He remembered how, in one of her frenzies, Mary Beaton had swept them down. He remembered his horror when all he could do was stand there and stare at all the coloured shards and splinters. He remembered how she had screamed and laughed, at the splinters of their marriage ... No, he could not tell Sir Pat any of that.

> Realising that she suffers from some sort of madness I closed up the castle for the last time and brought my wife here, where she can pursue her own style of living on the principle that in such a large town as Edinburgh, it will not be so immediately remarked.
>
> From time to time she becomes very ill, then partially recovers. The physician has diagnosed the onset of syphilis.
>
> I should not need to tell you above all, dear Pat, how much I hold myself to blame, not only for all this, but also and far, far worse, for letting down the only woman I ever truly loved, Lady Jean Gordon.
>
> Those fourteen letters of the alphabet which make up her name pierce me as I print them, like fourteen daggers. My heart is bleeding. I am truly in Hell.
>
> Alexander Ogilvie of Boyne.

One night when Abbie looked out she shuddered at a moon ringed with blood. 'I'm frightened, Donald,' she whispered. 'It means war.'

He tightened his arms around her. 'War or peace, you're safe with me. We have better things to worry about anyway,' he said as he made passionate love to her again. 'Little things, such as tiny feet pattering about this house, my Abbie.'

Lady Jean's next letter was from Holyrood Palace and dated 22 August 1565. It was delivered to Abbie only two days later by one of the Scottish Guard who had ridden north in a hurry to consult with what Gordon soldiers were left.

At six o'clock on the morning of 29 July Queen Mary and Henry, Duke of Albany, Earl of Ross, were married in the Chapel Royal. At her command we dressed her in her great black mourning gown with the black hood. She said that she felt compelled to wear it so that from the grave Francis could release her and give his blessing.

Bad omens attended the marriage. The sky was almost as black as her gown, thunder rumbled and the Queen had a nose-bleed just before she went into the Chapel.

She wears not just one wedding ring, but three, symbolising the Trinity. Darnley wears the diamond chain she gave him around his waist.

He is drinking heavily and plaguing the Queen for the Crown Matrimonial. So far she has refused to grant it. Next, he has insisted on having the King's apartments. Fleming, Seton and I have been removed to the west wing.

The citizens of Edinburgh caused a great tumult about the marriage when the royal heralds announced it at the Mercat Cross and posted up the proclamation. It reads, 'The Queen's beloved husband Henry, Lord Darnley, Duke of Albany, will henceforth be styled and honoured as Henry, King of Scotland.'

Another proclamation has just been posted declaring Lord James Stewart, Earl of Moray, an outlaw and rebel traitor to the Queen, and he has been put to the horn. Sir William Maitland has joined Lord James's faction, leaving the Queen without her chief adviser.

Now, beyond the gardens of Holyrood, Mary's army is gathering in the meadows below Arthur's Seat. The Royal Mile is crammed with soldiers. In Edinburgh Castle Erskine's cannon are trained on the town, at the ready for any invasion.

The Queen is determined to ride to war against Lord James and the rebels. Darnley and Riccio are going with her. Fleming, Seton and I have also been ordered to accompany her, to attend to her needs.

Abbie read the letter with mounting horror.

'What does Lady Jean say?' Donald asked, eyeing her white face.

'The Queen is going to war against Lord James and the rebels. She is gathering her army.'

'Yes. She sent a message to the Gordons by the same soldier who brought you that letter, calling us to arms.'

'*WHAT*? No, Donald!' Abbie cried. 'We are not to be separated again? Tell me it isn't true!'

'Don't worry, sweetheart. By the time she masses us all in Edinburgh it will be late in September. She's leaving it too late in the year. Besides, she is asking us to bring only fifteen days' provisions with us. It won't be a war. It can only be a runaround before the winter sets in.'

'But how can she expect the Gordons to go, when she had so many of them killed at Corrichie?'

'I'm afraid it was the Earl of Huntly who had them killed, by rebelling. The Gordons have always been loyal to the Crown. If Lord George were here, that is what he would expect of us. We must just try to carry on in his absence as he would wish.'

'Fleming, Seton and Lady Jean are riding with Mary, to attend to her, although Fleming must be heartbroken now that Sir William has joined Lord James, just another traitor.'

'Well, *you* will not be with them, Abbie. I forbid it,' Donald said sternly. 'You're going to no war. Just you stay here and wait for me. I shouldn't be away for much longer than five minutes, anyway. Mary is only playing another of her games, wait and see. And this time she can dress up in armour and a steel helmet, and carry pistols at her belt!'

'You are forgetting that as well as being headstrong and often very foolish, she is always very brave,' Abbie said sadly.

* * *

403

What was left of the Gordon fighting force, Donald and John McCracken and Geordie Brand at the head of them, rode away a few days later. Determined to keep busy and fill her mind with other things, Abbie's first thought was for the baking lesson Lizzie Sproat had promised her that morning.

'What shall it be today, Lizzie?'

'Well, I have a little fresh farm butter, some white flour and some rice. The only thing I lack for this recipe is sugar.'

'Wait,' Abbie said, and came flying back from next door with a large lump of it, to find Lizzie with her sleeves rolled up, grinding down the rice.

'Break off a bit of that sugar and grind it as fine as you can,' Lizzie instructed, handing over the rolling pin, 'and then we can start.' First of all she blended together the butter and the sugar with her hands. Then she added the flour and the ground rice. 'Notice that the minute it becomes oily I will stop,' she said. 'The less kneading, the shorter and crisper it will be. And I will not roll it out, only press it into this wooden mould. Now, watch me pinching the edges with my finger and thumb.'

'It's shortbread!' Abbie said, watching Lizzie pricking it all over with a fork before she put it into a slow oven. 'Donald's favourite, although he only tasted it once, at Wemyss Castle. He speaks of it as in a dream.'

Abbie and Lizzie chatted together for the next half-hour while they cleaned the kitchen and the glorious smell of the shortbread came wafting through the room.

'Yes, shortbread is every man's favourite,' Lizzie said when she took the flat golden cake out of the oven. 'I've never known a man to refuse it yet. What are you going to do next, Abbie?'

'I'm going out into the garden. Jack was telling me it's time to start tidying it up for the winter – and it's such a glorious day!'

Abbie didn't tell Lizzie that she suddenly felt so hot in her kitchen that she had got a headache. She just had to get outside for some fresh air, and she was bending down to pull out a dandelion that had had the temerity to invade her garden, when she felt her neck begin to get sore. In fact, she was feeling so ill all of a sudden that she thought she should go and lie down inside.

'What's the matter, lassie?' Jack asked. 'I'll go and fetch Lizzie.'

'Run down to the Gardeners' Cottage for Abigail,' Lizzie told Jack a few minutes later. 'Then stay with Johnny until she gets back.'

'It's my head, and my neck, Mother.' Abbie fingered the glands on the side of her neck.

'Mercy me!' Lizzie exclaimed. 'Look at those spots on her arms!'

'Are they anywhere else?' Abigail asked, pulling down Abbie's bodice to reveal her chest. 'Oh, yes! Here's some more! What are they, Lizzie?'

'They look like measles, but they're not any measles I've ever seen before. Look! The spots have disappeared from her arm, and they are coming and going in runs on her chest.'

'Let's have a look at your back, Abbie,' her mother said, but even as she and Lizzie turned her over a run of spots was fading away.

'I've never seen anything like it,' Abigail said.

'It's some kind of dirt she's picked up in Edinburgh,' Lizzie said scornfully. 'There are all kinds of wickedness and evil there.'

Abbie laughed. 'It's a long time since I was in Edinburgh, Lizzie! And anyway, I feel better now. The headache has gone. I'm going to get up and walk back down to the cottage with you, Mother.'

'You'll do no such thing, Abbie MacLaren,' her mother frowned. 'You'll stay in your bed for the rest of this day, anyway! And you mustn't come down to the cottage until you are completely better, for Johnny's sake. Those spots might be catching.'

But the following day, except for her neck which was still sore, Abbie had recovered, and a week later, when she went to see Abigail again, she had completely forgotten the whole little incident.

'Are you better?' her mother looked at her keenly.

'Oh, I was better from the spots the very next day,' Abbie dismissed them. 'But Mother, there is something else! I won't be better from it for another six months!'

'A baby, dearie? Does Donald know?'

'No. I wasn't sure when he went away. But oh! I am so happy! And when Donald knows he will be in seventh heaven, Mother. He has been so desperate for a child of our own.'

FIFTY-ONE

Three weeks later, Abbie took ill in the garden again. This time Jack Sproat found her clinging on to the fence between their gardens, while terrible pains ripped through her. He and Lizzie got her to bed, and once again summoned Abigail.

But this time, the pains only got worse, and Abbie didn't like the way the two older women were looking so worried. 'Tell me it's only cramps, Mother,' she begged Abigail, beginning to cry because she knew it was something far worse than that.

'I'll stay with you tonight, dearie. And Lizzie's here, as well. Jack's gone down to the cottage to stay with Johnny. Now, don't you worry about another thing.'

In the middle of the night Abbie was writhing in agony, and clutching both her mother's hands. 'What is it, Mother?' she cried between her screams. 'Am I losing the baby?'

Then there came the worst pain of all, and blood, and more blood, and Abigail was in tears when she replied, 'You've lost it, Abbie . . . Oh, I am so sorry, my poor wee lassie.'

And that was her child, a part of her and a part of Donald, that Lizzie was whisking away in a blood-soaked cloth. 'Was it a boy or a girl,' Abbie asked.

'We think it was a little boy,' Abigail answered sadly, 'but it was hard to tell. It was Nature's way, Abbie, to reject it. Try and think only of that, because the child would not have been normal.'

Abbie was far from recovered when Donald came back a few

weeks later. She knew she would never recover until he was by her side, and he saw at once from her face that something terrible had happened. When she told him she thought she had never seen anyone so distraught. They cried together, and they mourned together for a little light that had gone out of their lives, and would never come back again.

It was days before they felt even a little better, and could manage to talk about other things. Donald explained what had happened in the summer. 'What did I tell you?' Donald said. 'There was no fighting at all, only chasing about after Lord James and the rebels. Already they are calling it the Chaseabout Raid.'

'What happened in the end?' Abbie asked.

'We chased them over the Border into England. With Bothwell's help, of course.'

'*Bothwell?*' Abbie cried in horror, clutching at her breast.

'Oh, yes – he's back. He and his Borderers came crawling out of the woodwork of Hermitage Castle, so to speak.'

'So he had been hiding there . . .'

'Whatever, it was a brilliant stroke on his part. The Queen was forced to pardon him and give him back his job.'

'Where is he now?'

'At Hermitage, as far as I know. After all, he *is* Lieutenant of the Borders, Abbie. Why? What do you care about the Earl of Bothwell?'

'You know I hate him. But that has nothing to do with it. Oh God, Donald – what will happen to Lady Jean now?'

Within a week a letter came from Lady Jean herself:

So far, all is well with me. There were rumours that Bothwell had sneaked back from the Continent without the Queen's permission. Certainly, he turned up at the Borders with his men. It was he who threw Lord James and the rebels into England and into the hands of Queen Elizabeth. He is no longer an outlaw, and I believe remains at Hermitage. But I dare not ask.

I spend time with Mary Seton. Together we are illuminating a Prayer Book. She is a good friend to me, but she is not my dearest Abbie.

It sounded so calm that Abbie's fears were stilled . . . almost.

On All-Hallows Eve the north wind screamed down from the Highlands, tearing through trees, whining across heather moors. From north to south Scottish folk saw red fire on the hills and heard witches wailing on the wind.

In Edinburgh children shrieked and scuttered through the wynds and closes off the High Street with their turnip lanterns. Bonfires burned on Arthur's Seat, warning off vampires and goblins. Fox cubs rolled between the haystacks on the moonlit meadows, and in the stables of White Horse Close the horses neighed and whinnied and stamped their hooves, restless in the dark.

But inside Holyrood the Great Hall blazed with lights for a victory ball. The company talked of Mary's courage to have ridden from Edinburgh at the head of five thousand troops, and of Lord Bothwell's timely appearance further south with five thousand more to support her.

Now Lord James and the rest of the Protestant rebels were at a standstill at Newcastle and Sir William Maitland of Lethington had conveniently disappeared to his country estate. Queen Elizabeth ridiculed their failure. Between her scorn and the armed fury of Queen Mary they sulked, while Bothwell was pardoned and brought back to Edinburgh in triumph.

'They won't plague Scotland again in a hurry,' Bothwell said at a pause in the dancing. 'Forget that bastard brother of yours, and his scum. Be happy, madam.'

'Oh, I am,' Mary laughed and pirouetted in a white gown laced with scarlet ribbons, whirling in a froth of lacy petticoats. 'Thanks to you I feel ten years younger. I feel like a girl again.'

'Come then, lassie, and play with me,' Bothwell said,

catching her hand. 'What shall it be? Bobbing for apples? Or blind man's buff?'

'We shall play at fencing, my lord. You and I were always good at that –' Mary teased him with her golden eyes and ran off, reappearing in seconds changed into satin breeches and shirt and calling for a rapier.

While the dancers squealed and scattered they fenced skilfully, playfully, until he forced her up on a window seat.

'I give up,' she said, laughing, flushed, and throwing down her rapier. 'I submit to you, my lord.'

'Ah ... if only you would,' he whispered, catching her when she jumped down and holding her against his lean, hard body.

Very aware, Mary drew back. Her lashes dropped to veil her slanting eyes. 'Please excuse me. I must change to my gown and dance with the King.'

Bothwell glanced across at Darnley, who was filling his glass again at the wine buffet. 'Dance with him? When he can scarcely stand?'

'He is celebrating our victory,' she shrugged, and went to her bedchamber.

When she came back she was secretly overcome with disappointment to find Bothwell gone, but another visitor had arrived, so that she had no time to brood about it. Sir Nicholas Throckmorton had come from London, his blond good looks dulled by weariness. He looked far older than when Mary had seen him last at Calais.

'I am delighted to welcome you here, my good friend,' she said, extending both her hands for him to kiss. Then she led him to a quiet corner. 'Dear Ambassador, how is Elizabeth?'

'Heartsick, Your Majesty. Your last letter hinted that she conspired with Lord James and the rebels.'

'Perhaps she misunderstood,' Mary purred, and they went on to hedge around other prickly subjects, such as the Scots' piracy of English ships and the disappearance of shipments of English blue woollens.

410

'It is odd,' Throckmorton observed, 'that it coincides with a burst of blue in Bothwell's Liddesdale.'

'Odd indeed,' Mary smiled at him. 'The Borderers do not usually dress in wool. They prefer leather . . . But I will look into it. Will you be here long, Sir Nicholas?'

'Her Majesty allows me only two days, because she knows all too well how much I admire you, madam. I wish she would appoint me here permanently, but there is little chance of that. Still, I am your good friend, whatever she says, so may I be permitted to advise you?'

'You may.'

'Dismiss Riccio as fast as you can.'

'What?'

'Lord James has spread the rumour that Riccio is your lover, and because he saw you in Riccio's arms at Stirling you outlawed him in guilty and spiteful revenge. Madam, even the ballad pedlars have the tale, and are spreading it through both Scotland and England.'

'Why should I care? Scotland is united behind me, thanks to Lord Bothwell – and, of course, the King,' Mary added hastily.

They turned to look at Darnley, sprawled in a chair, staring at nothing and grinning foolishly. A goblet lay on the floor beside him in a puddle of wine.

'Madam,' Throckmorton said impulsively at the sight of him, 'in loyalty to my mistress I should not be telling you this, but Randolph told me half an hour ago when I arrived, that the King visited Knox this week.'

Mary's face went white. 'That is impossible.'

'With his own eyes he saw him enter Knox's house at dusk on Monday.'

Mary stared at him. 'My husband is a good Catholic. Knox could never convert him.'

'Then Knox must have had some other purpose, madam.'

'I shall find out what it is.'

'Be careful, madam. Tread as though on eggshells.'

* * *

Mary had never been so lonely in her life, and she was very tired. Usually she loved working at her embroidery, but now it lay on her lap, discarded. Her husband should have been at her side, but Darnley was absent most evenings. On the one hand she was thoroughly thankful for it, because he was always very drunk when he came home. On the other hand she resented that it left her so lonely with no one except Riccio to talk to about her troubles.

But there was always Riccio. He had never stopped loving her.

If Darnley arrived drunk in her bed he wanted her to do all sorts of strange things. They made her tired, and very unhappy about her personal life, and when she was unhappy the pain in her side always came back.

'I am the King,' he yelled on one of these occasions, when she was in bed, lying on her stomach, trying to ease the pain.

'Of course you are, Henry.'

Oh God, he was drunk again . . . Between the disgust of it and the pain in her side she felt sick.

'Then why was I not at the head of the army in a suit of golden armour? I will never be a proper king as long as you act like a man and enjoy it, as you clearly did on that Chaseabout Raid.'

'Don't be silly,' Mary sighed. 'My troops needed a leader, a sober leader, riding in front of them. And yes, I did enjoy that.'

He tore off his clothes, pushed her over to one side of the bed and got in. Then he grabbed her and lifted her on top of him. 'Well, let's see how you enjoy *this*,' he shouted, forcing his penis up inside her. 'You want to be a man? This is what it's like! Ride me! Rather, ride me against my will! It is better sport, that way.'

'You make a mockery of me and our lovemaking with such a foolish thought,' she said sickly, and tried to pull away. 'Let me go!'

'No, I will not. I am your husband. I am the King, in bed or out of it. You will obey my command.' He stared up at her, and she was suddenly frightened of the cold look in his eyes. She had never dreamed that his thin, stick-like arms possessed so much strength as when he flipped her over in the bed. 'We'll play another love game instead, then,' he said, and heaved her up so that she was on her hands and knees.

He came at her from behind, his hands grinding into her waist and hurting her sore side so viciously that the breath was knocked out of her in the sudden agony. She wanted to tell him that he was hurting her. She wanted to tell him that he was entering the wrong passage of her body, but she had no breath except to scream, and scream, and scream into the pillows for fear that someone would hear them and burst in. 'Now I'll ride *you*, the way all women deserve,' he slurred. 'Like a horse. Like a dog. Like a bitch.'

He was frantic with a strange excitement. She had never known him like this before, tearing at her, biting her shoulder, holding her in an iron grasp. He was like a madman, holding her victim while he satisfied his lust.

'You disgust me,' Mary said bitterly, lurching on to her good side when he had finished. 'Love games? Yes, that's all it ever was to you. As you say, a bitch, or a slut, or a hole in the wall, it would be all the same to you. You don't love me. You never did.'

For a minute he almost seemed to be sober again, breathless and penitent. 'Don't scold me, Mary,' he snivelled. 'I'm only young.'

She sighed sadly. Yes, he was young – and foolish – and warped. 'Why did you ever marry me?' she asked in despair.

'It wasn't my idea. It was –'

'Whose?' she ground out between teeth clamped together to stop her from screaming again. If the guards, or Riccio, or the Marys heard any of this they would send for Dr Bourgoing, and she would rather bear the pain than the shame.

He rolled out of bed and fell on the floor in a drunken stupor.

413

Mary had been having the pain in her side ever since, and now she was often sick in the mornings with the intensity of it.

'By all the signs, you are with child,' Darnley said moodily.

'You are counting chickens, Henry. I – I am not sure.'

'And how can *I* be sure of anything nowadays? For all I know, it could be Riccio's child.'

'Have a care! That is insulting!'

'Am I not insulted too? The nobles laugh at me when you are closeted with that boolie-backed Italian all day, and sometimes half the night! Knox says –'

'What does Knox say?'

'That he is a papal spy.'

Mary smiled at him. That wasn't it. He was hiding all manner of things. Determined to get to the bottom of them she kneeled beside him, smoothing back his golden hair. He was a big child, and she must pretend.

'Overburdened with matters of state, I *have* been neglecting you, haven't I, dearest husband? I must persuade Parliament to agree to the crown for you.' His eyes gleamed at that, and she rose up and fetched *aqua vitae*. 'Forgive me, Henry. Let's be friends again and have a drink together.'

Taking only a small sip herself now and then, Mary watched him drinking deeply, changing from the arrogance he had started with to pettishness and then to drowsy sentimentality.

'I will never love another woman,' he wept. 'Never! Oh, Mary, I didn't believe Riccio was your lover.'

'Who would believe such a lie?'

'Lord Morton . . .'

Morton? Once Lord James's friend, but too cautious and too frightened for his post as Lord High Chancellor of Scotland to join the rebels.

'Sir William Maitland,' Darnley was opening the floodgates of confession now. The whisky had loosened his tongue. 'Your dear Sir William! You never thought that, did you?' he smiled triumphantly, knowing things that she did not.

Sir William? Yes, she could believe that. As Riccio's fortunes rose, so Sir William's declined.

'Lord Ruthven,' Darnley babbled on.

That madman! Dying of consumption and said to be a sorcerer. 'And I suppose Knox believes it too?' Mary sighed.

'Knox sent for me,' Darnley whimpered.

'Knox sent for *you*? The King? And you went?'

'He said that Riccio is your lover. He wants me to spy on you. He says you have treated me shamefully. He says I must drive Riccio from power or I shall never have power myself.'

Then Mary knew that she had uncovered another Protestant plot. This time they wanted to get rid of Riccio and lay the blame on the King. But this poor arrogant King himself couldn't see that he was just a pawn in their game. With tears in her eyes, murmuring endearments, she continued to stroke his hair.

'And who told you that you must marry me, Henry?' she murmured as she soothed him.

'My mother,' he said drowsily. 'But it was really Queen Elizabeth. I hate them both.'

'Never mind, dearest,' Mary whispered, with loathing. 'You're here with me, now.'

What had possessed her to marry such a fool, such a weakling? Oh God, what a terrible blunder! And, she thought with a grimace of distaste, she must continue to pretend to be his nearest and dearest, to confound their enemies, especially now . . .

Because she suspected that she really was pregnant.

Gently, she laid Darnley's head on his pillow and making sure that he was deeply asleep, she slipped out of the bed-chamber and through to the antechamber where Riccio was still working at his papers.

'I should have Knox hanged,' she said, telling him about the plot, 'and I would, if I had not found out that Henry is implicated.'

'The fools should know that a woman such as you could

never look upon a hunchback with eyes of love,' Riccio said sadly. 'Not for long.'

'You know that isn't true.'

'You cannot afford another scandal, madam. You no longer need me as you did. I should leave Scotland.'

'Oh, no!' Mary said, and kneeled by his chair. 'I need you all the time, Davy. No one else is both capable and loyal, as you are.'

'But if I remain, the slander can only grow . . .'

Wind stirred the tapestries. The ashes fell in the fireplace, and suddenly it was very cold. Mary shivered as the last candle guttered out.

'Don't leave me, Davy, tonight or ever, I beg you!'

Riccio put his arms around her. 'I will never leave you,' he said.

But the following night, from the antechamber where he shuffled his papers, he could faintly hear her and Darnley talking together again in her bedchamber. Her voice was gentle, as always. His was raised, but his words were muffled.

'So you are alone?' Darnley was sneering.

'Yes, for now.'

'Ah-ha! You expect a guest? Well, you can dismiss him.'

'Him? What do you mean?'

'What do I mean? Who do I mean? You know who I mean!'

'I expect Seton. She has gone to get some oil, to rub on my side.'

'Seton be damned! It is Riccio you wait for. Come here!' He took her by the hair and dragged her out of bed.

Riccio could stand no more of it. Weeping, he flung out of the palace and into the Royal Mile.

'Get down on your knees and kiss my feet,' Darnley was yelling now. Having flung Mary onto the floor he pushed her head further down.

She pulled herself back, got to her feet and slapped him

416

hard across his mouth. 'You drunken bully!' she cried. 'How dare you come to me in this state again?'

'Because I am your husband. I am your lord and master. I can do as I like!' He made another grab for her, but she stepped to one side and he fell with a crash headfirst on the floor, moaning.

She went to the door and called the guards. 'Take the King away,' she said. 'I don't care where, so long as he is out of here.'

They dragged him out and threw him in a heap into the antechamber. Then Mary turned the huge iron key in the lock, something she had never done before. She would never open her door to that monster again.

Half sobered two hours later Darnley staggered to his feet and went to try the door. It was locked. He couldn't believe it. He heard nothing from inside except Mary's quiet weeping. But she often wept after love. Who was with her? Who had satisfied her to tears? It had to be Riccio. No wonder the nobles laughed. Tears blurred his own eyes as he made his way outside. There were women – and men – who *would* welcome him, the King. There were places in Edinburgh that never slept.

He got past the sentries easily at that time of night, or morning, he didn't know which, scaled the wall and landed unsteadily in the Canongate. All was dark. There were no lanterns still burning, and no sound except for the scurrying of rats.

Then, just in front of him, he thought he saw someone, and that someone stumbled and fell across the cobbles. Darnley jerked him up, and saw who he was, who he must be, with that hunched back.

'It's you, David Riccio! And you are looking for a house of comfort, as I am! Let me show you the way, my good fellow. I know them all.'

'No, no! I am only walking, trying to decide –'

'Decisions, decisions! I know all about them, too – whether

it shall be a he-house, or a she-house tonight. Come with me!'

Darnley dragged the little man along beside himself with glee. Now he had him where he wanted him!

If he couldn't punish Mary, he knew a way to crucify her lover instead.

FIFTY-TWO

'Turn left here,' Darnley told Riccio, and when they got around the corner there was a faint sound of voices in the silent darkness of the Royal Mile. 'This is it,' he said, and knocked on a low door.

Riccio waited with him, shivering with cold and besides that, with a tingle of excitement. A small shutter on the door was slammed back and an eye peered out.

'The password?' rumbled a deep voice.

Darnley giggled and shouted in his thin, reedy voice, 'Are we happy?'

'Ay, we're gay,' came a laughing chorus from inside.

'Let him in then, Bonzo,' someone shouted, 'or he'll freeze his balls off, standing out there.'

The door opened and the doorman jerked his thumb over his shoulder to point them into a dimly lit room. Riccio was becoming very lustful now and very desirous for a woman. Darnley pushed him onto a bench in front of a long table and then sat down himself, signalling to a serving boy to fetch ale.

When it arrived, they both took a long drink from their mugs and Riccio began to feel warmer and better. After a second mug he peered around at his surroundings and at all the men who were there. The place was full of men, men of all shapes and sizes, young and old. He supposed that this was where they waited their turn for the women.

'You've not come yourself tonight, Your Majesty,' a young man with a girlish face and long black ringlets was lisping in Darnley's left ear and peering past him at Riccio.

'No,' Darnley replied, and to Riccio's acute embarrassment, kissed the young man's cheek. 'I have brought a novice tonight.'

Two large burly men on Riccio's right who were sitting with their arms around each other, looked up at that.

'A novice, eh?' one of them said.

'*My* novice,' Darnley scowled at him. 'Remember that.'

'For initiation?' asked the other.

'All in good time.' Darnley waved his free arm regally. With his other he was hugging his companion now. His golden head bent over him while he kissed the young man passionately on the mouth. 'More ale,' he lifted his face long enough to yell.

There was something very far wrong here. In an agony of embarrassment Riccio knew it. He lifted his third mug and became more and more uneasy. Had he stumbled into one of those depraved houses that he had heard about? If he could have got out, he would have gone there and then. But there was no way, hemmed in as he was by all these men kissing and cuddling each other. It made him feel sick.

Then two of them stood up, climbed across the bench and went over to the wall. They both pulled down their breeches, and what happened next took Riccio's breath away.

The man facing the wall turned his head sideways. His nose was squashed by the force of the other man slamming into him from behind, and everyone stopped drinking to watch them, muttering and clutching each other. Suddenly the room was very hot and full of heavy breathing. Lust was in the very air.

When Riccio stood up to escape, it seemed that everyone else stood up too. The men were on their feet, pushing him towards Darnley, pushing him off the bench.

'Now!' cried Darnley, dropping his ringletted companion.

'Hold him down for His Majesty,' one of the big burly men shouted to the other, and they thrust Riccio over the table with his legs still on the floor.

'Oooh! Silken drawers!' someone laughed when his breeches were dragged off.

'Spread his buttocks for the King!' someone else yelled, and when Darnley stepped forward Riccio found himself in the same situation as the man with his nose pressed up against the wall had been.

'Ahhh –' he screamed in pain and terror, feeling with every stab how much Darnley wanted to tear him to pieces, to shame and humiliate him, to punish him savagely – and the King was doing all that, until at last he cried out in triumph, a high, shrill shriek.

'God! Look at all the blood!' said a voice in the silence after Darnley finally withdrew and collapsed on the bench again.

The men stood back and gasped at the sight of the little Italian's bloody buttocks. From somewhere there was a nervous titter. Riccio was crying. He didn't stop to pick up his clothes. He ran blindly to the door, heaved it open, and ran.

Next morning he was at his desk as usual, palefaced. He had scarcely been able to walk to the antechamber, and sitting down was sheer agony. But he said not one word to anyone. Lady Jean, at the Queen's side, thought he must be ill. There was no beautiful apricot colour this morning to flush his olive cheeks.

'My dear Davy, are you well enough today?' Mary asked anxiously.

'Just a little tired, Your Majesty,' he managed to smile, 'but otherwise perfectly well. When you are ready there are some documents here you should look over,' and he bent his head again.

It was afternoon before Darnley made his appearance, tipsy already and waving Riccio's breeches in one hand and his silken drawers in the other.

'And who might be the owner of these pretty things?' he sniggered.

'Go away, Henry!' Mary snapped. 'I cannot imagine what

silly game you are playing at next, but I forbid you to go into other people's rooms and steal their clothes. Take them back at once.'

'But they weren't in his rooms,' Darnley yelled. 'They were –'

'Go!' Mary said coldly. 'Or do you want the guards to throw you out again?'

Darnley walked right up to Riccio in a menacing manner and hissed in his face, 'You'll pay for this! You know now that I can make you pay.'

'Enough!' Mary ran to the door as if to call the guards, and Darnley scowled at Riccio as he shambled out.

Riccio only smiled back, but if the King had been sober enough he would have quailed, as Jean did, at the intensity of hatred in those dark Italian eyes, and trembled at the implacable promise of revenge in their depths.

Dr Bourgoing asked interminable questions, prodded Mary's stomach, frowned and then pulled on a pair of silk gloves.

'I'm sorry, madam,' he said, smearing the gloves with salve, 'but from the information you have given me about the irregularity of your courses, I must examine you internally.'

'Very well,' Mary sighed, and endured it.

'I would say your womb is about the size of an orange,' he announced at the end of it, 'but it is difficult at this stage to say when your baby will be born. It could be in June, but it is more likely to be in July.'

If it were in June, it might still be Darnley's, Mary thought. But if not . . .

She announced her pregnancy at a huge banquet the following night. It took far more courage than merely going to war to rise from one end of the banqueting table and smile down at the drunken Darnley at the other.

Nobody, not even Riccio, really knew how much she now hated the father of her unborn child. Nobody must ever know . . . At least, not until the child had been accepted by the nobles and the people as Darnley's legitimate son, the heir to the throne of Scotland and perhaps also the heir to the throne of England.

'Next summer,' she said, 'the King and I will present an heir to Scotland. I ask you all to pray with me in thankfulness for God's Grace.'

The court rose, heads bent, and afterwards there was a babble of congratulations and toasts.

Darnley lurched to his feet. 'Yes,' he crowed, 'I have succeeded where Francis failed! *And*,' he banged on the table, 'if any man says the child is not mine, I'll have his head!' Glaring around, he staggered and upset a jug of ale. The servants hastily mopped it up and fetched another jug. Still staggering, Darnley sloshed some of it into a mug and drank it in one gulp. 'God *knows* the child is mine.'

In an agony of humiliation and embarrassment, Mary hurried down the table and put an arm around him. 'Come, sire,' she said gently, 'we will go to the chapel and give thanks.'

Servants had to lead him away. Mary started to follow and then changed her mind. 'Remove the trestle tables,' she commanded, and signalled to the musicians in the gallery to play. 'We shall be merry,' she told the court. 'It is a happy occasion.'

But her smile was forced and fixed as she tried to chat normally to her ladies and courtiers, and tried to ignore their pitying faces. Inside, she was seething. Tonight was the peak of her humiliation. Tonight was unforgivable. How could she forgive such a public disgrace?

And how could she endure more hours of so-called revelry when her heart was breaking? She had loved Darnley at first sight, but now she knew that she had seen only his bright, golden veneer, and not his dark spirit.

Christmas and Hogmanay were not a very festive season for anyone in Huntly. Abbie and Donald were still grieving. With the old Earl dead, young Lord George Gordon in an English prison and old Lady Huntly somewhere in France, the people had fallen on hard times. There was no one left to pay wages.

Food was scarce. It was a struggle to survive, let alone celebrate.

Abbie and Donald and the McCracken family were harder hit than most because of the serious and lingering illness of young Johnny. Abbie spent a lot of time helping her mother to nurse him, and praying for his recovery.

Then she received another letter from Lady Jean. It was from Holyrood, and it was short and to the point.

> Lord Bothwell has been granted permission to marry me. Once again that dreaded date is set for 22 February, and afterwards we are to go to our future home of Crichton Castle. There is no way out of it, this time.

It was a savage bolt from the blue. Abbie had genuinely believed that after so long, Bothwell was no longer considered Lady Jean's prospective husband. But she should have known better, she thought bitterly, remembering the huge chest of money in Lady Jean's possession. Some of it, at least, would be her dowry. Lord Huntly would have promised him the money when his marriage to Lady Jean was first arranged.

Abbie was still sitting there with the letter dangling from her hand when Donald came in.

'What is it?' he asked. 'You look as if you had been struck by lightning.'

'I haven't, but poor Lady Jean has – *twice*!'

'Well,' Donald said, reading the letter, 'it's a *cri de coeur* all right. You want to go to her, Abbie?'

'I'll have to help her if I can. That means taking one of Queen Catherine's boxes with me, the one with the medicines. But what about you, Donald?'

'There is enough for you to worry about, without worrying about me. I shall go and live in the barracks while you are away, although we are not soldiers now. We are hunters and scavengers. I will have to be away a lot anyway, Abbie, scraping for food for the people, so perhaps this is a good time to go. But not alone. I'll take you to Holyrood. You

424

can send me word from Crichton when it's time to take you back.'

On the ride south Abbie begged Donald to tell her all he knew about the Earl of Bothwell, and what he told her chilled the blood in her veins almost to ice.

'In France we heard that he studied the black arts more than anything else. He is ruthless, and would not be above giving someone a sort of drug to get his own way.'

'Oh God,' Abbie moaned. Would it come down to her scant knowledge pitted against his? Her one weapon would be that Bothwell had no idea of the schooling she had received from Queen Catherine.

'He has had many mistresses,' Donald continued. 'There was Anna Throndsen. He didn't marry her – in fact, I've often wondered why her relations never killed him for that, descended as they are from the warlike and bloodthirsty Vikings. Then there was Janet Beaton.'

'Mary Beaton's aunt? Yes, I've heard her name mentioned.'

'He was twenty-four and she was in her fifties at the time,' Donald said, 'but they were soul mates, so the story goes, both artists in the practice of magic, which no doubt kept her looking so young and beautiful.'

'Does he have any children?'

'Dozens, I expect,' Donald said airily. 'All illegitimate. Of course he will take responsibility for none of them.'

'Poor Lady Jean,' Abbie sighed.

'And there is something else you should know about the Earl of Bothwell. Darnley is not the only one to consort with other men.'

'*Bothwell?*' Abbie asked, shocked.

'I am glad you will be at Lady Jean's side, my love. Believe me, Bothwell loves nobody and nothing except his own self-interest and his own gratification. Let's hope Lady Jean has her wits about her in such a terrible quandary – as you had, thanks be to God, when he abducted you to Hermitage Castle.'

'Don't remind me,' Abbie shuddered, and they rode on into the darkness, and at last into the eerily quiet Royal Mile at the dead of night.

FIFTY-THREE

'Go and see that my bed is turned down, Abbie,' the Queen said. 'I have had enough for one night. And send Flamina to attend to me.'

Upstairs, Abbie flattened herself against the wall when Darnley staggered past, supported by a young pageboy to whom he was slurring something suggestively, and giggling. She watched the pair going into Darnley's bedchamber and heard them both crash onto the bed. Horrified, she ran on to find Flamina, but someone else, also watching, didn't run away. He waited until he was sure that both King and page-boy were still in the bed, and playing games with each other. Then he hurried down to the Queen.

'Is there anything I can do, madam?' Riccio murmured, so suddenly at her side that Mary turned to him, surprised.

'I didn't know you were here, Davy. But no, thank you.' She got up stiffly, as she sometimes did if she had been sitting too long. She hadn't danced all evening. She hadn't had the heart. 'I had better go to the King before I sleep.'

She moved away, but he caught her arm. 'I've just seen the King as I passed his door. He is going to bed.'

'I should see that he is all right before I go to mine.'

But Riccio still held her back. 'Madam, you know he's mad-drunk. Please, I implore you –'

'There's something wrong, isn't there, Davy? Let me go!'

Mary flung off his hand as he had known she would. The more she was forbidden to do something the more she wanted to do it. He followed her up the stairs, at the top of which she summoned a guard to accompany her into the King's bedchamber, Riccio protesting every step of the way.

Inside, the room was dimly lit and the bed-curtains were drawn shut. Yet they fluttered with movements from the bed. Henry must be ill, Mary thought. It was not like him to be tossing and turning. Usually, he lay still, poleaxed, when he was drunk. Alarmed, she flung back the curtains.

And there was a sight she would never forget to her dying day.

Darnley and a young pageboy were both naked and doing things to each other on the rumpled velvet sheet that she could never have imagined in her worst nightmares. The guard's strong arms caught her as she fell to the rushes, Abbie arrived with Flamina, and Riccio backed out silently.

When Mary came to again she was on her own bed in her own bedchamber. Seton was pouring brandy between her lips, Abbie and Flamina were rubbing her wrists as they had done so often in the past, and Riccio was standing beside her bed. She closed her eyes again, willing herself to sink into everlasting darkness. If only she could die . . . But, she chided herself, she would only die when God decreed it. In the meantime she must live on, somehow.

'Is the pain in your side back again?' Seton asked anxiously.

Mary dragged herself up to sit. 'No, dear Seton,' she smiled wanly. 'You may leave me now, ladies. I wish to speak with Riccio alone.'

'You tried to prevent me from seeing it, didn't you?' she asked him sadly when her ladies went away. 'You knew what was going on. I would not have believed it if I hadn't seen it with my own eyes.'

'I'm afraid it was inevitable that you would find out sooner or later, madam. And now it is only right that you should know it all. It seems that it is not only with boys. He goes with sluts and serving wenches as well, and he demands strange services.'

Mary burst into tears. She could well believe all that; she had had personal experience. It was all true.

428

'Does he know that I saw him, Davy?'

'He saw you all right. He saw the guard picking you up and carrying you out.'

Too distraught to notice that Riccio himself had kept well in the background, Mary was only thankful that he was there for her to cling to at this lowest, most traumatic moment in her life. Dearest, dearest, Davy!

She didn't see the gloating satisfaction in his black eyes. She didn't know that for weeks he had waited and waited for such an opportunity, nor would she have believed that he had purposely engineered such a cruel exposure of Darnley.

Next morning Abbie helped Flamina to dress Mary in a plain grey gown. That she was still furiously angry was plain to see. Two spots of colour blazed in her white cheeks. Trouble was coming.

'Come with me, both of you,' she said. 'I may have need of your support,' and went directly to the King's bedchamber. She flung back the curtains again, and there was Darnley, sleeping like a baby. When she shook him his beautiful blue eyes flew open and he held out his arms to her.

If his actions last night had shocked her to the core, his innocent attitude this morning shocked her even more. He wheedled shamelessly. He cajoled. He promised, while she berated him unmercifully.

'He-bawd!' she spat. 'If you have any possible explanation for your behaviour last night upon this very bed, I should like to hear it.'

She endured an hour of his excuses, protestations of undying love for her, and finally his tears as he prostrated himself before her. 'Oh God, let me pray for forgiveness,' he wept. She left him praying on his knees before his oratory, signalled to her ladies to follow, and went to find Riccio.

She must shake off such dirt and shame, and deal with matters of State. She had still to decide who would benefit from the forfeiture of Lord James's lands and those of the other rebels.

'You may go,' she dismissed Flamina. 'Abbie, stay. I may need messages sent.'

And who had that pleasure all the time I was away? Abbie wondered sourly.

At the end of a whole day of it, off and on, Mary sighed and stretched. 'Davy,' she said, 'for all his debauchery, the strange thing is that I believe Henry really loves me.'

Abbie jumped awake at that. What rubbish! She expected an argument but Riccio surprised her. 'I think so, too, madam, but he has some inner terror which binds him.'

He certainly had some inner trouble, Abbie reflected.

'God will help Henry,' Mary smiled wearily. 'What will happen to Lord James, though? I have lost him now.'

'The only thing you have lost is your innocence, Majesty. You believed in him, and he was false.'

'I still miss his authority, Davy. A woman needs a strong right arm . . . Or is it Bothwell's I miss so much?'

Bothwell's? Abbie could not believe her ears. Surely the Queen was not still at that? Riccio also gazed at her in consternation and in despair. He might have been born with a hunched back, but could she not see that he had a strong right arm, too? What more would he have to do?

'It is nearly two o'clock in the morning. Abbie, I have kept you out of your bed too long. We are very late.'

With a taper Riccio led them out of the antechamber. The guard saluted but before he could open the door for them it flew open and Darnley stood there swaying and glassy-eyed, pointing accusingly at Riccio and Mary.

'Bitch!' he shouted. 'Whore! And you had the impertinence to criticise *me*?'

Abbie went to her bed that night beside the sleeping figure of Lady Jean and stared into the darkness, thinking of Donald and their marriage – so radiantly happy despite all their tribulations. She was lucky, very lucky . . . The Queen of Scotland was not as lucky as she was. And now, what sort of a marriage was Lady Jean going to face with that animal Bothwell?

* * *

The bridegroom arrived confidently at a small rented house in the Canongate. Surrounded by his henchmen and with his own tailor at his side, he was in buoyant mood. His tailor unpacked the boxes he had carried with him and later Bothwell stood preening himself before the mirror. His reflection told him that there was no doubt about it, he was a fine figure of a man in his wedding outfit.

His tailor tried to fasten the narrow lace ruff around his neck, tweaking its little gold studs.

'Damn it, man! It's too tight,' Bothwell growled. 'Rework it!'

'Very good, my lord. But the rest? Does it please you?'

'It'll do,' Bothwell said impatiently. 'I hate dressing up.'

But he couldn't help admiring the fine workmanship of his doublet, pale green pleated silk with its puffed sleeves, and the short cape of darker green velvet to swing over it, the same green velvet as his hat, the same green exactly as his eyes. It was all dashing, in the extreme. No woman could possibly resist him.

'You're a clever fellow,' he smiled, and clapped the tailor on the back. 'Run away now! I don't want to see you again until the great day, and by that time I expect everything to be perfect.'

The great day! He laughed softly and cynically, and then went whistling down the Royal Mile to Holyrood with his two most trusted Hepburns, Fobie Fingerless and Ill Will, a few steps behind him, as they always were. With a tiny gesture, and they knew every one, he let them understand that they would wait at the palace gates for him.

He went on alone and gained entrance to the Queen's apartments. Her ladies were all around her. Lady Jean, with that maidservant of hers beside her, was among them, looking as grave as ever, as boring as ever . . . He supposed she was attractive enough for any man who liked sandy hair and broad features and clever eyes that seemed to bore right through him, but he was not one of them.

However, there was her massive dowry . . . He smiled to

himself. She had it with her, so she said! Now, he hardly let his eyes rest on her, and certainly not on Abbie. The Queen was different, and he was pleased to see that she was all of a-flutter at the very sight of him.

'My lord,' she smiled and extended her hand. Bothwell shook it. He had never, never kissed it, and he was even more delighted to see the disappointment in those golden eyes of hers. He could play her like a fish.

'What do you here?' she stammered.

'I have come to speak with my Queen, Your Majesty,' he smiled.

Mary dismissed her ladies, keeping Abbie back, as usual. 'And I wish to speak with you, my lord,' she said, allowing her lashes to droop over her eyes. 'From now on I shall be needing you within close call, so I have decided that you must have a house in the Canongate, since you never accept my hospitality. Where are you housed at present?'

'In a small place at number thirty-seven, madam.'

'Then I shall buy it. It shall be yours.'

'But, I wonder, is it big enough for two?'

Mary's eyes widened. 'What do you mean?' she faltered.

'I mean, will it be big enough for me and my wife? You see, I am determined to marry. I am getting on in years and I should be married.'

'Yes ... I gave you permission ... But I did not really think —'

'You did not think I really meant to marry Lady Jean Gordon?' he laughed. 'I was prevented from marrying her because you outlawed me – remember? But now, at last, I shall fulfil that commitment.'

'You love her so much?' Mary asked coldly.

'I do not love her at all, madam, and she does not love me. She has told me that she will never love another man except Alex Ogilvie of Boyne. I admire her for her honesty.'

'But what about love, Lord Bothwell?'

'Oh! I shall never fall into that tender trap,' he laughed.

* * *

Later that day, having absorbed the shock, Mary summoned him back to the audience chamber along with Lady Jean, who came with Abbie.

'For such an important marriage we shall have the Chapel Royal made ready for you,' Mary told Bothwell.

'Certainly not, madam,' he said coolly. 'I intend to marry Lady Jean Gordon in the Protestant kirk of the Canongate.'

Lady Jean glanced up. She didn't say a word.

The Queen spoke for her. 'But Jean comes from a great Catholic family! You would wish to be married by Catholic rites, would you not, Jean?'

'Madam, it is of no account.' Jean kept her eyes downcast. 'It will be in God's sight wherever it is, I suppose.'

'Then I insist that I shall provide the banquet afterwards here at Holyrood.'

Again Bothwell refused. 'Mr Kinloch will provide it in Kinloch House, madam.'

'At least spend your honeymoon at Holyrood!' Mary cried.

'We shall be honeymooning at Crichton,' Bothwell told her.

'So – it only remains for me to wish you joy?' Mary gasped.

'Thank you, madam,' he smiled mockingly.

FIFTY-FOUR

The days and nights sped past and suddenly it was 21 February, the day before Jean's wedding, and Abbie still had not thought of any way out of the ceremony. Balthazzar came for the last fitting of the magnificent gown of cloth of silver. Everything else was ready.

As soon as he left Jean and Abbie went to find some air to cool their flushed, anxious faces. They paced along the corridors, back and fore, and found ways around the palace they had never seen before. Around one corner they came upon a back staircase that wound down and down like a well, with little alcoves on every floor of it.

From two flights down a young serving woman was ascending with a tray, and out of one of the alcoves Bothwell suddenly appeared. The sound of their voices travelled up the stairwell so that Abbie and Jean could hear every word they said. Silently they crept down so they could see as well.

'And who are you?' Bothwell asked. 'Why have I never seen *you* before?'

'Oh, my lord, you startled me, sneaking up on me like that! I'm new here. My name is Bessie Crawford.'

'Well, Bessie Crawford, I like sneaking up on people. I do it all the time. But it's not often I sneak up on someone as pretty as you,' Bothwell said, steering her into the alcove and looking down at her, blocking her way with one elbow propped against the wall.

Lady Jean and Abbie saw the slow, knowing smile spreading over Bessie's face and the come-hither invitation in her black, flashing eyes.

'What have you got on that tray, anyway?' he asked, taking it from her, setting it down on the floor and lifting the covers off the dishes. 'Ah, I see it's all cold. Then there's no hurry, is there?'

Bessie tossed her glossy black ringlets and laughed. 'I dare say ten minutes wouldn't make much difference, one way or the other, my lord.'

'The way I feel, ten minutes will do,' he said. 'Lie down quick, for God's sake!'

Bessie lay down obediently and pulled up her skirts. Abbie and Lady Jean watched the whole performance in fascinated horror as, humped over the girl like an animal, Bothwell took her there and then. And he had been right. In less than ten minutes he was reaching for his breeches again.

'I'll see you later, Bessie Crawford.' He wasn't even out of breath.

'I wish you could, my lord. But there's not much chance of that, with you going away so soon with your new bride, is there?' Bessie got to her feet, brushed down her skirts matter-of-factly and bent to lift the tray again. 'Worse luck, for me,' she added.

'Are you married, girl?'

'No, sir.'

'Have you a mother or father anywhere, dependent on you?'

'No. I'm alone in the world.'

'Then don't worry about it. Where there's a will there's a way.'

Bothwell and the servant went through a door into the corridor on the floor below. Abbie and Lady Jean remained transfixed for several minutes. 'And that's only one,' Lady Jean came to life, weeping. 'God knows how many more women, up and down the country.'

But no matter how badly she felt herself, Abbie wasted no time on tears. Her mind had jumped to more practical things.

'So you must face it, Jean. We only surmised it before, but now we have seen it with our own eyes. He is certain to be diseased. I have not been able to think of a way to get you out of this marriage, but I believe I can prevent you from even greater disaster. Come with me.'

In the bedchamber she would share with Jean this one last night, Abbie closed the door, went over to Catherine de Medicis' box, and searched for its key on the bunch at her waist. Kneeling down, she looked among the little bottles, reading their contents and instructions written in French on their labels, until she found the one she wanted. Next, she lifted off the tray of bottles and picked out a jar of ointment from underneath, also labelled with directions for use.

'Now, Jeannie,' Abbie said, with the bottle in one hand and the jar in the other, 'I must warn you that I have no real idea of what's in either of these. I only know what Queen Catherine told me. She said that this one will protect you from syphilis, and this other will prevent a child of the union.'

'Only remember this, Abbie – if they kill me, I would rather be dead than pregnant to Bothwell or tainted by any of his diseases. If you are willing to take a chance to help me, I am more than willing to try. Just tell me what I must do.'

'Well,' Abbie said, reading the labels minutely again, 'the directions are exactly as Queen Catherine told me at the time. There is a little pipette in the stopper of the medicine bottle. Two drops must be taken in water before intercourse. Not one drop, and certainly not three drops, which could be very dangerous. Let me see you try.'

Jean's hand was shaking so much that she bungled the first two attempts. Abbie looked at her sternly.

'It's only a little bottle, you know. You can't afford to waste the medicine like that! Calm down, Jeannie. This *really* is a matter of life and death,' she said, and it had the desired effect. The third time Jean managed perfectly.

'Leave the glass where it is,' Abbie said. 'It looks like water, but it's all measured out for you to take when I come to dress you in your nightgown tomorrow night,' and when

436

Jean shuddered at the very thought of it she added, 'Some of the Marys may come in to see you, and no doubt the Queen – so you can drink it when no one is looking. Just remember, one dose only in twenty-four hours. Look! It's on the label if you forget.'

'And the jar?' Jean asked. 'What is in it?'

'Ah ... You will have to learn to apply this ointment yourself.' Abbie took off the pigskin cover and showed it to Lady Jean. 'You must lie with your legs wide apart and insert it as far up as you can. And you must do it every single time before intercourse.'

'You mean, with my finger?'

Abbie thought of Bothwell's engorged penis before it was plunged into Bessie Crawford. 'No,' she sighed. 'You must try to get it in further than that. What we need is a round, smooth stick. I'll go down to the kitchen and have a look around while you look out some clean cloths.'

'What did you find?' Jean asked when she came back.

'A porridge spurtle. It's clean. Now we'll wrap it in a strip of linen and dip it into the ointment. Jeannie, I want you to practise it,' Abbie said anxiously. 'I'll stay with you, dearie, because your hymen may tear during this operation, and I don't want you to be frightened of the blood. It will only be a small show, anyway.'

No, Abbie thought sadly, the poor girl was frightened enough already. She had no idea of the joyous way the hymen could be ruptured, so that a husband could see for himself that his bride was a virgin. Bothwell would never notice. Bothwell wouldn't care.

Only *she* had cared for Lady Jean nearly all her life ... Sometimes, Abbie sighed, she had felt more like a mother to her than a friend, not four years her senior. But only she had been there to help her through those first difficult months of her adolescence when her courses had begun. She would not desert her now. Or ever.

When it was over, and Jean's blood had stopped flowing and been washed away, Abbie put her arms around the shaking bride-to-be and did her best to comfort her.

'Don't worry, Jeannie! Please don't worry any more. You saw for yourself he doesn't take long . . . And it won't be sore, now.'

'I don't know that I can go through with it, Abbie.'

'Yes, you'll go through with it, and no harm will come to you, God help us. Now, there's something I want you to promise *me*.'

'Anything. You know that.'

'Tomorrow you will be your usual calm self. Don't cry, don't argue, and above all don't let the Queen see that you are anything else but gloriously happy.'

'The Queen? Why?'

'Because she was only infatuated with Darnley – to the point of idiocy, as we all saw – but now the infatuation is over. She could have prevented your wedding tomorrow, but instead she chose to punish herself, and Bothwell, and you.'

'Why?'

'Because he is a staunch Protestant and she is a devout Catholic and neither of them will budge. But I have seen them together, Jean, when nobody else saw them – and it's Bothwell she's attracted to, believe it or not, although she is too frightened to admit it, even to herself. It will all come out in the end, believe me. But by that time, as his wife, you will have the upper hand. It's not the end of the world, Jeannie. It's a game, like a game of chess, and we will outwit them yet somehow or other – wait and see.'

FIFTY-FIVE

In the afternoon of 22 February the bells rang out for the
marriage of Lady Jean Gordon and the Earl of Bothwell.
They were still pealing when the bride and her attendants
arrived at the kirk door. Abbie slipped the gossamer veil over
the tight-fitting pearl cap on Jean's head and stood back to
admire her.

'The veil makes your silver gown shimmer like mother-of-
pearl. Oh, you look beautiful, Jeannie! You are a beautiful
bride,' she said, refusing to allow a single tear to well up in
her eyes.

But her heart was full of them, for Jean seemed more like
a nun than a bride, with her eyes cast down on the white
satin prayer book she held in her hand, the one she and Seton
had illuminated.

'Courage, dearie,' Abbie whispered when the bells stopped
ringing and, picking up her flowers, she followed Lady Jean
down the long aisle to join Bothwell at the altar in front of
the Bishop of Galloway.

Fleming and Seton walked behind them, their arms full of
the flowers Queen Mary had sent from her hothouses at
Holyrood. There had been a little card with them: 'The
Queen's bouquets for the Queen's bouquet', and their scents
filled the kirk.

She is here – she is all around us, Abbie thought uneasily,
and yet she could not relent long enough to attend the wedding, not in a Protestant kirk.

*   *   *

But that was not the only reason, as Queen Mary acknowledged to herself. Her throat was tight with pain. She had not dreamed that the hurt of this day would cut so deep. But she smiled with practised radiance as she waited with Darnley at Master Kincaid's house for the bride and groom to arrive after the ceremony.

Master Kincaid, a wealthy Edinburgh merchant, had hung the hall of his house with embroidered white satin and looped it up at intervals with white velvet ribbons tied around bunches of gilded wheat. More gilded wheat, symbolising fruitfulness and prosperity, decorated the oak chandeliers, blazing with a hundred candles, and under them the banquet tables sparkled with fine glass and golden plates.

The musicians were playing softly, too softly to drown the voices of the people who were crowding the Royal Mile outside hoping for a glimpse of the bridal couple.

To Mary's horror, Darnley strutted over to the window, pushed Riccio aside and leaned out, with a goblet of wine in his hand. 'See,' he shouted, 'they want to see me! They are waiting to see their King!'

'Drunk again?' a man in the crowd yelled back. 'You're not a king! You're a drunken bastard!'

But Darnley was too full of his self-importance to hear the words. He thought the people were cheering him and he persisted, laughing and waving his goblet, until he lost his footing and fell, sprawled on the floor. A roar of laughter came from the crowd.

'Put the bugger to bed, Mary,' the same man shouted. 'You would have done better with this same bridegroom coming up the Royal Mile today!'

As if she didn't *know*, Mary thought bitterly. There was nothing she could do to control Darnley, and how could she hide a man well over six feet tall? She only wished she could, instead of living in this constant anxiety over him, at a time when she should have had tranquillity, bearing his child.

She heard the bells ringing again, and soon the crowd were roaring, cheering and waving at Bothwell. He was a hero in their eyes, and they were still cheering when he ushered the new Countess of Bothwell through the garlanded doorway of Master Kincaid's house and bowed before his Queen.

Lady Jean dipped in a low curtsy, her gown billowing and shimmering around her, and Mary caught her breath with a savage pang of jealousy. She had not expected Jean to look so serenely beautiful when she looked up at her groom, and smiled.

Bothwell glanced down at Jean briefly, intimately. He looked devastating. There was no other word to describe his appearance in his green velvet with an emerald-hilted dagger tucked in his belt. He was ready from now on to defend his bride, Mary thought painfully, and extended her jewelled hand to him.

'We missed you, madam,' he said, holding it for a second.

Then the moment that Abbie had been dreading most for Lady Jean was upon them, when Bothwell led his bride round the hall to receive congratulations and they were face to face with Alex Ogilvie and his wife. But Jean remained calm as she curtsied to Alex and kissed Mary Beaton's cheek – rounder and plumper than ever, Abbie noted, whereas Alex himself seemed to have shrunk.

Master Kincaid led the Queen to an ornate carved chair under a blue velvet canopy spangled with stars. He seated Darnley at the other end of the table, Bothwell at Mary's right and Lady Jean at her left. Then he placed Fleming, Seton and Abbie right opposite the Queen and the bridal party, and smiled at them charmingly.

'I'll have your bouquets put in water,' he said. 'You three are flowers pretty enough yourselves to grace any table.'

Lady Jean stood up to cut the wedding cake. Bothwell stood with her, his hand over hers on the emerald-hilted dagger to help her. At first Fleming squealed with delight to find the Bride's Bean in her slice, and then her face became sad again. Sir William was still absent.

Abbie watched Mary toying first with a tiny strip of salmon and then with the powsowdie, the sheep's-head broth, and knew she could never eat any of it. It was all too heavy and laden with fat, and the Queen's stomach was often queasy now that her pregnancy was advancing. Bothwell watched her too, with side-long glances.

'I am still trying to like Scottish food, and to learn about Scottish things,' she smiled to excuse herself.

'And how will you manage that, madam, with that Italian Riccio always hanging round? Nobody likes him, you know,' Bothwell said.

'That's absurd.'

'It's the truth. Why did you bring him, anyway?'

'He is one of my household, as you know.'

'And so you just assumed that an honest Edinburgh trader would want to feed a foreigner?'

Abbie wondered why they were bickering about Riccio at a wedding feast, of all places, until she noticed that they were both casting nervous, flickering glances down the table at Darnley. Abbie understood then that they were both so worried at the sight of him that it was making them quarrel.

Bothwell confirmed these suspicions. 'What is he doing with *that* lot?' he demanded roughly, indicating the King. 'He is always whispering in corners with them. What have they got in common – tell me that, madam?'

Mary shook her head and continued to watch Darnley. He was eating nothing, but drinking hard, and speaking behind his hand first to Morton and Morton's cousin George Douglas on his right, and then to Andrew Ker of Fawdonside on his left. What they were talking about was quite obviously a secret, but Abbie noticed that every now and then they would turn around and glower at Riccio. It was something to do with David Riccio, Abbie was sure of it, but the small Italian was happily unaware of any of it as he sprinkled sugar on his cloutie dumpling.

Lord Balfour got to his feet and proposed a toast to the royal unborn child. 'To the future King of Scotland and England!' Everyone stood and drank, everyone except Darnley. In the reverent silence after the toast while the company

442

thought about the coming baby and wished him well, Lord Balfour asked, 'What shall he be called?'

Darnley began to shout. 'The child cannot be called Prince Henry, after me!' and followed that with a string of obscenities and accusations hurled at Riccio.

The silence continued, but now it was stunned. Prickles ran up and down Abbie's back. How would she ever have coped with a situation like this if she had been asked to impersonate the Queen again? As long as she was in Edinburgh there was always the danger of it, especially with Mary so unwell in her pregnancy.

Then it came to Abbie in a clear, cold light: it must be a godsend to the Queen to have her at Holyrood now – a sort of insurance – and suddenly Abbie wished she were many miles away, back with Donald again. Then she braced herself. She had work to do for Lady Jean before this night was out, and tomorrow, God willing, they would go to Crichton Castle. From there she would send word to Donald to come and fetch her.

No, Edinburgh was a dangerous place, just as Lizzie Sproat had denounced it – and never more so than when Bothwell half-lunged in Darnley's direction, his hand on his dagger.

But Mary proved that she was indeed a queen when she stood up to her full height and smiled at her husband, ignoring his words and putting a restraining hand on Bothwell's arm. 'It is my wish that you will all come to Holyrood later tonight for music and dancing to celebrate this happy event. But now,' she smiled, 'I must leave you.'

Two footmen behind Darnley's chair took hold of him disdainfully, as though he smelled, and escorted him out of the hall. As Master Kincaid helped Mary into her cloak the startled company heard the King yelling at the servants when they forcibly ejected him into the Royal Mile.

Outside, Mary dismissed the two guards who were waiting to accompany her down to Holyrood. 'No,' she smiled. 'I shall walk down to the palace alone. I am sorely in need of fresh air.'

She did not see Bothwell at the door behind her whispering to two of his Hepburns. 'Don't let her know you are following her, and don't let her out of your sight.'

Alone, as she thought, Mary walked slowly, placing her feet carefully, for the child was becoming heavy enough to affect her balance. By now it was dark on this February evening. Darnley was nowhere to be seen, of course. She had not expected him to be. He would have run off to one of his brothels. He was 'only young' as he kept telling her, and ever since she had discovered him in his bed with the pageboy she had denied him entrance to hers.

She had grown to hate him, and after that exhibition in Kincaid House she hated him more than ever.

The crowd had all gone home long ago, and the street was deserted. There was only one house lit up, the one that jutted out into the Royal Mile, John Knox's house. Peering up, Mary could see the flames of his candles on his table in front of the window.

He would be writing his sermon for Sunday. Or making up another plot to send to Elizabeth of England and Lord James, her own treacherous brother. Mary smiled bitterly into the darkness as she passed by. Whatever he was doing in his little house, John Knox would be happy, at least, in his own way. He had his wife, his children and his calling, while she, the Queen of Scotland, had nothing and nobody to make her happy . . . Less than ever now, without Bothwell.

'We shall have to spend our wedding night at Holyrood after all,' Lady Jean whispered to Abbie, 'now that she has arranged a ball for us there. It will be four o'clock in the morning at least, before it is over.'

'Thank goodness for that,' Abbie whispered back. 'Your medicines are still there, where we left them. I had been wondering what excuse I could make to transfer them.'

After the ball was over she helped Lady Jean out of her wedding gown and into her flowing, diaphanous nightgown, the medicines administered. Jean looked lovelier than ever.

444

Her gown bared her graceful shoulders and emphasised her breasts. Her hair – that terrible hair of her childhood which she and Queen Catherine had struggled so long with – now hung straight and shining down her back to meet the brighter gold of her girdle.

'Don't be afraid, dearie. You've got nothing to fear now.' Abbie kissed her gently and went out of the door as Bothwell came in.

Lady Jean Bothwell was still awake when daylight came in, lying rigidly on her side of the marriage bed. Abbie had been quite right. It had been short and sharp, but the worst pain she felt was to her dignity at being invaded.

'God,' Bothwell opened his eyes, swearing and blaspheming, 'what are you? A woman or a bloody block of wood?'

'You didn't find me as receptive as Bessie Crawford, then?'

'What do you know of Bessie Crawford?' he blustered.

'I saw you and her together less than forty-eight hours ago. I watched you taking her in the stairwell.'

'Whatever I do with Bessie Crawford is my business. It means nothing. What I want from you is an heir, a legitimate heir, to inherit our joint estates. He will be the most powerful man in the country.'

But some of Abbie's resourcefulness had rubbed off on Jean over the years, after all.

'Oh dear,' she smiled sadly, 'I'm afraid I can never bear your child. The physicians have told me that I am barren.'

'Barren? Barren?' Bothwell leaped out over the edge of the bed. 'Why was I not told?'

'Why did you not ask, my lord? When did you ever want to know anything about me, other than the dowry my father gave you? If you had taken the trouble you might have found out that I dislike fighting. I prefer to make bargains.'

'And what does that mean, pray?'

'That you are very welcome to all the Bessie Crawfords of this world. As for me, I will settle for Crichton Castle, and I want that in writing.'

'Jesus Christ! So not only have I married a frigid bitch, but a mercenary one as well!'

'It could be a very amicable arrangement. And you will always be made welcome any time you care to visit our home, my lord,' Jean said sweetly.

She actually enjoyed the journey when a subdued Lord Bothwell led his party out of Holyrood and over the twelve miles to Crichton later that day. Ladies, servants and Borderers wound in a considerable train behind them.

Abbie cantered up to Lady Jean. 'Well?' she asked.

'Don't worry, Abbie. Everything is all right.'

'Do you know that Bessie Crawford is here, as bold as brass, riding with the servants?'

'I have many things to be thankful for, Abbie. Bessie Crawford, for one. I shall deal with her later, in my own way, and in the meantime she can deal with Bothwell when he is feeling amorous.'

They arrived at Crichton Castle and Lady Jean took charge at once. The status of marriage seemed to have blossomed her. All the same, Abbie doubted that she could leave her just yet.

'You know that Donald will come shortly to take me back to Huntly, Jean. How can I leave you alone here without a reliable maidservant? I could never be happy unless I saw you settled with one.'

'We can look around, although there will never be another Abbie,' Lady Jean sighed, and they spent the rest of that day trying to pick out someone suitable from all the servants Bothwell had running about the castle.

'Well,' she added at the end of the search, 'there might be *one* girl here I believe I could take to.'

'And I know who it is. It's that fat little girl with the turned-up nose, isn't it? Her name is Hattie Hunter.'

'How did you know?'

'Ho! Because when she looked at you so longingly I found out her name,' Abbie laughed, and went to fetch her.

446

'Would you like to be my special maid, to look after me exclusively, Hattie Hunter?' Lady Jean asked.

'Would I not?' Hattie glowed, her two fat cheeks like rosy apples. 'I would like nothing better than to devote my entire life to you, my lady. It was what I was born for.'

'Not to be someone's sweetheart or wife?' Lady Jean teased her.

'Huh! I don't pay any attention to that Freddie Robertson.' Hattie tossed her head, so that the ribbons on her cap danced enchantingly.

FIFTY-SIX

Abbie was still at Crichton when another visitor arrived there. Though no longer the extravagantly turned out lady whom they used to know, she was still as haughty and still as imperious as ever.

'Mother!' Lady Jean cried, when Lady Huntly sailed in. 'Why did you not send me word from France that you were coming?'

'Even that would have cost money,' Lady Huntly said pointedly as she sank into the most comfortable chair in the room.

So, Lord Huntly hadn't told his wife where the Gordon fortune was, Abbie thought. If he had she would not be looking so run down and dowdy now.

'What has happened to all the Gordon money?' Jean asked, after she had sent Hattie scurrying away for refreshments. 'My father –'

'Oh, yes,' Lady Huntly smiled bitterly, 'your *father*! A fine mess he made of things! Strathbogie may be in ruins, but the money is still there somewhere, I can guarantee it!' Suddenly, she changed the subject. 'What sort of bread is this?' She spat out a mouthful and dashed the rest of her scone on the rushes. 'It is vile!'

'My lord does not seem to have given much thought to food,' Lady Jean agreed. 'The cooks and bakers here are very inferior. I have started to look around for someone better. But,' she returned to the subject, 'don't *you* know where the money is?'

448

'I only wish I did! Your father may have told George. He certainly didn't tell *me*,' Lady Huntly snorted. 'And, of course, George is still in prison.'

Ah ... So that is why she has come back from France, Abbie thought. To get her hands on George. And then, the money. George is the key to the treasure chest.

'The Queen pardoned George a long time ago, Mother.'

'Yes. Queen Mary pardoned him, but Queen Elizabeth will not release him. However,' the old cunning look was back in Lady Huntly's eyes, 'I hear that the Queen expects a child.'

'She does.'

'And I am the best midwife in Scotland, as everyone knows. I shall offer my services in exchange for a prod in Elizabeth's backside.'

'Mother!' exclaimed a scandalised Lady Jean. 'But you need not go at once. Crichton Castle will contain you for as long as you like.'

'Not with food like this! However, you will concede, daughter, that your father and I did very well for you! You know now what it is to be a countess. And I am the Countess of Huntly, don't forget! I shall not rest until I am back in Strathbogie, mistress of my own castle again, where the women of the district are renowned cooks. I shall send you one of them down – but to achieve all that, I must have money.'

Lady Jean smiled. 'At the rate the Earl of Bothwell is running through our money, I can let you have very little.'

'So long as it is enough to present myself in my usual style at Holyrood, that's all I ask. Abbie will come with me. I shall need a waiting-lady, and I shall go tomorrow.'

The most dangerous moment of her life was upon her. Abbie knew it. Lady Jean suspected it, and she jumped up in alarm. 'No, Mother! Her husband, Donald MacLaren, is coming for her, to take her back to Huntly!'

'Let him come,' Lady Huntly said calmly. 'Now that I am back in Scotland I will let him know that I am the chief of

449

the Clan Gordon until George is set free. Donald, Abbie and all the Gordons are in manrent to me, now.'

It was true, and as Lady Jean sobbed helplessly, Abbie's brain worked faster than it had ever worked before.

If Lady Huntly's real purpose was to get George out of prison, by hook or by crook, it would be to everyone's advantage. Lord George would be a kind Earl, who would look after his people, and if he really did know where the money was he would put an end to the misery and suffering in the district – not to mention what he might be able to do for her brother Johnny.

All she had to do was to accompany Lady Huntly until she achieved her purpose. It could solve so many problems, whereas if she went home now, Abbie thought, she would have achieved nothing. More and more Abbie became convinced that she must seize this chance, and it might not take more than a few weeks.

'Yes, my lady,' she said calmly. 'I shall accompany you, if Lady Jean will send word to Donald that I shall be delayed a week or two.'

Next day it was Queen Mary's turn to receive unexpected visitors. But, she felt, it was merciful that she had plenty to keep her mind occupied so she need not think of Bothwell and Lady Jean together. At the same time she was curious to find out if Lady Huntly would let something slip about the progress of the marriage, and she was surprised, but very thankful, to see Abbie with her at court again.

'You are welcome, Lady Huntly,' she came to the point at once. 'And you, too, Abbie.'

'Abbie will attend *me*,' Lady Huntly blustered her way into her first mistake. 'She is a Gordon servant.'

'Of course she will, when I can spare her,' the Queen said pleasantly but with authority. 'Abbie has always been my special messenger, all these years at court. But, Lady Huntly, I have been casting around for a midwife, since you were in France and unavailable.'

Lady Huntly was just as direct. 'I am back now, Your Majesty, and hope to return to Strathbogie as soon as possible – with my son, the Earl of Huntly, of course.'

'I shall write another letter on his behalf today. His continued incarceration is intolerable. But these things take time, as you know. In the meantime I hope you can forgive the mistakes of the past and stay with me at court at least until the birth.'

'The mistakes were my husband's, madam. It will be an honour to deliver the future King of Scotland into the world, just as I delivered you, his mother. Of course, I will stay.'

Another four months? Abbie had no intention of staying even as long as four weeks.

The relief of having Abbie back to impersonate her, when she was becoming more and more tired and jaded every day, was tremendous, but having Lady Huntly installed in Holyrood Palace overshadowed everything else in Mary's mind. At last she could sleep at night, without the nightmare of what might happen to Scotland if she lost this baby. She was now well into the fifth month of pregnancy, and the nearer the time came for her confinement, the more afraid she became for them both.

If the child died at the actual moment of birth, so would she, for few women she had ever heard of survived such an ordeal. Then Darnley would become King in his own right. It was an outrageous, intolerable prospect – and she had actually brought it all about herself by falling in love with the creature!

She worked on through the days with Riccio at her side, Abbie at her back and Lady Huntly in the antechamber with the other ladies, not noticing that Riccio himself was becoming as puffed up with pride as Darnley, not noticing how the nobles glared at Riccio behind his back, not noticing that they often stood about in small groups, whispering . . .

But Abbie noticed, and one day overheard Damiot, the

astrologer, talking to Riccio. 'Beware of the Bastard,' Damiot said.

'The Bastard? I shall take good care that Lord James does not enter Scotland again,' Riccio retorted.

'There are other bastards, and you are making yourself very unpopular.'

'Words! Words!' Riccio sneered. 'Nothing but words! The Scots will boast but rarely perform their brags.'

'Really, Damiot!' Mary said. 'We have no time for idle gossip today. Please leave. I expect Randolph at any minute.'

When Damiot went out and the English Ambassador, Randolph came in, Mary was furious. 'Your agents were caught supplying money to Lord James and the rebels. Bribing them, sir! My brother, who has rebelled against his Queen, and you, an ambassador for yours! You should be ashamed of yourself! You may take yourself out of Scotland today. I shall write to your Queen.'

A week later Elizabeth replied in a curt letter. Mary read it out. Elizabeth was sending Lord James a thousand pounds at Newcastle and she was taking Randolph back into her court. Furthermore, she was not disposed to release Lord George Gordon at the present time.

'I am sick and tired of it all,' Mary said, sinking into one of her depressions. 'I am tired, standing alone against all this hatred in a cold, hard country.'

Mary's depression lasted all that day. It was now 9 March. In three days the rebels would appear before Parliament. There was nothing to look forward to, except more trouble.

Only one thing relieved Mary's strain. Darnley actually invited Riccio to play a game of tennis.

'I suppose that he believes my influence with Your Majesty will win him the Crown Matrimonial,' Riccio laughed.

'He was never subtle,' Mary agreed. 'Oh, listen to that wind! Can you play tennis in it?' Without waiting for an answer she shuddered. 'I believe we shall sup in the turret room tonight, Abbie. Go and play your tennis, Davy. I shall expect you at seven.'

As soon as he left, the Queen put her hand to her side. 'The pain is back again, Abbie. Run and fetch Dr Bourgoing.'

The doctor told her what he always told her. 'You must rest, Your Majesty, and eat plenty of red meat and drink plenty of red wine for your supper. It is for your baby's bones, to make them strong. I shall see you in the morning.'

'Whatever he says,' Mary groaned, 'I feel worse than usual. I hope I am not going to lose this child,' and Abbie remembered – how could she forget? – the pain and sorrow of a miscarriage, and felt very sorry for her. 'Just in case I am not able to go into supper tonight, would you put on one of my black gowns and paint your face, to be ready to take over? I will send Flamina to help you.'

'I do not need her, madam. I can do it myself by this time.'

'Then, you may use my paints. And, if I do not recover in time, you have seen me conducting a supper party often enough. Be merry, and remember that the guests tonight are all relations of mine, or close friends.'

'And you do not think they will see through the disguise, madam?'

'They will not, and to make sure, place a little cushion under the gown to imitate the bump of a baby,' Mary said, her face as white as snow without any face paints.

Abbie saw her opportunity, and grasped it. 'Your Majesty, *please* beg Queen Elizabeth again for the release of Lord George Gordon, I implore you! The whole district of Huntly where my family lives is in desperate straits without him.'

'Any wish of yours should be my pleasure to grant, Abbie, after all you have done to help me, and indeed, many others at my court. But events in Scotland are so fluid that they change from day to day, and no one can guarantee now that Lord George Gordon, if he were free, would not raise the whole of the north of Scotland against me, to add to my troubles.'

'Madam, Lord George is the very opposite of his father. There is not a warlike bone in his body.'

'I shall give the matter my consideration, Abbie – but now,

I must lie down,' Mary said, trailing into her bedchamber.

Abbie curtsied, but now she knew that she was wasting her time here at Holyrood. Her mission had failed. All she wanted was to go back home. And she *would*, as soon as she could.

Just before seven the wind reached its peak, screaming around the tiny supper room adjoining Mary's bedchamber. Lord Robert Stewart, another illegitimate half-brother, and Lady Jean Stewart, the Countess of Argyll, an illegitimate half-sister, came in together, laughing and windblown.

Yes, Abbie thought, if they only knew, she and they were all illegitimate brothers and sisters together at this cosy little party . . . But she sat still, watching them all come in, one by one, and thinking that she knew why Mary's pain was back in her side again. In an unfortunate meeting in the corridor, Mistress Clarihew, the housekeeper, had been telling her another old wives' tale before anyone could stop her clacking tongue.

'A drunkard's wife gives birth to monsters,' she said gloomily, as they watched Darnley reeling downstairs. 'Or idiots. And always they are girls.'

Arthur Erskine, the Queen's equerry, had pooh-poohed it. 'Don't listen to anything Mistress Clarihew has to say,' he said. 'She is a silly old Edinburgh gossip, if ever there was one. I wonder that Your Majesty has not dismissed her before this.'

'She keeps the servants in order,' Mary had sighed.

But now the page, Anthony Standen, and Riccio were coming in, and Abbie saw that it was time to go into action. She put on her Mary voice. 'Squeeze in here,' she smiled at them from under the black gauze of the face veil of one of Mary's head-dresses. 'It's more fun this way,' and they all wiggled and pushed their way around the small table and giggled like children at a party.

Already the tension had eased.

Feeling a little more relaxed Abbie raised her glass to her

lips. Just then there was a rustle in the doorway of the private spiral staircase leading down to the King's bedchamber, the staircase the Queen had forbidden Darnley to use for months. In fact, she had got Arthur Erskine to post a guard to see that he didn't.

'Arthur,' Abbie whispered, 'there's someone there.'

She was still holding her glass halfway to her lips, and Arthur Erskine had got up with an exclamation, when Darnley materialised. He sauntered over to Riccio, patted his shoulder, admired his fur-trimmed russet doublet and lifted up the huge diamond the little man always wore on a golden chain around his neck to the light of the candles.

It cascaded a thousand glittering colours to dazzle their eyes, and when they looked again at another movement in the doorway, Lord Ruthven was standing there with a steel cap on, and with his armour shining through his nightgown. His face was the colour of old yellow rags and his eyes burned as red as fire.

It was a joke! The man was dying of consumption. But he must have got out of bed to play this joke on the Queen. Abbie couldn't understand it. 'My lord,' she said, stifling a nervous giggle, 'are you delirious?'

It was no joke when Ruthven croaked in his strange old-fashioned parlance, 'Let yonder poltroon Davy come out of your privy chamber! He has been there overlong.'

'Have you taken leave of your senses? Signor Riccio is here by my royal wish.'

'He has offended against the Queen's honour! Ask the King!'

'What is the meaning of this?' Abbie rounded on Darnley, in the most difficult role she had been forced to play so far.

'I know nothing,' Darnley muttered, shifty-eyed.

Riccio cowered into the window seat. Ruthven lunged at him with his dagger, and the Queen's stunned attendants came to life at last and leaped to restrain him.

'Lay not your hands on me,' cried Ruthven.

That must have been the signal for his followers, Andrew

Ker of Fawdonside, Patrick Bellenden, George Douglas –
Morton's bastard brother – Thomas Scott and Henry Yair
to rush up the spiral staircase and into the supper room.

They knocked over the table. Lady Argyll snatched up the
last candle and held it aloft over the splintered glass and
plates. Riccio fell to the floor, clinging to Abbie's skirts. Ker
prised his fingers open and wrenched him off her. It was real!
It was really happening!

Abbie screamed, 'For God's sake, spare him!'

Ruthven pushed her into Darnley's arms. 'Hold her, sire!'

Abbie broke away and turned to shield Riccio. Ker pressed
a cocked pistol to the cushion under her gown – to what
would have been Mary's womb. Bellenden held a dagger to
her back. She felt it prick her shoulder and thought: It is
Riccio's life or the Queen's child's life, now.

'Save me, madam!' Riccio screamed. 'For the love of God,
save me!'

Abbie begged for his life, saying anything that came into
her head. 'I will pardon you all! You shall have gold! I will
give you lands! If he has done wrong, let Parliament decide
it! I will send him away . . . Anything . . . Anything . . .'

George Douglas bent over Darnley and snatched his gold
dagger from its scabbard. He lunged over Abbie's shoulder
and drove it into Riccio's back. Darnley seized Abbie again
and, half-fainting, she remembered Damiot's warning –
'Beware the Bastard!' She had never dreamed it was Morton's
bastard brother he was meaning.

She saw Riccio dragged to the door and into the audience
chamber on his knees with Darnley's gold hilt sticking out
of his back and blood pouring through his russet doublet.
Shrilling, awful screams came from the audience chamber.
More men rushed up the staircase and through the supper
room headed by Morton, his red hair escaping from under
his helmet. Darnley was so unnerved that he let Abbie go
again.

At that moment Abbie was aware of long black skirts in
front of her. The Queen had got up out of her bed, and was

456

shielding her as she lay on the floor. 'Go into the bed-chamber,' she muttered. 'Nobody is looking at us. They are all looking at that carnage through there,' and Abbie crawled away.

The Queen tried to get to Riccio's side.

But so many assassins were around him, knifing him, that she couldn't see him. All she saw were daggers rising and falling, digging and hacking, until his cries grew fainter and finally died, as he bubbled and gurgled in his own blood.

Darnley vomited into the fireplace. Bells rang in Mary's head. Darnley caught her as she fell. She regained consciousness attended by Lady Argyll, and heard hoofbeats drumming over the drawbridge and the shouts, 'A-Douglas! A-Douglas!' the war-cry of Morton's kinsmen.

'Can we help Riccio?' she asked her half-sister, and Lady Argyll went to see.

She came back with a face like death. 'They have cut him into collops, madam. They even cut off his head.'

Mary sprang up to find Darnley and Ruthven had returned to the supper room.

'Give me wine,' Ruthven coughed, and spat blood.

Darnley scrabbled through the debris on the floor and found a bottle intact. He drank and passed it on.

'I hope to God it chokes you both!' Mary cried. 'God damn you to eternal Hell!'

Ruthven lifted terrified eyes. 'Do not curse me, madam. I shall meet my Maker very soon now. This was your husband's doing.'

'Traitor!' Mary turned on Darnley. '*Why?*'

'For the Crown Matrimonial. You would not give it to me, otherwise.'

'Your husband's plan was that you should be killed, madam, and your child, too. It was his doing,' Ruthven insisted. 'We have it in writing. Darnley's name is at the top of the bond.'

'*You?*' Mary almost laughed at Darnley. '*You* have my crown, and inherit Elizabeth's? Oh, I do not think so, sire.'

'In any case, you are now the King's prisoner, madam,' Ruthven gasped. 'He is to be your jailor. You are to have no ladies.'

'What?' cried Lady Argyll. 'In her condition? What about old Lady Huntly, her midwife? It will be a miracle if the Queen does not miscarry tonight after all this.'

'I suppose there can be no harm in Lady Huntly,' Ruthven smiled a ghastly smile before he left. 'Lord Huntly was a rebel, too.'

'Get out of my sight!' Mary spat at Darnley as Lady Argyll went to fetch Lady Huntly, and he crawled away with his tail between his legs.

The Queen returned to her bedchamber. 'Abbie,' she whispered, 'you may go. What I would have done without you on this bloody night, I do not know.'

Abbie crept out, thankful that she had trained herself for years to simply melt into the background. Nobody noticed her, and she reached the sanctuary of her bed safely.

The sights and sounds of the shocking murder she had just witnessed went on and on in her head. She thought she would never sleep again as she lay there rigid with terror and horrified at the plights of the Queen and her unborn baby.

Would the child ever be born? Shuddering, Abbie realised that tonight he had almost been slain in his mother's womb, or at least that had been the intention.

FIFTY-SEVEN

Outside, the Douglases were milling about in the courtyard. They were truly ready to kill her. Inside, Mary's baby fluttered restlessly in her womb. She felt sick and dizzy and very frightened.

Lady Huntly came into the bedchamber in her underclothes, her grey hair awry around her large, plump face. 'They've taken away my top clothes to search them,' she said indignantly. 'They think they will find some sort of message for your friends in them.'

A message!

'Oh God! I must lie down,' Mary groaned. 'I must stay calm, and think.'

Lady Huntly undressed her gently and laid her down in her bed. Mary could not believe that the widow of Lord Huntly was doing this for her. Why? Then she remembered Lord George Gordon, and she hadn't had time to do anything about him . . . Her head was going round and round.

'That's right, Your Majesty. You don't want to lose that baby, and I'm here to see that you don't,' Lady Huntly said grimly. 'You should rest now. But remember, I have a very ample bosom, and the bodice of my petticoat is ample too. I could hide a dozen letters inside it, if you like. Just let them try to search my bodice!'

In the morning Mary had made up her mind. She could get around Darnley if she promised him her body. She might even have to sleep with him again before she accomplished her plan of escape. The very thought of it nearly made her vomit. She went across to the chest she kept her face paints in, took out the white powder, mixed it with water and laid it thick on her face. Her face had been pale enough to begin with, but Darnley was stupid, and besides, he would be more than likely drunk.

'I hope you feel better than you look,' Lady Huntly said.

'Don't worry. Do you think you could get a letter to Lord Bothwell?'

'I *will* get a letter to Lord Bothwell, madam, if you wish it.'

'Then go, and send the King to me.'

She was forced to endure him in her bed once again that night, but she kept him dangling all day, while Lord James, Morton, Douglas and Sir William suddenly appeared in the audience chamber as if by magic. So, Sir William had been in the plot all along . . .

'Madam,' Lord James said, shocked, 'surely you will have this blood mopped up?'

'It will never be mopped up,' Mary vowed. 'It will sink into the stones and remind Scotland for ever of treachery, mayhem and murder.'

They were innocent, they assured her. They were very sorry that her favourite singer had been murdered by an unfortunate error. They craved pardon. Mary gazed at them, scarcely able to believe her ears.

But she kept calm, determined to act it out, and ran to Lord James.

'Oh, James,' she said, embracing him, 'if only you had been here, none of this would have happened! It is so good to have you back!'

'You will have to pardon everyone, the rebels who were with me, and those who murdered Riccio,' he said in the lordly manner she had expected. 'Then we can start all over again. We will draw up the documents for you to sign.'

'When?'

'Later today, madam.'

'Oh,' Mary groaned. 'I feel faint . . . I have pains . . .'

The lords looked alarmed, as though she would drop the baby on the carpet in front of them. Darnley took her to her bedchamber.

'When you come with the documents, give them to me,' he smirked at the lords. 'She is sleeping now, but I have my own ways of awakening her! I will guard her and see that she signs by tomorrow morning.'

Quickly, Mary removed the face paint. She heard the rough voice of Ruthven next door. 'Then may vengeance fall on your head, and on that of your children, if aught goes wrong!'

When they went away Darnley crept back. 'Did you hear that?' he whimpered. 'He cursed me!'

'Of course he did,' Mary said. 'He is an evil man. They are all evil men. They made you sign that document so that you are the one who will be blamed for everything. They even put your name on the top of it. They mean to kill us both, make no mistake about it. So, we must escape.'

'When? How?' he asked, immediately afraid for himself.

'You will go to your room and I will stay here. At two o'clock in the morning I will come for you, and we will make our way to where our rescuers will be waiting with horses.'

'You have arranged all that already?'

'Yes. Now, please go. I am so tired, and the baby is kicking.'

'It's not much further,' Mary encouraged Darnley through the passageways under the kitchens lined with sacks of apples, barrels of pickled herrings and casks of wine. 'There is a door here. It leads out into the burial ground.'

It was dark and cold and eerie as Abbie crept among the tombstones behind them. Suddenly Mary tripped over some fresh earth.

'Oh God, they must have buried Riccio here . . .' Mary whispered. 'There is something not far underneath the loose earth here! Oh, Davy, Davy,' she wept.

Darnley scrabbled in the earth. 'I wonder if they buried

461

that fine diamond he had around his neck with him?' he asked unconcernedly.

'Oh, how I hate him, hate him, hate him,' Mary muttered to Abbie, leading the way closer to the wall of the graveyard. Then they heard a voice. 'Bothwell!' she cried. 'Thank God! Thank God!'

'Come! Let us away!' Bothwell said. 'I'll take you up with me, Your Majesty,' and as his horse leaped forward Mary had to cling on tight, although her large belly made it very difficult. 'We'll go to Seton.'

Erskine took Abbie up with him, but when they got to Seton House Mary looked around fearfully, though a large number of Bothwell's men had gathered in support of her. 'It is not far enough,' she said. 'Where is a safer place?'

'Dunbar,' Bothwell said decisively. 'It's surrounded by the sea on three sides. But it's another thirteen miles. Will you be able –'

'Give me a horse,' Mary said, and after she was mounted she shouted to the men to follow.

Abbie was given a horse of her own and rode beside Mary. Darnley came up close. 'Go faster!' he shouted. 'We are being followed, I'm sure of it!'

'The baby –' Mary screamed into the wind.

'It's no matter,' Darnley shouted back. 'We can always make another.'

'Go!' she cried contemptuously. 'Save yourself, then!'

It was the end of everything for Mary. The bitter, stony, callous end. All she hoped was that the child would not be born long and fair. She hoped and prayed that it would not resemble Darnley, for any part of him was just pure filth. She would rather tear the child out of her womb right now. She could never love it as a mother should.

They reached Dunbar at daybreak, clattering along the High Street that wound downhill to the red sandstone castle on the shore. Erskine helped Abbie to dismount and Bothwell led them into what had been once the Great Hall. Now it was empty and cold. Mary looked around at the rock walls.

'I don't know who has been the keeper here, and I don't want to know. My Lord Bothwell, this castle is yours from now on.'

He signalled to his soldiers to make a fire. Others fetched blankets to make her a pallet. But Mary did not lie down. 'You have done well,' she smiled at them. 'Now, find me a pan and as many dozens of eggs as you can beg, borrow or steal in the town. We must eat.'

She was calmly frying the eggs when Darnley appeared.

His eye fell first on Bothwell. 'Fetch me wine,' he shouted.

'He is not your servant,' Mary snapped. 'He used to be, along with every noble and subject in the land. But no longer. From now on you give orders to no one except your own servants.'

'Oh, my Mary, you have changed since our last night together.'

'I am not your Mary, and that night I did what I had to,' she said, blushing.

'Those are not the words of a loving wife.'

'No,' she said, turning her back on him. 'They are not.'

'Do you feel ill?' Bothwell asked, propped up on his elbow on the pallet beside Mary, while they gazed into the fire.

'No, only tired.'

'Go to sleep,' he said.

'Stay here with me until I do, then. Let me lie and look at you. You are all I have now in the world. I trust you.'

And God knows I love you, desperately, shamelessly, more than my loyalty to God or Lady Jean. I want to touch that russet hair of yours. Is it soft, or does it spring through the fingers? I want to know your lips, your arms, every part of you. *And I will have them.* From now on I will snatch what happiness I can.

Bothwell sat beside her, well aware that he was at a crossroads in his life. Mary wanted him, he knew that. She had dropped so many hints and now, tonight, he could feel the heat of desire positively radiating from her body. This was the time to go slow, to tease her onwards. There were many obstacles ... But the goal in his sights was golden, in the shape of the crown.

Mary slept with a smile on her face that night, and five days later, heading the four thousand men Bothwell had summoned, she took the sulky Darnley and left Dunbar for Edinburgh. Abbie rode behind her, marvelling at another sudden change in fortune, followed by Bothwell, his Borderers and four companies of infantry. Despite her dislike of him, Abbie had to praise Bothwell for all he had done for the Queen in her hours of greatest need. Was it ungenerous, Abbie wondered, to suspect his motives?

The guns on the Castle Rock thundered a welcome to the Queen. Cheering crowds followed her through the streets where more people hung out of the windows and balconies of the tall timbered houses, all roaring their welcome.

'A royal welcome for their King,' Darnley said, bowing from the saddle and blowing kisses to the crowd, who jeered at him, screaming with laughter.

Mary gritted her teeth. *If only she were rid of him.*

In Parliament House the following day the Queen, accompanied by Flamina, Seton, Lady Huntly and Abbie, watched as Darnley protested his innocence of the murder of David Riccio.

'But your name is on this bond, sire.'

'Signed under duress, with a dagger at my heart.'

'We all know the part you played,' Mary said coldly, 'but a proclamation of your innocence will be nailed at the Market Cross. I command it. No one will believe it, but for the sake of our child we must try to protect your honour.'

'Nobody dares to judge *me*. I am the King. Nobody ranks higher.'

'I do,' Mary said, and turned to her nobles. 'My lords, you see before you a master of treachery –' *surpassing even yourselves* '– who betrayed me as Queen and wife, betrayed the Church he was sworn to defend and then betrayed even this miserable bond of conspiracy. From now on, unless at my command, he will attend no public functions nor councils and will sign no documents. Furthermore all coins bearing his image will be withdrawn from circulation.'

Darnley spluttered with rage, but she swept on.

'All those who were not actually present at the murder but who were indirectly involved – including Argyll, Boyd, Sir William Maitland, Rothes and Kirkcaldy – are ordered to absent themselves from court. Morton, Lindsay, Ruthven and the Douglases, both they and their partisans, are outlawed from Scotland. As an example to the exiled murderers we shall hang, draw and quarter their henchmen who held the gates and corridors of Holyrood,' and she read from a list of names.

'I understand that John Knox has been sensible enough to flee to Ayrshire,' Mary concluded, 'where I hope he rots.'

A few days later Mistress Clarihew admired the bloody heads decorating the tower of Holyrood and the Netherbow Port. 'It's just like old times, Your Majesty, when your father was alive,' she said cheerily. 'It comforts a body to look up at a death-grin. It makes you feel lucky to be alive.'

A few days later, Abbie got her passport for home, but though she was gladder than ever to leave the court it was in a form she never would have wished for. She curtsied to the Queen and said, 'Madam, I beg leave to go home. I have received a letter from Donald. My youngest brother, Johnny, has taken a turn for the worse. He is not expected to live.'

'Of course you must go,' Mary said, 'although I hope you will soon be back. Do you wish an escort?'

'Thank you, Majesty, but Donald says he will be here to fetch me this afternoon.'

Abbie went to pack her bundles and found Lady Huntly at her side. 'So you are going back to Huntly?' she said. 'Johnny McCracken is ill?'

'Yes, my lady.'

'Remember, when he dies, I want you back again.'

No, Abbie thought, when the tears sprang to her eyes, Lady Huntly hadn't changed. She never would. Those sabre teeth of hers could cut just as deep as ever.

'You have been closeted with the Queen for weeks, now,' Lady Huntly went on, unconcerned. 'What has she said about the release of George?'

'There was a letter of refusal from Queen Elizabeth, but I believe the Queen may try again.'

'She had better! I can see that it is going to be a case of an eye for an eye, and a tooth for a tooth. If she wants to be delivered of a son, she must deliver my son back to me,' Lady Huntly said grimly.

FIFTY-EIGHT

The news of Riccio's murder trickled through to Huntly, but by that time Abbie had too many troubles of her own even to think about it, let alone discuss it with anyone. She had just been helping her mother to bathe Johnny, and Abigail had turned away to get his porridge off the fire, when there was a strange sound, a rattle, from his bed.

Johnny was dead.

And then it was all as John McCracken had been dreading for years. Abigail was hysterical, inconsolable. She insisted on accompanying the coffin to the graveside, and when it was lowered into the ground she flung herself on top of it, sobbing and screaming.

Somehow, Abbie and her father got Abigail back to the Gardeners' Cottage, and somehow over the weeks, they calmed her down. Abbie dared to feel more cheerful about her mother's health, but her father was not convinced.

'It is a deceptive calm,' he confided. 'Your mother has not recovered. She only appears to be recovering. She is like a volcano, waiting to erupt. But I have made Jonathon and Jackson promise to visit her more often. That might help.'

So their two older sons came every week to visit now, instead of only once a month. They brought their sweethearts with them, Catherine and Edith, and they never came empty-handed. Sometimes they brought eggs, sometimes chickens, and as often as they could, they brought meat.

'You are my two dear, kind boys, to bring us so much,' Abigail smiled at them. 'We share it out with our neighbours as best we can, though there are very few Gordon soldiers here now.'

'We are trying to patch up a bit of the castle for when Lord George comes back,' John told his sons. 'Tomorrow we are going out to look for wood to make furniture. If there is any to be got, the people will give it to the Gordons.'

The wood-finding expeditions became a regular feature of her brothers' visits. Now that she had the time and space of her own to think about everything that had happened, Abbie felt restless, her mind full of death, the death of her brother, and the loss of her own unborn child. Abbie usually went to visit her mother then, to spend the day with her, and perhaps take her for a walk.

'You haven't been out for such a long time, Mother. Where shall we go? Lizzie Sproat has been baking, and has invited us to go and sample some of her scones,' she said one spring day.

'That'll be fine, dearie. Yes, I'd like to go for a walk,' Abigail said, 'although I'd rather be staying at home and looking after my Johnny.'

So her father was right, Abbie thought. It was going to take Abigail a long time, if ever, to get over his death. Perhaps it was like that for everyone. She suspected it was going to be like that for her, too.

Lizzie Sproat was her usual cheerful, bustling self. She spread her scones with butter and handed them round. 'You can say thanks to Jonathon and Jackson for both the scones and the butter,' she smiled.

She was chatting away to Abigail, and Abigail was smiling, when suddenly she broke off. Abbie was looking outside, and she had seen something. 'What is it, lassie?'

'Oh, my God,' Abbie said from the window. 'The Gordons are back already. Something is wrong!'

In a cold sweat she ran out of Lizzie's door, but the night-mare picture she had glimpsed from inside the window was just the same when she got outside. It was worse. It was the worst thing she had ever seen.

Donald was riding with his shoulders slumped over the body of a man lying across the saddle. And the man, as Abbie dreaded and didn't want to see, was her father.

'Donald!' she screamed up at him. 'Donald!'

He looked at her with tear-drenched eyes. 'It was so simple,' he said, shaking his head in disbelief. 'His horse just stumbled and threw him. When we got to him his neck was broken, and it was too late. Oh, Abbie, after all he's gone through . . . after all his battles . . . For it to end like this!'

But the grief was a thousand times worse when Abigail rushed out.

It was terrible.

For the second time the family attended the graveside, all except Abigail, who had never shed a tear since the day John McCracken was taken home. When they came back to the Gardeners' Cottage, she smiled around them all and, dressed in her nightgown, climbed into Johnny's bed still there in the living room. She said not one word, and then she turned her face to the wall.

Abbie didn't like that, not one little bit.

Jonathon clung to his Catherine and wept openly. Twice the size of her he might be, but it was clear to them all that Catherine would always have to prop him up through life.

Jackson's sweetheart, Edith, looked sad. 'It doesn't seem fair to leave you alone with her. I wish I could stay with you, Abbie.'

'No. I know you have to go, Edith. I'll be all right.'

'If you are not, I'll come back right away,' the plump, quiet girl offered shyly.

Abbie spent the next anxious days attending to her mother – washing her, talking to her, trying to get her to eat or drink, but all to no avail. One weary day she was trying to get her to take some beef broth when Lizzie Sproat knocked and came in.

'Don't, Abbie,' she sighed and gently held her arm. 'Your mother doesn't want any more food. It is only hurting her as much as it is hurting you to try. You see, she doesn't want to be here with any of us in this world any more. She is willing herself into the next one.'

Abbie's heart plunged to the ground. 'What do you mean, Lizzie?'

'I've seen it before, lassie, and always after someone has died. The one who is left turns to the wall, not wanting to see anyone again except the one who has gone before, and that is what has happened to Abigail. She only wants to see John, and we should not hold her back. But we will make her comfortable, at least, while she is waiting to depart.'

Lizzie Sproat helped Abbie faithfully day by day until Abigail, too, passed away. They all put on their black clothes again, and Abbie looked up at her husband on their way to the graveyard.

'Oh God, Donald, will this procession never stop? I am so tired.'

'Come home and rest,' he smiled bleakly, 'as long as there is peace.'

Peace there was, but it was more a state of suspended animation, of stunned shock, for Donald as well as for Abbie. She thought she could never recover from four deaths in her family, one after another. Then something happened to lift her spirits.

One Sunday just Jackson and Edith arrived.

'Where are Jonathon and Catherine?' Abbie asked.

'Enjoying the first day of their honeymoon, I expect,' Jackson said, 'the same as we are in our own way. The four of us had a double wedding yesterday, but after everything that's happened we kept it quiet, and there were no celebrations.'

'I'm so glad for you.' Abbie kissed Edith and then her brother in the first spark of animation she'd shown for weeks.

'And,' said Jackson, his fair young face so like his father's, just bursting with excitement, 'we've come to ask you something.'

'Ask us, then.'

'Who's going to live in the Gardeners' Cottage now?'

Abbie looked at Donald. He looked at her. Then they both shrugged their shoulders and spread out their hands.

'You mean, nobody?' Jackson gave a long sigh of relief.

'I *have* been worrying about it going to rack and ruin,' Abbie said.

'Then do you think that Edith and I could live in it?'

'But what will you do, Jackson?' Donald asked. 'How will you support yourselves?'

'Ho! Ho!' Jackson threw a cushion at him. 'Perhaps better than you, brother-in-law! I'd work the Home Farm again. Then at least we'd eat!'

'I would help him,' Edith said quietly, 'and I'd be very happy to look after the cottage and the garden.'

'Then it's yours,' Abbie said. 'You've got the right name. The McCrackens have been living there for all these years.'

'If you're going to work the policies, then I can't see any objection,' Donald agreed.

'We'll go now, and come back tomorrow.' Jackson sprang to his feet full of enthusiasm, and prepared to leave.

'You'll do no such thing.' Abbie pushed him back down in his chair. 'Unless you don't even want to try my shortbread? I have become an expert.'

'In that case I'll allow you to have another half-hour of my company,' Jackson grinned, and Abbie laughed genuinely for the first time for weeks.

Jonathon took Jackson and Edith and their few belongings in the farm cart, and deposited Edith and their boxes at the gate of the Gardeners' Cottage. Then he trundled on up to the old pigsty with his brother and his livestock.

'Donald was right,' Jackson said, jumping out and shutting the gate on the four squealing piglets he had brought, 'the whole place is in a hellish mess.'

471

'Well, you *would* come,' Jonathon said. 'Where are you going to put these hens?'

'God knows. In this old barn, just now. It looks as if the sooner I get to work here, the better.'

'And the best of luck to *you*, brother!' Jonathon laughed as he flicked the horse with his whip and the cart rumbled slowly away. 'I'm going back to our well-ordered farm and my honeymoon!'

Abbie shed floods of tears at last when she was supposed to be helping Edith to scrub out the cottage. Edith smiled in sympathy and now and then squeezed her shaking shoulders as she passed to and fro, but she said nothing and she never stopped working.

'I'm not much use to you, Edith,' Abbie sighed, 'and the strange thing is I haven't lived in this house since I was eight years old. I don't know what's the matter with me.'

'You're not crying for the house, Abbie, but for the people you loved who lived in it. It's only natural.'

'Well, now I've suddenly got two sisters,' Abbie said, wiping away her tears.

'You've got me, anyway,' Edith said, her kind face glowing.

'And Catherine?'

'Catherine will never leave the farm, Abbie. She's had her eye on it for years. When the old man dies, she'll push Jonathon into his shoes.'

'Were you sorry to leave it and come here?'

'No!' Edith laughed. 'It was Jackson I had *my* eye on! Wherever he wants to go will be home for me,' and she worked on placidly.

Abbie discovered that Edith never stopped working, inside the house or outside in the garden, and when she had got that all shipshape she took on the hens and then the pigs. Edith could run rings around anyone, and yet with her good nature there was always a pool of tranquillity around her wherever she was, whatever she was doing.

It was a gift, nothing short of it, and Abbie felt that with Edith's help she was beginning to rebuild her life at Huntly.

FIFTY-NINE

At the beginning of June, exhausted now nearing the end of her pregnancy, the Queen received Bothwell in her rooms.

Bothwell said, 'In the light of the flimsiness of the Holyrood defences, as proved in the recent murder, it is the Council's advice that you should repair to Edinburgh Castle for the birth of your child.'

Everything connected with it, each reference to it, struck more and more terror into Mary's heart, and the mere idea of hovering between life and death while giving birth and somehow miraculously surviving it, was all the more repugnant to her in the very rooms where Riccio's blood had been so cruelly shed.

She sat down immediately and made out her will. Her first concern was to provide for her child, to whom she left all her estates, although her true heart was for her French relations. They came next on the list for gifts. Then, her illegitimate brothers and sisters, their wives and husbands and in particular, their children, were each lovingly remembered.

Lady Huntly was specifically mentioned, Mary's attending nobles also, and one by one in loving detail she wrote down what she wanted her Marys to remember her by.

Then, with that attended to, the Queen took to her lying-in chamber in Edinburgh Castle ceremoniously on 3 June 1566, to await the birth, having provided Lady Huntly with a special black velvet dress for the coming occasion, hanging her own bed in blue taffeta and blue velvet, and furnishing the baby's cradle with ten ells of Holland cloth. She was prepared for birth – and death.

On 18 June bishops, priests and ambassadors hovered in the antechamber. Lady Reres, an established figure at Mary's court, settled her great bulk in the chair by Mary's bed, ready to help Lady Huntly and wet-nurse the baby. The afternoon slipped by. Mary dozed, hearing whispers and the telling of beads, and then she was sobbing and the room was full of people as the first pain slashed.

Bourgoing, her doctor, arrived and ordered everyone from the room except the midwives, and slipped a piece of barley bread beneath her pillow to please the fairies. The clock struck six.

Rain battered the castle walls and lightning streaked blue through the room. Mary lay, rigid with fear, and then the pains came in earnest. Lady Huntly threw something from the pocket of her velvet dress into the fire. The yellow flames changed to a violent blue-purple and clouds of purple smoke filled the room.

The fat face of Lady Reres hung over Mary. 'You should not have had that old hag here, madam,' she hissed. 'She is a witch.'

Lady Huntly elbowed her out of the way and made her sit at the other side of the room. 'Your time will come later,' she told her, and turned back to tie Mary's hands to the bedpost and wipe her forehead with damp cloths, for now the pains were grinding and tearing her apart, leaving her sweat-drenched and gasping for breath.

At midnight she was still conscious, racked with pain and screaming. She had gone to Hell. She wanted a priest. Bishop Ross was hastily summoned, but with her lips to his ear to confess her sinful love for Bothwell the words were smashed back in her body by raging, ravaging pain.

Lady Huntly held her calmly, murmuring instructions. 'No, don't push yet, my dear ... Wait ... Your time is nearly here.'

Lady Reres sobbed from the other side of the room. 'Help her, help her! Holy Mary, help her now!'

At dawn the curtains were drawn aside to admit a golden sunrise, and hours later, in the distance, Mary heard the chanting of the priests from the next room, the last Mass.

'Now,' Lady Huntly held her tight, '*push*, my dear Queen! Push!'

There was a shattering pain, and then another. The room went round and round. Mary smelled blood and incense. A few minutes later, at ten o'clock, she opened her eyes. Dr Bourgoing and Lady Huntly stood by the bed. Bishop Ross knelt beside it, offering thanks to God.

'A beautiful prince, Your Majesty,' Dr Bourgoing said. 'You have a son.'

Lady Huntly held up the slippery blue baby. A shining veil of gossamer was over his head. 'Don't worry,' she smiled down at Mary, stripping it away. 'I will preserve the caul and the good luck that comes with it. This little prince will have the gift of second sight. He will be free from the powers of fairies and witches, and he will never be drowned.'

Then she handed the prince to Lady Reres and took the back seat herself, resolving never again to act as midwife, whatever the loss to Scotland.

'Lady Huntly,' Mary's voice came weakly, 'this is June the nineteenth. The Prince's christening will be on December the seventeenth. You will stay with me at least until then?'

Well, she was in her sixties now and must preserve her health and strength. Lady Huntly reckoned it would be wiser to do that sitting on the silk cushions here at court than on the bare boards of Strathbogie while pressing for George's release.

'In the hope that we can secure the release of my own son, Lord George at last – I give you my promise, madam. You have a son of your own now, so you will understand a mother's love and longing for her child.'

That night the hills of Edinburgh blazed red with bonfires. The cannon boomed into the flaming skies. John Knox was not there to forbid it, and so the people danced around St Giles'.

Next day the houses in the Royal Mile were festooned with wild flowers, chains of daisies and bluebells and pinks. In the evening Lady Reres brought the baby to the Queen. 'You'll want to kiss him before I nurse him to sleep?'

'No,' Mary said. 'Take him away.'

She would kiss no spawn of Darnley's, now or ever.

Lady Reres, Lady Huntly and Abbie went with the Queen and her attendants to Alloa for a holiday and enjoyed the sea air on the way. They sat out on the castle forecourt in the sunshine with the cradle and enjoyed the peace, shattered when Darnley appeared, drunk.

They went to Traquair House in the valley of the Tweed. There Darnley could hunt and so stay out of Mary's way most of the day – but Abbie knew that he demanded his marital rights at least once during their stay there, and it was after one of those nights that Darnley again disgraced himself, and Mary had had enough.

'Dress the Prince for travelling,' she told Lady Reres. 'Pack all his things. I must take him to the safety of Stirling Castle, as I was taken once. And lock Lord Darnley up!' she screamed at the soldiers.

'Madam, he is the King!'

'Take him away,' Mary said contemptuously.

Mary hardly knew where to turn next. Bothwell was her strong right arm, but he was no diplomat. More and more she missed Sir William Maitland's cool head, his reasoning and his guidance through all the antics of her weathercock nobles. Flamina went to Lethington to visit him at some time every day in his town house and came back to gaze at her reproachfully. Mary could stand it no longer, and everyone at court was thoroughly relieved when, in September, she allowed Sir William to return. She received him coldly. But he was so repentant that she arranged his marriage to Flamina immediately, and at last there was music and dancing and laughter again at Holyrood.

So, the Spider is back, thought Abbie, and wondered, along with Lady Huntly, if he might approach Queen Elizabeth more tactfully on the subject of Lord Gordon. As time went on Lady Huntly, whose bark was proving much worse than her bite, confided in Abbie and conversed with her more and more. They even had a giggle, now and then.

'I go to Jedburgh, for the justice courts,' Mary said in October. Abbie, Seton and Lady Huntly accompanied her. Lady Huntly especially, found the ride there soothing in the yellow sunlight. The last vestiges of the summer still lingered. Now and then her eagle eye descended on the Queen, who was pale. Lady Huntly wrinkled her brows. Mary should not be riding after such a difficult birth, but she insisted. Worse still, from Abbie and Lady Huntly's point of view, since neither trusted them, she took Lord James and Sir William with her.

They had got as far as Melrose when one of Bothwell's soldiers approached Mary. 'Lord Bothwell is dead,' he told her.

When she didn't answer, Abbie saw it was because she couldn't.

'He was killed by one of the Elliots,' the man went on. 'Jock o' the Park. We took his body to Hermitage. Then I rode to tell you.'

'My daughter, his widow, should be informed,' Lady Huntly said.

Mary looked at her blankly, as if she had never heard of Lady Jean Bothwell. Then she collected herself.

'Oh ... yes,' she instructed the soldier. 'Go directly to Crichton Castle and tell Lady Bothwell.'

Whatever she was thinking and feeling, and Abbie believed it was a cut too deep to dwell on, Mary did not allow Lord James or Sir William to suspect it.

'We shall proceed to Jedburgh as arranged,' she said, and rode on with Abbie, leaving Lady Huntly to tell them.

477

Next day the Queen had been doling out punishments to the miscreants of the Borderlands all morning. To the disgust of Lord James and Sir William, she had sentenced none of them to death. They snorted behind her great chair of state until at midday Lady Huntly could suffer them no longer and made Mary stop to take some nourishment.

Mary only picked at the food on her plate. Then another of Bothwell's men was announced.

'I bring you wonderful news, Your Majesty,' he said. 'The Earl of Bothwell lives!'

Mary reeled back. Some colour returned to her ashen face, but apart from that she did not betray herself. 'We shall come and see him when the justice court is over,' she said calmly.

'You intend to ride sixty miles just to see Bothwell?' Lord James sneered. 'Thirty miles there and thirty miles back, all in one day?'

But they rode to Hermitage at her command and gained entrance to visit the invalid. Sir William smiled at him thinly. 'We are relieved to see that you were merely wounded and will soon be fighting fit again, and ready to tackle more of the Queen's enemies.'

Bothwell's lips stretched to a thin, grim line in his white face. *Merely wounded*, was he? Well, he would never let these men know of the huge wound in his side. He would never show weakness, and he pulled the bedcovers up more closely.

'Yes,' Bothwell replied, looking hard at Mary. It was the look of a lover. 'It's a pity she has so many,' he said wryly, and the Queen blushed and looked almost happy.

'They may be Protestants, but they hate Bothwell,' Abbie said to herself.

On the way back Mary's horse stumbled on a marsh in the dark. The men had to drag her out with her skirts sodden and filthy. She completed the journey, shaking with the cold, and it was past midnight when they arrived back at Jedburgh.

Abbie and Lady Huntly watched as over the next few days the Queen became delirious, and Dr Bourgoing pronounced that she was dying. Seton even opened the window, sobbing, to let her spirit fly to Heaven. Then Bothwell arrived, carried on a litter and, as usual, taking control of the situation.

'Shut that window!' he ordered Seton. 'It is chilling her to death. Pour spirits down her!' he yelled at Dr Bourgoing. 'Work on her! Rub her arms and legs!'

After three hours of it Mary's eyelids fluttered open and she tried to hold out her arms to Bothwell, but she was too weak. He held out his hand to her. She grasped it, covered it with kisses, and fell asleep.

'I wish all my Marys, past and present, to witness my son's christening,' the Queen told Lady Huntly at the end of November. 'It shall be in Stirling Castle. Lady Jean must come.'

On the appointed day it was Bothwell who acted as host. He and the Queen were together, like husband and wife. Mary received ambassadors and envoys under a white canopy starred with silver in a white satin gown encrusted with emeralds.

Abbie watched Bothwell ignoring Lady Jean as he hurried to speak to the Queen.

'All this is deeply insulting to you, Jean,' Abbie fumed. 'It is as if she has invited us here just so that she can flaunt Bothwell in front of you.'

'It would be insulting, if I cared. And if she is flaunting her affair with my husband under my nose, she is wasting her time. In fact,' Jean said, with a serene expression on her face, 'I am even delighted to see it, because it can only lead to trouble for him.'

The Bishop's deep voice rang out as the Comte de Brienne, Charles of France's representative, carried the six-month-old baby on a silver cushion to the great gold font sent by his godmother, Queen Elizabeth of England. 'I christen thee Charles James Stuart.'

At the feast the Earl of Bedford said, 'And is the child to be known as Prince Charles, Your Majesty?'

'Prince James, my lord, in honour of my father, King James the Fifth. One day, by the Grace of God, my son will be

James Sixth of Scotland and First of England.'

'A very special child,' Lady Jean murmured to Abbie.

It made Abbie think of all the very special children of King James V, so many of them unrecognised and in obscurity. More than that, it seemed somehow very unfair to her that this grandson of James V should inherit the crowns of two countries, while another little grandson of his had never even seen the light of day.

'A very special child in a world that is very poorly parted,' she replied, as Mary spoke again to the Earl of Bedford.

'You must remember to tell your mistress how magnificent her gold font is.'

'Queen Elizabeth is amazed at Lord Bothwell's new power,' he said, changing the subject to more interesting ground.

'Your mistress knows how much I value Lord Bothwell. He shall dance the royal galliard with me.'

'Surely that is the King's privilege?'

'Who knows that better than I?' Mary laughed.

When she heard that, and after all that she had seen, Lady Huntly lost no time in finding Lady Jean and Abbie in the crowd.

'Nobody will miss you if you go now,' she whispered urgently. 'You can be in Crichton by nightfall. Go home, both of you.'

'But what about the Queen?' Lady Jean objected. 'She was hinting that since there is only Seton left now, she would like Abbie and me to stay and attend her.'

'Never mind the Queen,' Lady Huntly said grimly. 'I will tell her that you became unwell and had to go home in a hurry, and since she is short of ladies to attend her, it will be a good opportunity to offer her my temporary services. I will keep hammering it home that I want George back. And I shall watch developments,' Lady Huntly said with relish. 'They spell nothing but trouble ahead.'

'Yes, Jean,' Abbie said. 'You should go back to Crichton, and stay away from any trouble. You will be safe there.'

'You are not coming with me, Abbie?'

480

'I will stay with Lady Huntly. While she takes your former place at court, I will go back to mine.' At that, Lady Huntly looked pleased. 'Together we can pursue a relentless quest for Lord George's freedom. Two heads must be better than one.'

Lady Huntly had been quite right. The trouble began that same night. When the dancing was over and Mary was in her bedchamber, a knock came at her door. Bothwell stood there. 'I dream of you,' he said hotly. 'I think of nothing else.'

Mary swayed towards him. 'I love you,' she said, and they made love all night long.

SIXTY

As often as she could, Abbie went to visit Lady Jean. Lady Huntly stayed at Holyrood. 'One of us must be here,' she said.

'Thank God to be home,' Jean said to Abbie during one visit, as they sat together on huge cushions before a blazing fire in Crichton Castle. 'I wouldn't like to be living at Holyrood these days.'

'Will Bothwell be home tonight?'

'He hardly ever comes home nowadays. Of course,' Jean laughed, 'he might change his ways when my mother sends me a cook from Huntly, as she promised.'

'She will have to get to Strathbogie first, and she doesn't show much sign of that. She is clinging like a leech to the hope that she can somehow get Lord George released. It's a terrible situation for you all to be in. And as for you, Jeannie, it is a life wasting. You love children so much – you might have had one of your own by now.'

'So long as it's not Bothwell's . . . But yes, I would have liked a child – Alex Ogilvie's child, for as you know I have always loved him, and always will.'

'You like Bothwell no better, then?'

'If only Bothwell were out of my life for ever! He is still the same man I was forced to marry, a brute of a man. The Queen does not have the faintest idea of how bad he is. But let them get on with it themselves.'

'Your mother will keep you informed of events at court,' Abbie sighed, thinking that Lady Huntly was in decline as the result of all the worry. And, she was getting old. 'But I hate leaving you alone again, Jean.'

'Don't worry. If there's any trouble I'll let you know. Any messages I send will be by Hattie Hunter's young man. You'll recognise him as genuine when he tells you his name is Freddie Robertson.'

Shocked that Bothwell lived openly at Holyrood now, Lady Huntly discussed this state of affairs with Abbie on her return. Mary dared not let him visit her chamber at night. The palace was too small and too heavily staffed for secrecy. The lovers were forced to meet outside.

They were not the only ones who knew, either. The sentry on duty every midnight, when Mary slipped out with a long cloak over her nightgown and a black wig hiding her hair, was alert to it. He kept a blankly correct face, but his eyes watched her avidly. He saw George Dalgleish, one of Bothwell's men, meeting her just beyond the gates and taking her away. He found out that it was to meet Bothwell in the darkened Exchequer House in the Cowgate.

He was still on duty when Dalgleish brought her back in the icy dawns and she crept back across the courtyard to her private staircase, too drugged by love to feel humiliated. Just a bitch in heat going after a dog, the sentry thought contemptuously, and spread the word.

Seton knew, too, and wept and prayed for her mistress endlessly. And Flamina, now Mary Maitland, when she came from her home at midday, found the Queen still dreaming in bed. No longer were her hangings pulled back at sunrise. It was always well after noon when Flamina bathed her and beautified her for hours on end, and since money was short after the christening, made over old gowns and nightrobes – nightrobes that were fit for a trousseau, transparent and jewelled.

And they were not for the King's benefit, Flamina reflected as she stitched. Darnley had departed to his father in Glasgow, and it was now an open secret that it was Bothwell who must be dazzled. Flamina understood that Mary wanted her beauty to blind him to visions of Lady Jean. It was a disgrace.

When Bothwell went to Crichton to go over the yearly accounts Mary carefully neither objected nor questioned him, although her ladies saw that she was sick with jealousy. She trusted him, she kept saying defiantly.

And when he came back he rewarded her with the Hepburn ring, a diamond horsehead, the neck bridled in emeralds, and inscribed with his motto – 'Keep Trust'. She wore it on a chain round her throat, hidden between her breasts as only he, in bed, and Flamina, when she bathed her, knew.

Lady Huntly was bursting with curiosity. If only her four cats had been with her, she might have been a fly on the wall of Exchequer House this very night! As it was she had to content herself with carrying piles of linen to and fro, dropping a pillowcase here or there in strategic places so that she could peep into rooms and listen at doors. In such a way she managed to eavesdrop one day in Holyrood and almost fainted at what she heard, as she reported to Abbie.

'I have a favourite daydream,' Mary told Bothwell in a low voice. 'To be your wife.'

'An impossible dream. You know that.'

'Not if Jean divorced you. Not if the nobles got rid of Darnley.'

'And how would they do that?'

'They can do it by any means they wish, so long as they don't involve me. You may tell them that.'

'Then I will tell you a secret. Lord James, Morton, Sir William and the rest have delegated the task of getting rid of Darnley to me, my love. We all want him gone. They will look through their fingers and say nothing.'

'Cowards, as usual!'

'You can help me, Mary. You can go to Glasgow and persuade Darnley to return here. You will have to arrange for a litter to bring him back. He is ill with syphilis.'

'*Syphilis?*' Mary shrieked in horror. '*Mon Dieu! Mon Dieu!* Then he will die, anyway.'

'We can't wait. There is something else you should know. He and his father, the Earl of Lennox, have conspired with the English to kill you and abduct the Prince. There is no time to waste. We want you to go this week.'

'I cannot. Not without you.'

'You can. Find out what Darnley is thinking, and send me word with my page, Paris. You can depend on him, as you can depend on me – with your life.'

At sunrise on 21 January Abbie and Lady Huntly, already in their riding habits, helped Flamina to dress the Queen in black breeches and pearl-embroidered boots of white kid. Next came the white leather jerkin that flared out from the hips, and lastly the black hat with the white curling plumes.

Mary took her pearl-handled whip from Flamina's hands, then sat down and buried her face in her hands.

'Your Majesty,' Flamina kneeled at her feet, 'do you feel faint?'

Mary shook her head, and her anguish continued. Abbie and Lady Huntly exchanged glances. They knew what she was thinking, for they had listened to her arguing with Bothwell for the past five days. But he had remained inflexible. It was a shockingly simple decision that the young Queen was having to make – she must choose between Darnley's life and Bothwell's love, and neither Abbie nor Lady Huntly had the slightest doubt which she would choose.

Seton came to the door and spoke timidly. 'Madam, may we help you to bed? Your face is as white as a sheet.'

'Bed?' Mary got up and gulped a glass of wine. She snatched up her whip. 'I am going to Glasgow. Flamina?'

'Madam, forgive me –'

'Do not concern yourself, Lady Maitland,' Lady Huntly said swiftly. 'Abbie and I will accompany Her Majesty, and if the King is ill I can help to deal with that, too, since I am a nurse.'

485

Lady Huntly had no experience of syphilis whatever, but she was not going to admit it, especially when she had no intention of nursing the King. He would have nurses and physicians of his own, she told Abbie, and she was not far wrong.

'The doctors want me to go to Craigmillar for the cure,' Darnley told them from behind his mask when they got to Glasgow. 'My nurses are coming with me.'

They saw that Mary was astonished at the speed of his acquiescence. In fact, he suggested the move to Edinburgh before she did. What was the meaning of that? Did Darnley have a plot of his own?

They were in Glasgow five days. During that time the Queen wrote four letters to Bothwell and sent them with Paris, his messenger. Abbie only hoped that Mary had included instructions to burn them as soon as he read them, for each one was written with the tears pouring down her face, and sealed with passionate kisses.

After the last one she laid her head on the desk in Darnley's room, so weary that she fell asleep. Lady Huntly tiptoed across to his bed to have a look at him. Darnley turned over in his sleep. The mask had caught on the corner of his pillow and slipped off. Lady Huntly gasped in horror and signalled to Abbie to come and look.

The closed eyelids were gutted with mucous. The pox had dug deep pits in his fair skin and mottled it with a red crust of scabs. His nose and cheeks were bloated. His lips were dry and cracked, and a stubble of golden beard poked out of his oozing chin. Even his ringlets were snarled with matter. No one had combed them for days.

They could not blame his servants, for the stench that came from him was overpowering, fetid, filthy. They put their scented handkerchiefs to their noses and woke the Queen.

'Come,' Lady Huntly said. 'He is sleeping. It is time to go back to our lodging,' and outside they all three gulped in the fresh air thankfully.

*　　*　　*

On 26 January they left Glasgow. Darnley lay in the litter on a velvet couch. His face was wrapped in a linen mask. Curtains of cloth of gold, cloth Lady Huntly recognised as having once been at Strathbogie, shielded him from the icy wind and prying eyes, and he was buried under piles of furs. It was bitterly cold in the swirling snow and when they looked upwards all they saw was a moving white mass of snowflakes.

Against that background a raven stood out, shiny and black. Abbie recognised it, and knew what Lady Huntly's reaction would be.

It was Nick – her Nick – from Strathbogie! He had found her again, at last!

He kept following the litter, to the dismay of the royal party. 'It means bad luck,' Mary said, crossing herself, but no matter how they tried the guards could not scare him away.

Lady Huntly guided her horse alongside the litter as they approached Edinburgh, fearful in case she never got another chance to speak to her familiar. She *must* speak to Nick. She had too many problems now possibly to solve them by herself, especially her son George, the largest problem of all. As she got up to the litter the raven actually flew down and perched on its canopy. He had come to her!

'Nick, Nick,' Abbie heard her murmuring softly. 'Speak to me.'

The guards became frightened for the King. They lifted their spears this time. The raven opened his beak as if to rip through the canopy. Then, croaking, snarling and thrashing his wings he glared at Lady Huntly with an evil eye and soared up into the sky and flew away to the east.

Sir James Balfour, a lawyer and close adviser of the Queen, met them on the outskirts of the city. Lady Huntly, thoroughly depressed now, had never liked him, nor his blackened teeth.

'There is a large crowd waiting to see you and the King at Craigmillar, Your Majesty,' Sir James addressed the Queen.

'Lord Bothwell's orders are that you should divert to Kirk o' Field.'

'And where is that?'

'If you would follow me down Blackfriars' Wynd, madam, it is just past Archbishop Hamilton's house.'

Lady Huntly sniffed. She didn't like Archbishop Hamilton either.

'Yes! Yes!' Darnley raised a muffled voice from the litter. 'Kirk o' Field! That's the place!'

From a distance Abbie and Lady Huntly saw that it was a two-storey house built of stone and sheltered by trees. The gardens in front of it were dotted with white clumps, bushes laden with snow. Servants appeared out of the door with torches. Their golden glow lit up the crow-stepped gables of the house – and that was not a weathercock on the roof-tree.

It was the raven.

Balfour got the King to bed in the largest bedchamber of the house.

'You will not leave me, my love?' Darnley quavered.

'Of course not, my husband,' Mary soothed him, but her soothing tone and the smile on her face were both false. Lord Balfour showed the ladies into small adjoining rooms, made freshly ready with glowing fires in the hearths.

'I see that you have had time to prepare this house for us, Lord Balfour,' Mary remarked, with raised eyebrows. 'I thought coming here was a last-minute decision.'

'It is my brother's house,' he replied obliquely. 'He doesn't live here now, but we keep it in a certain state of readiness.' He bowed, and went off in the direction of the King's room.

As soon as Abbie heard the Queen closing her door she crept past it, and far enough along the passage to hear what was being said.

'Is it in place?' Darnley was asking excitedly.

'Your Majesty!' Balfour's voice was reproving. 'It will take another two weeks to obtain the required amount of gunpowder! Men cannot openly bowl along the city streets with barrels of gunpowder, you know. Not in broad daylight. It must be done under cover of darkness.'

GUNPOWDER! Abbie's blood froze in her veins. If a guard had come and tried to arrest her at that moment, she could not have moved.

'Two weeks?' Darnley asked querulously. 'What date is that, then?'

'We shall have everything ready by Sunday, February the ninth, sire.'

'Well,' Darnley sounded pleased, 'in two weeks I shall be entirely cured. My beauty will be restored, that beauty which the Queen could never resist. It will be a simple matter to induce her to sleep with me.'

He giggled suggestively, and Balfour giggled with him. 'Dirty pigs,' Abbie said to herself.

'Now, about the fuses,' Darnley asked next.

'They will take a long time to run, Your Majesty. Two hours, anyway.'

'Good. That will give me plenty of time to make some excuse to leave the Queen alone while I escape on my horses. I will have them saddled and waiting to take me away. Be sure you give me the signal in plenty of time.'

'To assassinate a Queen is a grievous sin, sire. She seems most kind to you.'

'Ah, Balfour, things are not always as they seem, my friend! But one thing is certain. Scotland – and I am assured, England – will be better off without her.'

So Darnley was plotting to blow up Kirk o' Field, this very house, was he? Lady Huntly had heard bumps and thumps during the night from the cellar and now Abbie confided to her that the noises were made by men rolling casks of gunpowder. It would not go off until it was lit, but understandably, they both found it very difficult to sleep.

The next day Mary made an excuse to go to Holyrood to arrange for the King's own bed to be transported to Kirk o' Field, and if there had been fanfares of trumpets all the way in front of the furniture, she could not have made its transportation more public. Most days after that she spent in Holyrood, for which Abbie and Lady Huntly were truly thankful. Of course, Bothwell was usually there as well.

Now that she was so suspicious, it didn't take Abbie long to find out that Mary and Bothwell had a murder plot of their own, which also required gunpowder to blow up Kirk o' Field. The whole palace was seething with plots and counterplots, all with the same aim in view, the death of Darnley for certain – and possibly the Queen.

The Queen would leave Kirk o' Field in time to escape the explosion. To make doubly sure, she would attend the marriage festivities at Holyrood after the wedding of two of her household, Margaret Carwood, a tiring woman, and Bastion Pages, a Frenchman, on the Sunday night.

It was all a mess of confusion. Even Mary herself was confused, arguing with Bothwell one minute and kissing him frantically the next, behind closed doors. But about one thing she was crystal clear: she wanted Darnley dead.

'Oh, my love,' she said to Bothwell, 'then you shall be my King.'

Lady Huntly found the next two weeks almost unbearable. The intrigue on every hand deepened to out-and-out corruption, both at Holyrood and Kirk o' Field, but that only made it easier for her to watch Mary and Bothwell day and night.

Mary gave him a silver casket for his most private papers, asking him anxiously once again if he was sure he had burned all her love letters, especially the ones containing her desire to have Darnley killed. Then she sat for hours going through all her own papers and locking them away in an identical silver casket of her own.

Abbie watched the nobles muttering among themselves, then muttering with Bothwell, then muttering with Balfour. Holyrood, she had already decided, was a den of vice – when something worse began.

It started as a whisper here, a whisper there, but Lady Huntly heard the rumours. They were all about her own daughter, Lady Jean Bothwell . . . Lady Jean was a fool, a gawky. Lady Jean was ugly, so ugly that she couldn't keep a man, not even her own husband. Lady Jean allowed her husband to sleep with the serving-wench. Lady Jean was stuck-up and considered herself a *virtuous* woman. Bothwell had only married her for her money.

The whispers swelled to loud and vicious slurs and taunts. Try as she would, Lady Huntly could not find out who had started these rumours, but they were making her feel very angry. Abbie could do nothing to calm her, except to tell her to keep her mouth closed and her chin up, until they did find out. They weren't finished watching and waiting, not yet.

Sunday the 9th came and went, according to many plans. At two o'clock on the morning of the 10 February, Darnley woke up with the smell of burning in his nostrils. It was not wood burning, or straw, or his candle . . . Oh God! Someone had lit the fuse! And they had not warned him!

He jumped out of bed and stumbled over his manservant's cot, beside the window. 'Get up, Taylor!' he screamed. 'We must escape!'

'But I must get a rope, and warm clothes, and a chair, sire!'

Darnley could not wait. He jumped out of the window and landed in the snow, rolling over and over. He was unhurt. Behind him Taylor was struggling out with all his apparatus, and he was making a lot of noise.

Darnley took to his heels and ran across the lawns, until he bumped into something that was at once hard and soft in the darkness. It was a man, and he knew by his voice it was Archibald Douglas. Thank God it was not Bothwell . . . But Archibald Douglas was looking very menacing . . .

'No! No!' Darnley screamed. 'Remember, I am your kinsman!'

'Bothwell will get the blame. We have arranged for it,' and soon Darnley was dangling, limp, from Douglas's powerful hands. When Taylor struggled up, Archibald Douglas snapped his neck as well.

Douglas and his men laid the two bodies out beneath a pear tree, and arranged their belongings neatly beside them. A little distance away Bothwell was getting impatient. What had happened to the fuses? Had they gone out?

'I'm going to see,' he told Paris, but Paris held him back and suddenly a massive crack threw them to the ground in an explosion that was beyond their imagination. Kirk o' Field was lifted into the air as if by a giant's hand, and then scattered in debris far around.

When the debris had stopped showering down, Bothwell escaped, ran to Holyrood and climbed into bed. He got up again immediately when he heard so many people rushing along the corridors, screaming. 'What has happened?' he cried.

'Oh, my lord,' a guard replied, 'the King's house has blown up with the King in it! He is dead. Who will tell the Queen?'

'I will,' Bothwell said, and when she came to the door of her bedchamber he told Mary the terrible news in front of the court, Lady Huntly among them. The old countess was not deceived by their performance.

'Not dead,' Mary moaned. 'Oh no, not dead!'

'Dead,' Bothwell said, gazing into her eyes.

No one slept the rest of that night, and early next morning Mary, heavily veiled in black, propped up by Bothwell and accompanied by some of the court, including Abbie and Lady Huntly, tottered off to examine her husband's body and the scene of the crime. The crowd was thick and silent. The pantomime was not over yet.

The Queen uttered piteous cries and fell on her knees by Darnley's side. She lifted her veil and kissed his face over and over again. 'Who has done this dreadful deed?' She flung her arms wide, inviting an answer from somewhere, but none came.

The crowd remained silent and dour, their eyes darting

492

from her to Bothwell and back again. There were no ooohs and aaahs of pity or sympathy. Uneasily, Mary put down her veil again to hide her dry eyes.

Back in Holyrood, Lady Huntly chose her moment well. Most of the court stood around the antechamber shaking their heads and talking in low voices. The Queen sat beside Bothwell, a crumpled handkerchief in her hand, looking curiously unelated for one who had just engineered an unwanted husband out of the way.

'Your Majesty.' Lady Huntly's voice was deliberately loud in the hushed atmosphere. Everyone stopped talking. 'I wish to be excused from court at once. I am going home.'

'To your daughter, at Crichton?' the Queen asked, to enrage Lady Huntly further.

'No, madam. I will not impose on Lady Bothwell. She has troubles of her own.'

'Troubles?' Bothwell cast Mary aside and jumped up. 'What troubles?'

'She is the victim of cruel and unjust rumours and accusations, my lord, and they have come from this very palace.' Mary sat up and paid attention, glancing fearfully at Bothwell. 'I shall go to Strathbogie. I had hoped that I would go with my son, Lord George Gordon, but . . .'

Mary had the grace to look abashed. 'Oh dear – but you see, Lady Huntly, there has been so much to attend to here.'

'Indeed, there has, madam. And most of it has been so disgraceful that I am too disgusted to stay another moment. Accompanied by Mistress MacLaren I shall ride in half an hour.'

Complete silence had now fallen in the antechamber. Who would have thought that this old lady had the courage to voice their real suspicions?

Erskine, captain of the guard, cleared his throat. 'Not alone,' he said. 'A great lady like yourself, the Countess of Huntly, cannot ride all that way alone and unescorted.'

'It seems to me, sir, that I might be safer alone,' she said acidly.

'But fortunately, the last three Gordons are still here,' he said.

'How very convenient for you,' Mary sneered and turned to the court expecting a ripple of laughter.

But nobody laughed, and nobody spoke when Lady Huntly curtsied coldly to the Queen and made a regal exit with Abbie following her.

SIXTY-ONE

When Lady Huntly, still in a right royal rage, broke her journey that night, she did so with a flourish in no less an abode than Stirling Castle.

'Have *you* noticed the Queen going to see her son?' she demanded.

Abbie shook her head sadly. She had often wondered at the Queen's indifference towards her child, after all the trouble there had been to get an heir to the throne. She could hardly believe it was because Mary hated Darnley so much now that her feelings also included his son. He was only a baby, after all. Where were Mary's natural maternal instincts?

At the foot of the rock Lady Huntly stopped and asked one of her Gordons to volunteer to race on ahead through the night to Strathbogie, and warn of their coming.

Then, with the other two on either side of them they rode onwards and upwards. Lady Huntly became calmer, even pleasant, assured of a warm welcome by Lord and Lady Erskine, keepers of the castle, who had been the guardians of the baby Prince all this time.

Once inside she ran a professional eye over him. He was now eight months old, and had changed out of all recognition. 'What is that harness he is wearing?' she asked, watching him lolling on his mat on the floor, when by now he should have been sitting up with a straight back. She also took note of the ease with which he was fitting his playing bricks one into the other.

'Clever boy!' Lord Erskine laughed, swinging him up off the floor and kissing him.

'We thought he had a little curvature of the spine,' Lady Erskine said, 'but the harness has almost straightened it. We hope to dispense with it altogether soon.'

For a few moments Lady Huntly gazed at the Prince, wondering if the fairies had stolen the fair baby she had helped to bring into the world, and substituted this darker-skinned, darker-haired child instead ... Such things happened, she knew.

'We have just come from Holyrood,' she said, and introduced Abbie to them. 'Of course, the Prince will know his mother now. Do you think he looks forward to her visits?'

The Erskines laughed. 'The last time she was here he tore the earring out of her ear and made it bleed,' Lord Erskine told them.

'And she wasn't very pleased,' Lady Erskine added. 'She has never come since.'

'Hm!' Lady Huntly snorted. 'She wouldn't like her ear to be bleeding – no, she would not! It would spoil her beauty for Bothwell.'

'So the rumours are true?' Lady Erskine said.

'My daughter is married to the man, as you know, and yet he lives quite openly at Holyrood now. The Queen is totally obsessed with him.'

'That will cause more trouble,' Lord Erskine said. 'We all know that it is the crown he is after, and not necessarily the Queen. She is deluding herself. He has got rid of Darnley. Now, all Bothwell has to do is get rid of his own wife.'

'Yes, that's what I'm afraid of,' Lady Huntly said, and Abbie felt sick. She had been trying to deny to herself the possibility of such a plot ever since Darnley's death. But it was the next logical step.

Very early next morning, before the Erskines were even up, Abbie and the Countess collected the two Gordons and rode on.

'I didn't like that curvature of the spine,' Abbie said. 'If I were his mother, I should be very worried about it. But the Prince is obviously clever, even at this early age.'

'Darnley didn't have two grey cells to rub together,' Lady Huntly said bluntly. 'Believe me, that child was never Darnley's, although the Queen thinks he is.'

'Perhaps that's why she doesn't like him. You heard the Erskines. They said she never kissed him or cuddled him.'

'No . . .' Lady Huntly glanced at Abbie sideways. If it came to that, she hadn't liked her own daughter much either, as she was sure Abbie would remember, though her own mistake had only been over a name – Jean, instead of Mary.

Now she saw, because the Queen was so self-centred, that it would have made no difference to her treatment of Jean anyway, and she drooped on the saddle at the thought of all those wasted years of anguish.

'Are you well enough, my lady?' Abbie asked.

'I am tired, that's all. You have never had a child of your own, Abbie?'

'I suffered a miscarriage almost two years ago,' Abbie told her sadly, 'when I was twenty-five. I would dearly love another child, and so would Donald. But perhaps I'm too old now?' Abbie asked, thinking that not only had she come a long way in her relationship with the Countess, but also that she was consulting the best midwife in Scotland – as that lady was so fond of telling everybody.

'My dear child, I was thirty-nine when I had Lady Jean! But don't leave it much longer, all the same.'

Abbie saw that the nearer they came to Strathbogie the quieter and tenser Lady Huntly was becoming – in fact, frightened. She had wanted so much to return in triumph with George, but here she was now, with only one lady in attendance, her daughter's companion of yesteryear, and two Gordons.

But it turned out that she had been thinking something else altogether. 'Abbie, you have consulted me. Now it is my turn to consult you.'

'*Me?*' Abbie laughed.

'I have just been thinking that perhaps it isn't too late to make it up to my own daughter?'

Abbie had never heard of white witches as opposed to black witches, but she dismissed all witches in that moment.

'It's never too late for that,' she smiled at her as they rode up the long tree-lined avenue towards Strathbogie. 'And now, take heart, my lady. The people are all out to welcome you home.'

Lady Huntly straightened her back. The ghost of the imperious Countess arrived at her ruined castle convinced that her heart would break, as she gazed once more at her beautiful home almost in ruins. Only a small part of it had survived intact, including the magnificent front door.

But there was not the double row of servants lined up in front of it, as in the old days. Now, only a few Huntly folk, who had been giving their time and their loyalty to the broken Gordon stronghold, were there to give her a shy, silent welcome.

Donald rushed towards Abbie. Geordie Brand stepped forward to help Lady Huntly dismount, but she was very stiff after the long ride. She realised she was not the woman she had been when she left Strathbogie. Far from it.

Abbie looked at her in concern. In the years since she had left Strathbogie Lady Huntly's face was much thinner than it had been, with the result that all her upper teeth protruded now from her pale lips, and not just the two fangs which had made her look like a sabre-toothed tigress. She was thinner all over, to make her look shorter and more feeble.

'I have come home to die!' she announced dramatically, in ringing tones.

Oh dear, she hadn't changed all *that* much then, Abbie thought. 'Don't you believe her,' she muttered to Edith, Jackson's wife. 'She's got a long way to go yet before she dies! This is all an act.'

But Edith was not so sure. Not long ago she had looked after her own grandmother with loving care until she had died. Her eyes misted at the memory. She understood old people, especially old ladies. Those were genuine tears in Lady Huntly's eyes before she brushed them away impatiently, and Edith felt very sorry and quite sad.

'Where are my ladies?' Lady Huntly demanded in her old domineering manner, and the Huntly folk shuffled uneasily, not knowing what to do or to say.

'I'm afraid there are none here now, my lady,' Abbie told her, stepping forward. 'These are the only people left.'

Lady Huntly drew herself up to her full height. 'But I must have ladies-in-waiting,' she cried. 'I have *always* had ladies-in-waiting! I am the Countess of Huntly! Who will unpack me – wash me – dress me?'

Nobody moved. Her eyes searched the small group desperately. They fell on a tall, strong girl with a pleasant face, who had been standing next to Abbie. 'What about you, girl?' she said. 'Will you look after me?'

Again there was silence, and nobody moved until Edith detached herself from the group and to Abbie's horror, before she could stop her, walked right up to Lady Huntly. 'I might,' she said agreeably, 'if you are a very good girl, and do as you are told.'

There was a hiss of shock all round. Abbie could not believe her ears. For a servant, and a strange farm-servant at that, to dare to address a countess of Scotland in such a fashion! What was Edith thinking about?

Next, Abbie could not believe her eyes, either, for Edith had put an arm round the old, shaking shoulders and Lady Huntly's head was resting on her comfortable breast.

'I will,' she promised. 'But who are you?'

'This is Edith McCracken, my lady,' Abbie got back her breath far enough to say. 'She is married to my brother Jackson. They have come to live in the Gardeners' Cottage, and they are working the Home Farm and the policies.'

'Well, Edith,' Lady Huntly said, after a long pause, 'you will work the land no longer. I shall get men to help Jackson. Henceforth, your place is at my side.'

'If you wish it so, my lady,' Edith said calmly. 'But remember –'

'I remember. Now, take me to my rooms.'

'Oh, Donald! I love you, and I've missed you so!' Abbie said in his arms, when they got home. 'I stayed away so long, and I really tried – and so did Lady Huntly – but it did no good.'

'What did the Queen say?'

'Something I wouldn't dare tell Lady Huntly, I'm afraid! Donald, she fears that if Lord George got out of prison, he would raise an army against her.'

'I dare say all the other nobles in the land would raise an army against her if they could. Against Bothwell, at least. But not George.'

'That's what I told her, but she didn't listen. Oh, you're so thin, Donald! What have you been doing?'

'Not eating, I suppose. We're all thinner up here nowadays, even Lizzie Sproat. There's precious little to eat. It's real hardship now. Oh, Abbie, I didn't marry you to give you this kind of life, sweetheart! I wanted something a lot better for you and me. I don't know *what* we're going to do.'

SIXTY-TWO

If Lady Huntly's homecoming had been sharp and shocking, at least she had been spared the aftermath in Edinburgh of the King's murder. There had been no clamour, no shouting, but a long sustained murmur of fear, incredulity and horror in every house and tavern of the town.

And like a sign, once again the east coast haar descended. The night watchmen groped through the streets with lanterns. 'All's well . . .' their voices echoed dismally down the wynds and closes. But they knew better.

Sometime through the night sketches of a red-haired man, his hands dripping with blood, were nailed to the Tolbooth, the Tron, the Market Cross and Holyrood Palace, labelled 'Bloody Bothwell'. Next morning the Town Watch tore them down, but the following night and the night after that they were back again and the murmur of the people rose to a sullen roar.

It grew louder when Bothwell appeared in the Royal Mile with fifty Borderers and rode with perfect assurance into the courtyard of Holyrood Palace.

'I demand trial,' he told the Queen.

'You're mad! It will look like a confession! The lords will be only too delighted to convict you.'

'They want my blood, that's certain. They are frightened that I will wed you and strip them of all they have been stealing from you for the past twenty years and more. But they will never convict me.'

'And *will* you wed me?'

'How can I? I am married already.'

A week before the trial due on 12 April, five thousand of Bothwell's Borderers gripped Edinburgh in a ring of steel. Rough as the heather they came from, they roamed everywhere while they were waiting, good-naturedly poking and prying, for many of them had never been in a city before.

The Edinburgh men were wary of them. Douce Edinburgh matrons envied the whores in the whorehouses, and when the Earl of Lennox, Darnley's father heard about all this on his way from Glasgow with his three thousand followers, he stopped in his tracks at Linlithgow and advanced no further, although he was Bothwell's accuser.

Sir James Balfour beat a hasty retreat to his house in the country. Mary wondered cynically when her brother would do the same. Four days before the trial, Lord James came to see her.

'It's a pity I shall not be here to see the outcome,' he said, 'but I leave tomorrow for Paris and Rome.'

And whenever Lord James disappears, it always means he has hatched some new plot, Mary thought with a sinking heart.

But on the appointed day Bothwell set off confidently for the Tolbooth, dressed magnificently in black and silver, and riding his black horse caparisoned in black with silver fringes. A thousand of his men raised their spears and cheered as he entered the courtroom. He smiled sardonically when the jury was sworn in and he saw that most of them were friends of his bitterest enemies.

At the bar he denied the charge.

'Has the Earl of Lennox sent any witnesses?' Argyll asked.

'No, my lord.'

'Are there any other witnesses?'

There was no reply.

Bothwell's counsel stood up and addressed the jury. 'You cannot convict a man simply on the accusation of his enemy.

If you do, you convict yourselves of the grossest injustice before Scotland and before God.'

After five hours' deliberation the foreman of the jury delivered the unanimous verdict – Not Guilty. But nobody in Edinburgh was impressed. Nobody believed it.

By the end of April Mary was sure she was pregnant. The Queen of Scotland, unmarried and pregnant like some common slut! And the child could not possibly be Darnley's . . .

It would be her second child by Bothwell. A few months ago she had awakened in the middle of the night writhing in agony, her bed soaking with blood and something more solid. But only Flamina and Dr Bourgoing had known about that. She would not tell Bothwell her suspicions this time, either, not until she was sure – for, oh God! Most in all the world she wanted Bothwell's baby, right or wrong.

She discussed ways and means of marriage again with him. She spoke about it almost every day.

'I cannot marry you,' Bothwell repeated. 'I am a married man. Married to a cold, frigid woman who complains every day, it is true, but married all the same.'

'I could never be frigid, married to you . . . I would never complain. What can Jean find to complain about?'

'The food at Crichton. She cannot find a cook.'

'She cannot find a cook?' Mary almost wept with fury. Then her face changed. Her eyes gleamed with another emotion. 'Then I shall send her one, this very day. He has cooked for me since I came from France,' she said, putting her arms around Bothwell's neck and planting little coaxing kisses all over his face. 'There is nothing I would not do for your comfort.'

'No,' he laughed. 'I've noticed.'

'Or for the comfort of your family,' she added hastily, blushing. 'So would you?'

'Would I what?' he asked, drawing her to him and running his hands over her hungrily.

'Would you marry me, if you were not married already?'

503

He took her through to her bedchamber and flung her on her bed. Then he unbuckled his belt.

'Like a shot,' he grinned.

Inside Strathbogie Castle Lady Huntly found that the people had done their best to repair the dining hall. The great wide fireplace had been built up, the walls and ceilings patched up, and a replica of the original sturdy long table placed in the middle of clean rushes with eight matching chairs. She gazed at the bare walls, remembering the tapestries that had hung there once, and moved on into the Great Chamber which used to be her drawing room.

'Gilded vestments from Aberdeen Cathedral were stored here,' she told Edith, 'until Queen Mary took them away after my husband's rebellion.'

'I wonder what she did with them, my lady?' Edith asked, for the room was very bare now.

'Oh, I *know* what she did with them,' Lady Huntly laughed bitterly. 'The cloth was holy, yet I saw the King's litter had been hung with it, and what was left over had been made into a doublet for Lord Bothwell.'

'Did you say anything about it?'

'There was nothing I could say or do. The Queen owns every castle in the land and their contents.'

Edith led her through to her bedroom in the Inner Chamber. The bed was made up and Lady Huntly fell on it gratefully. 'Leave me, girl,' she said. 'I am very tired.'

When Edith returned in the morning Lady Huntly was only just waking up. 'I think I'll stay in bed today,' she announced.

'You'll do no such thing,' Edith said crisply. 'Here is some fine warm water. We'll get you washed and changed into clean clothes, for a start.'

So, with Lady Huntly grumbling loudly and Edith coaxing relentlessly, the day began. It took a week of the same treatment before Lady Huntly could be persuaded to go out into the fresh air, and the first place she headed for was the barn behind the kitchens.

'I used to have four cats here,' she said.

'There are still cats here,' Edith told her.

Lady Huntly's heart beat faster when, in the dim light of the barn, she saw that they were grey. She bent down and picked one of them up. Like lightning its paw shot out and its claws scratched her face as it squirmed and wriggled in her arms and finally slithered back down to the ground.

'They are not my cats,' she said, dabbing her cheek.

'It's only a little scratch,' Edith said cheerfully.

But Lady Huntly turned her face away to hide her tears. Everything she had ever had, and not so long ago, was gone – her husband, her sons, her magnificent castle, her pet raven and even her cats. All that was left was Lord George in prison and Lady Jean in Crichton Castle. She blamed the Queen for it all.

Jean would not come to visit her of her own accord, she thought sadly, and now her tears really flowed, when she thought back to the uproar her christening had caused, and the placid little child she had been. She had had so many ambitions, so many hopes for her daughter, but she knew that Jean only thought of her as a cruel mother. She had never meant to be!

'Is it very sore?' Edith asked.

'Yes, it's sore,' Lady Huntly said, but she meant her heart.

It wasn't long before, thanks to Edith's efforts, she felt much better. Abbie had come to the castle to lend a helping hand one afternoon, and she had brought with her a bottle of her green-grozet which she had made from the gooseberries in her garden. Lady Huntly sat down with them to try some.

'This is glorious,' she smiled. 'We must get your receipt for it – which reminds me, I really must get a cook soon. It is not fair that Edith should be doing all the cooking.'

'Donald and a few of the Gordons were at Crichton Castle yesterday,' Abbie said. 'Lady Jean has not been well.'

'*Ah*,' said her mother.

'No, she does not expect a child, my lady,' Abbie said in

505

sure and certain knowledge. 'She is vomiting a lot and has terrible cramps in her stomach. Her maid, Hattie Hunter, told Donald that it has been going on for a few weeks now, ever since you sent her the new cook.'

Lady Huntly reeled back. 'What new cook? I didn't send her a cook! My memory is not what it was, I know – but I didn't send her a cook, Edith, did I?' she appealed.

'As you said, my lady, you haven't even got one of your own yet.'

'That's very mysterious,' Lady Huntly said uneasily. 'Very mysterious indeed. In another week I shall have recovered sufficiently to go to Crichton myself and have a look at this new cook.'

But the very next day a young soldier in Bothwell colours came galloping up the long avenue and into the courtyard. Donald was in the barracks at the time and came out at once.

'Your name, and your business?' he asked.

'Freddie Robertson, sir, from Crichton Castle, with a letter from Hattie Hunter for Mistress Abbie MacLaren.'

'Come with me, then,' Donald said, and took him home.

It took Abbie some time to read the short letter. But even though the writing was childish and unformed, and the spelling undecipherable, its meaning was clear.

'lady b neerly dedd,' it said. 'poysind. Cum cwic.'

SIXTY-THREE

Darnley was interred in the vaults of Holyrood Abbey late at night. Mary held on to Bothwell's hand and listened to the Mass for the Dead like some idiot child who could not understand. When Bothwell was with her, her mind was fairly lucid. When he was away it hardly functioned at all, and she just spent hours mindlessly embroidering.

Bothwell was a worried man. He had tried every way he could think of to shake her out of her torpor, but none had worked. Now he resorted to shock tactics. 'I am going to Crichton to see Jean,' he said one evening.

She sprang from her couch. 'Why?'

'She is ill.'

'I knew it! She is with child.'

'Not by me, she isn't.'

'Then by Alex Ogilvie. She is sly.'

'He has never been near,' Bothwell said angrily, handing her a letter blotched with tears. 'She has sent me this.'

'Cramps! Vomiting! She is jealous, and wants you back,' Mary said desperately. 'It is another of her tricks.'

'It is you who are jealous, madam, to hold me back from my wife.'

'Your wife! Your wife!' Mary was wide awake now. 'How can you call her your wife, after all we have been to each other, you and I? In the eyes of God, I am your wife – or should be! You love her more than you love me!'

'I do not love Jean. I never have, and she has never loved me. It was an arranged marriage. But I respect her. I do not

507

wish anything to come over her . . . And I am going to Crichton,' he repeated coldly, and left.

Mary fell into a deeper slough of despond than ever. The black hangings of mourning intensified her depression. They seemed to be always hanging there dismally on the walls. Now, suffocated by them, she imagined she was in a casket herself. Dr Bourgoing became alarmed at her agitated, morbid state of mind. He ordered her to go to the seaside for the sake of her health.

The day Mary left Edinburgh was thick with fog again, and she rode with her black hooded mantle wrapped tight around her, looking neither to right nor to left, never seeing the placard near the Tolbooth,

> *The Abominable Earl of Bothwell*
> *Hath Killed Our King.*

She went to Seton and was welcomed there by Mary Seton's brother George, who had always been her unfailing friend. He threw the castle open to her. 'It is an honour to have you, Your Majesty. I hope your stay with us may be long. It will certainly be a happy one for us.'

The following morning she went out into the gardens which sloped down to the Firth of Forth and sat on a stone bench looking out unseeingly at the glittering waters. Lord George Seton approached her with a letter in his hand.

'It is from Queen Elizabeth,' he said. 'The messenger took it first to Holyrood and then brought it out here.'

'Preserve your honour! Take revenge!' was Elizabeth's advice.

Mary crumpled it up in her hand. It may be as straightforward as that in England, but in this tortured country of Scotland it was too complicated to begin to explain. Elizabeth could never understand.

She went back to Edinburgh only slightly restored, sick to her stomach to have to admit Lord James almost at once to the audience chamber. He was carrying a large paper, rolled up.

'What now?' Mary could have wept.

'The most damaging picture of all,' he gloated. 'Here it is!' Triumphantly he unrolled the paper. The gaudy picture painted on it would have caught anyone's eye. On the top half was a mermaid, naked to the waist, wearing a crown. The letters M. R. were beside it.

'A mermaid is how a whore is usually depicted,' he rubbed his hands.

Beneath the mermaid was a hare surrounded by a circle of spears with the letters J. H. beside it.

'The hare is James Hepburn's family crest,' James said. 'Only fools could mistake the meaning of this picture, and the Edinburgh folk are not fools. They have all seen this placard and they all believe that the Earl of Bothwell is your lover, and that he killed the King!'

When he left Mary ran through to her bedchamber, bolted the door and fell on her knees. She tried to pray, but she was convulsed with sobs and from somewhere deep inside her came a terrible scream, 'BOTHWELL! BOTHWELL!'

If she did not see him soon, she would die.

Abbie handed over Hattie Hunter's note to Donald speechlessly.

'Good God – poison!' he said. 'Well, we all know who to suspect! Abbie, we must go to her – and today, if it is not too late.'

'Who are you thinking of?' she gasped.

'Who wants to be rid of Lady Jean?' he whispered, so that Freddie Robertson couldn't hear. 'Who else, but that murdering husband of hers?'

'It could be the new cook,' Abbie said doubtfully, 'but there's no time to argue.'

Abbie went to pack a bag, all the time thinking about poisons and what Queen Catherine had taught her long ago.

'There are hundreds of deadly poisons, Abbie,' the Queen

had said. 'For some of them my scientists have found an antidote. The commonest poison, and the only one I hope you may ever come across is the one contained in contaminated food, so I'll give you a little bottle of the antidote for that.'

Unlocking Catherine de Medicis' medicine box once again, Abbie scrabbled through the bottles with shaking hands until she found it, and at the last minute threw it in the bag. Then they were off as fast as they could, but even so, it was almost dark when they approached Crichton Castle.

'Go on alone, Freddie,' Donald said, 'and warn the guards that Abbie and I are coming on foot. If Lady Bothwell is being poisoned, whoever is doing it must not know that we are here, if we are to catch him – or her – at it.'

'Yes, sir,' Freddie said and trotted off.

Donald tied their horses to a tree and they walked quietly over the drawbridge and into the courtyard. A round little figure cloaked in black was there to meet them. Without a word Hattie Hunter put her finger to her lips and pushed them back into the shadow of the walls when a door opened and a yellow light streamed out.

In its glow they saw a woman go over to the midden with a bucket of slops. Abbie recognised her. 'That's Bessie Crawford!' she breathed. 'Do you mean to tell me that *she's* the cook?'

'No,' Hattie whispered back, and they stood silently until Bessie Crawford walked back with her empty bucket and shut the door so that they were in darkness again. 'She only sleeps with him – or anyone else, for that matter.'

'*Him?*' Donald said. 'Is the cook a man, then?'

'And a horrible one at that,' Hattie snorted. 'But, since he was sent from Strathbogie, Lady Jean has been forced to put up with him. Now, follow me as long as the coast is clear.'

'Sent from Strathbogie?' Abbie questioned it.

Like shadows they flitted across the courtyard, into the building and at last to the door of Lady Jean's bedchamber. They could smell it before they saw it. The smell coming from the room was abominable, of vomit, of diarrhoea, of urine and of blood. Hattie opened the door and looked inside.

'Oh God,' she wrung her fat, fluttering little hands. 'She hasn't moved! Oh, she's dead!'

Abbie pushed her aside, and truly, Lady Jean was lying in a pool of filth, her face like white marble. At once Abbie sent Donald out of the room, and Hattie away for hot water and cloths.

'And hurry,' she said, before she tore back the covers. Jean looked more like a skeleton than a woman, lying with her knees drawn up to her stomach . . . Her dear Jeannie! Who would do this to her?

'I've changed her twice today already,' Hattie said, arriving with the water. 'And the bed. But it's as if the whole of her insides are pouring out.'

'Give me a spoon,' Abbie said grimly, tearing the pigskin cover off the little bottle from her bag. 'Now, Hattie, get up on the bed and prise open her mouth. She must swallow a dose of this medicine at once.'

Abbie poured it into Jean's mouth and Hattie pinched her nose to make her swallow. They saw her throat move.

'She's still alive,' Abbie said, and they removed all her soiled clothes and washed her down. 'Now we'll change the bed again.' A knock came to the door. 'I'll answer that,' Abbie said, while Hattie carried on working.

Outside Bessie Crawford was waiting with a tray in her hands and a grin on her face. 'How did *you* get in here?' she said, taken off her guard.

'That is none of your business. What do you want?'

'Here's her ladyship's fish.' Bessie tossed her black curls cheekily. '*Well*, her ladyship's parsley sauce, more like it! It's the only thing she will eat now. Is she worse?' She giggled and tried to peer around the crack of the door which was as far as Abbie had allowed it to open.

'Take it away.'

'But the doctor said she must eat something,' Bessie Crawford said.

'Take it away! I won't tell you again.'

The impudent look faded from Bessie's face. 'But I daren't take it back to the kitchen! I daren't!'

'Take it to the midden, then.'

'He'll find out. I daren't.'

'Eat it yourself, then,' Abbie said and shut the door in her face, at the same time wondering where Donald was, for he was nowhere to be seen.

'She hasn't been sick again,' Hattie said. 'And that's a whole half-hour.'

'It's too soon to tell.' Abbie looked at the maid's round little face, strained with worry. 'Fetch more hot water and more nightgowns. Then go to your bed. You haven't had much sleep lately, have you?'

Hattie shook her head and began to cry weakly.

'You were a very good girl to warn us of this, Hattie. I'll stay with Lady Jean tonight and look after her. Try not to worry any more.'

Abbie kept watch until, in the middle of the night, Donald crept back to join her. 'What are we going to do?' she asked him. 'We dare not give her anything to eat or drink, and we can't eat or drink ourselves until we find out what's happening.'

'Oh, I *know* what's happening,' Donald muttered angrily. 'Catching the bugger red-handed is another matter.'

Hattie was so relieved to see Lady Jean still alive and apparently sleeping normally the following morning that she burst into tears again. Then another thought struck her. 'But she'll still die,' she sobbed. 'She'll die of starvation next.'

'And she won't be the only one,' Donald growled. 'My insides are clapping together.'

'Then I'll have to see Freddie Robertson again,' Hattie said, and ran out of the room. In a few minutes she was back, with breeches and a doublet tucked under her cloak. 'This uniform is *his* idea, sir, so that the guards can smuggle you out and back in again in broad daylight. Go to the first cottage on the road to the right, where my family lives.

Freddie has gone to tell them to expect you and to give you a meal.'

'Do you have cows, Hattie?' Abbie asked.

'One cow, Mistress Abbie.'

'Then fetch back some fresh milk, Donald, and some clean drinking water.'

By early afternoon, after more medicine and a few sips of water Lady Jean had opened her eyes, smiled at them, and fallen asleep again.

'Can you manage yourself for an hour, Hattie?' Donald asked. 'There's something I want my wife to see.'

Outside the windows the sky was grey and there was a mizzling rain. Dusk was falling early. Hattie lit the candles and made up the fire, but still Abbie shuddered. This old castle was eerie, filled with gloomy foreboding. Donald grasped one of the candles and he and Abbie crept out into the empty corridor. Suddenly, at a corner, he pulled her into a hole in one of the walls.

'You'd never know there was a passage here, would you?' he whispered. 'I found it last night when I thought I heard someone coming and dived into this alcove.'

It reminded Abbie of the passageways to and from the kitchens at Holyrood. 'Where does it lead?'

'Nowhere. You'll see. Follow me, and when you are aware that I'm on my hands and knees, do the same. I'll have to douse the candle, Abbie, but just hold on to me.'

Soon, they seemed to be kneeling in the confined space of a cupboard or a small storeroom, on a wooden floor. But the slats of wood must have shrunk with the heat from below, for when Abbie looked through them she saw that they were right over the kitchen, and the only two in it were Bessie Crawford and a cook in a white apron and a tall, white hat.

'See the pallet of straw under the table?' Donald hissed. 'That's their love nest. I watched them at it last night, and believe me, if that was lovemaking, the animals in the fields are not so brutal.'

There was something familiar about the cook, Abbie was

thinking as Donald went on, 'First of all he beat her black and blue when she came back with that tray and he saw that the food was untouched. He yelled and cursed at her – in French – and then he ravished her cruelly.'

'In French . . .' Abbie repeated, watching Bessie Crawford cringing and snivelling in a corner now. There was a torrent of abuse from the cook. He stopped what he was doing to dart at her and aim a kick at her stomach. Not sure if he had hit his target, he turned around to kick her again, and that was when Abbie saw his face.

'It's Philippe,' she gasped. 'Donald, it's Philippe, from Queen Mary's kitchens.'

They watched the Queen's chef taking a chicken out of the oven and attack it with a hatchet, hacking it into little pieces. Next, with another dive, he brandished the hatchet in Bessie's face.

'Wait!' Donald held Abbie back, when instinctively she would have tried to get to the girl and help her. 'Now watch this. This is what he did last night.'

Philippe put a few bits of chicken on a plate. Then he turned to the white sauce he had made. Now for the herbs, Abbie thought.

But Philippe reached into his pocket and took out something Abbie recognised. It was a pod of laburnum seeds. There was a laburnum tree in Jack Sproat's garden in Huntly. The gloriously beautiful cascades of bright yellow blossom hung heavy on it in early summer.

'But when the flowers drop off like yellow dust and the pods appear, watch out for the seeds,' Jack had warned her. 'They're rank poison.'

Donald had been silently removing some of the wooden slats in front of him, but Abbie's fascinated eyes were glued to Philippe as he ripped open the pod. The vile dark green seeds lay on his chopping board. He ground them down and stirred them into his white sauce.

'Chicken in butter and parsley sauce, you may tell her ladyship,' he grinned evilly, and put a boot into Bessie Crawford again to chivvy her up. 'Get going,' he said. 'This should do the trick at last. Up to now it has been one seed at a time, but there's enough in here this time to kill a horse. Hurry up! I don't want to stay in this place in the back of beyond for ever! I want to get back to Edinburgh, or better still, Paris!'

What happened next was all so fast that it was just a blur to Abbie. Donald leaped down through the hole he had made in the slats and landed on Philippe's back. Bessie Crawford took to her heels, screeching, and ran out of the kitchen door. Ducking out of Donald's grasp, Philippe was behind her, running like a hare.

'Murderer!' Donald yelled, grabbing the hatchet on his way. 'You won't be going to Edinburgh – or Paris! You're going straight to Hell!'

Within seconds the kitchen was empty and silent. It was still all lit up, but it was empty, echoing, and all Abbie could do was watch, and wait, until Donald came back, silent and triumphant, to rescue her.

'Don't tell Lady Jean that it was Philippe in her kitchen all along,' Abbie begged him. 'I'll just tell her the cook has disappeared.'

Next morning Lady Jean was able to take a little warmed milk. In the afternoon the pallid look had gone from her face and she sat up. 'Stay with me, Abbie,' she whispered weakly.

'Of course I will,' Abbie said, after a quick glance at Donald. 'I'll stay until you are back on your feet. But Donald must return today.'

She walked with him over the lowered drawbridge. Lord Bothwell was riding in. He recognised Abbie, but not Donald, back in his Gordon uniform.

'Lady Bothwell?' He cast an anxious eye at Abbie. 'How is she?'

'Living and life-thinking, my lord. Thanks to my husband, Donald MacLaren here,' Abbie waved her hand, 'she is no longer dying of the poison the cook was feeding her.'

Donald kissed Abbie and got up on his horse. 'Think no

more about it, Lord Bothwell,' he flung over his shoulder. 'Once I found him out he didn't live to tell any tales. He'll never cook another cook! I saw to that.'

'Cook! Cook! What cook was that?'

'Philippe, my lord,' Abbie said sweetly. 'The cook the Queen must have sent from Holyrood. Didn't you know?'

With a face like thunder Bothwell burst into the Queen's chamber. She was alone. 'Madam,' he said, 'today Jean seemed so greatly improved that I believe she will recover.'

'Oh . . . I am pleased to hear it.'

'Liar! Cheat! Betrayer!' He was beside himself with rage.

Her golden eyes changed to black glass. Her hand went to her heart. 'What – what do you mean?' she stammered.

'Good God, woman! You know very well what I mean! You sent that French chef, Philippe, to Crichton to poison my wife!'

'No . . . no,' she moaned, and fainted at his feet.

He picked her up and laid her on the couch. She was as light and as fragile as a bird. The mass of her gloriously scented hair had fallen over her face, and he parted it so that she could breathe. Her hands were like ice, and he rubbed them between his own. But she didn't wake up, and he began to panic. Had she had a heart seizure? Would he be blamed for the Queen's death next?

'Mary! Mary, my love,' he whispered in her ear, more and more urgently. Still, she didn't wake up. And then he kissed her frantically.

She opened her eyes and put her arms around him wordlessly. They had made a pact not to see each other at such a delicate stage of events. In the company of others they had not even allowed their eyes to rest on each other. Now hers were filled with a world of longing. It had been so long . . .

'Bothwell, Bothwell,' she murmured, feeling his body resting on hers. She willed him to hold her. 'I want to touch your naked flesh again, to lie with you, to take you into myself until we feel nothing but ecstasy – until we forget all this.'

He carried her through to her bed and climbed in beside her, reaching out his arms to enfold her. 'Didn't you understand that if Jean had died, there would not have been a shred of doubt in Scotland that I had murdered her? Murdered her, to marry you?'

'Thank God she lives,' Mary said. 'Does that mean you *will* marry me? How much longer will this nightmare without you last?'

'Until we can be one, my love, however long that takes.'

'It mustn't be much longer. Did I faint again when you came in? You see, that is because I am carrying your child. Bothwell, we have made a child together . . .'

A child. He was shocked and angry. 'Get rid of it,' he said.

'Never! Get rid of your son? No, Bothwell, never!'

His son . . . A legitimate son, who would be King after him, if he married the Queen. Suddenly, the path before him was lit up with a great light. He must marry her, and as fast as possible. Jean would give him a divorce and later, Prince James would be easily got rid of, if he got in the way. But first things first. He must think of a foolproof plan.

Mary rolled over on him and began kissing him tenderly, so tenderly that along with these new ideas racing around in his mind, she was exciting him more than he had ever been excited in his life.

It was all he could do, with shaking hands, to tear off his own clothes and then hers before he sank into her with a shout of delight.

Then she began exploring his body with her lips, and he was drowning in pleasure again. 'I'm greedy, my love,' she whispered. 'I want you more and more. To lie together like this every night I would run away with you and leave it all behind. I would go to the ends of the world with you in a white petticoat, and think everything else well lost for the love of you.'

517

No woman had ever spoken words like that to him before, and he had known many – rich women, poor women, staid women, loose women, drabs even – and had never loved one of them in return. But perhaps, he thought as he took her again, the improbable might be possible, now.

'You will lose nothing, Mary. You and I together will have everything to gain,' he said, lying on his back afterwards. 'Already I have thought of a plan. Go to Stirling tomorrow to see the Prince, and return on the twenty-fourth. At Almond Bridge on the way back to Edinburgh I will seize you and abduct you to Dunbar where I will ravish you. Then you will have to marry me for your honour's sake, and when that time comes you will say that the shock of the episode brought on our child prematurely to silence idle tongues.'

Mary gasped at the audacity of it. Only Bothwell could have thought of such a plan. It was just the sort of adventure to appeal to her – but then, his mind matched hers. His body matched hers . . .

'But what about Jean?' she asked.

'Leave Jean to me. She will not hold me against my will.'

'*I wonder*,' Mary said to herself as dawn broke.

When Sir William Maitland presented himself later that morning, she looked at him coldly. She had never really forgiven him his transgressions.

'You may be seated, Sir William. And what I have to say must not be repeated to another living soul.'

'Your Majesty, I –' he began in self-defence.

'Silence, sir! I repeat, not to another living soul! You betrayed me once, remember!'

'It will not happen again, madam, on my soul.'

'What I ask will not be easy, but a way must be found. I wish to marry a Protestant – and I do not wish to be excommunicated.'

'Madam, you cannot mean Lord Bothwell? Lady Jean is recovering, I hear.'

Mary stood up and stamped her foot. 'Lady Jean! Lady Jean! She has nothing to do with it!'

'She *is* his wife.'

'That is the problem. She must be divorced from him. You were once of the Catholic faith yourself, before you became turncoat. You know the rules. Go back and study them. There must be one way out of that so-called marriage which would be acceptable to the Pope, so that it can be declared null and void.'

'Your Majesty . . .' For once, Sir William faltered. All his urbane suavity was gone. He was speechless.

'This is a matter of the most extreme secrecy, and of the most extreme urgency. I will see you again tomorrow with the answer.'

Of course, he told Flamina all about it as soon as he got home. 'Now she has gone too far,' he said. 'She must be mad.'

'Mad for love,' Flamina agreed, 'and there can be only one reason for all this haste.'

'She is bringing down Scotland with her madness. This will be my last task on her behalf. In the meantime, allow no one and nothing to disturb me until I have got a conclusion. Then I shall leave her service.'

With that he locked himself into his study and spent the rest of the day and the night wrestling with religious documents and the family trees of Scotland. Early next morning he went to see Archbishop Hamilton.

A few hours later the Queen granted him immediate audience. 'Well?' she asked impatiently.

'An annulment of the marriage can be granted by Archbishop Hamilton on the grounds that Lord Bothwell and Lady Jean Gordon were within the fourth degree of consanguinity. It appears that his great-great-grandfather married a Gordon –'

'Oh, thank God! Thank God!'

'Such an arrangement would of course be subject to Lady Jean's agreement, Your Majesty.'

'Yes . . . you have done well, Sir William.'

'I have always done my best for Scotland, madam, but now I wish to withdraw from public life. I ask you to accept my letter of resignation.'

SIXTY-FOUR

Bothwell had only told Mary the second part of his plan, the easy part. The first part would be far more difficult, to ensure the co-operation of all the nobles. First, he would prepare a bond. He sent Paris to fetch him a parchment, and while he waited he took off his doublet and rolled up his sleeves as he always did when contemplating a job of writing. Then, flexing his short, stubby fingers, he set to work.

> We, the undersigned, understand the noble and mighty Lord James Hepburn, Earl of Bothwell, to have been examined and tried by his peers for the heinous murder of the King, Her Majesty the Queen's late husband, and been found innocent and guiltless of the said odious crime.
>
> Moreover, considering that our Queen and Sovereign is now destitute of a husband, the common good of our native country may not permit Her Highness so to endure. Therefore, in case the affectionate and faithful service of the said Earl of Bothwell may move Her Majesty to take him to husband, every one of us permit the said marriage to be solemnised as soon as the laws permit.

That done, Bothwell looked at the clock. It was still not too late to visit Mr Ainslie in his tavern and order the most sumptuous feast that had ever been laid out on his tables. It would be arranged for the next night, after the final session of Parliament when all the nobles would be conveniently gathered together, and no doubt more than ready to accept Bothwell's invitation.

The following evening twenty nobles, including Privy Councillors and eight bishops attended his banquet, and Mr Ainslie had done him proud, providing huge platters of meat and most importantly, whisky – barrels of the stuff. By midnight, few guests were still able to stand up for the toasts, and Bothwell reckoned the time had come.

He rose and called for silence. From the pouch in his belt he pulled out a long white paper.

'My lords,' he said, 'I have prepared this bond which awaits your signatures,' and read it out loud.

The men stared at him dazedly, bleary-eyed and loose-lipped. Morton rose to his feet and spoke. His voice was very slurred. 'You said you would wed the *Queen*?' he asked incredulously.

'At present I cannot, sir. I am a married man, and even if I were free Her Majesty would refuse me on the grounds of religion.'

Morton narrowed his eyes. Between the drink and the shock they squinted horribly. 'But we thought she was enamoured of you.'

Bothwell laughed bitterly. 'I would not need your help tonight, if only she were.'

He moved the plates and goblets from his end of the table and unrolled the document, sending a servant for ink and a quill. 'Well, my lords,' he asked, 'who will be the first to sign?'

None of the lords moved. They mumbled to each other, and when he saw that, Bothwell went to the door and set it ajar. 'Let's have some air,' he said. 'It's hellish hot in here.'

Outside stood the Borderers, moonlight glinting on their steel bonnets and bristling spears, and five thousand voices were raised in song.

'Ho for the Sinclairs, the Armstrongs, the Elliots,
Ho for the Hepburns, and ho for the world . . .'

The lords looked through the door at a forest of spears. They looked at the barred windows. They looked at one another. Then Morton staggered forward. He tried to read the document, but it was hopeless when he was seeing three of everything. He signed his name and one by one the other nobles did the same.

Early next morning Morton visited Mary. She pretended to be furiously angry at Bothwell's presumption that she could ever want to marry him.

'I am outraged,' she said coldly. 'All those who signed such a bond may not appear at court for at least a week, or else I shall lose my temper and punish them severely. Pass on that message, my lord.'

When Morton slunk away she became very agitated. Bothwell was obviously carrying out his bargain and his part of the plan in his own way, but to help him she would have to go to Crichton and find out Jean's intentions regarding divorce. She was certain Bothwell had never asked her to divorce him. She had been too ill. If Jean refused, then she would have to warn him that the abduction would be both useless and dangerous.

She was sitting deep in thought when Flamina came to brush her hair and paint her face, and she sent her away. There was no time for that. Events were moving too fast. She would have to go to Crichton *now*, no matter how tired and ill she felt.

'Yes, Jean, it's a lovely day – but all the same, you will put on your cloak,' Abbie said sternly. 'You have just been very ill, and near to death. It would not do to catch cold now.'

They walked down to the hanging gardens, Lady Jean's pride and joy. She had planted roses when she first came to Crichton, and now they promised to bloom in banks right down to the outer walls.

'They will need to be tied up soon,' she said, 'and trained to grow horizontally for the best effect.'

'Tell me what colours they will be, then,' Abbie said as they walked along the paths in the balmy sunshine.

'The top row is all yellow. The next one down – what is it, Abbie?'

'Someone's coming.' They could see over the walls to the road outside, and along the road a small cavalcade was approaching in a cloud of dust. 'It's the Queen,' Abbie murmured, hurrying Jean back inside again.

They removed their cloaks and went into Lady Jean's small white-panelled parlour to wait for their visitor. Presently they heard the servants rushing out excitedly to welcome her, and minutes later the sound of her footsteps rustling the flower-strewn rushes as a butler showed her in.

'Your Majesty,' they greeted her, and curtsied low.

Jean offered her a chair. Abbie took her cloak and gave it to Hattie Hunter who was hovering near the door.

'Please, let us sit at that small table,' Mary said, eyeing her hostess uneasily, for Lady Jean had certainly changed.

She was slimmer and much more beautiful . . . much more beautiful . . . The planes of her face had hollowed so that her cheeks and her nose and her chin seemed delicately chiselled. To emphasise this transformation, she had learned to paint. There was grey shadow accentuating her clear grey eyes and rose paste outlined her lips. Yes, she had learned tricks to hold her husband, Mary thought jealously.

'May I get you some refreshments, madam?' Jean asked. 'My mother sent me an excellent cook from Huntly, after our previous chef disappeared.'

Mary changed colour at that, but she controlled her voice. 'Thank you. Perhaps a little wine.'

With a nod of her head Lady Jean sent Hattie scurrying off to fetch it, and while they were waiting she and Abbie studied the Queen, whom they had served so long, and loved so long, and knew so well – and saw that she was not as they remembered her. Her figure had thickened, her beautiful skin was mottled, and they had never seen her hair so unkempt.

524

Hattie curtsied and left the tray of wine and tiny fruit tartlets for Lady Jean to dispense. When the door closed behind her Mary stared pointedly at Abbie, sitting quietly back in the window seat.

'I wish to speak to you alone, Lady Jean.'

Jean smiled calmly. 'I cannot dismiss the other half of myself so easily, madam,' she said. 'As you know we have been together all through life, and now, since I was almost poisoned, my husband's instructions are that Abbie never leaves my side.'

'I will have no wine,' Mary said, waving it away, trying to cover the snub.

'No? It is my husband's favourite.'

The Queen positively quivered with anger. *Her husband. Her husband.* 'Your husband does not know that I am here,' she snapped, 'and I do not wish him to know.'

'Of course, madam.'

'You are aware of the relationship between your husband and myself?'

'I am.'

'We love each other. We shall wed.'

'He is wed to me.'

'Soon he will ask you to divorce him.'

'I took my vows very seriously, "Till death us do part". My marriage was made before God. Only He may dissolve it.'

'Lady Jean, I am with child. Bothwell's child. That is why I must wed, and quickly.'

'I see,' Lady Jean said calmly. 'Does Bothwell know of this?'

'Yes,' Mary sighed, looking ill as she told Jean about the Ainslie bond and the proposed desperate abduction.

'I feel deeply sorry for you, madam. That is a desperate plot, indeed.'

'I pray that it may succeed. If it does, only you stand between Lord Bothwell and me, Lady Jean.'

'So you have come begging, madam?'

The Queen rose and went to kneel in front of her. 'Yes, Jean. I am begging you, and humbly.'

Except to pray, Abbie had never seen the Queen on her knees before, and after all the damage she had done to Jean it was ironic to see her kneeling to her now. But strangely, it did not give Abbie any satisfaction. She should be feeling triumph that God was seeing justice done. Instead she felt only pity for this poor, dishevelled, distracted woman. And Jean must be feeling the same, for she was on her feet and raising Mary to hers.

'Please rise, Your Majesty,' she said quietly, 'and calm yourself. You must know that your Marys and Abbie and I have always loved you, and served you most of our lives until recently. It has been a way of life for us, the only life we knew. Although it goes against my beliefs, I will divorce Lord Bothwell with the greatest of pleasure.'

'You will?' Mary gasped.

'Yes. And because I love you, I implore you to remember that I have not spent one happy day – or night – with such a man. But since you are determined, I will not stand in your way, but only wish you well.'

Mary burst into tears and sat sobbing with relief.

'Please rest a little while, madam,' Abbie said, 'and refresh yourself. Now that Lady Jean has solved your problem, perhaps you may be able to drink some wine?'

'Yes. Thank you, Abbie. And my most heartfelt thanks to you, Lady Jean.'

After Mary left they sat for a long time in silence.

'Of course,' Abbie said, 'you will not mind divorcing him.' It was not a question, but a statement of fact.

'I shall set it in motion today as fast as I can, and I shall cite Bessie Crawford, no matter what other grounds they have thought up. Also, I shall demand that Crichton is mine exclusively, along with Hailes Castle which the Queen recently granted to Bothwell. I shall need all the revenues I get from them, since he has spent all my money on his Borderers, and wars, and left me penniless.'

Abbie smiled in relief. Lady Jean was back to normal again, looking at the world with her cool grey gaze, as hard-headed as ever, and the divorce went through in a record eleven days from start to finish.

'Now I can start to live my own life, at last,' Jean said.

But she had reckoned without her mother.

Three days later she received a letter from Strathbogie, showing that Lady Huntly was keeping up with the times.

> In the present scandals you are not safe so near to Bothwell and the Queen. All Scotland knows that his abduction of her is only a sham. The Lords will not accept it. There will be war again, and you may be in grave danger for agreeing to divorce him. Come home as quick as you can.

Bothwell's plot had succeeded, or so he and Mary thought when they barricaded themselves into Dunbar Castle.

'Stolen fruit is always the sweetest,' he told her. 'So far we have had only little bites of it here and there. Now we shall have a whole stolen week of pleasure, a honeymoon before our wedding.'

'Perhaps never again in our lives will we know such freedom,' Mary agreed.

She came to love Dunbar and the freedom it gave them to love through the long, delirious hours, the warm days when she stripped off her clothes and swam with Bothwell and played in the surf, or lay and loved in the tall grasses of the meadows. She was happy on the stormy days when she sat by the fire and embroidered baby dresses made of satin.

But such happiness on earth could not last. Mary's spies reported that another bond had been engineered by Lord James, who nowadays always called himself the Earl of Moray, and it had been signed by the nobles of Scotland who had gathered at Stirling, pledging the death of Bothwell.

Some weeks later Mary and Bothwell rode to Edinburgh

heavily armed, and at the West Port Bothwell ordered his men to drop their spears to their saddles, signifying that the Queen was no longer captive. Then he dismounted himself, and with bared head humbly led her horse up the steep rock to Edinburgh Castle.

Mary announced her intention to wed the next day. Her nobles heard her in silence, tight-lipped.

'They did not object,' she told Bothwell.

'Only because they know they are outnumbered. We must keep them outnumbered, but I am very short of money to pay our troops.'

'I have gold,' she said. 'I have Elizabeth's gold christening font. I shall have it melted down. And now we must post the banns for our marriage ceremony in the abbey –'

'Great God! You do not imagine that I would wed you in a Catholic church? My love for you has not softened my wits altogether.'

'*Mon Dieu*! You cannot do this to me! I would lose my self-respect! The Catholic world would become hostile! For the sake of our child, can you not turn Catholic?'

'And lose *my* self-respect? Never! If you want me I shall be at Hermitage.' He crossed the room and opened the door.

'Wait!' Mary cried. 'You cannot leave me! I'll bear no bastard!'

He was with her in four long strides. His kiss sent her reeling. Her arms went around him. We are indivisible, she thought. We are one, and lifting her head she caught her breath and met his eyes.

'We will marry,' he said, as slowly he bent his mouth towards hers.

'Yes! Yes!'

'In the Protestant faith.'

SIXTY-FIVE

The following day Mary slowly descended the staircase in Holyrood Palace, a crucifix in her hand. As she reached the Great Hall the clock struck four. She paused in the doorway. At the end of the room, in front of the altar borrowed from the kirk, stood Bothwell, the Bishop of Orkney and the wedding guests. Horrified, she counted them. There were thirteen.

There was no image of Christ, no Virgin Mary, none of the holy symbols to warm her heart. Crow-voiced, the Bishop droned on drearily, and Mary raised her head. All she saw were the browning petals of the flowers as the Bishop exhorted the couple to cleave together in the Eden of their kingdom, and all she thought of were the serpents in that Eden.

'Bothwell and I must cleave together or die,' she said to herself, 'and when I die I lose my immortal soul in Hell after the abomination of this marriage service. *Oh God, let me escape from here – now!'*

But Bothwell gripped her hand and looked into her eyes with such intensity that she was hypnotised. He is all I shall ever know of heaven, she thought, as they exchanged their rings.

They turned and faced the guests. 'My friends,' Mary said, 'greet my husband, His Grace the Duke of Orkney, King-Consort of Scotland.'

'Dearest Abbie,' Lady Jean said on the way to Huntly in response to her mother's letter, 'I am so glad for you that you are going home. Spare a thought for me. I hope I shall not have to stay at Strathbogie long.'

'Stay for a week or two – perhaps a month or two,' Abbie urged her, 'until you are properly recovered. There is no better place to convalesce than here in the clear Highland air. And besides, then I can see you every day!'

The smile was still on Jean's face when Lady Huntly accompanied by Edith came out to meet her, though it wavered a little at the change in her mother's appearance. But after a few words of greeting she discovered that her appearance wasn't the only thing to be so altered in Lady Huntly. Her whole personality was changed. She had softened out of all recognition, and it didn't take long to find out that this was entirely due to Edith, who treated her mistress like a beloved and rather spoiled child.

'I don't care how Edith has done it,' Jean reported to Abbie. 'The main thing is that my mother is liveable with now. I needn't be in any hurry to go back.'

At the end of the week Lady Huntly announced that a very special visitor was coming to Strathbogie.

'Who?' Jean asked.

'Never mind. It's a secret,' Lady Huntly smiled knowingly, more like her previous self. 'Anyway, he is coming tonight, in time to join us for a very special meal.'

'*He?*' Jean asked.

'Go on up to your bedchamber now, and put on your prettiest gown.'

Jean did not know if she was excited or frightened when she dressed. Her hands were trembling as she tied the bow of her sash, but summoning up all her courage she went downstairs. A man was standing in front of the fire speaking to Lady Huntly. He turned round when Jean came in.

'Jeannie,' he greeted her. 'Remember me?'

'Alexander Sutherland!' Jean smiled. 'My mother has been keeping you a big secret. I didn't know who to expect!'

'And is it a disappointment, Jean?'

'Oh no, my lord. It is a very great pleasure.'

*   *   *

'He has asked you to marry him?' Abbie asked incredulously, a month later. 'So soon?'

'He did ask me once before, you know, Abbie. And I did get to know him very well in those days. It isn't as if I only met him a month ago when I came home to Strathbogie.'

'And will you marry him?'

'I have said yes. Now, Abbie, don't ask me if I love him, next! You know the one and only man I ever loved or ever will love has been lost to me for years. And I am very fond of Alexander.'

'Enough to lie with him and have his children?' Abbie persisted.

'Enough to lie with him, and leave your medicines in the boxes,' Jean laughed. 'I won't need them ever again.'

'Then I'm happy for you, Jeannie. You deserve to be happy at last.'

But all the same, Abbie thought sadly when they waved the happy couple off to Dunrobin Castle, although Jean's second husband was a prince in comparison to her first – for everyone liked Alexander Sutherland – why could it not have been Alex Ogilvie of Boyne?

Alex Ogilvie moved his chair back a yard with the result that he now sat four yards from his wife's bedside. He held a handkerchief soaked in lavender water to his nose, and sighed. He went through this performance faithfully every morning and every evening for half an hour at a time, but it had been to no avail for months now, and he doubted if it would be to any avail ever again.

Her illness had first emerged years ago when she started to complain of excruciating headaches. This, he had told her coldly, was the result of her drinking habits. He had soon discovered it wasn't only that.

Then she had said her joints ached. Tight little bumps appeared on her forehead. To his horror the granular lumps spread to her cheeks. He began to suspect the truth, and when the physicians told him that there were irritations on her private parts as well, they diagnosed syphilis. They had wanted to examine him too, but he assured them there was no need for that. He had not had relations with her for years.

When all the symptoms disappeared she had laughed and gone back to her endless round of gaiety and parties which he cheerfully financed if only to keep her out of his way. All he wanted was to live his own life, and let her live hers, under the same roof and with no undue scandal.

But every now and again these incidents recurred and attacked her with increasing ferocity. At their height the physicians made her take hot baths with salt, as many as four daily. They applied dressings of oil of roses and camphor to remove the unsightly scabs which kept forming. Eventually the eruptions would dry up and the scars fade to pink and red. Then she would rub salve containing white clay on her face, and sally forth again.

The last time she had entered the whirl of society and court life had been her swan song before she had become unable to walk or eat or lead a normal life of any kind. All her so-called friends had deserted her three years ago and that was when he had got this attic cleared out and freshly painted. His servants had carried her and her bed up to it, and he was still paying two nurses to look after her, one by day and one by night.

He had seen to it that the attic window could open without causing a draught, to allow the terrible odours of her body to escape, and he had ordered clean rushes mixed with camphor to be laid down on the floor and changed thereafter every week. Then, of course, they were burned.

He moved restlessly on his chair, and reflected that a fire burned at the bottom of the garden non-stop nowadays. The ground floor and the first floor, which was his domain, had been fumigated. All hangings, carpets and any linen which she might possibly have touched with her diseased fingers were burned, along with any chair she had ever sat on, and the whole house refurbished – to *his* taste, since she would never be downstairs to see it ever again.

In short, he had done everything he could to eradicate all traces of her, but up in this attic Mary Beaton gloried on as large as life. She was his wife, and he was determined to look after her as long as she lived, although he hated every single stinking breath she breathed.

The thing he regretted most for her sake was the loss of her beautiful blonde hair. No woman liked to be bald. But he had got the best perukes that money could buy for her. Money could buy most things, he thought sadly, but it couldn't buy happiness, and it couldn't buy health.

And now, in spite of all his efforts, she had come to this, a travesty of a human being, just rotting away. She wore a taffeta mask all the time now to hide the livid purple of her face, but she couldn't mask the awful festering smells of her body.

There was never a word spoken during his visits to the attic, but he was used to that. She twitched and jerked, and always she muttered away to herself behind her mask in mad, incoherent yelps.

The physicians assured him every day that it wouldn't be long now. Soon she would die. *But not that night.*

She was still twitching and muttering when he left.

In the morning, she was dead. Until then Alex Ogilvie had managed somehow to hang together, but now he collapsed. The strain had been too much, and he cried day and night. Everyone thought he was distraught at the death of his wife – and so he was, in a way.

He was distraught at the whole sorry mess of it from start to finish. He blamed himself for it all when he thought of the tragedy of Lady Jean's life, which he had caused as well, and his misery intensified when he heard that she had divorced Bothwell and had since married the Earl of Sutherland.

The shock of the news almost finished him, and the physician ordered him to get away, to go abroad. He sent a brief note to Sir Patrick Spence and dragged himself off to Italy.

Once there he was startled to find that Sir Pat had not

bought a villa, as he had imagined. It was a small castle, called the Castel Randolfo, and at its door to greet him was Sophia, Sir Pat's wife, slim and beautiful with huge black eyes. Laughing, she held out their baby for him to take.

'His name is Alissandro, after my dearest friend,' Sir Pat smiled at him, and after that he was simply wrapped in the love of his friends in their happy home, something Alex had never known before.

The castel was set in very large grounds on a rolling hill where labourers were digging up acres of soil. 'All this was once a vineyard,' Sir Pat told him, 'and it's going to be a vineyard again. The trouble is, all this soil must be cleaned. It is a very slow job, and a hard one, as well as being very expensive. I will need an outdoor oven in which to steam the soil.'

'There will be no difficulty about the money,' Alex said.

Bit by bit Alex was drawn into another life, a soft golden life, a placid life, working in the fields stripped to the waist while the sun beat down and time drifted past.

Alissandro was his parents' pride and joy, and Alex's pride and joy. He was the one who taught him to walk, who played with him, who gave him piggybacks all around the estate. Soon, Sophia had another baby, this time a girl.

'Lucia,' she said proudly, and as the tiny infant grew to be a year old, Alex was convinced she wasn't a human child at all, but one of those adorable cherubs who had just happened to fall down off her cloud. He simply worshipped her, and she, him.

Sophia's wonderful food, and eventually Sir Pat's wine, were almost curing him – almost. But there was only one cure for guilt and sense of failure that periodically brought him low – to be reunited with Lady Jean Gordon.

SIXTY-SIX

The Queen and Bothwell sat down with their small company for the wedding banquet, but without music and masques and dancing it was a miserably silent and cheerless affair. 'Marry in May, rue it for aye,' Mistress Clarihew had gone around muttering for days. Utterly distressed, Mary could hardly lift her eyes from her plate.

There had been no rich presents for Bothwell as her bridegroom, such as there had been for Darnley, only some genet fur from one of Marie de Guise's old black cloaks to trim his dressing gown, and for herself only an old yellow dress relined with white taffeta and an old black gown done up with gold braid. She had hated this squalid, hurried wedding without any of the preparations she so loved.

And now that the marriage was a *fait accompli* the magnitude of her offence against her own religion hit her full force. Later in their bedchamber she couldn't stop crying except when from time to time she flung herself on her knees and tried to pray for forgiveness.

But nobody was forgiving her on earth either. There had been no wedding presents from Elizabeth or from Charles of France, and Philip of Spain was treating the whole thing as so sordid as to be beneath his dignity even to remark it. Mary was still in a state of stupefied horror the following morning when Bothwell lost his temper.

'I can suffer no more of this,' he shouted at her. 'I am going to Hermitage.'

'Hermitage . . .' Mary whispered, appalled, and when she

had recovered sufficiently from this cruelty, sent for John Leslie, the Bishop of Ross. In floods of tears she told him how much she repented her marriage, and when Melville, who had replaced Sir William Maitland, and Erskine joined them she began to scream.

'Fetch me a dagger, for the love of God! Let me put an end to this misery here on earth! I want to kill myself!' she cried, throwing herself first against one wall and then another and another until she exhausted herself. Her self-control had completely vanished.

'Only God decides when you shall die. If you take your own life you will be in eternal damnation,' the Bishop told her.

'I am there now,' Mary sobbed, and did not calm down until Bothwell came back and made frantic love to her. She was under his spell.

But in the days that followed, her tears and lamentations rang through Holyrood again and again because of his jealousy if she so much as looked at another man, berating her in language so filthy that her nobles and courtiers crept away, ashamed for her. He insisted on dictating to her Privy Councillors, was present at every meeting and even posted two of his Borderers at her chamber door.

Yet her inner self secretly thrilled at his domination of her. This was why she had married him! To have a strong man at her side at last to control the quarrelsome nobles. Lord James, although he was carefully not of their number, was constantly whipping them into a frenzy of jealousy by reminding them that one of their own kind had succeeded by foul tricks in becoming the King of Scotland.

They congregated at Stirling, and at the end of another two weeks the animosity towards Bothwell was such that by 10 June he decided to take Mary and flee once again to Dunbar.

But they only got as far as Castle Borthwick, about twelve miles south of Edinburgh.

*　　*　　*

'Abbie,' Donald said when they heard of this, 'we must make one last desperate appeal for Lord George's release before the Queen loses her head altogether, one way or another. This time we'll go together.'

'When?'

'If we leave at dawn tomorrow we should be there by nightfall, riding hard. We'll take Geordie Brand and the best of the Gordons with us.'

Queen Mary welcomed Abbie with open arms. 'My dear Abbie!' she said. 'Providence has sent you! The soldiers will take charge of the Gordon troop and give them food and a bed after such a long ride. Come with me!'

The rooms in Castle Borthwick were small, mean and very inhospitable, as Abbie soon discovered, trembling to imagine what the soldiers' quarters must be like. She was left to hope for the best, for Donald, as she sat at the side of the narrow 'Great Hall' watching the Queen poring over maps of the district with two of her military advisers, and making plans.

Before long Bothwell marched in, grunted, and then took himself off to the far end of the hall with a full bottle of wine, well away from all these calculations. He was a man of action and such calculations were not for him. Abbie was dead beat, and the Queen seemed to have forgotten her until the clock chimed loudly in the silence and she looked up with an exclamation.

'You must go to bed, Abbie,' she said, waving a hand at an antechamber to one side. 'But before you do,' pointing to her paint box at her side, 'I must ask you to paint your face like mine, once again. I should have asked you when you arrived, ages ago. It is only in case our enemies pursue us this far, and perhaps break in. Then you can decoy them away, making them think that you are me!'

Just like that! It didn't matter that she would be put in danger, Abbie thought sourly. To Mary it was just another adventure, another crisis. The woman lurched from one crisis to the next, always digging herself deeper and deeper into a hole. 'Yes, madam,' she said, half fainting with fatigue and splashing on some white paint down the centre of her face. It stung, but she was too tired to care.

'That will do,' the Queen said, as Abbie fell onto the couch. 'Loosen your hair and pull it down over your face. Now sleep, my dear.'

But it took her a long time to fall asleep, overtired as she was. The Queen and her advisers droned on in the hall. Bothwell's armour clanked to the floor somewhere else, and Abbie dozed off.

Suddenly Bothwell was on the couch beside her. Abbie opened outraged, disbelieving eyes. Oh God ... Oh God ... She trembled from head to foot at the very worst, most frightening moment of her life. And the Queen must have known this would happen. Of course she did. The white paint was for Bothwell, not for her enemies. She didn't care what might have happened when Bothwell lay down beside her. How could she have encouraged one of her own ladies to be in the same bed as him? And where was Donald when she needed him most, anyway?

Donald, had she but known it, was at present in chains, he and the rest of the Gordons, overpowered by Bothwell's Borderers when all they were expecting was a bed and something to eat.

By a miracle, Bothwell slept. Then Abbie realised from his hoarse snoring and puffing that he must be dead drunk, and thanked God. If she was ever to get away, and to Donald, it must be now. She crept out of bed, twisted the coverlet on the couch into a rope and tiptoed into the hall with it. Mary and her advisers slept where they sat, their heads on the table. There wasn't a sound except for a lone night bird calling from the heather.

Then, to hear it so clearly, a window must be open. Abbie saw that it was the window beside the chair where Bothwell had sat. She tied the end of her rope to the iron window jamb and flung herself out, clinging to it, without any idea of how high up she was.

She swung out and slithered to the end of the rope. The ground was not far below. She remembered that when jumping from a height you should keep your knees bent. Donald had taught her that, when as a child she had jumped off a horse.

She landed in a ball on the ground. Nothing seemed to be broken. Her arms were working. Her legs weren't sore, and her body was only slightly jarred. She got to her feet shakily. Just then two iron arms enfolded her, and fingers were missing on one of the hands. It was Fobie Fingerless.

'And where do you think you're going?' he asked, marching her around to a tiny room like a cell, where he clanged shut a heavy door, and turned the key.

It was still pitch-dark, and it seemed she had been in that cell for hours when she heard his voice again. This time he was speaking to Bothwell, but she couldn't hear what they were saying. Then came the sound of two horses riding away at top speed. So Bothwell had gone, and left Mary to hold the fort alone!

His flight without her must have jolted the Queen back some way to her senses. She gathered her small escort around her, and began a search for Abbie.

'Oh, Abbie,' she said when they found her, 'what a stupid mistake! I suppose it was one of those Borderers, who didn't know you, who locked you in here!'

And that was all! Not a word of explanation! Not a word of apology! Abbie was furiously angry when Mary and her supporters set off on horseback to follow Bothwell to Dunbar, but long before they got there her anger had turned to sadness to think that after all these years of service she was a prisoner, even if not in chains, with no hope of escape.

And Donald and the Gordons had vanished. The remaining soldiers swore they had not seen them leave. All Abbie knew was that, as so often in the past, she was alone and in danger.

The Queen was happy again, back in Dunbar Castle, her previous romantic haunt. She seemed prepared to stay there with her husband for ever if need be. However, it was soon time to move on.

'There is a message here from Lord Balfour,' Bothwell told Mary after a few days, 'to go back to Edinburgh Castle where he is now in command. His cannon will be at our disposal, and we shall be safe.'

'What? The same treacherous James Balfour who organised Darnley's murder? I do not trust him.'

'But you can trust me.' Bothwell kissed her, and after that she was prepared to do anything he said. She was smiling when she waved goodbye to her ladies. Only Abbie, by this time very rebellious, was kept behind.

'We have very few soldiers,' Mary said nervously as they all set off for Edinburgh.

Perhaps this was where Donald was, waiting for them, Abbie hoped, not knowing that he and the Gordons were not very far away from her at that very moment, riding with their hands tied behind them, and gagged, surrounded by Borderers, so tight in their grip that they might as well still be in prison. The only advantage was that Donald could still see Abbie. He knew what was happening to her.

'I shall pick up more soldiers on the way. That is not for you to worry your beautiful head about,' Bothwell told Mary. 'The Scots will rally to me, their mighty King.'

But they picked up only a few more soldiers, after all. The people of Scotland thought very little of their new 'King', as Abbie could have told him. In their opinion he was a jumped-up, thieving, murderous Border bastard who had somehow entranced their Queen before he stole her from her senses, killed her husband and now posed a threat to the baby Prince.

When on the morning of Sunday, 15 June the confederate lords marched out of Edinburgh to meet him, the people saw their banner and rallied to it instead, for it showed a green tree with the corpse of Darnley lying underneath it, and his infant son kneeling before him crying, 'Judge and avenge my cause, O Lord.'

The two armies met at Carberry Hill at the height of a blazing hot day, where a tent was hastily erected to shelter Mary and Abbie, and where there was no water for Bothwell's soldiers to quench their thirst. They were none too keen to fight this battle, anyway, and they lay on the hillside, sweltering, while Bothwell swaggered about, posturing and posing in his armour, and demanding one-to-one combat with anyone who felt like committing suicide. His Borderers grew tired, and bored. There was not enough action here for them, and gradually they began to drift away.

The sun is stronger than Bothwell, Abbie thought.

The challenges went on all day. The parleys went on all day, and in ones and twos Bothwell's army melted away all day. Donald and the Gordons escaped when their captors slunk off, and watched from a distance, hidden by some bushes.

Abbie could see that the battle was won by the lords before it had ever begun. It had been a terrible farce. 'Madam, if this is not stopped it will be wholesale slaughter,' she said in the tent.

The Queen looked at her strangely. 'Fortunately, you have not been out in the sun,' she said. 'Your face paint has not melted. You may have need of it yet.'

Then she rode out on her horse, a lone woman, and positioned herself between the two sides although she looked desperately ill, exhausted and sick in the oppressive heat and glare of the sun.

'This must be the most gruelling battle never fought,' she said wearily, 'but it has meant, thank God, that there has been no bloodshed. A pact, gentlemen, if you please!'

Kirkcaldy detached himself from the confederate lords. 'Madam, your husband is guaranteed safe-conduct for twenty-four hours on condition that you are never to see him again, nor will he make any attempt to see you.'

He handed Bothwell a paper. Bothwell examined it, nodded and put it in his pouch.

'On condition of his absolute freedom,' Mary begged.

'No. Twenty-four hours of absolute freedom,' Kirkcaldy

insisted. 'Thereafter he will be a hunted outlaw.'

'I accept,' Bothwell said, and Kirkcaldy went back to tell the lords.

Then Bothwell slipped a paper into Mary's hands, and she quickly stuffed it into the bodice of her gown. It was the bond of Darnley's murder signed by Bothwell himself, Balfour, Sir William Maitland, Morton and his cousins.

'But I cannot use it without harming you!' she protested.

'Use it, should anything befall me, Mary.'

'Nothing must befall you – my lord, my love, my life!' Mary clung to him.

He kissed her once, fondly and firmly. Then he was yards away, nodding to Kirkcaldy mockingly. Mary rushed over to him, flinging her arms around him and kissing him so passionately that she almost caused him to lose his balance in his heavy armour.

'I will wait for you for ever!' she cried to the man for whom she had sacrificed her honour and her reputation, as he mounted up.

'I love you, wife of my heart,' he said, spurring his horse and galloping away into the sunset.

They had been married for only five weeks.

Mary knew she would never see him again.

She watched as he disappeared from sight without a backward glance on the road to Dunbar. Then she stared at the slowly tarnishing sky over the bracken of the hills.

She stared at the empty world, at the beginning of her end.

SIXTY-SEVEN

It was cooler now in the tent. When Abbie lifted the flap to look out the soldiers were retreating from the battlefield and the Queen had disappeared. Now was the time to escape. No sooner had this thought come to her mind than Kirkcaldy's men were swarming into the tent and swarming all over her. They lifted her bodily over the field and on to a horse.

'I am not the Queen,' Abbie screamed in her own voice, over and over. 'She has gone.'

'The Queen must be seen to be captured and brought back,' Kirkcaldy said.

So, it was another plot ... And the lords were all in it. They had spirited Mary away, and left someone who looked like her to face the outcome of this terrible day.

It was a nightmare as she moved with the lords in an endless grey-gold twilight back to Edinburgh. From Musselburgh onwards it was a slow press through angry crowds in every village and town.

'Harlot! Jade! Whore!' the people shouted and spat at her.

'Justice!' The crowds swarmed about her at Kirk o' Field. The house lay like a stone monster, squashed under red, red roses, red roses that seemed to her like spilled blood. 'Drown the murderess! Avenge the King! Drown her in the loch!'

Abbie's face was wet with spittle and tears and sweat. Market women hurled rotten fruit and she put up an arm to defend herself. The mob raged at her for deserting her son. 'You'll not kill the Prince as you killed the King!'

'Burn her!' shouted a magistrate from his window in the High Street. 'Burn her alive!'

'Yes, burn her!' the mob took up the roar. 'Burn her at the Market Cross! Gather wood to burn her! Burn her! Burn her!'

Kirkcaldy rode up beside her as she slumped half fainting in the saddle, and shook her shoulder. 'We're taking you to the Provost's house over there,' he shouted above the crowd and pointed across the street, 'and it will be none too soon. Hurry, or they will tear you to pieces!'

But Abbie went limp. She was only vaguely aware that Kirkcaldy lifted her from her horse and carried her up a garden path. An iron door clanged shut behind her and she lost consciousness.

When she revived she found herself lying on a hard cot by a barred window that faced the Market Cross, and the room must be on the ground floor. She could see people crowding around right outside. Eight armed soldiers stood between her and the bolted door, and when she looked down her bodice had been slit from throat to waist. Somebody must have thought that she was really Mary, and that she had the bond of Darnley's murder.

The room spun, and Abbie closed her eyes. It seemed like only seconds later that sunlight was beating on her eyelids, and she opened her eyes again. It was morning.

The crowd was still there, yelling and jeering. She pulled herself up to stand on her cot and grasped the bars of her window to look out at them, to plead with them, a madwoman with her face streaked, her hair in strings and her bodice ripped, her naked breasts exposed. Abbie realised that to them Mary was no longer their young and beautiful Queen, but an adulteress – and an adulteress who had become the willing bride of a murderer.

'Help me! Help me!' Abbie screamed in the stunned silence that greeted her appearance.

The mob murmured in pity. The women began to cry for her shame. 'Save her! Save her! For God's sake, save our

544

Queen!' Then Abbie caught a glimpse of Sir William Maitland in the crowd. Thank God! Thank God! Oh, thank God for the Spider, after all! He would save his Queen. She called to him in Mary's voice but he pulled his hat down over his face, and melted away in the crowd.

'We will never get in this way,' Donald muttered to Geordie Brand as they sat on their horses behind the milling mob in the Royal Mile.

'A house that size is bound to have a garden at the back,' Geordie agreed, and they trotted down a wynd followed by a dozen Gordons.

But the Edinburgh folk had thought of that already. Donald and Geordie located it by the shouts and screams of another mob who had burst down the large wooden gates in the eight-foot-high walls of the garden, and were now massed around a barred window shouting and swearing at the poor half-naked woman clinging to the bars, crying to them for help.

With an agonised cry Donald recognised his Abbie under the streaked white paint. He positioned his horse against the wall and then he was up on the top of it with his dirk drawn. The other Gordons did the same to stand alongside him.

'For Christ's sake!' he roared. 'Does that little lady look like your long skinny Queen to you? Are you blind, the lot of you? She is only five feet tall! The Queen is six! She is not the Queen – she is my wife!'

The crowd was hushed. The Gordons presented a fearsome sight. Donald, spitting fury, was the most fearsome of all, and when he leaped down off the wall laying about him with his dirk, the crowd disappeared like smoke.

Then the Gordons were inside the Provost's house, yelling for blood. One of their own was threatened. 'We take no prisoners!' Geordie Brand promised grimly in the Gordon battle cry, and there was a short, bloody battle. Afterwards the eight guards lay dead. Donald took the keys from one of them, unlocked the door, flung a blanket over Abbie's shoulders and carried her out to the horses.

On the road to Huntly Abbie had never seen or heard him so angry. It was a good job that he didn't know the half of it, she thought, and she would never tell him. He was swearing one minute and hugging her to him the next, and she understood that he had got the shock and the fright of his life.

She understood also, with a lurch of her heart, that he wasn't going to leave it at that. Sooner or later there would be more to come.

Queen Mary was in her own Holyrood Palace again with her ladies. Mary Seton was there and so was Mary Livingston Sempill who had come from her country home. The two Marys who had gone from her service had been replaced by the two young tiring women, Jane Kennedy and Marie de Courcelles – and ah! the luxury of a warm scented bath again ... The silken whisper of her black gown ... And then the Great Hall where a table was laid for supper, although she could eat none of it.

She asked for a glass of milk, mindful of the child she carried. Morton himself, standing behind her chair, acted as the taster for fear of poison. *So they weren't going to kill her, then. At least, not yet.* She sipped her milk thoughtfully, and he bent down and whispered in her ear.

'Madam, prepare to leave at once. We are sending you on a journey.'

In vain and in tears her Marys begged to accompany her. Only Jane Kennedy and Marie de Courcelles were permitted to do so, along with Dr Bourgoing, who said anxiously, 'I trust it is not a long journey. She has not eaten and she is exhausted. I pray you consider her health, as I have been doing for years.'

Morton looked at the clock. It was midnight. 'A thirty-mile ride? It is nothing. You should be there by daybreak. I can tell you now that you are going to Kinross-shire, to be the guest of Lady Margaret Douglas.'

Mary gasped. Then it was straight into the nest of vipers! Lady Margaret Douglas was Lord James's mother and Morton's sister, and lived with her husband in the most isolated castle in Scotland, a desolate island fortress in the middle of a deep loch. Lochleven . . . She knew it well.

Bothwell had got clean away, but the lords found some of his henchmen and had them hanged. One remained, the tailor who had sewn Bothwell's wedding suit when he had married Lady Jean, and they caught him skulking in Edinburgh Castle.

When he protested that he had only come back for some of his master's clothing, they tortured him until he confessed where a silver casket containing Bothwell's secret papers was to be found. Morton took charge of it and the lords continued to question the poor tailor about the Darnley murder, but by the time the subject of the casket letters, containing evidence of Mary's part in the murder was raised in England the tailor had long since been executed.

The goings-on in Scotland had not gone unnoticed in England. Queen Elizabeth was keeping her eye on events, utterly outraged at such unmannerly treatment of queens north of the Border.

What could *she* get out of this situation, she asked Cecil, and between them they schooled Throckmorton as to the line he would take when he went to see the Scottish lords for himself. First and foremost he must ask for wardship of Prince James, and invite him to be brought up in England.

The French had the same idea, and sent their ambassador to remind the lords of Queen Mary's happy upbringing in France.

Throckmorton reported back to a horrified Elizabeth that the next Scottish plot was to eliminate the Queen, and after that it would be easy to get rid of the baby Prince. The House

547

of Hamilton would then rule supreme, with Châtelherault at the head of it. Another Catholic.

In Strathbogie Lady Huntly crumpled at the news of Mary's imprisonment. There was no other word for it. Edith became alarmed.

'I don't understand it, Edith,' Abbie said. 'There was little love lost between her ladyship and the Queen latterly. On the other hand, Lady Huntly *did* bring Mary into the world. That might explain it.'

She went up to the castle to help Edith with the nursing of the old lady. Now it was heavy nursing, and nonstop. Sometimes Jackson and Donald were there too, waiting for Edith and Abbie to hand over to the night nurses, and they were all there when Lady Huntly, in the middle of her rambling, spoke a few words quite clearly.

'My husband and my other sons – all dead. My daughter, Jean, hundreds of miles away in Dunrobin Castle. I am alone. The Queen, a prisoner in Lochleven, with no more powers left to her. She can never free my George now. He will die in that English prison. There is no more reason to live.'

Edith refused to go home that night. She held her mistress's hand to the end, and the Huntly people, so critical of their Lady in life, showed her the utmost respect in death when they crowded the graveyard where she was laid to rest.

Lady Jean Sutherland arriving at her childhood home for her mother's funeral, pressed Abbie's hand.

She was thriving on her new settled life, Abbie was glad to see it, but still she detected a shadow, a secret sadness in Jean's large grey eyes. Well, everyone had secrets, didn't they? Not even to Lady Jean could Abbie confide her own little secret. That special moment belonged to Donald alone. But seeing her friend again brought back many memories of the past. It must have been the same for Jean. So many of them had been painful, Abbie thought, and none more painful for Jean than memories of Alex Ogilvie.

*   *   *

Alex Ogilvie of Boyne woke up one morning to find the sunshine was too bright. It was making him see everything more clearly than he had for a very long time. He had been taking Patrick Spence's hospitality for granted for far too long, and he knew that his long convalescence was over.

'Dear Pat and Sophia,' he said later that day, taking their hands in his, 'you have been just what my doctor ordered. When I came here I didn't care whether I lived or died.'

'After the way you poured money into my venture,' Sir Pat teased, 'we had to keep the goose that laid the golden eggs living!'

'Your kindness and care have given me back my life,' Alex said. 'No amount of money can pay for that.'

It was hard to tear himself away from his friends, especially the children, but he left shortly afterwards with one of the visiting English courtiers, a distant relation of Sir Pat's, who had invited him to spend some time with him at Queen Elizabeth's court.

Eventually, he divided his time between there and Boyne House in Edinburgh, fascinated by the ever-changing colours of the politics he observed in both countries. A quiet, self-effacing man, he soaked them all up, grateful to have been given another chance at life, a second bite of the cherry.

And he was a patient man, a good listener.

He soon discovered that events in Scotland were reported in London within a week of their happening, and that Elizabeth knew of them long before most of the people of Scotland did. She kept her finger firmly on the pulse of the British Isles, and far beyond. Alex Ogilvie compared events to a long, absorbing game of chess, and Queen Elizabeth was controlling the game with great skill.

SIXTY-EIGHT

Strangely, Donald was the one who seemed to be the most affected by Lady Huntly's death. He was not recovering, and the more he flung himself about and moped the more puzzled Abbie became, until the night came when she knew before she woke up that he was no longer in their bed.

It was cold without him beside her. She sat up in bed and saw him silhouetted, head on knees, in an attitude of utter despair on the window seat. She lit her bedside candle and spoke to him, holding out her arms to him.

'Come back to bed, my dearest. Whatever is wrong, let me help you.'

'Oh, Abbie,' he said, creeping back in beside her, just frozen, 'this is a terrible business.'

'But you never liked Lady Huntly, Donald! She was very cruel to you when you were a boy. It is not her death which has upset you like this. What is it? Was it something she said?'

'It was.'

'About Lord George?'

Abbie knew what was coming. She had been dreading it, for Donald had been preoccupied and worried for months, long before the funeral.

'Abbie, how do you think *he* feels, all this long time?'

'He must be hating it as much as I hate what you are going to say and do next. You want to go and free him, don't you?'

'I would have tried long ago, but –'

'But for the money it would cost . . . I know,' Abbie sighed.

The whole Gordon world was marking time, waiting for the next Gordon chief to come and take charge of the clan. Until he did there was no work, no money, nothing. And the gold Lord Huntly had given Donald at the time of his wedding had long since been spent on food for his family and friends. Everything was at a standstill. 'But why has Elizabeth kept him in prison all this time, anyway? Mary pardoned him long ago.'

'He's a Gordon, and except for Lord Huntly's moment of madness when he rebelled, the Gordons have always been faithful to the Scottish crown. Queen Elizabeth is frightened to let George go in case he raises another army for Mary here in the north. And then, there are all these rumours that Philip of Spain wants to marry Mary next. All the Catholics in Europe will unite and crush England between them. Elizabeth is a very frightened lady.'

But why did the problem have to come to a head at this particular, very inconvenient, moment? Why could it not have waited another four months or so? Abbie sighed again. Men were not made to play a waiting game, like women. With them it was all action, all immediate.

For that reason she could not hold Donald back, and that meant she could not tell him that she was pregnant again, a couple of months by her reckoning, a fact she had been concealing from him until she was sure she was going to keep the baby this time. She had intended to tell him tomorrow, but now she couldn't.

'Lie still,' she said, 'and wait. I have something to show you,' and taking the candle and her bunch of keys with her, she went over to Queen Catherine's boxes and unlocked the top one. The little black velvet box was still there, slipped down amongst the bottles of oils and perfumes. 'Look at this,' she said, climbing back into bed with it.

'What's in it?'

Abbie snapped it open. The ruby and pearl brooch glowed up at them. 'It was a gift from Catherine de Medicis. Now I am giving it to you.'

'*Abbie!* Why have you never worn such a gorgeous jewel?'

'Because I didn't like her or trust her. I thought the brooch was unlucky. To tell you the truth, I'll be glad to see it going out of this house. Perhaps all the bad luck around Strathbogie will go with it. Sell it in Edinburgh. Its true worth would be appreciated there, and the money you get for it should take you to England and back again with Lord George, God willing.'

He sat up straighter. She could feel him quivering with excitement. His eyes began to sparkle in the candlelight, and they hadn't done that for a long, long time. Abbie felt like crying.

'I've only one more thing to say to you,' she said. 'The sooner you go, the sooner you'll get back. How long do you think it will take?'

'Ho!' Donald laughed confidently. 'A few weeks – a month at most. I'll go tomorrow.'

Donald hadn't told Abbie everything that was in his mind. He never did, to save her from worry, but as he galloped south he realised that he had no real idea of where he was going or how to get there. His burning ambition had been fulfilled suddenly and surprisingly. Quite clearly, arguing and pleading about Lord George was getting nowhere, and now that he was hellbent on doing something about it himself he had no clear plan of action.

He needed a friend he could rely on, and he needed him urgently. He had heard that Alex Ogilvie was back from Italy. It didn't take him long to locate Boyne House, once he got to Edinburgh, and fortunately found that Alex was there. He greeted Donald warmly, took him inside, sat him down and sent his servant for refreshments.

'We were all sorry to hear of your wife's death,' Donald began, thinking that the tragedy hadn't left the scar on him that he would have expected, for now Alex looked fitter and bronzed, although his eyes were very sad.

'I'll tell you no lies, Donald. Our marriage was a catastrophe. Her death was a merciful release from a terrible illness for her. For me, it was a release from hell on earth. But in Italy I recovered, as far as I ever shall.'

'So there is no question of you marrying again?'

'I would never marry again, except to the right woman, the woman I always loved and should have married in the first place,' Alex groaned.

'Lady Jean.'

'Yes, Lady Jean. What news of her? Is she well?'

'She is well, and expecting a child. We saw her at Lady Huntly's funeral . . .' Donald paused, and took a different tack. 'In fact, it was that death that triggered my journey here. You see, there is absolutely no one at Strathbogie now. Lord George is still in prison.'

'Good God! I had completely forgotten about Lord George!'

'You are not alone, Alex. So have many other people, including Queen Elizabeth and Queen Mary. They have their reasons for deliberately forgetting him. Anyway, I have come to you for advice,' Donald said, taking out the black velvet box, 'because I want to realise the value of this jewel, and I thought you would know where to do that in Edinburgh. I shall need all the money I can get to find Lord George and get him out.'

'This is Saturday evening, old chap. There will be no more business done in Edinburgh until Monday morning. John Knox has seen to that. But you'll stay here with me, and first thing on Monday morning I'll take you to the right place. In the meantime, do you still play chess?'

'Yes,' Donald laughed.

That was the first problem solved, but in the evening over supper he tried to unravel a few more with Alex Ogilvie's help.

'No one could ever trust James Hamilton, Earl of Arran, or Duc de Châtelherault as he is called,' Alex told him. 'Mary of Guise said of him that he was "a simple and inconstant man who changed purpose every day." Anyway, Lord Huntly had sent George to consult him, being his second cousin. That was when George was arrested and thrown into an English prison, and nobody in Scotland has much doubt that Châtelherault helped to put him safely there.'

'What prison?' Donald asked eagerly, thinking that now he was getting somewhere, and this whole thing might be a lot easier than he had supposed.

'Well,' Alex said sadly, 'it would probably be one near Dover. That's where Châtelherault was at the time, living in Hamilton House, Dover. But don't get your hopes up, Donald. The English have a habit of constantly moving important political prisoners from keep to keep and castle to castle. Goodness knows where Lord George may be now.'

On Monday Donald prepared to set off again, better fed than he had been for many a long day, and with a bag of large gold coins and smaller silver ones they had got for Abbie's brooch strapped firmly around his waist under his doublet.

'I'll go to Dover first,' he said, shaking Alex's hand and thanking him. 'I'll find him, never fear.'

'Be careful,' Alex warned him. 'You are riding into danger. There is more intrigue than ever, now that the Queen is in Lochleven.'

It had taken Mary weeks to become accustomed to the poverty and harshness of her surroundings in Lochleven, the dusty coldness of her mean rooms, the complete lack of her wardrobe and jewels, and the close surveillance under hostile, suspicious Douglas eyes.

Then one day Lady Margaret introduced her grudgingly to her youngest son, George Douglas. She could hardly get out of it, since they all met together face to face on the same path, when Mary was allowed out under guard for one of her brief walks.

His unbelievably long, curling black eyelashes ringed his blue, blue eyes, and his skin was so fair and his hair so blue-black that Mary found it a welcome relief to allow her eyes to linger on him, after all these red-haired Douglases of whom she was thoroughly sick and tired.

Startled, George stared back at her, the beautiful young Queen he had heard so much about, and instantly he was her slave, although not one word was spoken between them.

So, she had made another conquest! Mary laughed for the first time for weeks. She felt almost light-hearted as she delved into her latest parcel as a prisoner-of-war. It contained sweets, pins, lengths of Holland cloth, Spanish silk, and gold and silver thread for her embroidery.

Far more importantly, there was scented soap, and some of her perukes, and face powder. But instead of using them that day to charm George Douglas, terrible pains in her stomach forced her to go to bed. She recognised them for what they were and fought against their crunching agony, trying to keep her child, her last link with Bothwell.

At midnight Dr Bourgoing stood over her with tears in his eyes.

'Madam, you have lost twin boys.'

They would have been princes of Scotland. 'Let me see them,' Mary said, and touched each tiny dead thing with her fingers.

'Your Majesty,' Seton said with a shudder, 'they will throw them in the loch.'

'We will bless them ourselves before they get the chance, and shroud them in the best cloth we have,' Mary sobbed. 'It should have been cloth of gold. Oh, Bothwell, Bothwell . . .'

He should have been here with her at this agonising time. Now there was absolutely nothing of him left to her. She was quite alone again.

Because she had lost so much blood with the miscarriage Mary was still lying in bed a fortnight later, weak and wearied of the lords who kept trying to make her sign a deed of abdication. She had adamantly refused, over and over.

The door of her room burst open, and there stood Lindsay Douglas's son-in-law and the ugliest of all her captors, tower ing in the doorway. He marched over to her bed, and waved papers under her nose. She did not need to ask what they were.

'So you won't sign?'

'I cannot sign. I am the Queen of Scotland.'

'You cannot rule, you mean. Even your infant son could do better.' He dragged her out of bed and flung her onto the chair in front of her desk. He shoved a quill into her hand. Then he stood with the point of his dagger at her throat. 'Sign, bitch,' he yelled, 'or I will slit your throat!'

'No. I will not sign.'

Lindsay lowered his dagger to her breast and scratched a cross on it. Blood was trickling from it when he yelled, 'Come in here!' Melville and Ruthven and the young George Douglas emerged from the stairwell where they had been hiding. 'Still the whore will not sign,' Lindsay roared, 'but I am going to make her. Hold her down!' Then he put his great, crushing paw over her hand and made it write 'Marie R.' once, twice and three times. The papers were signed. 'It is done!' he cried triumphantly, and marched out with the others following.

George Douglas bowed his head in shame.

John Knox waited inside the Protestant kirk at the gates of Stirling Castle. When the Lords of the Congregation escorted Prince James from his nursery to be crowned King of Scotland and Lord of the Isles, Knox knew he had reached the very zenith of his ambition. He had been asked to preach the sermon on this wonderful Protestant occasion.

His dreams had all come true. The Catholic whore was gone. This was a glorious new beginning. The Bishop of Orkney anointed the Prince with holy oil, and then the Earl of Atholl placed the crown on his little head.

Now Knox's time had come. Full of fire, he bellowed out his text. His sermon was a long one, but strangely, the Lords did not seem moved by the brilliance of it. Instead, they knelt before the child and did homage, and to the sound of trumpets as the new King's titles were being proclaimed, they went slowly away.

In the afternoon of that same day Mary, his mother, was looking out of her prison window at the quiet waters of the loch, trying to find some peace and tranquillity when events were moving so fast in Scotland that they were positively dizzying. She was trying not to remember the terrible scene in her bedchamber when Lindsay had hurt her arms in his bullying grasp and scarred her breast with his dagger.

Of course, she told herself, that had been nothing short of torture. If she could escape from here, no signature extracted under such duress would hold water. The abdication papers were worthless.

As she stared out she saw the Douglases gathering together on the little pier. They were lighting a bonfire! It burned up brightly, and the Douglases danced around it, laughing and cheering. And next, there was a crashing boom, and another, and another, so loud that the very floor shook under her. They were firing the cannons from the castle walls! She jumped up in fright. What had happened?

Lord William Douglas came to report.

'We are saluting a glorious day for Scotland and for the Douglas family,' he told her. 'Your son has been crowned King James, and we have recalled Lord James, Earl of Moray, to be Regent.'

Then he became quite alarmed. Mary was alternately mumbling and shrieking in French, with her eyes starting from her head. Then she fell to the floor, frothing at the mouth.

SIXTY-NINE

As Mary recovered her health, so she recovered her courage, as always. She lived now for only one thing – to get out, to escape, and she would never do that alone. She needed someone to help her, and preferably a man.

She bathed in scented water. With a few face paints Mary Fleming Maitland managed to include in her parcels, she tinted her face delicately. She took care to wear the best in her scanty, shabby wardrobe, and gently chastised Jane Kennedy and Marie if her gowns were not at all times absolutely fresh.

She looked at George Douglas and then looked away again tantalisingly from under her shadowed, lowered eyelashes. It had always worked before, and it did this time. George became more interested than ever.

She had not lost her touch! She could still attract any man she chose! And soon George was whispering to her to meet him on the causeway down by the pier where the guards were at their slackest, frozen by the winds off the loch.

'Laundresses come here every Tuesday,' he whispered. 'All you have to do is don the garments of one of them and cover your head.'

The following Tuesday they put their plan into action, and it went like a dream. Mary couldn't believe that she was actually sitting in a boat heading away from the castle . . . The plan had almost succeeded when a gust of wind blew her hood over her eyes. She put up a hand to push it back and one of the guards rowing her to freedom saw that such a long, fine white hand didn't belong to a washerwoman. They rowed her back.

'Madam, it is my charge to restrain you here,' Lord Douglas said as he helped her out of the boat at the landing pier.

'And before God, it is my charge to free myself, sir, by whatever means I can,' she replied. 'This attempt may have failed, but there will be others.'

After that George Douglas was nowhere to be seen on the island. Her best friend had been banished, and she was in despair, alone again.

But she had reckoned without a youth called Willie Douglas, some illegitimate brat of Lord Douglas's. Young Willie, aged fifteen, with short, horrible red hair, took over where George had left off. He was even more passionately in love with Mary than George had been, and with all a young man's confidence didn't remotely consider that any plan of his could possibly fail. He would get her out. Mary doubted it. She was tired, disappointed and just not interested.

'I have been ordered to arrange a revel,' he told her, kneeling before her. 'I am to be Lord of Misrule, and everyone must do as I do, or do as I say, no matter how stupid.'

'Yes, Willie,' Mary sighed wearily. 'I have attended revels before.'

'Not like this one, Your Majesty. I have a foolproof plan.'

She smiled at last at his boyish enthusiasm. 'You have?'

'I can get into the wine cellar the night before and lay by many extra flagons in a place of my own. At the revel I will keep everyone leaping about and dancing while they get drunker and drunker, especially Lord Douglas.'

'Yes?'

'Every night the gateman comes to the supper table and lays the keys of the castle beside the master's plate. I will steal them when he isn't looking, when he's too drunk to notice, anyway.'

'Oh, Willie! How can you do *that*?'

'I know a way, don't worry about it. All you must worry about is seeing that you, Jane and Marie get servants' disguises

– gowns, and cloaks with hoods – because when I steal the keys that will be the signal for you to cross the courtyard as if you were three maidservants. Nobody will pay any attention to three maidservants. In the meantime I will unlock the gates and wave to you when it is safe to run out and jump in my boat.'

'But we would be followed by all the other boats here!'

'No. I will disable the other boats first, so they cannot follow us.'

'Oh, Willie! It is a very impertinent plan!'

'Well, I am an impertinent fellow, Your Majesty,' Willie grinned.

The suspense all the way through the revel was almost too much for Mary and her ladies to bear. But sure enough, Willie was keeping the wine flowing and everyone was becoming drunker and drunker by the minute, just as he had promised, and under Mary's fascinated gaze the keys of the castle were beside Lord Douglas's plate one minute, and the next were gone, scooped up in the napkin Willie had dropped over them so carelessly.

The noise of music and laughter followed the three ladies as they wandered outside casually for a breath of air. Quickly they removed their gowns to reveal servants' dresses underneath. Jane found the blue cloaks she had rolled up and hidden. Willie waved to them from the gates.

'Don't run.' Mary held Jane and Marie back to a walking pace.

Then at last – *at last*! – they were all outside the gates!

Willie locked them again from the outside and flung the keys in the loch. 'Let them dive for them!' he laughed. 'Now *they* are prisoners!'

The blood coursed very fast through Mary's veins and turned her pale cheeks pink with excitement. An adventure! Another adventure, on this balmy, breezy, wonderful night! She grabbed the other set of oars.

'Madam!' Willie frowned.

'Whose escape is it? I can row if I like for my own escape!'

560

'Pray God,' he said, as they struck out strongly for the mainland.

George Douglas was waiting. George Seton was waiting. All her dear friends were waiting . . . And she was free! Free! Tears of happiness were blinding her as she embraced them.

George Douglas lifted her onto the saddle of her horse. Willie lifted Jane and Marie onto theirs, and then he came to kneel before her.

'Farewell, madam, and Godspeed,' he said.

Mary gasped. 'But surely you are coming with us? Of course you must come! You and George shall be in my service for life. I will not ride without you.'

'There are no horses for us, madam.'

'Then you shall ride with Marie, Willie, and George with Jane.'

Heading the little cavalcade Mary clattered through the village of Kinross. When her hood flew back the villagers recognised her, cheering her on and blessing her. Exultantly, she waved back, allowing her glorious hair to stream in the wind.

Bad luck and a chapter of accidents dogged Donald's footsteps all the way south. If he had not loved and respected horses so much he would have ridden the one he had into the ground in his tearing anxiety to get to Dover, but as it was, the poor beast must be fed, watered and rested before they could go on again the following morning.

On the third day the horse went lame in spite of him. He managed to exchange it for another at the inn he stayed in overnight, but it turned out to be frisky and troublesome. On the fourth day it threw him and then bolted, kicking up its heels.

He had been thrown on his head, but except for a blinding headache when he came to, he thought he was quite able to trudge groggily along the road until he came to another inn. He was gazing up at the sign of a Black Swan swinging in the night breeze when he suddenly fell down. To his amazement he couldn't get up again, try as he might. Two men passing thought he was drunk, helped him up and threw him in at the door of the inn. This time Donald blacked out altogether.

The landlord sent for the barber to have a look at him. As soon as he came Donald emptied the contents of his stomach, groaning in apology, with his face cold and wet.

'Ah, yes, me boyo,' said the barber. 'You've got a nasty bump there on your head, to be sure.'

'Well, I can't lie here. I've got to get to Dover in a hurry.'

'Take your pick, lad. It's all the same to me. Either rise up out of that bed and quite possibly collapse and die, or else do the sensible thing and lie still for at least three days.'

'*Three days?*'

'Three days, indeed. A bang on the head is not to be trifled with.'

'But that means it will be Saturday before I can go!'

'Ay, well, you can still count, I see. You haven't lost your senses altogether. Think yourself lucky so far, and don't be tempting the Devil.'

Far from happy, Donald did as he was told. He was forced to, anyway, because every time he lifted his head the room began to spin around sickeningly. He, who had never been ill before in his life, had not allowed for this. By Saturday it would be a week since he had left Huntly and Abbie, and he was still nowhere near Dover.

Six weeks later Donald did not dare allow himself to think of Abbie. If he dwelt on her he would be sorely tempted to turn around and go back home. All he knew was that it seemed like a lifetime since he had said goodbye to her, since last he had seen her dear face, and because it grieved him so much to think of her, he must try not to dwell on it.

This quest of his had been a miserable round of sleeping rough, eating where and when he could, washing in rivers and streams, and trying to preserve his money. So now his mind was made up.

He had drawn a blank at Dover. He had snooped around every castle and keep that he could find in the proximity. This next one was the very last castle he was going to investigate.

He would have to put up in an inn for his last few days in the south of England, and there he would clean up, rest up, and fill his belly for a change. His horse could do with a rest, too. Donald was in a very bad mood indeed, admitting defeat at last, when he had never, never admitted defeat before. It was completely foreign to his sanguine, optimistic nature, and he went downstairs to the taproom, very disconsolate.

None of the customers looked promising company, either. They were mostly men, but there were a few women, rough working women, at that. But then, it was a shabby inn he had chosen in an effort to save his money.

Also, he thought next morning when he arose from the first night's soft, normal sleep for months, it was a very small town for such a very large castle. He skirted around it, noting that the different parts of the castle where the prisons were likely to be were quite far apart, too far to jump from one roof to another. He couldn't get into it that way. This was the most impregnable castle yet.

The outside wall was also very high, and it must be wide, to allow two guards to walk along it as they did, side by side. They looked a lazy pair, to him. One was very stout with a huge belly – a beer-belly, Donald decided instantly, for it hung and wobbled over his belt. The other guard was thin, with a sour mournful face.

The weather held, and Donald packed a crusty loaf, a hunk of cheese and a flagon of ale in his fishing basket, and made his way to a spot under the castle walls in full view and within speaking distance of the guards. He opened the basket and prepared to enjoy a leisurely midday meal, while out of the corner of his eye he saw that the guards were watching him.

'Fancy a drink?' he asked, holding out the flagon.

'God, yes,' Beer-belly replied, and Donald went right up

to them and handed it over. They both took a deep swig and rubbed the backs of their hands across their mouths.

'Thank you, sir,' Mr Mournful said. 'Come again.'

Donald repeated this exercise every day from then on until the guards were chatting away to him quite freely. He had been on a fishing holiday, he explained, but now he was going back home.

'I *had* hoped to see a friend of mine,' he added one morning, withholding a larger flagon than usual in the meantime. 'He's in a prison somewhere around here, but God knows where. His name is George Gordon.'

'You've struck lucky, then,' Mr Mournful said. 'He's here.'

Donald's heart did a somersault. 'I dearly wish I could see him,' he said.

'Well,' Beer-belly said, looking longingly at the flagon, 'I dare say we could let you. For a consideration, of course.'

At that Donald handed over the flagon. 'When?' he asked.

The ale was having the desired effect already. 'Why not now?' Beer-belly reeled a little. 'There's nobody about in the middle of the day.'

'Might as well,' Mr Mournful said. 'We'll let you in and leave you for an hour. We might even get a little nap.'

They marched him down passages and more passages and then suddenly stopped outside the barred door of a cell.

'Back in an hour,' Beer-belly said, unlocked the door and marched off with his mate.

'George! George!' Donald said softly to the bearded figure hunched up in a corner of the cell. 'It's me – Donald! I've come to get you out!'

George couldn't speak. He put his arms around Donald and wept.

That night Donald felt more frustrated than ever when he went into the taproom. Lord George was well, and delighted to see him, but there was no way that he could think of to escape, either. 'And believe me, Donald,' he sighed, 'I've thought of little else.'

Moodily, Donald ordered some rabbit stew, and glanced at the two men at the table next to him. He couldn't help overhearing their conversation. From it he gathered that they were brothers, and one had been to collect and drive cattle down from Scotland, where they were cheaper.

'All they talk about up there is the Scottish Queen,' he reported. 'She was shut up in an island prison for a long time until an admirer tried to get her out.'

Donald pricked up his ears.

'How?' asked his brother. 'Will you have some stew?'

'I will that. I haven't had a decent meal for days. Well, this admirer got an idea that she would dress up as one of the laundry-women who came and went across the water in a boat every week.'

'And did it work?'

'That plan didn't. But later, someone else came up with another one, and she escaped to fight another battle. At Langside, I think the place was called.'

'Who was she fighting?'

'Her brother. Her bastard brother, who has always wanted the crown. In fact, they call him the Bastard, in Scotland.'

'Man, that must be a terrible place, Scotland! Full of bastards, and battles amongst themselves! Did she win?'

'Freezing cold, as well, I can tell you! No, she didn't win. She had to escape again, this time over the Solway to a place called Workington. Then, of course, Elizabeth had her moved to Carlisle Castle, and that's the last I heard of her.'

'Poor thing! Perhaps it's the last we'll ever hear of her. One thing is sure, she'll never see Scotland again.'

Donald finished his rabbit and his ale and called for another pint to while away the time until he went to bed. He drank it slowly, thanking Providence that, after what he had heard, Abbie had been nowhere near Queen Mary, or she might have been pressed into impersonating her again. *She* might have been the one shut up on that island. He was brooding over it when the two brothers left and the same two rough

565

women who came in every night took their places, and he was forced to listen to them next.

They didn't like their husbands. He got that message as soon as they opened their mouths.

'All Claud Wilkins thinks about is booze,' said the little one, knocking back half a glass of ale in one gulp. 'Ah,' she added, with a loud burp, 'that's better! Lil, he sits in that cobbler's shop all day, just waiting for a drink.'

'You'd be worse off if you had a prison guard to put up with, Pansy,' said her companion, and Donald, sitting with his back to them, pricked up his ears again. 'That man's belly is going to burst one day soon. All he ever did in his life was drink ale and give me five sons. Now that they've all grown up and gone I've a good mind to run away myself.'

When he turned his head a little Donald could see that Lil was the large, stout one, in her forties.

'It's a good job we have work, or else we would never get a drink ourselves,' Pansy grumbled. 'Certainly, not from those greedy bastards.'

'Ay – some work!' Lil sniffed. 'There's none so bad as being a washerwoman, God help us,' and she gave a deep sigh. 'I could do with another drink. I've got the glooms tonight. Got any more money, Pansy?'

'No.'

'Oh God . . .'

They whispered together, so that Donald couldn't hear. They giggled. Out of the corner of his eye he saw them nudging one another, and then Lil spoke up.

'He looks a nice, kind gentleman.'

They cackled together again. Donald turned round. Now that he saw them close up he couldn't blame their husbands for taking to drink. But that didn't matter, and neither did their large red, rough hands. As far as he was concerned he was looking at two goddesses.

'Excuse me, ladies. Did I hear you say that you took in washing?'

'We're ladies, you're right,' Pansy said belligerently. 'We

566

don't take in just any washing either. We're laundresses for the prison.'

Lil poked her in the ribs to be quiet. 'But we would do yours, sir,' she said, 'for a consideration.'

And where had he heard those very words? From Beer-belly, only this afternoon. Lil must be his wife. Donald smiled at them and offered to buy them another drink. Then he bought them another, thinking that sometimes Fate was just marvellous. Bloody marvellous.

SEVENTY

Donald took his 'considerations' with him, and the guards allowed him in again the next day.

'You can have no idea how wonderful it is to be speaking to a friend at last,' Lord George said, holding up a little hand mirror, and peering into it. 'The barber has been this morning, and shaved me.'

'Good. A beard doesn't suit you, any more than it suits me,' Donald observed.

'But what has he done to the back of my hair?'

Donald moved behind him. 'Cut it very short. Much shorter than –' He stopped, staring into the mirror. Both faces were reflected in it, and now that they were clean-shaven the likeness was there for all to see.

Lord George laughed. 'That was a little trick I played on you. People might say, "They could be brothers!" The fact is, we *are* brothers. Your father was my father, too. Who else but a brother would have moved heaven and earth to find me? Your name should always have been Donald Gordon.'

'Donald MacLaren I was born. Donald MacLaren I shall die, George.'

'You are a brother to me, whatever you say – and the only one I've got left. But don't forget I am the Earl of Huntly now, and you are only my younger brother. I could force you to do my will!'

Donald barked with laughter. 'You? Force anyone? I don't think so, George. You wouldn't force a fly out of its way.'

'Of course not,' Lord George said, clapping him on the

back. 'But I want you to stop being a soldier when we get back to Strathbogie. I want you by my side. I'm going to need your help.'

'You shall always have that. But Abbie would never want to live in a castle. She's seen too many.'

'If not in Strathbogie, what about Flowers?'

'Flowers? They knocked it down as well! It's a ruin.'

'It may be a ruin, but it's only a stone's throw from the castle. I shall have both places renovated . . .'

'Now, *that's* very interesting, George! And what do you propose to use for money, may I ask?'

'Ho! Get me out of here, and the first thing I'll show you is money! Don't tell me that Abbie wouldn't like Flowers! Such a gracious house it was! And set in beautiful gardens – of course, that's how it got its name. There used to be a painting of it in the castle somewhere . . .'

'I'll think about it,' Donald said briskly, doing his best to exert a little pressure on his gentle, dreamy friend – or half-brother. 'But first things first. To business, George. Last night I got an idea about how to get you out. Tell me, who are your visitors?'

'Nobody, except the priest, the barber once a month, and the guard who brings me my food. Sometimes he brings paper and charcoal so that I can write and draw. Look – here are a few sketches for Strathbogie –'

'*George*! Do you have any other visitors? It's important.'

'Only the washerwomen.'

'Oh, it's like pulling out teeth, trying to extract information from you! But that's what I wanted to know. When do they come?'

'On Mondays.'

'Three days away, then.'

Three days, Donald thought, as he walked back to the inn. There was a lot to do in three days, and the first thing to attend to was Lil.

Never had a lover been more impatient to see his lady than Donald was that night to see Lil. He heaved a huge sigh of relief when she came clumping in, as gloomy as ever. The gloom soon wore off after a few drinks, and when Donald walked home with her he felt as nervous as though he were about to propose marriage. 'Lil,' he said, 'you could do me a big favour.'

'Oh, yes? First you would have to show me the colour of your money.'

'No, Lil. I didn't mean that.'

'Huh! What else does a man ever want from a woman?'

'I want something different. If you give me it, this is the colour of my money.' He held up a gold coin.

'Jesus!'

'I want you to go into George Gordon's cell and take off your clothes next Monday.'

'I knew it! I knew it!'

'No, Lil,' Donald said patiently. 'I want you to let him put on your dress and cloak, and walk out as if he were you.'

'Ah ha! An escape, is it? Oh, I'd need a lot of gold for *that*.'

Donald's face was white with anxiety on Monday morning when he slipped Lil three gold coins, muttering that three more were waiting for her inside. By now his gold coins were dwindling rapidly.

He'd had to buy another horse, for Lord George. Now he led it and his own into the first narrow street down from the castle and waited with his heart in his mouth. If this went wrong . . .

Of course he had not confided all his fears to Abbie. There was no need for her to know about Elizabeth's huge network of spies all over England. Donald was sure that a visitor for the Earl of Huntly on a daily basis would have been reported by this time. Would the English Queen be cruel enough to allow them to escape, and then easily pounce on them? Just for sport? He believed she would – and then George would be executed.

He began going over everything in his mind. He was sure

he had judged it right. He agonised, pacing up and down. Lil and George were about the same height. He was broader in the shoulders, of course, and only half her width, but the cloak would hide that. When would they raise the alarm? That was something he had never contemplated, but he contemplated it now. When the guard came with George's next meal, he supposed. Midday. By that time they could be far away.

Far away . . . If it all went right. He looked up and saw a figure walking towards him, head bent.

Was it? Was it?

Then Lord George's cool, calm voice spoke in his ear. 'So far, so good. Let's go. But I'm sorry for that poor woman in that freezing cell in her underwear. However, I did put my doublet around her shoulders.'

Speechless, Donald mounted his horse, handed Lord George the reins for his, and together they galloped off.

Abbie was now more than eight months pregnant. She had not been able to hide the fact from Lizzie next door almost from the time Donald left. And Edith was just as concerned. They visited her at least six times a day on the slightest pretext. They took her for walks. They brought her titbits which she couldn't eat . . .

She was far too worried.

'Now then, Abbie, this won't do,' Lizzie said sternly. 'Today, you'll polish a floor. It's the very best thing you can do in your condition,' and stood over her with a woollen cloth and some oil until she got down on her hands and knees. 'Keep busy, dearie. Waggle your hips as you go. Give it plenty of effort. You'll be glad you did when you go into labour.'

Edith was more concerned about her state of mind.

'I know you can't stop worrying about Donald, Abbie. There's no use asking you to, or expecting you to. But Jackson has utter faith in him. Please, dear, just be patient a little while longer, and hang on. Remember, it was a very difficult task that Donald took on. It's just taken him longer than he thought, that's all.'

Abbie smiled at her. Jackson had faith in Donald, but no more than she had herself. It was just this never-ending waiting, waiting, waiting.

Donald and Lord George only realised the danger they were in when they reached the first town on the way north. They thanked their lucky stars that they had thrown away the washerwoman's dress and cloak. The militia were everywhere. They were on the lookout for an escaped prisoner disguised as a woman.

'Here's some money,' Donald muttered. 'Buy yourself another doublet before you freeze to death, and then go your way, and I'll go mine. I'll meet you at the first inn on the north road out of here.'

And so it continued, day after day, night after night, when sometimes they managed to meet and ride on together, but mostly they forged on separately, on parallel lines.

A week later they had got as far as York when they both landed together at the Black Swan. Another Black Swan, Donald thought sourly, when saddle-sore and weary he limped in to find Lord George on the other side of the dining room calmly eating his supper and deliberately ignoring him.

Good old George! Donald had to smile. He cheered up immediately just to see him safely there. They were coming near the north of England now, and once over the Border the danger was halved. When George left to go upstairs without a glance at him, Donald followed and nipped into his room.

'Well?' Lord George asked. 'You're the seasoned campaigner. What now?'

'We should stay here for a few days and get our breath back. We'll rest and get fresh horses. From now on it's all moors, miles and miles of them, and there will be soldiers all over the place because Queen Mary is being held in Carlisle Castle, so I found out. They'll be watching for possible rescuers, so until we meet again in Carlisle itself, we'll have to be careful.'

'Where, in Carlisle?'

'There's bound to be a Black Swan! The English don't seem to be able to think of any other name,' Donald said gloomily.

'The Black Swan it is, then. Where else?' Lord George started to laugh. He went into such gales of laughter that Donald had to join in.

'Oh, I feel better now,' he gasped. 'But oh! My backside!'

'And mine. How are we off for money?'

'We'll have just enough to get to Edinburgh,' Donald told him. 'Then we'll go and see a friend of mine, Alex Ogilvie of Boyne.'

Once over the Border at Gretna, and up through Hawick and the other Scottish border towns they began to breathe easier. They got to Edinburgh, and in Boyne House were attended to royally. Rested, fed, watered, bathed and shaved, they were attired in new suits.

'We can never thank you enough, Alex,' Donald said. 'We owe you a huge debt of gratitude, for everything you've done to help us.'

'I'm the cause of all this,' Lord George said, 'so I'll be the one to pay back the debt. Donald and I will not leave here unless you promise to come to Strathbogie whenever you can, for as long as you can.'

'I will, my lord,' Alex said sadly. 'I only wish I had, years ago.'

Now, on the last leg of their journey home, the weather became colder and powdery snowflakes began to fall.

'Snow?' Lord George laughed. 'I had forgotten what it looked like! What date is it, Donald? I'm afraid I've lost all track of time.'

'It's Christmas Eve.'

And that meant he had been away from home for five months, Donald thought wearily. Goodness knows what Abbie must have been thinking all this time. On and on they

573

galloped. The snow became heavier and stuck to the capes Alex Ogilvie had insisted they should take with them. It lay softly on the ground and muffled their horses' hoofbeats when they cantered up the long avenue from Huntly to Strathbogie Castle. All was quiet, and the moon came out, yellow and bright.

Lord George had his first shocking glimpse of the damage that had been done to the castle. The once-beautiful towers and peaked roofs of it had gone, leaving jagged rocks behind, silhouetted monstrously in the moonlight like huge rotten teeth.

'No, no,' he kept muttering. And then, 'Oh, Donald, it is all worse than I thought! What, if anything, is left?'

He pushed the huge front door. Amazingly, it opened, grating on its hinges, and they flitted silently inside. They paced about the few rooms hurriedly thrown together by the Huntly folk, all brilliantly lit by the moon, all quiet, all ghostly, sadly eloquent of times gone by.

'Yes,' Lord George whispered, 'it will take a lot of money to put all this right. And I promised you, my brother, that I would show you what real money is, and where it is, for in my eyes you have as much right to it as I have – or Lady Jean, for that matter. Follow me!'

He led the way to what had once been Lord Huntly's bedchamber. One side of it had been blasted out, but not the side that George went to unerringly, and where he opened a small wooden door into a tiny room. Donald saw that it was a privy, still with its wooden toilet-seat over the open chute.

'This is where the Earls of Huntly did their most important business.' George's smile flashed briefly. 'Not a place where people would be inclined to linger. For that reason, secret passages in Scottish castles are traditionally entered from the privy, and this one is no exception.'

He pushed at one side of a large stone in the wall, and after a lot of effort and with Donald's help it swivelled back with a crunching sound to reveal a large gaping black hole.

'It sounds promising,' George said, 'as if no one has tried

574

it for a long time. Well, the moon's not going to penetrate inside here, Donald. We'll have to strike a light. Wait here until I look in the press behind the front door. The night lanterns used to be kept there.'

In a few minutes he was back, delighted that he had found a lantern with its wick intact, and that there was still some oil in the bottom of it. By that time Donald had opened the tinderbox that he always kept handy in his pocket, and when he rubbed his dirk across it he lit the wick from the spark.

George put one leg in the hole and fished around with his foot. 'Ah! It's all right! Nobody can have been here since my father and I were last in it. The box to step on is where we left it. But be careful. There's a drop of two feet after that.'

Cautiously, Donald followed him into the gloomy passage. The walls were slimy, running with water, and the only way he could have described the smell was that of a grisly opened-up grave. When the passage widened into a sort of cave the sound of rushing water and gurgling became louder and louder until it was thunderous.

'Where are we?' Donald asked.

George shouted above the noise. 'The river's just beyond that wall, but don't worry. It's been rushing past for hundreds of years, and that strange gurgling sound you hear is the Whirling Pool.'

'I know the Whirling Pool. Everyone does. No man ever came out of it alive.'

'It's supposed to exist because the rock bottom of the river takes a plunge just there. Anyway, it ensures that nobody can come into this passage from the other end.'

Natural outcrops of rock made uneven shelves around the cave, and on every one were strongboxes. There were hundreds of them, from the dripping roof down to the floor. After trying two or three of them George managed to lift the lid of one with his bare hands, and Donald staggered back. It was full of golden church ornaments, precious holy relics, worth a fortune. The next box was full of coins.

'Have you seen enough to convince you?' George asked,

showing him the glitter of precious stones in another. 'The Gordon fortune is intact, after all.'

One of the guards on duty in the barracks roused Geordie Brand. 'Intruders in the castle, sir,' he reported.

Geordie was alert at once, flinging on his uniform and barking orders at the sleepy soldiers before handing out the weapons. They found the main door of the castle standing open.

'Who was careless enough to leave it like that?' he hissed, but nobody answered as they filed in silently.

It was as much of a shock to the Gordons as it was to the two intruders when they met face to face in the fickle moonlight.

A shot rang out. And then another.

Donald leaped into the shadows behind the open front door. When he looked back Lord George was lying on the floor, bleeding profusely. Oh God, they had come through all that together, and now he was dead, shot by his own soldiers.

'It's the new Earl!' Geordie Brand was saying, with the soldiers clustering around him. 'We've killed Lord George ... One of you, take a horse and fetch the apothecary here! Hurry! Hurry!'

As soon as the soldier rushed out and jumped on a horse Donald crept out of the door and began what seemed like an endless nightmare journey back down the long avenue on foot to get to Abbie, not attempting to mount one of the horses he and Lord George had left among the shrubs. His leg was hurting him so much that it was not possible to get up on a horse, anyway. It was hurting so much that it was all he could think about. He lost all sense of logic, that after all this time he was safe with friends. He only knew he was hurt, and he had to see Abbie again before it was too late.

SEVENTY-ONE

Abbie had been sitting in the rocking chair all day, refusing to move, refusing to eat, and refusing company.

'No. Please leave me alone,' she pleaded with Lizzie, Edith and Jackson. 'If the baby starts, if anything happens, I promise to call.'

But she locked the doors behind them. She had no intention of calling anyone. She was desperate. She had had no word from Donald, he had been away so long and his mission had been so dangerous. By now she was convinced something had gone terribly wrong. She had never felt so low, so unhappy and unwell in her life. The terrible nightmare of last night was still vivid in her mind in every detail. If she closed her eyes she was still in it.

Once again the red-haired boy was knocking at the door crying, 'Mother! Mother!' Once again Flamina, her bright hair dimmed and turning grey, was rushing out of the drawing room and leading him back upstairs to soothe him to sleep. Once again Sir William was crouching over letters spread out over the table, and when Flamina returned he pointed to this one and then another.

'One more sentence inserted here, and again there,' he said, 'and the task is done.'

But Flamina was looking very unhappy. 'Are you sure about this?' she asked, her eyes filling with tears.

Abbie didn't blame her, for Sir William was having such difficulty in breathing, and his face was quite yellow under his sparse grey hair. When he got up to consult another book from the shelves he was dragging one leg painfully past the other.

'Dearest wife,' he gasped when he sank back in his chair, a broken old man, 'you know it must be done, or else my whole life's work will have been wasted. You know that all I ever wanted was peace for Scotland, and that will never be as long as Marie Stuart continues to live and to plot. You know that Queen Elizabeth must believe she has committed treason against her, and this is the only last desperate way. I have tried everything else, and now there is not much time left for me.'

'Please, William, don't say that,' Flamina sobbed.

'Well then, since no one can tell your handwriting from hers . . .' He paused and coughed, gasping for breath.

'Just tell me what to write and where, my darling,' she said. 'Then you are going to your bed.'

That scene dissolved, but then another appeared. At first Abbie hadn't believed that the tall woman robed in black with a veil of white gauze flowing from her coif could possibly be Queen Mary. Her figure was thicker, her high ruff could not hide her wrinkling throat, and the fine skin of her long hands was branched with veins of violet.

No, it must be her mother, Marie de Guise, entering this trial chamber, supported by Dr Bourgoing and Melville. A noble came forward and led her to a scarlet velvet chair. Above it on a dais stood a chair of State under a canopy emblazoned with the arms of England.

So – it was an English courtroom, and these must be English nobles on the benches to right and left, and English judges at a round table in front of the Queen.

A noble spoke. 'We are gathered here at Her Majesty Queen Elizabeth's commission to examine the Queen of Scots. Madam, you will hear the indictment.' So it *was* Mary! But it was a very different Mary from the young and beautiful Queen she used to serve.

They were accusing her of conspiring with a man called

Anthony Babington to kill Queen Elizabeth. It was ludicrous. Bits and pieces of the argument afterwards were still clear in Abbie's mind when letters were read out, first from this one and then from that one, along with those purported to be written by Mary herself. They were the most damning of all. Time and time again the Queen leaped from her chair wincing with pain, and denied she had ever written them.

'Forgeries! Forgeries!' she cried.

'Madam, Sir William Maitland himself has vouched for them!'

It was the death knell, Abbie knew.

'Sir William . . .' Mary reeled back, her face stricken. She knew it, too.

And then, as in the way of dreams, a young girl, beautiful, beguiling, with her red-gold curls massed in tendrils and ringlets was somehow there, and laughing, with a quill in her hand and treachery in those blue eyes of hers.

Flamina, with her gay, mocking laugh. Flamina, who could copy Mary's handwriting so perfectly.

Shocked, Abbie became aware that a man was speaking. 'Guilty of conspiring against the life of Queen Elizabeth . . . Condemned by the Parliament of this country to die . . .'

On all sides the shout was taken up. 'Guilty! Guilty! You will die!'

Abbie had awakened trembling and sweating and looking around wildly, unable to comprehend that she was in her own bed and not in some terrible courtroom far away.

All her life her sleep had been short, and light. Now and then she had dreamed, but she had never had a nightmare like that. And now that she was fully awake, it wouldn't go away, as dreams usually do, almost instantly. Fearfully she wondered about it all that day, and then became convinced that it had been an omen.

Now it was getting dark, but Abbie was still shuddering at the treachery so cruelly exposed in her nightmare. It was a short step from there to think of all the treachery and cruelty she had seen herself during her own lifetime.

Her lifetime, she thought bitterly, as she lit one small candle and set it down on the table. It had been a short one, and without Donald, best ended. Best ended for the child, too – for who would willingly bring a child into the world without a father? She had been lucky herself, as well as Abigail, to have been looked after by John McCracken, and nobody appreciated that more than she did. Sighing, she looked beyond the candle-flame, her eyes drawn to Queen Catherine's boxes still lying one on top of the other in the corner.

Well, she thought, this would be the third and last time that she would ever open them. With trembling hands she drew out the blackest little bottle, the one with white skulls and crossbones all over it, and set it down on the table beside the candle. Then she went back to her rocking chair and gazed steadily at the bright little flame. When it died, she would die. There was no longer any point in living.

And as she gazed tiny phantom figures began to move. They came and went around the flame, all the people she had ever known. Donald first, Donald when he was only a boy, Donald when he became her lover. Then her mother, her father, her brothers, Lord and Lady Huntly and their sons, Lady Jean, Alex Ogilvie, the four Marys – the flowers in the Queen's bouquet – Queen Catherine, dear little Francis, Darnley, Riccio, Bothwell and Sir William Maitland of Lethington . . . Sir William the Chameleon, Sir William the Spider.

There were more and more going round and round, and one by one they dropped out. Only Donald was left. But Donald was dead and gone.

She must stop dreaming. The candle was guttering now, its flame leaping up and then almost dying out. It was time to act.

And then her child – Donald's child – kicked her violently and moved. Her sickness intensified as cruel, grinding pains started in her back, a terrible spasm was in her stomach, her waters broke and her baby was demanding to be born. She thought of his little arms, his legs, his face so like his father's – how could she ever have thought of killing herself? She would kill him, too. It had been a moment of madness.

With a terrible sob Abbie took the bottle, unlocked the front door, reached the gate set in its iron railings at the bottom of the garden and flung the bottle as hard as she could onto the cobbles of the street. It smashed to pieces and the black contents oozed out. It would have taken only one drop of that...

Then something attracted her attention, something awful, a long shape crawling along towards her, like some large bloated snake. She was rooted to the spot in terror.

But it couldn't be a snake. It had arms, and one of them was holding on to the railings and pulling its body along. And it had a face.

'*DONALD!*' Abbie screamed.

At once a candle flared in the window next door. Seconds later Jack Sproat was running down his path with his nightcap all askew to bend over Donald. Then came Lizzie in her nightgown with a shawl wrapped around her. She dragged Abbie back inside and led her to her bed.

'Take off your clothes, dearie. You've started, have you?'

Abbie nodded, dumb with shock, and did as she was told. Lizzie ran back out to help her husband lift Donald in and lay him on the couch. 'My God, Donald,' she said, 'what's happened to your leg?'

'I must have been shot.' He gazed at her in a daze before his eyes rolled up and he fainted.

'Run and fetch the barber, Jack,' Lizzie said, 'and don't be long about it. I'll get the fire going again for hot water. But first I'll have to get some of our old sheets to tear up. We're going to need them in this house tonight.'

Jack ran to the house where a red and white pole stuck out of the wall and hammered at the door. Almost at once an upstairs window was flung open.

'What next?' John MacTavish demanded. 'Is there to be no peace at all tonight? What do *you* want, Jack Sproat?'

'Donald's come home, shot.'

'Another one? I've just this minute come from the castle. Lord George is back. He was shot too.'

The window slammed down and Jack was left shuddering in the snow, jumping up and down on his spindly shanks and wondering if John MacTavish had just gone back to bed . . . But no. Out he came with his bag of scissors and knives and bandages.

'Lead on,' he groaned.

Donald was coming round again when they arrived at the house.

'So what about Lord George?' Jack asked. 'Is he dead?'

'No, his shoulder was only grazed. But you would think he was dead, with the fuss up there! Look at all the lights! Half the women of Huntly are up there, running around and wringing their hands.'

'So he'll be all right?' Donald asked, grimacing with pain.

John MacTavish laughed and examined Donald's leg. 'Yes, but the Gordons won't be able to lift their heads for a long time! They've all got gey red faces, after shooting their chief!' Then he turned to Jack. 'Hot water and clean cloths, if you please,' he said, snipping off the leg of Donald's breeches before he set to work, poking into Donald's raw flesh and bringing out a bullet with his tweezers. 'He's been lucky, too. It's only a flesh wound. Have you got any whisky, Jack?'

'I wouldn't be seen dead in my house without a bottle of whisky,' Jack said, black affronted.

'Well, go and get it. I'll pour a drop into this wound to clean it. There's nothing like the water of life to preserve life.'

'You're right there,' Jack agreed, speeding off again, while all this time Lizzie was closeted with Abbie, and they were battling it out together while the pains got fiercer and fiercer.

'How long will this go on?' Abbie panted. 'Is the baby coming now? Oh, it *must* be coming, now!'

Lizzie mopped her brow with a cool cloth. 'It won't be long, dearie,' she said encouragingly. But she knew it would be hours.

John MacTavish poured the raw whisky into the gaping hole in Donald's leg. He screamed with the pain of it, opened his eyes briefly, and passed out again. Satisfied that the wound was clean John bandaged it firmly, quite unconcerned.

'Och, he'll sleep it off,' he informed Jack. 'He'll get over it, although it may be a day or two before he's hopping about again.'

'Ay, well,' Jack said, 'Abbie's having their bairn at this very minute, through the house.'

'That could take the rest of the night.'

'So what do you say we have a wee dram out of this bottle to wet the baby's head, John?'

'By God, a splendid idea! There won't be any sleep tonight now anyway, so we might as well,' John MacTavish agreed, and the two old men poured themselves a dram, and then another dram, and another, while Abbie and Donald hovered between life and death, and gradually the grey light of a northern dawn came in.

With it came another blast of snow and hail, rattling on the window, but Jack and John MacTavish slumbered on happily in their chairs while the fire died down to ashes and their patient lay as one dead.

Suddenly there was the thin cry of a new-born baby. Perishing cold hadn't wakened any of the men, nor snow and hail. But that little wail did. Donald shot up on the couch. 'What's that?' he asked.

'It's your bairn, laddie,' Jack Sproat told him, 'a gift for you on Christmas Day.'

Donald forgot his leg and tried to leap out over the side of the couch in his normal fashion. 'Bairn? Bairn?' he cried, and fell flat on his face. 'I never knew about this,' he added, lurching to Abbie's side, and gazing down at her, 'otherwise I could not have left you.'

'That's why I didn't tell you, Donald,' Abbie wept.

'Well, you've got a beautiful little daughter,' Lizzie informed him.

'Oh, Abbie, Abbie!' he said, tears pouring down his face.

He put his arms around both her and the baby, for once lost for words, and kissed their faces over and over again. 'Thank God you are both safe! It's all right, now.'

But Abbie remained tearful. 'It's *not* all right, Donald. I had a name all picked out. It was going to be Donald, after you.'

'When will you learn to trust me, my Abbie? I always make things right, don't I?'

'You always do. But how are you going to manage that, this time? Donald won't do for a little girl.'

'She's not just a little girl, Abbie. She's a gift from God.'

Abbie gazed up at him. He couldn't possibly know all that had happened . . . How their child almost never was . . . How God had certainly watched over their daughter's entrance into the world.

'Gifted by God,' Donald repeated, 'our little Donata. How does that sound to you?'

'Donata MacLaren, daughter of Donald MacLaren,' Abbie sighed and smiled – and then she laughed. 'I might have known you would give her the best name. You were always the best at everything, simply the best.'

SEVENTY-TWO

As soon as Lord George was well enough he searched the remains of Strathbogie, unearthed the old painting of Flowers and, using it as a pattern, had the house rebuilt. Donata was eighteen months old when the MacLarens moved in, and Lord George took Donald aside.

'Now the workmen can concentrate on the castle full time,' he said. 'Can I leave you to supervise them?'

'With pleasure. Why? Where are you going?'

'It's high time I went to have a look around all our other Gordon strongholds. By rights, you should be coming with me, but I could be away for three months or more, so I won't ask you.'

'Well, you should see a difference when you come back, but not much in only three months.'

'No. Perhaps you'll see a bigger difference in me by that time,' Lord George smiled mysteriously, and set off on his tour.

When he came back, he came back with a lady and a twinkle in his eye. 'Donald,' he said, 'let me introduce you to Lady Helen Gordon, daughter of a distant kinsman.'

'I'm so pleased to meet you, Donald,' said the small fair-haired girl. Perhaps she wasn't a raving beauty, but the warmth and the sincerity shining out of her stopped Donald in his tracks. 'I've heard so much about you – and Strathbogie, of course! George is going to show me around.'

'It will be her home one day, if I can persuade her to marry me,' Lord George said.

Lady Helen laughed. 'Afterwards, will you take me to meet Abbie and Donata, Donald? That's really why I've come.'

'Oh, so you're not really on your way to Paris with me?' Lord George teased her. 'We're going to Paris tomorrow,' he explained to Donald. 'Lady Helen's sisters will chaperone her and we are all to meet up in Aberdeen.'

Donald and Abbie waved them goodbye. 'They'll bypass England altogether, going by sea,' he told her. 'England is a dangerous place.'

Abbie shuddered. After the Battle of Langside Queen Mary had actually *asked* to be transported across the Solway to Workington, against the advice and earnest pleas of her loyal nobles. However, as far as the Scottish people knew, she was being properly entertained in Carlisle Castle, after abdicating and seeming to desert them.

All they could do now was to turn to the little King James who was remarkably clever, so they were told, and being brought up in the Protestant faith.

When Donata was nearly four years old, Donald and Abbie decided the time was right for her to learn to ride. They got her a Shetland pony called Floss, and detailed Robin MacDonald, a stable-boy, to teach her to ride.

One perfect day the following July Abbie went up to her favourite place in the gardens of Flowers. It was a flat plateau of grass, with a bower amongst the rioting flowerbeds in front of the tapestry hedge, and from there she could keep an eye on her daughter in the meadow below.

Nobody could possibly be happier than she was, but even to think so rang warning bells in her head. Yet it was true. She was married to the best man in the world, living in the most beautiful house in the world with the most adorable child in the world – *and she was expecting another*. She would have it in four months' time. And now, here was Donald, climbing up the little hill to see her. It didn't even occur to her to wonder why.

She had never looked more beautiful, Donald thought,

586

walking towards her. Sometimes, fleetingly, he would catch the resemblance between her and her half-sister, Queen Mary. But not today. Today she was his own dainty, perky Abbie, her face flushed with happiness and love just to see him.

She was wearing blue skirts bunched to the back over a short white petticoat, the bodice laced at the waist with crimson silk, a very provocative costume that revealed her slender ankles in red-heeled slippers.

'I love you, Abbie,' he said and patted her stomach, 'and I hope you're keeping another little girl, just like you, warm in there.'

Abbie laughed. 'Well, there's no doubt whose child Donata is! She grows more and more like you every day. Look at her!'

They stood together watching her in the paddock below, her sturdy little legs scampering after Robin MacDonald, who was striding away in an effort to escape her. But Donata caught up with him. She took his hand and smiled up into his face, running along beside him.

'I don't know if Robin MacDonald was a very good choice,' Donald said doubtfully. 'She's becoming altogether too fond of him.'

'She's in love with him, you mean.'

'Behave yourself, Abbie! How can a child of four be in love?'

'Very easily. I was a child of four when I fell in love with you, ran after you just like that, and I've loved you ever since. But I don't suppose you've come to hear me say that?'

'Yes, and no. I've brought you a letter from Lady Jean. Freddie Robertson, Hattie Hunter's young man, is in our kitchen having a meal and waiting for an answer.'

'I didn't know Jean had taken them with her to Dunrobin.' Abbie looked surprised, and opened the letter.

'Well, what is it?' Donald asked and put an arm around her when her face paled.

'It's Alexander Sutherland. She says this could be his last illness. She fears he will die this time. And Lady Jean never

587

says anything she doesn't mean. Oh, Donald –'

'She wants you to come to her. And you want to go. I know.'

'But I don't want to leave you.'

'Don't worry about me, Abbie. I've got more than enough to occupy me up at Strathbogie. One good thing about it is, it will take Donata's mind off Robin MacDonald. I think you should go.'

Two days later, having insisted that his wife and child should make the journey in a litter, Donald became a soldier again long enough to head the Gordon escort to Dunrobin Castle. He had pacified Donata by allowing Floss to travel with them, tied on behind the litter, and she had been entertaining herself by peering out of the curtains and chatting to her little pony all the way.

'There will be other children to play with when we get to Dunrobin,' Abbie reassured her daughter.

Lady Jean was there to meet them when they arrived with her sons John and Robert. Donata smiled and dimpled at them so that they took her hands and led her inside immediately.

'I see she's a proper little flirt,' Lady Jean smiled at Donald.

'She takes after her father,' Abbie agreed, 'but he's hoping this next one will be more like me.'

There the old, easy bantering ended.

'Is Alexander fit to see me?' Donald asked.

'There's no doubt that all the privations he suffered at the hands of the Earl of Caithness when he was younger has brought this about,' Lady Jean said, and led them inside.

Ten minutes afterwards Abbie and Donald were in no doubt that she was right. The mark of death was on Alexander's face, although he tried to rally and talk to them. Later, Donald put his arms around him and with tears in his eyes patted his shoulder in farewell. Then he said his goodbyes to Abbie.

'If I hear no word from you I'll be back in late September,' he said. 'I want to be with you in plenty of time for our child's birth.'

'What is your date?' Lady Jean asked as they watched the Gordons riding away.

'November the third, God willing,' Abbie said.

Ten days later, Alexander Sutherland died. A month after that the news of his death trickled through to Alex Ogilvie in London. The original leopard who couldn't change his spots, never one to make up his mind in a hurry, he sat and thought about it for another month. Then he arrived at the perfect solution to his problem. The young Earl of Huntly had invited him to go to Strathbogie Castle. Perhaps the time had come to call in old debts.

The following month, he went.

'I had been dreading Alexander's death for so long,' Lady Jean told Abbie, 'but when it happened the shock was no less great. I'm sorry if I have seemed to be in a trance, ever since. I became very fond of him, you know,' she said, dabbing at her eyes. 'He was a lovely man.'

'Do you think you are well enough to be up, even yet?' Abbie asked anxiously. 'I have been helping the nursemaids with the children. They don't really understand.'

'Perhaps John does,' Lady Jean said, 'although he says nothing. He will be the next Earl of Sutherland, but his father has left very little money, through no fault of his own. I must see what I can do.'

'But Jean, there is the Gordon money!'

'No,' Lady Jean said quietly. 'I have never begged, and I will not do so now, not even from my own brother. George will need all he has for Strathbogie, and besides, I would not let my husband's memory down by pleading poverty now, as much as to say he left me penniless. In a way, he did not. Come into the library with me.'

She cleared the large table in the middle of the room and spread a large map out on it.

'Alexander discussed this with me and our factor the last time he was well enough,' she said, poring over it. 'He believed that up here in the north-west of our lands,' she pointed, 'there is coal. He intended to sink a mine.'

'That should not be a woman's concern, Jean. Surely that is too technical?'

'It was not too technical for Alexander, though,' Lady Jean smiled. 'He left full instructions. I'll take the factor and ride there tomorrow.'

Abbie didn't argue. Lady Jean had always had a shrewd head on her shoulders, already owning large tracts of land around Edinburgh. She had done some hard bargaining with Bothwell over those.

A week later she came riding back again. 'I've left the factor to engage miners,' she said. 'The work will begin at once. I shall go every week from now on to supervise it. Fortunately, the weather is holding.'

The long, hot summer persisted through August. September came in golden and sunny, and Abbie began to feel restless.

'Perhaps Donata and I should go home soon,' she said, looking at her friend. 'The roses are back in your cheeks with all this galloping about. You don't need me any more, Jeannie.'

'The time will never come when I wouldn't want you at my side, dearest Abbie, but it is for your own sake that I will not allow you to go now, in your seventh month. In fact, I sent word to Donald to tell him so, yesterday. You will have your baby here.'

A week later a message came back from Strathbogie, to prepare for four visitors. Lord George was coming to stay with his sister, and he was bringing Lady Helen to meet her. Of course, Donald was coming too, along with another friend who happened to be staying at Strathbogie.

'What is Lady Helen like?' Jean asked Abbie.

'Small, blonde and not especially beautiful. But you only have to be in her company five minutes when you think she is completely lovely. It's her nature. She's so very pleasant! She and Lord George are well suited.'

After the middle of September the weather changed little by little. It was still very mild for the north of Scotland, but now and then the wind sprang up and there was a shower of rain.

'It's beautiful here, Jean,' Abbie said, looking out of the window over the gardens and right out to sea. 'The leaves are beginning to change colour.'

'You'll see them better out of the window on the other side of the room, where the trees line the drive.'

Abbie crossed the room. This was the way Donald would be coming. 'When do you expect them, Jean?'

'Any day now. Perhaps today.'

Perhaps today . . . Abbie felt the old familiar lift of excitement at the prospect of seeing Donald. 'In fact,' she said, 'the leaves are beginning to fall. They're swirling in a cloud of dust down there at the gates.'

'Horses are making them swirl.' Lady Jean came to stand at her side. 'Our visitors are here.'

'Donald's out in front,' Abbie said, 'and that's Lord George and Lady Helen behind him.'

'I suppose George's friend is bringing up the rear.' Lady Jean turned away. 'Of course, being George, he forgot to tell me his name. Well, I'll go and warn the servants.'

'I think you'd better stay here instead, Jeannie. Come and have another look at Lord George's friend. Don't you recognise him?'

Lady Jean's face went white, then red, then white again. 'Oh, Abbie . . .'

'Yes, it's Alex Ogilvie! He's come to you at last.'

SEVENTY-THREE

It was a long, lively house-party for the next two weeks. Alex Ogilvie got to know Lady Jean's sons, who took to him immediately and trusted him. He accompanied her on her visits to the coal mine. Sometimes Lord George and Lady Helen went with them, but Donald remained at Dunrobin, never far from Abbie's side.

He was such a good father ... Abbie smiled at him, and loved him more than ever, watching him playing with the children, throwing balls for them, taking them for little rides on their ponies and afterwards, in the nursery, splashing them in their baths and pretending to eat supper with them, squeezing his large frame onto their pint-sized chairs.

'Abbie,' Lady Jean said one day, 'I want you to be the first to know. Alex has asked me to marry him, and I have accepted.'

Abbie flung her arms around her. 'Oh, Jean! Truth is stranger than fiction, after all! Who could have invented such a fairy-tale ending for your sad, hard life? At last you can be happy. No one deserves it more.'

'He will come and live here at Dunrobin when we are married. He says he is going to rebuild the dower house for us to move into when little John comes of age.'

Jean and Abbie looked at each other and started to laugh. They rocked with laughter.

'Oh, Abbie,' Jean gasped, 'do you think he'll manage to get it ready in time?'

'Let me see ... In seventeen years? Yes, I really think he

might. Don't make me laugh any more, Jean! I might easily drop this baby on the floor. I think I'm going to burst.'

'Come and help me arrange the table for supper, instead.'

The children were all sleeping when the grown-ups sat down that evening to a relaxed and cosy meal, laughing and chatting. It was all happy talk, of weddings and plans for the future, and Donald was in his element teasing Lord George and Alex Ogilvie. The jokes came fast and furious.

And then, the conversation took a different turn.

'Come on then, Alex,' Lord George said, 'tell us the latest news of Queen Mary. You heard it all in London, did you not?'

'She's been sent to Sheffield, now.'

'Always nearer and nearer to London,' Donald said, 'for some purpose of Queen Elizabeth's. But she will never meet her face to face, I bet.'

'The Earl of Shrewsbury is looking after her. Although he is so much older than Mary, and married to the jealous Bess of Hardwicke, they say –'

'Oh, they *say*, they *say*!' the rest groaned.

'– they say he's in love with her. But then, many men are in love with her, it seems. She even accepted a diamond engagement ring from the Duke of Norfolk.'

'But she's still married to Bothwell,' Lady Jean said.

'Jean,' Alex Ogilvie said gently, and covered her hand with his, 'the marriage was annulled. Lord Bothwell is insane.'

The whole atmosphere of the supper party changed.

'He is incarcerated in Malmoe prison and will never be free now.'

Abbie felt sick. Bothwell, the daring, dashing, hard-bitten fighting man – to come to such an end! Again the vision of him achieving the impossible, swinging out over the murderous rock of Edinburgh Castle and escaping, floated before her eyes.

'Of course, you know that the Bastard was killed?' Alex asked them, all of them silent now. 'One of the Hamiltons shot him dead in the main street of Linlithgow. Everyone thought he got his just deserts.'

'Only in Hell,' Donald said, 'for all the damage he did to his sister, our little Queen.'

Abbie felt worse still.

In an effort to lighten the sombre response around the table, Alex went on.

'Well, at least Shrewsbury allows Mary her court, although it has dwindled to only thirty now. Bourgoing is still her physician and Balthazzar still her tailor. She has a French secretary, Claud Nau, and Bastion Pages provides whatever entertainment is allowed and possible. Willie Douglas is with her, and Jane Kennedy and Marie de Courcelles – and, of course, the faithful Mary Seton.'

Abbie and Lady Jean glanced sadly at each other. Seton, the faithful Seton, the only one of the four Marys still with the Queen. Seton, 'the weed,' as she used to call herself, 'in the Queen's bouquet.'

'But nothing changes,' Alex said. 'It's still all plots, plots and more plots – and truly suffocating.'

Abbie stood up. She must have air. Donald rose with her and put his arm around her.

'Are you all right, dear?' Lady Jean looked across at her in concern.

'Not very,' Abbie admitted.

Lady Jean rushed around the table and took her other arm. 'There's a room all ready for her along this corridor,' she told Donald, and led the way. 'The physician and the midwife have been alerted. They will be here in minutes.'

So Abbie found herself on her second bed of labour with the pains coming and going, coming and going, and never coming to any natural conclusion.

'She's waiting for something,' the physician told Lady Jean. 'I can't think what's holding her back. Look! She seems to be falling asleep. I've never seen anything like it.'

*   *   *

594

Abbie was back in the nightmare again, but this time it was much, much blacker than before.

Bitterly against her will, she was floating up a mean stone stair and into an even meaner crude chamber as the clock outside in the tower struck six on a perishing cold February morning.

A woman – and now Abbie knew she was Queen Mary – rose from her bed.

'Madam, what may I do?' Jane Kennedy asked.

'I shall dress.'

Jane fetched her a relieving vessel, and afterwards removed it with its purplish contents, the colour of Burgundy wine.

'I'm sorry, Jane,' Mary said. 'The royal water is very royal today.'

Her ladies brought her a basin of water, and she bathed. They slipped a dark red camisole over her shoulders and helped her into a velvet petticoat of the same colour.

'My blood against this colour will not be so conspicuous,' Mary said.

Blinded by tears they dressed her in a black velvet gown stamped with gold. The puffed upper sleeves were purple velvet, the lower sleeves black lined with sable and falling to her feet. There was a high pleated ruff for her throat, a brown wig for her hair, and Jane placed a peaked white coif on her head, its lace-edged veil sweeping to the floor.

Sobbing helplessly, Jane and Marie fell on their knees and kissed the hem of her dress. Then they fastened a golden crucifix and a golden pomander around her waist, placed an ivory crucifix in one hand and a gold-bordered handkerchief in the other, the one she had chosen to blindfold her eyes. At the last minute, sensing that his mistress was going out, Mary's little white Skye terrier crept under her skirts as he always did, to run along close by her side.

The narrow, broken stairs outside were difficult enough for a fit, healthy person to descend. For Mary, they were almost impossible, as Abbie saw when Marie held her skirts up out of the way. Her legs were so swollen that they were as stiff as boards. Slowly and gently, Jane helped her down, and she shuffled across the courtyard and into the Great Hall of Fotheringay Castle, leaning on her ladies, one on either side of her.

Mary stood stock still at the door. The hall was draped in black from side to side, and near the fireplace stood a scaffold.

'I am glad that my death in the True Faith will be witnessed by so many,' she said, gazing at the packed benches all around as she painfully ascended the wooden steps of the scaffold.

It was at that moment that once again the ghosts of those who were not there, but should have been there, appeared to Abbie. The shadow of Queen Elizabeth was sitting on the chair of state raised on a dais, presiding. Her face was painted, her skin raddled, and she wore the Crown of England on top of a brilliant scarlet wig. Her nose was more like a beak than a nose. Her youth was gone.

And her eyes were frightened.

King James, a grown man of twenty-one, slack-mouthed, with hard avaricious eyes which he averted from his mother, turned his back both on her and on the map of Scotland hanging on the wall, and smiled at Elizabeth.

Even in her dream Abbie understood his reasons. When had Mary ever treated him as a beloved son? Had she not put him into someone else's care when he was only a few months old? He could have no love for the mother he hardly knew, who had been more interested in herself than in her country or her son, and who was dying penniless . . . Whereas Queen Elizabeth would give him another country, with all its power, with all its gold. Compared with that, his mother and Scotland were nothing.

Mary stood erect, courageous and proud. Jane and Marie wept and crossed themselves continually as they removed her magnificent top clothes to expose her underclothes of red, and bound her eyes with the gold-bordered handkerchief.

But King James, her son, did not put out a hand to help her.

'Into Thy hands, O Lord, I commend my spirit,' Queen Mary said.

The headsman raised his axe high and brought it down with a smash. But he missed. He had cut only half of her neck.

'Sweet Jesus,' Mary's head whispered.

Angry and ashamed the man sawed away at the last quivering ligaments, and the head rolled away, the lips still moving in silent prayer. The wig fell off, to reveal a few wisps of white hair on an almost bald head. The body flopped over, the neck still spurted, and the little dog crept out and stood beside it, looking puzzled and lost.

'Sweet Jesus!' Abbie screamed suddenly, with her hands around her neck in a clamp.

Try as he might the physician could not move them, as Abbie's face turned blue. Abbie's pain was indescribable, sawing, sawing at her neck. Then Lady Jean was beside her, loosening her fingers, one by one from around her neck. 'No, no,' she said gently. 'The pain is not there, Abbie.'

'Queen Mary,' Abbie croaked, trying to explain.

'Queen Mary is in Sheffield, dear. Don't worry about Queen Mary. Your pain is down here.' Lady Jean placed Abbie's hands gently over her lower stomach. 'Your baby is coming. Help the little child.'

'Now you may go, my lady,' the physician said as the clock struck midnight and Abbie's body suddenly arched. 'She's started again, at last, and she won't be long.'

Outside in the corridor no one thought of going to bed. Donald paced up and down. At one o'clock Lord George could stand it no longer, and joined him. At two, Alex paced with them.

'It isn't always a bed of roses, you know,' Donald told them. 'No marriage is. But I have been very lucky, surrounded by flowers since ever I knew Abbie. Flowers at the Gardeners' Cottage. Flowers in France. And now even in my home, the House of Flowers.'

At the end of every hour Lady Jean sent for refreshments, and Lady Helen fought a losing battle trying to persuade anyone to try a little cake off one of the plates.

Shortly after three o'clock Donald heard the first cry of his second child. Lord George and Alex Ogilvie held him down firmly between them until the door opened and the midwife said, 'You can come in now.'

Donald rushed in and kneeled by the side of the bed. Abbie lay with a face like marble and her eyes closed, while the midwife wrapped the baby in a shawl.

'Abbie, Abbie,' he whispered, and kept on whispering in her ear. And as he whispered her startled eyes flew open and her tears began to flow. How did he know? How could he possibly know all she had seen of the future?

But as he whispered she realised that he had guessed along the same lines as she had herself – there could be no happy ending for Mary, Queen of Scots, the beautiful, courageous, exasperating, generous, selfish enigma whom they had all loved.

They must bow to the inevitable, when King James would sell himself to Elizabeth for five thousand pounds a year, and was greedy for more. He wanted all she had, her throne as well. James VI of Scotland was desperate for his other title, James I of England, and all the money that went with it. Elizabeth and England had won.

But Donald was proud, and gallant and unrepentant in Scotland's defeat.

'Just look at that little flower face, Abbie,' he said and kissed her, whispering again.

Abbie smiled and nodded her head.

Then Donald took the baby in his arms as Lady Jean, Alex Ogilvie, Lord George and Lady Helen tiptoed into the room, and held up their loving tribute to their Queen.

'This is Flora,' he announced her, 'another little flower for the Queen's bouquet.'